SelectEditions

SELECTED AND EDITED

SelectEditions

BY READER'S DIGEST

VOLUME 1 1999
THE READER'S DIGEST ASSOCIATION, INC.
PLEASANTVILLE, NEW YORK

READER'S DIGEST SELECT EDITIONS

Editor-in-Chief: Tanis H. Erdmann
Executive Editor: Marjorie Palmer
Volume Editor: Angela Plowden-Wardlaw
Book Editors: Anne H. Atwater, Madeline Tracy Brigden
Volume Copy Editor: Charles Pendergast
Copy Editors: Daphne Hougham, Marilyn J. Knowlton
Art Director: Angelo Perrone

CONTENTS

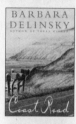
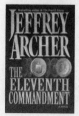

The
Loop

Nicholas
Evans

His kind have been here before. They were hunted and destroyed a hundred years ago.

Now they have returned, protected by law. And the struggle between man and wolf is about to begin anew.

SUMMER

One

THE scent of slaughter, some believe, can linger in a place for years. They say it lodges in the soil and is slowly sucked through coiling roots so that in time all that grows there bears testimony.

Perhaps, as he moved silently down through the forest on that late afternoon, the wolf sensed it. And perhaps this vestige of a rumor in his nostrils—that here a hundred years ago so many of his kind were killed—should have made him turn away.

Yet on and down he went.

He had set out the previous evening, leaving the others in the high country where even now, in July, snow lingered in gullies shy of the sun. He followed a rocky canyon that wound down to the valleys below. When the sun rose, he stopped to drink, then found a shaded nook and slept through the heat of the day.

He was a prime four-year-old, the alpha of the pack, almost pure black. In this descent to the valley he would pause to sniff a bush or a tuft of grass, then lift his leg and make his mark, reclaiming this long-lost place as his own. At other times he would stop and tilt his nose to the air, and his eyes would narrow and shine yellow as he read the scented messages that wafted from below. Cattle, dogs, the acrid tang of man's machines. And though he must have known, without ever being taught, the peril of such things, on again he went.

The valley ran some ten miles due east in a widening glacial scoop toward the town of Hope. Its sides were ridged and thick with pine and reached out to the great sun-bleached plains that stretched from the town's eastern edge to the horizon.

All of this could be surveyed from where the wolf now stood on a limestone crag that jutted from the trees. Below, the land fell away sharply in a scar of tumbled rock and then gave way grudgingly to pasture. A straggle of black cows and calves were grazing. Beyond them, at the foot of the meadow, stood a small clapboard ranch house, painted oxblood. There were barns to one side and white-fenced corrals. Along the house's southern side ran a porch that was bathed in a last throw of golden light. The windows along the porch had been opened wide, and lace curtains stirred in the breeze.

From inside floated the babble of a radio, and maybe it was this that made it hard for whoever was at home to hear the baby crying. The buggy on the porch rocked a little, and a pair of pink arms stretched out, craving for attention. Then, distracted by the play of sunlight on his hands, the baby began to coo.

The only one who heard was the wolf.

KATHY and Clyde Hicks had moved here to the red house two years ago, right after they got married. If Kathy were honest with herself, she hated it. Well, the summers were okay. But even then, you felt you were too far away from civilization. The winters didn't bear thinking about.

Kathy had hoped having the baby might change how she felt about the place, and in a way it had. At least she had someone to talk to when Clyde was out working the ranch.

She was twenty-three and had married straight out of college. She had a degree in agribusiness management from Montana State. The only use she'd ever made of it was shuffling her daddy's paperwork down at the main ranch house three days a week. When she got into the car to come back up here, she would feel a sort of dull regret. She would push it aside by jabbering to the baby in the back or by finding country music on the radio.

She had music on now, and as she stood at the sink shucking corn and looking out at the dogs sleeping in the sun by the barns, she felt better. Really, she should count her blessings. She had a fine husband and a beautiful, healthy baby, and this place was their own. She was tall, had great hair, and even though she hadn't quite got her figure back since having the baby, she still looked good. And she was Buck Calder's daughter. Around these parts that was about as big a thing to be as there was. Her daddy's ranch was one of the largest spreads this side of Helena.

It was getting on for six. Clyde and her daddy were down in the hayfields. They and her mom were all coming over for supper around seven. Kathy put the corn into a pan on the stove.

The wolf by now was at the foot of the meadow. A pair of magpies came toward him in fluttering swoops, scolding him. The wolf ignored them. But from his buggy the baby, Buck Junior, did a passable imitation of the birds and shrieked with delight at how it sounded. Inside, a phone started to ring.

It was Kathy's mother. "Luke says he'll come, if that's okay."

"Of course it's okay."

Luke, Kathy's brother, had just turned eighteen. He was sweet with the baby, but he and Clyde didn't get along too well. As kids, Luke and Kathy had never really been close. But no one was close to Luke except their mom. She was the only one who could handle his stutter. Since he'd graduated from high school a couple of months ago, Kathy had hardly seen him. He was always off on his own in the wilderness on that horse of his.

It was just as she hung up that the dogs started barking. Kathy looked out the window. Maddie, the old collie, had her tail tucked under her and was slinking off around the side of the barn. Prince, the yellow Labrador, was pacing to and fro with his hackles up, and he punctuated his barking with worried little whines.

Kathy frowned. She'd better go see what was spooking them. When she stepped down into the yard, Prince started to come to her. Then he changed his mind and took off in full cry around the side of the house.

Then the thought struck her. The baby. There was something getting the baby. She started to run. It must be a bear. Or a mountain lion. As she came around the corner of the house, Kathy saw, directly below the porch, what at first she took for a big black dog.

"Get out of here! Git!"

The animal glanced at her, and she felt the yellow flash of his eyes upon her and knew in that instant this was no dog.

Prince lowered himself before the wolf, his chest inches from the ground. He had his teeth bared and was snarling and barking but so timidly that it seemed he might at any moment roll over and submit. The wolf stood very still. He towered over the dog, his tail bushy and raised high. Slowly he curled back his lips and snarled, and his long incisors showed white.

Then, in a single lunge, he had his jaws on the Labrador's throat and swung him through the air as if he were a rabbit. The dog yelped, and Kathy had a sudden image in her head of the wolf having already done the same with her baby. She screamed, jumped onto the porch and ran toward the buggy.

Oh, God, please. Don't let him be dead. Please don't let him be dead. The thought of what she would find made her sob.

When she got there, she forced herself to look, and saw the child staring up at her, his face breaking into a gummy grin. She cried out and snatched him up with such sudden violence that the child began to cry. She turned, pressing her back to the wall.

The wolf was standing with his head lowered over the Labrador. The dog was dead. His throat had been torn out, and his belly gaped like a gutted fish. Kathy screamed again.

"Get out of here! Go on! Get out!"

She looked around for something to throw at him, but the wolf was already running off. He ducked under the fence and loped up among the cattle in the meadow, then vanished into the forest.

THE offices of the U.S. Fish & Wildlife Service wolf recovery team were on the third floor of a red brick building in Helena. There was no sign outside that told you this. People around here didn't much like any federal agency, least of all one whose purpose was protecting the most loathsome creature God ever made. Dan Prior and his team knew from experience to keep a low profile.

In the outer office stood a glass case from which a stuffed wolf, informally known as Fred, looked benignly on their labors.

Dan had gotten into the habit of talking to Fred, particularly on those long nights when everyone else had gone home, leaving him to unpick yet another political tangle in which Fred's more animated brethren had snagged him.

Tonight was not going to be one of those nights. Dan was leaving early. He had a date. As he came out of his office, everyone chanted in rehearsed unison, "Have a nice time, Dan!"

"You're all fired." He was at the door when the phone rang.

"I'm gone," he mouthed to Donna, his assistant.

He waited at the elevator while the cables clunked and whirred.

"Dan!" Donna hurried down the corridor toward him. "I'm sorry, but that was a rancher called Clyde Hicks from Hope. He says a wolf just tried to kill his baby boy."

TWENTY minutes and half a dozen phone calls later Dan was on his way to meet predator control agent Bill Rimmer in Hope to do a necropsy on the dog.

It was about an hour's drive from Helena to Hope, and as he swung west off the interstate toward the mountains, Dan reflected on why it was that anyone who worked with wolves ended up getting nailed by them. He'd met a lot of biologists who specialized in other animals; on the whole they seemed able to stumble through life like the rest of humanity. But wolf biologists were walking disaster areas in every league—divorce, nervous breakdown, suicide.

By these standards Dan himself had nothing to be ashamed of. His marriage had lasted nearly sixteen years. And even if Mary, his ex, didn't speak to him, Ginny, their daughter, who was fourteen, adored him, and it was mutual. But apart from Ginny, what, really, at the age of forty-one, did he have to show for all these years of devotion to the welfare of wolves?

To avoid answering his own question, he switched on the radio for the local news. The last item did little to improve his mood.

It was about a "wolf attack" on a ranch near Hope and how the baby grandson of one of the community's most prominent figures, Buck Calder, had only escaped certain death because a pet Labrador had bravely laid down his life instead.

Until recently, the only wolves in the region had been the few that had ventured down from Canada. Then the federal government decided to give wolf recovery a boost. Sixty-six Canadian wolves were trucked to Yellowstone Park and central Idaho and released. Ranchers who lived in these areas were allowed to shoot any wolf they found attacking their livestock. But the released wolves had multiplied and spread to places where shooting them earned you a hundred-thousand-dollar fine and even a spell in jail. Hope was one of these places. What's more, it was wolf-hater heartland.

In the far distance now, Dan saw the town looming—one straight street, a couple of hundred yards long, with a few side alleys. At one end stood a run-down motel and at the other a school, and in between, a gas station, a grocery, a hardware store, a diner, a Laundromat and a taxidermist. There were two churches and two bars. There were also two gift shops, which said more about optimism than sound business sense.

One of these shops (and by far the better) had a cappuccino bar. The shop was called Paragon, and the woman who owned it was a handsome New Yorker called Ruth Michaels. From their two or three encounters Dan had so far established that she used to run an art gallery and had come to Montana on vacation after her marriage broke up. She'd fallen in love with the place and stayed.

The locals mostly preferred their coffee weak and stewed, as they did it at Nelly's Diner, and as he drove by, Dan was sad but not surprised to see Ruth had a FOR SALE sign stuck in the front window.

He could see Bill Rimmer's pickup parked where they'd arranged to meet, outside a forlorn bar named the Last Resort. Rimmer got out to greet him. He was a born-and-bred Montanan and at six foot six, with his Stetson and droopy blond mustache, looked it.

Dan got out of his car, and Rimmer slapped him on the shoulder. "How're you doing?"

"Well, I had a better date than you lined up for tonight."

"You could break a man's heart, Dan Prior."

They climbed into Rimmer's pickup and drove down Main Street. He and Rimmer both had started their jobs three years ago. Their predecessors had been involved in the release program and had quit not long after. They were wolfed out—tired of being yelled at by ranchers for not doing enough to control the spread of wolves and by environmentalists for not doing enough to help it.

Rimmer worked for Animal Damage Control, a division of the Department of Agriculture, and was usually the first person to get the call when a rancher was having trouble with predators. He was judge, jury and, where necessary, executioner. A trained biologist, he kept his love of the animals to himself. And that, along with his skill with rifle and trap, had helped him earn the respect even of those who harbored a natural mistrust of all federal employees. To ranchers, Dan Prior would always be an East Coast outsider and the man who'd caused their problem.

They swung off the last stretch of blacktop and onto the gravel road that led up the valley toward the mountains.

The gateway to the Calder ranch was a massive structure of weathered lodgepole pine, its crossbar mounted with the skull of a longhorn steer. They followed the road for another mile, winding among small scrub-covered hills, until the ranch house loomed ahead of them. Built of stout whitewashed timber, it stood assertively on a low bluff that afforded a commanding view of the Calder domain. Below it lay an imposing set of white barns and three silver feed silos, which towered above a network of corrals.

They forked left, and two miles farther up they saw, in the gathering dusk, the Hicks house. There were six or seven vehicles parked in front, and though partly obscured by the house, a small crowd could be seen around the rear porch. Someone had a spotlight on, and every so often there was the flash of a camera.

They parked and made their way to the back of the house.

Up on the porch, in a flood of light, a young TV reporter was interviewing Buck Calder. He towered above her.

He was tall and powerfully built. He wore a light-colored Stetson and a white snap-button shirt that set off his tan. His eyes gleamed a pale gray-blue in the TV lights.

Alongside him were Kathy and Clyde Hicks. Kathy was holding the baby. There was a table beside them with something bulky and yellow on it. It was the dead dog.

"The wolf is a killing machine," Calder was saying. "He'll take anything he can. And if it wasn't for this poor, brave dog here, he'd have taken my little grandson, Buck Junior."

There were about a dozen people there. Dan kept going back to two faces: a graceful woman in her mid-forties and a tall young man, probably in his late teens, beside her.

"Calder's wife and his son, Luke," Rimmer whispered.

The woman had thick black hair, streaked with gray and loosely pinned up to show a long, pale neck. She had a kind of melancholy beauty that was echoed in the face of her son.

"Thank you Mr. Calder," the TV reporter was saying, "very much. That was really really . . . great."

From the open door of Kathy's barn, Luke Calder looked out across the yard to where they were doing the necropsy. He was kneeling beside Maddie, the old collie, and stroking her.

Rimmer had the Labrador laid out on clear plastic sheeting on the tailgate of his pickup. He'd rigged up some lamps so he could see what he was doing with his knife. The other guy who'd come with him, the wolf expert, was videoing it, while Luke's father and Clyde stood looking on in silence. His mother and Kathy were inside, getting supper ready. Everyone else had at last gone home.

They were skinning him like a deer, Rimmer talking all the while for the video. "Severe internal hemorrhaging and more bite marks here at the base of the neck. Real deep puncture wounds. Can you see that, Dan? Here, I'll measure them. Incisor holes, nearly two inches apart. That's a big animal."

It must have been the alpha male, Luke thought, the big black one. Luke had known for months that there were wolves up there. He'd first heard them when he was out on his skis. He'd found tracks, followed them and found the carcass of a fresh-killed elk.

One icy day in April he'd seen the black one. Luke had climbed to the top of a high ridge and stopped to rest on a rock. Gazing down into the next valley, he saw the wolf trot out from the trees. It made its way up a snowy meadow to a slope cluttered with sliprock and blowdown. The wolf vanished into it.

It was where the mother had denned. In the weeks that followed, Luke saw the others. When the snow melted, he rode up there, making sure to stay downwind, tying his horse, Moon Eye, a good way off and climbing to the top of the same ridge.

He told no one.

Then, in the first week of May, he saw the pups, still fluffy and dark. All five of them had come stumbling out from the den, blinking in the sunshine. Their mother, with her drooping teats, stood proudly by while the father and two younger adults nuzzled the little ones as if welcoming them into the world.

Toward the end of June he found them again in a meadow filled with flowers. Luke watched the pups chasing bees and butterflies and learning how to hunt mice. Sometimes, when their mother or their father lay dozing in the sun, the pups stalked them, creeping on their bellies through the long grass. When they got close, the pups pounced, and the whole pack chased around the meadow until they all collapsed in one big, exhausted heap of wolf.

Witnessing this, Luke silently said a prayer that the wolves stay up there where they were safe and not venture down to the valley.

But now it had happened. One of them had come.

Across the yard, the necropsy was over now and Dan Prior was helping Rimmer clean up. Luke stood up and walked out of the barn, hoping that no one would spot him.

"Well, there's no doubt it was a wolf," Rimmer said.

Calder laughed. "Was there any doubt before? I reckon my daughter can tell a wolf from a woodpecker." Luke's father saw him, and he cussed himself for leaving the barn. "Gentlemen, this is my son, Luke. Luke, this here's Mr. Prior and Mr. Rimmer."

Fighting an instinct to turn and run, Luke walked over and shook hands with them. They both said hi, but Luke just nodded. As usual, his father steamed right on with the conversation. Luke knew the reason his father always stepped in so smartly; he didn't like folks knowing he had a stutterer for a son.

"So, how come you fellas never told us there were wolves around here?"

Prior answered. "Mr. Calder, we've had no indication, until today, of any wolf activity in this area. This one may be a disperser—a single wolf who's broken away from some other pack. Maybe he's hanging out with others that are radio collared. That's what we're going to try and find out tomorrow morning."

"What are you planning on doing once you've found them?"

"I think we need to know a little more before we decide on that," Prior said. "I appreciate how upset you must be, but if it's any consolation, there's never been a case in North America of a healthy wild wolf killing a human being. In all probability this one was only after the dog. It's kind of a territorial thing."

"Oh, is it? Mr. Prior, where do you come from originally?"

"Pittsburgh."

"Pittsburgh. Grew up in the city. That's *your* territory?"

"Well, in a manner of speaking, yes, I guess it is."

"Well, let me tell you something, Mr. Prior. This here is *our* territory, and we've got 'kind of a territorial thing' about it too. We don't want wolves here."

BUCK Calder was baptized Henry Clay Calder III, but he had never been too keen on the idea of being third or even second to anyone, and to those who liked him and to those who didn't, he'd always been much more a Buck than a Henry.

The nickname came when, at fourteen, he carried off every prize at the high school rodeo, revealing only when all was safely won that he had two broken fingers and a cracked collarbone.

Even back then the name's carnal connotation was not lost on the more knowing of his female classmates. Had any of these girls seen fit to share such secrets with their mothers, they would perhaps have found that a previous generation of Hope schoolgirls had flushed with similar feelings for his father, Henry II.

Of Buck's grandfather, Henry I, no such intimate detail endured. History bore witness only to his great resilience. In 1912 he loaded a few cows and chickens, a young bride and her upright piano onto a train in Akron, Ohio, and headed west.

When they got to Montana, Henry filed a claim way out by the mountains. And while countless others gave up, driven out by drought, wind and winters, the Calders somehow survived.

Henry I bought the land his neighbors couldn't make pay, and little by little the Calder ranch spread down the valley toward Hope. With dynastic ambition he named his first son after him and set about making the HC brand something to be proud of.

Henry II never went to college, but every moment he wasn't chasing women he read everything he could lay his hands on about rearing cattle. His father thought some of the articles the younger Henry read to him too newfangled, but the more he handed over decisions, the more the herd thrived.

Buck grew up with all the confidence and not a little of the arrogance such status can give a child. No ranch was bigger than theirs, no rancher smarter than his daddy. There were some who secretly hoped that the legendary Calder drive might dissipate in this third Henry's veins. Instead, it seemed to redouble.

Buck went to college in Bozeman and learned all about genetics. When he came back, he started keeping a file on every animal they reared, charting its performance in detail. The progeny of those who made the grade flourished; those found wanting went to the wall. Weeding out poor stock was hardly revolutionary, but the rigor with which it was applied on the Calder ranch was. Buck's changes improved performance dramatically and had stock growers talking across the state. The first Henry died content.

With the old man gone, Buck argued with his father that they should switch to Black Angus. Within a few years Calder-bred Black Angus bulls and the richness of their seed were renowned throughout the West and beyond.

With his own seed the young Buck Calder was somewhat less discriminating. He would boast that a real man had three inalienable rights: life, liberty and the pursuit of women. There were two kinds of women he pursued, and the ones he dated knew nothing of the ones he paid, which allowed Buck to be seen, throughout his twenties, as nothing worse than what was still quaintly called a ladies' man.

By the time he turned thirty most women his age had found husbands elsewhere and Buck was dating their younger sisters. His eyes at last settled on a young woman ten years his junior.

Eleanor Collins was the daughter of a hardware store proprietor from Great Falls and had just finished her training as a physical therapist. Buck was one of her first patients.

He had strained a shoulder hauling a broken hay wagon from a creek. At the clinic he saw this young goddess step through the door of the consulting room. She wore a white coat that fitted close enough to show Buck's practiced eye a lithe, full-breasted figure. She had skin like ivory and long black hair. She fixed him with her wonderful green eyes and told him to take off his shirt. Buck left the clinic with both his shoulder and his heart aglow. He had met, at last, the woman he would marry.

She refused to sleep with him before they were married, but on their wedding night she dutifully conceived. It was a boy. His name was not up for discussion. Two daughters, Lane and Kathy, followed at intervals of roughly two years.

"Only breed your best cow every other year," Buck said to his pals at the Last Resort. "That's the way to get prime beef."

It was a description that he could honestly apply to the first three of his children. Henry IV was a firstborn Calder to the core, and sometimes when the two of them were out hunting or rounding up cattle, Buck would shake his head with pride.

And then he'd look at young Luke. It had taken Eleanor four years to have him, and during that time something seemed to have happened to the Calder genes. The boy was the image of his mother—the pale Irish skin, the dark hair, the same watchful green eyes. Even in front of the boy, he'd referred to Luke as "your son."

It was said in jest, but secretly he felt his genes had somehow been denied access to the boy, even before Luke began to stutter.

"Ask for it properly," Buck would tell Luke at the table. He'd say it gently but firmly. "Say 'please may I have the milk.'"

And Luke, just three, would sit there and try and fail and keep trying and keep failing until he cried, and Eleanor would give it to him and Buck would yell at her. How was the boy supposed to learn if she did that every time, for Pete's sake?

As Luke grew, so did his stutter. More than ever he became Eleanor's son, and soon he was to be her only one.

On a snowy November day, when Luke was seven, his older brother and his grandfather, Henry II, were killed in a car wreck.

Young Henry, just fifteen years old, was learning to drive, and it was he at the wheel when a deer sprang out before them. The road was like greased marble, and when he swerved, the wheels locked and the car launched itself into a ravine. Three hours later the rescue team found the frozen bodies in a tree.

The older Henry's death was the more easily absorbed, but the loss of a child is an abyss from which few families return. Like shipwrecked strangers, the Calders each struck out for shore alone, as if fearful that in helping others they might be dragged beneath the waves of grief and drown.

Lane and Kathy fared best, escaping as often and for as long as they could to the homes of their friends. Their father meanwhile, like a brave pioneer, strode forward in manly denial. And sought sexual solace wherever he could. His philandering, only ever briefly curtailed by his marriage, took on new zeal.

Eleanor retreated to a distant inner land. She would sit glazed for days before the TV. When she grew tired of that, she tried drink. But she could never quite get the hang of it and stopped.

It was Luke who felt her distance most keenly. She often forgot to come and kiss him good night and rarely hugged him anymore.

She still protected him from his father's rage, but wearily, as if it were a duty whose purpose she had forgotten.

And so the boy's quiet harvesting of guilt went undetected. On the day of their death his brother and grandfather had been on their way to fetch him from his speech therapist in Helena. And with seven-year-old logic this made the accident his fault. With one stroke he had slain his father's father and best-beloved child.

THE red-and-white Cessna 185 banked steeply against a cobalt dome of morning sky above the rim of the mountains. Dan pointed the nose for the twentieth time toward the east. Beside him in the narrow cockpit Bill Rimmer sat with the radio receiver on his lap, going methodically, again and again, through the list of frequencies of every collared wolf there was from Canada to Yellowstone, while both men strained their ears for the unmistakable cluck-cluck-cluck of a signal.

It wasn't the easiest country for spotting wolves. All morning they'd combed the peaks and the canyons, using their eyes as much as their ears, squinting into the shadowed spaces between the trees, scanning ridges and creeks and lush green meadows for some tell-tale sign: a carcass in a clearing, a flock of ravens, a sudden flight of deer. Once, they startled a grizzly bear feeding with her cub. Here and there they came across cattle, grazing the allotments— high summer pastures that many ranchers leased from the Forest Service. But of the wolf or wolves there was no trace. Dan knew the chances weren't great that the wolf was wearing a radio collar.

As a matter of policy, over the past couple of years they had scaled down the number of wolves they'd collared. The idea of restoring a viable breeding population to the region was that the animals should be truly wild. Every time you captured a wolf and handled him, you made him a little less of a wolf. However, if a wolf started killing cattle or sheep or people's pets, you needed to get a collar on him before someone beat you to it with a gun.

If any wolf down there was wearing a collar, they should have found him by now. Finding an uncollared wolf in country like this was much tougher. The trouble was, this was more than just a trap-and-collar job. With the town's deep hatred of the wolf, whoever Dan sent in would also have to be a skilled communicator, sensitive to local feelings yet strong enough to stand up to bullies like Buck Calder. Hope could turn out to be the most severe test yet for the recovery program.

Dan glanced down at the fuel gauge. There was just enough juice to get back to Helena. "Time we were headed home."

"Yep. Looks like a job for the trap man."

Somewhere below, in a wild place that was still a young man's secret, the wolves heard the drone of the plane's engine fade and die.

HELEN Ross hated New York. And she hated it even more when it was ninety-four degrees and the air was so humid you felt like a clam being baked in traffic fumes.

Sitting at the cramped table on what the SoHo restaurant manager called the terrazzo—a hedged display pen on the sidewalk—Helen looked for her father's face among the crowds along the street. Everyone looked impossibly cool and beautiful. Tanned young businessmen in linen suits chatted to women who had perfect teeth and long legs. Helen hated them all.

It wasn't that she was, by nature, mean-spirited. Quite the contrary, she lived her life normally at the danger end of generosity. Today, however, several factors had conspired, among them the city and the weather, to put her out of sorts. Not least was that her twenty-ninth birthday was tomorrow, and when it dawned, she would still be unemployed, unmarried and unhappy.

It had become a ritual that her father took her out for a birthday lunch, no matter where either of them was living at the time. It was always Helen who did the traveling, because her father was always so busy. She loved her father, and their birthday lunch was about the only time she ever got to see him nowadays.

Her parents had been divorced when she was nineteen. Her sister, Celia, two years younger, had just gone away to college, and Helen was studying biology at the University of Minnesota. Both girls came home to Chicago for Thanksgiving, and after the meal, their parents calmly announced that now that their job of bringing up their children was done, they were going their separate ways. The marriage, they revealed, had been wretched for years, and they both had someone else with whom they would rather live. To Helen it was devastating. Her parents had always rowed, but Helen had assumed that everybody's parents did this. And now it turned out that all these long years they had suffered each other's company only for the sake of their children.

Celia had behaved perfectly, as Celia always had and always would. She wept and hugged them both, which made them both weep, while Helen stormed out of the house.

Helen had never since been able to rid herself of the notion that she was to blame for all the mutual pain her parents had endured. Had it not been for her, and Celia, of course, her parents could have gone their separate ways years ago.

Their divorce confirmed her long-held suspicion that animals were infinitely more reliable than people. And, on reflection, it seemed no coincidence that around that time, she had begun to develop a passionate interest in wolves. With their devotion and loyalty to each other, the way they cared for their young, they seemed superior to human beings in almost every respect.

Ten years had allowed her feelings about the divorce to mellow, and she was pleased that her parents had at last found happiness.

Her mother had remarried immediately and now lived a life of golf, bridge and apparently galvanic sex with a short, bald and hugely attentive real estate agent called Ralphie. It turned out Ralphie had been her Someone Else for six years.

Her father's Someone Else didn't see out six months and had since been superseded over the years by a string of Other Someone Elses, each younger than the last. His work as a financial consultant had taken him from Chicago to Houston and, last year, to New York City, where he had met Courtney Dasilva.

And this was the other main factor that had helped render Helen's mood today less than ebullient. Because this coming Christmas,

Howard Ross and Courtney Dasilva were to be married. Helen was about to meet her for the first time.

Her stepmother-to-be, her father told her on the phone last week when he'd broken the news, worked for one of the biggest banks in America. She was also, he said, a Stanford psychology major and the most gorgeous human being he had ever laid eyes on.

"I'm so happy for you," Helen had said, trying to mean it.

"Baby, I feel so . . . so *alive*. I'm dying for you two to meet. Is it okay if she joins us for lunch?"

"Of course. That'd be . . . wonderful."

"Helen, there's just one thing. She's twenty-five."

And there she was, locked onto his arm, her great mane of black hair shining in the sun. Helen's dad seemed to have lost about thirty pounds and had a different, shorter haircut. Courtney was wearing a black linen shift with a wide red belt. Her high-heeled sandals were red too and made her taller than he was, which was about five ten. Her lips and nails were painted to match the belt and the shoes.

Helen was wearing a dress too, her best in fact: a mud-colored cotton print dress bought two summers ago at the Gap. She briefly considered crawling under the table.

Her father saw her and waved and pointed her out to Courtney, and Courtney waved too. Helen stood up and cranked her face into a smile. He opened his arms, and she let him hug her.

"How's my baby girl?" He kissed her. He stood back so that he could inspect her. "You look fabulous," he lied.

Helen shrugged. She had never known how to react to his compliments. Nor anyone else's, come to that. Her father turned to the lovely Courtney, who stood to one side, looking warmly on.

"Baby, I want you to meet Courtney Dasilva."

Courtney held out a tanned and elegant hand.

"Hi," Helen said, shaking it. "Great nails."

"Why, thank yoooou," Courtney said.

After a couple of glasses of Champagne, Helen started to feel better. They talked about the weather, New York in the heat and about SoHo, where Courtney wanted to get a loft.

When they ordered, Helen went first, opting for pasta. Then Courtney said all she wanted was an arugula salad with lemon juice. Her new svelte father ordered the striped bass, grilled, no oil.

While the waiter heaped a mortifying amount of spaghetti carbonara onto her plate, her father leaned nearer and said, "Guess where we're getting married?"

Helen wanted to say Vegas? Or Reno, or wherever it was you could get divorce papers out of a machine the very next day.

"I have absolutely no idea."

"Barbados." He took Courtney's hand, and Courtney smiled.

"Wow," she said. "Barbados. Wow."

"But only if you promise to come," said Courtney.

"Well, sure. I'm often cruising around down there, so why not?" Helen saw a flicker of hurt in her father's eyes and told herself to be nice. "You pay, I come." She beamed at them both and went on, "No, seriously, I'd love to. I'm really happy for you both."

Courtney seemed touched. "You're a biologist," she said. Boy, she was trying hard.

"Technically, at the moment, I'm, as they say, between jobs."

"And you're still up on Cape Cod?"

"Yup. Stranded on the Cape. Good a place as any to wash up."

"Why do you always put yourself down so much?" her father said. He turned to Courtney. "She's a brilliant wolf biologist. This Ph.D. thesis she's finishing is groundbreaking stuff. Helen lived among the wolves in Minnesota for a number of years."

"Not lived among, Dad. You make me sound like Mowgli. You hardly ever got to see the damn things. I just did research."

In fact, her father wasn't far wide of the mark. Whether her research was groundbreaking was debatable, but it was certainly one of the most intensive studies ever carried out into why some wolves kill livestock and others don't. It was about the issue of nature versus nurture, which had always intrigued her, and seemed to suggest that cattle killing was more learned than inherited.

"Anyway, enough of that," Helen said. "Courtney, tell me about you. You're a banker, right?"

"Uh-huh."

"And you're a psychologist."

"Well, I never practiced."

"Practice makes perfect, and you seem pretty perfect to me."

"Helen . . ." Her father put a hand on her arm. He was about to say something, then gave her a sad little smile instead.

Courtney said she needed to go to the bathroom. When she had safely gone, Helen's father said, "What's the matter with you, baby? There's no rule that says you have to hate her, you know."

"Hate her? What on earth do you mean?"

He sighed and looked away.

Helen felt her eyes suddenly fill up with tears. She reached out and put a hand on her father's arm. "I'm sorry," she said.

He took her hand in both of his and looked with great concern into her eyes. "Are you okay?" he said. "I worry about you."

She sniffed and fought back the tears. "I'm fine."

"Have you heard from Joel?"

She nodded and took a deep breath. "Yep. He wrote me."

No, she wasn't going to cry. Joel was thousands of miles away and it was all over, anyway. And here came dear Courtney, smiling with freshly glossed lips. She wasn't so bad. In fact there was something tough and sassy about her that Helen found appealing. Who knows, she thought, some day they might even be friends.

HELEN flew back to Boston that evening. It was getting on for ten o'clock by the time she'd driven down from Logan Airport in her ancient Volvo station wagon and swung east onto Route 6, which would take her up the Cape to Wellfleet.

The house she had lived in for the last two years was a rental on the bay side, a mile or so south of Wellfleet village. She still thought of it as Joel's house. She stopped beside her mailbox, but there was nothing in it. He hadn't written for over a month.

There was a light on at the Turners', who looked after Buzz when she was away. Buzz was a neutered scruff that Helen got from a dog pound in Minneapolis. His coat was shaggy now, but when she first saw him, he'd had a crew cut to rid him of a frightful infestation. He'd been the ugliest dog in the pound. Helen had to have him.

"Hiya, Trouble. How're you doing? Get down now. Get down."

Buzz jumped into the car while she thanked Mrs. Turner. Then Helen and Buzz drove down the last quarter mile to the house.

It was a big old place, clad in rotting white clapboard that rattled when the wind blew. It stood on its own like a beached ocean liner at the water's edge. It seemed yet more like a ship inside, paneled in narrow, darkly varnished tongue and groove. Upstairs, gable windows surveyed the bay like portholes.

Helen dumped her bag outside the door. She would take a quick walk along the shore to give Buzz a run. It was also an excuse to delay going inside. The house seemed so big and silent now that it was only she and the dog who lived there.

SHE and Buzz first came to the Cape on vacation in early June the summer before last. Her sister had rented a house for the season, a million-dollar place set high above the water, with its own staircase down to the beach. She invited Helen to stay.

Celia had married her college sweetheart, bright but boring Bryan, whose software company had just been bought out by a computer giant for a mind-boggling amount of money. Even before that they had been predictably happy and had produced a boy and a girl, Kyle and Carey. They lived in Boston.

Helen had spent the previous five years in the wilds of Minnesota. She had planned to stay for a week, then go back to Minneapolis to work on her thesis. But the week became two weeks, then the two weeks a month. They got on well, though her sister remained the enigma she always had been.

Nothing seemed to faze Celia. Not even Buzz eating her best straw hat. She did charity work, played elegant tennis and cooked like a dream. She never had headaches or sleepless nights.

One night after supper, when Bryan wasn't there and the kids were in bed, Helen asked her if their parents' divorce had been as traumatic for Celia as it had been for her.

Celia shrugged. "Oh, I was mad at them for a while. But you can't let these things get to you. It's their life after all."

After a month of swimming and reading on the beach, Helen grew restless. A friend in Minneapolis had given her the number of a friend called Bob who was working at the Marine Biological Laboratory at Woods Hole, down the Cape, and Helen called him.

He sounded nice and asked her if she would like to come to a party that weekend. She noticed Joel Latimer as soon as she walked into the party.

He looked like a Californian surf bum from the '60s, tall and thin and tanned, with a mop of sun-bleached blond hair.

It was a help-yourself-in-the-kitchen kind of dinner, and Helen found herself at the vegetarian lasagna alongside him.

"So you're the woman who runs with the wolves," he said.

"Actually it's more of a flat-footed stumble."

He laughed. He had the bluest eyes and the whitest teeth she'd ever seen. She felt something contract in her stomach and told herself not to be ridiculous. He wasn't even her type.

He helped her to some salad. "You're on vacation here?"

"Yes. I'm staying with my sister. Up at Wellfleet."

"Then we're neighbors."

Joel was from North Carolina, and she could hear it in his accent. He was doing a Ph.D. on horseshoe crabs, which he said weren't really crabs at all, but arachnids, distant cousins of the spider. They had been around for four hundred million years without changing.

"Sounds like my supervisor," she said. He laughed.

He told her that horseshoe blood had all kinds of important medical applications, even to diagnose and treat cancer. But they were a species under pressure, and here on the Cape eel fishermen killed them for bait. His research was to find out how serious an impact this was having on the local horseshoe populations.

When they said good-bye, he asked if she would like to meet some horseshoe crabs, and far too promptly she said she would. He said how about tomorrow, and she said fine.

Within a week they were lovers, and a week later Joel asked her to live with him. He said they were soul mates, that if she moved in, they could spend the winter side by side, writing their theses. Helen had never heard anything so romantic in all her life.

It was as close to shocking Celia as she had ever come.

"You're going to live with him? After knowing him only two weeks?" she said, watching her pack.

"Sister, if a girl can't find Mr. Right, sometimes she's got to settle for Mr. Right Now."

Since her parents' divorce, Helen seemed to have this uncanny knack of picking the most unsuitable men available. Quite why she chose so badly, Helen had never been able to figure out. Perhaps because deep down she was sure no man could ever possibly see anything in her. For it was rarely Helen who ended the affair. She stuck in there, striving desperately for their approval, until they drifted off or started cheating on her.

For weeks after she'd moved in, she was certain that tomorrow this gentle, golden man would tell her it had all been a mistake and would she please pack her bags, take her dog and get out of his life.

But it didn't happen. And after a while she relaxed. And soon it seemed as if they weren't even separate people.

She found herself telling Joel more about her work than she had ever told anyone, and he made her realize that she was good; hell, she was brilliant.

As fall gave way to winter, she came to accept that Joel loved her and she must therefore be lovable. He told her she was beautiful, and for the first time in her life she felt she was.

Joel had just discovered opera, which Helen had always claimed to hate. Then he caught her one day humming something from *Tosca* in the bathtub, and she was forced to admit that some of it was bearable. Not as good as Sheryl Crow, but not bad.

They moved the long kitchen table into the living room, by the big bay window, setting up their laptops on it and piling it high with papers.

That winter, for the first time in years, snow fell heavily and stayed for the best part of a month. The bay froze over, and from the frosted window they watched it stretching away like tundra to a gray horizon. Joel said they were like Zhivago and Lara, marooned in their palace of ice. All they needed, he said, were some of her Minnesota wolves to howl for them at night.

The spring and summer were the happiest of Helen's life. Sometimes at night they would hike through the woods to a freshwater pond and swim naked, the black water still warm from the sun.

Then, the second fall, things began to change.

They had long disagreed about the issue that lay at the heart of Helen's research: nature versus nurture. Joel believed the actions of any living creature were almost entirely conditioned by its genes, while Helen thought learning and circumstance often counted just as much. They had debated the subject endlessly and amicably. Now when it arose, Joel would get impatient, and one evening he shouted at her and said she was stupid. He later apologized, and Helen made light of it. But she felt hurt for days.

As the new year settled in, Helen became aware of a growing restlessness in him. She felt that everything she did was being silently judged and found wanting. He would suddenly get up and say he was going for a walk, and Helen would sit there, wondering what she had done and blaming herself.

In bed one night, staring at the dark ceiling, Joel said he wanted to do something worthwhile with his life.

"Saving a few crabs isn't really going to change things. Helen, all over the world people are starving and slaughtering each other. What do a few crabs mean alongside all of that?"

She suddenly felt very cold.

One night in late April he told her over supper that he had applied to a foreign aid charity to go and work for them in Africa. They wanted to interview him. Helen tried not to look hurt.

"Oh," she said. "That's great."

"It's only a year, Helen. It'll go so fast." He wouldn't look at her.

The following week he flew to Washington for the interview, and they called the next day to say they wanted him to start in June.

It was a long while before they could talk about it or about anything. Outside, the air was growing warm, but in the house winter endured. A cool politeness had settled, under which Joel stifled his guilt and she her anger.

Then anger gave way, and creeping upon her came that same old sense that, yet again, she had failed. She had given all and still been found wanting.

Two

H E HAD been gone, now, for nearly two months.

Helen called Buzz and walked back along the shore.

She picked up her bag outside the back door and nudged Buzz into the kitchen. She didn't turn the lights on. There was too much of Joel everywhere. Books, a pair of boots, all his opera CDs. Since he had gone, she hadn't trusted herself to listen to music of any kind.

The answering machine showed there were three messages. She listened to them in the dark. One was from her father, hoping she'd gotten home safely. The second was from Celia, just to say hi. And the third was from her old wolf buddy, Dan Prior.

They'd had a brief fling one summer when they were tracking together in northern Minnesota. He'd been a rare exception to the catalog of jerks she normally dated, but it had still been a mistake. They were cut out to be friends, not lovers. And like all the best men, Dan was happily married.

They hadn't talked in about three years, and it was good to hear his voice. He said he had a job for her in Montana. Would she please give him a call. Helen looked at her watch. It was a quarter of one. And she remembered that it was her birthday.

DAN Prior stood looking toward the gate, unaware of the giant Alaskan brown bear that towered behind him. The first disgruntled passengers from Salt Lake City were emerging. The flight had been delayed, and Dan had been there an hour, which wasn't as long as the bear, who'd been shot in 1977, stuffed, and set here on his hind legs to scare all visitors to Great Falls.

Dan had spent most of the weekend cleaning up the cabin in which Helen would be living and trying to fix the carburetor of an old Toyota pickup he'd found for her to use. The cabin belonged to the Forest Service and stood beside a small lake way up in the wilderness above Hope.

Dan wondered if Helen still looked the same. He'd dug out a photograph the other night, taken five years ago in northern Minnesota, when they were working together. She was sitting in the front of a canoe and giving him one of those slow, sly smiles of hers. Her eyes were a clear golden brown. She was wearing that old white T-shirt with DANGER: ALPHA FEMALE in red letters on it. Her long brown hair had gone blond in the sun. Dan had forgotten how stunning she was and sat staring at the picture for a long time.

He had always been attracted to her. It wasn't just her looks. He loved her quick wit, that spiky sense of humor. She also happened to be the smartest wolf biologist he'd ever worked with.

What had happened between them didn't really qualify as an affair. At the time, he'd been running a wolf research program at the university and Helen was a volunteer. That one night, camping by a lake under a star-riddled sky, was the only occasion Dan had been unfaithful to Mary since they'd been married. It had taken him a while to get over Helen, but he had, and they'd remained friends.

Now he wondered if there might be a chance of rekindling things, at the same time telling himself not to be stupid.

Then he saw her coming out of the gate. Helen saw him and waved. She was wearing jeans and a baggy beige army shirt. The only real change was the hair, which was cut short, like a boy's.

They gave each other a hug. "Welcome to Montana," he said.

"Thank you, sir." She leaned back, still holding on to him, and inspected him. "You're looking okay, Prior. Power and success don't seem to have changed you."

"It's good to see you, Helen. What happened to your hair?"

"Don't. I did it last week. Big mistake."

They picked up Helen's bags at the baggage claim area—two duffel bags and a battered trunk—and loaded them onto a cart.

"Is that it?" Dan asked.

She gave him a guilty look. "Well. Almost."

An airline employee was making his way toward them with a crate that was barking loudly. Helen bent down and opened the cage door, and one of oddest-looking dogs Dan had ever laid eyes on came out and started washing Helen's face.

"This is Buzz."

"Funny, Helen, I don't recall you mentioning Buzz."

"I know. Sorry. Isn't he cute?"

"Yeah, well. Let's hope that wolf thinks so."

SHE kept the window down in Dan's car as they headed south on the interstate toward Helena. Buzz sat blinking and licking at the hot wind with his head out the window, behind her head.

"How's Mary?"

"She's fine. We got divorced three years ago."

"Oh, Dan, I'm sorry."

"I'm not and she sure isn't. Ginny's fourteen now. Mary's living in Helena, so Ginny gets to spend time with us both." He paused. "How about you? I mean, have you . . ."

"Don't be shy, Prior. You mean how's my love life?"

"No. Okay, yeah."

"Well, we've been together just over two years now. He's got long sandy hair, brown eyes, doesn't say a whole lot. And he's got this thing about thwacking the back of your legs with his tail."

Dan smiled.

"No. I was living with a guy for a couple of years on the Cape. But he's, well, I guess you'd say it's on hold."

She swallowed and looked out the window. Dan, bless his heart, changed the subject. He filled her in on all that had happened since the wolf had first shown his face in Hope almost a month ago. Since then, he said, things had quieted down, but just two days ago a Forest Service ranger hiking east of Hope had reported finding tracks.

At the office he introduced Helen to Donna, who said it was great that at long last Dan had seen sense and hired a woman.

Dan sent out for sandwiches, and he and Helen spent the next couple of hours going through what she would be doing. Helen's job was to trap wolves, fit collars and then track to find out what was going on. Bill Rimmer had volunteered to help her set the traps. The other important thing was to try to build a rapport with the local ranchers.

"Do I get a truck or is it just a bicycle?"

He laughed. "I'll show you. Want to take a drive out to Hope and have a look at the town? We can do the cabin tomorrow."

"Sounds good."

They went out to the parking lot and stopped by the old Toyota pickup. In the sunshine it didn't look too bad. He slapped the hood affectionately, and the side-view mirror fell off. Helen laughed.

Dan picked up the mirror and handed it to her. "I can only give you mileage. Thirty-one cents a mile."

"Gee, Prior, you sure know how to spoil a gal."

She drove, following Dan's directions, heading toward the mountains. On either side of the road the land stretched away as far she could see, cropped a pale gold and scattered with hay bales. Both sky and earth seemed immense, the roads ran straight and purposeful to ranches confidently placed. She found herself both thrilled and daunted and somehow inconsequential to it all. And she thought of Joel, as she still did a dozen times each day, and wondered whether he felt anchored in his new world or detached as she now was in hers.

As the mountains loomed larger, the land before them crumpled into a badlands sprawl of rocky bluffs, sliced by scrub-filled creeks. Cresting a hill, she saw a line of cottonwoods converging from the south and, through their foliage, the glint of water.

"That's the Hope River," Dan said.

The blare of a horn made them both jump. Looking at the river, Helen had let the pickup wander, and in the mirror now she saw there was a black truck right behind them, pulling out to pass. As it drew alongside, Helen turned and beamed her sweetest apology at the two inscrutable young cowboy faces that surveyed her. Dan gave a friendly wave. The passenger touched the brim of his hat and almost smiled, while the driver just shook his head and drove on by.

"You know them?"

Dan nodded. "They're Abe Harding's boys. They ranch a little spread up near the Calder place. You'll be neighbors."

Helen looked at him. "There's me off to a great start."

"Don't worry, it's not your driving they'll hate you for. See the bumper sticker?"

Leaning forward, she could make out a wolf's head crossed out in red and the words NO WOLVES, NO WAY, NO WHERE.

"Terrific."

The road followed the river for another four miles until Helen saw a white clapboard church on a low hill, then other buildings above the trees. A narrow bridge crossed the river, and there was a sign saying HOPE (POPULATION 819), after which some cryptic soul had added three clean bullet holes of perfect punctuation, consigning both town and people to a state of perpetual suspense.

Crossing over the bridge, Dan pointed ahead. "Take that turn."

She pulled off the road and stopped in a gravel parking lot.

"Come on," Dan said. "I'll show you something."

They left Buzz in the pickup and walked into a small park that stretched beside the river. It was a pretty place, its grassy slopes kept lush by sprinklers making rainbows in the sun. There were swings and a climbing frame for children, but those there now were playing chasing games through the sprinklers.

Dan led the way along a path that snaked from the parking lot to the church on the hill at the end of the park. He stopped and picked up something small and white and handed it to her.

"It's like a piece of shell or something."

He shook his head and pointed to the ground. There were flecks of it along the edge of the path, like a snowy residue.

"Sometimes you can find bigger pieces," he said. "The soil must be full of it. I guess that's why the grass grows so well."

"What is it then?"

"It was from an old road that was here once. It's wolf bone. The road was paved with wolf skulls."

She looked at him, thinking he must be kidding.

"It's true. Thousands of them."

And while the children played on among the sprinklers, Dan told her how there came to be a road of skulls.

THE valley had been a special place for wolves since ancient times. Honored as a great hunter by the Blackfeet, who had long lived here too, the wolf knew it as a winter shelter for deer and elk and as a passage from the mountains to the plains where, in great packs, he trailed herds of buffalo. By 1850 the white man had begun his grand massacre of these herds. At first this made life easier for the wolf, for all the hunters wanted was mainly the hide. Wolves could dine in style on what was left.

Then, from across the eastern ocean, came a great demand for wolfskin coats. Like thousands of others all across the West, the trappers of Hope turned to wolfing.

A bottle of strychnine crystals cost seventy-five cents, and it took two to lace a buffalo carcass. In the right spot it could kill fifty wolves in a single night. A winter's poisoning might net you two or three thousand dollars.

A line of bait might stretch for many miles and was laid in a circle. When they rode its circumference the next morning, the wolfers would find it littered with the dead and dying of any bird or beast that had happened across it.

When winter tightened its grip and the daily harvest froze too hard for skinning, the wolfers stacked the bodies in the snow like firewood. The year of 1877 saw one of the longest freezes Hope had ever known. By March more than two thousand unskinned wolves were piled above the wolfers' caves and around the cabins where they lived.

Then one morning there came a whisper of warmth in the air. The wolfers, frantic with the fear of a whole season's loss, set to work with their snicker-snack knives. By sunset every stockpiled wolf in the village was skinned and not a pelt lost, and the wolfers of Hope, giddy with triumph, danced in a mire of melted snow and blood.

For years they had dumped their skinned carcasses beside the river to be picked clean by ravens and buzzards, many of which promptly died from the strychnine. Now, as a monument to their brave day's doing, the wolfers raked all the bones together and, along with the headless remains of those just skinned, laid the footings of a road. Then they took the heads and boiled them and cobbled the road with clean white skulls. From that day forth the skull of every wolf they killed was added, eventually winding their way more than half a mile.

By now the valley was filling with the moan of cattle, and the town grew proportionate with every herd that came. Blacksmith, barber, hotelier and whore, all thrived in their several ways. So too did Hope's wolfers.

Wolfing now was better paid than ever. There was a state bounty of a dollar for every wolf killed, topped up by cattlemen whose hatred of the species needed no prompting. For now that the buffalo was gone and the deer and elk grown scarce, wolves had acquired a taste for beef. Cows, moreover, were easier to kill.

In truth, the elements were always better and more brazen in their killing than the wolf had ever been. Yet why curse the weather or God when the devil himself was at hand? You could hear him each night out stalking the range and howling the stars from the sky. So the wolf became Hope's scapegoat.

The livestock industry gained huge political clout, and spurred by a rancher-president, the government took over the anti-wolf crusade. In 1915 the U.S. Biological Survey, the agency entrusted with nurturing the nation's wildlife, methodically went to work on a well-funded policy of absolute extermination. Just as the wolves had followed the buffalo across the plains, they now followed the buffalo, in a few short years, to the brink of extinction. Most of the wolfers drifted away. There was no longer a living to be made.

In Hope, however, with its great hinterland, some wolves lingered on. They hid high in the forests, too wise and wary to be caught by a crassly poisoned carcass. They could smell a poorly set trap from half a mile. To catch these animals, a man had to be more than cunning; he had to think like a wolf.

And there was only one left in Hope who did.

Joshua Lovelace first came to the valley from Oregon in 1911, attracted by a new state law that increased the bounty on wolves to fifteen dollars. He was so much more skilled than any of his rivals that the local cattlemen's association hired him full-time.

He was a taciturn man who guarded closely the secrets of his profession, but was known for two trademarks. The first was that he never used poison, saying it was only for imbeciles who didn't care what they killed. Wolfing, to him, was an art of the utmost precision. His second trademark was a working illustration of this, a device he had invented and for which he had applied, unsuccessfully, for a patent. He called it the Lovelace loop.

It consisted of a circle of thin steel wire, some fifty feet in length, to which were attached, on traces of thinner wire, a dozen spring-loaded hooks. Each hook was baited with a bite-size piece of meat—Joshua's personal preference was chicken. The loop would then carefully be laid around the outside of the den and anchored with an iron stake.

For optimum results the loop needed to be laid between three to four weeks after the mother had given birth in the spring. At the age of three weeks a wolf pup's milk teeth broke through. Then he would venture out into the world ready to eat small morsels of meat. Joshua prided himself on knowing the exact moment that the loop should be laid. He wanted his chicken to be the pups' first taste of meat. And their last.

He would lay it as the sun was starting go down, then retire to some high place and keep watch with an old army telescope. Normally they came out of the den when it was too dark to see, and you only knew you'd got one from the squeal they made when the triple-hook snapped open in their throats. At dawn you would find five or six pups, hooked like fish, around the den. More often than not their mother would be there, nuzzling and licking them, all her wariness lost in distress.

And therein lay the beauty of the loop. For if you were smart and didn't go blundering in at first light, you could shoot the adults one by one as they came home from their night's hunting. Then go in and finish the pups off with an axe or the butt of your gun.

Lovelace eventually married a woman much younger than himself, who died a year later, giving birth to their only child. The boy was christened Joseph Joshua but was known simply by his initials.

By the time J.J. was born, Lovelace had virtually put paid to Hope's wolves, and his reputation had spread. He had offers of work from far afield, wherever wolves persisted. Almost as soon as J.J. could walk, Joshua took him on his travels and taught him about killing. For the next seventeen years the two of them went wherever there was a wolf that no one else could catch. When the traveling became too much for his father, J.J. worked alone and, once wolves were protected by law, in greater secrecy.

The site of the old wolfers' camp in Hope remained so toxic that for many years the county fenced it off. Then bulldozers came to level the land for a park.

Indian folklore had it that the spirits of all America's slaughtered wolves lived on, gathered on some far-off mountain beyond the white man's reach. Awaiting a time when they might safely walk again upon the earth.

Three

LUKE Calder leaned back in his chair and waited while his speech therapist rewound the videotape. She had just taped him reading a page of *This Boy's Life*. He had managed it with only one block, and although it was a big one, he felt pleased with himself.

"Okay, kiddo, let's have a look."

Joan Wilson had been helping him with his stutter for about two years now. She was a tall, genial woman, maybe a few years older than his mother. Luke looked forward to her weekly visits. She covered some of the more remote schools in the area, but during school vacations he came to see her. Every Wednesday morning he drove himself to this private clinic.

On the video screen, Luke was doing pretty well, sailing through words that often knocked him flat—M words and P words like music and Paris. But as he came up to the M of Moulin Rouge, he took a great gulp of air and his mouth pushed forward and he started to blink.

"Okay, let's stop it there." Joan pressed PAUSE and froze Luke in mid-blink. "You saw the words coming."

"Yeah. It's no b-big deal. I just wish I didn't b-blink like that."

She played the tape again and showed him where he was tensing up. She got him to say the phrase several times over and think about what his tongue and his jaw were doing as he said it. Then she got him to read the whole thing again, and although there were a couple of blocks and repetitions, he didn't blink once.

"See?" Joan said. "You were right. No big deal."

He shrugged and smiled. Talking with Joan didn't count. Just like it didn't count when he talked with animals. It wasn't like the real world where words had such terrifying importance. Where his father would ask him a simple question, and he would completely seize up. Where a little word like milk or butter or bread could raise a hurricane. Apart from Joan there was only one person in the world he could talk with easily, and that was his mother. She was the only one who didn't look away when he got into trouble. She just waited patiently, and the tension would slip out of him like water from a tub. It had always been like that.

After the video work it was ten o'clock, and the session was over. They both stood up, and she walked him out to the lobby.

"Are you still planning on putting college off till next year?"

"Uh-huh. My dad thinks it's a g-good idea."

"And what do you think?"

"Oh, I don't know. I g-guess so."

Joan peered at him as if something in his face might show this to be a lie. She knew about him and his father, and she clearly believed his father was largely to blame for his stutter. When Luke had first told her he wasn't going straight to college that fall, she'd gotten all worked up and said that the sooner he got away, the better he and his stutter would be.

She was probably right. He knew full well why his father wanted him to do a year's work on the ranch before going to college. Luke had his heart set on studying wildlife biology at the University of Montana in Missoula, a place his father thought infested with liberals and "bunny huggers." He wanted Luke to follow Kathy's example and do agribusiness management at rancher-friendly Montana State, in Bozeman, and was hoping that a year of practical ranching might make his son see sense.

Luke was happy enough to go along with it, though for an entirely different reason. It meant he could go on watching the wolves. And if the need arose, as he feared it might, perhaps he would be able to protect them.

THERE was no one to be seen when he got back to the ranch, though everyone would soon be coming in for lunch. Wednesday, after his session with Joan, was now the only day he got to eat with the others. Every other day, since his father had given him the job of riding the herd up on the allotment, he just took sandwiches and ate them on his own. It suited Luke just fine.

He headed up to his room to change so he could ride out directly after eating. It was really two rooms knocked into one. The other half, through an open archway, had been his brother's. Over the years Luke had colonized some of it, but Henry was still very much present. Some of his clothes still hung in the closet. There were shelves crammed with his high school photographs, sport trophies and hunting magazines.

The shelves in Luke's half of the room were cluttered with things he had picked up in the mountains: rocks, gnarls of old wood, fossilized fragments of dinosaur bone, bear claws, feathers and skulls.

There were books about animals of almost every kind. Hidden among them were the ones about wolves.

Luke had an hour to kill before the others showed up for lunch, so he decided to do some of Joan's voice exercises. He lay down on his bed and closed his eyes and began to let words, any words, whatever came into his head, float out into the world.

After a while his voice grew slow. He fell asleep, and the silence regathered, stirred only by the lowing of a distant calf.

It was how the house mostly was nowadays. Silent and empty of all but memories. It had been that way since Luke's sisters had moved out—first Lane, who had married a real estate agent from Bozeman, then Kathy.

You noticed it most of all in the living room. It was a large room, with a broad-plank cedar floor, walls of swirled white plaster and a stone hearth at its far end. The walls were hung with samplers and tapestries, stitched by Luke's Calder grandmother and her mother before her. Here too, as well as photographs of all the Henry Calders, were the antique wall clocks that Luke's mother had once collected. All of these clocks were now silent. They had been that way since Henry's death.

Of greater significance, for Luke at least, were the mounted heads of animals killed by four generations of Calders, all of whom had been great hunters. His brother had shot his first elk at the age of ten, which was both illegal and a great source of pride to his father. One of Henry's favorite tricks was to toss his hat onto its antlers from across the room. It hung there still.

Luke had always found these trophies disturbing. He wasn't afraid of them. He'd never been afraid of any animal. All that Luke had ever feared in animals was their judgment. He saw the wrongs they suffered at man's hands and knew, by virtue of his own strictured tongue, how it felt to be unable to speak out against oppression.

He helped with jobs that his conscience abhorred, such as holding calves down at branding time while the smoke of their seared flesh filled his nostrils with nausea. He ate meat, although its taste and texture often made him want to gag.

To find favor with his father, he had even gone hunting and in so doing achieved the opposite.

Luke was thirteen when his father asked him if he wanted to try for his first elk. He had been dreading the invitation, while at the same time feeling hurt that it had taken so long to come.

His father carried the .270 Winchester, the same weapon that Henry had used to fell his first elk. In practice a few days earlier Luke had hit the target time after time. His father had been thrilled.

"You shoot darn near as straight as your brother," he said.

At the lip of the canyon they crawled into the sheltered hollow of an old pine and peered between its lowest branches. His father handed him the binoculars.

Across the canyon there was a herd of maybe twenty elk cows. A solitary bull with five-point antlers was nibbling bark in a stand of quaking aspen. He was less than two hundred yards away.

"Not a six-point like Henry's, but he'll do," his father whispered, as Luke handed the binoculars back.

"M-m-maybe we should w-w-wait till we find a s-s-six-point."

"Are you crazy? That's a fine animal. Here." His father carefully passed the rifle. "Take your time, son. Take it real slow now."

His father helped him ease the barrel out through the gap. Luke pressed the butt of the rifle into his shoulder and put his eye to the scope. The eyepiece felt clammy against his skin. Then he saw the bull. He was tugging a piece of bark from a sapling. The intimacy of the scope was shocking. Luke could see the grinding of the jaws as the elk chewed, the liquid black eyes, droplets of melted snow on his nose.

"He looks k-k-kind of young to have his own herd. M-m-maybe there's a b-b-bigger bull around somewhere."

"Hell, Luke, if you won't take him, I will."

Half of Luke's brain screamed at him to hand his father the gun. But the other half assessed this moment for what it was, a final chance to *be* something in his father's eyes. He must take this creature's life for his own to have any value.

He was breathing fast, and his heart was pumping so hard he

could feel his blood pulsing against the eyepiece of the scope. The crosshairs moved on the elk's head and body like a yo-yo.

"Easy now, son, easy. Take a deep breath."

He felt his father's eyes on him, judging him. Comparing him, no doubt, with how Henry had been that day.

"You've still got the safety on, Luke."

With twitching fingers Luke clicked it off. The elk turned his head and seemed to look directly into the lens of the scope.

"Has he seen us?"

His father was looking through the binoculars. "He's sure gotten a whiff of something. If you're going to do it, Luke, do it now. Take him just behind the shoulder."

Luke swallowed. "I know." The blood was roaring in his ears. It was as if the elk was staring into the darkest corners of his heart. And finding there perhaps a glimpse of death, the animal jerked in alarm and began to move away. Luke pulled the trigger.

The elk jolted and stumbled. The herd of cows erupted and headed as one for the cover of the trees.

"You got him!"

The bull was on his knees, but then he stood again and moved off in a broken, uncertain run through the aspens. Luke's father was pushing himself headfirst out of the tree hole. "Come on!"

Luke followed. His father took the rifle and set off down the slope, wading strongly through the snow with the rifle held high. Luke followed in his tracks, half-blinded by the sun, and all the time saying to himself, Oh, God, please don't let me have done this, and if I have, please let him live. Please let him get away.

When they got to the stand of aspen, they followed the bull's blood up into a ribbon of pine that fringed the foot of the canyon wall.

They heard the elk before they saw him, a low, throaty scream, like a broken door creaking in the wind. From the tracks it seemed that the elk had stumbled and disappeared over a ledge of rock. Luke's father edged his way along it and peered down.

"Here's your baby, Luke. You got him in the neck."

Luke felt his chest contract. The elk's screaming was so terrible

that he had to fight not to block his ears. Dreading what he was going to see, he came alongside his father and peered down. The
ground fell away steeply in a tumble of sliprock. About halfway
down, a dead tree had snagged the elk's fall, and he lay wedged there,
watching them, his hind legs thrashing in the air. There was a dark
hole in his neck, and his shoulder and chest ran slick with blood.

His father racked another bullet into the chamber and handed
him the rifle. "There you go, son. You know what to do."

Luke took it and, as he did so, felt his mouth quiver and the tears
flood in his eyes. He tried to stop it but he couldn't, and his whole
body started to shake with sobs. "I c-can't."

"You've got to do it. He won't be yours unless you do."

"I don't w-w-want him!"

"Come on, Luke. He's in pain—finish the job."

"I can't!" He handed back the rifle.

"A hunter finishes what he's started."

"I'm not a hunter!"

His father looked down at him for a long moment. Then, in what
looked more like sadness than anger, his father shook his head and
took the rifle. "No, Luke. I don't think you are."

His father shot the elk through the neck again, and they watched
it jerk and kick its legs in the air. Then, with its eyes never leaving
them, it stiffened and gave a long, gurgling sigh and was still.

But that wasn't the end of it. They got a rope on the carcass and
pulled it out of the tree from below. And there his father made him
help skin it out and field dress it. They sawed off the head and then
cut the body into pieces so that they could pack it out. And Luke
wept in silence all the while.

They hung what they couldn't carry from a high branch. And
when they left the place, Luke looked back and saw the gut piles
and the snow soaked wide with blood, and it occurred to him that
if there were indeed such a place as hell, this was how it must look
and where surely now he belonged.

The elk's head was never hung on the wall with the others. Perhaps his mother forbade it, after hearing what had happened. Even

now, five years later, he sometimes conjured it in his dreams, and he would wake whimpering and soaked with sweat.

THAT Wednesday morning Eleanor made her way along Hope's Main Street with her two sacks of groceries to where she had parked. She dumped the groceries into the back of her car and got in, wincing at the scald of the seat through her cotton dress. She was about to start the engine when she noticed the FOR SALE sign was still in the window of Ruth Michaels's gift shop across the street.

It was about a month ago when Kathy mentioned that Paragon was for sale and suggested Eleanor should consider buying it. Finding projects for her mother to get involved in was one of her favorite pastimes.

"Ruth doesn't want out," Kathy said. "She's just borrowed too much. You could buy into the business and let her go on running the place. Be involved as much or as little as you wanted."

Eleanor had thought about it. With both girls married and Luke soon off to college, she could do with something to fill the void.

She didn't know Ruth Michaels, except to say hello to, but had always thought she seemed bright and pleasant. On the few occasions Eleanor had gone into the shop, she had been impressed. It wasn't the usual western tourist trash—plastic dream catchers, snowshakers and jokey cowboy T-shirts. Ruth had taste. You could see it in the selection of jewelry, books and artwork.

Before she had finally made up her mind, Eleanor found herself crossing the street. There were bells on the door that clanked when it opened and closed. In the shadowed clutter of the shop it was cool and calm, and soothing music floated on the air along with a rich smell of coffee. There was no one to be seen.

There were clunking and hissing noises coming from the rear of the shop, where the cappuccino bar was, and as Eleanor got nearer she heard Ruth's voice.

"Do it, you stupid jerk! *Do* it!"

Suddenly the huge chrome coffee machine on the counter erupted with a terrifying squall of steam.

"Hello?" Eleanor said tentatively. "Is that Ruth?"

"Not if you're from the bank or the IRS, it isn't."

Ruth's head lifted into view above the machine. When she saw Eleanor, her eyes seemed briefly to fill with panic, then she beamed.

"Mrs. Calder! Hi! I'm sorry, I didn't hear you. What can I do for you? Can I make you a coffee?"

"Not if it's going to explode."

"Oh, he only behaves badly when he thinks no one's here."

"Do you have decaf?"

"You bet. Please, take a seat."

Eleanor sat on a stool while Ruth coaxed two cappuccinos from the machine. She was wearing faded jeans and a baggy purple T-shirt emblazoned with the shop's name. Her black hair was bundled up in a red bandanna. Eleanor guessed she must be in her mid to late thirties and was struck by how attractive she was.

"So have you found a buyer yet?" Eleanor asked. "Kathy said you were hoping to find a partner to come in with you."

Ruth placed Eleanor's coffee in front of her. "Nobody's interested."

Eleanor sipped her coffee. It tasted good. Go on, she told herself, say it. She put the cup down. "Well," she said. "I might be."

BUCK figured the calf must have been dead a few days. There wasn't a whole lot left of it. The remains were lying exposed at the top of a steep gully, and what the birds and varmints hadn't taken, the sun had baked stiff. Nat Thomas, the local vet, was having a hard time working out what had happened.

He was kneeling beside it, probing with his knife and forceps. Nat and his father before him had been vets to the Calder ranch, and Buck had called him right away. He wanted to get an independent opinion before the feds got their hands on the carcass.

Buck didn't like the guy from Fish & Wildlife, Prior. The other one, Rimmer, the predator control fellow, seemed okay, but when it came to the crunch, feds were wolf lovers, every one of them.

Buck was standing with Clyde, his son-in-law, looking over Nat's shoulder. Buck was sweating in the shimmering noon heat.

It was Clyde who had found the calf this morning. What riled Buck was why Luke hadn't found it earlier. He had given the boy the job of riding the herd up here on the allotment as soon as Prince, Kathy's dog, got killed. If there were wolves around, someone needed to keep an eye on the cattle, and as Luke knew the lay of the land up here and wasn't a whole lot of use at much else, it might as well be him. How Buck was ever going to make a half-decent rancher out of him, he had no idea.

"Well, Nat, how long's he been dead?"

"Oh, three, four days maybe."

"Reckon it was a wolf?"

"Well, he's been chewed up real good. Could be he was already dead, or he could have been struck by lightning, anything—"

"Struck by lightning. Give me a break, Nat." Buck felt a surge of anger. He knew in his bones that a wolf was to blame, probably one of those varmints the feds had let loose in Yellowstone.

"So Nat, are you prepared to back me on it being a wolf?"

The vet stood up and scratched his head. Buck could see how uncomfortable he was, being put on the spot. "It's a tough call."

Buck put his arm around the vet's shoulders. "Nat, I don't want to put words in your mouth. But you know these bunny huggers. They'll do all they can to pretend it isn't one of their precious wolves that did it. All I want is a little ammunition."

"Well, maybe."

"What are you saying, ninety percent certain it was a wolf?"

"That's pushing it, Buck."

"Eighty?"

"Well, I dunno. Maybe."

"Seventy-five, then. Okay." Buck took his arm off the vet's shoulders. "Well, thank you, Nat. I appreciate it, old buddy."

Nat said he was running late and had better go. Buck knew the poor fellow didn't fancy being around when the feds got here. Buck slapped him on the back, and they set off down the hill.

"I'll drive you down. Come on, Clyde, let's go call the bunny huggers."

"LUKE? ARE YOU coming to eat?"

Luke opened his eyes and saw his mother standing beside the bed. He sat up and swung his legs off the bed.

"Yeah. I must have dropped off."

He could see in her eyes that something was wrong. "What's the matter?"

She looked away and sighed. "Clyde found a dead calf. Your father's making a big thing of it."

"W-where? Up on the allotment?"

She looked at him and nodded.

"And he thinks it's a w-w-wolf?"

"Yes. So does Nat. Come on, let's get it over with."

He followed her out. How on earth had Clyde found it?

Luke had come across the carcass two days ago. There were fresh wolf tracks in the dust and some scat too. He dragged the calf to the gully and covered it with rocks. He brushed away the tracks, then got rid of the droppings. He figured no one was going to know anything until the fall, when the cattle came down and got counted.

As he walked toward the kitchen doorway, Luke could hear them all chatting. Clyde was laughing with Ray and Jesse, two hands who were helping with the haying, but he stopped as soon as Luke stepped into the room. Everyone looked up at him. His father was sitting at the head of the table.

"Hi, Luke," Clyde said. "Come and eat. It's getting cold."

Luke sat next to Ray, who gave him a nod. Luke knew his father was looking at him, but he kept his own eyes on his plate.

"So, Luke," his father said. "You heard we found a dead calf."

"Yes, sir. W-w-where did you f-f-find it?"

"The gully over by Ripple Creek," Clyde said.

The hands were concentrating hard on their food, sensing this was family business. His father's eyes hadn't once left him.

"I thought you said you checked along there every day," he said. "Nat Thomas reckons it was a wolf. That Prior fella's trying to get hold of Bill Rimmer to come up this afternoon. What bothers me is how many more dead calves have we got up there?"

"I d-d-don't think there are—"

"You wanted that job, Luke. If you're going to do it, you're going to have to do it properly. Okay?"

Luke nodded. "Y-y-yes, sir."

DAN had told Helen a lot about Buck Calder, but nothing he'd said had quite prepared her for the shock of the real thing. Dan had introduced them down at the house, and she and Buck had shaken hands. His hand was huge and cool, and he had held on to hers just a little too long, fixing her with those pale eyes. The gaze was so direct, so intimate, that Helen had found herself blushing.

Calder's son-in-law had called the office in Helena just as Helen and Dan were about to set off up to the cabin. They were packing the Toyota with Helen's gear and the ton of provisions they had bought at the supermarket. It was still all stacked in the back.

Now they were standing around this supposed wolf-kill. Bill Rimmer was on his knees, inspecting it, and Dan was videoing it. Facing them across the carcass, Calder and his son-in-law Clyde stood waiting for the verdict.

It was a farce. The calf was so far gone nobody could possibly say how it had met its end.

A horse snickered somewhere below them, and Helen looked down into the gully and saw Calder's son riding up toward them through the rocks. They had passed him on his horse coming up here, and Dan had told her who he was. She was struck immediately by how good-looking he was.

Luke got off his horse when he was still some way off and stayed there. Helen caught him staring at her with those intense green eyes and she smiled, but he looked away.

Rimmer stood and took a long breath. "Well, I don't see how Nat can say this animal was killed by a wolf."

Calder shrugged. "Experience, I guess."

Rimmer ignored the insult. "There's not enough to go on."

"With all due respect, I reckon Nat Thomas's opinion is a sight more objective than others around here. You government fellows let these wolves loose, let them kill our pets and now our cattle, and then try and pretend they're not to blame."

"Sir, I—"

"Don't make an enemy of me, Prior. It's not a good idea." He looked away, and for a long moment no one spoke.

"Okay," Calder said at last and looked at Dan. "Okay. You tell me this young lady here is going to be working full-time on this." He tilted his chin in her direction.

"Yes, sir."

"Then she'd better do a good job and do it quick. Because I tell you, Mr. Prior, if I lose another calf, we may have to do something about it ourselves."

"Well, I don't need to remind you of the law—"

"No, sir, you sure don't."

IT TOOK Helen two days, with Dan's help, to unpack and get the cabin into some kind of livable condition. Compared with some places she had to stay in, it wasn't too bad. It was twelve feet square and built of logs, with a screened window in each wall. In one corner stood a potbellied stove with a top you could cook on. Dan had filled a box with firewood and given her a chain saw to cut more. There was also a Coleman gas stove with two burners.

"Hey, I can throw dinner parties," she said.

"Yeah, for your new friend Buck Calder."

On rickety shelves beside the stove were assorted cups, bowls and plates, all of them chipped and emblazoned with the Forest Service logo. The cracked enamel sink was rigged with a pitcher pump and drained into a slop pail below. The water was stored in a five-gallon plastic container you had to fill from the stream. In the opposite corner were two bunk beds. The only other pieces of furniture were an old wardrobe and a plain wooden table with two chairs.

The one luxury was the neat little Japanese generator that Dan had rigged outside the door so she could recharge her laptop, stereo and the cell phone Dan had supplied her with. Dan also set up a voice mail number for her.

Around back was a log-built outhouse and, beside it, a kind of improvised shower—a metal bucket with holes in the bottom.

The second afternoon Dan showed up with all the radio collars, trapping gear and some mapping software. That night he took her to Nelly's Diner. The diner was wallpapered with huge photo panoramas of the Rocky Mountains. Tablecloths of red-and-white check strove bravely to make the place cheerful.

The only waiter was a friendly giant named Elmer, with blue-tinted aviator glasses and long gray hair tied in a ponytail. The tattoos and the black T-shirt with BIKERS FOR JESUS emblazoned on the front proclaimed him the owner of the Harley outside. When Helen and Dan had first walked in, he'd said, "Angels on your body." It took them a moment to realize it was a greeting.

They had spent most of the meal reminiscing about the good old days in Minnesota. No mention had been made of that one time they had briefly become more than just friends, and for this Helen was grateful—until Dan took a drink of beer and sat back.

"After Mary and I broke up, I nearly called you," he said.

"Oh?"

"Yeah. I thought about you a lot. And how, you know, that summer, if I hadn't been—"

"Dan, come on."

"I'm sorry."

"Don't be sorry." She took his hand across the table and smiled at him. "We're friends," she said softly. "And, right now, I really need a friend more than, well, more than anything else."

"I'm sorry." He let go of her hand.

Elmer loomed to the rescue, and they asked for coffee.

"You're the new wolf lady, huh?" he said.

"That's me. How did you know?"

He shrugged. "Whole town knows."

BUCK checked to make sure the road was clear both ways. If he ever saw another car when he reached her driveway, he would just keep on up the road.

Some time ago they had worked out a system. If she closed the curtains in the little window nearest the road, it meant she had company and he should drive on by. He was glad to see that tonight they were open.

Buck never had trouble finding an excuse to be away from home. There was always a meeting to attend or a neighbor to visit or a deal to do in town. On those rare occasions when things got tricky, there were always friends he could count on for cover. Mostly he didn't even have to lie, because Eleanor never asked where he was going, and she was always asleep when he got home.

The road was clear, and he parked around the back. The door to the house opened as he was getting out, and he saw her in her black bathrobe leaning against the doorframe, waiting for him. When he reached her, he kissed her.

"Ruth Michaels," he said. "You're the sexiest woman this side of the Missouri River."

"Oh, yeah? So who is it you're seeing on the other side?"

LATER, at home, as he shed his clothes for the second time that night, Buck wondered what in heaven's name Eleanor thought she was playing at, offering Ruth the money.

Ruth seemed to find it amusing. She'd broken the news about half an hour after he arrived, when they were lying sleepy and sated and he was thinking, for no particular reason, about that pretty young biologist all alone up there in the forest and wondering what his chances might be in that direction. As if to punish him for his thoughts, Ruth had said, almost matter-of-factly, that Eleanor was going to bail her out and become her business partner.

"Your business partner!"

Ruth laughed. "You know, when she came in, I was so nervous. I thought, Uh-oh, here it comes. She knows. But then she sits there with her cappuccino and offers me the money."

"Ruthie, I've told you, I'll give you the damn money."

"I couldn't take your money."

"But hers is okay?"

"Yes."

"Well, I don't get it."

"Well, Buck honey, you think about it."

He stood in the shower now while he considered things. He couldn't say a word, of course, until Eleanor chose to tell him. And after all, it was her money; her daddy had left it to her. But if it happened, it was bound to make life more complicated. Ruth, to his amazement, didn't seem to think it was a problem.

He dried himself in front of the mirror, routinely admiring his body and checking it for any mark she might have made on him. He was all clear. Then he flashed himself a smile, walked back to the bedroom and slipped into bed beside Eleanor.

As always, she was turned away and didn't so much as stir.

"Good night," he said softly. But there was no answer.

ELEANOR listened to him sighing and shifting and knew that in about five minutes he would settle on his back and start to snore. Sometimes, when she was sure he was asleep, she would turn quietly and lie studying him. Slackened by sleep, his upturned face was oddly childlike, almost touching. Eleanor would search her heart for some vestige of love and try to remember how it was to feel more for him than pity or contempt.

He was a skilled and thoughtful deceiver. Those he lay with never called him at home or smeared makeup on his clothes. And Eleanor, being spared much of the routine ignominy of the cheated wife, was a willing host to denial.

It was Kathy's birth that changed things.

Eleanor's waters broke two weeks early, when Buck was at a live-stock conference in Houston. Everything happened in such a rush that it wasn't until late that night, with the baby swaddled in her arms, that she called his hotel from her hospital bed and was put through to his room. A woman answered the phone, one to whom he obviously hadn't had time to explain the rules. Buck came home and came clean. For the sake of the children, Eleanor was prepared to forgive him for what he promised was his only transgression.

Then two commiserating friends made the mistake of thinking she should now hear about others Buck had bedded in the past few years, including some Eleanor had counted as friends.

She should have followed their advice and left him. But in some diminished corner of her heart she felt that Buck might yet be saved, though it would be three years before she allowed him to make love to her again. Not that she didn't want him. There were times when it took all her strength not to reach out and wake him.

It was in precisely this way that Luke was conceived. And during the months that followed, as their last child grew in her womb, Eleanor and Buck found a passion in their coupling that seemed to surprise and excite her as much as him. He was the only man who had ever made love to her, but not until then had she fully woken to him.

But, with the arrival of Luke, their passion ended. For Buck, she thought, it probably seemed merely like the end of another affair.

She lay listening to him now, wondering in whose bed he had been earlier. And doing her best, after all these years, not to care.

DAN escorted Helen to her pickup. She thanked him for a great evening and gave him a kiss on the cheek.

"Angels on your body," she said as she drove away.

"And on yours."

She headed out to where the pavement ended and turned onto the gravel road that led up the valley. It was the first time she had driven the route in the dark, and after leaving the main road near the top of the valley, there were no signs. At last, at the forest's edge, she found the row of five mailboxes, her own among them. Here the gravel road turned to dirt and wound through the forest for another four steep and rutted miles to Eagle Lake.

The lake lay in a shallow bowl of meadow half a mile long. The cabin stood on the bowl's western rim, some thirty yards from the water, at the top of a gentle slope that was divided by a stream.

Helen parked the old pickup beside the cabin, and while Buzz went off to forage, she leaned her back against the hood and looked up at the star-filled sky. There was no moon.

Tomorrow she would start the search for the wolf. She wondered where the animal was right now. Hunting somewhere, no doubt, stalking like a liquid shadow through the forest.

Perhaps she should howl, she thought, and see if she got an answer. Dan had always said that no wolf in Minnesota could resist returning her call. She hadn't howled in years, but she cleared her throat and tilted her face to the sky. The first and second howls sounded like a donkey with a sore throat. Then, on the third attempt, the low start rose in a slow, expanding, mournful curve and tailed away into the night.

All it found was an echo in some remote recess of the mountains. But the sound made Helen shiver. For in it she heard the cadence of her own bereft soul.

FALL

Four

THEY reached the ridge and stood shielding their eyes against the sun and squinting into the canyon that stretched away in a crooked arm below them. It was three weeks since Helen and Bill Rimmer had laid the traps. In this remote canyon where they now were, they had found wolf tracks and scat, though neither fresh. It seemed the most promising place, a rocky funnel down which any wolf traveling the divide might go, and they set ten of the twenty traps in and around it. The rest, with Buck Calder in mind, they laid along the two most likely routes down through the forest toward the allotments Calder and his neighbors leased for summer grazing.

Each trap was attached by a cord to a radio collar hidden nearby. As soon as the trap was dragged from the ground, the cord pulled a little magnet off and the collar would start to transmit a signal.

Helen set half of the traps and Rimmer the other half, and they bet a beer on who would catch the first wolf.

The result so far was that neither of them had.

She started to think that maybe she was doing something wrong. So after about ten days she moved the sets around and tried different kinds of places, not just alongside trails, but high on the ridge and down by the creek. It made no difference.

She'd loaded into her computer all the G.I.S. (Geographic Information System) software Dan had given her, and could now call up maps of the whole area. Onto these she entered the precise location of every trap and other useful information, such as sightings or signs of elk or deer or any other animal a wolf might be preying on—including the cattle on the allotments.

She knew it was important to keep busy. Whenever she stopped, thoughts of Joel might steal up behind her and grab her.

The nights were worst. It was usually dusk when she got back from checking the traps, and if her cell phone had recharged—it often didn't seem to want to—she would check her voice mail. Every time she hoped, foolishly, that she might hear Joel's voice.

She would feed Buzz, take a shower, cook supper and spend the evening on the computer, making notes and reading. And as it got dark and silence lowered itself like a murderer's pillow over the forest, it became harder and harder to keep Joel at bay.

He would creep into her body and hang like a deadweight inside the cavity of her chest until she couldn't bear it any longer. She'd storm out of the cabin and down to the lake, and sit there sobbing and hating herself and him and the whole wretched world.

By now she had visited with most of the local ranchers and done her best to charm them. Mostly those she met had been courteous and welcoming, and most gave her permission to go on their land if she needed to.

She had managed to see almost everyone except Abe Harding.

She had tried phoning his ranch but got no reply. Then she saw him in town one day and smiled and said hi, and he walked right past her as if she didn't exist. Harding's two boys were loading something into the back of their truck. She could see them smirking.

"Oh, don't worry about Abe Harding," Ruth Michaels said when Helen told her what had happened. "He's like that with everyone." Ruth said that Abe bought his place after coming back from Vietnam. Whether it was the war that gave him his wary, hunted look, Ruth could only guess.

Helen liked Ruth. Her wicked sense of humor always got Helen laughing, which was a good tonic. It was useful too to have someone who could fill her in on all the town characters.

As the weeks went by, Helen's failure to catch the wolf was becoming something of an embarrassment. People were starting to make wisecracks. Then yesterday she had found three traps sprung, and that's when she called Bill Rimmer and asked him to come out with her this morning.

The first two traps they checked in the canyon were just as Helen had left them last night. The next one had been sprung. She had set it at the side of a narrow dust trail. Rimmer picked it up carefully on the end of a stick and examined it.

"There's nothing wrong with the trap."

He put it down again and walked away, about twenty yards along the trail, his eyes fixed on the ground. Then he came back and went the same distance the other way.

"Come and have a look," he said. Helen walked over, and Rimmer pointed down at the trail. "See these deer tracks and how they just stop? Now look over here."

They walked past the trap to where Rimmer had first stopped. "See how the tracks start again here? That's the same animal, going in the same direction."

"Are you sure?"

"Yep. Whatever sprung the trap brushed the trail clean afterward. I've met some pretty smart wolves, but none that smart."

It was the same at the next trap. Then, at the third, they found wolf tracks and fresh scat right on top of the sprung trap.

Helen whooped. "Well, at least he's still around."

Rimmer frowned at the ground. "Yeah. But it was sprung before he came along. See these tracks here? Looks like he's just sauntered up, sniffed it, done his business, then gone on his way. The dust's been brushed. That's why you can see his prints so well."

Then Rimmer found a freshly broken piece of sagebrush, covered in dust. He held it up for her to see.

"Here's his broom. Somebody around here's playing games."

HOPE'S fairground had known better days. In times gone by the place had been busy all around the calendar with craft markets, gun shows and various parades and rodeos. The only event of any consequence that survived was the Hope Labor Day Fair and Rodeo, and even this had shifted to a Saturday in mid-September.

The fair had always climaxed with a concert, and this year's top of the bill was Rikki Rain and the Ragged Wranglers.

Eleanor sipped her iced tea beside one of the concession stands and watched her husband across the crowd. He had his arm around Rikki, and she was tossing back her peroxide curls and laughing raucously at something he'd said.

"Finest set of dentures I ever did see," Hettie Millward said, following Eleanor's gaze. They laughed. Hettie was her best friend, the only one who came close to understanding how it was between her and Buck. Doug, her husband, was a friend of Buck's and one of Hope's most popular and respected ranchers.

Eleanor changed the subject and asked Hettie about her daughter's wedding plans. Lucy was getting married next spring, and all of Hope was going to be invited. Hettie told her the latest idea was to have the whole ceremony conducted on horseback; then she left to find her two boys.

Eleanor finished her tea, then strolled along the row of exhibit booths. It had been her idea that Paragon should take a booth, and she was proud that one of her first suggestions as Ruth's new business partner had worked out so well. They had sold as much here in one day as they did in the shop in a whole week.

As she came up to the booth, she saw Ruth staring across the crowd, a strange almost angry expression on her face. Eleanor followed her gaze and saw that it must be Buck she was looking at. He was still making a fool of himself with that singer woman.

It was touching, Eleanor thought, that Ruth should care.

BUCK wished Rikki and the Wranglers all the best and said he'd see them after the show, although he wasn't so sure he would. Rikki had looked a whole lot better from a distance. And with his wife and his mistress like best buddies at the booth over there, life was complicated enough, thank you very much.

Buck saw Abe Harding's troubled face heading through the crowd toward him. That's all I need, Buck thought.

They'd been neighbors for thirty years and in all that time had never really gotten to know each other. You could fit Abe's place twenty times into the Calder spread. The land was a lot poorer too, and it was well known that Abe had borrowed too much money on it and was always on the brink of bankruptcy.

"Hi there, neighbor. How ya doin'?"

Abe nodded, eyes peering out from under a frowning shelf of eyebrow. "Buck, you know that wolf that killed your Kathy's dog?"

"Uh-huh. Reckon he had one of our calves too."

"So I heard. This wolf. He was a big black fella, right? Well, we've seen him again. And he had two others with him."

"Where?"

"Up on the allotment. We were up there and we heard this howl and then we saw them. This big fella and two gray ones."

"Were they going for the cattle?"

"No, but they sure as hell were thinking about it. If I'd had my gun with me, I'd have had 'em."

"Abe, you go shooting them, you could wind up in jail."

Abe didn't reply, just narrowed his eyes. "Thing is, we're going to bring the herd down early where we can keep a better eye on them. I was wondering if you'd mind lending a hand."

"Sure I will."

"Appreciate it. There'll be hell to pay if there's any missing."

LUKE HAD ONLY COME DOWN to the fair because he'd promised his mother he would. He didn't plan on staying long. Rikki Rain and the Ragged Wranglers were one good reason to leave. Another good reason was that Luke had just spotted a group of kids he had graduated with, including Cheryl Snyder, who he'd had a thing about all through high school. She was the only girl he'd ever properly kissed. Which at his age was downright pitiful.

She was one of the nicest and definitely the prettiest girl in the school. As a result, she was usually surrounded by the worst kind of guys, four of whom were now showing off to her and her friend Tina Richie outside the fortune-teller's tepee.

Luke was on his way back to the Paragon booth with some sodas for Ruth and his mother when he heard her call out.

"Luke! Hey, Luke!"

"Hi, Ch-Ch-Cheryl."

Tina and the others came up alongside her.

"I haven't seen you all summer," said Cheryl.

"Oh, well, I've been w-w-working on the ranch, you know." He watched their eyes, as he always did when he stuttered, for any hint of laughter or pity, which was the worst.

"Hey, Cooks, we saw you on the TV, when that wolf got your sister's dog," Tina said. Luke's nickname—some preferred Cookie or Cuckoo—came from the stabbing stutter he often got into when asked to say his name.

One of the boys, a loudmouth called Jerry Kruger, gave a howl.

"Have you seen it again?" Cheryl said.

"No. He was p-p-probably just p-p-passing through." Luke held up the sodas. "I'd better be g-g-going."

"Okay," Cheryl said. "See you around."

As he went off, Luke heard Kruger laugh and say, "P-p-probably just p-p-passing through" and the others telling him to hush.

IT WAS cooler now, and Helen wished she had brought a sweater. She was wearing hiking shorts and boots and a T-shirt.

Most of the people she had met over the past weeks were here at the fair, and with the exception of the Hardings, she'd chatted with all of them. Everyone had made a fuss of Buzz, who was having the time of his life.

She knew she should go, but she was reluctant to leave. It was partly, she realized, a simple hunger for human contact.

Observing the people of Hope on this sun-washed September afternoon, she had found herself moved by their sense of community, by the roots that seemed to hold them to this place and to a way of life that, despite years of tribulation and all the mad rushings of the world, endured in its essence unchanged.

The crowd was thinning now, and some of the booths were packing up. As she walked along, she spotted Luke Calder talking with his friends. She watched and listened unseen. His stutter came as a surprise. And when that idiot imitated him, she felt like slapping the kid. She was sure Luke must have heard. He was heading off through the crowd, and because it was the same way to the parking lot, she found herself following him. He stopped at the Paragon booth to say good-bye to his mother and Ruth. Then he went on toward the parking lot.

"Luke?"

He turned, and when he saw her, his eyes seemed to show alarm. Then he smiled nervously and touched his hat to her. "Oh, hi."

As she walked up to him, she realized he was a good six inches taller than she. Luke hunkered down to stroke Buzz.

"We haven't really had a chance to meet yet," Helen said. "I'm Helen." She held out her hand to him.

"Yeah, I kn-kn-know." He noticed her hand just as she was about to let it drop. "Oh, sorry, I d-d-didn't . . ." He straightened up and shook hands.

"And your new friend here is Buzz."

"B-Buzz. He's . . . cute."

"You're not staying for the music?"

"Oh. No. I've g-g-got some th-things to do. Do you like it?"

Helen frowned and scratched her head. "Well . . ."

Luke laughed, and his big green eyes softened, giving Helen a glimpse of what he might really be like. But his shy defense was quickly back in place. He turned his attention to Buzz again.

"Well, I'm afraid I still haven't managed to find your wolf."

"Why *m-m-my* wolf ? I never saw him."

Helen could see his cheeks coloring up. "I know. I was just—"

"I'd b-b-better be g-g-going now. Bye."

Helen stood there a moment, wondering what she'd said wrong. They made their separate ways to their cars. She waved as Luke drove off, but he didn't wave back nor look in her direction.

At the turning up to the lake she stopped at the mailboxes. Since coming to Montana she'd had letters from her mother, her father and her sister. But none from Joel. In all those long weeks she must have written him five or six times. Perhaps he hadn't received them? Or perhaps he couldn't get letters out?

Buzz watched dolefully from the pickup while she opened the lid of her mailbox. It was empty.

HE HAD watched her ever since she arrived.

Even those first couple of days when Dan Prior was helping her unpack her things and get the cabin into shape. And that next night when she'd come back late and did that amazing howl down by the water. He had stood in the cover of the trees across the lake, where he was standing now, and had prayed no wolf would answer. If he walked north along the fringe of the forest, he might get a glimpse of her through the open doorway, sitting at the table with all her charts and her computer or talking on the phone.

Luke tried to persuade himself that he wasn't spying. All he was doing was trying to stop her getting the wolves. But he was finding it harder and harder to think of it that way.

She seemed so sad. The way she came down and sat by the lake, crying. He'd wanted to go down there and put his arms around her and tell her to stop and that everything was okay.

Across the lake the lights were on, her truck was parked outside and her dog was barking. She was home, and that was all he needed to know. It meant he could safely go about his night's work.

He turned and slipped quietly back into the forest.

Moon Eye was grazing where he had left him, at the southern end of the lake. Luke put his face against the white crescent on the horse's face, for which he had named him. Then he swung into the saddle and headed across the creek and down through the forest toward the first of the traplines.

It wasn't that he thought she meant to harm the wolves, but once she got collars on them, they could be found and got rid of whenever anyone chose. These biologist people didn't get it.

At the start Luke had treated the trap thing almost like a game. He had enjoyed shadowing her and the predator control guy, Rimmer, seeing where they set the traps.

He'd bought some green crystals from a pet store. They were supposed to stop cats and dogs pooping on your lawn. Then he bought bug repellent, ammonia and pepper, and mixed them into a gooey liquid with the crystals. The result, when he sniffed it, nearly made him pass out, and it worked like a dream on the ranch dogs. He even gave his new product a name: Wolf Stop.

The two traplines she'd laid down toward the allotments were a breeze. Both places were like corridors, and he sprayed a three-line barrier of Wolf Stop at each end. But the traps in the high canyon were a different matter. All he could do was spray around each trap, and if she moved one without him seeing her do it, he could lose hours trying to find it.

Even worse, a couple of nights ago he'd lost his bag with all the Wolf Stop in it, and ended up having to spring some of the traps, which you had to do without activating the radio collars.

His excuse for being away from home all night was simple. He had suggested to his father that he camp up on the allotment so he could ride the herd through the night. His mother said it was ridiculous, but his father had backed the idea.

The only night he regularly went home was Tuesday, so he could get a shower and a shave and some decent sleep before his speech therapy the next morning.

Tonight the sky was clouding over, but there was a moon and he hardly needed to use his flashlight to locate the forest traplines. He urged Moon Eye up the steep route to the canyon.

Exactly where the wolves were at the moment, he didn't know. A few nights ago he had heard them howl, and though the mountains played tricks with any sound, he figured it was somewhere up above Wrong Creek, a mile or so to the north.

He reached the canyon and tied Moon Eye to a bush. She had set three traps alongside a deer trail that skirted a thicket of juniper. Below it the ground fell away in a steep slope covered with buffaloberry, where Luke stopped, a few yards short, he thought, of the first trap.

The moon was permanently masked by cloud now. Luke took out his flashlight and walked slowly through the buffaloberry bushes. He saw wolf scat and knew he'd found the right spot. There, behind it, was the telltale tuft of grass, and buried between the two, sprinkled with dirt and debris to disguise it, would be the trap. He hunkered down to spray the scat.

"Just what the hell do you think you're doing?"

The voice gave him such a jump that he lost his footing and found himself sprawled on his back among the berry bushes. He'd dropped the flashlight, and he could hear someone charging out of the trees toward him. Quickly he rolled over, scrambled to his feet and launched himself down the slope.

"Oh no you don't, pal!"

With one leap Helen cleared the trail. Whoever it was had about a ten-yard start on her and was crashing through the bushes.

"You're in big trouble, buddy. *Big* trouble!" Thunder boomed, and the bushes thwacked against her legs as she ran.

As he reached the trees, she heard his boot crack against a rock, and he tripped and disappeared headfirst into the undergrowth. Without thinking, Helen dived like a football tackler and landed on his back. He flattened beneath her in a great oomphing grunt.

She rolled off him and got to her knees, too out of breath herself to speak. Then the thought occurred to her: Now what? She had just attacked a total stranger out in the middle of nowhere. She must be out of her mind.

She got to her feet. "Don't you try anything. I'm a federal agent. In fact, you're under arrest."

She realized he was in no state to try anything. He was on his side, with his knees doubled up, gasping for breath. In a flash of lightning she saw his face, all contorted and covered in dust.

She couldn't believe it. "Luke? What on earth . . ."

She knelt beside him while he tried to get the air back into him. And when at last he succeeded, she made him sit up, then brushed the dirt and twigs from his back. With her flashlight she saw there was blood on his forehead. She took out a handkerchief.

"You've cut yourself."

He took the handkerchief and wiped the wound himself.

"Is it you who's been doing this all along?"

He nodded, still looking down.

"Why? Don't you want me to catch the wolf? Your dad does."

He gave a little humorless laugh. "Oh, yeah. *H-h-he* does."

"But you don't?"

He shrugged, looking away, still avoiding her eyes.

"You know, Luke, we're not trapping him to kill him or take him away. Just to put a radio collar on him. It'll protect him."

"There's m-more than one. There's n-nine, a whole p-p-pack."

"You've seen them?"

He nodded. "And collars won't protect them. It'll just make them easier to g-get rid of."

"That's not true."

"You wait."

For a while neither of them spoke. And then, at last, he looked at her. And something in his eyes startled her. Something lonely and lost, like a mirrored fragment of herself.

HE SAT on a chair beside the cabin stove, with Buzz curled up at his feet and his forehead tilted up so she could see to clean the wound. He watched her face while she worked, noting the way she frowned and bit her lip in concentration. Their clothes were still soaked from the rain. She had lit the potbellied stove when they came in, and in the warmth she smelled wonderful, not of perfume or anything, just of her.

"This is iodine. It's going to hurt a little, okay?"

He couldn't help wincing as she dabbed it into the wound.

"That'll teach you to go messing with my traps."

He looked up at her and smiled.

It was amazing how well she'd taken it. She'd scared him half to death, but afterward, walking down through the dripping forest, with her backpack strapped to Moon Eye's saddle, she had actually laughed about it. She'd made him get the bottle of Wolf Stop out and taken a whiff of it that nearly knocked her out.

He explained how he had first come across the wolves and how since then he had watched them. And when she tried to convince him that collaring them was the right thing to do, he could see she cared just as much as he did about their survival.

She was sticking a Band-Aid on him now. "There you go."

"Thanks."

The pan of water she was heating on the Coleman stove was boiling, and she went over and started to make hot chocolate. While she busied herself, he looked around the room. It was cramped, but in the light of the hissing gas lamps it looked warm and cozy.

She came over with the hot chocolate, putting the mugs down on the table.

"Are you sure you don't want to change out of that wet shirt? You'll catch cold."

"You sound like my m-m-mother."

"I do? Catch cold, I don't give a damn."

Luke laughed. He was starting to relax a little.

"But *I'm* not going to." She went over to the wardrobe and, facing away from him, started taking off her T-shirt.

He tried desperately to think of something to say, something casual that would make it seem like it was no big deal to have a woman take her clothes off in front of him.

"Am I still un-un-under arrest?"

"I'm thinking about it." She put on a pale blue fleece shirt that made her face look all golden, then came back and sat down at the table. She picked up her mug of chocolate and took a thoughtful sip. "It depends," she said.

"On what?"

She placed one of the maps in front of him.

"On you showing me where to catch those wolves."

Five

BUCK Calder sat, resting his horse, in the early morning sun on a bare bluff that leaned out from the forest above his allotment. He looked down over the trees at the pasture and the valley stretching away toward Hope. He and Clyde were about to head over to Abe's allotment to give him a hand gathering his herd. They had come up to fetch Luke first, so he could help too.

Below him now, Buck could see Clyde riding up out of the trees toward him. "Find him?" he called down to Clyde.

"Nope."

Buck shook his head, his good humor spiked, as it so often was, by thoughts of Luke. Clyde rode up the slope to join him, and they set off up the logging trail to the Harding lease.

It had seemed like a good idea to have Luke keep an eye on the herd, but now he wasn't so sure. Whenever Clyde came up here, the boy was nowhere to be seen.

Sometimes Buck despaired of the boy. He couldn't help comparing him to the son he'd lost, and he wondered what would happen to the ranch in years to come. Buck was thinking more and more that Clyde and Kathy should take over when he let go. That the Calder place be run by one who bore a different name was for Buck a source of shame. He had failed to produce a decent living male heir to continue the line, and the whole world knew it.

The trail was too narrow for the horses to go side by side, so Clyde rode behind, keeping his thoughts to himself, for which Buck was grateful. Conversation wasn't Clyde's strong suit; indeed, it was sometimes hard to tell what was. There was something doglike about him that Buck found irritating. He was always just a little too eager to please. But, hell, Kathy had enough brains for both of them, and the young fellow doted on her and the baby. And one day he might even make a decent rancher.

As the trees opened up before them, he saw Abe on his horse at the foot of the pasture. He gave them a nod as they rode up.

"Howdy, Abe. Sorry we're late. We were looking for Luke."

"Seen him as we was coming up here, 'bout an hour ago," Abe said. "Heading over toward Wrong Creek with that wolf woman."

"What the hell's he doing with her?" Clyde said.

"Don't ask me," Abe said grimly.

It was a while before anyone spoke. Buck didn't want his voice to show how mad the news made him.

At last he said, "So how's it going?"

"Four cows so far with no calf. Bags are all dried up."

"Reckon it's the wolves?" Clyde said.

"What else would it be?"

Buck and Clyde made themselves useful, and within the hour every living cow and calf was gathered at the foot of the pasture. Abe's count of dried-up cows had gone up to six. Of their calves there was no trace. Abe had grown pale and quivered around the eyes, as if he was having trouble keeping the lid on things.

Once they were down from the higher trails, the going got easy enough for Abe and his sons, Wes and Ethan, to manage the rest of the way without help. Buck and Clyde cut off along a trail that wound up through the forest to the lake where the wolf woman had her cabin. Buck thought it was worth checking if Luke was there. Even if he wasn't, they could leave a message on her door, telling him to get back home right away. The boy had some explaining to do.

IT HAD taken them a day and a half to reset the traps, and now they were out checking them. Luke was fairly sure that the wolves had been at Wrong Creek when he'd heard them howl. It was the first place he and Helen Ross had come. They'd found fresh wolf scat and tracks and the carcass of an old bull moose.

The previous afternoon he had taken her up to the abandoned den. She put on a little headlamp and slithered right down into the hole. She was gone so long he started to worry, but then her boots appeared, and she wriggled out, babbling with excitement and covered in dust, and handed him the headlamp.

"Your turn."

Luke shook his head. "Oh, no. I d-don't—"

"Go on, I dare you."

So down he went, into the hillside for about fifteen feet. It was so narrow he had to use the toes of his boots to inch himself along.

In the beam of the headlamp the walls looked pale and smooth. There was no sign of wolf at all except a few pale hairs snagged in the tree roots. The end of the tunnel broadened into a chamber about three feet across, and Luke stopped there and lay still. He thought of the mother wolf curled in this womb of cold earth, giving birth to her pups. Then he switched off the lamp. Enfolded in the silence and the darkness, he remembered something he'd read, about how life was a circular trip from the tomb of the womb to the womb of the tomb. He had never understood why anyone should fear the perfect nothingness of death. He would happily have died right there and then.

When he emerged blinking into the sunlight, he just blurted out what was in his head, which was really dumb. But she simply nodded, and he could see in her eyes that she understood.

He watched her now, ahead of him along the trail, holding the antenna above her head while she thumbed through the frequencies on the little radio receiver that hung from her shoulder. Suddenly she stopped and stiffened, and he knew she'd heard something. Then she gave a whoop. "Yes!"

"W-w-which one is it?"

"Five-sixty-two. That's the one you reset. Down by all that willow scrub, remember?"

Helen drove so fast it seemed to Luke they were lucky to get there at all. All the way she kept teasing him about beginner's luck. Luke laughed and promised not to tell anyone.

They parked at the edge of a clear-cut, left Buzz in the pickup and set off up the creek.

As they got to the trail beside the willow thicket, Helen could see the hole where the trap had been torn from the ground and a long furrow carved by the hook of the drag as the wolf had headed for cover. But still there was no sound or movement.

Then she heard the clink of the drag chain and knew they had him. He was somewhere in the willows, maybe thirty feet from where they were standing. Helen whispered to Luke to stay where he was, then slowly followed the drag mark toward the thicket.

She had already explained to him that if you'd trapped an alpha, you had to be careful. They could come right at you and get their teeth into you. Knowing how securely they were snagged and how far they could reach was crucial.

The chain clinked again, and this time the bushes rustled, and she saw a flash of pale fur. Luke had told her that the alpha female was almost white. Helen turned to Luke and mouthed, "I think it's Mom."

She stopped at the very edge of the thicket. Slowly she lifted her foot, thinking maybe if she took a step into the thicket, she might see her, when the bush in front of her erupted.

Suddenly there was the wolf's head, all snarling teeth and yellow eyes, lunging at her through the branches. It gave Helen such a shock that she jumped away, lost her footing and fell flat on her back. She saw the head jerk and disappear as the drag hooks held fast. She looked up and saw Luke's grinning face.

"I think it *is* Mom," he said.

"That's standard practice, by the way. Always fall over. It makes them feel at ease."

Luke laughed and helped her to her feet. He pointed to a rock a little way along the thicket. "Maybe we could see better from there."

He was right. She should have gone there in the first place.

"Okay, smarty pants."

The two of them perched precariously on the narrow rock, peering over the thicket. The wolf was looking right at them, about twenty feet away, curling her lips and growling.

"Isn't she beautiful?" Luke whispered.

"She is." Helen could see the trap jaws clamped on the wolf's front left foot. "She's not going anywhere. Looks like it's best to come at her from the far side there."

Helen took out her jabstick and loaded the syringe with Telazol. Then they circled around the wolf and walked slowly through the thicket toward her from the far side.

When they parted the last shield of bushes and saw her, she tried to make another lunge at them. But the chain held fast. The wolf snarled and lowered herself slowly to the ground.

"Hi, Mom," Helen said gently. "Hey, aren't you gorgeous?"

She was in prime condition, her coat lustrous and almost fully thickened for the coming winter. Helen figured she was maybe three to four years old and must weigh almost eighty pounds. Her eyes glinted a pale greenish yellow in the sunlight.

"It's okay, baby," Helen cooed. "We're not going to hurt you." Softly she asked Luke to walk slowly around to the other side, and as she hoped, the wolf turned to keep her eyes on him.

It gave Helen her chance. She reached out and plunged the jabstick into the wolf's rear end. The wolf snarled and whipped around with her jaws. But Helen kept the jabstick pressed home until the syringe had safely delivered its shot. Then she and Luke watched from a distance while the wolf's limbs slackened, until at last she slumped like a drunk in a doorway.

Half an hour later they were almost done. They'd blindfolded her, weighed her, taken samples and checked her all over from teeth to tail. She was free of lice and seemed in perfect health. The trap had made a small flesh wound on her leg, but there were no bones broken. Helen smeared it with some antibiotic.

Luke was kneeling beside her, running a hand along the wolf's silvery side. He had been a great assistant, taking notes and marking the samples and passing anything she needed from the kit box.

Helen sat back on her heels and watched him stroking the wolf, his eyes gentle and full of innocent wonder.

"Isn't her coat amazing?" she said. "The different layers?"

"Yeah. And the colors. From a d-distance, she looks white. But up close there are browns and blacks, even a t-tinge of red."

He looked at her and smiled, and Helen smiled back and felt something connect between them. It was she who broke the moment and looked down at the wolf.

"This old girl's going to be waking up soon."

Helen clipped the ear tag on, then slipped the collar over the wolf's neck, making sure that the signal still worked. She then removed the blindfold and took some photographs. By the time they had packed up all the gear, the wolf was starting to stir.

"Let's go," Helen said. "It's best to give her some space."

From the other side of the meadow they watched the wolf get groggily to her feet. She licked her front paw. Then she delicately sniffed the air and caught their scent. She turned and stared right at them. Then, with all the disdain of a slighted movie star, the wolf turned her back, flounced her tail and trotted away up the canyon.

HE COULDN'T take his eyes off her. She was strolling barefoot down beside the stream, talking on the cell phone. Luke wondered if she had any idea how beautiful she was. He was sitting on the ground in front of the cabin, where they'd eaten a picnic when they got back from trapping. Beside him, Buzz lay sprawled on his back in dog heaven while Luke rubbed his tummy. She had caught him staring at her, but she just smiled back at him as though it were the most natural thing in the world.

Helen was talking with her boss, who was obviously teasing her. "What do you mean *luck?*" she said. "It's skill, Prior, and brilliance. When have you ever caught two wolves in one hit?"

It had happened right after they watched the alpha female trot away. Scanning the frequencies again, they heard another signal and, in a trap they set a few hundred yards farther up the same trail, found a second wolf, this time a young male.

To begin with, Luke had stuttered badly, but she hadn't seemed to notice, and soon he'd managed to relax. She was real easy to be with. The thing he liked best was how she sometimes touched him when she was telling him something, just put a hand on his arm or shoulder. When they heard that second signal and knew they'd caught another wolf, she gave him this massive hug. Luke started blushing like an idiot.

Moon Eye suddenly stopped his grazing by the stream and lifted his head to look down toward the lake, his ears twitching forward. The next second Buzz was off down the hill, barking. Two riders were coming out of the trees, and Luke's heart sank.

He and Helen had agreed they would keep his role in the trapping a secret. She hadn't even mentioned it to Dan Prior. And now they'd blown it. He looked at her and saw she was thinking the same. She was finishing her phone call. Luke stood up and watched his father and Clyde steer their horses around the water's edge and up the slope toward them, Buzz barking alongside.

"Morning," Helen said brightly.

She told Buzz to hush. Luke's father tipped his hat at her and gave her one of those smiles he always used when he knew he had you cornered. "Ma'am."

Clyde just stared at Luke while they stopped in front of the cabin. Luke saw his father's eyes travel from the picnic remains to Helen's bare feet, then all the way up to her face.

"Mighty fine life, working for the U.S. Fish and Wildlife."

"Oh, it is," Helen said. "Beats being on vacation anytime. And, wow, you should see the size of our paychecks."

Buck hadn't so much as glanced Luke's way. He always liked to keep you waiting before he hurt you. Now he turned his head, and Luke felt the pale eyes fix upon him, cold and critical.

"Well, son, I'm glad we've found you at last. You know, we were all supposed to be helping the Hardings gather their herd this morning. Like I told you. Clyde and I rode up to the allotment to find you, and you weren't there."

Luke had clean forgotten. "I w-w-was there."

"So how come Abe saw you with this young lady here, in her truck, driving up Wrong Creek?"

"I w-w-w—" Luke's tongue was nailed to the roof of his mouth; he didn't know what to say anyway. A few moments ago, alone with Helen, he'd felt for once almost like a man. Now he was a stupid tongue-tied kid again. He glanced at Helen, to confirm this was how she now saw him too. Instead, she took his look as a call for help.

"He was with me because I asked him for help," she said. "And, thanks to him, you'll be pleased to know, this morning we caught and collared two wolves."

"You caught two wolves?"

"That's right. Thanks to Luke here. He helped me find them."

Luke's father was silent for a moment. "So where are they?"

Helen frowned. "Sorry, what do you mean?"

"Well, have you already shipped them out or what?"

"Mr. Calder, I think you know what—"

"You just turned them loose again."

"Yes, but—"

"Let me get this straight, young lady. I've just been with a good friend and neighbor of mine, Abe Harding, gathering his herd. And this man, who, unlike your bosses back in Washington, D.C., doesn't have a barrel of tax dollars to burn, finds six of his calves missing. That's a loss to Abe of, what, three thousand dollars? And you tell me you've just caught two of the varmints responsible and then let them go again? And I should be *pleased*?"

Luke could see Helen was angry. But scared too. There was nobody, in the end, who his father wasn't able to scare.

"Mr. Calder, the whole idea—"

"Thank you, ma'am. I've heard enough." He gathered his reins. "Luke, when you've finished here, I'd appreciate it if you'd come down to the house. There's one or two things you and I need to clear up." His father touched his hat at Helen. "Miss Ross."

He loped away down toward the lake, with Clyde at his heels. Luke felt too small and shamed even to look at Helen. As he picked up his bag, she put her hand on his shoulder.

"Luke, it's my fault. I'm really sorry."

"It's no b-big deal."

Without another word he walked to the stream to collect Moon Eye and swung himself into the saddle. And he rode off without once looking back, but feeling her eyes upon him all the way.

HELEN spent the rest of the afternoon radio tracking the two collared wolves. Mercifully the signals stayed high up Wrong Creek and well away from any livestock.

When she came back to the cabin, it was almost dark. As she drove nearer, she could see something lying in the road, and she stopped so that the headlights were on it and got out. It was her mailbox. The metal stake had been twisted to the ground and the box itself flattened. It looked as if someone had smashed it with something and then for good measure driven over it. The other mailboxes in the row were unscathed.

For an instant she thought she saw a flicker of something pale in the gray gravel where her shadow reached the blacker black of the night. But then it was gone.

She turned and walked back toward the pickup. The letter jigged again, this time unseen. Then it scuttled away in the wind.

AS HE tried to hold the Cessna steady in the bruising north wind, Dan could see that word of Abe Harding's alleged losses to the wolves had spread. All along the mountain front, herds were being gathered from their summer allotments.

Helen sat beside him, scanning the radio frequencies. They'd picked up the first signal a couple of miles southwest of Hope. The signal belonged to the young male, and Helen soon found the mother's. Both were strongest as the plane crossed Wrong Creek, which was good news, because it meant they were away from the cattle, on the north side of the canyon.

They reached the end of the canyon again, and Dan banked into another turn. He went lower this time, tilting the plane so Helen could get a better view. Suddenly Helen pointed. "There she is. The alpha. And there are four, no, five others." Helen had the binoculars on them now.

"You say the Calder boy thinks there are nine in all?"

"Four adults, five pups."

"Any sign of the alpha male down there?"

"No. Looks like four pups and the two we collared."

Helen got out her camera, and Dan circled again so she could take some pictures on a long lens. The wolves were lounging in the sun and seemed none too bothered about the plane. Dan flew the canyon and the surrounding area for a while longer, but there was no sign of the other three. On the way back to the airfield Helen made notes. Dan wondered if something was bothering her. She seemed a little sad and distracted.

"I'd feel a whole lot happier if the alpha male had been up there with them," he said. "My guess is he likes to be lower down, near all those tasty young steers."

"Come on, Dan. You don't believe Abe Harding's calves were killed by wolves, do you? We're not talking about the world's greatest rancher here. I bet he loses that many every summer."

"If these wolves *are* killing cattle, we're going to have to take them out. They jeopardize the whole recovery program."

"What do you mean, take them out? Relocate them?"

"There's nowhere to put them. No. I mean lethal control."

"Shoot them." Helen shook her head and looked away.

"Helen, wake up. It's the real world. Read the control plan."

They landed in silence, then drove to his office.

Dan walked her to her pickup. He'd been looking forward to seeing her again, but it had all gone wrong. He felt bad about what he'd said just now. He'd been harsh with her, and it was probably because he felt rejected by her. It wasn't going to happen between them, and he'd better get used to the idea.

Helen climbed into the pickup.

He noticed something on the passenger seat. "What's that?"

"My ex-mailbox. I have to get a new one."

She told him what had happened.

"That's not good, Helen. Any idea who did it?"

She shrugged. "Nope."

Dan frowned at it for a moment. "Listen, promise you'll call me if something like that happens again. Promise."

"I promise, Dan."

"Angels on your mailbox."

She smiled and drove off. He turned and went up to the office.

Dan could tell from Donna's face, as soon as he walked in, that something had happened.

"I've had the press on the phone," she said. "And that TV reporter. She said some ranchers out in Hope are spitting blood. Say they've lost a whole load of calves to the wolves."

"How many?"

"So far, forty-three."

"What! Did they say which ranchers?"

"Yeah. And one of them's Buck Calder."

THE meeting wasn't due to start for another half hour, but already there was a steady procession of trucks coming into town. Some pulled up outside Nelly's Diner, but the more popular destination was the Last Resort, which didn't bode well for the meeting. It was starting to rain.

Helen was spying from the window of Ruth Michaels's gift shop. Stuck to the door glass was one of the yellow posters that were all over town.

WOLF KILLS!

PUBLIC MEETING

HOPE COMMUNITY HALL

THURSDAY, 7 P.M.

Two nights ago, after Buck Calder and his neighbors had gathered their herds, Buck had announced the meeting on TV, saying that "those federal government fellas who let all these wolves loose in the first place" might care to come along and explain themselves to the people who paid their wages. Trying to restore calm, Helen had visited every rancher who claimed to have lost calves—and gotten short shrift from all of them.

Dan and Bill Rimmer seemed remarkably cool. They were sitting at the little bar at the back of the shop, chatting with Ruth.

Helen walked back to join them.

"Come on, Helen," Dan said. "It'll be fine."

"Thanks, Prior." She'd tried to get Dan to front the meeting, but he insisted it was her show.

In case things got out of hand, Dan had taken precautions. Hope had a deputy sheriff, Craig Rawlinson. There was no mistaking him for a wolf lover; he was the son of a rancher and married to the daughter of another. So Dan had asked for extra police, along with a couple of plainclothes special agents from the Fish & Wildlife Service.

Dan stood up and paid for the coffees. "Well, I guess we'd better be getting down there." He put an arm around Helen's shoulders. "Anyone pulls a gun, I'm right behind you."

"Thanks, Dan. I'll remember to duck."

AN HOUR later Dan's joke about guns seemed even less amusing. Helen had been trying to make her speech for about twenty minutes, and the heckling was starting to get to her. Among the loudest were Wes and Ethan Harding. Abe Harding didn't seem to be there. Neither did Luke. She hadn't seen him since the day they caught the wolf. She'd worried about him and been surprised by how much she missed his company.

The place was packed. There was seating for about a hundred, but easily as many again were standing at the back, which was where most of the heckling was coming from.

Helen was standing behind one end of a long trestle table on the rostrum at the front of the hall. Dan and Bill sat huddled beside her like war criminals. At the other end, leaning back in his chair and regally surveying the crowd, sat Buck Calder.

His opening speech had been masterful. He began by recounting how his baby grandson had been snatched from the jaws of death. Then he went on to catalogue the terrible losses he and his neighbors had since sustained. Then he'd introduced Helen.

Helen had gone through what was known so far about the wolves, which wasn't much, except that there were nine of them and that early DNA tests showed no relation to any wolves released in Yellowstone or Idaho. Then she'd explained about the Defenders of Wildlife scheme that compensated ranchers for any verified wolf-kill. "To recap, any proven killers of livestock will be removed or destroyed. I understand how strongly some of you are feeling. All we'd ask is that you give it a little time."

"What more proof do you need? Wolves kill cattle, period."

"Well, sir, there's a fair amount of evidence that wolves *can* live in close proximity with livestock and not bother them—"

"So how come they killed forty-three calves here?" Ethan Harding called out. There was a loud murmur of support.

"Well, we're trying to get verification on precisely how many of those losses were in fact caused by wolves."

"You calling us liars?"

"No, I certainly am not."

Buck Calder leaned forward in his chair. "Maybe you could tell us, Helen, how many you have verified as wolf-kills so far?"

It was the question she'd dreaded. Of the forty-three alleged losses, only five carcasses had been found, and not one of them was recent enough for the cause of death to be established.

"We've still got work to do on that. The evidence is thin—"

"But how many for sure?"

The whole room went quiet, waiting for her answer.

Helen swallowed. "Well, so far—none."

There was an uproar. Everyone started shouting at the same time. Calder held up his hands and called for quiet. But it had little effect. Helen looked at Dan, and he shrugged guiltily. The TV cameraman was clambering up on a chair to get a better shot.

Helen could see someone at the entrance of the hall. The crowd out in the lobby slowly parted to let him through, and the hecklers stopped their shouting. It was Abe Harding.

He was carrying something, a bundle of some kind, over his shoulder, heading down the aisle. He was wearing a yellow slicker that glistened with rain and swished as he walked.

Everyone was silent now. As he made his way toward the rostrum, he was staring at Helen with a kind of crazed intensity. Helen hoped Dan's special agents had their guns handy.

It wasn't until Harding stopped right in front of her that Helen noticed the blood rivering down his slicker and realized at last what the bundle of black fur on his shoulder was.

"Here's your damn verification," Harding said.

And he dumped the dead wolf on the table.

BY THE time Helen and Bill Rimmer got out of the hall, Main Street looked like a war zone. It was blocked by four flashing police cars. The rain was coming down like a monsoon. Dan and the two special agents were arguing with one of the cops who had arrested Abe Harding. With his hands cuffed behind his back, Abe was being ushered into the back of one of the police cars. His sons were yelling at two other cops.

Helen and Bill Rimmer headed across the street to him.

"You don't have to do this!" Dan was saying to the cop.

"The man assaulted a police officer. Listen, it was you who asked for police backup in the first place."

"Yeah, but why take him away? This'll make a martyr of him."

It was too late anyway. The car Abe had been bundled into was already moving off through the dispersing crowd.

In its lights Helen suddenly caught sight of Luke. "Luke!"

He turned and saw her and looked very sad. When he came up to her, he tried to smile. "I w-w-was looking for you."

"Me too. I mean, in there. Did you see what happened?"

He nodded. He fished something from his coat pocket and handed it to her. "I f-found this. By the side of the road."

Helen took it. It was a letter. The envelope was mud-stained, and the ink had run a little. But she could still recognize the handwriting as Joel's. Her heart gave a little flutter. "Thank you."

"I'd better g-go now."

She suddenly realized how he must feel about what had happened to the wolf. "Will you come and see me?"

He shook his head. "I c-can't."

And he walked away in the rain and was lost in the crowd.

Six

> Mwanda Hospital,
> Kagambali
> 16 Sept.
>
> My dear Helen,
>   So did you catch them yet? No? Okay, well here's what you do: you get a BIG metal pail. Next, you rig a pole across the top with a revolving oil drum on it, onto which you then strap one dead moose. This method has the Latimer seal of approval and has been used in North Carolina for centuries.

HELEN laughed out loud. She was sitting in bed, reading the letter by the light of her headlamp. As soon as she could, she had driven back to the cabin, with her heart singing. He had written at last. Cocooned in her sleeping bag, her back pillowed against the cabin wall and the letter propped on her knees, Helen sat listening to the rain and feeling something close to bliss.

> The A.C.L. have started a new round of ethnic cleansing about eighty miles north of here, and every day we're getting over a thousand new refugees, all of them in pretty bad shape.
>   And of course, there's nothing like enough medicine or food to go around. Some of the kids that get here (hundreds, maybe

even thousands, don't make it) haven't eaten for weeks. It's pitiful. The amazing thing is, some of them still know how to smile.

Actually, it's not all bad. Mainly because of the incredible
people I'm working with. And Helen, that's really the main purpose of writing this letter. It isn't going to be easy to say.

Helen felt something turn inside her chest. Oh, Joel, she begged
in her head. Don't. Please don't say it.

Marie-Christine has been out here six months. She's Belgian
but lives in Paris. By training, she's a pediatrician.

She sat there for a moment, staring at the circle of light her headlamp made by the door. Her breathing made it rise and fall, idioti-
cally. Then she read on.

When we met—oh, Helen, this is so hard to tell you—but it
was like we already knew each other.

That sounds familiar, Helen thought. She scanned ahead, searching for any reference to soul mates, but couldn't see it, which was
just as well, for she would probably have screamed.

Anyway, we ended up working together, running this mobile
unit that made rounds of the refugee camps, and I got to see how
amazing she was with these kids. They just all adore her. Perhaps
I shouldn't be telling you all this, but I feel I can, Helen, because
of our being so close and sharing so many good times.

The bottom line is, in two weeks, Marie-Christine and I . . .

"No," Helen sobbed. "Don't, Joel. Don't say that."

. . . are getting married.

Helen scrunched the letter up and threw it across the room.
She kicked off the sleeping bag and stood up, holding her hands
over her face. Buzz was on his feet too. He started barking.

"Shut up, you stupid animal!"

She ripped off her headlamp and threw it at him, and he whimpered and slunk away while she stumbled in the darkness to the cabin door and ran blindly out into the rain.

Her bare feet slipped on the mud, and she fell heavily and lay there for a while with her face pressed into the wet earth, panting and cursing him and herself and the day she was ever born.

BUCK was in the Last Resort, with a cigar between his teeth. For the last hour he had been holding court at the bar, where everyone had adjourned when the fun outside was over.

The meeting had gone better than he could ever have dreamed. And then old Abe, pulling that stunt with the wolf. Hell, what a performance. Money couldn't buy that kind of publicity.

He handed Lori behind the bar a fifty-dollar bill to buy everyone another drink and said good night. Buck had other business.

It was nearly two whole weeks since he and Ruth had been able to steal so much as a kiss. She always seemed to have some excuse not to see him, and often as not it had to do with Eleanor, going through accounts or whatever. Well, he was going to put that right tonight. Rabble-rousing always got his juices flowing.

As he drove by her house, he saw the curtains were open, and he swung the car into the driveway and parked in his usual place. She was opening the door as he got out of the car.

"Buck, you've got to go. Eleanor's coming over."

"What's she doing, coming here at this time of night?"

"There's a meeting with the accountants tomorrow, and we need to go over the figures. Now, go!"

"Gee whiz." He stalked sulkily back toward his car and heard her shut the door on him. Buck flung his half-smoked cigar angrily away across the driveway, got into the car and slammed the door. Scowling through the rain, he drove home.

The house was silent as a morgue when he got there. Luke must have already turned in. He opened a beer, took it to the living room and sat down heavily on the couch.

He'd hardly settled when the phone rang. He picked up.

"Is that Calder?"

"Buck Calder speaking. Who's this?"

"Never mind who it is. Scum like you deserve to die. I saw you on the TV and saw what your psycho pal did to that wolf. And we want you to know, we're going to kill your cows."

The line went dead. Buck put the phone down. He noticed there were four messages on the answering machine. He pressed PLAY.

"So the wolves killed your calves, huh? Oh, dear!" It was a woman's voice. "Before *you* had a chance to kill them. That's so unfair! You're a dying breed, pal, and the sooner, the better."

Buck heard a noise and looked up to see Luke standing at the top of the stairs. "Did you hear that?"

Luke nodded.

"And the others? Are they all like that?"

"Yes."

Buck took a drink of beer. "Did you see it on TV?"

"Y-y-yes."

"Did they show Abe dumping the wolf?"

"Yes. Th-the whole . . . thing."

"Did it say what's happening to him?"

"He's in j-j-jail, in Helena."

"Guess he'll need someone to stand bail for him. Who the hell are all these crazy people, calling me like that?"

"I d-d-don't know. I'm g-g-going to bed now."

Buck sighed. "Okay, Luke. Night then."

"G-good night."

Buck thumbed through the phone book to find the number of the jail in Helena.

Maybe Abe should have just followed the old rule: shoot, shovel and shut up. Well, he hadn't, and now they had a war on their hands.

Buck was damned if he was going to be frightened off by a bunch of pot-smoking bunny huggers, but they'd got him wondering. Maybe he wasn't playing this wolf business the right way.

"I'VE been doing some thinking," Buck said at breakfast, "and I reckon maybe I've been a little hard on those Fish and Wildlife guys.

Maybe it'd be better if we cooperated a little more, help sort this wolf thing out. You know, finding them, keeping an eye on them and all."

Luke didn't say anything. He was always wary when his father came on all reasonable like this.

"You know what that Helen Ross girl was saying the other day? How much she appreciated your help catching that wolf, saying how you had a real feel for that kind of work."

He paused, waiting for a reaction, but got none.

"And it got me thinking, once we've shipped the calves off to the feedlot, maybe you should give her a hand. It's okay by me."

Luke couldn't wait to break the news to Helen. He went right out and saddled up. His father probably had some sneaky motive, but Luke wasn't going to argue.

He coaxed Moon Eye out of the trees toward the lake. The cabin door was open, and Buzz stood on the doorstep, staring at something inside and barking uncertainly.

Helen's truck was there. Buzz turned and saw him and Moon Eye and came bounding down the slope to greet them.

"Hey, Buzz dog. How're you doing?"

Luke expected Helen to emerge from the cabin, but there was no sign of her. He got off his horse and walked to the door.

"Helen?" There was no answer. "Helen? Hello?"

Buzz, beside him, barked again, then brushed past his legs and ran inside. Luke followed him. It was dark inside and across the room, he could just make out Helen, lying on the bed.

One of her arms was dangling down. A mug lay on its side in a pool of spilled liquid. There was an open bottle of pills there too. She lay perfectly still, even when Buzz nuzzled her and whimpered. Luke took a cautious step toward her.

"Helen?" he said softly.

He could see there was mud on her arm and on her face. Her eyes were open, and she was staring blankly ahead.

"Helen? Helen?"

Then something flickered in her eyes, like life itself being switched on. She looked at him without moving her head.

"Helen, what is it? Are you okay?"

She blinked. Maybe she was sick. He reached down to touch her forehead. Her skin felt cold as stone. He lifted the edge of her sleeping bag and saw her T-shirt was dirty and soaking.

"Helen, what happened?"

Silently she started to cry. The tears made tracks through the mud on her face. He couldn't bear to see such wretchedness, and he sat beside her and hoisted her up in his arms and held her. She was so cold and wet. He tried to warm her and just let her cry. When she stopped, he wrapped her in a blanket, then lit the stove.

Behind the door he saw a screwed-up piece of paper. It was that same pale blue as the airmail letter he'd found and given to her last night. He picked it up and put it on the table, then heated some water and made tea. And all the while she sat hugging her knees, with the blanket over her, shivering and staring at nothing.

He soaked a washcloth with some warmed water and gently cleaned the mud from her face and from her arms and hands. Then he found her blue fleece shirt and said maybe she should put it on, but she didn't seem to hear him. So he sat behind her and pulled the wet T-shirt over her head. As he pulled the fleece shirt down over her, he noticed the notches of her spine and the faint curve of her ribs, and it made her seem fragile, like a wounded bird. He had to lift each arm in turn, feeding them like a doll's into the sleeves.

He made her drink the tea; then he stayed beside her, holding her in his arms, for a long time.

It must have been an hour or more before she spoke. Her head lay against his chest, and her voice sounded small and faint. "I'm sorry. I'm not worth the effort."

He knew better than to ask what had happened. Perhaps it was something to do with the letter. All he knew at that moment, or cared to know, was that he loved her.

As IF in revenge for the killing of the alpha male in Hope, wolf packs throughout the region seemed suddenly to be wreaking havoc. A sheep farmer north of Yellowstone lost thirty-one lambs to wolves that had wandered out of the park. Another pack killed a pair of Thoroughbred foals east of Glacier National Park. A lone disperser from a pack in Idaho killed three calves near the Salmon River.

Bill Rimmer was hardly ever out of his helicopter. In ten days he shot and killed nine wolves and darted fifteen more, mainly pups, who were relocated. It was Dan who had to sign the death warrants, and he did so each time with a sense of personal failure. He had little choice, however. And because of what had happened in Hope, the media was watching his every move.

Abe had been charged with killing an animal listed as endangered, namely, one wolf, and of possessing the remains and transporting them. A further charge of assaulting a police officer was dropped. He was released by a federal magistrate without bail.

Schumacher and Lipsky, the two Fish & Wildlife special agents who had been at the meeting, had gone with a search warrant to the Harding ranch, accompanied, at his own insistence, by Deputy Sheriff Craig Rawlinson. He caused nothing but trouble by siding with Harding's sons, who had yelled abuse for the duration of the visit. The agents found the Ruger M-77 rifle with which Abe had admitted shooting the wolf. It was duly confiscated.

At the Fish & Wildlife forensics lab in Ashland, Oregon, DNA tests showed the wolf had no connection with the wolves released in Yellowstone or Idaho. An ear tag showed he had traveled from British Columbia. He was also missing a toe on his right foreleg and had a scar there that suggested he had once been trapped and torn himself free. This might have affected his ability to hunt deer or elk, and led him to the easier option of cattle.

Abe at first claimed he'd shot the wolf when it attacked a calf. He later admitted it hadn't yet attacked, but he knew it was going to. He said he was not guilty and refused any legal representation.

Secretly Dan thought Abe may have done them all a favor by killing the most likely troublemaker. It had taken some of the sting out of the ranchers' anger over lost calves and, at the very least, had bought Helen some breathing space. With luck she could keep tabs on the rest of the pack and avert further trouble.

He hadn't seen her since the meeting and had become a little concerned. For three days she neither phoned nor replied to any of the messages he left for her. Then she called to say she'd had the flu but was now okay. Calder's son, Luke, had been taking care of her, she said, and had been really sweet.

Dan couldn't help feeling a twist of jealousy.

"Isn't it a little like sleeping with the enemy?"

"He's just helping me out. You ought to be grateful."

"I'm sorry," he said.

She didn't reply.

"Listen, I've found you a snowmobile. You're going to be needing it soon. Could I bring it up on the weekend?"

"Sure."

After hanging up, he sat there awhile, thinking about her. He would take her out to dinner again, somewhere nice.

BUCK always enjoyed coming to the Billings public auction yards. It was a little after twelve, and the two young bulls he'd brought over in the trailer this morning were up next.

Forty minutes later he towed his empty trailer out onto the highway, pleased with the price he'd got for his bulls. Now it was time to get rid of the wolves.

The first part of his plan was already in place: Luke was working for Helen Ross. And though Buck hadn't yet managed to glean any information from the boy about where the varmints were, it was only a matter of time. When he got it, he would need someone who could act upon it. And, along with selling bulls, that was what he intended to see to today.

He'd remembered an old trapper who used to live up on the Hope River. Buck's father used to hire him whenever they had varmint trouble, usually coyotes, but sometimes a mountain lion or a grizzly. Buck recalled the guy having a son in the same line of business, but he couldn't remember the name. Then, two nights ago, in the Last Resort, he'd asked old Ned Wainwright, who was ninety if he was a day, if he could remember it.

"Josh Lovelace. Passed away, must be thirty years ago."

"There was a son too, wasn't there?"

"Uh-huh. J.J. Moved down Big Timber way."

Buck found a J.J. Lovelace in the phone book and called several times. There was never a reply. So Buck decided to stop by on the way back from Billings and see if he could find him.

He saw the sign for Big Timber and pulled off the interstate. He stopped at a gas station and asked for directions. Ten minutes later his truck and trailer were bouncing the potholes of a winding dirt road. It was getting dark. After about three miles his headlights found a rusty green mailbox that said LOVELACE.

The driveway looked too treacherous for his trailer, so he parked and set off on foot along the rutted track. After about half a mile he saw above him a low wooden house set among trees. There was a light on inside. Parked nearby was a silver trailer.

He expected dogs to bark. But the only sound as he climbed toward the house was the wind. There were no drapes, and Buck could see the light was coming from a lightbulb above the kitchen table. He knocked on the kitchen door. While he waited for an answer, he turned casually around—and nearly had a heart attack.

He was looking down the barrel of a 12-gauge shotgun.

The man at the other end of it was wearing a long black parka with the hood turned up. In the shadow of the hood Buck could make out a bony, graybearded face and hostile black eyes.

"Mr. Lovelace?"

The man didn't admit or deny it, just let Buck hang there.

"Hey, I'm real sorry just dropping by like this. My name's Buck Calder, from Hope. Your daddy, Joshua, used to do some work for my daddy when I was a kid."

"You're Henry Calder's boy?"

"Yes, sir, I am."

"What are you doing here?"

"Well, I understand you're in the same line of business as your father was. Or used to be."

Lovelace looked at him for a moment. Then he whisked the barrel in the air, clicked the safety on and strode past Buck into the house. He left the door ajar, and Buck followed him inside.

LOVELACE put the gun down on the table. The house was cold, so he kept his coat on. Since Winnie died, he could never be bothered to light the stove in the living room. He headed to his trap room at the back and heard Calder following him.

The trap room was really no more than a garage, but nowadays that was where he spent most of his time. He'd rigged up a little electric fire and even slept there at night on a mattress.

Lovelace sat down on a stool by the fire, dragged a pail with a deer head in it between his legs and got back to work. He'd been skinning it out when he'd heard Calder's truck. Not bad hearing, he thought, for an old buzzard of sixty-nine.

Calder told him about the wolf trouble they'd been having up in Hope. As he talked, his eyes kept roaming the room, festooned with traps and wires and snares and the skins and skulls of animals.

Lovelace remembered the man's father, Henry Calder. He had no recollection of meeting the man yakking away at him here, but back in '56 he'd married Winnie and moved to Big Timber, and after that he'd rarely visited Hope.

"So what do you think?"

"Killing wolves is against the law."

Calder smiled knowingly. There was something smug about him which Lovelace didn't care for. "Who's going to know?"

"They'll be watching them like hawks."

"That's true." Calder winked and grinned. "But you'd have inside information. My boy's helping this biologist woman out. He knows where the wolves are."

"Sounds like you don't need no help, then."

"No. Except the boy sees things more their way than mine."

"So how come he's going to part with the information?"

"Oh, I'll find some way of getting it. So, Mr. Lovelace, what do you say? Will you help us out? You can name your price."

Lovelace had finished the deer head. He stood up, picked up the pail, took it over to the sink at the other end of the workbench and poured the blood away while he thought it over.

After nagging him for ages to retire, Winnie had at last persuaded him. And then, just when he was getting used to it, even starting to enjoy it, six months ago she'd gone and gotten cancer. Found her riddled with it. Within three weeks she was dead.

The truth was, he now needed to keep himself busy. This was the first offer of work he'd had since the funeral.

"What's that wire thing over there, with all those little bits of metal on it?" Calder said. "If you don't mind my asking."

He was pointing to the far wall, where Lovelace hung his drag chains and hooks and coils of steel wire.

"For catching wolf pups. My father's idea. He called it the loop."

THE two hunters trudged up the trail. They were wearing full combat gear, their magnum rifles slung over their shoulders. The general hunting season started the next day, and these two clearly didn't want to miss a minute of it.

Luke and Helen were coming down through the trees above the trail, with the traps they'd collected slung over their shoulders. They had to collect all the traps; it wouldn't be good for business if a hunter stepped into one. They walked onto the trail just as the hunters came alongside. Buzz suddenly sat up in the Toyota, barking and growling. Helen hushed him.

The hunters were eyeing the traps that they were dumping, along with the others already collected, into the bed of the pickup. Both of them started to laugh.

"Rambo idiots," she said as they climbed in.

Luke started the engine and drove off. "D-did you never hunt?"

"No. But I know plenty of good biologists who do. Dan Prior for one. What about you? You don't hunt?"

"Once. When I was thirteen." He told her about killing the elk and how his father had forced him to help butcher it.

Since that cold morning when Luke had found Helen lying wet and filthy in her cabin bed, there was a closeness between them unlike any friendship she'd ever known. Without him, she knew, she would not have survived. While she clawed her way out of the pit, he had taken care of her, making sure she ate and slept and kept warm. He would leave late at night, and he would be there again at dawn to let Buzz out and make her coffee.

Only later did he mention that his father had said it was okay for him to help her if she wanted him to. And while she lay in the cabin, he got to work, checking the traps and tracking the signals of the collared wolves. In the evenings he would give her his notes and, while he cooked her supper, tell her all he had done. Through the mists of her own misfortune, she saw he was in his element.

At times now his stutter seemed to have vanished, returning only when he talked about his father or got excited. Such as on the morning he had come racing back to tell her there was a wolf in one of the traps. "You've g-g-got to come."

"Luke, I can't—"

"You've g-got to. I don't know w-what to do."

He made her get dressed and gather her gear; then he'd driven her up to a narrow canyon high above the Millward ranch.

The wolf turned out to be one of the pups, a female. Under Helen's instruction, Luke did all the measuring and noting, leaving her only to give the shots and take samples. The pup still had some growing to do, so they fitted her with an adult-size collar and padded it out with foam rubber and duct tape.

For Helen that day was a turning point. Luke's elation woke in her a glimmer of hope that life might again be bearable.

She still cried herself to sleep most nights or lay awake, with her head playing movies of Joel at the altar with his flawless Belgian bride. She told herself again and again that it was idiotic to feel this way, because it had been all over with Joel from the moment he applied for that job. But she couldn't avoid the conclusion that his marriage confirmed her worthlessness.

On the evening Dan had brought the snowmobile, he'd planned to take her somewhere fancy over in Great Falls for dinner, but she said she couldn't face it. He'd been hurt and tried to talk her into it, and she'd ended up yelling at him. With Luke, however, her moods didn't matter. He seemed to understand whenever she was ambushed by a sudden rush of rage or tears. He would simply gather her up and hold her, as he had done that first morning, until she stopped.

Now, listening to the story of the elk, she marveled at how the son of such a father could have learned such tenderness.

Telling the story had brought Luke's stutter back.

"My f-f-father g-got real mad. He w-w-wanted me to b-b-b-be like my b-brother. He shot a six-p-pointer when he was t-ten."

"I didn't know you had a brother."

Luke swallowed and nodded. "He d-d-died. Al-most eleven y-y-years ago. In a c-c-car wreck. He was f-f-fifteen."

"Oh, I'm sorry. That's terrible."

"Yeah." He shot her a grim little smile, and she got the message that he didn't want to talk anymore about it.

THAT evening it started to snow while, inside, Helen and Luke cooked and ate supper. Before he went home, they wrapped up warm and took the snowmobile high into the forest. Luke sat behind her, holding on, with his arms encircling her, and it felt warm and comforting to be held that way. They drove to where they thought the wolves might be, and just as they got there, the snow stopped and the clouds opened on a sliver of moon.

They took the flashlight and the radio receiver and walked along the trail. They found the signals clucking clear in the crystal air, and they knew the wolves were very close. In the beam of the flashlight they found tracks no more than minutes old.

Helen turned off the light. "Howl," she whispered.

He had heard her do it several times, without success, but had never yet attempted a howl himself. He shook his head.

"I c-can't. It w-wouldn't . . . " He gestured toward his mouth, and she realized that he was afraid his voice would betray him.

"It's only me, Luke."

For a long moment he looked at her. And she saw in his sad eyes what she already knew he felt for her. She took off her glove and reached out and touched his cold face and smiled. And as she lowered her hand, he put his head back and opened his mouth and howled, long and plaintively, into the night.

And before the note had time to die, from across the snow-tipped trees of the canyon, the wolves replied.

WINTER

Seven

NOBODY witnessed the wolfer's return to Hope. His silver trailer slid into town, like a ghost ship in the dead of the night, before Thanksgiving, when the plowed snow lay like unmarked graves along the roadside.

J.J. Lovelace sat in the old gray Chevy pickup he always used for hauling the trailer. At the junction by the old school was the graveyard where the mother he'd never known was buried. But Lovelace didn't look that way or even think of it. He no special feelings for Hope. To him it was just another faceless town.

He remembered the route to the ranch well enough. It would take him past his father's old house on the river. The gateway to the house was overgrown with scrub and drifted deeply with snow. He could see the house plainly enough and could tell it had long been derelict.

He headed on up the valley. At last he saw the epic gateway of the Calder ranch with the steer's skull looming above it, watching all who approached. A mile farther he saw the ranch house and veered left on up the road toward the Hicks place.

He parked the trailer, as instructed, under some high trees at the back of the barns, where Calder said it couldn't be seen, not even from the air. Hicks and his wife were the only others who knew he was coming, Calder had assured him.

There was a woodstove in the trailer, but he hadn't the energy to get it going. The trailer was built for work, not comfort. It was like a smaller version of his trap room at home, with a narrow aisle of linoleum running from the bunk and galley at the front to a table and workbench at the rear. His gear was concealed behind secret panels in wooden cupboards he'd fitted all around the interior.

He lay down on the bunk, still wearing his coat, cap, boots and gloves, and heaped himself with his wolfskin rugs and the quilt Winnie had sewn for their bed. Then he turned off the lamp.

He tried to distract himself from his shivering by thinking about the job that would start in the morning. He could do it, even though he was getting old. His heart wasn't in it, like it had been before, but the work would keep him busy.

TODAY was Wednesday: speech therapy. It was quarter to eight. Luke had already heard his mother's car leave. With Christmas coming up, she was helping Ruth in the store every day.

His father's office opened directly onto the living room. As Luke came down the stairs, he could see him in there in front of the computer, a cigar stuck between his teeth.

"Morning, Luke."

"M-morning."

His father put down his cigar. "Not out with Helen today?"

"No, sir. It's m-my c-clinic day."

"Gonna have some breakfast?"

"Yes, sir."

"I'll join you for a coffee."

His father led the way into the kitchen, filled a cup from the coffee machine and took it to the table. Luke poured himself some cereal and sat down opposite him.

He knew what was coming. These cozy father-and-son chats about his work with Helen had been happening a lot lately. The other day his father had asked a load of questions about radio-collar frequencies. It was comical. If the guy had shown any interest in Luke's life before, he might have stood a better chance.

His father took a drink from his cup. "So how'd the tracking go yesterday?"

"G-good.

"Where are they mainly hanging out now?"

"Oh, they m-m-move around all th-the time."

"Yeah, but I mean, like yesterday, for example?"

Luke swallowed. When it came to straightforward lying, he was hopeless. His stutter nearly always betrayed him.

"They were way b-back. Right up b-by the divide."

"Uh-huh?"

"Yeah. Ab-b-bout ten miles s-south of the b-big w-wall."

"Is that so?"

Luke saw his father's face harden. For salvation he looked up at the clock. "I'd b-b-better be going."

He got up and took his hat and coat from the pegs by the door. He knew his father's eyes were on him the whole while.

He opened the door and fled.

THE session with Joan went well. He'd hardly stuttered once in the whole hour. When they said good-bye, she said how happy he looked. It was true. He'd never felt happier in his whole life.

He drove to the supermarket to pick up some things Helen had asked him to get. He parked and, as he got out, saw Cheryl Snyder and Jerry Kruger heading toward him. Kruger had his arm around her, presumably to let the world know he and Cheryl were an item.

"Hi, Luke."

"Hey, Cooks! Congratulations!"

Luke frowned at Kruger.

"Hear you got yourself laid at last."

"What?"

Luke could see Cheryl jabbing him in the ribs, telling him to shut up. But Kruger took no notice.

"Aw, come on. The wolf babe! Everybody knows." He howled. Cheryl broke away from him. "Don't take any notice, Luke."

"I'm just h-h-helping her. That's all."

"Yeah, right," Kruger said. "Oiling her traps, huh?"

Cheryl gave him an angry push. "Jerry, just shut up, okay?"

Luke walked the aisles of the supermarket in a state of shock. He prayed that Helen didn't get to hear about it.

ELEANOR fixed the star to the top of the Christmas tree in the shop window and stood back.

"It looks beautiful," Ruth said. "Whenever I do Christmas trees, they always end up looking Jewish."

Eleanor laughed. "How can a tree look Jewish?"

"I don't know. They just do. You're a Catholic, huh?"

"Born, raised and lapsed."

"It shows. The born and raised bit. Catholics do good trees."

Eleanor laughed again, and while Ruth served some customers, she got on with decorating the rest of the store. It had been years since she had put up Christmas decorations at home, and it gave her a nostalgic, almost childlike, pleasure.

When the customers had gone, Ruth came to help her hang a big gold streamer across the front of the store. Ruth held one end while Eleanor went up the stepladder to tack the other.

"So is Luke still helping Helen Ross out with the wolves?"

"Yes. We hardly ever see him."

"I like her."

"I do too. I think Luke's got a bit of a crush on her."

They moved the ladder to the other side of the shop, and up Eleanor went again. For a while they were silent.

"So how come you lapsed? If you don't mind me asking."

"Well, all my life I'd been a regular churchgoer. Buck used to tease me about it. But then he's not a Catholic, so he never understood. After our boy Henry was killed, I started going more than ever. You know, you're looking for a sign that the one you've lost is somewhere else and happy. And then one day I realized that He wasn't there."

"You mean, your son?"

"Oh, no. He's there all right. I mean *He,* with a capital H."

"So you believe in heaven, but you don't believe in God?"

"Exactly."

By now the streamer was in place. Eleanor came down the ladder to inspect it. "What do you think?" She looked at Ruth and was surprised to find she was staring at her and not the streamer.

"You're a great woman, Eleanor. Do you know that?"

"Don't be silly."

"I mean it."

"Well, I think you're pretty good too."

Ruth gave a little mock curtsy. "Thank you, ma'am."

"Can I ask *you* a personal question now?" Eleanor said lightly. It wasn't fair, she knew, and she felt a little mean doing it. But there were moments in life that you couldn't let go by unused.

"Of course."

"How long have you been sleeping with my husband?"

KATHY had been up awhile but was still in her pink quilted dressing gown, sitting on the couch, idly flicking through the pages of *People* magazine, while the baby had his feed. It had snowed again, and Clyde was out with the plow. The morning sun was flooding in through the doorway from the kitchen. Suddenly Kathy heard two sharp knocks on the kitchen door. She got up and made herself decent, and right away the baby began to cry. She put him over her shoulder and patted his back while she walked into the kitchen.

The face she saw when she opened the door gave her such a shock she almost dropped the baby. Everything about it was gray, from the fur of the cap to the frosted tips of the beard. All except the eyes, which glared at her like a pair of angry black bugs.

It was the first time she had met the wolfer, though he'd been there more than two weeks. She had caught a glimpse of him now and then, heading up toward the forest on his snowmobile. Clyde said he was weird and grouchy and she shouldn't bother him.

Little Buck was bawling in her ear, and the wolfer was staring at him as if he'd never seen a baby before. Then he seemed to remember Kathy was there too and touched his cap.

"Ma'am."

"You're Mr. Lovelace. Come in. Nice to meet you."

He stepped into the kitchen, his eyes fixed on the baby.

"Is he yours?"

Kathy laughed. Whose baby did he think it was? "That's right."

"How old?"

"He'll be one come the end of January."

Lovelace nodded, considering this. Then, abruptly, he took his beetle eyes off the baby and fixed them on Kathy. "Your husband said I could borrow the chain saw, cut me some firewood."

He looked down. The chain saw was right by the door. Clyde had filed and oiled the chain at the kitchen table last night while lecturing her on how she shouldn't go telling anyone about the wolfer.

"Can I take it?"

"Oh, yes. Please."

He picked up the chain saw. "Won't trouble you again."

Before Kathy could say it was no trouble, the wolfer had gone.

LOVELACE had been looking for the wolves for fifteen days now, starting from the north, where Calder said he reckoned they were, methodically combing the canyons and forest. But he'd seen no sign of them, nor heard a single howl. He knew that the biologist woman and Calder's son would be out radio tracking, so he always chose the routes he figured they'd be least likely to use.

The weather was a curse. It had snowed almost every day since he arrived, as if God was trying to hide the wolf tracks from him.

He lay now in his sleeping bag, looking at the map with his flashlight, working out where he'd go when the blizzard blew itself out. It was nearly twenty below outside his tent. On the map, he saw he was above a place called Wrong Creek. High above it, he noticed the crossed pickax symbol of a mine, no doubt disused. It might be somewhere for dumping the wolves, assuming he ever caught them. He killed the flashlight and lay on his back, staring at the tent roof.

All day he'd been thinking about the Hicks woman's baby. The noise, the energy, the sheer, explosive life in the little thing, had quite shocked him.

He had known the young of many species, but he'd never known a human baby. Nor had he ever smelled that warm, sweet, puppy smell he'd smelled that morning.

He and Winnie weren't able to have children. She'd been keen to adopt, but he didn't like the idea of rearing another man's child. Whenever possible, he had avoided any contact with children. Perhaps he feared they might touch some painful spot within him.

Suddenly and for no apparent reason Lovelace thought about that last evening he'd spent with Winnie at the hospital.

The doctors had told him out in the corridor that she was slipping away. He went in and sat down beside the bed. Her eyes were closed, and she looked so frail and pale. After he'd been sitting there some time, she opened her eyes and saw him and smiled.

She started to talk, so softly he had to lean in real close to hear her, and it was as if she were in the middle of a conversation.

"I was thinking, Joseph. About all those animals. How many it must be. How many do you think?"

"Winnie, I . . ." He took her hand in both of his.

"It must be more than thousands. Tens of thousands, maybe. Do you think it's that many, Joseph?"

"Winnie," he said softly. "What animals, dear?"

"The ones you've killed. I was trying to add them up. It's so many, Joseph. All those lives, every one of them a separate life."

"You shouldn't be fretting about things like that."

"Oh, I'm not fretting. I was wondering, that's all."

She suddenly frowned and looked at him with great intensity. "Do you think, Joseph, their life is the same as ours? I mean, what it's made of, that little flicker or spirit or whatever it is, inside them. Do you think it's the same as what we have inside us?"

"No, dear, of course it's not. How could it be?"

She closed her eyes with a faint smile on her lips. "You're right," she sighed. "How silly I am. How could it be?"

THE blizzard had come from the northeast, straight across the lake. Helen listened to it wailing around the cabin, like a choir of the unforgiven. She levered the lid from the stove and dropped in another log, setting off a small volcano of sparks. The noise roused Buzz where he lay sprawled on the cabin floor. He gave Helen a look of disapproval, and she knelt and ruffled his head.

Luke was sitting at the table with his back to her, putting the last of the day's tracking notes into the laptop. He knew his way around the G.I.S. software by now as well as she did. Helen had never known anyone learn so fast. It was the same when they were out tracking. He was a born wildlife biologist.

Helen watched him now from where she knelt, still stroking Buzz. She treasured these evenings together. It was always dark when they came back from their tracking. One of them would bring in the skis and the rest of the gear from the snowmobile, while the other lit the lanterns and got the stove going. Helen would check her voice mail and return any calls, and then one of them would cook supper while the other started transferring the day's tracking notes into the computer.

Tonight, when he'd finished entering the last of the notes, he would be heading home, and Helen would feel the usual lonely hollowing within her. And she would slide into a pit of self-loathing and recrimination over Joel.

Luke clicked on SAVE and sat back.

"All done?"

"Uh-huh. Come and look."

Helen went to stand behind his chair. He had set up a new sequence of maps, showing all the locations where he and Helen had found scent posts—places where the wolves regularly urinated to mark the borders of their territory. In the snow you could spot them easily, and they were finding more every day. His new map sequence showed how the wolves had established a clearly defined territory of about two hundred square miles, which they patrolled every few days. Its most northern tip was Wrong Creek, and it spread from there, south and east, to the western edge of Jordan Townsend's ranch.

All the time she'd been standing there, her hands had been resting on his shoulders. "Well. Nice work, professor."

He tilted his head back, and she had an urge to lean down and kiss his forehead and only just stopped herself in time.

"You'd better be getting home," she said.

While he got himself ready, Helen went around tidying things, hoping to conceal her confusion. What kind of kiss, exactly, had she had in mind? Was it sisterly? Or motherly? Or was it something else entirely? She told herself not to be ridiculous. He was a friend, that was all. A friend who—unlike Joel—never judged her or criticized, who'd hauled her back from the brink.

She knew how Luke felt about her. It was obvious from the way she sometimes caught him looking at her. And there were times, she had to admit, when she felt something not wholly dissimilar for him. But the idea of anything happening between them was absurd. He was eleven years younger than she was. Well, perhaps that wasn't such a good line of reasoning. At his age she had dated men much older than she was now.

Luke was at the door now, ready to go. "G-good night."

"Night, professor."

The instant he opened the door a pile of snow fell in on him, followed by a howling blast of wind. The blizzard hadn't died. Luke had to shove hard to shut the door, and when he'd done it, he stood with his back to it, laughing and covered in snow.

"Back so soon?" Helen said.

LUKE woke in total darkness and took a moment to remember where he was. He lay on his back, on the lumpy mattress of the top bunk, listening to the muted moan of the wind and wondering what had woken him. He looked at the luminous dial of his watch. It was a little after three.

"Luke?" Helen whispered. "Are you okay up there?"

"Sure, I'm fine."

"I never thanked you," she said, "for looking after me."

"You don't need to thank me."

"Why have you never asked me about what happened?"

"I figured, if you w-wanted to tell me, you would."

And now she did. And he listened, trying to picture the face of this man she had loved. Sometimes he could hear her swallow and knew she was fighting tears. Only when she got about halfway through telling him about the letter Luke had found in the road did her voice start to crack, and he knew she was crying.

"I'm sorry," she said, when she was done. "I really thought I could do that without blubbering. I hope they'll be very happy." She paused. "Actually, I hope they rot in hell."

Luke wanted to say the guy didn't deserve her anyway and that she was well rid of him, but it wasn't his place to say it.

For a long time neither of them spoke.

"What about you?" she said at last.

"How do you mean?"

"I mean, girlfriends and all that. I remember I saw you talking with that really pretty girl at the fair."

"Cheryl. Oh, she's not a g-girlfriend. She's nice, b-but girls . . . Well, with my s-stutter and all, it never k-kind of . . ."

He felt his cheeks coloring up and was glad she couldn't see him. He couldn't bear the idea that she might feel sorry for him.

He heard the rustle of her bedclothes, and suddenly she was on her feet and her pale face was right beside him in the dark.

"Luke? Hold me. Please, hold me."

Her voice was an urgent whisper, on the edge of tears. He pulled off his sleeping bag and slipped down from the bunk. She put her arms around him, and he put his around her and held her head to his chest. The feel of her body against him almost took his breath away.

"Y-y-you're . . ."

He blocked. He couldn't say it, couldn't tell her that she was the only one he had ever loved or ever would love. Then he felt her arms release him and her hands reach up and softly take hold of his face. She kissed his forehead as if in blessing, then lightly traced the tops of his cheeks and kissed the lids of his closed eyes. She rested her cheek against his, and they stayed like that, quite still. Then he opened his eyes and kissed her face in the same way. He could taste the salt of her tears on her cheeks.

And when at last their mouths met, he felt his whole body quake, and he breathed the smell and the taste and the feel of her, drinking her down into his lungs as if he would willingly drown.

THE Christmas bazaar and pie sale at the community hall looked as if it was still going strong when Buck got into town after feeding the cattle. Eleanor was in there now; at least, that's what Buck was counting on. He'd had a job getting her out of the house, what with her fretting all night about Luke being lost in the blizzard. Just after breakfast, the boy had phoned to say he was fine and had been holed up with Helen Ross all night in her cabin. What a waste, Buck thought.

He slowed as he drove past Paragon to see if he could get a glimpse of Ruth, but the window was too cluttered. He parked a little short of Nelly's Diner and walked back, glancing casually around in case anyone was looking. Today everyone seemed to be down the street at the bazaar.

There were no customers in the store. Ruth was at a counter. He hadn't seen or spoken with her in over a month. She was wearing a tight brown sweater. She looked fabulous.

"Buck, what the hell are you doing here?"

"And a Merry Christmas to you too."

"Don't play games."

"I'm not playing games."

She stopped and stood scowling at him from a safe distance, with her arms folded. "Buck, in case the message hasn't gotten through that hat of yours, it's all over with us. Okay?"

"Ruthie, I miss you so bad—"

"After all that's happened, I can't believe you'd do this."

"What do you mean, 'after all that's happened'?"

Ruth narrowed her eyes. "You mean, she hasn't told you?"

"Told me what?"

"She knows everything, you stupid idiot! About us."

"You *told* her?"

"I didn't need to. She knew anyway."

The door clanked, and they both looked around.

"Mrs. Iverson!" Ruth called. "How are you doing?" She looked at Buck and hissed through her teeth, "Go. Now."

Buck left without saying good-bye.

IT WAS Tuesday, the one evening in the week when Luke came home early. They were having fish pie, for two good reasons: It was one of Luke's favorites, and his father couldn't stand it.

Eleanor had no idea where Buck was. He was probably hiding somewhere, trying to work out how to play it when he came home. The thought made her smile.

Ruth had told her about his coming by this morning. The poor woman still couldn't quite fathom Eleanor's attitude. Betrayed wives were supposed to be vengeful about "the other woman." In fact, Ruth's affair with Buck hadn't even been mentioned since the day Eleanor broke the news that she knew about it. She felt a little ashamed of the way she had brought the matter up, for she was fairly sure the affair had been already over by then.

To her credit Ruth hadn't tried to deny a thing. But she did ask how Eleanor had found out.

"Ruth, I'm afraid to say, I've had a lot of practice."

Eleanor spared her the details of how she'd found out this time. Of how, on that first day when she'd come into the shop and offered to get involved in the business, she'd found Ruth's scent oddly familiar and later realized it was the same one she sometimes smelled when Buck came home. Of how she'd seen his car that night outside Ruth's house and then found one of his cigars in the driveway.

"There's always some woman somewhere," Eleanor went on. "And frankly, Ruth, I don't really care anymore."

Poor Ruth had been quite shaken.

It was another hour before Eleanor heard his car. When he came in, she was busy laying the table. She glanced up and saw that he looked contrite and edgy and gratifyingly pale.

"Something smells good," he said.

Eleanor smiled and told him they were having fish pie.

LOVELACE SNIFFED THE NIGHT air like a wolf. The wind would be drifting the smell of the deer's blood down the canyon, where he wanted. The night of the blizzard, when the wind had died, he'd heard them howl, and when it got light, he'd found tracks a hundred yards from his tent, as if they'd come to check him out.

It was nine o'clock. He'd been waiting nearly four hours.

He was lying on his belly in his sleeping bag, wedged under a high fissured shelf that ran along the wall of the canyon.

Through the rifle's nightscope he scanned the canyon again, down the creek and the trail beside it, which the wolves would likely use if they came. Then he panned the scope back up the creek until he found the rock where he'd laid out the young deer. A fraction to the right Lovelace saw a shadow step right into his invisible spotlight.

There were two of them—three now, four—trotting in single file around a bend in the trail. The one in front must be almost white. From its size and prime position and from the height of its tail, Lovelace guessed it was the alpha female. He could see the collar on her neck and on the neck of the one behind her too. The other two were slighter, not quite full-grown.

Lovelace's heart started to thump. He couldn't believe his luck. Silently he slid the safety and switched on the laser sight.

According to Calder, there were eight in the pack, so he kept his eyes on the trail, waiting for the others to show. But they didn't. It was strange, he thought, for them all not to be hunting together, but at least he had two to go for. He was going to leave the collared wolves until he'd killed all the others. So long as their signals kept chiming, the woman would likely think the whole pack was okay.

The white one stood quite still with her nose raised, and then came on again, more slowly, and the others followed to the rock where the deer lay. Lovelace wanted them all to eat enough of it for anyone finding it to think they'd killed it.

Only when they had feasted did he get ready to shoot. The two uncollared wolves were side by side, their heads deep in the deer. Lovelace leveled the laser dot on the nearer one. The wolf lifted its head to swallow. He pulled the trigger.

The impact of the bullet lifted the wolf backward, clean off the rock and into the creek. He'd only reckoned on getting one. The others, he thought, would spook and run. But they didn't.

He shot the second clean through the head, and it dropped stone dead beside the deer. This time the other two wolves leaped through the water and crashed off through the trees.

He loaded the dead wolves onto the snowmobile and drove up to the mine he'd found the previous day. One at a time he hoisted the wolves over the edge of the shaft. They tumbled down in a clatter of rocks and landed with a splash in the belly of the mine below.

He stood there a moment, listening to the silence.

"Do you think, Joseph, their life is the same as ours? I mean, what it's made of, that little flicker or spirit or whatever it is, inside them. Do you think it's the same as what we have inside us?"

"No, dear, of course it's not. How could it be?"

It was snowing again. By dawn his tracks would be gone.

THEY had only kissed. Kissed and lain in each other's arms on her bunk and talked until dawn. Where was the wrong in that?

It was the question Helen had harassed herself with ever since. Joel once told her she must have majored in guilt rather than biology. Luke, it emerged, was the same.

In their huddled confession that night she had told him of the guilt she felt for her parents' loveless marriage. And Luke had then told her of his own for his brother's death.

It was still hard to believe she was going away. Helen had gotten a letter from her father, enclosing a plane ticket and a formal invitation to his wedding in Barbados. She was going for Christmas and would be away for ten whole days.

Her flight was due to leave at six o'clock the following morning. Despite her protest, Luke had insisted he was going to drive her to the airport.

Luke was going to stay up at the cabin to look after Buzz and keep the tracking going. His parents were okay about it, and Dan said it was fine, provided it was all unofficial.

Buzz started barking. He'd probably sniffed some passing animal outside the cabin. Helen told him to hush. She folded the dress she'd bought in Great Falls for her father's wedding and packed it.

"I wish you weren't going," Luke said.

"I don't want to go. I'll miss you." She put her arms around his neck, and he held her.

"I love you, Helen."

"Oh, Luke. Don't say that."

"But I do." He held her away from him and looked into her eyes. She frowned. "It isn't right."

"W-why isn't it right? You still love J-Joel?"

"No."

"He hurt you. I could never hurt you."

"But I . . . I might hurt you."

He drew her toward him and kissed her. For an instant he thought she was going to pull away, but she didn't, and he felt her fingers tighten on his arms.

"I don't care," he breathed.

An hour later, when they said their good-byes and Luke left for home, it was snowing heavily. Had he looked, he might still have deciphered the half-filled footprints outside the cabin window. But his head was soaring elsewhere with his heart.

Eight

COURTNEY and Howard were married on Christmas morning, a few days after Helen arrived. The ceremony took place in a flower-clad gazebo overlooking the bay.

It was good to see Celia again and to have time alone with her, for Celia's husband, Bryan, spent most of the time swimming or sailing with their children, while Helen and Celia lazed on their recliners, reading and talking. At the end of each day the sisters would swim to a small pontoon to watch the sunset. Christmas Day, with the wedding party still going strong onshore, they swam out clutching glasses and a bottle of Champagne.

"You don't like her, do you?" Celia said, pouring the wine.

"Courtney? She's okay. I don't know her."

"I like her. And I think she really loves him."

"Whatever the hell that means." Such a remark would normally elicit some gentle reproof from Celia, but Helen had told her two nights ago about Joel's letter, and perhaps that was why she now made no reply. The silence soon had Helen feeling a little ashamed. She looked at her sister and smiled. "Sorry. Sour grapes, I guess."

"It'll happen," Celia said simply.

Helen laughed. "What, me? My prince will come, you mean?"

"I know it."

"Actually, I already met him."

Celia didn't say anything. Helen stirred the darkening water with her legs. She turned and saw Celia staring at her, waiting.

"Well, you can't just leave it at that."

"Okay, he's tall, dark and slim. He has beautiful green eyes. He's the son of a big rancher, and he's sweet and caring. He's completely besotted with me. And he's eighteen years old."

"Oh. Well." Celia had her schoolmarm face on. "Did you . . ."

"Did I sleep with him?"

"Helen! You know darned well I didn't mean that. Why do you always assume I'm going to be shocked by such things? I know you think Bryan and I are just boring, narrow-minded little yuppies and that you're the one who really lives."

"I don't think that. Really, I don't—"

"Yes, you do. And it's always, like, you're the only one who knows about passion and pain, the only one who suffered when Mom and Dad broke up. But Helen, sometimes the rest of us feel and get hurt too, you know. Two years ago, I had breast cancer."

"You *what?*"

"Don't worry, it's fine. I caught it early. I'm all clear."

"Celia, you never said—"

"Why should I? You get on with your life. I only told you now to make you see that you don't have some sort of monopoly on pain. Things didn't work out with Joel, and that's very sad. But maybe you're darned lucky to have found it out now. Mom and Dad lost nineteen years of their lives finding out."

Helen nodded. She was close to tears, not of self-pity, but of shame. About Celia having had cancer, about every other item of truth she'd spoken. "I can't believe you never told me."

"Why worry everybody? I'm okay." She pulled down the top of her swimsuit to reveal a small pink scar. "Bryan says it's sexy."

"You're amazing."

Celia laughed. She covered herself up and put her arm around Helen's shoulders. "What's his name?"

"Luke."

"Does he have cool hands?"

"He has beautiful hands."

Celia cradled her, stroking her hair. In silence they watched a pelican come gliding in to land farther along the beach.

Celia said, "You know, Courtney's twenty-five, Dad's, what, fifty-six? Okay? What's all the fuss about? If they make each other happy. Last night he said to me, 'Courtney has given me the secret of life. She's taught me to *be*.' To live in the moment. And she's right. And if anyone in the whole world needs to do that, it's you."

"You think so?"

"I *know* it. I say, give yourself a break. Just let things be. Go back to Luke and, well, you know . . ."

"Sleep with him?"

"Helen, you're impossible."

That night Helen lay listening to the swish of the waves on the beach. It had been a revelation. She felt stupid for having always underestimated Celia and daunted at finding herself so accurately understood. As to Celia's advice about Luke, Helen was less sure. It took account of Helen's needs, but not Luke's.

Until now Helen had been the one waiting to get hurt and rejected. With Luke all this had changed. She had not the slightest foreboding that he would hurt or reject her, only the other way around. Yet when she had tried to warn him, he had told her he didn't care. So why should she? Was it not enough to love and be loved? For she did love him, she knew, and not simply for rescuing her from despair. She loved him for himself.

SINCE Luke had been staying on his own in the cabin, he had gotten into the habit of putting on some music when he came back from tracking. Normally he chose one of the albums Helen usually played—Sheryl Crow, Van Morrison or Alanis Morissette—which somehow made him feel she was there. But today he had found her box of opera discs and put on the first that came to hand, *Tosca*.

She had called her voice mail on Christmas Day and left him a long message, telling him funny things about the wedding. She'd ended by saying she missed him and wishing him a Merry Christmas.

Christmas at the Calder ranch had been about as merry as it ever managed to be. His father was in a bad mood, and Luke spent most of the time playing with the baby, until he felt he could make an excuse of having to feed Buzz and escaped back up to the cabin. He'd played her message a dozen times.

She hadn't called since. There was only one message now, from Dan Prior. They were going flying in the morning. Dan also said he'd at last got the results of the DNA test on the young collared male: They showed he had different genes from the others, which meant he was a disperser.

By the time Luke had made himself some tea and the cabin had warmed up, the opera was in full swing. The Italian lady was really letting it rip, and even though Luke couldn't understand a word, he found himself enjoying it.

He had just sat down to untie his boots, when he heard a note that, at first, made him think someone in the orchestra had goofed. Buzz had clearly heard it too and seemed oddly excited.

"It's *Tosca*," Luke confided. "In Italian."

It was only when he heard the sound a second time that he recognized it. He went to the window and looked out. There was still enough light for him to see the wolf.

It was the alpha female. She was at the edge of the forest on the far side of the frozen lake. Her white coat stood out against the dark of the trees. He could see her collar clearly, and as he looked, she lifted her head and howled. It was different from every other howl he'd heard, starting with a series of barks, just like a dog's. Luke quickly went to fetch Helen's binoculars.

Luke decided to try to get a better view by opening the door a little. He'd barely opened it an inch when Buzz pushed past him and headed hell for leather down toward the lake.

Luke stepped out after him. "Buzz! No!"

The wolf stopped howling and stood still, with her tail held high, watching the dog cross the ice of the lake. Luke started running down the slope, but he broke through the snow to his knees. He struggled to his feet and looked through the glasses.

The dog was bounding up the far slope now, and suddenly the wolf started wagging her tail. Buzz slowed and went the last few yards getting lower and lower, until he was slithering on his belly. When he got to her, he flipped over and lay on his back beneath her, and the wolf just kept on waving her tail to and fro like a flag, looking down her nose at him.

Luke was waiting for her to pounce and rip the dog's throat out. But she didn't. Suddenly she flattened down and put her head on her paws, still wagging her tail. She wanted to play. And as soon as Buzz got the message, she was off, running in crazy circles around him, the dog trying in vain to catch her. Then the wolf stopped and crouched down again, and Buzz did the same, and then off they went again, only this time it was the wolf's turn to do the chasing.

Then, abruptly, the wolf veered away and headed for the trees. Buzz stood there a moment, looking a little lost. Luke called him, but off he went in hot pursuit and vanished into the forest.

Behind, in the cabin, *Tosca* boomed on. Night was falling fast. Suddenly the wolf's game didn't seem so funny anymore.

THE wolfer heard the music too. He was higher up the valley, on his way to the place where he'd killed the third wolf, on Christmas

Day. For several days he'd followed the boy's tracks, taking care to place his skis and poles precisely inside them. On Christmas Eve, unwittingly, the boy had led him to a wolves' cache of meat from an old bull elk. Lovelace set foot snares on the likely approaches.

He spent the night camped a mile downwind, and when he skied back in at dawn, he found not just one wolf, but a pair: a female pup and a young collared male. He took off his skis and pulled his axe and two black sacks from his pack.

As he came toward them, he crooned to the pup in a soothing singsong. "Ain't you a pretty thing? Ain't you just?"

He stopped a little way short of her and raised the axe above his head. The pup looked up at him, and something in her golden eyes made him hesitate. But he slammed his mind shut to whatever he'd seen there and with two swift blows cleaved her skull. He quickly wrapped her head in one of the sacks, so her blood wouldn't stain the snow, and took the snare off her leg.

He looked down at the collared wolf. It was bleeding heavily from where the wire of the snare had worked into its front leg. It was a sorry affair, on Christmas Day of all days, to look a gift wolf in the mouth, but he'd already decided to leave the collared ones till last.

He threw his second sack over the wolf's head and roped its muzzle so it couldn't bite him. It took him a while to pull the wire from the wound, but he managed it. Then he untied the rope, stood clear and pulled off the sack. The wolf scrambled to its feet and fled into the trees, limping badly. He reset the snares, then took the dead wolf directly to the mine and sent her down the shaft to join her brothers. Three dead, five to go.

That was two days ago now. Since then, each time he'd checked the snares he found them empty. The place by now was too spoiled by his scent, and it was time to remove them. He was on his way to do that when he heard the music. Then he heard the wolf start to howl along with it. It was a strange duet. Then he heard the boy calling the dog and sensed something was wrong.

When he got near to the kill site, he heard the yelping. The dog had run into the same snare that had snagged the wolf pup two days ago. The mutt saw him and started wagging its tail. Then he heard the boy calling somewhere in the forest below him. Peering down through the trees, he caught a glimpse of a moving flashlight. If the dog barked now, he was in trouble.

There was only one thing to do. He clicked the bindings of his skis and stepped out of them. The dog gave a little whine.

SHE looked for him as she came out of the gate and saw him standing in front of the giant stuffed bear. He stared right at her and for a moment didn't seem to recognize her.

"Luke?"

"Hey!"

They stood shyly facing each other, the crowd streaming by.

"Y-y-your hair's gone all b-blond."

She put a hand through it. "Yeah. It's the sun."

"It looks nice." He took her bag. "Let's go."

They didn't say another word all the way to the parking lot.

Buzz was in the front seat of the Jeep, and when he saw her, he started to go crazy. When she opened the door, he almost knocked her over. She saw the bandage on his front paw.

"Hey, dog, have you been messing with bears again?"

"W-wolves."

"Are you serious?"

As they headed out onto the interstate, he told her what happened and how he'd been following the tracks up into the forest with his flashlight when the dog came limping down toward him.

"I figured the wolf must have b-bitten him. But Nat Thomas said it looked like it was a wire wound. He reckoned Buzz had gotten himself caught in a snare or something."

"A snare? Do people set snares up there?"

"Yeah, sometimes. P-poachers, folk like that. I was g-going to have a look the next day. But it snowed in the night, and by morning all the tracks were gone. I g-got the feeling, that night, that there was someone up there. I've felt it once or twice lately."

He changed the subject and told her how he and Dan Prior had gone flying and seen five wolves, including three who were collared. Dan had said the other three were probably around too, but they were deep in the timber, so it was hard to get a proper look.

"And g-guess what? I applied to M-Minnesota."

"You did? For the fall? Luke, that's terrific!"

Dan and he had talked about it when they got back to his office, he said. The university had a Web site, and the two of them had gone on a virtual tour of the campus on Dan's computer. They'd downloaded the application, and Luke had sent it off.

She stared at him, thinking how good it felt to be with him again and to see him cheerful. He took his eyes off the road for a moment and beamed at her.

"What are you grinning at?" she said.

He shrugged and said simply, "You c-came home, that's all."

She didn't know where or what home was anymore. If it was about belonging, all she knew was that, at this moment, she felt she belonged here with Luke more than anywhere else.

FOR three weeks it thawed and rained. The forest roads transformed themselves into rivers of mud. Three times Lovelace had ventured up into the forest and on each occasion been forced to turn back. He spent days alone in his trailer, thankful of the rest.

He was dog-tired. But try as he might, he couldn't sleep. He would lie awake all night, fighting thoughts he'd rather not let into his head.

The only thing that passed the time was carving his antlers. He'd done it for years. He liked to use a whole elk antler and carve animals chasing each other along it: big ones at the base, like bears and elk, then smaller ones, like wolves, and at the tips of the tines little bitty chipmunks and mice. The one he was finishing now wasn't too bad. All he had to do was carve the name on the underside.

An hour later he was knocking on the Hickses' kitchen door. In a few moments the woman came to the door.

"Mr. Lovelace, I'm afraid Clyde's not back yet."

"That's not why I came." He held the antler out to her. "It's for the boy. You said his birthday was coming up."

"Yes, it's tomorrow. Why, that's really so sweet of you."

She took it from him. "Please, come in."

"No. I got things need doing. Just wanted him to have that."

She held the antler up. "It's lovely. Did you do this yourself?"

He shrugged. "See, it's got his name on it."

"Oh, that's so pretty. Thank you."

He gave her a nod and walked away.

BUCK sat waiting in the driver's seat while Clyde hauled the last of the hay bales from the bed of the truck and spread it out on the ground in front of a row of forlorn-looking cattle. The rain was beating on the cab roof. The clock on the dash read five thirty. They were an hour late for Buck Junior's birthday party.

It took twenty minutes to get back to the Hicks house. Kathy, Eleanor and Luke were all waiting for them. There were balloons and streamers hung across the kitchen. Buck Junior was hungry, and as soon as they'd got their boots and coats off, Kathy put him in his high chair and lit the single candle on his birthday cake. It was in the shape of a six-shooter. She'd made it herself.

They all stood around him and sang "Happy Birthday." Kathy helped him blow the candle out, and eventually everybody got a cup of coffee and a slice of gun.

"So what'd this son of a gun get for his birthday?" Buck asked.

Kathy went through the list while the baby tried to shovel choco-late cake into his mouth. "And Lane sent him a fabulous romper suit, all white and silver. Clyde said he looks like Elvis in it. And Mr. Lovelace, would you believe it? He brought over this weird antler thing with animals carved on it."

There was a moment of silence. Clyde darted a look at Buck.

"Who's Mr. Lovelace?" Eleanor asked.

Kathy suddenly realized what she'd done and seemed to be try-ing to think of something to say. Clyde beat her to it.

"Just an old guy we've got doing some joinery work for us."

Eleanor frowned. "That name rings a bell. Where's he from?"

"Oh, he's from over Livingston way. Used to do a lot of work for my uncle. Hey, Kathy, look! That cake's going all over the place."

The danger passed. Luke didn't seem interested, and Eleanor didn't ask another question. She told Luke to fetch some milk and went to the other end of the kitchen to make more coffee.

"What do you think you're doing?" Clyde hissed at Kathy over the baby's head.

"I just forgot, that's all."

"It's okay," Buck said quietly. "No damage done."

He walked over to join Eleanor and Luke. What with the boy's wolf work, Buck had hardly seen him lately. He looked different somehow, more grown up. But kids his age were like that. Look away and they grew an inch taller.

"Well, stranger," Buck said. "How're you doing?"

"I'm f-fine."

"Getting much wolf tracking done in this weather?"

"It's a little m-muddy."

"So what are you and Helen finding to do up there?"

Clyde sniggered. Luke turned to look at him.

Kathy groaned. "Clyde, don't make a fool of yourself."

Buck had heard the gossip himself, about how Luke and Helen Ross were supposed to be having an affair. It was preposterous. Luke had never shown the slightest interest in girls. His dead brother was the one who'd gotten all those particular Calder genes.

The boy ignored Clyde and turned again to Buck.

"We're c-c-collating all the tracking data we've got so far."

Buck took a mouthful of cake. "So where are they hanging out?"

Luke looked him right in the eye. The boy plainly didn't trust him at all, and it stirred Buck's temper to see it. "Oh, they g-g-go all over the place."

"Think I'll go tell Abe or something?"

"N-no, sir."

"Well, why the hell can't you tell your own father?"

Eleanor, infuriatingly, as always, came to the boy's rescue. "He can't give away classified information. He's working for the U.S. government. Now who's going to eat the rest of this cake?"

Curiously, Buck hadn't thought of it that way before. His own son working for the damn feds. It did little to improve his mood.

"I hope that Ross woman knows you're going to be needed here full-time once calving starts," he said.

Luke started trying to speak. Buck cut him off. The sight of the boy's stuttering face enraged him.

"That's not a suggestion. It's an order."

And he clacked his plate down on the table and left.

AFTER the death of the old black wolf, killer of dog and calf, there was never a doubt over who should succeed him, for there was only one other adult male: the collared disperser who had joined the pack as a yearling two falls ago.

It was the new leader's right and duty to mate with the white alpha female. Only the alpha pair of any pack could breed.

But the new king was now a cripple. The month-old wound made by the wolfer's snare had festered, and the wolf had lain for many days in a cluttered creekside crevice, licking his swollen, seeping paw and daily growing thinner and weaker.

Perhaps because the alpha female and the three remaining pups knew that their survival as a pack depended on him, they tended him and brought him food back from their hunts.

In the first week of February, with the windless world again freezing hard and the snow falling in feathered flakes, the white queen coupled with her maimed king.

ON THAT same night, away across the blanketed forest, Luke and Helen lay entwined in the candlelit cabin. She was sleeping, her head on his chest, and he could feel her breath, warm and soft and slow, on his skin. He reached over and snuffed the candle out.

He thought of that day in early fall when he'd taken her to where the wolves had denned, and he remembered lying there alone in the hole in total darkness and thinking it was a perfect place to die.

Now he knew he was wrong. Here—in darkness just as black, with this other living creature in his arms—was the perfect place.

THE TRIAL OF ABRAHAM EDGAR Harding took place in late February, and its third and final day was drawing to a doleful and predictable close. Sleet angled on the Harding supporters who trudged up and down outside the Helena federal district court building.

On the first morning there had been fifty or sixty of them, corralled by police at a safe distance from a smaller but equally voluble band of pro-wolfers. To the satisfaction of photographers and TV reporters, the two sides heckled, chanted and brandished placards.

But Abe was beyond help. He proudly declared in his final speech to the jury that he had deliberately killed the wolf—which was pretty well all the prosecution had to show.

Abe Harding was found guilty on all counts. Sentencing would come later, but the magistrate left the court in no doubt that Abe faced several months in jail and probably a fine as well.

Harding's sons, Wes and Ethan, turned and glared venomously at Helen, but either she didn't notice or pretended not to.

"Let's go get a drink," Dan quietly said to her.

They both had cars and drove separately to a bar Dan thought none of the Harding supporters would be likely to choose for drowning their sorrows. Everything the place served was organic, the clientele was mainly students, vegetarians or both.

They found a booth and ordered two wheat beers on tap.

"Has Luke heard back from the university?" he asked.

"Not yet. He sent them this great paper about the G.I.S. work he's been doing."

"They'll take him okay."

Dan took a long draft of beer and put down his glass.

"Helen, there's something I have to tell you."

"Going to fire me? It's okay, I quit."

He smiled. "No." He paused. "It's just that we've been getting these calls at the office. I'm sure it's just somebody trying to stir up trouble. It's about Luke."

He saw her stiffen slightly. "What about him?"

"Well, I know he has to spend a lot of time up at the cabin, but some folks are saying you and Luke are having an affair."

"And you want me to tell you if it's true or not?"

"No," he lied. "You know that's not what I'm saying."

His cell phone started to ring. "Rats." He tugged it out of his coat pocket. The call was from Bill Rimmer. Some wolves had killed three calves near Boulder, he said, and it was important that Dan come at once to try to calm things down. "Helen," he said. "I'm sorry. I've got to go. I'll call you in the morning."

"Fine," she said, watching him put on his coat.

He felt guilty over what he'd said. "I'm sorry. I got that all wrong."

"Hey, no problem." She looked hurt—and beautiful.

"In case you're wondering," she said. "It is."

"What?"

"True."

He drove to Boulder with his heart sinking.

HELEN was at the bottom of her second beer and thinking about a third when she heard the voice behind her.

"Sure is a sorry thing when a pretty woman has to celebrate on her own."

That's all I need, she thought. She turned and saw Buck Calder standing by the booth, leering down at her.

"Why should I be celebrating?"

"You got the verdict. I figure that's what you wanted."

Helen shook her head and looked away.

"Mind if I join you?"

"Mind if I ask what you're doing in here?"

"Well, I was heading home, and I saw your pickup parked out there and thought I'd stop and say hi."

The waitress appeared, and Buck ordered two wheat beers.

"Thanks, but I ought to be going."

He eased himself into the other side of the booth. Helen warned herself to go easy. However much she might dislike the man, he was Luke's father.

"I wanted to talk about Luke," he said, with a knowing smile. "I want you to know, whatever idle tongues may be wagging—"

The waitress arrived with the beers. He thanked her and waited for her to leave before he went on.

"What I wanted to say was, just how grateful Eleanor and I are for all you've done for the boy, letting him work with you and all. Of course, I'm going to need him around now we're getting into calving, which I hope you'll understand."

Helen nodded.

"But his mother was saying only the other night that she's never seen the boy so happy. He seems at last to have grown up a little. Even his stutter seems to have gotten better. So thank you."

Helen didn't know what to say. He had taken her by surprise.

He took a drink. "You know, I reckon if you and I hadn't gotten off on the wrong foot, we might have been friends."

"Hey, we're friends, as far as I'm concerned."

"Okay, then. More than friends."

She pretended to look puzzled. He gave her a slow smile. Then he reached beneath the table and put his hand on her leg. "Why settle for a boy when you can have a man?" he said.

Helen took a deep breath and stood up. "I'm going home." She put her coat on and walked away.

It was snowing hard. Hurrying across the parking lot, she was so shaken and angry that she slipped and nearly fell. How *dare* he?

Helen climbed into the pickup and slammed the door. Thank heavens, the engine fired first time. She hit the gas, and the Toyota slithered off, showering wet snow from her wheels as she went.

THEY finished supper in silence. Luke could tell something was wrong as soon as she came in, but whatever it was, she wasn't letting on. Luke had figured on telling her his worries that something weird was going on with the wolves, but it didn't seem the right time. He took both her hands in his. "What's the matter?"

She sighed. "I don't think you should stay here anymore."

"W-why?"

"You know what people are saying."

He nodded. "I d-didn't know if you knew."

She gave a wry laugh. "Oh, I know all right." She told him about the anonymous calls to Dan's office.

"So are you saying we should stop seeing each other?"

"No. Oh, Luke, I couldn't bear not seeing you."

"Does what other p-people think change what we have?"

"I don't know, Luke. There are just some people who always try and destroy what they don't understand or what they can't have."

"B-but if you listen to them, they win. And I love you."

"Oh, Luke, please—"

"It's okay. Y-you don't have to say it too."

"The last guy I said it to left me. For a Belgian bimbo."

"I don't know any B-Belgian b-bimbos."

It almost made her laugh.

"I'm not going to be able to c-come here much anyhow for a few weeks. My f-father wants me to help with the calving."

"He told me."

"You spoke with him? What did he say?"

She shrugged. "Just that."

THE wolf lay halfway up a narrow gully. His nose was stretched out on his paws, and his eyes were open and frozen a solid, dull yellow. How long he had been dead, it was hard to say.

They had picked up the signal shortly after dawn, a single sustained note that told them something had happened.

It took them a long time to lever him out from the rocks without damaging him further. They laid him down beside the creek.

"Look at his foot," Helen said. "That's what's killed him."

The paw was stripped of fur and was swollen to three times the size of the other. There was a deep gash all the way around it.

"You poor old fella. It looks like he's been caught in a trap."

"Or a snare, like Buzz," Luke said. "Same f-foot too."

Helen took off the collar and stopped the signal. She stood up and sighed. "And then there were seven."

"I don't reckon there's that m-many. When Dan and I w-went flying, we only saw five of them. He said the others were p-probably in the trees, but these last few days, while you've been in court, I've g-gotten the feeling that's all there is now. When the tracks separate, it looks like there's only three or four of them."

They took the dead wolf back to the cabin. Helen called Dan, and he said he would have his assistant, Donna, drive out and pick it up.

"Luke thinks someone's trying to get rid of them," she said.

"Poachers set snares for all kinds of animals. I think the boy's being a little fanciful."

Helen told him about Luke's never seeing more than four sets of tracks. When Dan replied, his voice had gone hard.

"Helen, you're the biologist. We're paying you, not Luke."

It was stupid of her, but until that moment, it hadn't occurred to her that Dan was jealous. She'd lost him.

As A young girl, Kathy had always loved calving time. Now, since moving up to the red house, she didn't like it at all. It meant that for more than a month Clyde would be sleeping down at the main house, working his shifts on the calving crew.

The calving had been going for little over a week now, and already she was bored and lonely. So if she saw a light on in the wolfer's trailer, she would find an excuse to go over and visit with him. She would take him some leftovers. And if the baby was awake, because she knew the old man liked him, she would take him along too.

The trailer smelled worse than a hogpen, but she got used to it, simply for the sake of having someone to talk with. And despite his grouchy way, there was something about the old man she liked.

He'd been away for a couple of days, up in the forest, and after she'd noticed he was back, she'd carried over a bowl of stew. He'd shoveled it down and was now mopping the bowl clean with some bread she'd also brought.

Kathy sat on a stool, with Buck Junior on her knee, on the other side of the narrow table. Little Buck sat still and silent, his eyes following every move the wolfer made.

"That was good." He poured himself some coffee, and they sat in silence while he stirred sugar into it, all the while watching the baby.

Sometimes he barely said a word, and Kathy ended up doing all the talking. At other times though, you couldn't stop him, especially when he got on to the subject of his daddy.

"You know you told me about that thing your daddy invented?"

"You mean the loop?"

"The loop, that's it. What exactly was it?"

He went on stirring his coffee. "Want to see it?"

"You've still got it? Really?"

"Still sometimes use it."

He got up and went to one of his cupboards. He pulled out a coil of wire with small, slender cones of metal attached to it, brought it back to the table and stood uncoiling the wire. The baby reached out toward one of the metal cones.

"No, honey," Kathy said. "Don't touch."

"That's right, don't you go touching. These things may look like toys, but they ain't. I'll show you."

There was a piece of bread left on the table, and he picked it up and started to slide it carefully over the point of one of the cones.

"My daddy used to say chicken was best, but pretty much any kind of meat'll do. You lay the loop of wire outside the den, just when the wolf pups are about three weeks old and thinking about venturing out into the world. And then . . ."

He stopped, and Kathy, who'd been watching his hands, looked up at his face and saw he was staring in a strange way at the baby.

"Mr. Lovelace? Are you okay?"

His eyes shifted up to look at Kathy, and it was as if he had no idea who she was. He looked down at his hands again, and it seemed to make him remember what he'd been saying.

"The pup smells the bait. And cos he don't know better, he takes this into his mouth, narrow end first. That's important, cos you don't want him triggering it till it's gotten right down."

He was looking at the baby again.

"Right down?" Kathy prompted.

"Right down . . . right down into his throat. Then, the moment he closes his mouth on this wide bit, just here . . ."

He gave it a little squeeze with his fingers, and there was a sudden loud snap. Three barbed hooks, like a small grappling iron, shot out through the bread, making it explode all over the table.

Buck Junior jumped in fright and started to bawl. Kathy stood up and held him to her, patting his back, but he wouldn't stop.

"I'm sorry, I better take him home."

The old man didn't reply. He just stood there, staring at the hook in his hands.

"Mr. Lovelace?"

The baby's hollering was becoming unbearable. Kathy went to the door and turned to say good night. But he didn't seem to hear.

She would never be sure, for the lamp was behind him and half his face was in shadow, but as she closed the door, Kathy thought she saw, on the old wolfer's cheek, the glint of a tear.

In the dead of night, lying in bed, with the baby asleep beside her, she heard his snowmobile. She went to the window and saw its light going away across the meadow and up into the forest.

It was the last time she would ever see him.

IN THE second week of calving they were coming at a rate of around twenty a day, and the men worked through the night in two- and three-hour shifts, none of them getting more than four hours sleep. Luke had taken over from Ray at four a.m. and had a fairly easy time of it. The only drama had been when he spotted a pair of coyotes sniffing around the corrals, and he just chased them off, thanking his lucky stars that they weren't wolves. He headed down to the corrals to have another look at one of the heifers who was overdue. In the last hour she'd been looking troubled, and Luke was starting to think something might be wrong.

He stood on the fence and searched over the rail with his flash-light for the heifer.

"How's it going?"

He looked around and saw Clyde, who was taking the next shift.

"Okay. There's one here I'm a little w-worried about. I think she may have got a t-twisted uterus or something."

Clyde asked him to point her out.

"No way," Clyde said dismissively. "She's okay."

Luke shrugged. He told Clyde about the coyotes, then went back to the house to get an hour of sleep before sunup.

He overslept. The others were already having breakfast in the kitchen. He could tell right away that something had happened. Ray and Jesse, the hands, were eating in silence. His father had a face like a thunderhead, and his mother caught Luke's eye in warning. For a while no one said a word.

"So how come you let that heifer die?" his father said at last.

"W-what? Which heifer?" He glanced at Clyde, but Clyde was keeping his eyes on his plate.

"Clyde found a dead heifer in the corral. Had a twisted uterus."

"B-but I showed her to you." Clyde looked up briefly, and Luke could see the fear in his eyes. "Y-y-you said she was okay."

"You did not, Luke!"

"Come on, boys," Luke's mother said. "We always lose one or two—"

His father cut her off fiercely. "You keep out of this."

"I even t-told you what I thought was wrong with her. And you said she was okay!"

"Hey, look, kid. Don't you try and pin this on me."

Luke stood up. His chair grated on the floor.

"Where do you think you're going?" his father said.

"I-I-I've had enough."

"You have? Well, I sure as hell haven't. You sit down."

Luke shook his head. "No, sir."

Ray and Jesse got up and quietly left the room.

"You stay put till I've had my say. Your mother tells me you think you're going off to college in Minnesota, is that right?"

Luke's mother stood up. "Buck, for heaven's sake, not now—"

"Shut up. To study bunny hugging or something. Is that true?"

"B-b-biology."

"So it is true. And you don't consult your father about this?"

Luke's legs started to shake. But for the first time in his life he wasn't afraid of the great bull face glaring across the table at him. All he felt was anger. It was almost exhilarating.

"Have you lost your tongue?"

He took a deep breath and felt a strange calm rising in his chest. "No," he said simply.

"Then you'd better damn well explain yourself."

He took another breath. "I didn't think you'd be interested."

"Oh, really?" His father smiled sarcastically.

"I knew you w-wouldn't approve."

"Well, I *am* interested, and I don't approve. You'll go to Montana State, boy, and see if you can learn how to be a good enough rancher not to let good heifers die."

"If Clyde's too much of a c-coward to admit it, I don't care. And I'm not going to M-Montana State, I'm going to M-Minnesota."

"Oh, you are, huh?" His father stood up and came toward him, and for a moment Luke felt his courage falter. "And who the hell do you think's going to pay for it?"

"I'll f-f-find a way."

"I'll pay." His mother said, and they both turned to look at her.

"I told you to keep out of it."

"Wh-wh-wh . . ." Oh, God, Luke thought, don't desert me now.

"Wh-wh-wh . . ." his father mimicked.

Luke felt a river of cold anger sweep the words out of his mouth. "Why do you have to go on b-bullying everyone? Haven't you done enough damage? Anything you c-can't understand, you have to hurt. Is it because you're scared or something?"

"Don't you dare talk to me like that." His father hit him hard across the face with the back of his hand. His mother screamed.

Luke could taste blood inside his mouth. He stared at his father, who stood glaring back at him, his massive chest heaving and his neck flushed with anger. The sight no longer scared him.

"I'm going now," he said.

"You do, and you'll never set foot in my house again."

"I don't b-belong in it anyhow. I never did." And he nodded to his mother and walked out of the room.

Upstairs, he fetched two canvas bags from the closet and packed some clothes and a few favorite books and one or two other things he thought he might need. He heard the kitchen door slam and out the window saw his father stomping through the snow to the corrals, with Clyde at his heels. It was getting light.

As he came to the top of the stairs, he looked through the open doorway of his parents' bedroom and saw his mother packing a suitcase. He put his bags down and walked to the door.

"Mom?"

She turned, and after a moment she came toward him with her arms outstretched, and he went to her and put his arms around her too. He didn't speak until he felt the shudder of her sobs subside.

"Wh-where are you going?"

She was wiping her eyes. "I called Ruth. She said I could stay with her for a while. You'll go to Helen's?"

He nodded.

She kissed his cheek. "Promise you'll come see me?"

"I promise."

He dumped his bags in the living room and went to the gun rack in his father's office and took down the .270 Winchester that had become his when his brother died. He took a box of cartridges and put them with the rifle in one of the bags. In the kitchen he collected his coat and hat and slicker and a spare pair of boots, then carried everything out to the Jeep.

When he drove under the skull of the gateway, he looked over his shoulder toward the ranch. His father and Clyde were moving some heifers up to the barn. Clyde turned and stood there a moment, watching him go. But his father kept on walking.

BEFORE he died, the wolfer wanted to say sorry, but there was no one to say it to. The only person who'd understand was Winnie, and she was dead. He wondered how long she'd known about that little flicker, as she'd called it, and why she hadn't told him before, though he knew in his heart he'd never have listened.

He thought of saying sorry to the biologist woman. But it wasn't just this he needed to apologize for. It was a whole lifetime. In the end, he came to the mine. It was as good a place as any.

Now he sat naked, with his back against a tree. He'd thrown all his clothes down the air shaft and imagined them lying on top of the wolves. His withered skin was almost as pale as the snow. He watched the stars disappear one by one in the dawn sky.

The cold was taking possession of him. He felt it creep up his legs and up his arms, closing in stealth upon his heart, while his breath slowed and froze and stiffened in his beard. A strange, dreamy kind of peace was settling on him. In his reverie he saw a baby's face by the light of a candle, staring at him. Perhaps it was the baby down at the house, though it seemed somehow different. Perhaps it was the child he and Winnie had never had.

Then, suddenly, the wolfer knew it was his own young self. And in that moment the shadow of his unknown mother leaned toward the candle flame and gently blew it out.

SPRING

Nine

As THE snow retreated like a tide up the valley, the white wolf found a deserted coyote den at the foot of a clear-cut, and while her two surviving pups looked on bemused, she dug for hours on end until it was remodeled to her taste. Her belly bagged heavily now, and she found it ever harder to hunt. The two pups were full-grown yearlings, but they lacked the wiles and wisdom of adults, and with their mother grown so slow, the pups were a poor match even for the weakest winter-wasted deer.

The smell that wafted from the valley ranches was more tempting by far. The main herds were calving now, and the wolves had already found those places where the ranchers dumped their dead.

Now the white wolf's hour was approaching, and she disappeared alone into her den, all night and all the next day. The two yearlings paced to and fro for hours, watching the mouth of the den. Sometimes they would put their heads into the hole and whine, and a growl from below would warn them to keep out. On the second evening, while their mother bore six new pups, they followed, hungry, in their dead father's footsteps and slew their first calf: a purebred Calder Black Angus.

HELEN had told Luke she was going into town to pick up some supplies. She was pretty sure he wouldn't like the idea of her going to see his mother. But Helen felt she owed the woman some kind of explanation. What she was going to say, she didn't know. She found it hard enough to explain it to herself, how she'd felt when he'd shown up at the cabin and said he'd left home and could he maybe "stay for a few days?" She had put her arms around him, and they'd stood there for a long time.

To live with him in that tiny place, which was their world and no one else's, seemed the most natural thing imaginable.

With Joel there had been passion and pleasure and friendship too, but there had never been real intimacy. She had always been the kind of woman she thought he wanted. With Luke she could be simply herself. He made her feel wanted and beautiful and for the first time in her life, completely unjudged.

But how could she begin to say this to his mother?

The door of Paragon clanked loudly as she went in. There were no customers, just Eleanor at the till.

Helen was struck again by how like Luke she looked—the same pale skin and beautiful green eyes. Eleanor smiled.

"Hello, Helen. What can I do for you?"

"Hi, Mrs. Calder. Uh. Well, I . . ."

"Come back here, and we can sit down."

Helen followed her to the coffee bar and perched on a stool. Eleanor went behind the counter. "Can I make you a coffee?"

"If you're going to have one."

Helen watched while Luke's mother deftly made their coffees.

"I came to explain about me and Luke—not *explain* exactly, just to . . . let you know that . . . Oh, rats."

Eleanor Calder smiled. "Let me make it easier for you." She put Helen's coffee in front of her. "You've made Luke very happy. As far as I'm concerned, you've done him nothing but good." She came around the counter and sat down.

Helen was stunned. "Thank you," she said fatuously.

"As to him moving in with you, all I'd say is, some of the folk around here are a little old-fashioned. But that's your decision. And in all honesty, I don't know where else he'd go."

"You moved out too, Luke says."

"I should have years ago. I only stayed because of Luke."

They talked about Luke's college application and then about the wolves. Helen said there were only three or four of them left now.

"What's happened to the others?"

"Don't know. Someone's killing them off, maybe."

Eleanor frowned. "You know, maybe I shouldn't say a word. But my son-in-law has someone called Lovelace working for him up at his place. I couldn't figure out where I'd heard the name, but then I remembered. A famous old trapper called Lovelace used to live here. A wolfer, they called him."

LUCKILY, this time Calder and his son-in-law hadn't called the TV station, but Clyde Hicks had his video camera rolling as soon as Dan Prior and Bill Rimmer arrived to check the two dead calves.

"You government people can edit stuff and have the pictures say whatever you want," Hicks said. "We're gonna make our own record."

Calder hadn't even said hello. His silence was deafening. When he'd called Dan to tell him what had happened, he'd stuck to facts. And added a warning not to bring Helen Ross. He didn't want her on his property, he said. Dan left a message on her voice mail.

Rimmer had the second calf on the tailgate of his truck. Besides the tracks and the scat, the teeth marks and hemorrhaging left no doubt that the first had been killed by a wolf.

Calder stood watching with his arms folded. He looked pale and had the dark rings under his eyes that most ranchers got during calving time. He kept clenching the muscles in his jaw.

"Well," Rimmer said at last. "They certainly fed on this little fella too. But they didn't kill him. The calf was stillborn."

Calder looked at him for a moment. "We don't have stillborn calves," he said icily.

"This one was. His lungs haven't opened. I can show you—"

"Get out of here."

Dan tried to mediate. "I'm sure Defenders of Wildlife will give full market price compensation for them both—"

"Get the hell off my property."

Luke almost got lost in the labyrinth of logging roads. He had set off as soon as Helen got back and told him about the wolfer. Kathy would be at the big house, cooking lunch for the calving crew. She normally went home about three. He only had about half an hour.

At last he found the trail he was looking for, and he knew, from the lay of the land, that he was above Kathy's house. He parked and went the rest of the way on foot.

There didn't seem to be anyone around. There was a silver trailer and an old gray Chevy tucked away behind the barn. He knew neither belonged to Clyde and Kathy. When he got down to the house, he knocked on the kitchen door and called out around the barn. There was nobody there. He walked quickly around the back to the trailer and knocked on the door, and when there was no reply, he tried the handle. It wasn't locked.

The smell alone told you it wasn't the home of any carpenter. Then he found the hidden cupboards. Two were packed with traps and wires and snares and things he'd never seen before. In another one he found bottles. He uncorked one. Wolf pee.

Then he heard a car pulling up. He quickly put the bottle and one of the snares in his coat pocket. He stepped down from the trailer and tried to shut the door quietly, but it made a loud click.

"Mr. Lovelace?"

Luke froze. It was Clyde. He was coming around the barn. When he saw Luke, his face switched in an instant from friendly to hostile. Kathy appeared behind him, holding the baby.

"What are you doing here?" Clyde said.

"I w-wanted to see my sister."

"Oh, yeah? How did you get here, fly?"

Luke nodded up toward the forest. "I p-parked up there."

"You've got a nerve, snooping around other people's property."

"Clyde, for Pete's sake," Kathy said.

Clyde's eyes flicked to the trailer. "Get out of here."

"Clyde!" Kathy said. "He came to see me!"

"Shut up."

"It's okay, Kathy. I'll g-go."

He walked past them, and when he reached the meadow, he started to run. And he didn't stop till he got to his car.

When he arrived at the cabin, he saw Dan's car parked outside. From the tense silence he knew as soon as he stepped inside that they had been arguing.

"Dan wants to kill the rest of the wolves," Helen said.

Dan sighed. "They killed one of your father's calves."

"So Dan's going to let himself be bullied into doing exactly what your father wants: Get rid of the wolves."

"Helen, sometimes you have to lose a battle to win the war."

"That's bull, Dan. Remember what you said about Hope being the real test? If you don't take a stand against people like Calder, you'll never win the war."

"Helen, just face it. Hope isn't ready for wolves."

"You do this and it never will be. I don't know why you ever asked me to come here in the first place."

"You know something? I ask myself the same question."

They stood glaring at each other. Luke brought out the snare and the bottle of wolf pee. He put them on the table.

"Does this m-make any difference?"

BUCK HAD DRIVEN RIGHT UP AS soon as Clyde called him. The two of them went straight to Lovelace's trailer.

"How long since you last saw him?" Buck asked.

"Must be near on three weeks. Kathy saw him going off on his snowmobile in the middle of the night. He's never been gone that long before. She thinks something's happened to him."

They checked inside the trailer. It didn't look as if Luke had been in here, but for him to have come sneaking around, he must have had his suspicions. The boy might tell Dan Prior, and in no time there'd be feds coming up the driveway.

"We'd better get rid of the trailer," Buck said.

"Shouldn't somebody be looking for Mr. Lovelace?" Kathy said, back at the house.

"Sure they should. I'll have a word with Craig Rawlinson about it. But, sweetheart, we've got to be careful." He said he and Clyde were going to move the trailer out, just in case Luke had gone blabbing to his Fish & Wildlife pals. If anyone came while they were gone, she was to say she didn't know a thing.

They hitched the wolfer's Chevy to the trailer, then took off. Buck drove the wolfer's truck, while Clyde followed in his own.

They dumped both pickup and trailer at a big truck stop some forty-five miles west of Hope.

WHEN Kathy first heard the sound, she thought it must be Clyde and her daddy come back, but a few seconds later, through the kitchen window, she saw a beige-colored truck pull up across the yard next to her daddy's. There were two men in it, wearing hats.

They got out and headed to the house. Kathy went to the door, and as she opened it, one of them showed her some ID.

"Mrs. Hicks?"

"Yes?"

"I'm Special Agent Schumacher from U.S. Fish and Wildlife Service Law Enforcement Division. This is Special Agent Lipsky."

Kathy tried to look casual. "So what can I do for you?"

"May I have a word with your husband, please?"

"He's not here right now. Is there something wrong?"

"Ma'am, we've received information that someone's been doing some illegal trapping work on Forest Service land, possibly taking endangered animals. The informant had reason to believe the person involved was operating out of here."

"Really? I'm sure there's some mistake."

Then she saw Clyde's truck come over the ridge, followed by Deputy Sheriff Rawlinson's car. Her daddy was sitting beside him.

As Clyde got out, Kathy could see anger in his eyes, and she was thankful her daddy was there. Schumacher went through it again.

Her daddy heard him out in silence. "I think someone must have gotten their wires crossed," he said.

"Mind if we take a look around?"

Clyde erupted. "Yes, I damn well do."

The agent reached into his pocket and pulled out a piece of paper. "Sir, this is a warrant that says I can search the premises."

"You'll do it over my dead body," Buck said in a low voice.

Kathy saw Craig Rawlinson gulp; then he stepped forward. "This is my jurisdiction, as sheriff. You guys had better leave. Right now."

Schumacher pointed at Craig Rawlinson. "You're the one who's out of line, mister," he said. "I'll be calling your boss."

"You do that, pal."

The agents got back in their car, and no one said a word until they'd disappeared over the ridge.

Clyde punched the air. "Yes!"

Kathy's daddy grinned and clapped Craig on the back. "Son, I'm proud of you." He turned to Kathy. She was close to tears, not of relief, but of rage. "You okay, sweetheart?"

"No, I'm not! You men can tell your own damn lies in future."

And she turned her back on them and headed for the house.

"VARMINTS at two o'clock!" the pilot called.

The helicopter was chasing its own shadow into a wide clear-cut, scarred with sliprock and a crisscross of felled lodgepoles. Then she saw them. Two of them were sunning themselves on an outcrop of rock. Helen could just make out a collar on the paler one. They scrambled to their feet and started to trot, then lope, up toward the trees. Bill Rimmer already had the barrel of his gun sighted on one.

He fired, and she saw the uncollared wolf cartwheel as he was hit, and then the pilot wrenched the helicopter into a steep climb, missing the tops of the trees by inches.

Rimmer grinned. "Nice flying. Hey, Helen, don't look so worried! It's only a dart."

Dan had only granted the wolves a reprieve at the last minute. Even after Luke had shown him the wolf urine and the snare, he'd still been adamant that all the remaining wolves except the alpha female must be killed. She and any new pups would be evacuated to Yellowstone. It was only when Dan heard from Schumacher what had happened up at the Hicks place, that he'd changed his mind.

Buck Calder's open defiance of federal agents sent him ballistic. It was time to make a stand. Instead of killing however many wolves remained, they would dart and collar them, then monitor their every move. And if anyone so much as sneezed on them, he would personally throw the bastard into jail.

The pilot was now taking them in a wide circle so they could keep an eye on the wolf. The den was exposed and could easily be seen from the logging road that ran along the top of the clear-cut. Helen saw Dan and Luke in Dan's car stopping there now.

Just as he reached the trees, the wolf tottered and fell. The collared one had already fled ahead into the forest.

"Okay, boys and girls. Going down."

It took Helen and Rimmer half an hour to do all that was necessary with the wolf. Dan and Luke walked down and stood by, watching.

"Looks like he's having a hard time of it," Rimmer said.

"Yeah. His sister's probably the same."

Once they'd tested his collar, Rimmer went back to the helicopter. They wanted it out of the way so as not to frighten the wolf again when he woke up. Helen walked back up the slope with Luke and Dan. The air between her and Dan was still strained, and neither spoke. Luke looked through the binoculars. "He's g-getting up."

The wolf staggered a little, then shook himself. At last he trotted off into the trees, the way his sister had gone.

Dan drove them back to the cabin. No one spoke the whole way. Then Luke got out and said he had to go into town. Helen knew he was only making himself scarce so she and Dan could have a few words alone. He walked to his car and drove off.

"I'd better be getting along too," Dan said, not looking at her.

"Okay." She opened the door and got out. "Dan?"

He turned and looked at her. His eyes were hard. "Yeah?"

"I'm sorry."

"Sorry for what?"

Helen shrugged. "For everything. It feels like we're not friends anymore. I know you disapprove. Of me and Luke, I mean."

"Hey, Helen. It's your life." He gave her a sad smile and restarted the engine. She reached into the car, and he took her hand in his and held it a moment.

"You know where I am," he said.

"I know where you are."

THE days were growing warm, and there was easy prey to be found. Several times the two collared yearlings felled a young or weakened deer and bore proud morsels back to the den.

When Helen and Luke witnessed this, unseen, from higher ground, they knew that the mother and her litter must be in the rocks.

Down in the cool dark earth, the white wolf suckled her six pups. The scraps of meat the yearlings brought were barely enough to keep milk flowing, and her pups were smaller and weaker than last year's litter. In a day or two their milk teeth would be breaking through and they would start to need meat. Only then would she let them wander from the den.

IT WAS after eight, and Kathy was about to shift from irritated to downright mad. Buck Junior was in bed, supper was in the oven, but where was Clyde? Calving was all but over, and it was their first

evening alone together in over a month—or supposed to be. Clyde
had probably gone for a drink with the calving crew first.

Things had been cool between them since that trouble with the
federal agents. Kathy was still angry, but it was time to make up.

To keep herself from smashing something, she was wrapping Lucy
Millward's present. Her wedding, to a man named Dimitri, was tomorrow. She had just finished writing Lucy's card when Clyde came
in. He looked so sheepish that she almost forgave him on the spot.

Then he had to spoil things by bringing up wolves again. Earlier
on, down at the Last Resort, he'd been talking with two of the guys
from the post and pole company, who'd told him they knew where
the wolves were denning. "So unless someone does something about
it, there'll be a whole new pack of critters."

Kathy didn't want to hear another thing about wolves. And it
made her think of poor old Mr. Lovelace and those federal agents.
Clyde got up and went into the living room. She could hear him
rummaging around for something in the closet.

When he reappeared, he had something in his hands. Kathy realized it was the wolfer's loop. "Where did you get that?"

"It's the thing he showed you, right?"

"You stole it from his trailer?"

"I just borrowed it. Show me how it works."

He laid it on the table and came and put his arms around her.
"Come on, honey. Help me. I want to do it for your daddy."

THE letter came that morning from the University of Minnesota,
offering Luke a freshman place that fall.

Helen screamed and hugged him. Luke wanted to tell Dan right
away, and because the cell phone had again refused to recharge, they
drove into town to call him. He insisted they come on into Helena
so he could buy them lunch to celebrate.

It was Lucy Millward's wedding day. Both Luke and Helen had
been invited, but neither of them fancied bumping into Luke's
father or Clyde. They accepted Dan's offer.

He took them to the Windbag, and they all ate and drank far

more than they needed. Dan seemed to have patched up his quarrel with Helen. Luke and Helen drove back out to Hope, into the lowering sun, feeling dreamy and good and together.

EVERYONE was in the corral, sitting on pews of baled hay. At the western end, beneath a high gateway entwined all around with red-white-and-blue ribbon that fluttered in the evening breeze, Lucy and Dimitri were declaring their love. Their horses stood side by side, facing the minister's mare. Lined up on either side were the bridesmaids and the page boys, three of each, all mounted. Apart from the video cameras, the whole thing was like a living tableau from the Old West.

It was the first time Eleanor and Buck had seen each other since she'd walked out, and it wasn't as awkward as she'd feared.

"Eleanor," Buck said.

"Buck." She smiled, but he just gave her a nod. And that was all. It was fine by her. She hadn't felt so good for many years.

"You may kiss the bride," Eleanor heard the minister say.

"He'll fall off his horse," little Charlie Millward muttered, and all around him laughed. Lucy leaned across and spared poor Dimitri the risk, and the congregation cheered.

The wedding party posed for photographs while everybody else adjourned to the next corral for a drink. There were tables and benches and a wooden dance floor in the middle.

Then it happened. The bellowing scream of cattle in distress.

A THREE-QUARTER moon threw their shadows down the slope as they loaded their gear into the pickup. It was twenty-three days since the alpha female had denned, and Luke was convinced that tonight they would get to see the pups. Helen was locking the door when she saw the beam of headlights angling up through the trees.

The car was traveling fast. Only when it came right up to them and stopped did Helen recognize Ruth Michaels at the wheel and Luke's mother beside her.

"Mom?" Luke said, going to her. "What's going on?"

"The wolves have killed some of Doug Millward's calves. Your father shot two of the wolves. He just grabbed a gun from one of Doug's ranch hands and shot them both. Doug tried to stop him, but he wouldn't listen. And now he's getting a whole crowd together, and they're going up to the den to kill the rest of them."

"They know where the den is?" Helen said.

"Clyde says it's up above the Townsend place."

"I'll call Dan." Helen opened the cabin, snatched up the cell phone and punched in the number. She waited, then realized that she had been listening to silence on the phone.

"It still hasn't ch-charged?"

"No." She thought for a moment. "Luke, you go down to the clear-cut with your mom and Ruth and try and talk some sense into them. I'll go try and get the pups out."

"I'll g-get the pups out," Luke said.

"You've never done it before. You have to crawl right down into the den. With the mother down there, it can be dangerous."

"Helen, I can do it!"

She hesitated. He was probably right.

"You'll need something to carry them in—those canvas bags of yours. Ruth, could you go into town and call Dan?" Helen scribbled his number on a piece of paper and handed it to her. "Call the police and the Forest Service emergency line too. Tell them we're at the big clear-cut."

"You bet." She was off at once, running to her car.

Luke had the two bags. He was loading his rifle.

"You won't need that."

"No, but you might." He held the rifle out. "Take it."

She did as she was told. She picked up the chain saw, locked Buzz in the cabin and followed Luke and his mother to the cars. Ruth was already driving away. Helen dumped the gun and chain saw in the pickup and took the jabstick and another flashlight over to Luke, who was climbing into his Jeep.

"Go down into the den slowly. And keep the jabstick out in front of you. She'll threaten you, but in the end she'll make a break for it."

"Okay. Shall I bring the p-pups back here?"

The cabin would be the first place anyone would look.

"Take them to Ruth's house," Eleanor said.

"And Luke," Helen said. "Be careful."

He nodded, then slammed the door. As he swung the car around, Helen and Eleanor climbed into Helen's pickup. Soon she'd caught up with Luke and was following his taillights.

"Thank you," Helen said. "For coming to tell us."

Eleanor reached across and gently touched her on the shoulder.

THE white wolf paused in the mouth of the den while the two biggest and bravest of her pups tottered out into the moonlit world. There was something near at hand that smelled good.

The mother had smelled it too, all day. Perhaps the humans had left it there. She had caught their scent long before she heard the scuffle of their feet outside. She'd heard the clink of something too, and could smell it out there, mixed with the waft of fresh meat.

All the two pups smelled was the meat. All day they had tried to leave the den, and time and again she had stopped them and carried them back. But after so many hours of waiting in vain for the year-lings to bring food, she was starving and at last relented.

The first of the pups staggered toward the smell, and his mother followed, nudging the other pup before her to his first proper meal. There was a lump of pale meat, and now she could smell and see others a few yards to either side. The tang she had smelled came from a line, a thing of humans, that ran between them.

The pup nudged the meat with his nose and nipped it. As he tugged, his mother saw the line move, and she shied. There was danger here, she now knew. In a bound she was beside the pup.

But the meat was already inside his mouth, and he bit on it.

LUKE left the car, took the bags and the jabstick and headed off through the trees. He kept the beam of the flashlight low and ran in the pool it made among rocks and tangles of blowdown.

At last, through the trees ahead, he saw the moonlit glow of the clear-cut. He turned off the flashlight and fished out Dan's infrared nightscope. Just as he found focus, the wolf started to bark.

It was the alpha female. She was a few yards from the entrance to the den and barking right at him. There was a movement behind her. The pups were scurrying down into the den. The mother didn't seem to want to follow them. When the last one had gone, she lifted her head and barked, ending each burst of barking with a howl. Luke willed her to shut up. She was telling the whole world where she was.

He put the nightscope away and stepped into the clear-cut. As he got closer, she kept running off, then coming back, barking and howling at him. In the moonlight Luke could see something dark in the place that she kept returning to.

As he walked the last few yards, the mother ran off. She stopped about twenty yards away and stood watching him. There was a whimper. He switched on the flashlight.

"Oh, God," he murmured.

HELEN had parked the pickup across the road. She'd cut down a tall Douglas fir in front of it. Now she was cutting a second, and the chips were showering into the beam of Eleanor's flashlight. The tree leaned and creaked and toppled exactly where she wanted it.

They were a mile and a half north of the clear-cut. Helen had chosen the place for its view of the road that wound up from the valley. Any approaching headlights would be seen a long way off.

Helen put the chain saw in the bed of the pickup. Eleanor handed her the flashlight. The two women stood in silence for a while beside the pickup, staring at the moon.

Something in the valley caught Helen's eye. "Here they come."

A pair of headlights was coming around the first bend. Another vehicle, then another came into view. There were more trucks coming now. Five, six . . . eight in all, winding up the road in convoy.

"Well, here we go," she said.

BUCK figured there were about twenty of them, including a few he'd rather not have had along. The two Harding boys and some loggers were pretty far gone. On the other hand, there was safety in numbers. No one was going to put the whole damn town in jail.

He and Clyde were leading in Clyde's truck, with one of the loggers sitting wedged between them to make sure they didn't get lost. He was one of the guys who'd come up here with Clyde last night to lay that damn fool loop thing. They should have just stuffed some poison down the hole or poured gasoline in it. Anyhow, they'd put that right when they got there now.

"Hey, look," Clyde said. He was peering up ahead. "There's somebody already got here."

A couple of hundred yards ahead of them, there was someone with a flashlight. Then, in the headlights, they saw trees had been felled across the road and a truck parked behind them.

"It's the wolf woman," Clyde said. "Who's with her?" Then Clyde looked at Buck. "What's Eleanor doing here?"

Buck didn't answer. She must have gone and told Helen Ross what was happening. His own wife. "Stop here."

They stopped about fifteen yards short of the roadblock, and as they did, Helen Ross climbed over the trees and came toward them, shielding her eyes against Clyde's headlights. Buck got out and walked around to the front of the car. All the other guys were piling out of their trucks. Abe Harding's dogs were barking.

"Hello, Mr. Calder."

He just stared at her. He could tell she was scared.

"I'm afraid, sir, this road has been closed."

"Uh-huh? On whose authority?"

"The U.S. Fish and Wildlife Service."

"This is a public road."

"I know that, sir."

Eleanor was coming up behind her now. No doubt thinking she could make a fool of him in front of everyone.

"Craig?" he called out, keeping his eyes on Helen Ross.

"Yeah!" Craig Rawlinson pushed his way through the crowd.

"Does this woman have the authority to close a public road?"

"Not unless she's got a piece of paper to prove it."

"Buck," Eleanor said. "Please. It's time to stop."

"Stop?" He laughed. "Honey, I haven't even gotten started."

The Ross woman turned to Craig Rawlinson. "I can't believe you're going to help these men commit a crime."

"You're the only one committing a crime around here. Now get your truck out of the way or I'll arrest you."

He reached out to take her by the shoulder, but she lashed out and gave him a shove in the chest that made him stagger back.

"Feisty little thing, ain't she?" Wes Harding called out.

Eleanor stepped forward. "What's the matter with you boys?"

The sound of her voice made Buck's blood seethe. "Clyde, get those trees off the road."

LUKE had tried to get the hooks out of the pup's mouth, but all three barbs were deeply bedded in, and he couldn't loosen them without doing more damage. He got all the meat out of the poor little thing's throat, so it didn't choke, but that was all. He knew it was going to bleed to death, and if he wasted any more time, maybe the others would be lost as well, so he put the pup back on the ground, attached to the line like a drowning fish.

All the while, the mother wolf had been barking and howling at him from across the clear-cut. He could even hear her now that he was down in the den, inching along the tunnel on his belly, pointing the flashlight ahead of him.

Then he heard whining and saw the pups in the beam of the flashlight. They were in a dark furry huddle at the far corner of the nesting chamber, squinting and mewing at the light.

"Hey," he said softly. "It's okay. Everyone's going to be okay."

He put down the jabstick and the flashlight and pulled the canvas bag out of his shirt. He opened it up and elbowed his way toward the pups. There were five of them. The tunnel was narrow, and he didn't want to risk hurting them. He decided to take three first, then come back for the other two. He reached out and plucked one. Its fur was soft and all fluffed up. It mewed at him.

"I know, I know. I'm sorry."

"MOVE YOUR TRUCK," Buck Calder said.

"No."

Helen stood facing him, her back to the driver's door, her arms folded, trying to look tough and official. Her head came about half-way up his chest. She could feel her knees going wobbly.

Clyde was supervising the removal of the second tree. The first had already been towed off the road by the Harding boys.

Helen saw that some of the men had guns out now.

"Give me the keys." Buck held out his hand, and Helen only just resisted the urge to spit in it. Over his shoulder she could see Eleanor talking to Abe Harding. He wasn't listening. The second tree was being dragged away behind his sons' truck, in the back of which the two dogs were tethered, still hollering.

"Clyde? Get a rope on this thing," Buck shouted.

"On her or the pickup?" Ethan Harding called out.

They all laughed. Someone handed Hicks a rope, and he started to walk toward the pickup. Helen turned and wrenched open the door. She reached behind the seat and pulled out Luke's rifle.

She pointed it at Hicks and cocked it. He stopped in his tracks, and everything went quiet. Helen swallowed hard. "Go home. All of you."

Everyone stood frozen, staring at her. For the first time, Eleanor looked frightened. Calder was frowning at the gun, and as he stepped toward her, she swung the barrel so it was pointing at him instead. He faltered. But he walked right up to her, until the barrel was an inch from his heart.

"You dare," he whispered. "You *dare* point my dead son's gun at me?" He closed his hand over the barrel and took it from her.

THE mother wolf was at the mouth of the den when he came out with the first bag of pups. She backed away, barking and snarling at him, showing her teeth and gums. Luke yelled and swung the jabstick at her, and she ran off twenty yards or so, still barking. Luke worried that if he left the bag of pups outside the den she might come and carry it off while he was down getting the others.

He wedged the bag of pups into a crevice between the rocks. It wouldn't stop her getting at them, but it might buy him enough time. All the while he tried to block his ears to the screams of the pup who was hooked to the wire that, he now discovered, stretched in a wide circle all around the den.

What kind of mind, he wondered, could have devised such a thing?

Then Luke heard a distant rumble of engines and a dog barking. Looking up the clear-cut, he saw headlights pan the sky. He grabbed the flashlight and the empty bag and dived back down into the den.

THE cars and trucks all pulled up in a line along the top of the clear-cut, and everyone climbed out. Most of them had guns, and those who didn't were holding flashlights. Abe had his dogs on leashes now. They were barking more crazily than ever.

Buck stood by Clyde's truck with Henry's gun in his hands. His blood was still simmering at the sight of that woman pointing it at him. He'd felt like smashing her face in. It was just as well Craig Rawlinson had been there to take her aside while they shunted her heap of a truck off the road. He'd felt pretty much the same about Eleanor, siding against her own husband like that.

Tactfully, Rawlinson had said he'd stay down there with the two of them. Buck knew he'd then be able to plead ignorance about what they were all about to do.

"So where is it?" Buck said.

Clyde pointed down the clear-cut. "Plum in the middle there. See the rocks? Den's right under there."

"Look!" Wes Harding yelled. "There's one right there!"

He was pointing toward the edge of the clear-cut. Every flashlight they had was at once pointed the same way, enough to see a white wolf, brazen as day, standing there staring at them.

Buck was just lifting his rifle when three or four others beat him to it, and a volley of shots rang out. It was enough to lift her clean off her feet. She was dead before she landed.

"Listen up!" Buck called out. "I've got a job to finish here. I've killed me two of these critters today, and if anyone's going to jail, it's me, okay? If another one shows, it's mine. Understand?"

There was mumbled agreement.

"Okay. Got the shovels and the gasoline?"

The loggers called out to confirm that they had.

"Then let's go."

Buck let Clyde lead the way with the flashlight. He kept the safety catch of Henry's rifle off and his eyes locked on the den. He wasn't going to have one of these drunken jerks beating him again if another wolf showed its face.

They were about halfway down the clear-cut now, and he could see the black hole of the den clearly in the pale moonlit earth. Suddenly he saw its shape alter. It was another wolf. He didn't want to yell because he knew, despite what he'd told them, all the others would take a shot. Instead, he whispered to Clyde to stop. "There's one coming out. When I tell you, shine your light."

He raised his gun and centered the crosshairs on the moving shape emerging from the mouth of the den. "Now!"

At exactly the same moment that the flashlight beam found its mark, Buck pulled the trigger and the shot rang out.

There was a cry. Sharp and terrible.

And Buck and all who heard it knew that it wasn't from a wolf.

"LUKE? Luke?"

It was the moon calling him, and he couldn't understand why.

"Luke? Oh, God. Luke?"

It sounded like his father, but it couldn't be, because his father didn't want anything to do with him anymore. There were other voices, and sometimes their shadows loomed across the moon.

When he blinked, one of his eyes felt funny. It seemed to have something wet and lumpy in it.

Where was Helen? Just for an instant he thought he heard her voice, among all the others, calling his name; then the moon flooded with red clouds. It wasn't clouds. It was red curtains closing across the sky. Maybe when they opened again, she would be standing there.

SUMMER

Ten

ELEANOR sat alone in the mall café, sipping a soda and watching the crowds go by. It was the Fourth of July weekend, and the place was teeming. The café was on a corner by the escalators.

She looked at her watch. He was ten minutes late. Perhaps he was having trouble finding the place. He'd always hated malls, but when he'd called she hadn't been able to think of anywhere else to meet. It was right across the street from her apartment.

The prospect of seeing Buck again after all these weeks didn't make her nervous, only sad. The last time had been at the hospital. They hadn't been able to look at each other, let alone speak.

She saw him now, walking with his head slightly bowed, his face half hidden by the brim of his hat. He was wearing a pale blue snap-button shirt and black jeans that seemed baggy on him. As he got nearer she saw how thin he'd grown.

Buck stood by the café entrance. She waved to him.

"I'm sorry I'm late," he said as he sat down. "I got confused with all the different entrances."

Eleanor smiled. "That's okay."

He ordered coffee from the waitress. When she went, they sat in silence, neither one of them knowing what to say.

Buck's coffee arrived, and he stirred it for a long time, though he always took it black, no sugar. It gave her time to study him. He looked almost haggard. "So," he said at last. "Kathy was telling me the house you're buying down in Bozeman is real nice."

"It's lovely. Small, you know. But I don't need a big place," she said. "You heard Ruth's moving to Santa Fe?"

"Yeah, I heard that." He paused. "You know, Eleanor. That thing between Ruth and me, it was never really—"

"Buck, don't. It's gone. It's all gone."

He nodded and kept his eyes on his coffee.

"How are things on the ranch?"

"Pretty good. I've handed a lot of stuff over to Kathy."

"She told me."

"That girl's something. Twice the rancher Clyde'll ever be."

"Little Buck's growing so fast."

Buck laughed. "Yeah! Yeah, he's coming along good."

Eleanor asked if he'd heard when his trial might take place.

"September, so they reckon. Kathy tell you about Clyde?"

Eleanor nodded. They'd found his fingerprints on that horrible loop thing, but probably because Buck was pleading guilty to everything, charges against his son-in-law had just been dropped.

"Do you have any idea yet what kind of sentence you'll get?"

"Nine months, a year. Tell you the truth, I don't really care."

"Oh, Buck."

She saw his face clench up as he tried to fight his tears. As if he hadn't been punished enough, she thought. He forced a laugh. "Anyway, Abe's boys say it's like summer camp. Apparently the old guy's having the time of his life."

Eleanor smiled. A young couple with twins were leaving. She watched Buck's face as he watched the babies being wheeled past. One of them gave him a glorious smile, and it seemed to start the tears welling again in his eyes. He looked at her.

"All I wanted to say was . . . I'm sorry. I'm so sorry."

BY THE time they had driven high into the mountains, as far as the last road would take them, a thin band of pink had risen in the eastern sky. The van Dan had hired was unmarked except for a spattering of mud. When they were finished, they were going to take it down to the cabin and load it with all the things Helen didn't want. By nightfall the cabin would be empty.

The road was getting rough now. Helen could hear the faint rattle of the cages in the back. She hadn't been up this high since the day Luke had shown her the wolves' first den. She remembered the look on his dusty face when he came crawling out and what he'd said about being happy to die down there.

"I figure this is as about as far as we can get," Dan said.

The road seemed to peter out in a short plateau of rock. To the east it fell away sharply in a narrow, rock-strewn funnel through the trees. Dan turned off the engine and looked at her.

"Just like old times, huh? Prior and Ross, alpha wolf team."

She smiled. "What are you going to do?"

"With my life? Get a proper job, I guess. Mom always said I should work with people, and I'd say, okay, I'll be a mortician."

"So even back then your jokes weren't any good."

Dan had resigned the day after Luke was shot. They'd asked him to stay on and insisted he was in no way to blame for what happened, but he said he'd had enough; he was "wolfed out."

Dan peered at the sky. "It's getting light. Better get this show on the road."

They got out and walked to the back of the van. Then he pulled the handle and opened the rear doors wide.

They pulled off the tarpaulins, and Helen's flashlight glinted on two aluminum cages standing side by side.

"I hope someone's told these guys what happens to wolves around these parts," Dan said.

"I thought you said these were vegetarian wolves?"

"They are. But, you know, it could be just a fad."

Helen wasn't going to ask Dan where they'd come from. All she knew was that they were an alpha pair, gray, untagged, uncollared and untraceable. She and Dan had picked them up just before midnight at a remote spot about ten miles south of the Canadian border. The crates had just been there, waiting for them, covered with the tarps and a few branches.

Helen went behind the first crate and slid the handles out.

"Ready? One, two, three, lift."

They put it down at the top of the slope, then did the same with the other one. Then they slid up both front doors. Behind each was an inner door of vertical square bars through which, now, they could see two pairs of amber eyes, warily surveying them.

Dan said, "One, two, three . . ."

On the count of three they opened the inner doors, and the wolves launched themselves out of the cages, landed in a clatter of sliprock and plunged headfirst down the slope.

Halfway down the funnel they stopped and seemed to look back up toward the van. Helen started to sob.

Dan put his arms around her. "Hey, it's okay."

"I know, I know. I'm sorry."

When she looked again, the wolves had vanished.

WHEN they pulled up outside the cabin, the sky had brightened to a perfect, cloudless blue and the sun was drying the dew from the flowers that smothered the slope down to the lake. Buzz came bounding to them, barking loudly. As they walked toward the cabin, they could smell breakfast cooking.

Luke was standing in the doorway.

He was smiling and squinting in the sunshine with his one good eye. The black patch over the other still gave Helen a shock.

He came to meet them and put his arms around them both. They stood in unspoken communion while Buzz bounced around them.

The bullet had hit him in the side of the neck. It had passed right through, then hit a rock, sending a splinter of it, the size of an arrowhead, into his left eye. By the time he was helicoptered to the hospital, he had lost a lot of blood. That he had survived was little short of a miracle.

The neck wound had done almost no damage. They had operated on his eye for many hours and managed to save it, though Luke would never see much with it. The first thing he wanted to know, when he came around, was what had happened to the pups.

Only the hooked one had died. The others had been taken to Yellowstone and successfully fostered. Luke's father had told the police where they could find the wolfer's trailer. And sometime later a ranger discovered his snowmobile in a clearing above Wrong Creek. No trace of the old man himself was ever found.

They sat on the grass outside the cabin and ate eggs and bacon and hash browns and washed the food down with coffee and orange juice. They talked about Alaska and some of the places Helen and Luke were going to visit in the next two months before he started college. Beyond that they hadn't made plans.

Luke wanted her to come to Minnesota with him, and while he went to classes, she could finish her thesis.

Maybe she would. For the first time in her adult life the future didn't seem to matter. It was as though all that had happened here had purged the part of her that had always yearned and worried. All that mattered was *now* and that she was with the person she loved best in all the world.

After breakfast they loaded the last few things, along with Buzz, into Luke's Jeep. Helen gave Dan the keys to her old pickup.

None of them wanted to make a big issue of saying good-bye, so they just gave each other hugs and wished each other well. Dan stood beside the car while Helen and Luke got in.

"Angels on your body," he said.

"Yours too, Prior."

They saw no one they knew when they passed through town. They turned east and headed out toward the plains.

As they came over the bridge, Helen stopped the car, and they looked one last time at the church above the river.

"Look," Luke said. He was pointing at the sign on the other side of the road, the one that said HOPE (POPULATION 819). Three narrow beams of sunlight were shining through the bullet holes.

NICHOLAS EVANS

At first glance it might seem a long leap from Nicholas Evans's life as a London-based screenwriter to Big Sky country, the setting of his best-selling first novel, *The Horse Whisperer*, and now *The Loop*. But Evans has always been a lover of the outdoors. Raised in rural England, he grew up riding horses, watching TV westerns, and reading Jack London. Later he roughed it in Africa with the Volunteer Service Overseas (the British Peace Corps). His subsequent writing career has not slaked Evans's thirst for adventure. Just recently, for instance, he climbed to the summit of France's Mont Blanc. Who knows where the call of the wild will take him next?

IS FOR NOOSE

Sue Grafton

Welcome to Nota Lake, California, where the views are spectacular and the air is crystal-clear. And where secrets can be hazardous to the health of someone who asks too many questions—someone like private investigator Kinsey Millhone . . .

CHAPTER ONE

SOMETIMES I think about how odd it would be to catch a glimpse of the future, a quick view of events lying in store for us at some undisclosed date. Suppose we could peer through a tiny peephole in Time and chance upon a flash of what was coming up in the years ahead? Some moments we saw would make no sense at all, and some, I suspect, would frighten us beyond endurance. If we knew what was looming, we'd avoid certain choices, select option B instead of A at the fork in the road: the job, the marriage, the move to a new state, childbirth, the first drink, the elective medical procedure, that long-anticipated ski trip that seemed like such fun until the dark rumble of the avalanche. Time, of course, runs in only one direction. Here in the blank and stony present we're shielded from the knowledge of the dangers that await us, protected from future horrors through blind innocence.

Take the case in point. I was winding my way through the mountains in a cut-rate rental car, heading south on Highway 395 toward the town of Nota Lake, California, where I was going to interview a potential client. The roadway was dry, the view unobstructed, and the weather conditions were clear. The client's business was unremarkable, at least as far as I could see. I had no idea there was any jeopardy waiting, or I'd have done something else.

I'd left Dietz in Carson City, where I'd spent the last two weeks playing nurse/companion while he recovered from surgery. He'd been scheduled for a knee replacement, and I'd volunteered to drive him back to Nevada in his snazzy little red Porsche. I make no claims to nurturing, but I'm a practical person and the nine-hour journey from California seemed the obvious solution to the problem of how to get his car back to his home state. I'm a no-nonsense driver, and he knew he could count on me to get us to Carson City with no irrelevant conversation. He'd been staying in my apartment for the two previous months, and since our separation was approaching, we tended to avoid discussing anything personal.

For the record, my last name is Millhone, first name Kinsey. I'm female, twice divorced, seven weeks shy of thirty-six, and reasonably fit. I'm a licensed private detective, currently residing in Santa Teresa, California, to which I'm attached like a tetherball on a very short cord. Occasionally business will swing me out to other parts of the country, but I'm basically a small-town shamus and likely to remain so for life.

Robert Dietz is a Nevada-based private investigator I once hired as a personal bodyguard. Our relationship became something more. In his late forties, he's five ten, maybe a hundred and seventy pounds, with medium-length hair showing gray around the ears. His surgery, which was scheduled for the first Monday in March, proceeded uneventfully, so we can skip that part. He was out of the hospital by Friday morning of that week. The ensuing recovery involved a lot of sitting around his condominium with his knee wrapped in bandages as thick as a bolster. We watched trash television and played gin rummy. The first three days I did all the cooking, which is to say I made sandwiches, alternating between my famous peanut butter and pickle extravaganza and my much beloved sliced hot hard-boiled egg confection with tons of Hellmann's mayonnaise and salt. After that, Dietz seemed eager to get back into the kitchen, and our menus expanded to include pizza and take-out Chinese.

By the end of two weeks Dietz could pretty well fend for himself.

He had a long way to go, but he could drive to his physical therapy sessions and otherwise tend to his own needs. By then I thought it entirely possible I'd go mad from trailing after him. It was time to hit the road before our togetherness began to chafe. I kept my farewells perfunctory—lots of airy okay-fine-thanks-a-lot-I'll-see-you-laters. It was my way of minimizing the painful lump in my throat, staving off the embarrassing boohoos best left unexpressed. Don't ask me to reconcile the misery I felt with the nearly giddy sense of relief. Nobody ever said emotions made any sense.

So there I was, barreling down the highway in search of employment and not at all fussy about what kind of work I'd take. I wanted distraction. I wanted money, escape, anything to keep my mind off the subject of Robert Dietz. I'm not good at good-byes. On the other hand, I'm not that good at relationships. Get close to someone and next thing you know, you've given them the power to wound, betray, irritate, abandon, or bore you senseless. My general policy is to keep my distance. In psychiatric circles there are names for people like me.

Just north of Topaz, I crossed the state line into eastern California. Further south, to my left, was Mono Lake. To my right, through a forest of pines, was Yosemite National Park, with its rugged canyons, lakes, and thundering waterfalls, and the towering peaks of the Sierra Nevada.

The prospective client I was traveling to meet was a woman named Selma Newquist. Dietz had done work for her in the past, helping her extricate herself from an unsavory first marriage. There'd been a subsequent marriage, and the recent death of this second husband, Tom, had apparently generated questions his wife wanted answered. She'd called to hire Dietz, but since he was temporarily out of commission, he suggested me. Dietz had vouched for my integrity, and by the same token he'd assured me that she'd be conscientious about payment for services rendered. It made sense to stop long enough to hear what the woman had to say. If she didn't want to hire me, all I'd be out was a thirty-minute break in the journey back to Santa Teresa.

I reached Nota Lake (population 2356, elevation 4312) in slightly more than three hours. The town didn't look like much, though the setting was spectacular. Mountains towered on three sides, snow still painting the peaks in thick white against a sky heaped with clouds. On the shady side of the road I could see leftover patches of snow, ice boulders wedged up against the leafless trees. The air smelled of pine, with an underlying scent that was faintly sweet. The chill vapor I breathed was like sticking my face down in a half-empty gallon of vanilla ice cream, drinking in the sugary perfume. The lake itself was no more than two miles long and a mile across. The surface was glassy, reflecting granite spires and the smattering of white firs and incense cedars that grew on the slopes. I stopped at a service station and picked up a one-page map of the town.

The prime businesses seemed to be clustered along the main street. I did a cursory driving tour, counting ten gas stations and twenty-two motels. Nota Lake offered low-end accommodations for the Mammoth Lakes ski crowd. The town also boasted a number of fast-food restaurants, including my personal favorite, McDonald's. Additional restaurants of the sit-down variety were divided equally between Mexican, Bar-B-Que, and "family" dining.

The address I'd been given was on the outskirts of town, two blocks off the main highway, in a cluster of streets named for Indian tribes: Shawnee, Iroquois, Modoc, Chippewa. Selma Newquist lived on Pawnee Way, her house a replica of its neighbors—frame siding, a shake roof, with a screened-in porch on one end and a two-car garage on the other. I parked in the driveway beside a dark Ford sedan, climbed the two porch steps, and rang the bell—*dingdong*—like the local Avon representative.

The woman who came to the door was in her late forties, with a small compact body, brown eyes, and short dark tousled hair.

"Hi. I'm Kinsey Millhone. Are you Selma?"

"No, I'm not. I'm her sister-in-law Phyllis. My husband, Macon, was Tom's younger brother. Can I help you?"

"I'm supposed to meet with Selma. I should have called first. Is she here?"

"Oh, sorry. I remember now. She's lying down at the moment, but she told me you'd be stopping by. You're that friend of the detective she called in Carson City."

"Exactly," I said. "How's she doing?"

"Selma has her bad days, and I'm afraid this is one. Tom passed away six weeks ago today, and she called me in tears. Poor thing looks like she hasn't slept in days. I gave her a Valium."

"I can come back later if you think that's best."

"No, no. She wants to see you. Why don't you come on in."

"Thanks."

I followed Phyllis across the entrance and down a carpeted hallway to the master bedroom. In passing, I allowed myself a quick glance into doorways, garnering an impression of wildly overdecorated rooms. In the living room the drapes and upholstery fabrics were coordinated to match a pink-and-green wallpaper that depicted floral bouquets, connected by loops of pink ribbon. The cut-pile carpeting was pale green and had a scent that suggested it had been recently laid. There were storm windows in place everywhere, and condensation had gathered between the panes. The smell of cigarette smoke and coffee formed a musky domestic incense.

Phyllis knocked on the door. "Selma, hon? It's Phyllis."

I heard a muffled response, and Phyllis opened the door a crack, peering around the frame. "You've got company. Are you decent? It's this lady detective from Carson City."

I started to correct her and then thought better of it. I wasn't from Carson City and I certainly wasn't a lady, but then what difference did it make? Through the opening I caught a brief impression of the woman in the bed: a pile of platinum-blond hair framed by the uprights on a four-poster.

Apparently, I'd been invited in, because Phyllis stepped back, murmuring to me as I passed, "I have to get on home, but please call me if you need anything. We live two doors down."

I nodded my thanks as I moved into the bedroom. The curtains were closed, and the light was subdued. There was a surplus of ruffles, bold multicolored prints covering walls, windows, and puffy custom bedding. The motif seemed to be roses exploding on impact.

I said, "Sorry to disturb you. I'm Kinsey Millhone."

Selma Newquist, in a faded flannel nightie, pulled herself into a sitting position and straightened the covers. I estimated her age on the high side of fifty. Her skin tones suggested dark coloring, but her hair was a confection of white-blond curls, like a cloud of cotton candy. At the moment the entire cone was listing sideways. She groped on the bed table until she had her cigarette pack and lighter. Her hand trembled slightly as she lit a cigarette. "Come over here," she said. She gestured toward a chair.

I pulled the chair in close before I took a seat.

"I'm sorry you had to see me this way," she said. "Ordinarily I'm up and about at this hour, but this has been a hard day."

"I understand," I said. Smoke began to settle over me like the fine spray from someone's sneeze.

"I don't know if you've ever lost anyone close," she said, "but there are days when your whole body aches and your head feels so stuffy you can't think properly." She tended, in speaking, to keep a hand up against her mouth, apparently self-conscious about the discoloration on her two front teeth, which were markedly gray. "How do you know Robert Dietz?" she asked.

"I hired him myself a couple of years ago to handle my personal security. Someone threatened my life, and Dietz ended up working for me as a bodyguard."

"How's his knee doing? I was sorry to hear he was laid up."

"He'll be fine. He's tough. He's already up and around."

"Did he tell you about Tom?"

"Only that you were recently widowed."

"I'll fill you in, then, though I'm really not sure where to start. You may think I'm crazy, but I assure you I'm not." She took a puff of her cigarette and sighed a mouthful of smoke. I expected tears, but the story emerged in a Valium-induced calm. "Tom had a heart attack. He was out on the road, about seven miles out of town. This was ten o'clock at night. He must have had sufficient warning to pull over to the side. A California Highway Patrol officer—a friend of ours, James Tennyson—recognized Tom's truck with the hazard lights on and stopped to see if he needed help. Tom was slumped at the wheel. I'd been to a meeting at church and came home to find two patrol cars sitting in my drive. You knew Tom was a detective with the county sheriff's department?"

"I wasn't aware of that."

"I used to worry he'd be killed in the line of duty. I never imagined he'd go like he did." She drew on her cigarette.

"It must have been difficult."

"It was awful," she said. The tears began to well in her eyes. "I mean, as far as I know, he never had any symptoms. Or let's put it this way: If he did, he never told me. He did have high blood pressure, and the doctor'd been on him to quit smoking and start exercising. You know how men are. He went right on doing as he pleased."

"How old was he?"

"Close to retirement. Sixty-three," she said. "Lately he wasn't sleeping well. I'd hear him up at two, three, five in the morning, doing heaven knows what. His weight had begun to drop in the last few months. The man hardly ate, just smoked and drank coffee and stared out the window at the snow."

"Sounds like he was under some kind of strain."

"Exactly. But I don't know why, and it's driving me nuts." She took a deep drag from her cigarette. "Anyway, that's why I called Dietz. I feel I'm entitled to know."

"I don't want to sound rude, but does it really make any difference? Whatever it was, it's too late to change."

She glanced away from me briefly. "I've thought of that myself, but I don't think I should have to wonder for the rest of my life. I don't even know where he was going that night. He told me he was staying home."

"He didn't leave you a note?"

"Nothing," she said.

"I don't mean to pry, but were you happily married?"

A little burble of embarrassed laughter escaped. "I certainly was. I don't know about him. He more or less took life as it came. I was married before . . . to someone physically abusive. I have a boy from that marriage, Brant."

"Ah. And how old is he?"

"Twenty-five. Brant was ten when I met Tom, so essentially Tom raised him."

"And where is he?"

"Here in Nota Lake. He works for the fire department as a paramedic. He's been staying with me since the funeral, though he has a place of his own in town."

"You and Tom were married for what, fourteen years?"

"Coming up on twelve. We were fine for most of it, but recently things began to change. I mean, he did what he was supposed to, but his heart wasn't in it. Lately I felt he was secretive . . . tight-lipped or something. Why was he out on the highway that night? I mean, what was he doing? What couldn't he tell me?"

"Could it have been a case he was working on?"

"It could have been, I suppose." She thought about the possibility while she stubbed out her cigarette. "Tom seldom said a word about work. He took his job very seriously, almost to a fault."

"Someone in the department must have taken over his workload. Have you talked to them?"

"You say department like it was some kind of big-city place. There were only two investigators, Tom and his partner, Rafer. I did talk to him. Rafer's always nice enough on the surface, but for all of the chitchat he managed to say very little."

I was having trouble understanding what she wanted. "Do you think there's something suspicious about Tom's death?"

"Not at all, but it upsets me to think he was withholding something when it clearly bothered him so much. I was a good wife to him, and I won't be kept in the dark now he's gone."

"Have you been through his personal effects?"

"The coroner returned the items he had on him when he died, but they were just what you'd expect. His watch, his wallet, the change in his pocket, and his wedding ring."

"Did he have an office here at the house?"

"Well, yes, but his desk is a mess. Papers piled up everywhere. It could be staring me in the face, whatever it is. I can't bring myself to look, and I can't bear to let go. That's what I'd like you to do. See if you can find out what was troubling him."

I hesitated. "I could certainly try. It would help if you could be more specific. You haven't given me much."

Selma's eyes filled with tears. "I've been racking my brain and I have no idea. Please just do *something*. I can't even walk in his den without falling apart."

Oh boy, just what I needed—a job that not only was vague but felt hopeless as well. I should have bagged it right then, but I didn't, of course. More's the pity, as it turned out.

CHAPTER TWO

TOWARD the end of my visit with Selma the Valium seemed to kick in, and she rallied. Somehow she managed to pull herself together in a remarkably short period of time. I waited in the living room while she showered and dressed. When she emerged thirty minutes later, I was amazed at the transformation. With her makeup in place she seemed more confident, though she still tended to speak with a hand lifted to conceal her mouth.

For the next twenty minutes we discussed business. It was clear by then that Selma Newquist was capable of holding her own. She reached for the phone, and in the space of one call she not only booked my accommodation but insisted on a ten percent discount on the off-season rate.

I left Selma's at two o'clock, stopping off in town long enough to flesh out my standard junk-food diet with some Capt'n Jack's fish and chips and a large Coke. After that, it was time to check into the motel. The Nota Lake Cabins consisted of ten rustic cottages set in a wooded area just off the main highway, about six miles out of town. Tom Newquist's widowed sister, Cecilia Boden, owned and managed the place. When I pulled into the parking lot, I could see that the area was a bit too remote for my taste. I'm a city girl at heart and generally happiest close to restaurants, banks, liquor stores, and movie theaters, but since Selma was paying, I didn't think I should argue the point. Silly me.

Cecilia was on the telephone when I stepped into the office. I pegged her at sixty, as small and shapeless as a girl of ten. She wore a red plaid flannel shirt tucked into dark stiff blue jeans. The reception area was a pine-paneled cubbyhole hardly large enough for one small upholstered chair and a rack of pamphlets. The reception desk was a twelve-inch writing surface mounted on the lower half of the Dutch door of the office, where I could see her consulting a big reservations book. She seemed ever so faintly annoyed with the questions she was being asked. "You want fish cleaning and freezing, try the Mountain View. . . . Uh-huh. . . . I see. . . ."

While I waited for her to finish, I pulled out several pamphlets at random, reading about midweek ski lift and lodging packages closer to Mammoth Lakes and Mammoth summit. I'd missed February's big fishing show. Well, dang.

I looked up to find Cecilia Boden staring at me with a flinty expression. "Yes, ma'am," she said.

I told her who I was, and she waved aside my offer of a credit card. Mouth pursed, she said, "Selma said to send her the bill direct." She took a bunch of keys from a hook and opened the Dutch door, leaving me to follow as she headed through the front door and down a path packed with cedar chips. The air outside was damp and smelled of loam. I could hear the wind moving in the trees and the chattering of squirrels. Ahead of us the cabins were spaced about seventy-five feet apart, separated by sufficient Douglas firs to resemble a cut-your-own Christmas tree farm.

"We're close to full up," she remarked. "Unusual for March."

"Really," I murmured, for lack of anything better. "Why do they call it Nota Lake? Is that Indian?"

Cecilia shook her head. "Nope. Ancient times, nota was a mark burned into a criminal's skin to brand him a lawbreaker. That way you always knew who the evildoers were. Bunch of desperadoes ended up over in this area—scoundrels deported to this country from England back in the mid–seventeen hundreds. All of them were branded. Killers, thieves, and fornicators—the worst of the worst. Half the people in this town are related to them."

We'd reached the first of the cabins, and she inserted her key. "This is Willow."

Willow was spacious, a pine-paneled room with a fireplace made up of big knobby boulders. The inner hearth was black with soot, with wood neatly stacked in the grate. The room was pungent with the scent of countless hardwood fires. Against one wall was a brass bedstead with a mattress shaped like a hillock. The quilt was a crazy patch and looked as if it smelled of mildew.

Cecilia opened a door on the left. "This here's the bath and your hanging closet. We got all the amenities. Iron, ironing board, cof-feemaker, soap."

"Very nice," I said.

She handed me a key. "There's more wood around the side. Watch for black widder spiders if you fetch more logs. Pay phone outside the office. Saves me the hassle of settling up for calls. We got a café down the road about fifty yards in that direction. Open six o'clock in the morning until nine thirty at night."

"Thanks."

After she left, I returned to the parking lot and retrieved my duf-fel, along with the portable typewriter I'd stashed in the rental car. I'd spent off-hours at Dietz's catching up on my paperwork. My wardrobe, in the main, consists of blue jeans and turtlenecks, which makes packing a breeze. In the cabin again, I put my few articles of clothing in a crudely made chest of drawers. Home sweet home, barring the black widders.

I set the typewriter up on a wooden table under the side window. These days most P.I.'s use computers, but I can't seem to get the hang of 'em. With my sturdy Smith-Corona I don't require an elec-trical outlet, and I don't have to worry about head crashes or lost data. I pulled a chair up to the table and made myself some notes.

Essentially Selma Newquist had hired me to reconstruct the last four to six weeks of her late husband's life on the theory that whatever had troubled him probably took place within that time frame. I'd agreed to give her a verbal report every two to three days, supplemented by a written account. The other issue we'd discussed was my fee. Selma had assured me she had money to burn, but frankly, I felt guilty about eating into Tom's estate.

We'd agreed on two hundred and fifty bucks a day. Using a boilerplate contract I'd borrowed from Dietz, I'd penned in the details, and she'd written me a check for fifteen hundred dollars. I intended to run that by the bank to make sure it cleared before I got down to business. While I sympathize with all the widows and orphans in the world, I think it's wise to make sure sufficient funds are in place.

I closed the cabin and locked it, hiked back to my rental car, and drove the six miles into town. The highway was sparsely strung with businesses: tractor sales, car lot, trailer park, country store. The wide sweep of sky had turned from strong blue to gray, a thick haze of white obscuring the mountaintops. Wind rattled the trees. I adjusted the heater in the car, flipping on the fan until tropical breezes blew against my legs.

The clothes I'd packed for Carson City were too light and insubstantial for this area. So downtown, I cruised the streets until I spotted a thrift store, where I bought a bulky brown leather bomber jacket and a faded blue flannel shirt. On my way out I spotted an office-supply store across the street. I stocked up on paper supplies, including a couple of packs of index cards. Two doors down I found a branch of Selma's bank and came out with a wad of twenties in my shoulder bag. The town already felt familiar, neatly laid out and clean, the atmosphere vaguely western. I noticed most of the vehicles were pickups and utility vans with ski racks across the tops.

When I arrived back at Selma's, the garage door was open. The parking space on the left was empty. On the right I spotted a late-model blue pickup truck. As I got out of my car, I noticed a uniformed deputy emerging from a house two doors down. He crossed the lawns between us, walking in my direction. I waited, assuming this was Tom's younger brother, Macon. I placed him in his late forties, but his looks might have been deceptive. He had dark hair, dark brows, and a pleasant, unremarkable face. He was close to six feet tall and compactly built.

"Are you Macon?" I asked.

He offered me his hand, and we shook. "That's right. I saw you pull up and thought I'd come on over and introduce myself."

"I'm sorry about your brother."

"Thank you. It's been a rough one, I can tell you." He hooked a thumb toward the house. "I believe Selma went off to the market a little while ago. You need in? Door's open most times, but you're welcome to come to our place."

"I should be fine. I expect she'll be home in a bit, and if not, I can find ways to amuse myself. I would like to talk to you sometime in the next day or two."

"Absolutely. No problem. I'll tell you anything you want, though I admit we're baffled as to Selma's purpose. Tom was as decent a fellow as you'd ever hope to meet. Everybody in town looked up to him, including me."

"This may turn out to be a short stay, in that case."

"Where'd Selma put you? Someplace nice, I hope."

"Nota Lake Cabins. Cecilia Boden's your sister, as I understand it. You have other siblings?"

Macon shook his head. "Just three of us," he said. "Tom's three years older than Cecilia and close to fifteen years my senior. I've been trailing after them two ever since I can remember. I ended up in the sheriff's department years after Tom hired on." His eyes strayed to the street as Selma's car approached and slowed, pulling into the driveway. "Here she is now, so I'll leave you two be. You let me know what I can do to help."

Selma pulled into the garage and got out of the car. She and Macon greeted each other with an almost imperceptible coolness. While she opened the trunk of her sedan, Macon and I parted company. Selma lifted out a paper sack of groceries and two cleaner's bags and slammed the trunk lid down. Under her fur coat she wore smartly pressed charcoal slacks and a shirt of cherry-colored silk.

"Let me give you a hand," I said, reaching for the groceries.

"I hope you haven't been out here long," she said. "I decided I'd spent enough time feeling sorry for myself."

"Whose pickup truck? Was that Tom's?" I asked.

Selma nodded as she unlocked the door leading from the garage into the house. "I had a fellow tow it the day after he died. I can't bring myself to drive it." She pressed a button, and the garage door descended with a rumble. "You met Macon, I see."

"He came over to introduce himself," I said as I followed her into the house. "One thing I ought to mention. I'm going to be talking to a lot of people around town, and I really don't know yet what approach I'll take. I may bend the facts a bit."

"What about Cecilia? What will you say to her?"

"I don't know yet. I'll think of something."

"She'll fill your ear. She's never really liked me. Whatever Tom's problems, she'll blame me if she can. Same with his brother. Macon was always coming after Tom for something—a loan, advice, good word in the department. If I hadn't stepped in, he'd have sucked Tom dry. You can do me a favor: Take anything they say with a grain of salt."

The disgruntled are good, I thought. They'll tell you anything.

I SPENT the rest of the afternoon working my way through Tom Newquist's insufferably disorganized home office. I'm going to bypass the tedious list of documents I inspected, the files I sorted, the drawers I emptied, the receipts I scrutinized in search of some evidence of his angst. In reporting to Selma, I did (slightly) exaggerate the extent of my efforts so she'd appreciate what two hundred fifty bucks a day was buying in the current marketplace.

Tom was apparently compulsive about saving every scrap of paper, and his desk was a jumble of folders, correspondence, bills paid and unpaid, income tax forms, newspaper articles, and case files he was working on. In the bottom drawer I found some of his equipment—handcuffs, nightstick, the flashlight he must have carried. Maybe Macon would like them. I'd have to remember to ask.

I went through two big leaf bags of junk, taking it upon myself to throw away paid utility stubs from ten years back. I kept the office door open, conducting a conversation with Selma in the kitchen while I winnowed and pitched. "I'd like to have a picture of Tom."

"What for?"

"Not sure yet. It just seems like a good idea."

"Take one of those from the wall by the window."

I glanced over my shoulder, spotting several black-and-white photographs of him in various settings. "Right," I said. I set aside a lapful of papers and crossed to the largest frame. An unsmiling Tom Newquist and the sheriff, Bob Staffer, were pictured together at what looked to be a banquet. I lifted the framed photo from the hook and held it up to the fading light coming in the window.

Tom Newquist was a youthful sixty-three years old, with small eyes, a round, bland face, and dark, thinning hair trimmed close to his head. His expression was one I'd seen on cops ever since time began—neutral, watchful, intelligent. It was a face that gave away nothing of the man within. I wondered what he could have seen in Selma. She seemed too brassy and emotional for a man skilled at camouflage.

I glanced up to find her standing in the doorway, watching me. I held up the picture. "Is this one okay? I'd like to have it cropped and copies made."

"All right. That's nice of him. How's it coming?"

I shrugged. "So far there's nothing but junk."

"Do you need help?"

"Not really. I'm about to wrap it up for this afternoon. I'll come back tomorrow and take another run at it." I jammed a fistful of catalogues and advertising flyers into the trash bag. "At some point we'll have telephone records to go through. That's a big undertaking, and I'm saving it for last. We'll sit side by side and see how many phone numbers you can recognize."

"Well," she said reluctantly, "I'll let you get back to work."

WHEN I HAD FINISHED FOR THE day, Selma gave me a house key, though she assured me she generally left the doors unlocked. She told me she was often gone, but she wanted me to have the run of the place. I told her I'd want to look through Tom's personal effects, and she had no objections.

It was fully dark when I left, and the streetlights did little to dispel the sense of isolation. Once I was out on the highway, vast tracts of land bore no evidence of human habitation. The mountain ranges were as black as jet, and the pale slice of moon scarcely brushed the snowy peaks with silver. The temperature had dropped, and I could smell the inky damp of the lake. I felt a flicker of longing to see Santa Teresa with its red tile roofs, palm trees, and the thundering Pacific.

I slowed when I saw the sign for Nota Lake Cabins. Maybe a crackling fire and a hot shower would cheer me up. I parked my car in the lot. A few low-voltage lights along the path cast a circle of dim yellow on the cedar chips. I let myself into the cabin and felt for the light switch. The overhead bulb came on with its flat forty-watt wash of light. I clicked on the table lamp, which offered forty watts more.

The room felt drab and chilly. I checked the wood in the grate. There was a stack of newspapers close by meant for kindling. Of course, there was no gas starter, and I suspected the fire would take more time to light than I had time to enjoy. I went around the room closing cotton curtains. Then I peeled off my clothes and stepped into the shower. I'm not one to waste water, but even so, I rinsed the last of the shampoo from my hair a split second before the cold water descended full force. This was beginning to feel like a wilderness experience.

Dressed again, I locked the cabin and headed back toward the road, walking briskly along the berm until I reached the restaurant. The Rainbow Café was about the size of a double-wide trailer, with a Formica counter, red Naugahyde booths, a waitperson (female), and a short-order cook (also female). I ordered breakfast for dinner. There's nothing so comforting as scrambled eggs at night—soft cheery yellow, bright with butter. I had three strips of crisp bacon, a pile of hash browns sautéed with onion, and two pieces of rye toast dripping with jam. I nearly crooned aloud as the flavors blended in my mouth.

On the way back to my cabin I paused to use the pay phone outside the office. I used my credit card to call my landlord, Henry Pitts, eighty-six years old. His would be the cover photo if the AARP ever did a calendar of octogenarian hunks.

I caught Henry on his way out the door. "Where you off to?" I asked.

"I'm on my way to Rosie's. She and William need help with the dinner crowd tonight," he said. Rosie ran a tavern half a block from my apartment. She and Henry's older brother, William, had been married the previous Thanksgiving.

"What about you? Where're you calling from?"

I filled Henry in on my current situation. I gave him both Selma's home number and that of the office at the Nota Lake Cabins in case he had to reach me. Once he rang off, I placed a call to the law firm where I have an office and left a message, again giving my location and Selma's number. I couldn't think of any other way to feel connected. The notion of spending the evening in the cabin seemed depressing. I pictured myself huddled under that damp-looking quilt, spiders creeping from the woodpile the minute I relaxed my vigilance. It was a sorry prospect.

I crossed to the motel office and peered in through the glass door. A light was on, but there was no sign of Cecilia. I let myself in. I bypassed the desk bell and knocked on the door marked MANAGER. After a moment Cecilia appeared in a pink chenille bathrobe and fluffy slippers. "Yes?"

"Hi, Cecilia. Could I have a word with you?"

"Something wrong with the room?"

"Not at all. Everything's fine. More or less. I was wondering if you could spare a few minutes to talk. Has Selma said anything about why I'm here in Nota Lake?"

"Said she hired you is all. I don't even know what you do."

"Ah. Well, I'm a field investigator with California Fidelity Insurance. Selma's concerned about the liability in Tom's death."

"Liability for what?"

"Good question. Of course, I'm not at liberty to discuss this in detail. You know, *officially* he wasn't working, but she thinks he might have been pursuing departmental business the night he died. If so, it's possible she can file a claim."

She stared at me blankly and held the door open. "You better come in. I don't mind telling you the subject's painful."

"I can imagine it is, and I'm sorry. I met Macon earlier."

"He's useless," she remarked. "No love lost between us. Of course, I never thought of Selma as family either."

Cecilia Boden's apartment was on a par with my cabin, which is to say, drab, poorly lighted, and faintly shabby. The prime difference was that my place was icy cold, whereas she seemed to keep her place somewhere around preheat.

We took a few minutes to get settled in. While my story didn't give me much room to inquire into Tom's character, Cecilia didn't question my purpose, and the longer we chatted, the clearer it became that she was perfectly comfortable discussing Tom and his wife, their marriage, and anything else I cared to ask about.

"Selma says Tom was preoccupied with something in the past few months. Did he say anything to you?"

Cecilia narrowed her eyes. "He didn't confide anything specific," she said cautiously.

"Any hunches about what was going on?"

She hesitated for a moment. "I think Tom was unhappy. He never said as much to me, but that's my belief."

I made a sort of *mmm* sound, verbal filler accompanied by what I hoped was a sympathetic look.

"Far be it from me to criticize Selma. *He* married her. I didn't. If you want my opinion, my brother could have done a lot better for himself. Selma's a snob, if you want to know the truth."

"Really," I murmured.

"She has no spiritual foundation even if she does go to church.

She's a mite materialistic. She seems to think she can use acquisitions to fill the void in her life, but it won't do."

"For example," I said.

"You saw the new carpet in the living room?" Cecilia shot me a glance filled with satisfaction. "She had that installed about ten days ago. I thought it was in poor taste, doing it so soon. She's also considering having those two front teeth capped, which is not only vain but completely trivial. Talk about a waste of money."

What's wrong with vanity? I thought. Given the range of human failings, self-absorption is harmless compared to some I could name. "I got the impression she was devoted to Tom."

"As well she should have been. Tom spent his life trying to satisfy the woman. First she had to have a bigger house in a better neighborhood. Then they had to join the country club. And on it went. Anytime she didn't get what she wanted? Well, she pouted and sulked until he broke down and got it for her."

I said, "My goodness." This is the way I talk when I cannot for the life of me think of where to go next. "He was a nice-looking man. I saw a picture of him at the house," I said, vamping.

"He was downright handsome. Why he married Selma was a mystery to me. And that son of hers?" Cecilia pulled her lips together like a drawstring purse. "Brant was a pain in the grits from the first time I laid eyes on the boy. He had a mouth on him like a trucker, and he was bratty to boot. Did poorly in school, too. Problems with his temper and what they call his impulse control. Of course, Selma thought he was a saint. Poor Tom nearly tore his hair out. I guess he finally managed to get the boy squared away, but it was no thanks to her."

"Do you happen to know where Tom was going that night? I understand he was found somewhere on the outskirts of town."

"A mile north of here."

"He didn't drop in to see you?"

"I wish he had," she said. "I was visiting a friend down in Independence and didn't get back until shortly after ten fifteen or so. I saw the ambulance pass, but I had no idea it was meant for him."

CHAPTER THREE

TUESDAY morning at nine I stopped by the offices of the Nota County coroner. I hadn't slept well the night before. The cabin was poorly insulated, and the night air was frigid. I'd moved the thermostat up to seventy, but all it did was click off and on ineffectually. I'd crawled into bed wearing my sweats and a pair of heavy socks. I curled up under a comforter, a quilt, and a wool blanket, with my heavy leather jacket piled on top.

When I woke up at seven, my nose felt like a Popsicle and my breath was visible. I showered in tepid water, dried myself shivering, and dressed in haste. Then I dogtrotted down to the Rainbow Café, where I stoked up on coffee, sausages, and pancakes saturated with butter and syrup. I told myself I needed all the sugar and fat to refuel my depleted reserves, but the truth was, I felt sorry for myself and the food was the simplest form of consolation.

The coroner's office was located on a side street in the heart of downtown. In Nota County the coroner is a four-year elected official, who in this case doubled as the funeral director for the county's only mortuary. Wilton Kirchner III, generally referred to as Trey, had occupied the position for the past ten years.

Kirchner & Sons Mortuary appeared to have been a private residence at one time, probably built in the early '20s. The architectural style was Tudor with a façade of pale red brick trimmed in dark-painted timbers. Thin, cold sunlight glittered against the leaded glass windows. Selma had called, and Trey Kirchner came out to the reception area, extending a hand in greeting. He was in his mid-fifties, tall and broad-shouldered. His smile was pleasant. There was something solid about him—a man who, by nature, looked like he could absorb all the sorrow, confusion, and rage generated by death.

I followed him down a long corridor. The office we entered

seemed designed for the public—not a book, a file, or a piece of paper in sight. "Have a seat," he said, indicating two matching upholstered chairs arranged on either side of a small table. His manner was relaxed, friendly, curiously impersonal. "I take it you're here about Tom's death." He reached over and opened the drawer, pulling out a flat manila folder. "I ran a copy of the autopsy report in case you're interested."

I took the folder. "Thanks. I thought I might have to talk you into this."

He smiled. "It's public record. I could have popped it in the mail and saved you a trip if Selma'd asked for it sooner."

"Tom's death was classified as a coroner's case?"

"Of necessity," he said. "You know he died out on Highway 395 with no witnesses and probably not much warning. We figured it was his heart, but you never really know until the post. Could have been an aneurysm. Anyway, Calvin Burkey did the autopsy. He's the forensic pathologist for Nota and Mono counties. Nothing remarkable showed up. Tom died of a massive acute myocardial infarction due to severe arteriosclerosis. You'll see it. It's all there. Sections of the coronary artery confirmed ninety-five percent occlusion."

"Nothing else came to light?"

"In the way of abnormalities? Nope. He'd eaten recently. According to our report, he'd stopped off at a café for a bite of supper. The toxi report was clear. What makes you ask?"

"Selma said he'd been losing weight. I wondered if he knew something he wasn't telling her."

"No, ma'am. No cancer, if that's what you mean. What's Selma's worry?"

"It's hard to say. I think she feels he was holding out on her, keeping secrets of some kind. She didn't press him for answers, so now it's unfinished business and it bothers her a lot."

"I don't think you'll turn up anything scandalous. Tom was churchgoing, a good soul. Well liked, well thought of in the community, generous with his time. If he had any faults, I'd have to say he was straitlaced, too rigid. He didn't believe in bending the rules, though I've seen him do it from time to time. He was a real straight-ahead guy, but that's good in my opinion. We could use a few more like him. We're going to miss him around here."

"Did you spend any time with him the past few weeks?"

"Nothing to speak of. Mostly, I saw him in the context of his job. Not surprisingly, the county sheriff's department and the coroner's office are just like that," he said, crossing his fingers. "Fellow you ought to talk to is his partner, Rafer LaMott."

I SAT in the rental car in the Kirchner & Sons parking lot, leafing through Tom Newquist's autopsy report. The typewritten pages detailed the facts as Trey Kirchner had indicated.

I'd been hoping the explanation was obvious, that Tom Newquist was caught in the grip of some terminal disease, his preoccupation as simple as an intimation of his mortality. This was not the case.

I started the car. The next logical move would be to talk to Tom's partner, Rafer LaMott. I checked my map of Nota Lake and spotted the sheriff's substation, which was part of the civic center about six blocks west.

The Nota Lake Civic Center had once been an elementary school. I know this because the words NOTA LAKE GRAMMAR SCHOOL were carved in block letters on the architrave. I could have sworn I could still see the faint imprint of construction-paper witches and pumpkins where they'd been affixed to the windows with cellophane tape—the ghosts of Halloweens past. Personally, I hated grade school. It was a minefield of unwritten rules that everyone but me seemed to sense and accept. My parents had died in a car crash when I was five, so school felt like a continuation of the same villainy and betrayal. I'd beg to go home, my teachers rebuffing every plaintive request. By the time I was eight, I learned to quit asking. I simply left when it suited me, and suffered the consequences later. What were they going to do? Shoot me down in cold blood?

The entrance to the civic center opened into a wide corridor that served as a lobby. I found the sheriff's substation, which consisted of several interconnecting offices that were a hodgepodge of wall plaqués, glossy paneling, and office machines. The civilian clerk was a woman in her thirties who wore running shoes, jeans, and a sweatshirt over a white turtleneck. Her name tag identified her as Margaret Brine. She had chopped-off black hair, oval glasses, and a dusting of freckles under her blush.

I took out a business card and placed it on the counter. "I wonder if I might talk to Rafer LaMott."

She picked it up. "Will he know what this is about?"

"The coroner suggested I talk to him about Tom Newquist."

"Just a minute," she said. She disappeared through a door in the rear. I could hear a murmur, and moments later Rafer LaMott appeared, shrugging himself into a charcoal brown sport coat. He was an African American in his forties, probably six feet tall, with a caramel complexion, closely cropped black hair, and startling hazel eyes. The sport coat he wore looked like cashmere.

He had my card in his hand, reading out the information in a slightly cocky tone. "Kinsey Millhone, P.I. from Santa Teresa, California. What can I help you with?"

I could feel a prickly sensation at the back of my neck. Technically, he wasn't rude, but he certainly wasn't friendly. I tried a public smile, nothing with any sincerity or warmth. "Selma Newquist hired me. She has some questions about Tom."

He regarded me briefly and then moved through the gate at one end of the counter. "I have to be someplace, but you can follow me out. What questions?"

I had no choice but to trot along beside him as he headed toward a rear entrance. "She says he was upset about something. She wants to know what it was."

He pushed the door open and passed through, picking up his pace in a manner that suggested mounting agitation. I passed through after him. I had to two-step to keep up. He pulled his car keys from his pocket, walked briskly across the parking lot, and slowed when he reached a white compact car, which he proceeded to unlock. "Listen, here's the truth, and no disrespect intended. Selma was always trying to pry into Tom's business, just in case the poor guy had a fleeting thought of his own. Repeat that and I'll deny it."

"I appreciate your candor—"

"Then you can appreciate this," he said. "Tom never said a word against Selma, but I can tell you from experience, she's exhausting to be around. Tom was a good guy, but now that he's gone, it's a relief not to have to see her. My wife and I never really wanted to spend time with Selma. We socialized when we had to, out of affection for him. If that sounds spiteful, I'm sorry, but that's the bottom line. My best advice to you is leave the man in peace. He's barely cold in his grave, and she's trying to dig him up again."

"Could he have been worried about a case?"

He glanced away from me then with a quick smile of disbelief. I could see him rein himself in, struggling to be patient. "He had as many as ten, fifteen files on his desk when he died."

"Who's taken over his workload?"

"I took some files. A new guy just hired on, and he's taking the rest. None of that information is for public consumption."

"Do you think Tom had personal problems he didn't want Selma to know?"

"Ask somebody else. I don't want to say anything more."

"What's the big deal? If you'd give me some help, I'd be out of here," I said.

By way of an answer, he got into the car and pulled the door shut. He turned the key in the ignition, pressing a button in the console. The car window slid down with a mild whir. When he spoke again, his tone was more pleasant. "Hey, this may sound rude, but do yourself a favor and let it drop, okay? Selma's a narcissist. She thinks everything's about her."

End of subject. End of Q and A. He put the car in reverse, backed out of the space, and took off. Belatedly I sensed a stinging heat rise in my face. I raised a hand to my cheek as though I'd been slapped.

I GOT in my car and headed to Selma's, still completely unenlightened. I couldn't tell if Rafer knew something or if he was simply annoyed at Selma's hiring a private detective.

A note taped to the porch door said she'd be at the church until noon. The door was unlocked, so I let myself in, calling a hello in case Brant was on the premises. There was no call in response, though several lights in the house were on.

I went into Tom's office and sat down at his desk, wondering what secrets he might have kept from view. It could have been anything: drink, drugs, pornography, gambling, an affair, an affinity for young boys. Most of us have something we'd prefer to keep to ourselves. Or maybe there was nothing. I didn't like to admit it, but Rafer's attitude toward Selma was already having an effect. A small touch of doubt was beginning to stir.

Feeling restless and bored, I went out to the kitchen. There was a plate of what looked like raisin-oatmeal cookies on the counter, with a note that said, "Help yourself." I ate several and wandered into the hall. The phone seemed to ring every fifteen minutes, but I let the machine pick up messages. Selma was much in demand, but it was all charity-related work—the church bazaar, a fund-raising auction for a Sunday school wing.

I turned my attention to the master bedroom. Tom's clothes were still hanging in his half of the closet. I began to go through his pockets. I checked the top shelf, his shoe boxes, dresser drawers, his change caddy. I found a loaded Colt .357 Magnum in one bed-table drawer, but there was nothing else of importance, just that embarrassing assortment of junk everyone seems to keep somewhere: ticket stubs, matchbooks, shoelaces. I looked under the bed, slid a hand along under the mattress, peeked behind picture frames, tapped the walls in the closet. I checked the medicine cabinet in the master bath, all the while wondering how soon I could decently quit.

I went back into the den, where I finished going through the remaining junk on Tom's shelves. I checked his credit card receipts for the past twelve months, but neither his Visa nor his MasterCard showed anything unusual.

I heard a car pull into the drive. If this was Selma, I'd tell her I wasn't wasting any more of Tom's hard-earned money. The front door opened and closed. I called "Hello" and waited.

I got a manly "Yo!" in response, and Selma's son, Brant, appeared in the doorway. He was wearing a red knit cap, a red sweat suit, and pristine white leather Reeboks, with a white towel wrapped around his neck. Brant, at twenty-five, was the kind of kid matronly house-wives in the supermarket turned around and checked out in passing. He had dark hair and brows over serious brown eyes. His complex-ion was flawless. His jaw was boxy, his cheeks honed. His posture was impeccable—square shoulders, flat stomach, skinny through the hips. If I were younger, I might have whimpered at the sight of him.

"My mom's not here yet?" he asked, removing his knit cap. His smile showed straight white teeth.

"Should be any minute. I'm Kinsey. Are you Brant?"

"Yes, ma'am." I shook hands with him across the littered expanse of his father's desk. His palm was an odd gray. When he saw that I noticed, he smiled sheepishly. "That's from weightlifting gloves. I just came from the gym. How's it going so far?"

"Well enough, I guess."

"Mom comes, tell her I'm in the shower."

"Sure thing."

Selma got home at twelve fifteen. I heard the garage door grum-ble up and then down. Soon afterward I could hear the clattering of dishes, the refrigerator door opening and shutting. She appeared in the den doorway wearing an apron. "I'm making chicken salad sandwiches if you'd like to join us. You met Brant?"

"I did. Chicken salad sounds great. You need help?"

"No, no, but come on out. We can talk while I finish up."

I followed her to the kitchen, where I washed my hands. "You know what I haven't come across yet is Tom's notebook. Didn't he take field notes when he was working an investigation?"

Surprised, Selma turned from the counter. "Absolutely. It was a little loose-leaf notebook with a black leather cover, about the size of an index card. He always had it with him." She began to cut sandwiches in half, placing them on a platter with sprigs of parsley around the edge. "What about his truck?"

"Good suggestion. I should have thought of that myself."

I opened the connecting door and moved into the garage. I skirted Selma's car and opened the door to the pickup on the driver's side. The interior smelled heavily of cigarette smoke. The glove compartment was tidy, bearing only a batch of road maps, the owner's manual, registration, and proof of insurance. I looked in the side pockets in both doors, looked behind the visors, scanned the space under the bucket seats.

I returned to the kitchen. "Scratch that," I said. "Any other ideas?"

"He could have left the notebook at work, though he seldom did that. I'll call Rafer and ask him."

"Won't he claim the notes are department property?"

"Oh, I'm sure not," she said. "He told me he'd do anything he could to help. He was Tom's best friend, you know."

Brant reappeared, wearing the blue uniform that identified him as an emergency medical technician. B. NEWQUIST was embroidered on the left. His skin radiated the scent of soap, and his hair was shower damp. I allowed myself one small inaudible whine of the sort heard only by dogs; neither Brant nor his mother seemed to pick up on it. I sat at the kitchen table, just across from him, politely eating my sandwich while I listened to them chat. Midway through lunch the telephone rang. Selma got up. "You two go ahead. I'll pick that up in Tom's den."

Brant finished his sandwich without saying much, and I realized it was going to be my job to initiate conversation.

"I take it Tom adopted you."

"When I was thirteen. My . . . I guess you'd call him a birth father . . . hadn't been in touch for years. I'd consider Tom my real dad whether he adopted me or not."

"You must have had a good relationship."

He reached for the plate of cookies on the counter, and we took turns eating them while we continued our conversation. "The last couple of years we did. Before that, we didn't get along all that great. Tom came down real hard on the side of obeying rules. He encouraged me to get involved with Boy Scouts—which I hated— karate and track, stuff like that. I guess I did just about anything I could think of to challenge his authority. Eventually he shaped up," he said, smiling slightly.

"How long have you been a paramedic?"

"Three years. Before that, I went to school for a while, though I wasn't any great shakes as a student back then."

"Did Tom talk to you about his cases?"

"Sometimes. Not lately."

"Any idea why?"

Brant shrugged. "Maybe what he was working on wasn't that interesting."

"What about his field notes? Have you seen those?"

A frown crossed his face. "His field notes are missing?"

"I think so. Or put it this way, I haven't been able to lay hands on his notebook."

"That's weird. When it wasn't in his pocket, he kept it in his desk drawer or his truck. All his old notes he bound up in rubber bands and stored in boxes in the basement. Have you asked his partner? Might be at the office."

"I talked to Rafer once, but I didn't ask about the notebook, because at that point I hadn't even thought to look."

"Can't help you on that one. I'll keep an eye out around here."

After lunch both Selma and Brant took off. Brant had errands to run before he reported for work, and Selma was involved in her endless series of volunteer positions. A silence settled on the house, and I felt a mild ripple of anxiety climb my frame. I was running out of things to do. I went back to the den and pulled the phone book out of Tom's top drawer. Given the size of the town, the directory was no bigger than a magazine. I looked up James Tennyson, the California Highway Patrol (CHP) officer who Selma said had found Tom that night. James W. was listed on Iroquois Drive in this same development. I checked my map, grabbed my jacket and my handbag, and headed out to the car.

JAMES Tennyson was fair-haired, clean-cut, and slender, the kind of earnest young man you want assisting you on the highway when your fan belt goes funny or your rear tire's blown. He answered the door dressed in civilian clothes: jeans, a sweatshirt, and a pair of sheepskin slippers.

"Kinsey Millhone," I said as the two of us shook hands. "I'm a private investigator. I have some questions about Tom Newquist's death. I'm sorry to bother you at home."

"Not a problem."

He moved aside to admit me, and I stepped into the entrance.

"I work nights, so I was just eating breakfast," he said, closing the door behind me. We proceeded to the kitchen. He sat at the table, indicating a seat. "What can I do for you?"

While James ate his cereal, I laid out Selma's concerns. "I take it you knew Tom personally?"

"Yeah, I knew him. Mean, we weren't real good friends, but everybody in Nota Lake knew Tom. I tell you, his death shook me. He was like a fixture around here."

"Can you tell me how you found him? I know he had a heart attack. I'm just trying to get a feel for what happened."

"Well, this was five, six weeks ago and really nothing unusual. I was cruising 395 when I spotted this vehicle off to the side. Hazard lights were on, so I pulled in behind. I recognized Tom's pickup. At first I thought he might be having engine problems or something like that. Both the doors were locked, but once I got close, I could see him slumped over the wheel."

"How'd you get in?"

"Well, the window on the driver's side was open a crack. I had a wire in my car and popped the lock up with that. I could see he was in trouble. He looked awful. I hauled him down out of the truck onto the side of the road and did CPR right there. I got an ambulance out there as fast as I could, but there was nothing for it. Doc in ER declared him dead on arrival."

"You think he knew what was happening and pulled over?"

"That'd be my guess. He must have had chest pain."

"Did you happen to see Tom's notebook? Black leather, about this big?"

He thought back for a moment, shaking his head slowly. "No, ma'am. I don't believe so. Of course, I wasn't looking for it."

"I thought maybe you turned it in to the department."

"I'da probably done that if I'd seen it. Anyway, I can't imagine there's anything to investigate about him. You couldn't meet a nicer fellow. He's the best. A good man and a good cop."

"So I gather."

I WENT back to the motel. I couldn't face another minute of sitting in Tom's den. I hadn't slept in my own bed for weeks. I was homesick and wanted out.

I let myself into the cabin, noting with approval that the room had been done up. I sat down at the table and rolled a piece of paper in my Smith-Corona. Selma Newquist was just going to have to make her peace with Tom's passing. Death always leaves unfinished business in its wake. I could sit here and type till I was blue in the face. Tom Newquist was gone, and I suspected no one would ever know what his final moments had been.

CHAPTER FOUR

I FOUND myself that night in a bar called Tiny's Tavern. Cecilia had indicated this was a popular hangout for off-duty law enforcement, and I was there trolling as much as anything. I was also avoiding the cabin, with its frigid temperatures and depressive lighting. Tiny's had rough plank walls, sawdust on the floor, and a bar with a brass footrail that stretched the length of the room. The place was gray with cigarette smoke. The jukebox was gaudy green and yellow with tubes of bubbles running up the sides and stocked with country music. Occasionally a couple would clomp around on the ten-by-ten dance floor while the other patrons looked on.

I wasn't sure about the unspoken assumptions in a place like this, but after an hour on the premises no one seemed to take any particular notice of me. I perched on a barstool, sipping bad beer and shelling peanuts, and I chatted with the waitress named Alice, who had bright orange hair.

At ten o'clock Macon Newquist came in. He was in uniform, moving through the bar at a leisurely pace, checking for any form of trouble in the making. He spoke to me in passing but didn't seem inclined to small talk. Shortly after he left, my idleness paid off when I spotted the civilian clerk from the sheriff's substation. I couldn't for the life of me remember her name. She came in with a fellow I assumed to be her husband and another couple. The four found an empty table on the far side of the room. I stared at her dark hair cropped short above her ears, dark brown eyes glinting behind her small oval glasses. The other woman was auburn-haired, top-heavy, and pretty. The two shed their jackets, took up their purses, and left the table, heading toward the ladies' room. I made a beeline for the facilities myself, and the three of us reached the door at just about the same time. I allowed them to enter first.

The clerk was saying, "Oh, honey, Billie's taken up with that trashy fellow from the video store. The one with the attitude. I told her she ought to think more of herself. . . ."

The two continued to talk as they passed through the door and into the first two toilet stalls. I entered the third and eavesdropped my tiny heart out. Three toilets were flushed in succession, and we reassembled at the sinks so we could wash our hands. Miraculously, just then my brain supplied the clerk's name. I caught her eye in the mirror and flashed her a smile. "Aren't you Margaret?"

She looked at me blankly and said "Oh, hi" without warmth.

"Kinsey Millhone," I prompted. I held out my hand, and she was too polite to decline a handshake.

She said, "Nice seeing you again."

I turned and gave a little wave to the other woman. "Hi. How are you? Kinsey Millhone," I said. "And you're . . ."

She seemed to hesitate, glancing at Margaret. "Earlene."

"My best friend," Margaret interjected.

"Well, isn't that nice," I said. I was acting like a salesperson, forcing chitchat to gain a foothold in the conversation.

Margaret wasn't fooled. "I don't know what you said to Rafer, but he was ticked off all day, and I was the one had to take the flak."

"Really? I'm sorry to hear that. I didn't mean to set him off."

"Everything sets him off since Tom passed away. They worked together for years, long before I hired on."

"I can see where he'd be upset." I was making myself sick with all this conciliatory garbage, though it seemed to be having the desired effect.

Margaret rolled her eyes. "He'll get over it, but I wouldn't advise you to cross paths with him if you can help it."

"I'm only in town for a couple of days, and I'm not sure where else to get information. Maybe you can help. Honestly, I'm not looking for any dirt on Tom Newquist. I've heard he was a great guy, and everybody seems real sorry that he's gone."

"Well, that's true," she said grudgingly. "But Rafer says Selma's stirring up trouble, meddling in Tom's affairs."

"It's hardly meddling," I said. "She told me Tom was worried about something. He slept badly. He brooded. She kept hoping he'd confide in her, but he never said a word. Now she's heartsick she didn't barge in when she had the chance. That's why she's hired me. She hopes to make amends. You'd do the same thing, wouldn't you?"

Margaret said, "Well." I could see she was having trouble marshaling an argument.

I decided to pull Earlene in. "What do you think, Earlene? What would you do?"

"Same thing, I guess. I can see your point." She flicked a look at Margaret. "You said yourself Tom was a bear the last few weeks before he passed. You know, moody and—"

"*Earlene.*"

"Well, it's the truth."

"Do you have any idea what was bothering him?" I asked.

Margaret was indignant. "I most certainly do not. If he was hard to get along with, that's hardly a crime."

"But who'd know? Who should I talk to if not Rafer?"

Earlene raised her hand. "Wouldn't hurt to ask Hatch."

"Would you butt out?" Margaret snapped.

"Who's Hatch?" I asked Earlene.

"Hatch's her husband. He's sitting right out there," she said.

Margaret snorted. "He won't help, and I give you odds Wayne won't either. Wayne hasn't worked for Tom in years, so what's he know about anything?"

"Hatch worked for Tom?" I said to Margaret.

"Uh-huh. Him and Wayne are sheriff's deputies, only Wayne covers Whirly Township and Hatch works down here."

"It couldn't do any harm," I said.

Margaret frowned. "I don't guess I can stop you."

The three of us left the ladies' room together.

"I'll grab my beer and be right back," I said.

I hustled over to the bar, grabbed my beer mug and jacket, and moved over to their table. I went through another round of introductions, trying to seem winsome as I shook hands with both men. Winsome is not a quality I normally project.

Hatch was a big, rangy man, with a thatch of blond hair shorn close along the sides. Earlene's husband, Wayne, was dark-haired, with a receding hairline and the pretty-boy handsomeness of a small-time thug. He avoided my eyes.

Hatch at least *seemed* friendly, so I focused on him. "I understand you knew Tom. Can you tell me about him?"

Hatch regarded me uneasily. "You're not going to get me to say anything bad about the man."

"Absolutely not. How long did you know him?"

"Little over fifteen years, since way before I joined the sheriff's department. I'd moved up here from Barstow, and first thing you know, someone broke in and took my stereo. Tom was the one showed up when I dialed nine one one."

"What was he like? Was he smart? Was he funny?"

Hatch tilted his head, allowing one shoulder to creep up toward his ear. "I'd say Tom was a good cop first, last, and always. Small town like this, somebody breaks the law, they might have lived down the street from you way back when. In Tom's mind it wasn't personal. He wasn't mean or anything like that. Business was just business, and you had to respect him for his attitude."

"Can you give me an example?"

"I can't think of one offhand. Wayne, you know what I'm saying. What's the kind of thing Tom did?"

Wayne shook his head. "Hey, Hatch. This is your party."

Hatch scratched at his chin. "Well now, here's one I remember. We had this good ol' boy named Sonny Gelson. Remember him, hon? This was maybe five, six years ago, I guess. He used to live over by Winona in a big old falling-down house. His wife shot 'im one night—pumped a big hole in his chest. About six months before, she'd reported a prowler, and Sonny got her a Smith and Wesson. So one night he's out of town, and she hears someone in the downstairs hall and pops the guy as he comes in. Problem was the gun misfired and blew up in her hand. Sonny'd packed the reload himself, and I guess he'd done it wrong, or that's what it looked like at any rate. Bullet still hit him smack in the chest. I think he died before Judy could even dial nine one one. See, but now here's the point. Tom got it in his head that the whole thing's a setup. So here's Judy Gelson crying her heart out for her terrible mistake. D.A. was going to let her plead out and let it go at that. Tom just kept digging, and pretty soon he comes up with this hefty insurance policy. Turns out Judy had a lover and the two of 'em concocted this plan. She's the one jimmied the cartridge with an overload of fast powder. Tom's the one nailed her, and he'd went *steady* with her once upon a time. Cut no ice with him, and that's the point I'm trying to make."

"What happened to Judy Gelson?"

"She's doing twenty-five to life somewhere. Lover dropped out of sight. In fact, nobody ever figured out who he was. Maybe somebody local. Tom was always trying to get a line on the guy."

"He liked to work old cases?"

"Everybody does. Always the chance you'll crack one and make a name for yourself. Anyway, it's more than that. It's putting paid to an account. Closure they call it nowadays, but it's the same thing."

I glanced at Margaret, saying, "That's all Selma wants."

Hatch shook his head at the mention of her name. "Well, now Selma. She's something else. Tom was crazy about her, worshiped the ground she walked on, and that's no lie."

Margaret chimed in. "The rest of us find Selma pretty hard to take."

"How so?"

"Oh, you know, she's easily offended, imagines slights where there's none intended. Tom tried his best to reassure her, but it was never enough. You'd run into the two of 'em out in public, and he'd always make sure she was included in the conversation, didn't he?" she said, turning to Earlene for confirmation. "I think he knew people didn't like her."

"That's right. Everybody liked him and hadn't any use for her."

"So in a way, her insecurity was justified," I said.

Earlene laughed. "Sure, but if she wasn't so self-centered, people might like her better. Selma's convinced the sun rises and sets on account of her. On top of that, she's a social climber. Selma has to be right out in front."

I thought Earlene's husband, Wayne, seemed irritated that she was talking to me. "What about you, Wayne? Anything to add?"

He smiled, but more to himself than at me. "Ask me, them three are doing pretty good."

"You agree with their assessment?"

"Basically, I don't see Tom's marriage as any of our business. What him and Selma worked out is between them."

Earlene tossed a crumpled paper napkin in his direction. "You old sourpuss," she said. "Loosen up. Honest to Pete."

"Say what you want. You're not drawing me into this."

"Let him be," I said. I was suddenly feeling tired. The combination of tension and smoke-filled air was giving me a headache. I'd asked for general information, and that's what I'd received. "I think I'll head on back to the motel," I said.

"Don't go away mad. Just go away," Wayne said, smiling.

"Very funny. Ha ha," Earlene said to him.

"We'd best be off, too," Margaret said, glancing at her watch. "Oh, jeez, look what time it is. Eleven forty-five, Earlene, and you still have to drop us off."

The four of them began to gather their belongings.

"Catch you later," I said.

Various good-bye remarks were made. I watched them depart and then returned to the bar, where I settled my tab. Alice, the orange-haired waitress, was just taking a break. She pulled up a stool beside me and lit a cigarette. "You a cop?"

"I'm a private investigator."

"Well, that explains," she said, blowing smoke to one side. "I heard you're asking around about Tom Newquist."

"Word travels fast."

"Oh, sure. Town this small, there's not much to talk about," she said. "You're barking up the wrong tree with that bunch. They're all law enforcement, loyal to their own. You're not going to get anyone to say a bad word about Tom."

"So I discover. You have something to add?"

"I try not to judge others, but it's hard not to have *some* opinion. Everybody's down on Selma, and it seems unfair. I just wish she'd quit worrying about those silly teeth of hers." Alice put a hand to her mouth. "Have you noticed her doing this? Anyway, I grant you Selma's abrasive, but you know what? Tom got to look good by comparison. He'd never dream of getting in your face about anything, and why should he? He had Selma to do that. She'd take on anyone."

"Interesting," I said.

"Well, you know, it's just my reaction. I get tired of hearing everyone trash Selma. Tom was passive—pure and simple—so why blame her for taking over? You'd have done it yourself."

"Selma says he was very preoccupied in the last few weeks. Any idea what it was?"

She paused to consider, drawing on her cigarette. "I never thought much about it, but now you mention it, he didn't seem like himself. Tell you what. Let me ask around. It's not like people around here are dishonest or secretive, but they protect their own."

"You're telling me," I said. I took out a business card and jotted down my home number in Santa Teresa and the motel where I was staying. "Thanks for your help."

I headed out into the night air. The temperature had dropped, and I could see my breath. The parking lot was only half full and the lighting just dim enough to generate uneasiness. I took a moment to scan the area. There was no one in sight, though the line of pine trees on the perimeter could have hidden anyone. I shifted my car keys to my right hand as I moved to the rental car, and let myself in.

I slid under the wheel, slammed the car door, and locked it, listening to the locks flip down with a feeling of satisfaction. The windshield was milky with condensation, and I wiped myself a clear patch with my bare hand. I turned the key in the ignition, suddenly alerted by the grinding that indicated a low charge in the battery. I tried again, and the engine turned over reluctantly. There was a series of misses, and then the engine died.

I caught a flash of headlights in the lane behind me and checked the source in my rearview mirror. A dark panel truck was passing at a slow rate of speed. The driver, in a black ski mask, turned to stare at me. The eyeholes in the knit mask were rimmed with white, and the opening for the mouth was thickly bordered with red. The driver and I locked eyes in the rearview mirror. I could feel my skin prickle, the pores puckering with fear. I thought male. I thought white. But I could have been wrong on both counts.

The truck slowed and finally came to a halt. I could hear the engine idling against the still night air. I realized I was holding my breath. I wasn't sure what I'd do if the driver got out and approached my car. After an interminable thirty seconds the truck moved on, reached the end of the aisle, and took a left.

I tried starting my car again. "Come *on*," I said. The engine seemed, if anything, a little less energetic. The panel truck was now passing from right to left along the lane in front of me, the two of us separated by the intervening cars, parked nose to nose with mine. I could see the driver lean forward, the masked face now tilted in my direction. It was the blankness that unnerved me, the shapeless headgear wiping out all features except the eyes and mouth, which stood out in startling relief. Terrorists and bank robbers wore masks like this, not ordinary citizens concerned about frostbite. The panel truck stopped. The black ski mask was fully turned in my direction, the prolonged look intense. The driver extended a gloved right hand, index finger pointing at me like the barrel of a gun. Two imaginary bullets were fired at me, complete with recoil. I flipped him the bird in return, then wondered if I should have kept my snappy metacarpal retort to myself. In Los Angeles, freeway shootings have been motivated by less. For the first time I worried he might have a real weapon down by his feet.

I pumped the gas with my foot and turned the key again, uttering a low urgent sound. Miraculously the engine coughed to life. I put the car in neutral and applied pressure on the accelerator, flipping on the headlights while I gunned the engine. The panel truck was just turning out of the lot at the far end.

I backed out of the slot, shifted gears, and swung the car into the lane heading in the opposite direction, peering through the dark to see what had happened to the panel truck. I could hear my heart thudding in my head, as if fear had forced the hapless organ up between my ears. I reached the marked exit and eased forward, searching the streets beyond for signs that the panel truck was rounding the block. The street was empty as far as I could see. I patted myself on the chest, a calming gesture designed to comfort and reassure. Nothing had actually happened. Someone passing in a panel truck had turned and looked at me, firing symbolically with a pointed index finger and a wiggle of his thumb. I didn't think the incident would make the national news.

It wasn't until I was midway through town that I caught a glimpse of the truck falling into line half a block back. I checked in all directions, but I could see no other traffic and no pedestrians. At this late hour Nota Lake was deserted. Even the gas stations were shut down.

Shuddering from some internal chill, I turned on the heater. I was desperate to get warm, desperate for the sight of another human being. Didn't people walk their dogs? Didn't parents dash out for milk? I wanted the driver of the panel truck to see that I had help.

I turned left at the next street and drove on for three blocks, eyes pinned to the rearview mirror. Within seconds the panel truck came around the corner behind me and took up its surveillance. I continued west for six blocks and then turned left again. Ordinarily I keep a gun in the well behind my VW's back seat. But this car was a rental, and when I'd left Santa Teresa, I was with Dietz. Why would I have needed a weapon? The only jeopardy I'd imagined was living in close quarters with an invalid.

I was checking the rearview mirror compulsively every couple of seconds. The panel truck was still there. If the driver was trying to psych me out, I didn't want to give him the satisfaction of any overt reaction. I refused to speed up. I refused to play tag. I turned left again, driving at a measured rate as the blocks rolled by. Ahead of me, close to the intersection, was the Nota Lake Civic Center, with the sheriff's headquarters. Next door was the police station. I wasn't sure the place was even open at midnight. I coasted to a stop and idled the engine. The panel truck rolled up even with my car, and the driver turned, as before, to stare. I could have sworn there was a smile showing through the red-rimmed knit mouth. The driver made no other move, and after a tense moment he drove on. I checked the rear license plate, but it was covered with tape and no identifying numbers showed. The truck began to speed up, turned left at the intersection, and disappeared from sight. I felt my insides turning luminous, as adrenaline poured through me.

I waited a full five minutes, though it felt like forever. I studied the street on all sides, lest someone approach on foot. The feeling of apprehension was as palpable as a fever. I caught a glimpse of headlights behind me again, and when I checked the rearview mirror, I saw a vehicle come slowly around the corner. I leaned on the horn. A howling blare filled the night. The patrol car eased up beside me, and James Tennyson, the CHP officer, rolled down the window on the driver's side. "You okay?" he mouthed.

I pressed a button on the console and opened the window on the passenger side of my car, saying, "Someone's been following me."

"Hang on," he said. He pulled his car over to the empty curb, walked around to my side of the car, and hunkered so we could talk face to face. "What's the story?"

I explained the situation, trying not to distort or exaggerate. I wasn't sure how to convince him of the alarm I'd felt, but he seemed to accept my account.

He was in his twenties by my guess, and I suspected I'd seen more in the way of personal combat than he had. Still, he was a cop in uniform, and the sight of him was reassuring.

"Well, I can see where that'd worry you," he said. "It seems creepy to me, too. Might have been a guy in the bar. Sometimes the fellows around here get weird when they drink. Sounds like he was waiting for you to come out to the lot."

"I thought so, too."

"Police station's locked up for the night. You want me to see you home? I'd be happy to."

"Please," I said.

He escorted me the six miles to the motel, driving ahead of me so I could keep my gaze fixed on the sight of his patrol car. There was no sign of the panel truck. Once at the Nota Lake Cabins, we parked side by side, and he walked me to the cabin. I intended to check the premises, but he held out an arm like the captain of the grade school safety patrol. "Let me do this."

"Great. It's all yours," I said.

I DIDN'T sleep well, but in the early morning light I felt better.

I was blessed with a full three minutes of hot water before the pipes began to clank. I walked out to the highway into a morning filled with icy sunlight and air clear as glass. I could smell loam and pine needles. There was no sign of the panel truck. Nobody in a ski mask paused to stare at me. I had breakfast at the Rainbow and watched the short-order cook, a young black girl working with remarkable efficiency and concentration.

Afterward I returned to Selma's.

Her sister-in-law Phyllis was in the kitchen. The two of them were at the table, which was covered with paperwork. They were determining the seating for some country-club event.

Selma looked up at me. "Morning, Kinsey. What's on your plate today? Are you about finished in the den?"

"Almost," I said. I glanced at Phyllis, wondering if this was a subject to be discussed in front of her.

Selma caught my hesitation. "That's fine. Go ahead. You don't have to worry about her. She knows all this."

"I'm drawing a blank. I don't doubt your story. I'm sure Tom was worried about something. Other people have told me he didn't seem like himself. I just can't find any indication of what was troubling him. It's frustrating."

I could see the disappointment settle across Selma's face. "It's only been two days," she murmured.

"Well, that's true," I said. "And there's always the chance something will pop up, but so far there's nothing." I debated whether to mention the business with the panel truck, but I couldn't see the point. "See you in a bit," I said, and moved into the den.

I stood in the doorway staring at the disarray that still littered the room. I was down to the dregs, and it was hard to know just where to go from here. I'd lost all enthusiasm for the project, which felt dirty and pointless. I did have six banker's boxes stacked along one wall, containing files that I'd labeled: previous income tax forms, warranties, insurance policies, telephone bills, and credit card receipts. Still no sign of his field notes.

I folded together a fresh banker's box and began placing papers in it. Once I tidied the desk, I could see now that his blotter was covered with scribbles: doodles, telephone numbers, what looked like case numbers, appointments, names and addresses. I panned across the surface item by item. The drawings were much like the ones sixth-grade boys seemed to favor in my elementary days—daggers and blood and guns firing fat bullets. The only repeat item was a length of thick rope fashioned into a hangman's noose. He'd drawn two of those; one with an X'd-out phone number in the center, the second with a series of numbers followed by a question mark. In one corner of the blotter was a hand-drawn calendar for the month of February, the numbers neatly filled in. I did a quick check of the calendar and realized the numbers didn't correspond to February of this year. The first fell on a Sunday, and the last two Saturdays of the month had been X'd out. I paused long enough to make a detailed list of all the telephone and case numbers.

Intrigued, I retrieved the file of telephone records from the past six months, hoping for a match. I was temporarily sidetracked when I spotted seven calls to the 805 area code, which covers Santa Teresa County, as well as Perdido County to the south and San Luis Obispo County to the north of us. One number I recognized as the Perdido County Sheriff's Department. There were six calls to another number, spaced roughly two weeks apart. The most recent of these was in late January, a few days before his death. On impulse I picked up the phone and dialed the number. After three rings a machine clicked on, a woman's voice giving the standard answering-machine message. Her voice was throaty and mature, but that was the extent of the information I gleaned. I quietly replaced the handset. Maybe she was a friend of Selma's.

I made a note of the number and went back to comparing the numbers on the phone bills with the numbers on the blotter. That netted me a hit. It looked as if Tom had completed a call to the number I'd seen X'd out in the center of one noose, though that number had been noted without the 805 area code attached. I tried the number myself.

"Gramercy. How may I direct your call?"

"Gramercy? This is the Gramercy Hotel in Santa Teresa?"

"That's correct."

"Sorry. Wrong number."

I disconnected. Well, that was odd. The Gramercy Hotel was a fleabag establishment down on lower State Street. Why would the Newquists call them? I circled the number in my notes, adding a question mark, and then continued packing.

At ten o'clock I paused to stretch my legs. I still had a lower storage cabinet to unload, which was enclosed by wide doors spanning the width of the bookshelves. I got down on my hands and knees, inserted my head and shoulders into the commodious space, and heaved two boxes into view, then sat on the floor going through the contents.

At the top of the second box I came across two blue big-ring loose-leaf binders. Apparently, Tom had photocopies of the bulk of the reports in the sheriff's department case books. This was the log of unsolved crimes kept on active status, though many were years old, copies yellowing. I leafed through with interest. This was Nota County crime from the year 1935 to the present.

"Kinsey?" Phyllis was standing in the doorway.

"You scared me," I said. "I didn't hear you come in."

"I'm sorry. I'm just on my way home. Can I talk to you?"

"Sure. Come on in."

"In private," she added, and then turned on her heel.

CHAPTER FIVE

I SCRAMBLED to my feet and followed her down the hall. Behind us I could hear Selma chatting on the phone. We reached the front door and moved out onto the porch. The cold hit like a blast. The sky had turned hazy, with heavy gray clouds sliding down the mountains in the distance. I crossed my arms.

"Aren't you cold?" I asked. There Phyllis stood in a skimpy cotton blouse, her skirt blowing against her bare legs.

She made a careless gesture, brushing aside the bitter chill. "I'm used to it." Then she continued. "You know Macon and Tom were always close, and of course when Tom married Selma, we wished him all the best. Tom was a wonderful man."

"So everybody says. In fact, most people seem to prefer him to her," I said.

"Oh, Selma has her good points. I wouldn't say we're friends, but you can see somebody's weaknesses and still like them for their better qualities."

"Absolutely," I said, mentally begging her to hurry. I felt like making that rolling hand gesture that says, "Come on, come on."

"In September, Tom and Macon went to a gun show in Los Angeles, and I tagged along. Selma wasn't really interested—she had some big event that weekend. Anyway, I happened to see Tom with this *woman,* and I remember thinking, Uh-oh. Know what I mean? Something didn't look right to me. This gal was interested."

I felt a flash of irritation. "Phyllis, I wish you'd mentioned this before *now.* I've been in there slogging through that mess, and what I hear you saying is that Tom's problem didn't have anything to do with paperwork."

"Well, that's just it. I don't really know. I asked Macon about the woman, and he said she was a sheriff's investigator over on the coast. Perdido, I believe. Macon told me to keep my mouth shut. Selma was planning this big anniversary party, and I kept thinking if Tom was . . . well, if he was *involved* with someone."

"So you told her," I suggested.

Phyllis made a face. "Well, no, I didn't. At any rate, the next thing I knew, Tom had passed away and Selma was beside herself. I've felt terrible ever since. If I'd told her what I suspected, she could have confronted him right then."

"You know for a fact he was having an affair?"

"Well, no. That's the point."

The front door burst open, and Selma popped her head out. "*There* you are. I thought the two of you'd gone off and left me."

"We were just jawing," Phyllis said without missing a beat. "She was nice enough to walk me out."

"She's frozen. Let the poor thing come in, for Pete's sake!"

Gratefully I scurried into the house while the two of them discussed another work session the next morning. I headed for the kitchen, where I washed my hands. I should have considered another woman in the mix. It might explain why Tom's buddies were being so protective of him. It might also explain the six 805 calls to the unidentified woman whose message I'd picked up.

A few minutes later Selma came in, agitated. "Well, if that doesn't take the cake. I cannot believe it. She was just telling me about a dinner party coming up in the neighborhood, but have I been invited? Of course not," she said. "When Tom was alive, we went everywhere. We were always included in the social scene. Now I sit here night after night, and the phone hardly rings except for things like this. Scut work, I call it. Good old Selma's always up for a committee."

"But Selma, it's only been six weeks. Maybe people are trying to show their respects, giving you time to grieve."

"I'm sure that's their version," she said tartly, then seemed to shake off her mood. "Enough of this. Would you like a bite of lunch? I'm fixing soup and some grilled cheese sandwiches."

"Sounds great," I said. By now familiar with the kitchen, I opened the cupboard door and took down soup bowls and plates. "Will Brant be joining us?"

"I doubt it. He's still in his room, probably dead to the world. He goes to the gym three days a week, so he likes to sleep in on the mornings between. Let me go check." She disappeared briefly and returned nodding her head. "He'll be right out," she said.

While she heated the soup and grilled sandwiches, I filled her in on activities to date. My efforts sounded feeble in the telling. Because of what Phyllis had said, I now had a new avenue to explore, but I was unwilling to mention it when I was only dealing with suspicions. Selma had never even suggested the possibility of another woman.

Brant appeared just as we were sitting down to eat. He was wearing jeans and cowboy boots, his snug white T-shirt emphasizing the effectiveness of his workouts. Selma ladled soup into bowls, cut the sandwiches, and put one on each plate.

We began to eat in the kind of silence I found mildly unsettling. "What made you decide to become a paramedic?" I asked.

I had caught Brant with his mouth full. He smiled, embarrassed, tucking half the food in his cheek. "I had a couple of friends in the fire department, so I took a six-month course. I think Tom was hoping I'd join the sheriff's department, but I enjoy what I do. You know, it's always something."

I nodded, still eating. "Is the job what you expected?"

"Sure. Only more fun," he said.

I might have asked him more, but I could see him glance at his watch. He wolfed down the last of his soup and sandwich, pushed back from the table, and gave his mother's cheek a quick buss.

"I think I'll drive down to Independence and see Sherry," he said.

"Will you be back tonight?" Selma asked.

"I wouldn't count on it," he said.

"You drive carefully."

"Twenty-five whole miles. I think I can handle it." He snagged the four remaining cookies from the plate, placing one in his mouth with a grin. "Better make more cookies. This was a short batch," he said. "See you later."

SELMA left the house after lunch, so I didn't broach the subject that was beginning to tug at me—a quick trip to Santa Teresa to pick up my car. The rental cost was mounting daily, and besides, I could dig into the issue of the female sheriff's investigator once I got home. Meanwhile, it was time to have a chat with the Nota Lake Police Department. I shrugged on my leather jacket, took my shoulder bag, and headed off.

The police department was housed in a plain one-story building with a stucco exterior. The desk officer was M. Corbet, a fellow in his forties with a smooth, round face. I gave him my business card, hoping to establish my credibility before I launched into a description of the events involving the driver of the panel truck. Officer Corbet was polite, but I could tell that the issue of someone in a ski mask staring at me real hard wasn't going to qualify as a major case. He took my report, then tapped with his fingers on the counter. "I know someone with a truck like that."

"You do?" I said, surprised.

"Yes, ma'am. Sounds like Ercell Riccardi. He lives right around the corner. Keeps his truck parked in the drive. You might want to have a look. Ercell leaves it sit out any time it's not in use."

"With keys in the ignition?"

"Yes, ma'am. He started doing it maybe five, six years back. We had us a rash of break-ins—bunch of kids taking tape decks, going joyriding. Ercell got tired of replacing the stereo, so now he leaves the truck open, keys in the ignition, and a note on the dash saying, 'Please put back in the drive when you're done.' "

"So people take his truck anytime they like?"

"Occasionally somebody borrys it, but they always put it back."

"I'll take a look," I said.

Out on the street again, I shoved my hands into my jacket pockets and headed for the corner. As soon as I turned it, I saw the black panel truck. I approached it with caution, moved around to the rear, and ran a finger across the license plate, scrutinizing the surface, where I could see faint traces of adhesive. I reversed my steps and returned to my parking spot.

When I reached the rental car, Macon Newquist was waiting, his black-and-white vehicle parked behind mine. He smiled. "Hi. I figured this was your car. How's it going?"

"Fine. For a minute I thought you were giving me a ticket."

"Don't worry about that." He crossed his arms and leaned a hip against the side of the rental. "I hope this doesn't seem out of line, but Phyllis mentioned that business about the gun show."

I calculated my response. Phyllis must have felt guilty about telling me and blabbed the minute she got home. "She said something in passing. I really didn't pay that much attention."

"I didn't want you to get the wrong impression. The woman Tom was talking to—that was strictly professional."

"Not surprising. You know her name?"

"I never heard it myself. She's a sheriff's investigator."

"You happen to know what county?"

He scratched at his chin. "Not offhand. Could be Kern, San Benito. I forget what he said. I could see Phyllis put the hairy eyeball on the two of them, and I didn't want you to be misled. Last thing Selma needs is some kind of gossip about him."

"I couldn't agree more. Trust me, I'd never be irresponsible."

"That's good. I'm glad to hear that. People admired Tom, and if there was something tacky in his life . . . well, they aren't going to want to know about that. Take somebody like Margaret's husband. I believe you talked to him at Tiny's. Hatch was a protégé of Tom's, and the other fellow, Wayne, was somebody Tom rescued from a bad foster care situation. See what I mean? You can't run around asking those fellows what Tom was *like*. They don't take to it that well."

"I appreciate the warning."

"I wouldn't call it a warning. All I'm saying is, let's not be hasty and cause trouble for no reason."

"I wouldn't dream of it."

I WENT back to the motel, making a brief detour into the Rainbow Café, where I picked up a pack of chips and a can of Pepsi. I was eating for comfort, but I couldn't help myself. I hadn't jogged for three weeks, and I could feel my butt getting larger with every bite I ate. The young black woman who handled the griddle had paused to follow the weather channel on a small television at the end of the counter. She was trim and attractive, with loopy corkscrew curls jutting out around her head. I saw a frown cross her face. "Hey now," she said to no one in particular. "Whatever happened to spring?"

The radar showed areas of storm activity. I'd been hoping to hit the road for home tomorrow, but a heavy snowstorm could force the mountain passes to close. Nota Lake was technically out of the reach of such blockades, but the rental car had no chains, and I had scant experience driving in hazardous conditions.

Back in the cabin, I finished typing up my notes, translating all the pointless activity into the officious-sounding language of a written report. I neatly omitted the as-yet-unidentified female sheriff's investigator, who may or may not have been interested in Tom Newquist and he in her.

At two o'clock I locked the cabin and headed for my car. Cecilia must have been peering out the office window, because the minute I walked by, she rapped on the glass and made a beckoning motion.

She came to the door, holding a piece of paper aloft. "Alice wants you to get in touch. I took the number this time, but I run a motel here, not an answering service."

Her aggrieved tone inspired a matching complaint. "Oh, hey, now that I've got you, do you think I could get some heat? The cabin's almost unlivable, close to freezing," I said.

An expression of annoyance flashed across her face. "March first is the cutoff date for heating oil out here. I can't just whistle up a delivery because a couple of short-term visitors make a fuss."

She gave the door a little bang as she withdrew. Good luck to me, getting any other messages. I crossed to the pay phone and dropped in some money. Alice picked up on the fourth ring.

"Hello, Alice? Kinsey Millhone. I got your message. Are you at work or home?"

"Home. I'm not due at Tiny's until four. Listen, this might not be helpful, but I thought I'd pass it along. The waitress who works counter over at the Rainbow is a good friend of mine. Her name's Nancy. She says Tom came in that night about nine. You can talk to her yourself if you want."

"Is she the black girl?"

"Uh-uh. That's Barrett, Rafer LaMott's daughter. Nancy doubles as a cashier. Brown hair, forties."

"What else did she say? Was he alone or with someone?"

"She says he was alone. Said he ate, then left about nine thirty, just as she was closing out. She said she'd never known him to come in at that hour. You know the night he was found, he was out on 395, heading toward the mountains instead of home to his place."

"I remember that," I said. "The coroner mentioned his having eaten a meal. According to Selma, he was in for the night. You ever hear rumors about Tom and any other woman?"

She barked out a laugh. "Tom? You gotta be kidding. He was stuffy about sex. What makes you ask?"

"He might have been at the Rainbow for a rendezvous."

"Oh, a *rahndezvous*. That's rich. Listen, if you're fooling around in this town, you'd best meet somewhere else unless you want everyone to know. Why take the risk his sister'd show up? Cecilia's not that fond of Selma, but she'd have told on him anyway. That's how people around here operate."

"I take it word's gone out about me. Anybody seem upset?"

"Oh, grumbles here and there, but nothing serious that I've heard. Some of the guys were wondering if you're married. I guess they noticed no wedding ring."

"Actually, I took my ring off to have the diamond reset."

"Yeah. Right."

"No, really. My husband's *huge.* He's always pumped up on steroids, so he's touchy as all get-out. He'd tear the head off anyone who ever laid a hand on me."

She laughed. "I bet you've never been married a day in your life."

"Alice, you would be surprised."

As PREDICTED, the weather was turning nasty as the front moved in. The sky changed from blue to a misty-looking dark gray, which made the day seem as gloomy as a solar eclipse.

Here's what I did with my afternoon. I went to the copy shop, where I made copies of my typewritten report and several five-by-seven photocopy enlargements of the head shot of Tom Newquist. I dropped the original photograph and report in Selma's mailbox. And I still had hours to kill before I could decently retire. In the meantime I was bored and I wanted to get warm. Nota Lake didn't have a movie theater, a library, or a bowling alley. I went to the lone bookstore and picked up two paperbacks, returned to the cabin, crawled under a pile of blankets, and read to my heart's content.

At six o'clock I hunched into my jacket and walked over to the Rainbow. I ate a BLT on wheat toast, then chatted with Nancy while she rang up my bill, making sure Alice had reported accurately. At six thirty-five I went back to the cabin, finished the first book, tossed that aside, and reached for the next. At ten o'clock, exhausted from a hard day's work, I got up, brushed my teeth, washed my face, and climbed back into bed, where I fell promptly asleep.

A sound filtered into the tarry dream I was having. I labored upward, slow swimming, my body weighted with dark images and all the leaden drama of sleep. My eyes opened, and Nota Lake crept back into my consciousness, the cabin so cold I might as well have slept outside. What had I heard? The tiny scrape of metal on metal—not the sound of a key. Possibly a pick being worked into the door lock. Fear shot through me like a rocket. I flung the covers aside and shoved my feet into my shoes.

I stood where I was, tuned now to the silence. Even in the depths of the country the dark wasn't absolute. I could see the blocks of gray that were the windows on three sides. I glanced back at the bed. Hastily I arranged the pillows to form a plump body shape, covered with blankets. This always fooled the bad guys. I eased over to the door, trying to pick up the scratchings of my intruder over the pounding of my heart. I felt along the doorjamb. There was no security chain, so once the lock was jimmied, there was nothing else between me and my night visitor. The cabin, though dark, was beginning to define itself. I surveyed the details in memory, looking for a weapon somewhere among the homely furnishings. Bed, chair, soap, table, shower curtain. On my side of the door I kept my fingers on the thumb lock to prevent its turning. Maybe the guy would assume the lock was stiff. On the other side of the door I could hear a faint chunking across woodchips as my visitor retreated in search of some other means of ingress. I tiptoed to a wooden chair and eased the top rail under the knob, jamming the legs against the floor. It wouldn't hold for long, but it might slow him down.

Were the windows locked? I couldn't recall. I moved from window to window, feeling for the latches. All of them seemed to be secured. A slight parting of the curtains allowed me a thin slice of the exterior. No traffic on the highway. No lights in neighboring cabins. To the left I caught movement as someone disappeared around the cabin toward the rear. I crossed the room in silence and entered the darker confines of the bathroom. I felt for the shower curtain, hanging by a series of rings from a round metal rod. I let my fingers explore the brackets, which were screwed into the wall on either side of the shower stall. Carefully I lifted the rod from the slots, sliding the curtain off, ring by ring. Once in hand, I realized the rod was too light, too easily bent. I needed a weapon, but what did I have? I glanced at the frosted glass of the bathroom window. Framed in the center was the intruder's head and shoulders. It must have been frustrating for him to discover the dark was too dense to penetrate. I stood without moving. A snippet of sound, perhaps a claw hammer being eased into a crack between the frame and the glass.

Feverishly I reviewed the items in the cabin, hoping to remember something I could use as a weapon. Toilet paper, rug, clothes hangers, ironing board. Iron. Taking care not to make a sound, I set the curtain rod aside, moved to the closet, and lifted the iron from the shelf. I held the end of the plug while I unwrapped the cord. Blindly I felt for the outlet near the sink, inserted the prongs, and slid the heat lever as far to the right as it would go. I set the iron upright on the counter. I glanced back at the window. The head-and-shoulders silhouette was no longer visible.

I eased my way to the door, where I pressed my ear to the lock. I could hear the key pick slide in again. The tiny torque wrench joined its mate as the two rods of metal crept across the tumblers. Behind me I heard a ticking from the bathroom as the iron picked up heat. I longed to feel the weight of the iron in my hand, but I didn't dare yank the plug from the socket yet. I could feel pain in my chest where the rubbery muscle of my heart slapped the wooden pales of my rib cage. I'd never known anyone who could use a lockpick wearing gloves, so the chances were he was using his bare hands.

I placed my right hand lightly on the knob. I could feel it turn under my fingers. With the chair still in place, I did a quick tiptoe dance to the bath. I could feel heat radiating from the iron as I pulled the plug from the socket. I wrapped my fingers around the handle and returned to the door, taking up my vigil. My night visitor was now in the process of easing the door open. As stealthily as a spider his fingers crept around the frame. I lunged, iron extended, but he was quicker than I expected. I made contact, but not before he'd kicked the door in. The chair catapulted past me. I could smell the harsh chemical scent of scorched wool. I pressed the iron into him again and sensed burning flesh this time. He uttered a harsh expletive—not a word but a yelp.

At the same time, he swung and his fist caught me in the face. I staggered backward, off-balance. The iron flew out of my hand and clattered heavily across the floor. He was fast. Before I knew what was happening, he'd kicked my feet out from under me. I went down. He had my arm racked up behind me, his knee planted squarely in the middle of my back. I knew I'd black out within minutes if he didn't ease up. I couldn't fill my lungs with sufficient air to make a sound. Any movement was excruciating. I could smell stress sweat, but I wasn't sure if it was his or mine.

Now you see? This is precisely the kind of moment I was talking about. There I was, face down on a braided rug, immobilized by a fellow threatening serious bodily harm. Had I foreseen this sorry development the day I left Carson City, I'd have dumped the rental car and flown home. But how was I to know?

Meanwhile, the thug and I were at a temporary impasse while he decided what kind of punishment to inflict. This guy was going to hurt me; there was no doubt of that. He was supercharged, juiced up on rage, his breathing labored and hoarse. I tried to relax and, at the same time, steel myself for the inevitable.

He half lifted himself away from me and slammed his knee into my rib cage, knocking the breath out of me. He grabbed the index finger of my right hand and in one swift motion snapped it sideways, dislocating the finger. The sound was like the hollow pop of a raw carrot being snapped in two. I heard myself emit a note of anguish as he reached for the next finger and popped the knuckle sideways in its socket. I could sense that both fingers protruded now in an unnatural relationship to the rest of my hand. He delivered a kick, and then I heard his heavy breathing as he stood staring down at me. I closed my eyes, fearful of provoking further attack.

I kept my face down against the rug, feeling absurdly grateful when he didn't kick me again. He crossed the cabin in haste. I heard the door bang shut behind him and then the sound of his muffled footsteps. In due course I heard a car engine start.

I rolled over on my back, cradling my right arm. I could feel my hands tremble, and I was making noises in my throat. I'd broken out in a sweat, so much heat coursing through my body that I thought I'd throw up. At the same time, I began to shake. It had been a long time since I'd been hurt, and I'd nearly forgotten how it felt to be consumed by suffering.

I held my hand against my chest protectively while I eased onto my side. From there I struggled to my feet, mewing like a kitten. I turned on the overhead light and looked down at my hand. Both fingers jutted out at thirty-degree angles. The sight of it was sickening. I found my bag near the bed. I picked up my jacket and laid it across my shoulders like a shawl. Tidy little bun that I am, I righted the chair, picked the iron up, and returned it to the closet. Now I had only myself to accommodate.

CHAPTER SIX

CECILIA dialed 911. The dispatcher said he'd send an ambulance, but Cecilia assured him she could get me to the hospital in the time it would take the paramedics to arrive. She threw on her sweats, a coat, and running shoes, and put me in her boat-size Oldsmobile. To give her credit, she seemed properly concerned about my injury, patting me occasionally and saying things like, "You hang on now. You'll be fine. It's just down the road."

I no longer felt pain. Some natural anesthesia had flooded through my system, and I was woozy with its effect. I leaned my head back against the seat. She studied me anxiously.

"You're dead white," she said. She depressed the window control, opening the window halfway so that a wide stream of icy air whipped against my face. The highway was glossy with moisture, snow blowing across the road in diagonal lines.

The hospital emergency room looked like every other emergency room I'd ever been exposed to: beige speckled floor glossy with wax, acoustical ceiling tile. I crawled up on the examining table, where I lay and stared at the ceiling. I was shivering. The lights seemed unnaturally bright, and the room oscillated. I laid my left arm across my eyes and tried to think about something nice, like sex.

I could hear a low conversation in the corridor, and someone came in. "Miss Millhone?" I opened my eyes.

The ER nurse was black, her name tag identifying her as V. La-Mott. She had to be Rafer LaMott's wife, mother to the young woman working as a short-order cook over at the Rainbow Café. Like her daughter, V. LaMott was trim, her skin the color of to-bacco. "I'm Mrs. LaMott. You've met my husband, I believe."

"We spoke briefly."

"Let's see the hand."

I held it up. A newfound talent allowed me to point in two direc-tions simultaneously—index and middle fingers going northwest, ring finger and pinkie steering east northeast. She was careful to make only gingerly contact. She took my temperature and then my blood pressure, making notes on my chart.

"What's the V stand for?" I asked.

"Victoria. You can call me Vicky. We're not formal around here."

Ever the professional, I took advantage of the opportunity to quiz her about the Newquists while we waited for the doctor. "I gather Rafer and Tom were good friends," I said.

"That's right."

"Did the four of you spend much time together? You might as well be honest. I've heard it all by now. Nobody likes Selma."

Vicky smiled. "We spent time together when we had to. There were occasions when we couldn't avoid her, so we made the best of it. I swear, she once said to me—these are her exact words—'I'd have invited you over, but I thought you'd be more comfortable with your own kind.' I had to bite my tongue. And just to compli-cate matters, our daughter, Barrett, was going out with her son."

"She must have loved that."

"She could hardly object. She was always so busy acting like she wasn't prejudiced. If it wasn't so pitiful, it'd have cracked me up. The woman has no education and no intelligence to speak of. Rafer and I both graduated from U.C.L.A. He's got a degree in criminology; I've got a B.S. in nursing and an R.N. on top of that."

"Selma knew the kids were dating?"

"Oh, sure. They went steady for years. Tom was crazy about Barrett. I know he felt she was a good influence on Brant."

"Does Brant have a problem?"

"Basically, he's a good person. He was just screwed up back then, like a lot of kids that age. I don't think he ever did drugs, but he drank quite a bit and rebelled every chance he had."

"Why'd they break up?"

"You'd have to ask Barrett. You want my assessment, I think Brant was too needy. He tended to be all mopey and clinging. This was years ago, of course. He was twenty at that point. She was just out of high school and didn't seem that interested in getting serious."

Her comments were cut short when the doctor came in. Dr. Price was in his late twenties, thin and boyish, with bright blue eyes. He took one look at my fingers and said, "Oh wow! Keen." I liked his enthusiasm.

We had a chat about my assailant and the job he'd done. He studied my jaw. "He must have clipped you good," he said. "Any other abrasions or contusions?"

"He kicked me twice in the ribs."

"Let's take a look," he said, pulling up my shirt.

My rib cage on the right side was swiftly turning purple. He listened to my lungs. He palpated my right arm, wrist, hand, and fingers. We trooped into the other room, where a rumpled-looking technician took X rays. I returned to the table and lay down again, feeling thoroughly air-conditioned as the room spun.

When the film had been developed, Dr. Price tucked the various views onto the lighted screen. My ribs were bruised, but not cracked, likely to be sore for days, but requiring no further medical attention. Roentgenographically speaking, the two pesky fingers were completely screwed, though no bones were broken.

With a merry whistle Dr. Price stuck a needle repeatedly in the joints of both my fingers. While I stared at the wall, he maneuvered my digits back into their original position. When I dared to look at my hand, I saw that while the injured fingers would now bend, they were fat and reddened. With a roll of adhesive tape, a packet of gauze, and a metal splint—for which my insurance company would be charged in the neighborhood of five hundred dollars—he taped the two fingers together and affixed them to the ring finger.

I could hear another conference in the hallway, and a deputy appeared at the door. This was a fellow I hadn't seen before—a tall, skinny kid with a long face and shiny metal braces on his teeth. Well, I was filled with confidence.

"Ms. Millhone, I'm Deputy Carey Badger. I understand you had a problem. Can you tell me what happened?"

I said, "Sure," and went through my sad tale of woe again.

There was more conversation outside the door, and Rafer LaMott appeared. He looked freshly showered and shaved, natty in a pair of tan corduroy trousers and a soft red cashmere vest with a dress shirt under it. His expression was neutral. He put his hands in his pockets, leaning casually against the wall. He looked like an ad in a menswear catalogue. "Cecilia was tired, so I told her to go on home. As soon as you're finished here, I'll take you anywhere you want."

IT WAS six a.m. by the time Rafer finally put me in the front seat of his car. The offer of a ride was as close to an apology as I was likely to get. No doubt his true motivation was to quiz me about the current state of my investigation, but I really didn't care. The sun was not officially up, and I was at a loss where to have him deliver me. I couldn't bear the idea of being in the cabin. As if reading my mind, Rafer said, "Where to?"

"I guess you better drop me at the Rainbow. I can hang out there until I figure out what to do next."

"I'd like to check the cabin. I've got a print tech from Independence coming up at seven, as soon as he gets in. Maybe we'll get lucky and find out your intruder left his prints."

"Perform an exorcism while you're at it. I don't expect a good night's sleep until I'm out of there."

He was silent for a while, turning his attention to the road. Finally he spoke up. "You have a theory about last night's attack? Anything taken?"

"I didn't even bother to look," I said. "And I'm assuming this was the guy who followed me from Tiny's."

"I heard about that. We got a copy of the report."

"Anyway, I doubt the motive last night was theft. I think the point was to discourage my investigation."

"Why?"

"You tell me. I guess he feels protective of Tom Newquist. That's the best I can do."

"You could be mistaken, you know. You're single and you're attractive. That makes you a natural target—"

"For what? This was plain old assault and battery. The guy wanted to cause me great bodily harm."

"What else?"

"There's nothing else," I said. "Here's a question for you: Where's Tom's notebook? It's missing. No one's seen it since he died."

He shot me a look and then shook his head blankly. I could see him casting back in his mind. "He usually kept it close, but I know it's not in his desk drawers. We cleaned those out."

"The CHP officer doesn't remember seeing it in the truck. I know it must irritate you that I'm pursuing the point—"

"Look. I was out of line on that. I get huffy about Selma. It has nothing to do with you."

I could feel the distance between us easing. There's nothing as disarming as a concession of that sort. "It may not be relevant in any event," I said. "What's the procedure on reports? Wouldn't most of his notes have already been submitted?"

"Possibly. Old-timers like me and Tom tend to do things when we get around to it."

"Would there be any way to work backward by checking to see what reports were missing?"

"It wouldn't tell you much. You'd have no way of knowing where he'd been and who he'd talked to. Besides, it might have been a case that he was reworking for some reason."

"Such as?"

Rafer shrugged. "He might have picked up a new lead."

"My point exactly. I mean, what if Tom was privy to something he didn't know how to handle."

"He'd have told me. We talked about everything."

"Suppose it concerned you?"

He made a little move that indicated agitation. "Let's get off this, okay? We can talk further, but let me think about it some."

"One more thing. And don't get testy on me. Is there any possibility Tom might have been involved with another woman?"

"No."

I laughed. "Try to keep your answer to twenty-five words or less," I said. "Why not?"

"He was a deeply moral man."

"Well, couldn't that explain his brooding? A man with no conscience wouldn't be at war with himself."

"Objection, Your Honor. Purely speculative."

We pulled in at the Rainbow Café. Rafer put the car in park. "Come on. I'll buy you breakfast. I got a daughter works here."

I struggled with the handle and then gave up. I sat while he walked around the car and opened my door. "Thanks. I can see this is going to be a pain."

"It'll be good for you," he said. "Force you to deal with your dependency issues."

"I don't have dependency issues," I said stoutly.

He smiled in response.

He held the café door open, and I entered ahead of him. The place was bustling—all men, clearly the stopping-off place of early risers, ranchers, cops, and laborers on their way to work. The brown-haired waitress, Nancy, was taking an order from a table full of fellows in overalls, while Barrett, behind the counter, was focused on pancakes and omelettes in the making. Rafer took the lead and found us an empty booth. As we passed the intervening tables, I could see we were attracting any number of stares. I was guessing the jungle drums had already spread the news about my assailant.

Two tables over I caught sight of Macon with his gaze fixed on me. He leaned forward, making some comment. The man with him made one of those casual turns, pretending to glance idly around the room. I picked up a menu, pretending I didn't notice him. Margaret's husband, Hatch.

"Know what you want?" Rafer asked. "I do the works myself."

"I'm with you," I said. "Your daughter's name is Barrett?"

"That was Vick's idea. The job is temporary, by the way. She's applied to med school. She wants to be a shrink. This allows her to live at home and save her money till she goes."

"Where'd she do her undergraduate work? U.C.L.A.?"

"Where else?" he said, smiling. "What about you?"

"I hated school," I said. "I made it through high school by the hair of my chinny-chin-chin, then did three semesters of junior college, but that's as far as I went. Well, I graduated from the police academy, but that was more like boot camp than academia."

"You're a cop?"

"I was. But I was too rebellious."

Nancy appeared with a coffeepot in hand. She had large brown eyes and a beauty mark high on her right cheek. "You're out early," she remarked to Rafer. We both pushed our mugs in her direction, and she filled them.

"You met Kinsey?"

"Not formally, but we've chatted a bit. I'm Nancy."

"How are you?" I said. "I'd shake hands if I could."

"Yeah, I heard about that. Cecilia stopped by when we were opening. She says you took quite a hit. I can see your jaw turning blue."

I put a hand to the place. "It must look terrific."

"Gives you character," she said. She glanced at Rafer. "What's for breakfast?"

"Well, I'm trying to keep my cholesterol up, so I think I'll have the blueberry pancakes, sausage, scrambled eggs, and coffee.

"Make that two," I said.

"Back in a flash," she said.

I saw Rafer's gaze flicker to the window. "Excuse me. I see the print tech. I'll take him on back to the cabin and get him started."

I had to use two hands to hold my coffee mug, given that three fingers on my right hand were taped together like an oven mitt. The doctor had told me I could remove the tape after a day or two, as long as it felt comfortable. He'd given me four painkillers in a small white envelope. I glanced out the window, watching Rafer head toward the cabin in the company of a young man carrying a black case, like a doctor's bag.

"Miss Millhone, can I talk to you?"

I looked up. James Tennyson was standing at the table in his tan CHP uniform, complete with all its creaking paraphernalia: nightstick, flashlight, keys, holster, gun, bullets.

"Sure. Have a seat."

He put a hand against his holster, securing his gun as he slid into the booth. I thought he was ill at ease, but I didn't know him well enough to be certain. He pointed at my hand. "I just heard about the fellow coming after you last night. You all right?"

"More or less."

"He meant business."

"I'll survive," I said.

"The reason I came over . . . I didn't even think about this until yesterday. The night Tom died? When I spotted his truck . . . you know, with the hazard lights on? There was a woman walking along the road, heading toward town."

"A woman?"

"Yes, ma'am. I'm almost sure."

"And she was facing you?"

"That's right, but she veered off shortly before I passed, so I didn't get a good look at her. She was bundled up pretty good."

"Is it unusual to see someone walking out there?"

"Yes, ma'am. There's very little in the way of houses out there."

"Do you think she was *with* him?"

"I suppose it's possible," he said. "If he was having chest pains, she might have been on her way to find help."

"Why not flag you down?"

"Beats me. I don't know what to make of it," he said. He glanced toward the front of the café. "My breakfast is here. You have any more questions, give me a call."

WHEN Rafer and I reached the cabin after breakfast, the door was standing open. I could see smudges of powder along the edges of the sills. Rafer introduced me to the technician, who rolled a set of my prints for elimination purposes. He could have saved himself the trouble. The cabin yielded nothing useful in the way of evidence.

The interior seemed dank, the bed still lumpy with the pillows I'd tucked under the pile of blankets. A rivulet of revulsion trickled over me. I was embarrassed at my inadequate attempt to defend myself. Anxiety whispered at the base of my spine, a reminder of how vulnerable I was. A memory burbled up. I was five years old again, bruised and bloodied after the car wreck that killed my parents.

While Rafer and the tech conferred outside, I hauled out my duffel and began to pack my things. I was suddenly aware of Rafer in the doorway. "You're taking off?" he asked.

"I'd be crazy to stay here."

"I agree with you on that, but I didn't think you were finished with your investigation."

"That remains to be seen."

His gaze rested on me with concern. "You're going to quit?"

"I didn't say that."

"Look, I can see you're upset. I'd offer you protection, but I don't have a deputy to spare. We operate on a shoestring. You know anybody who could pitch in on personal security?"

"Oh, please. Absolutely not. I wouldn't do that. I hired a bodyguard once before, but this is different."

"How so?"

"If that guy meant to kill me, he'd have done it last night."

"Well," he said. He paused, silent, hands in his pockets. I zipped the duffel, picked up my jacket and my handbag, looking around the cabin. I'd forgotten about the Smith-Corona, still sitting with the lid half closed. I snapped the cover into place.

"Thanks for the ride and thanks for breakfast."

"I have to get in to work, but let me know if there's anything I can do to help."

"You can carry this," I said, passing him the typewriter. He did me one better, carrying both the duffel and the Smith-Corona to the car. Snow had begun to fall, big lacy flakes that settled on my face. I waited until he'd pulled away, and then headed for the office and stuck my head in the door. There was no sign of Cecilia. Her door was shut, and I imagined her catching up on the sleep she'd lost taking me to the emergency room. I got into my car and headed back to Selma's. By ten a.m. I was on the road for home.

CHAPTER SEVEN

SHORTLY after leaving Nota Lake, I caught a glimpse of a county sheriff's cruiser keeping me company from half a mile back. The effect was to make me feel I was being ushered across the county line. When we reached the junction of 395 and 168, the patrol car turned off. Whether the escort was deliberate or coincidental, I couldn't be sure. Nor could I determine whether the intention was benign or belligerent.

After that, the desert landscape sped by in a monotonous repetition of scrub-covered low hills, and I spent the rest of the journey in a haze of road-induced hypnosis. The intervening towns were few—Big Pine, Independence, Cartago—small enclaves that consisted of gas stations, wooden cottages, coffee shops, perhaps a pizza restaurant or a Frosty Freeze, boarded over for the winter.

Gradually I let my thoughts drift back to events I'd left behind. I'd spent an hour at Selma's before I'd departed Nota Lake. So far, given my four days' work, I'd earned a thousand dollars of the fifteen hundred she'd paid me in advance. That meant that I would owe *her* money if I decided to quit. She'd been properly upset by what had happened, and we'd gone through the predictable litany of horror and remorse. "I feel sick. This is my fault. I got you into this," she'd said.

"Don't be silly, Selma. It isn't your fault. If nothing else, it gives credence to your hunch about Tom's secret."

"But I never dreamed it'd be dangerous."

"Life is dangerous," I said, feeling oddly impatient. "Look, we can sit here and commiserate, but I'd much prefer to use the time constructively. I've got a big pile of phone bills. Let's sit down together and see how many numbers you recognize."

Which is what we'd done, eliminating more than three quarters of the calls for the past ten months. Many were Selma's, related to her church work and assorted friendships. Some were business calls, a fact confirmed by judicious use of Tom's Rolodex. I'd placed the entire file of phone bills in my duffel, and then I'd gone down to the basement to take a look at the storage boxes Brant had mentioned. There, in the dry, overheated space, a curious order prevailed.

At least Tom Newquist was systematic where work was concerned. On a shelf, in a series of cardboard boxes, he'd placed bundles of field notes going back twenty-five years. Once a notebook had been filled, his method was to remove the six-hole lined pages, apply a wrapper showing the inclusive dates, and then secure them with a rubber band. Bundles of notes that pertained to the same case were packed in separate manila envelopes, again labeled and dated. I could walk my fingers back through his investigations, year after year, without gaps or interruptions. Occasionally, on the outside of an envelope, he'd penned a note indicating an update. Missing were notes from June of last year until the time of his death. I had to assume the missing notebook covered the previous eight months, so essentially I was back to square one.

The snow turned to rain as I drove south. At Rosamond, I found a McDonald's and picked up a big cola, a large order of fries, and a QP with cheese. I downed a painkiller while I was at it. Twelve minutes later I was on the road again. The closer I came to Los Angeles, the more my spirits lifted.

When I reached Highway 5, I turned north as far as the junction with Highway 126, where I cut west again through Fillmore and Santa Paula. Route 126 spilled into 101, and I nearly whimpered aloud at the sight of the Pacific. I rolled the window down and let raindrops blow on my face. The scent of the ocean was dense and sweet. The water was silken, endless reams of gray taffeta with churning lace at the edge. While I can spend brief periods in landlocked locations, I'm never as happy as I am when close to deep water.

I powered through the final few miles into Santa Teresa. By that time I'd been on the road for five hours. My foot felt as if it were welded to the accelerator. My bruised fingers were deadened by drugs, yet somehow managed to throb with pain.

My neighborhood looked the same, a short street a block from the beach: palms, tall pines, wire fences, crooked sidewalks, and stucco houses with aging tile roofs. I found a parking spot across the street from my apartment, once a single-car garage, now a two-story hideaway attached by a sunporch to the house where Henry Pitts, my landlord, lives. This month marked the fifth anniversary of my tenancy, and I treasure the space I've come to think of as mine.

It took me two trips to unload the rental car, passing in and out Henry's squeaking gate. I unlocked the front door, left the typewriter by the desk, and hauled my duffel up the spiral stairs to the sleeping loft. I stripped off my clothes, removed the bandages from my hand, and treated myself to a long, hot shower, wherein I washed my hair and sang a medley of show tunes. The luxury of being clean and warm was almost more than I could bear. I did a left-handed toothbrushing and anointed myself with an inexpensive drugstore cologne that smelled like lilies of the valley. I put on a fresh turtleneck and jeans, clean socks, Reeboks, and pronounced myself whole. After that, all I had to do was spend twenty minutes getting my fingers splinted and retaped. This was going to be obnoxious.

At a quarter to five I ducked out my door and splashed across the patio in the rain. I peered through the window in Henry's back door while I rapped on the glass. Henry Pitts is lean-faced, tanned, and long-legged, a gent with snowy white hair, blue eyes, a beaky nose, and all of his own teeth. At eighty-six he's blessed with intelligence, high spirits, and prodigious energy. He came into the kitchen wearing a navy T-shirt and white shorts, covered by a big baker's apron. He hurried to unlock the door, his face wreathed in smiles.

"Well, Kinsey. I didn't expect you back today. Come on in. What happened to your hand?"

"Long story." I gave him a hug. "Something smells wonderful. What's cooking?"

Henry smiled. "A surprise for Rosie's birthday—a noodle pudding with a Hungarian name I hope you won't ask me to pronounce. I'm also making a Hungarian apple pie."

"Which birthday?"

"Last I heard, she was claiming sixty-six, but I think she's been shaving points for years. You'll be joining us, I hope."

"I wouldn't miss it. I'll have to sneak out and find a gift."

"I'm not going over till six. Sit, sit, sit and I'll fix a pot of tea."

He settled me in his rocking chair and put the kettle on while we filled each other in on events during the weeks I'd been gone. In no particular order we went through the trip, Dietz's surgery, and news from the home front. I laid out the job as succinctly as I could, including the attack the night before. While I finished my tea, Henry put together the pie crust. "I better whiz out and find a present. Are you dressing for the party?"

"I'm wearing long pants," he said. "You look fine as you are."

As it turned out, Rosie's entire restaurant had been given over to her birthday party. Some of her patrons had decorated the place with crepe paper streamers, balloons, and hand-lettered banners that read WAY TO GO, ROSIE! There was a huge bouquet of flowers, a keg of bad beer, a stack of pizza boxes, and an enormous birthday cake. The partygoers had seeded the jukebox with high-decibel hits from the 1960s, and they'd pushed all the tables back so they could do the twist and the Watusi. Rosie looked on with an indulgent smile. I'd spent the better part of an hour at a department store, finally selecting a red silk chemise I thought would tickle her fancy. Henry and I ducked out at ten and scurried home through the rain.

I locked the door behind me and moved through the apartment, marveling at the whole of it: walls of polished teak and oak, cubbyholes of storage tucked into all the nooks and crannies. I had a sofa bed built into the bay window for guests, two chairs, bookshelves, my desk. Up the spiral stairs I had a double bed and a bathroom with a sunken tub and a window looking out toward the ocean. I was so thrilled to be home I could hardly bear to go to bed. I crawled, naked, under a pile of quilts and listened to the rain tapping on the Plexiglas skylight.

The next thing I knew, it was six a.m. I tuned in to the sound of rain, bypassed the thought of jogging, and went back to sleep again. I roused myself at eight and went through my usual morning ablutions. I had breakfast, read the paper, and then set the typewriter case and my notes on the desktop. My first chore of the morning would be to return the rental car. That done, I'd take a cab to the office, where I'd put in an appearance and bum a ride home. In the meantime I'd begin the painful hunt-and-peck addition to my progress report. It wasn't until I opened the typewriter case that I saw that someone had twisted the middle two rows of typewriter keys into a hopeless clot. Some of the keys had been broken off, and some were simply bent sideways, like my fingers. I sat down and stared with a sense of bafflement. What was going on?

I DECIDED to skip the office and concentrate on running down the one or two leads I had. In my heart of hearts I knew perfectly well the trashing of my typewriter had taken place in Nota Lake before I'd left. Nonetheless, the discovery was disconcerting and tainted my sense of security and well-being. Annoyed, I flicked through the yellow pages and made calls until I found someone equipped to handle my vintage Smith-Corona.

Next I took out Tom's phone bills and punched in a number. When I'd dialed this same number from Tom's den, the call had been picked up by an answering machine. I was operating on the assumption that the woman I'd heard was the female sheriff's investigator Phyllis claimed she'd seen flirting with Tom. Now, as I listened, once again an answering machine picked up, and the same throaty-voiced woman told me what I could do at the sound of the beep. I left my name, my home and office numbers, and a brief message indicating that I'd like to talk to her about Tom Newquist.

I tucked Tom's photograph into my handbag, grabbed my jacket and an umbrella, and headed out into the rain. I used my left hand where I could, fumbling with car keys, transferring items. The simplest transactions were consequently slowed, since the splint on my right hand forced me to proceed by awkward degrees. I made a second trip for the typewriter. I dropped it off for repair, returned the rental, and took a cab back to my apartment. I picked up my car, which—after a series of stutters—finally coughed to life.

I drove into downtown Santa Teresa. The Gramercy Hotel was a chunky three-story structure on lower State Street, a residential establishment favored by the homeless when their monthly checks came in. The stucco building was painted the sweet green of a crème de menthe frappé. A marquee spelled out the rates.

SGL RMS $9.95   DBL RMS $13.95   DAILY*WEEKLY*MONTHLY

The hotel must have been considered elegant once upon a time. The floor was green marble, with a crooked path of newspapers soaking up all the rainy footsteps. I approached the long front desk, located beneath an archway decorated with white plaster scrolls. The fellow behind the counter was leaning forward on his elbows, clearly interested in my intentions. This felt like one more fool's errand, but it was the only thing I could think to do at this point.

"I'd like to talk to the manager. Is he here?"

"I guess that's me. I'm Dave Estes. And your name?"

"Kinsey Millhone." I passed him my business card.

He read it with serious attention. He was in his thirties, a cheerful-looking fellow with an open countenance, glasses, a slight overbite, and a hairline that had receded to reveal a long, sloping forehead, like an expanse of empty seashore when the tide is out.

"What can I help you with?"

I placed the photograph of Tom Newquist on the counter. "I'm wondering if you've seen this man. He's an investigator for the Nota County Sheriff's Department. His name is Tom—"

"Hold on, hold on." He held a hand up, motioning me to wait a moment, during which time he made the kind of face that precedes a sneeze. His expression cleared, and he pointed at me. "Newquist. Tom Newquist."

I was astonished. "That's right. You know him?"

"Well, no, I don't know him, but he was in here."

"When was this?"

"Oh, I'd say June of last year. Probably the first week. I'd say the fifth if forced to guess."

I was so unprepared for the verification, I couldn't think what to ask next.

Estes was looking at me. "Did something happen to him?"

"He died of a heart attack a few weeks back."

"Hey, too bad. Sorry to hear that."

"Can you tell me what brought him in here?"

"Oh, sure. He was looking for some guy who'd just been released from jail. We seem to get a lot of fellows here in that situation. Don't ask me why. Classy place like this."

"Do you remember the name of the man he was looking for?"

"Hang on." He went throught the same procedure, face screwed up. He paused. "You're probably wondering how I do this. I took a course in mnemonics, the art of improving the memory. Trick is you come up with these devices that help fix an item in the mind."

"That's great. I'm impressed."

"Reason I remember the time frame for your Newquist's visit is I started my study just about the time he came in. He was my first practice case. So the name Newquist? No problem. New because the fellow was new to me, right? Quist, as in question."

"That's good," I said. "And the other guy? The one he was in-quiring about?"

"Oh, yes. It had to do with dentists. His last name was Toth. That's tooth with an *o* missing. His first name was Alfie."

"So Tom Newquist was here on business."

"That's correct. Trouble is, he missed him. Toth'd been here two weeks, but he moved out June one."

"Do you have any idea why he was looking for Toth?"

"Said he was developing a lead on a case he was working."

"Did Toth leave a forwarding address?"

"Well, no, but I have his ex-wife's address, under 'nearest relative not living with you.' That's not confidential information as far as I'm concerned. People check in, I tell 'em the hotel files are open to the authorities."

"I'm sure the police appreciate your attitude, but don't the hotel guests object?"

Dave Estes shrugged. "I guess the day I get sued, we'll change the policy. You know, another fellow came in, too. Plainclothes detective. This was maybe June one. I wasn't working that day, or I'd have filed it away in the old noggin. I told Peck, the assistant manager, he better take the same course I did, but so far I haven't talked him into it."

"Too bad," I said. "So who was this other detective?"

"Can't help you there, and that's my point. If Peck took this course, he could recall in detail. Since he didn't? No dice."

"Could I talk to Peck myself?"

"You could, but I can tell you exactly what he's going to say. He remembers this investigator came in—had a warrant and all, but Toth wasn't on the premises. In fact, he checked out later that day. Detective called back the next morning, and Peck gave him the address of Toth's ex-wife, same as I would."

"What about the warrant? Was that local?"

"Can't answer that. Peck doesn't pay attention the way I do."

"Did you tell Tom Newquist about the other detective?"

"Same way I'm telling you."

"Did you tell him how to get in touch with Toth's ex?"

"Sure did. That's why I'm giving it to you. I don't show favorites.

Why say yes to one and no to someone else is the way I look at it."

"You haven't given me anything yet," I said.

He reached for a piece of scratch paper and jotted down a woman's name, address, and telephone number, apparently off the top of his head. He passed it across the counter.

I took the paper, noting the Perdido address. "Sounds like Alfie Toth was suddenly very popular. What's Peck's first name?"

"Leland. Number's unlisted. Now *that* I wouldn't give out without getting his permission."

I thought about it for a moment, but couldn't think what other ground I should cover. "Well, thanks for the help."

"Don't you want to hear the rest of it?"

I hesitated. "What rest?"

"The guy's dead. Murdered. Some backpacker found his body up near Ten Pines couple months ago. January thirteen. Reason I remember is it's my great-aunt's birthday."

I stared at him, remembering a brief mention of it in the paper. "*That* was Alfie Toth?"

"Yep. Coroner figured he'd been dead six, seven months—since right about the time everybody came looking for him."

AT THE public library, I turned up the relevant paragraph in a copy of the Santa Teresa *Dispatch* for January 15.

BODY FOUND IN LOS PADRES THAT OF TRANSIENT

The decomposed remains discovered by a hiker in the Los Padres National Forest January 13 have been identified as a transient, Alfred Toth, 45, according to the Santa Teresa County Sheriff's Department. The body was found in the countryside five miles east of Manzanita Mountain. The case is being investigated as a homicide. Anyone with information is asked to call Detective Clay Boyd at the Sheriff's Department.

I found a pay phone, scrounged a couple of coins from the bottom of my handbag, dialed the Santa Teresa County Sheriff's Department, and asked for Detective Boyd.

"Boyd." The tone was flat, professional, all business.

"Hi. My name is Kinsey Millhone," I said, trying not to sound too chirpy. "I'm a local private investigator working on a case that may connect to the death of Alfie Toth."

Pause. "In what way?"

"Well, I'm not sure yet. I'm not asking for confidential information, but could you give me an update? The last mention in the paper was back in January."

Pause. "What's the nature of your interest?"

"Ah. Well, that's tricky to explain. I'm working for the widow of a sheriff's investigator up in Nota Lake. Tom Newquist. Did you know him by any chance?"

"Name doesn't sound familiar."

"He drove down last June to talk to Alfie Toth, but by the time he reached the Gramercy, Toth had moved out. Do you have any record Newquist contacted your department?"

"Hang on." He put me on hold, then clicked back in. I could hear him flipping pages. "Tom Newquist didn't get in touch with us, but I do show we've been in communication with Nota Lake."

"Really. I wonder why he didn't let you know he was coming."

"Gosh, I don't know. That's a stumper," he said blandly.

I could feel my frustration mount. How could this man be so pleasant and so obtuse at the same time? I switched gears. "Was Alfie Toth wanted for some crime at the time of his death?"

"Not that I'm aware of."

"The desk clerk at the Gramercy says a plainclothes detective came in with a warrant for his arrest."

"Wasn't one of ours."

"You don't show any outstanding warrants?"

"No, ma'am, I don't. Why don't you talk to Nota Lake and see what they have to say. I'm not going to reveal the substance of an ongoing investigation to any yahoo who asks. I don't mean to cast aspersions, but you could be anyone . . . a journalist."

"God forbid. Surely you don't think I'm anyone that low."

Detective Boyd laughed. "Have a good day."

CHAPTER EIGHT

OLGA Toth opened the door to her Perdido condominium wearing a bright yellow outfit that consisted of formfitting tights and a stretchy tunic, cinched with a wide white bejeweled plastic belt. The fabric clung to her body like a bandage that couldn't quite conceal the damage time had inflicted on her sixty-year-old flesh. Her hair was a dry-looking platinum-blond, her brown eyes heavily lined. I could smell the vermouth on her breath before she said a word.

I'd driven the thirty miles to Perdido in drizzling rain. The roadway was slick and the driving hazardous. Under ordinary circumstances I might have delayed the trip, but I was worried the cops would somehow manage to warn Alfie's ex-wife of my interest, urging her to keep her mouth shut if I knocked on her door.

"Mrs. Toth?" I showed her my card. "Could I talk to you about your ex-husband?"

The smile she'd greeted me with faded with disappointment. "Honey, I'm sorry to be the one to tell you, but he's deceased, so if you're here about his unpaid bills, the line forms at the rear."

"This is something else. May I come in?"

"You're not here to serve process," she asked cautiously.

"Not at all. Your record's clean as far as I'm concerned."

She studied me, considering. "No funny business," she warned.

"I'm never funny," I said.

I followed her through the small foyer, watching as she retrieved a martini glass from a console table. "I was just having a drink in case you're interested."

"I'm fine for now, but thanks."

We entered a living room done entirely in white; trampled-looking white nylon cut-pile carpeting, white nylon sheers, white leatherette

couches. The glass-and-chrome coffee table bore a large arrangement of white lilies and a pitcher of martinis.

"What sort of work do you do?" I asked.

She motioned me to a seat at one end of the couch while she settled at the other end. Her nails, I noticed, were very long and pink.
"I'm a cosmetologist, and if you ever get interested in a makeover,
I could do wonders. Now what's this about Alfie? I thought all his
problems were over and done with, the poor guy."

I filled her in on the nature of the job I'd been hired to do, thinking that as a widow, she might appreciate Selma Newquist's concern
about her husband's mental state before he died.

"I remember the name Newquist. He was the one called me a
couple days after Alfie took off."

"How long was Alfie here?"

"Two days, maybe three."

"What made him leave the Gramercy?"

"I got the impression he was nervous, but he never said why. He
was looking for a place to hole up, and I wasn't having it. Alfie was
a sweet man. He was twenty years younger than me, though you
never would have guessed. We were married for eight years. Of
course, he was in and out of jail for most of it."

"What was he in jail for?"

She waved the question away. "It was never anything big—bad
checks or petty thievery. His problem was he was just born dumb.
He tended to take up with some loser with a harebrained scheme,
but he never seemed to learn. You had to love that about him. He
was good-looking, too, in a goofy sort of way. What he did, he did
well, and the rest you might as well write off as a dead loss."

"What was it he did well?"

"He was great in the sack."

"Ah. So he was here last June," I said, trying to steer her back
onto neutral ground. "Where'd he go when he left?"

"Your guess is as good as mine. Last time I saw him, he was gathering up his things. Next thing I know, they're asking about his
bridgework, trying to identify his body. This was the middle of Jan-

uary, so he'd been gone six months. The cops seemed to think he'd been killed shortly after he took off."

"How'd they pinpoint the time?"

"I asked the same thing, but they wouldn't give me any details. I'd reported him missing—oh, I'd say early September. His parole officer had somehow tracked down my address and telephone number, and he was in a tiff because Alfie hadn't been reporting."

"Did the police have a theory about what happened to him?"

She shook her head. "I'll tell you this. He wasn't killed for his money, because the man was stone-broke."

"Why was Newquist looking for Alfie in the first place?"

"That was in regard to a homicide in Nota County. He'd heard Alfie was friends with a fellow whose body was found back in March of last year. I guess they had reason to believe the two were traveling together around the time of this man's death."

"Alfie was a suspect?"

"Oh, honey, the cops will never say that. They think you'll be more cooperative if they tell you they're looking for a potential witness to a crime. In this case, probably true. Alfie was a sissy. He was scared to death of violence. He'd never kill anyone."

"How did Tom Newquist find out Alfie was in Santa Teresa?"

"I don't know. He never said a word about that."

"What about the victim? Did Newquist give you his name?"

"He didn't have to. I knew him through Alfie. Fellow by the name of Pinkie Ritter. He and Alfie met in prison six years ago at Chino. Ritter was vicious, a real s.o.b., but he protected Alfie's backside. After they got out, Alfie wanted him to stay here, but I said absolutely not. Ritter was a convicted rapist."

"And no one else called or came looking for Alfie?"

"I was off at work most days, so I don't really know what Alfie did with himself. He might have had friends. He usually did. Like I said, he was a sweet guy. You know, horny, but kind."

"He sounds like a nice man," I murmured, hoping God wouldn't strike me dead.

"Well, he was. He never got in bar fights or said a cross word to anyone. He was just a big dumb Joe," she said, voice wavering. "Alfie was a bumpkin, and he didn't always show good sense. Someone could have killed him for the fun of it."

I DROVE back to Santa Teresa, trying not to think much about the information I'd gleaned. I let thoughts wash over me without trying to put them in order or make any sense of them. I was getting closer to something. I just wasn't sure what it was. One thing seemed certain: Tom Newquist was on the same track and maybe what he'd found caused him untold distress.

I reached my apartment shortly after three o'clock. The rain had passed for the moment, but the sky was overcast. I unlocked my door and flipped on the lights. My hand was beginning to ache. I went into the kitchenette for water, and took some pain medication. I removed the gauze wrap from my fingers and tossed the splint but left the tape in place. The gesture was symbolic, but it cheered me up.

I checked the answering machine, which showed one message. I pressed REPLAY and heard Tom's contact at the sheriff's department. "Colleen Sellers here. Home until five."

I tried her number. She picked up quickly, almost as though she'd been waiting for the call. Her hello was careful. No infusion of warmth or friendliness.

"This is Kinsey Millhone," I said. "Is this Colleen?"

"Yes. You wanted to get in touch regarding Tom Newquist."

"That's right. I appreciate your getting back to me. Actually, this is awkward. I'm assuming you've heard that he passed away."

"So I heard."

That was as much as she gave me, so I was forced to plunge on. "Well, I'm a private investigator here in Santa Teresa—"

"I know who you are. I checked it out."

"Well, good. Anyway, for reasons too complicated to go into, I've been hired by his widow to see if I can find out what was going on the last two months of his life."

There was a momentary pause. "Why?"

"Is there any way we can do this in person?" I asked.

COLLEEN LIVED IN SANTA Teresa, not far from me, and she suggested we meet in the kiddy park. I spotted her sitting on one of the swings in a yellow slicker with the hood up. "Why don't we walk?" she said.

Up close I placed her in her late forties. She had a square face, oversized glasses set in square red frames, and shoulder-length blond hair. Her eyes were a warm brown. She was large-boned and tall, with a shoe size that probably compelled her to shop out of catalogues.

"You don't work today?" I asked.

"I'm taking a leave of absence."

"Mind if I ask why?"

"You can ask anything you want. Believe me, I'm experienced at avoiding answers when the questions don't suit. I turn fifty this coming June. It does make you take a long, hard look at your life. Suddenly I don't know what I'm doing or why I'm doing it. My parents are both gone . . . my mom just last year. It's a very strange sensation to be out on the front lines alone."

"You have any kids?"

She shook her head. "Nope, and that's another thing I question. I mean, it's way too late now, but I wonder about that. Not that I ever wanted children. What about you? You have kids?"

"No. I've been married and divorced twice, both times in my twenties. At that point I wasn't ready to have children. I wasn't even ready for marriage, but how did I know?"

"Know what I regret? I wish now I'd listened more closely to family stories. Or maybe I wish I had someone to pass 'em on to. I worry about what's going to happen to the family photographs once I'm gone. They'll be thrown in the garbage. . . . All those aunts and uncles down the tubes." Her voice dropped away, and then she changed the subject briskly. "What'd you do to your hand?"

"A fellow dislocated my fingers. You should have seen them . . . pointing sideways. Made me sick," I said.

We strolled on for a bit. To the right of us a low wall separated the sidewalk from the beach. "How are we doing so far?" I asked.

"I assume you're sizing me up, trying to figure out how much you want to tell."

"Yes, I am. Tom confided in me, and I take that seriously. Even if he's dead, why would I betray his trust?"

"That's up to you. Maybe this is unfinished business and you have an opportunity to see it through for him."

"This is not about Tom. This is about his wife," she said.

"She's entitled to peace of mind."

"Aren't we all?" she said. "I never met the woman, so I don't care about her peace of mind."

That was as much as I got out of her. By the time we'd walked as far as the wharf, the rain had begun again. "I think I'll peel off here. If you decide you have more to tell me, why don't you get in touch."

"I'll think about that," she said.

I trotted home and retrieved my car. It was time to quit horsing around and go visit Santa Teresa Hospital.

I CAUGHT Dr. Yee on his way out. I'd parked across from the emergency room, and I was circling the hospital to the main entrance when Dr. Yee emerged from a side door. I called his name and he turned. I waved, and he waited until I'd reached his side.

In Santa Teresa County, autopsy work is done by various forensic pathologists under contract to the county. Steven Yee was in his forties, a third-generation Chinese American, with a passion for French cooking.

"You looking for me?" He was easily six feet tall, slender and handsome, with a smooth, round face. His hair was a straight glossy black, streaked with exotic bands of white.

"I'm glad I caught you. Are you on your way home? I need about fifteen minutes of your time if you can spare it."

He glanced at his watch. "I'm not due at the restaurant for another hour," he said.

"I heard about that. You have a second career."

He smiled with pleasure, shrugging modestly. "Well, it's restful to chop leeks instead of . . . other things. So what's up?"

"I'm looking for information about a man named Alfie Toth. Are you familiar with the case?"

"Should be. I did the post," he said. He hooked a thumb in the direction of the building. "Come on back to my office. I'll show you what we have."

"This is great," I said happily as I followed him. "I understand Toth's death may be related to a suspected homicide in Nota Lake. One of the sheriff's investigators there was working on the case when he died of a heart attack a few weeks back. Tom Newquist. Did he get in touch with you?"

"I know the name, but he didn't contact me directly. I spoke by phone to the Nota Lake coroner, Trey Kirchner, and he mentioned him. What's your connection?"

"Newquist's widow hired me. She says her husband was stressed out, and she wants me to find out why. Law enforcement's been very tight-lipped on the subject."

"I'll bet." We reached the elevator, he punched the DOWN button, and we descended into the bowels of the building.

Dr. Yee's office was a small bare box down the hall from the morgue. The anteroom was lined with filing cabinets, the office barely large enough for his big rolltop desk, his swivel chair, and a chair for guests. His medical books were placed in a bookcase, and the top of his desk was reserved for a neat row of French cookbooks, trussed on either side by a large jar of murky formalin, in which floated something I didn't care to inspect. "Hang on a second and I'll pull the file," he said. "Have a seat."

The chair was stacked with medical journals, so I perched on the edge, grateful that Dr. Yee was willing to trust me. He returned with a file and a manila envelope and took his seat.

"Are those the photographs? Can I see?"

"Sure, but they won't tell you much." From the envelope he extracted a set of eight-by-ten color prints showing views of the scene where Alfie Toth had been found. The terrain was rugged: boulders, chaparral, an ancient live oak. "Toth was identified through skeletal remains, largely dental work. Pinkie Ritter's body in Nota

Lake was found in much the same circumstances—same MO and a similar remote locale."

I paused, staring at one close-up with perplexity, not quite sure what I was looking at, probably the lower half of Alfie Toth's body crumpled on the ground. The pelvic bones appeared to be still joined, but the femur, tibia, and fibulas were tangled together in a heap. The haphazard skeletal assortment looked like a Halloween decoration badly in need of assembly.

Dr. Yee was saying, "Ritter's body was found fully clothed with various personal items in his pockets—expired California driver's license, credit cards. Identification was confirmed by his fingerprints, which had to be reconstituted. Ritter'd had his prints in the system since 1972. Real scum. The first presumption was of suicide, though Kirchner said he had big doubts and the county sheriff did, too. Keep in mind there wasn't any suicide note at the scene, but there was also no sign of trauma on the body. Same thing with Toth."

"So what are we looking at?" I asked.

"To all appearances, both guys tied a rope around a boulder, put a noose around their necks, pushed the rock through the Y of a tree limb, and hung themselves."

I stared at him. "That's odd." I glanced down at a photograph, in which I could see the crisscross of rope circling a rock the size of a large watermelon. Toth's lower torso and extremities had separated, falling in a tumble on one side of the tree, while the upper half of his body, pulled by the weight of the boulder, had fallen on the other.

"Nothing remarkable about the rope, in case you're wondering. Garden-variety clothesline." Dr. Yee watched my face. "Not to be racist about it, but the method's more compatible with an Asian sensibility. Some dude out in Nota County, how'd it even occur to him? And then a second one here? I mean, it's possible Toth heard about his pal's alleged suicide and imitated his methodology, but even so, it seems off."

"Really. If Alfie Toth wanted to kill himself, you'd think he'd blow his brains out."

Dr. Yee shifted in his chair. "A more plausible explanation is that both victims were killed by the same party. The reason the cops are so paranoid is to avoid all the kooks and the copycats. You don't want anyone but the killer in possession of the details."

"What's the estimated time of death for Ritter?"

"Oh, he'd been there five years from Kirchner's estimate. A gasoline receipt among his effects was dated April 1981."

"Quite a gap between deaths," I said. I ran the scenario through my head like a piece of film. "There's no way two men on opposite sides of California would have independently devised the same method."

"Probably not," he said. "Though, given the fact they were friends, it's possible they overheard someone describe the technique. If you're intent on suicide, the beauty of it is once you topple the boulder through the fork in the tree, there's no way back. Also, death is reasonably quick. Not instantaneous, but you'd lose consciousness within a minute or less."

"These are the only two deaths of this kind that you know of?"

"That's right. I don't think this is serial, but the two have to be connected."

"Isn't there a chance Toth killed his friend Ritter, hoping to make it look like suicide instead of murder, and then ended up killing himself the same way?"

"It's possible," he said dubiously, "but what's your picture? Toth commits a murder, and five years pass before he finds himself overwhelmed with guilt?"

"Doesn't make much sense, does it?" I said.

WHEN I got home at five o'clock, I stopped by to have a cup of tea with Henry. At six I headed for Rosie's tavern. Once again the rain had eased off, but cold saturated the air, making me grateful to step inside. Rosie's was quiet, the air scented with the pungent smell of garlic, bacon, and simmering beef. There were two patrons sitting in a booth, but the occasional clink of flatware on china was the only sound I heard.

Rosie was sitting at the bar, absorbed in the evening paper, which was open in front of her. I pulled out the stool next to hers and perched. "Something smells good."

"Lot of somethings," she said. "I got my husband fixing hot pickled beef, and beef tongue with tomato sauce."

"My favorite," I said dryly.

Behind us the door opened, and a foursome came in. Rosie eased down off her stool and moved across the room to greet them, playing hostess. The door opened again, and Colleen Sellers was suddenly standing in the entrance. What was *she* doing here?

WE SAT in the back booth I usually claim as my own. I poured her a glass of wine. Her glasses had fogged over, and she held them by the frames while she pulled a paper napkin from the dispenser and cleaned the lenses. Without the glasses she looked vulnerable, the misery palpable in the air between us.

"When did you first meet Tom?"

"At a conference up in Redding a year ago. I never did meet his wife. I gathered she was a bit of a pain, but he always spoke of her like she was some kind of goddess." She tucked her hair behind her ears and put on her glasses again.

"Did you meet by chance or by design?"

Colleen rolled her eyes, and a weary smile played around her mouth. "I knew he was going to be there. How's that?"

I smiled back at her. "You want to tell it your way?"

"I'd appreciate that," she said. "Until Redding, I only dealt with him by phone. He sounded terrific, so naturally, I wanted to meet him in person. We hit it off right away, chatting about cases we'd worked, talking department politics, the usual stuff."

"Someone seemed to think the two of you were very chummy."

"Chummy?"

"That you were flirtatious. I'm just telling you what I heard."

"There's no law against flirting. Tom was a doll. I never knew a man yet who couldn't use a little boost to his ego, especially at our age. Who's telling you this stuff? Someone trying to make trouble, I can tell you that."

"How well did you know him?"

"I only saw him twice. No, correction. I saw him three times. It was all work at first, starting with the case he was on."

"What case was that?"

"County sheriff up in Nota Lake found an apparent suicide in the desert, an ex-con named Ritter, who'd hung himself from a branch of a California white oak. Identification was confirmed through his fingerprints, and Tom tracked him back as far as his release from Chino in the spring of '81. Ritter had family in this area—Perdido, to be precise. Tom talked to them by phone, and they told him Ritter'd been traveling with a pal."

"Alfie Toth," I supplied. "I know Tom drove down here in June to look for him."

"That's right. I was the one got a line on the guy. I called Tom, and he said he'd be down within a day. This was mid-April. I guess he got caught up in work, and it was June by the time he made it down here. By then Toth was gone."

"So Tom never talked to him?"

"Not that I know of. As it turned out, Toth's body was the one found in January of this year. The minute the ID was made, I called Tom. The MO was the same for both Ritter and Toth, and that was worrisome. The two deaths had to be related, but it was tough to determine what the motivation might have been."

"From what I hear, the murders were separated by a five-year time gap. You have a theory about that?"

I could see her mouth pull down, and she wagged her head to convey her ambivalence. "This was one time Tom and I didn't agree. It could have been a double cross. You know, a bank heist or burglary with Ritter and his sidekick betraying an accomplice. Fellow catches up with them and kills Ritter on the spot, then takes five years to hunt down Toth."

"What was Tom's idea?"

"Well, he thought Toth might have been a witness to Ritter's murder. Something happens in the mountains and Pinkie Ritter dies. Toth gets away, and eventually the killer catches up."

I said, "Or maybe Alfie Toth killed Ritter, and someone else came along and avenged Ritter's death."

She smiled briefly. "I suggested that myself, but Tom was convinced the perpetrator was the same in both cases."

Dr. Yee's assessment was the same as Tom's. "It would help if I knew how to get in touch with Ritter's family."

"I can give you the phone number later if you like."

"That'd be great. One other thing. I know this is none of my business, but were you in love with Tom? Because that's what I'm picking up, reading between the lines," I said.

Her body language altered, and I could see her debate with herself about how much to reveal. "Tom was completely devoted to his wife, which he let me know right off the bat. But I'll tell you something. We had real chemistry between us. It's the first time I ever understood the term soul mate. It was like finding myself in this other guise—my spiritual counterpart—and that was heady stuff. There wasn't anything I couldn't say to him. And laugh? God, we laughed."

"You go to bed with him?" I asked casually.

A blush began to saturate Colleen's cheeks. "No, but I would have. I was so crazy about him I broached the subject myself. I was shameless. I'd have taken him on any basis." She shook her head. "He wouldn't do it, and you know why? He was honorable. He made a promise to be faithful, and he meant it."

"You miss him," I said.

"I've cried every day since I heard about his death. I never even had the chance to say good-bye to him."

"It must be tough."

"Awful. It's just awful. At least his wife has the luxury to mourn in public. Is she taking it hard?"

"That's why she hired me, trying to find relief."

Colleen looked away from me casually, trying to conceal her interest. "Did she love him?"

"Very much, I'd say. It was probably a good marriage. Maybe not perfect, but it worked. She doesn't like his dying with unfinished business."

Colleen's gaze came back to mine. "You thought it was me. That we were having an affair."

"It crossed my mind." I was silent for a moment. "Do you know why Tom was so distressed?"

"I might."

"Why so protective?"

"I have to go," she said abruptly, gathering up her coat. "I'll call you later with the phone number for Ritter's daughter."

I held a finger up. "Hang on. I have something for you if you're interested." I reached into my shoulder bag and pulled one of the black-and-white photographs of Tom at the April banquet. "I had these done up in case I needed 'em. You might like to have something to remember him by."

She took the picture without comment, a slight smile playing across her mouth as she studied it.

I said, "I never met him myself, but I thought it captured him."

She looked up at me, tears rimming her eyes. "Thank you."

CHAPTER NINE

WHEN I returned from my run Saturday morning, there was a message from Colleen Sellers on my answering machine, giving me the Perdido address of a woman named Dolores Ruggles, one of Pinkie Ritter's daughters. As soon as I was showered and dressed, I gassed up the VW and headed south on 101.

On my right the bleak Pacific thundered against the shore. I took the Leeward off-ramp and crossed over the freeway in search of the street where Dolores Ruggles lived. The neighborhood was a warren of low stucco structures and narrow intersecting streets. The house was a plain box, sitting in a plain treeless yard with scarcely a bush or a tuft of grass. I rang the bell.

The man who opened the door was drying his hands on a towel.

Easily in his sixties, he was maybe five feet eight, with hair the color of wood ash. "Keep your shirt on," he said irritably.

"Sorry. I thought the bell was broken. I'm looking for Dolores Ruggles."

"Who the hell are you?"

I handed him my card. "I'm a private investigator," I said.

"I can see that. What do you want with Dolores? She's busy at the moment and doesn't want to be disturbed."

"I need some information. Maybe you can help me and we can spare her the imposition. I'm here about her father."

"The little scumbag was murdered."

"I'm aware of that. I'm trying to find out what happened."

"What difference does it make? The man is d-e-a-d dead, and not soon enough to suit my taste. I've spent years coping with all the damage he did."

"Could I come in?"

He stared at me. "Help yourself," he said abruptly, and turned on his heel. I scurried after him through the living room: dark hardwood floors, a tired couch, a sagging upholstered chair. Not to sound sexist, but the room looked as if it had been designed by a man. The walls were lined with books packed two deep on some shelves, three deep on others.

"I'm doing dishes out here," he said as he moved into the kitchen. "By the way, I'm Homer, Dolores's husband. Mr. Ruggles to you. Grab a towel and you can pitch in."

His tone had shifted from outright rudeness to something gruff, but not unpleasant. I could see he'd been rather good-looking in his day. Not wildly handsome, but something better—a man with a certain amount of character and an appealing air.

He turned on the water and was back washing plates and glassware. I picked up a clean dish towel and reached for a wet plate. "You can stack those on the kitchen table."

I glanced at the table. "Um, Mr. Ruggles, the table needs to be wiped. Do you have a sponge?"

"Skip the Mr. Ruggles bit. It sounds absurd."

"Yes, sir."

That netted me half a smile. He wrung out the cloth and tossed it in my direction. I wiped the tabletop. "So what's your interest in Pinkie Ritter? Nice girl like you should be ashamed."

"I didn't know anything about him until yesterday. I've been tracking down a friend of his who may have been— Could we just skip this part? It's almost too tricky to explain."

"You're talking Alfie Toth."

"Thank you. Everybody seems to know about him."

"Yeah, well, Alfie was a birdbrain. Women thought he was attractive, but I couldn't see it myself. I think he hung out with my father-in-law for protection, which just goes to show you how dumb he was."

"You knew Alfie was dead."

"You bet. The police told us about it when his body turned up. They asked the same question you probably want answered, which is, what's the connection and who did what to whom? I'll give you the same answer I gave them. I don't know."

"I take it you didn't think much of Pinkie."

"That's a gross understatement. I hated his guts. Whoever killed Pinkie saved me life in prison. Pinkie had six kids—three sons and three daughters—and mistreated every one of them from the day they were born. Nowadays there's all this talk of abuse, but Pinkie did the real thing. He punched them, burned them, locked them in closets, starved 'em. He molested every one of 'em. Pinkie was the meanest s.o.b. I ever met."

"Didn't anybody intervene?"

"People tried. Lot of people blew the whistle on him. Trick was trying to prove it." He shook his head. "Pinkie knew how the game was played. He kept a clean house—the kids saw to that—and he did like to cook. Social workers came around and everything looked fine. Kids didn't open their mouths. Dolores says she can remember the six of them lined up in the living room, answering questions nice as you please. Pinkie was always somewhere close. Kids knew better than to rat on him or they'd be dead by dark. They'd stand there and lie. Only thing saved 'em was his getting thrown in jail."

"What about his wife? Where was she all this time?"

"Dolores thinks he killed her, though it couldn't be proved."

"Pinkie sounds like a very nasty piece of work."

"The worst."

"So anybody could have killed him, including one of his kids. Is that what you're saying?"

"That would cover it," he said. "Of course, by the time he died, the rest of the kids had scattered and gone. Couple of 'em still in California, though we don't see 'em all that much." Homer finished the last dish and turned the water off.

"When did you see him last?"

"Five years ago in March. The minute he got out of Chino, he headed straight up here. Dolores was the only kid of his still living in the area, so naturally, he felt she owed him room and board."

"Didn't you object?"

"I did, but that was an argument I couldn't win. She's a great gal, and what she's endured, believe me, you don't want to know. But the upshot is, she wanted that man's love. He was still Daddy to her, and she couldn't turn him away. I finally got fed up and told him to clear out."

"Toth was with him at the time?"

"Off and on. I think Alfie's ex-wife lived in town somewhere. The two left together as far as I know."

"And where were they headed?"

"Los Angeles. You piece it together later, and it turns out they stole a car in Los Angeles and drove up to Lake Tahoe."

"You think someone could have been after them?"

"I wouldn't know," he said. "Pinkie didn't act like he was worried. Why? You think someone was trailing them?"

"It's possible," I said.

As we were speaking, on an almost subliminal level I could hear an odd series of voices from another room. At first I thought the sound was coming from a radio, or television set, but the phrases were repeated, the tone lifeless and mechanical. Homer heard it, too, and he tilted his head as though toward a back bedroom. "Dolores's back there. You want to talk to her?"

"If you think it's okay."

"She can handle it," he said. "Give me a second and I'll tell her what's going on."

He moved down the hall to the door, tapping before he entered. A few minutes later the door opened again, and he motioned me in.

At first sight I thought Dolores Ruggles couldn't have been a day over twenty-one. Later I found out that she was twenty-eight, which still seemed too young to be married to a man Homer's age. Slim, petite, she sat at a workbench in a room filled with Barbie dolls. Floor to ceiling, dressed in an astonishing array of styles, these bland plastic women were decked out in miniature suits, furs, shorts, capes, pedal pushers, baby doll pajamas—each outfit complete with appropriate accessories. I confess I found myself at a loss for words. Homer leaned against the open door, watching for my reaction.

"Amazing," I said in what I hoped was a respectful tone.

Dolores glanced at me shyly. She had a doll in her lap, not a Barbie but some other type. With a little hammer and an X-Acto knife she was cutting open its stomach. There was a box of identical little plastic girls, sexless, unmarred, standing close together with their chests pierced in a pattern of holes like those old-fashioned radio speakers. "Chatty Cathys," she said. "It's a new hobby. I fix their voices so they can talk again."

"That's great."

Homer said, "I'll leave you girls. You have a lot to talk about."

"How many Barbies do you have?" I asked, feigning enthusiasm for the little proto-women.

"A little over two thousand." Her speech was uninflected, her manner without affect. She addressed most of her comments to the doll as she worked. "Did you have a Barbie as a kid?"

"I can't say I did." I picked one up and examined her. "She looks like she's suffering from some sort of eating disorder, doesn't she? What prompted you to get into Chatty Cathys?"

"Most of the Chatties aren't mine. I'm repairing them for a friend who runs a business doing this. It's not as far-fetched as it seems. Anyway, I'm sure you didn't drive down here to talk about dolls. You're interested in my father."

"Homer filled me in, but I'd like to hear your version. I understand he and Alfie Toth spent some time with you just after they were released from Chino."

"That's right. After they left here, Pops tried to spend a night with my brother Clint—he lives down in Inglewood, by the L.A. airport. Clint refused to let him in, but he told him he could sleep in the toolshed. Pops was furious. Him and Alfie waited till Clint was gone; then they stole his cash and busted up all his furniture."

"Did Clint report it to the police?"

Dolores seemed startled. "Why would he do that?"

"I've heard there was a plainclothes detective trying to serve a warrant against Toth around the time of his death. I'm wondering if it dated back to that same incident."

Dolores shook her head. "I'm sure not. Clint might not want Pops in his house, but he'd never snitch on him."

"Why do think he went from Clint's to Lake Tahoe?"

"My sister lives up there. Or one of them, at any rate. Not in Lake Tahoe exactly, but that vicinity."

"How long was he with her?"

"A week or so. Mame told me later him and Alfie went off to go fishing and that's the last anyone ever saw Pops."

"Do you think I could talk to her?"

"Oh, sure. She isn't hard to find. Mame works as a clerk in the sheriff's department up there."

"Up there where?"

"Nota Lake. Her name is Margaret, but everybody in the family calls her Mame."

WHEN I got home, Henry was in the backyard, kneeling in the flower bed. I crossed the lawn, pausing to watch him at work. He was aware of my presence but seemed content with the quiet. His feet were bare, long, and bony, the high arches very white against the faded grass. I sat down on a wooden lawn chair while he turned the soil with a hand trowel.

"I have to go back to Nota Lake," I said.

"When?"

"Sometime next week. I'd like to hang out here long enough to get my hand back in working order."

"Why go at all?"

"I have to talk to someone."

"Can't you do that by phone?"

"It's too easy for people to tell lies on the phone. I like to see faces," I said. I was silent, listening to the homely chucking of his trowel in the dirt. I pulled my legs up and wrapped my arms around my knees.

Henry looked up. "You have bad vibes?"

"The worst." I held up my right hand and tried flexing the fingers, which were still so swollen and stiff I could barely make a fist.

"Don't go. You don't have anything to prove."

"Of course I do, Henry. I'm a girl. We're always having to prove something."

"Like what?"

"That we're tough. That we're as good as the guys, which I'm happy to report is not that hard."

"So what worries you?"

"What worries me is I got my fingers dislocated before I knew squat. Now I'm getting closer, what's the guy going to do?"

"Phone's ringing," he remarked.

"Henry, how can you hear that? You're eighty-six years old."

"Three rings."

I was off the chair and halfway across the yard by then. I left my door open and caught the phone on the fly, just as the machine kicked in. I pressed STOP. "Hello, hello, hello."

"Kinsey, is that you? I thought this was your machine."

"Hi, Selma. You lucked out. I was out in the yard."

"I'm sorry to have to bother you."

"Not a problem. What's up?"

"Someone's been searching Tom's study. I know this sounds odd, but I'm sure someone came in here and moved the items on his desk. It's not like the room was trashed, but something's off."

"How'd they get in?"

She hesitated. "I was only gone for an hour, maybe slightly more. I hardly ever lock the door for short periods like that."

"What makes you so sure someone was there?"

"I can't explain. I'd been sitting in Tom's den earlier, before I went out. I was feeling depressed, and it seemed a comfort just to sit in his chair. You know how it is. Anyway, when I got home, I set my handbag on the kitchen table and went back to the car. I'd picked up some boxes to pack his books. The minute I walked into his den, I could see the difference."

"What about Brant? How do you know he wasn't in there looking for something on Tom's desk?"

"He was at Sherry's until a few minutes ago." There was a tiny pause while she changed tacks, her voice assuming a faintly injured tone. "I must say, I've been upset about your lack of communication. I've been waiting to hear from you."

"Sorry. I was going to call, but I haven't had the chance."

"Now that I have you on the line, could you tell me what's happening? I assume you're still working."

"Of course." I controlled my desire to bristle, and I filled her in on the past day and a half, sidestepping the personal aspects of Tom's relationship with Colleen Sellers. Telling a partial truth is much harder than an outright lie. Here I was, trying to protect her, while she was chiding me for neglect. Talk about ungrateful. "Tom came down here in June as part of an investigation. Do you remember the occasion? He was probably gone overnight."

"Yes," she said slowly. "What's the relevance?"

"There was a homicide down here Tom felt was connected to some skeletal remains found in Nota County last spring."

"I know the case you're referring to. He didn't say much about it, but I know it bothered him. What about it?"

"If we're talking about an active homicide investigation," I said,

"I don't have authority. I'm a private investigator. I can't, even on your say-so, stick my nose into police business."

"Surely there's no law against asking questions."

"I *have* asked questions, and I'm telling you Tom was stressed out about matters that had nothing to do with you."

"But if this is strictly professional, then why would someone go to all the trouble to search the house?"

"How do I know?" She was backing me into corners, and it was annoying me no end.

"Kinsey, I am paying you to get to the bottom of this. If I'd known you weren't going to help, I could have used that fifteen hundred dollars to get my teeth capped."

"I'm doing what I can. What do you want from me?" I said.

"Well, you needn't take *that* attitude. All I'm hearing are excuses. When are you coming back?"

I had to bite my tongue. "I'm not sure yet. Maybe Tuesday."

"Next *week?*" she said. "What's wrong with today? You still owe me five hundred dollars' worth of work. For that kind of money I would think you'd want to get here as soon as possible."

"Selma, I'm not going to sit here and argue. I'll do what I can."

"Wonderful. What time shall I expect you?"

"I have no idea."

"Surely you can give me *some* idea when you might arrive. I'll be gone all day tomorrow. I go to ten-o'clock services and then spend some time with my cousin down in Big Pine. I can't sit around waiting for you to show any time it suits. Besides, if you're coming, I'll need to make arrangements."

"I'll call when I get there, but I'm not going to stay at the Nota Lake Cabins. I hate that place. It's dangerous."

"Fine," she said. "You can stay here at the house with me."

"I wouldn't dream of imposing."

"It's no inconvenience. Brant's in the process of packing up and moving back to his place. The guest room is always ready. I'll have supper waiting and no arguments about that, please."

"We'll talk about it when I get there," I said. Of course, I noticed

I'd already started revising my mental timetable, preparing to hit the road as soon as possible. Having consented, in effect, I now found myself wanting to get it over with.

The minute I replaced the receiver, I picked it up again and placed a call to Colleen Sellers. She didn't sound that thrilled to hear from me, but I was through pussyfooting around.

"Colleen, I just spent thirty minutes with Dolores Ruggles and her husband. Turns out Pinkie Ritter has another daughter, in Nota Lake, which is why he and Alfie went up there in the first place."

"And?"

"This is someone I've met, a woman named Margaret who works for the sheriff's department. I'm going to have to go talk to her again, but I have to know what I'm up against."

"Why call me? I can't help. Frankly, I'm annoyed you keep pressing the point."

"Well, *frankly,* I guess I'll just have to risk your irritation, Colleen. You have to level with me."

"Why?"

"Because my life may depend on it," I snapped. "Come on, you're a professional. You know better. You sit there doling out little tidbits of information, hanging on to crumbs because it's all you have. This is serious stuff. If Tom were in your position, do you think he'd withhold information in a situation like this?"

"Probably not." Grudgingly.

"Then let's get on with it, for heaven's sake. Let's have it."

She seemed to hesitate. "Tom was facing a moral crisis. I was the easy part, but I wasn't all of it. I think he could do the right thing with me, and it was a comfort to him. The other problem he was facing was more complicated."

"You're just guessing at this, or do you know for a fact?"

"Well, Tom never came out and said so, but he did allude to the issue. To not knowing how to reconcile his head and his gut."

"In regard to what?"

"He felt responsible for Toth's murder."

"Tom felt *responsible?* How come?"

"A breach of confidentiality. I gave him Toth's address at the Gramercy. Tom thought someone took an unauthorized look at his notes to track down Toth. It was driving him crazy."

I felt myself blinking at the phone, trying to make sense of what she'd said. "But his notebook is missing."

"Well, it wasn't back then."

"Who did he suspect? Did he ever mention a name?"

"Someone he worked with. And that's my guess, by the way, not something he said to me directly. Why else would it bother him if it wasn't someone betraying the department?"

I felt myself grow still. I flashed on the officers I'd met in Nota Lake: Rafer LaMott; Tom's brother, Macon; Hatch Brine; James Tennyson; Earlene's husband, Wayne. Even Deputy Carey Badger, who'd taken my report on the night of the assault. All of them connected with the Nota Lake Sheriff's Department or the CHP. At the back of my mind I'd been flirting with the suspicion that my attacker had been trained at a police academy. I'd been resisting the notion, but I could feel it begin to take root in my imagination. He'd taken me down with an efficiency I'd been taught once upon a time myself. "Are you telling me one of Tom's colleagues was involved in a double homicide?"

"I think that was his suspicion and it was tearing him apart. Again this wasn't something he said. This is my best guess."

I was silent for a moment. "I should have seen that. How stupid of me."

"What will you do now? You can't do this on your own."

"Who'm I gonna call? The Nota Lake Sheriff's Department?"

"I'm not sure I'd do that," she said, laughing for once.

"Yeah, well, if I figure it out, I'll let you know," I said.

"I'd proceed with care."

"Trust me," I said. "One more question while I have you on the line. Were you ever in Nota Lake yourself?"

"Are you kidding? Tom was too nervous to see me there."

I replaced the receiver, distracted. My anxiety level was rising ominously, like a toilet on the verge of overflowing. The fear was like something damp and heavy sinking into my bones. I have a thing about authority figures, specifically police officers in uniform, probably dating from that first encounter while I was trapped in the wreckage of my parents' car at the age of five. I can still remember the horror and the relief of being rescued by those big guys with their guns and nightsticks. Still, the sense of jeopardy and pain also attached to that image. Being on the side of the law was, no doubt, my attempt to cope with that old anxiety. Most of the officers I'd known since had been decent, caring people, which made it all the more alarming to think that one might have crossed the line. I couldn't think when anything had frightened me quite as much as the idea of going up against this guy, but what I could I do? If I quit this one, then what? The next time I got scared, was I going to quit that job, too?

I went up the spiral stairs and dutifully started shoving items into my duffel.

CHAPTER TEN

I TOOK Highway 126 through Santa Paula and Fillmore until I ran into Highway 5. I doglegged over to Highway 14, driving through canyon country—balding brown hills, tufted with chaparral.

I'd tucked my semiautomatic in the duffel. Given the state of my bunged-up fingers, I doubted I'd be capable of pulling the trigger, but the gun was a comfort.

Little by little I was giving up my irritation with Selma. I regretted that I hadn't had time to contact Leland Peck, the clerk at the Gramercy Hotel. I'd taken his co-worker's word that he had nothing to report. Any good investigator knows better. I should have quizzed him about his recollections of the plainclothes detective with the warrant for Toth's arrest.

In the meantime, secure in my ignorance of events to come, I thought idly of the night ahead. I truly hate being a guest in someone's home. I don't want someone across the table from me while I'm eating my breakfast. I don't want to share the newspaper, and I don't want to talk to anyone at the end of the day. If I were interested in that, I'd be married again by now and put a permanent end to all the peace and quiet.

By the time I arrived in Nota Lake at six forty-five, night had settled on the landscape and the weather was truly nasty. The drizzle had intensified into a stinging sleet. My windshield wipers labored, collecting slush in an arc that nearly filled my windshield. I parked out in front of Selma's, snagged my duffel, and hurried to the front porch, head bent, as if to avoid the biting rain and snow. I knocked politely, waiting until she opened the door. We exchanged the customary chitchat. I eased out of my shoes, conscious of the pristine carpet. The house was toasty warm, hazy from the cigarette smoke sealed in the winterproof rooms. I padded after Selma to the guest room. "Take whatever time you need to freshen up and get settled. I'll be out in the kitchen."

"Thanks."

Once the door closed behind me, I surveyed the room with dismay. The carpet here was hot pink, a cut-pile cotton shag. There was a four-poster bed with a canopy and a puffy, quilted spread of pink-and-white-checked gingham. The wallpaper was pink and white stripes with a floral border across the top. The room smelled as though it had been closed up for some time, and the heat here seemed more intense than in the rest of the house. I could feel myself start to hyperventilate with the craving for fresh air.

I crossed to the window, like a hot prowl thief trying to escape. I inched up the sash, only to be faced with a seriously constructed double-glazed storm window. I worked at the latches until I loosened all of them. I gave the storm window a push, and it fell out of the frame and dropped into the bushes below. Oops. I stuck my head through the gap and let the sleet blow across my face. The storm window had landed just beyond my grasp, so I left it where it was, resting in the junipers. I lowered the sash again and adjusted the ruffled curtains so the missing storm window wasn't evident. At least at bedtime I could sleep in a properly refrigerated atmosphere.

I washed my hands and brushed my teeth in the guest bath; then I stood in the bedroom and did a quick visual scan. I removed my handgun from the duffel and hid it between the mattress and the box spring, near the head of the bed. This would fool no one, but it would allow me to keep the gun close. Finally there was nothing for it but to present myself at the supper table.

Selma seemed subdued. Her attitude surprised me, given the fact that she'd gotten her way. "I kept everything simple. I hope you don't mind," she said.

"This is fine," I said.

She took a moment to stub out her cigarette, blowing the final stream of smoke to one side. This, for a smoker, constitutes etiquette. We pulled out our chairs.

Given my usual diet, a home-cooked meal of any kind is an extraordinary treat. Or so I thought before I was faced with the one she'd prepared. This was the menu: iced tea with Sweet 'n Low already mixed in, a green Jell-O square with fruit cocktail and an internal ribbon of Miracle Whip, iceberg lettuce with bottled dressing the color of a sunset. For the main course, instant mashed potatoes and a stout slice of meat loaf, swimming in diluted cream of mushroom soup. As I ate, my fork exposed a couple of dried mashed potato flakes. I knew for a fact she didn't feed Brant this way.

Selma was quiet throughout the meal, and I didn't have much to contribute. I felt like one of those married couples you see out in restaurants—not looking at each other, not bothering to say a word. The minute we'd finished eating, she lit up another cigarette so I wouldn't miss a second of the tars and noxious gases wafting across the table. "Would you like dessert? I have a nice coconut cream pie in the freezer. It won't take a minute to thaw."

"Golly, I'm full. This was great."

"I didn't ask you about your fingers."

I held up my right hand. "They're a little stiff yet, but better."

"Well, that's good. Now that you're back, what's the plan?"

"I was just thinking about that," I said. "I think I have a line on what was bothering Tom."

"Really."

"After we spoke this morning, I made another phone call. Without going into any detail, it looks like Tom suspected a fellow officer in that double homicide he was investigating."

She took a deep drag of her cigarette. "I don't believe it."

"I know it sounds incredible, but apparently, he believed one of his colleagues lifted Alfie Toth's address from his field notes. Toth was murdered shortly afterward. Tom must have gone crazy thinking he played a role in Alfie's death. Worse yet, suspecting someone in the department had a hand in it."

"But you don't really *know*," she said. "This is just a guess."

"How are we ever going to *know* anything unless someone fesses up? And that seems unlikely. I mean, so far this someone has gotten away with it."

"Who told you this?"

"Someone with the sheriff's department. A confidential source."

"Confidential, my foot. You're making a serious allegation."

"You think I don't know that?" I said. "Look, I don't like the idea any better than you do. That's why I came back, to pin it down."

"And if you can't?"

"Then frankly, I'm out of ideas. There is one possibility. Pinkie Ritter's daughter, Margaret . . ."

Selma frowned. "That's right. I'd forgotten their relationship. Why didn't she speak up when you were here before?"

"I didn't know about Ritter until yesterday."

"I think you better talk to Rafer."

"I think it's best to keep him out of this for now." I caught the odd look that crossed her face. "What?"

She hesitated. "I ran into him this afternoon and told him you'd be back this evening."

I felt my eyes roll in despair, and I longed to bang my head on the tabletop for emphasis. "I wish you'd kept quiet. It's hard enough as it is. Everybody here knows everybody else's business."

"Don't be silly. He was Tom's best friend. What will you do?"

"I'll talk to Margaret Brine tonight and see what she knows. Unless something develops, I'm at a dead loss."

"I see. Then I suppose that's it." Selma stubbed out her cigarette and got up to clear the dishes. "I hope I didn't make a mistake in hiring you."

I glanced at her sharply. "I never offered you a guarantee."

"That's not what I meant."

I was having trouble tracking the change in her demeanor. Maybe she thought I was giving up. "I'm not saying I'll quit," I said.

"I understand. You're saying you're out of your league."

"You want to go up against the cops? Personally, I've got more sense."

She banged a plate down so hard it broke across the middle into two equal pieces. "My husband *died*."

"I know that. I'm sorry."

"No, you're not. Nobody gives a damn."

"Selma, you hired me to do this and I'm doing it. Yes, I'm out of my league. So was Tom, for that matter. Look what happened to him. It broke his heart."

She stood there, her shoulders shaking. Tears coursed along her cheeks. I patted her awkwardly, making little murmurings. I pictured Tom doing much the same thing in his life, probably in this very spot. Finally she pulled herself together. We did the dishes, and she retreated to her room. I fled the house as soon as it was decently possible. Nothing like being around a self-appointed invalid to make you feel hard-hearted.

MARGARET and Hatch lived close to the center of town on Second Street. I'd called from Selma's before I left the house. I'd scarcely identified myself when she cut in, saying, "Dolores said you came to see her. What's this about?"

"I'm trying to figure out what happened to your father," I said. "I wondered if it'd be possible to talk tonight."

She'd seemed nonplussed at my request, conceding with reluctance. Twice she put a palm across the mouthpiece and conferred with someone in the background. I assumed it was Hatch.

The drive over was uneventful despite the treacherous roads and the continuous sleet. But I did note the close proximity of the Brines' house to the parking lot at Tiny's Tavern, where I'd been accosted. Once Wayne and Earlene dropped the Brines off at home, Hatch could easily have doubled back.

I entered a tract of brick ranch houses and slowed when I spotted the house number. The Brines had two cars and a pickup truck parked in or near the drive. I found a parking spot two doors down and sat at the curb wondering if there was a party in progress. I didn't like the idea of walking into a social gathering, especially since I could always talk to Margaret tomorrow. On the other hand, meeting with her tonight would delay my return to Selma's. I still had a key to her place, and the plan was for me to let myself in whenever I got back.

I got out of the car and locked the doors. The sidewalks must have been warmer than the streets. Snowflakes melted instantly, leaving shallow pools. I knocked on the door, hoping I wasn't walking in on a naughty lingerie party. Maybe that's why she'd invited me, in hopes I'd purchase a drawerful of underpants.

Margaret opened the door wearing blue jeans and a thick red sweater with a Nordic design. "Hi. Come on in."

"Thanks. I hope I'm not interrupting. I saw cars in the drive."

"Hatch's poker night. The boys are in the den," she said. "I'm on kitchen detail. We can talk out there."

I followed her to the kitchen at the end of the hall. She was preparing food—platters of cold cuts on the wood-grained Formica counter, bowls of chips, dip. "If you'll help me move these snacks to the dining room, we can get 'em out of the way and we can talk."

"Sure thing."

She picked up two bowls and shoved the swinging door open with a hip, holding it for me while I moved through with the tray of sliced cheeses and processed meats. Of course, it was all so unwholesome I was immediately hungry, but my appetite didn't last long. Through an archway to my left I saw Hatch and his five buddies sitting at the poker table in the den. There were countless beer bottles and beer mugs in evidence. To a man the entire gathering turned to look at me. I recognized Wayne, James Tennyson, and Brant; the other two fellows I'd never seen before. Hatch made a comment, and James laughed. Brant raised his hand in greeting. Margaret paid little attention to the lot of them, but the chill from the room was unmistakable.

I placed bowls on the table and moved back to the kitchen, trying to behave as though unaffected by their presence. I picked up a platter from the counter and intercepted Margaret as she reached the swinging door. "Why don't I pass these to you and you can put them on the table," I said, feigning helpfulness. I couldn't bear subjecting myself to that collective stare.

She took the platter without comment. Once we'd assembled the eats, she sighed with relief. "Lucky they don't play more than once a month," she said. "I told Hatch they should rotate, but he likes to have 'em here."

She leaned against the kitchen counter, crossing her arms in front. "So what can I help you with?" The question suggested cooperation, but her manner was all business.

"I'm just wondering about Pinkie's last visit. I'm assuming he and Alfie Toth came to the area to see you that spring."

"That's right," she said. "I hope you don't think this is disrespectful, but my father was a loser and we all knew that."

"Was he a problem on this visit?"

"Of course. Mostly chasing women," she said. "He'd just gotten out of jail, and he was itching to go."

"Was he after anybody in particular?"

Margaret shrugged. "A waitress at the Rainbow and one at Tiny's. Alice, the one with red hair."

"I know her," I said.

"That's all he talked about, how horny he was. I was embarrassed. I mean, what kind of talk is that coming from your dad? He couldn't have been more obnoxious. He got in fights. He borrowed money. He dinged the truck. It drove Hatch insane, so of course, the two of us were fighting."

"So what finally happened?"

"After a week we sent him and Alfie off on a fishing trip. Anything to get them out from underfoot for a couple of days. Hatch lent 'em a couple of fishing rods he never did get back. Anyway, something must have gone wrong. Next morning Alfie showed up and said they'd decided to take off and he'd come for their things."

"Where was your father?"

"Alfie told us Daddy was waiting for him and he had to get a move on or Pinkie'd be furious with him. I didn't think anything about it. I mean, it did sound like him."

"Did Tom know all this?"

"I told him last March when Daddy's remains turned up."

"Didn't it strike you as odd that no one in the family ever heard from him once he supposedly left here?"

"Why should it? Bad news travels fast. We figured if something happened to him, someone would contact us. He always carried ID. Besides, we heard from Alfie now and then."

"Why did he call?"

Margaret shrugged. "To see how we were doing is what he said."

"Did he ever ask about your dad?"

"Well, yes, but it wasn't like he wanted to get in touch. You know—'What do you hear from your dad?' That sort of thing."

"So he was wondering if Pinkie ever showed up again."

"I guess. Tom thought Daddy might have been murdered the very day Alfie left, though there was never any way to prove it."

"It's possible," I said. "Judging from Alfie's behavior, he was either trying to create the impression that Pinkie was alive or he really wasn't sure himself."

Saturday night at Tiny's was a rowdy affair: two alternating live bands, line dancing, whooping, hollering, and much thumping of cowboy boots on the wooden dance floor. Six waitresses worked in a steady progression from the bar to the crowded tables. I spotted

Alice with her gaudy orange hair half a room away and pushed my way through jostling three-deep bystanders. I had to yell to make myself heard. She got the message and pointed toward the ladies' room. I watched her deliver a sloshing pitcher of beer and six tequila shooters, then angle in my direction. The two of us burst into the empty ladies' room and pushed the door shut. The quiet was remarkable, the noise in the tavern reduced by more than half.

"Sorry to drag you away," I said.

"Are you kidding? I'm thrilled. It's hell on earth out there, and the tips are lousy." She took a pack of cigarettes out of her pocket. "What are you doing here? I thought you went home."

"I left. Now I'm back."

"That was quick."

"Yeah, well, I know a lot more now than I did two days ago."

"That's good. More power to you. I hear you're investigating a murder. Margaret Brine's father, or that's the word."

"It's slightly more complicated, but that's about it."

Alice snorted. "He hustled my butt off, the randy little turd. I pinned his ears back, but he was hard to shake."

"Who else did he hustle? Margaret tells me he was—"

Alice held up a hand. "Mind if I interrupt? I don't know how to say this, but people around here seem to be concerned about you."

"Why? What'd I do?"

"Grapevine has it you're into drugs."

"I am not! How ridiculous. That's ludicrous," I said.

"Also you shot a couple of fellows in cold blood."

"Where'd you hear *that?*" I said, laughing in startlement.

"You never killed anyone?"

I felt my smile start to fade. "Well, yes, but that was self-defense. Both were killers coming after me—"

Alice cut in. "Look, I don't really give a hoot, but folks around here take a dim view of somebody coming in here starting trouble."

"Alice, I promise. I've never shot anyone without provocation. The idea's repugnant. I swear. Where did this come from?"

"Who knows? I overheard the fellows talking earlier tonight.

I guess someone did some digging and came up with the facts."

"*Facts?*"

"Don't get so defensive. I'm telling you for your own good. You better watch your step is all I'm saying."

"Somebody's trying to discredit me," I said hotly.

"Hey, it's not up to me. I don't give a hoot. You can whack anyone you want," she said. "The point is, people are getting fed up. I thought I should warn you before it went too far."

"I wish you could tell me where it's coming from."

Alice shrugged. "I'd avoid crossing paths with the cops if I were you."

I felt a pang of anxiety, like an icicle puncturing my chest wall. "What makes you say that?"

"Tom was a cop. They're mad as hell."

I STOOD at the side exit, my hands in my pockets, though the chill I felt was internally generated. I searched the empty rows of cars, checking the dark. The music from the bar behind me was reduced to a series of dull, repetitive thumps. I caught a flash of light and saw a car pull in. I stepped back into the shadows. Macon pulled up in his black and white. I walked to the window on the driver's side. He rolled it down as I approached.

"How's it going?" he asked. "I'm glad you came back."

"Alice tells me there's a rumor going around that I'm some sort of dope-crazed vigilante."

He looked off to one side and stirred restlessly, tapping the steering wheel with his gloved hand. "Don't worry about gossip. Nobody pays attention to that stuff. Why don't I see you home? I got a call to check out."

"Thanks." I got in my car, and he followed me as far as Selma's driveway, his engine idling while I crossed the front lawn. The porch light was on, and my key turned easily in the lock. I waved from the doorway, and he took off. I slipped out of my shoes and carried them down to the guest room. Selma had turned on a bed-table lamp, and the room was washed in cheery pink. On the nightstand she'd left me a plate of homemade chocolate chip cookies secured in plastic wrap. I ate two, savoring the flavors of butter and vanilla. I ate two more to be polite.

Apparently, Selma was not in the habit of turning down the furnace at night, and the room felt close with heat. I crossed to the window, pushed the curtains aside, and raised the sash. Frigid air poured through the gap left by the storm window, still resting against the bushes three feet down.

I stared out at the portion of the street that I could see. A car passed at a slow speed, and I pulled back out of sight. I hated being in Nota Lake. I hated being an outsider, the target of local gossip that misrepresented my actions. I hated my suspicions. Where once the badge and the nightstick had been symbols of personal safety, I now thought of them with trepidation, as if stung by electric shocks.

Why couldn't I just hop in my car and barrel home tonight? If I left within the hour, I could be in Santa Teresa by four a.m. I pictured my snug platform bed with its blue-and-white quilt, stars visible through the Plexiglas dome overhead.

I stepped away from the window, effectively breaking the spell. The only road home is through the forest, I thought.

I peeled off my clothes and pulled on an oversized T-shirt. I washed my face and brushed my teeth with the usual difficulty. I took the file from the duffel and got into bed, adjusting the reading lamp so I could review the notes I'd typed. The only item that leaped out at me was James Tennyson's report of the woman walking down the road the night Tom died.

Was he lying about that? Had he invented the woman in an attempt to throw me off? I wondered what kind of woman would have walked off and left Tom in the throes of death. I didn't believe he was having an affair, so if the woman existed, why conceal her presence?

For the second time I wondered if Tom had gone to the Rainbow Café to meet someone. He'd been there at an unaccustomed hour. I'd asked Nancy about it once, but it might be time to press.

I woke to the sound of the phone ringing in the kitchen. On the eighth persistent ding-a-ling I flung off the covers and trotted down the hall. There was no sign of Selma, and the machine had been turned off. I lifted the receiver. "Newquists' residence."

Someone breathed in my ear and then hung up.

I replaced the receiver and stood there for a moment. The silence extended. I reactivated the answering machine and then checked Selma's calendar, posted on the refrigerator door. There was nothing marked, but this was Sunday morning and I remembered her mentioning a visit to a cousin after church.

I padded back to the guest room, where I brushed my teeth, showered, and dressed. I didn't look forward to another day in this town, but there was nothing for it except to get the job done. Like a dutiful guest, I made my bed and ate the remaining three cookies to fortify myself. I grabbed my leather jacket and my shoulder bag, locked the house, and went out to the car. The gas gauge was close to E, and since I was heading toward the Rainbow, I stopped for gas on my way out of town.

I pulled up to the full-serve pump and glanced over at the office windows, where I could see two attendants chatting. Both turned to look at my VW and then resumed their conversation. I waited, but neither came forward to assist me. I opened the car door and moved toward the office.

"Hello?"

Nothing. No one. The office had been deserted.

I started the engine and slid into the flow of traffic. I drove six blocks before I spotted another station and pulled in. There was a car at the adjacent pump, and the attendant was in the process of removing the nozzle from the tank. He glanced at me briefly, and then I saw the alteration in his gaze.

I said, "Hi. How're you?"

He took the other woman's credit card, disappeared into the office, and returned with her receipt. The two chatted for a moment. When she pulled out, he went back to the office and that was the last I saw of him. What was going on?

I could see an off-brand station three doors down. I drove into that gas station, and this time I saw an attendant in the service bay and I pulled in there first. I rolled down the window on the passenger side and said, "Hi. Are you open for business?"

His blank stare sparked a moment of uneasiness. I tried the best smile I could manage. "Do you speak English? *Habla inglés?*"

His return smile was slow and malevolent. "Yeah, lady, I do. Now why don't you get the hell out of here? You want service in this town, you're out of luck."

I shifted my gaze, keeping my expression neutral as I drove out. Under my jacket the sweat was soaking my shirt.

CHAPTER ELEVEN

NCE out of sight, I pulled over and parked on a side street to assess my situation. The word had clearly gone out, but I wasn't sure whether these guys were cueing off my car or my personal description. I removed my bomber jacket and tossed it in the back seat, then rooted through the assorted garments I keep for just such emergencies. I donned a plain red sweatshirt, a pair of sunglasses, and a Dodgers baseball cap. I took out the five-gallon gasoline can I keep in the trunk. I locked the car and hiked over to a service station I hadn't tried so far.

The attendant in the office was maybe nineteen, with a bleached-blond crew cut and green-painted fingernails. He stared through the plate-glass window, watching me without expression as I filled the container at the self-serve pump. The total was $7.45. I went over to the office and handed him a ten, which he tucked in his pocket without offering change. Nice to know that regardless of how low you sink, someone's always willing to make a profit at your expense. I returned to my car, where I emptied five gallons of gasoline into my tank.

My heart was beating as though I'd run a race, and perhaps I had. I was already on unfamiliar turf and depended on ordinary day-to-day pleasantries for my sense of well-being. Now I was being shunned, and the process was scaring me.

Six miles out of town I pulled into the parking area of the Rainbow Café. I sat for a moment, trying to get "centered," as Californians say. I've no idea what the term means, but in my present circumstance it seemed applicable. If I was being banished from the tribe, I better make sure I had a grip on my "self" before I went any further. I took a couple of deep breaths and got out.

The café was sparsely occupied. I did a quick visual sweep. James Tennyson was sitting at the counter with a cup of coffee. Rafer's daughter, Barrett, with her back to me, was working the grill. Rafer and Vicky LaMott sat in a booth midway down the line of empty tables. They appeared to have finished eating. James caught sight of me and nodded. I headed for a booth in the far corner, murmuring a greeting to Rafer and Vicky as I breezed by. I was afraid to wait for a response lest they cut me dead.

Nancy caught my attention. She seemed distracted but not unfriendly, crossing toward the counter to pick up a side of oatmeal. "I'll be with you in just a minute. You want coffee?"

"I'd love some." Apparently, she wasn't a party to the boycott. Alice, the night before, had been friendly as well. Maybe it was just the guys who were shutting me out—not a comforting thought. It was a man, after all, who'd dislocated my fingers.

While I waited for service, I studied James in profile. He was certainly first at the scene the night Tom died, giving him the perfect opportunity to lift Tom's notes. I was still toying with the possibility that he'd invented the walking woman. It wasn't Colleen. She'd assured me that she'd never visited the area, a claim I tended to believe. Besides, if she'd been in the truck with Tom, she wouldn't have deserted him.

The LaMotts emerged from their booth, hunching into overcoats. Vicky crossed to the counter to chat with Barrett while Rafer paid the check. James rose at the same time, leaving his money beside his plate. He and Rafer exchanged a few words, and I saw Rafer glance my way. James pulled on his jacket and left the restaurant without a backward look. Vicky joined her husband, who must have told her to go out and wait for him in the car. She nodded and then busied herself with her gloves and knit cap. I wasn't sure if she was ignoring me or not.

Once she was gone, Rafer ambled in my direction, his hands in his coat pockets, a red cashmere scarf around his neck.

"Hello, Detective LaMott," I said.

"Rafer," he corrected. "How's the hand?"

"Still attached to my arm." I held my fingers up, wiggling them as though the gesture didn't hurt.

"Mind if I sit down?"

I indicated the place across from me, and he slid into the booth. He seemed ill at ease, but his expression was sympathetic, and his hazel eyes showed disquiet, not the hostility I'd half expected. "I had a long talk with some Santa Teresa fellows about you."

I felt my heart start to thump. "Really. Who?"

"Coroner, couple cops. Homicide detective Jonah Robb. From the perspective of the sheriff's department you're okay, but I've heard rumbles I don't like." His voice dropped a notch. "Listen, I know about your suspicions. Why don't you tell me what you have and I'll do what I can to help."

I said, "Great," wondering why I didn't sound more sincere. "I'll tell you what concerns me at the moment. A plainclothes detective— or someone posing as one—showed up at a fleabag hotel in Santa Teresa with a warrant for Alfie Toth's arrest. The Santa Teresa Sheriff's Department has no record of an outstanding warrant in the system, so the paper was probably bogus."

"I can check that," he said smoothly. "What else?"

"I think the guy was a phony, too. He might have been a cop, but I think he misrepresented himself."

"What name did he give?"

"I asked about that, but the clerk I talked to claims the fellow on the desk that day didn't get a name."

"You think it was someone in our department," he said.

"Possibly."

"Based on what?"

"Well, doesn't the timing seem a tiny bit coincidental? Tom wanted to talk to Toth in connection with Pinkie Ritter's death. The other guy got there first, and that was the end of poor old Alfie. Tom was a basket case starting in mid-January, when Toth's body turned up, right?"

"That's Selma's claim." Rafer's manner was now guarded.

"So isn't it possible this is what Tom was brooding about?"

"Tom was a consummate professional for thirty-five years. He was the investigating officer in a homicide matter that I would say, yes, captured his interest, but no, did not in any way cause him to lie awake at night and bite his nails. It didn't cause his heart attack. The idea's absurd. This was his *job*."

"He felt responsible."

"For what?"

"Toth's murder. Tom believed someone gained access to his notebook, where he'd jotted down Toth's temporary address and the phone number at the Gramercy."

"How do you know what Tom *believed?*"

"Because that's what he confided to another investigator."

"Colleen Sellers. And Tom told her this?"

"Well, not explicitly. But that's how the killer could have found Toth and murdered him."

"You still haven't said why you suspect our department."

"Who else had access to his notes?"

"Everyone," he said. "His wife, his son, Brant. Half the time the house was unlocked. Add his cleaning lady, the yard man, his next-door neighbor, the guy across the street. Any one of them could have opened the front door and walked right in. And what makes you so sure the leak didn't come from Santa Teresa?"

I stared at him. "You're right," I said. He had a point.

His manner softened. "Why don't you back off and let us handle this? We haven't been entirely idle. We're developing a lead."

"Are you saying you have a line on Alfie's killer?"

"I'm saying you'd be smart to go home and let us take it from here." He glanced at his watch. "I got Vick in the car and we're late for church," he said, taking his leather gloves from his coat pocket. I watched him smooth them into place, and thought, inexplicably, of his early morning arrival at the emergency room, freshly showered and shaven, nattily dressed, wide-awake. "Did anyone ever fill you in on local history?"

"Cecilia did. The nota of Nota Lake."

"Bunch of convicts literally branded for the heinousness of their behavior. What you're dealing with now are their descendants. You want to watch your step."

I laughed uneasily. "What is this, a western? I'm being warned off? I have to be out of town by sundown?"

"Not a warning. A suggestion. For your own good," he said.

I watched him leave the restaurant. I had that low-level dread that acted as an appetite suppressant. Breakfast didn't sound like such a hot idea. Nancy hurried in my direction with a menu. She filled my mug with hot coffee. "You have any idea what you want to eat?"

"I'm not hungry," I said. "Why don't I move to the counter so we can talk?"

"Sure thing."

I picked up my mug and moved to the counter, where she set a place for me between the griddle and the cash register. Barrett was in the process of cleaning the grill with a flat-edged spatula. Bacon fat and browned particles of pancake and sausage were being pushed into the well. Nancy wiped the surface of the counter clean. "Alice says you've been asking about Pinkie Ritter."

"You remember him?"

"Every woman in Nota Lake remembers him," she said tartly. "He attacked me one night when I got off work. He waited in the lot and grabbed me as I was getting in my car. I kicked his rear end between his shoulder blades, and that was the last of that."

"Did you report it?"

"What for? I took care of it myself. What's the law going to do? Come along afterward and smack his hand?"

Barrett had now come over to the small sink just below the counter in front of us and was rinsing plates. She had her father's light eyes, and she made no secret of the fact that she was listening to Nancy's tale and enjoying her attitude.

I caught her attention. "Did he ever come on to you?"

"Uh-uh. No way," she said, a blush creeping up her cheeks. "I was close to jailbait at that point, barely eighteen years old."

I turned to Nancy. "Could I ask you about something else?"

"Sure."

"The night Tom Newquist died, he was in here earlier, wasn't he?"

"That's right. He came in about nine o'clock. Ordered a cheeseburger and fries, sat around and smoked, looking at his watch like he was killing time. I couldn't figure it out. He never came in at that hour. I figured he was meeting someone, but she never showed up."

"Why do you say 'she'? Couldn't it have been a man?"

Nancy seemed surprised. "I never thought about that."

"Did he use the telephone?"

She shook her head. "Not that I saw."

Again I directed a question to Barrett. "Did you get the impression he was here to meet someone?"

Barrett shrugged. "I guess."

Nancy spoke up again. "You know what I think it was? He was freshly shaved. He looked sharp, like he'd gussied himself up. He wouldn't do that if he were here to meet some guy."

"You agree with that?" I asked Barrett.

"He did look nice, now you mention it," she said.

"Did he seem annoyed or upset, like he'd been stood up?"

"Not a bit of it," Nancy said. "Nine thirty, got up, paid his check, and went out to his truck. I never saw him afterward. I did closing that night, so I was stuck in here." She turned to Barrett. "Did you see him out there? You took off shortly before he did."

Barrett thought about it, frowning slightly before she shook her head. "Not me. Maybe he was parked around back."

"Where were you parked that night?" I asked.

"Nowhere. I didn't have a car. My dad was picking me up."

"She just lives over there on the other side of that subdivision, but her folks don't like her walking home at night. They're real protective, especially her dad."

Barrett smiled, her dark skin pink with embarrassment.

The place began to fill with the after-church crowd, and I was hoping to avoid further confrontation with any irate citizens. I hunched into my jacket and went out to the car for my briefcase, then crunched along the berm to the Nota Lake Cabins.

The office lobby was unlocked, and there was a flat plastic clockface hanging on the doorknob with the hands pointing to eleven thirty. The sign said BACK IN A JIFFY. I went in.

"Cecilia? Are you here?" No answer.

I sat down in an upholstered chair and opened my briefcase. Along with my notes I'd tucked in the packets of index cards. I began to read through my notes, transferring one piece of information to each card with a borrowed ballpoint pen. In some ways this was busywork. I could feel productive and efficient while sheltered from public scrutiny. Transcribing my notes had the further advantage of diverting my attention from the state of discomfort in which I found myself. Yet I couldn't picture turning tail and running on the basis of Rafe's veiled "suggestion" about my personal safety. So what was I doing? Trying to satisfy myself that I'd done what I could. Following leads until the trail ran out.

I went through a pack and a half of index cards without any startling revelations. I shuffled them twice and laid them out like a hand of solitaire, scanning row after row for telling details. For instance, I'd made a note that Cecilia'd told me she got home around ten fifteen the night Tom died. She said she'd seen the ambulance but had no idea it had been summoned for her brother. Could she have seen the woman walking down the road? It occurred to me the woman might have been staying at the Nota Lake Cabins, in which case her stroll might not have had anything to do with Tom. Worth asking, just to eliminate the issue.

CECILIA WAS LATE GETTING back. It was close to twelve fifteen when she finally walked in the door. She was dressed for church in a baggy blue tweed suit with bumblebee scatter pins on the lapel. She opened the half door to the office, put her handbag on the desk, and turned to look at me. "What can I do for you? You're staying at Selma's, so it can't be a room you've come to ask about."

"I'm still working on this business of Tom's death." I tucked the index cards into the briefcase. "Do you happen to remember who was staying here that weekend?"

"At the motel? That's easy." She reached for the registration ledger, paged back through the weeks, ran a finger down the names. "A party of skiers, maybe six of 'em. Complained a lot. Nothing suited them," she said, shooting me a look.

"Anyone else? Any single women?"

"Meaning what?"

"Not meaning anything, Cecilia," I said patiently. "Tennyson says he saw a woman walking down the road that night. I'm hoping against hope she was staying here."

She checked again. "Nope. One other family with a couple of kids. Wife was in a wheelchair, so I doubt he saw her."

"What about you? When you came back, was there anyone on the road? This would have been between ten and ten thirty."

Cecilia seemed to give it some thought and then shook her head. "The only thing I remember is someone using the phone out there. I try to discourage strangers stopping off to make calls, but it was only Barrett calling her dad to pick her up. I offered her a lift, but she said he was already on his way."

She closed the ledger. "Now, I hope you'll excuse me. I have someone joining me for Sunday lunch."

"Sure. No problem. I appreciate your help."

I shrugged into my jacket, grabbed my handbag and the briefcase, and returned to my car at the Rainbow. So here's the question I asked myself: If Barrett left work at nine thirty, why did it take her forty-five minutes to call her dad? I sat in the car, watching the clouds gather in a dark gray sky. It was only one o'clock in the afternoon, but the dark was so pervasive that the photosensor on Cecilia's exterior lights popped to life. Snow began to fall, big airy flakes settling on the windshield like a layer of soapsuds. I waited, watching the rear of the Rainbow Café.

By two thirty the lunch crowd was all but gone. I sat with the inborn patience of the cat watching for a lizard to reappear from the crevice between two rocks. At two forty-four the back door opened and Barrett came out, wearing her apron and carrying a large plastic garbage bag intended for the trash bin. I rolled down the window. "Hi, Barrett. You have a minute?"

She dumped the bag and came over. "I thought you were gone."

"I was visiting Cecilia. Why not take a break? I'd like to talk to you."

She hesitated, looking toward the Rainbow. "I'm really not supposed to, but it's okay for just a minute." She got in the car, slammed the door, and crossed her bare arms against the cold.

"Your dad says you're on your way to med school."

"I haven't been accepted yet," she said.

"Where're you thinking to go?"

"Did you want something in particular? Because Nancy doesn't know I'm out here and I really don't have a break until three."

"I should get to the point, now you mention it," I said. "I was curious about something." Please note she didn't ask what. "Wasn't it you Tom Newquist was here to meet that night?"

"Why would he do that?"

"I have no idea. That's why I'm asking you," I said.

She made a show of frowning, then shook her head in bafflement. "I don't think so," she said, as though racking her brain.

I could feel a fib start to form. "I have to tell you, he made a note on his desk calendar. He wrote 'Barrett' plain as day."

"He did?"

"I ran across it today, which is why I was asking earlier who he was here to meet. I was hoping you'd be honest, but you dropped the ball," I said. "I would have let it pass, but then the story was confirmed, so here I am. You want to tell me how it went?"

"Confirmed? Who confirmed it?"

"Cecilia."

"It wasn't anything," she said.

"Well, great. Cough it up, in that case. I'd like to hear."

"We just talked a few minutes, and then he started feeling bad."

"What'd you talk about?"

"Just stuff. Chatting about my dad. Just idle conversation. Me and Brant used to go steady, and he was asking about the breakup. He always felt bad that we didn't hang in together. I knew he was leading up to something, but I didn't know what. Then he started feeling sick."

"Did he say he was in pain?"

She nodded, her voice wavering when she spoke. "He was clutching his chest, and his breathing was all raspy. I said I'd go back to the motel and get help, and he said, fine, do that. He told me to lock the truck door and not mention our meeting to anyone. He was real emphatic about that, made me *promise*." She fumbled in her pocket and found a tissue. She swiped at her eyes.

I waited until she was calmer. "Did he say anything else?"

She took a deep breath. "Stay off the road if cars came along. He didn't want anyone to know I'd been talking to him. He didn't want to put me in any danger, he said."

"He didn't say from whom?"

"He didn't mention anyone by name," she said.

"He didn't give you his notebook for safekeeping?"

She shook her head mutely.

"Are you sure? I thought he gave you the little black book where he kept his field notes."

"Well, he didn't."

"Barrett, tell the truth. Please, please, please? Trust me, I won't say a word to anyone about your having it."

"I'm telling you the truth."

I shook my head. "I hate to contradict you, but Tom always kept it with him, and yet nobody's seen it since he died. Now it turns out you were in his truck. Where else could it be? He was anxious to protect the notebook, so he must have given it to you. That's the only way it adds up."

The silence was exquisite. I let it drag on.

Barrett looked out the window. "You don't have any proof."

"Well, yeah, I know. I mean, except for the fact that Cecilia saw you on the motel porch that night."

Nancy poked her head out of the Rainbow's back door. Barrett opened the door and leaned out. "I'll be right there!"

"So where's the notebook?"

"In my purse," she said glumly. "He told me to hide it till he could decide what to do with it."

"He didn't know he would die."

"What a bummer," she said.

"Look, if you'll give it to me now, I'll make a copy first thing tomorrow and give it back to you."

After an agonizing moment she said, "All right."

She got out of the car on her side, and I got out on mine, locking the doors quickly before I followed her in. She kept her handbag in the storage room to the left of the kitchen door. Barrett took the notebook out of her bag and passed it to me. She seemed irritated that I'd managed to outmaneuver her somehow. "The other thing he said was the key's on his desk," she said.

"The key's in his desk?"

"On, I think. He said it twice. I have to go."

"Thanks. You're a doll." I put my finger to my lips. "Top secret. Not a word to anyone."

"Great. Then why did I tell you?"

Nancy stuck her head in the kitchen door. "Oh, Kinsey. You're here. Brant's on the phone," she said.

I went out into the café proper, which was virtually deserted. The receiver was face down on the counter. "Brant, is that you?"

He said, "Hi, Kinsey. I'm at Mom's. I drove past the Rainbow a while ago and saw your car. I just wanted to check and make sure you're okay."

"I'm fine. Is your mother home yet?"

"She won't get back till nine," he said. "You need anything?"

"If you have a way to call her, would you tell her I got it?"

"Got what?"

I curled my fingers around the mouthpiece, feeling like a character in a spy movie. "The notebook."

"How'd you manage that?"

"I'll be home in a few minutes. Can you wait?"

"Not really. I'm filling in for someone at work. I just stopped by for some stuff I'll be taking to Sherry's later. We'll talk tomorrow."

"Right. I'll see you then," I said.

I LET myself into Selma's house and headed out to the kitchen. The house was dim, silent. Everything was much as I'd left it, except for a plate of brownies with chocolate frosting on the counter with a note attached: "Help yourself." The condensation on the wrap suggested the brownies had been refrigerated or frozen until recently. Brant must have assumed the note was meant for him because a plate and fork, showing telltale traces of chocolate, were sitting on the table at the place he occupied. I was sorry I'd missed him. We could have put our heads together.

I went into Tom's study and sat down in his swivel chair. I started going through the notebook. The cover was a pebbly black leather, soft with wear. I took the obvious route, starting at the first page—dated June 1—and working through to the last, which was dated February 1, two days before he died. Here at last were the eight months' worth of missing notes. The scribbles, on thin-lined paper, identified each case by a number in the left margin and included complaints, crime-scene investigations, names, addresses, and phone numbers of witnesses. In a series of nearly indecipherable abbreviations, I could trace the course of successive interviews on any given matter. I read about the discovery of Pinkie's body, the findings of the coroner. By copious squints and leaps of imagination I could see that he'd worked backward from Pinkie's death to his incarceration in Chino and his friendship with Alfie Toth, a fact confirmed by "MB," Margaret Brine. I took "C" to refer to Colleen Sellers, who'd called to report Alfie Toth's jail time in "ST." As I'd learned earlier, he'd talked to Dave Estes at the Gramercy on 6-5. Later he'd talked to Olga Toth. By the time C called again to report the discovery of Toth's remains, Tom's notes had become cursory, circumspect, reverting, I suspected, to a code of some kind. The last page of notes contained only some numbers—8, 12, 1, 11, and 26— writ large and underlined with an exclamation point and question mark.

I sat and stared at the numbers until they danced on the page. What did they signify? A date? The combination to a safe? I thought about Tom's telling Barrett about the key in or on his desk. I'd been working at his desk for a week and hadn't seen any key. What kind of key? The key to what?

Maybe he had a lockbox. Maybe he had a cupboard secured by a small combination lock. How many bags full of garbage had I thrown out? How could I be sure I hadn't tossed the key he was referring to? I felt a wave of panic at the idea.

One by one I emptied the contents of each drawer, then removed the drawer itself, checking the back panel and the bottom. In the drawer with his handcuffs and nightstick, I came across his flashlight and used that as I felt along the drawer rails. Did he mean a key that explains something else? I put the drawers back together and moved everything off the top of the desk. I ran a finger across his blotter, looking among the notes he'd scribbled. The numbers were there—8, 12, 1, 11, 26—appearing in the noose. What if I'd discarded the critical information? Had the trash been picked up? I was in a white-hot sweat. The house, as usual, felt like an oven. I crossed to the window and lifted the sash. I loosened the catches on the storm window and pushed the glass out unceremoniously, watching with satisfaction as the window dropped to the ground below. I swallowed mouthfuls of fresh air, hoping to quell my anxiety.

I sat down at the desk again and cleared my mind of emotion. The point was to keep searching as calmly as possible. Again I went through each drawer, looking carefully at the contents. I checked each item in Tom's file folders, looked in envelopes, opened boxes of paper clips, and peered at labels. At the back of my mind I kept returning to the notion that the numbers were a code of some kind. On or in his desk.

I found a piece of paper and wrote out the alphabet in sequence, attaching the numbers 1 through 26 underneath. If the numbers 8, 12, 1, 11, and 26 were simple letter substitutions, then the name or initials would be HLAKZ. Which meant what? Nothing on the face of it. I tried the same sequence backward. The numbers spelled out SOZPA. If the numbers represented letters and this was a word, then all I knew for sure was that the five letters were different. Someone's name? Brant, Macon, Hatch, Wayne, James, Rafer. I looked at the exclamation point and the question mark. Which said what? Consternation? Dismay?

I realized I was famished—a manifestation of my anxiety, no doubt. I went to the kitchen in search of sustenance. It was now four fifteen. I looked in Selma's refrigerator, greeted by plastic-wrapped leftovers from last night's dinner. Not worth re-eating. I glanced at her note and helped myself to several brownies on the counter. The texture was off—a bit dry—but the icing was nice and gooey, only a faint chemical taste suggesting she'd used a boxed mix. I drank some milk from the carton, figuring to save a glass.

Thus fortified, I went back to Tom's swivel chair and swiveled. What if 8, 12, 1, 11, and 26 were page numbers, referring to the notes themselves? I tried that approach, but the contents of the pages seemed in no way related. The afternoon was stretching toward evening, and I was getting nowhere. I went back to the original premise. Selma had hired me to find out why Tom was distressed. If someone he knew had violated his privacy, reading his notes and using the information to get to Alfie Toth to kill him, that would certainly do the trick. But why would Hatch's involvement—or James's or Wayne's—have generated a moment's uneasiness or hesitation. Tom played by the rules. If he'd suspected any one of them, he'd have acted at once. Wouldn't he?

My gaze dropped to the blotter. I pushed a stack of files aside. Down in the right-hand corner Tom had drawn a grid, penning in the days of the month of February. The first fell on a Sunday, the twenty-eighth on a Saturday. The last two Saturdays of the month were crossed out. Was the year 1908, 1912, 1901, 1911, or 1926? I got up and went to the bookshelf, where I took down a copy of his almanac. I thumbed to the index and found the perpetual calendar. In a table beside each year was a number corresponding to a numbered template representing all the variations in the way the months could be laid out.

I flipped on the desk light and studied the series of calendar pages, looking at the Februaries laid out like the one he'd drawn. Calendar number 5 was like that. I checked the years that corresponded, starting with 1900: 1903, 1914, 1925, 1931, and so on. The year couldn't be relevant, could it? And why had he crossed out the last two Saturdays of that month? Eliminating two Saturdays cut the number of days to twenty-six—the number of letters in the alphabet. I lined up the letters with the days of the month. The answer was now HLAKY.

Still rocking in his desk chair, I swiveled toward the window. It was nearly five thirty, fully dark outside. The room was decidedly chilly. I leaned forward and closed the window. What did those numbers mean? I could feel a draft from somewhere. Curious, I got up and walked along the front hall to the living room, where I turned on the table lamps. The drapes were wavering as though pushed by an unseen hand. The front door was closed and locked, as was the door to the garage. I poked my head into Selma's bedroom. All was undisturbed. Down the hall, all the windows in Brant's old bedroom were closed.

I stopped where I was. The door to my room was ajar. Had I left it that way? I pushed it open with apprehension. Curtains flapped and fluttered. The room was a shambles. There were jagged shards of glass on the carpet. The window, which I'd oh-so-carefully locked, had been shattered by a hammer that someone had left on the floor. Pebbles of glass the size of rock salt were spread out across the sill. The sash had been pushed up, probably from the outside. Someone had clearly entered. I moved to the bed and slid my hand between the box spring and mattress. My gun was missing.

CHAPTER TWELVE

GLANCED at my watch. Five thirty-six. I walked back to the kitchen prepared to dial 911. I hesitated, my hand on the receiver. Who was I going to call? Rafer? Brant? Tom's brother, Macon? I wasn't sure I trusted any one of them. I stood there, trying to determine whom I could confide in at this point. A chill went through me. Surely there wasn't anybody in the house *with* me. I felt disembodied, my mind having been separated from my flesh by the harrowing sensation of fear.

The phone shrilled with extraordinary loudness, setting off a surge of nausea. I snatched up the receiver. "Hello?"

"Hey, Kinsey. Brant here. Is my mom home yet?" He sounded young and carefree, relaxed, unconcerned.

My stomach churned in response. "You need to come home."

His tone shifted. "Why? What's going on?"

"Someone's broken in. There's glass on the bedroom floor, and my gun is gone."

"Stay where you are. I'll be right there."

I replaced the receiver. I turned and leaned my back up against the wall, making little mewling sounds. A town full of cowboys, and someone was coming after me. I held my hands out in front of me. I could see my fingers tremble, the recently dislocated digits looking all puffy and useless. My gun had been stolen. I had to have some way to defend myself. I started opening kitchen drawers in search of a knife. I could feel tears stinging my lids. What good would a serrated steak knife do against a speeding bullet?

Hours seemed to go by.

I could hear the second hand on the kitchen clock tick each passing second in turn.

Outside, I heard the squeal of brakes, and then a car door

slammed shut. I turned and stared at the front door. What if it was someone else? What if it was them? The door flew open, and Brant moved toward me with all the comforting bulk of a battleship. I put a hand out and he took it.

"You look awful. How'd the guy get in?"

I pointed to my room and then found myself following as he moved down the hall. His assessment was brief, the most cursory of glances. He turned away from the guest room and toured the rest of the house methodically, looking in every closet, every nook and cranny. He went down to the basement. I waited, one hand plucking at the other. Where was my gun?

Brant returned to the kitchen. "Did he get the notebook?"

I found myself grinding my teeth. "Who?"

"The guy who broke in," he said sharply.

"It was in my bag," I said.

"Tell me exactly what you did today. How long were you gone?"

I felt burbling and incoherent, spilling out the story of the gas station attendants, my stop at the Rainbow to talk to Nancy. I told him I'd run into Rafer and Vick, that I'd talked to Cecilia and Barrett. My brain was moving at twice the speed of my lips, making me feel sluggish and stupid. What was wrong with me? I knew I'd felt like this before—this scared—this out of it. . . .

Brant was staring at me. "You actually talked to him?"

What was he talking about? "Who?" I sounded like an owl.

"Rafer."

What had I asked? What had he said before this? "What?"

"Rafer. At the Rainbow. I'm asking if you talked to him."

"Sure."

"You *talked* to him?" His voice had risen with alarm.

"I brought him up to date," I said. My voice was delayed, like something in an echo chamber.

"Who do you think started all the rumors?"

"Who?"

Brant took me by the shoulders and gave me a little shake. "Kinsey, wake up and pay attention. This is serious," he said.

"You're not saying it was him?"

"Of course it was him." He seemed angry. "Who else could it be? Think about it, dummy."

"Think about what?" I asked. I was relying on him for help, but his anxiety was pushing mine into the danger zone.

His voice pounded on, pleading and cajoling. "You told Mom it was someone in law enforcement. Do you honestly think my father would have lost even one night's sleep if it was anyone but Rafer? Rafer was his best friend. The two of them worked together for years and years. Now Dad finds out Rafer killed two guys? He must have freaked. Isn't this in his notes?"

"The notes are in code. I can't read them."

"Where? Can you show me? Maybe I can crack it."

"In there." My brain worked lickety-cut. It was my mouth that fumbled. "I talked to Barrett. She was with Tom in the truck just before he died," I said.

"What did they talk about? Why did he do that?"

"Something. I can't remember."

"Didn't you press her for answers? You had the girl right there in the palm of your hand," he said. His words appeared in the air, written in big capital letters.

"Quit yelling."

"I'm not yelling. What's the matter with you?"

"Barrett never said a word about Rafer." I remembered then. She did say Tom had asked about her father.

"Why would she? She doesn't know you from Adam. She's not going to confide. She wouldn't tell you something like that. Her own father? She'd have to be nuts," he shrilled.

"But why give me the notes?"

"Barrett doesn't have a clue. She has no idea."

"How do you know what he did?"

"Because I can add," he said, exasperated. "I put two and two together. Listen, Tom met with Barrett. He was probably trying to find out about Rafer's whereabouts when Pinkie was murdered. Same with Alfie Toth. He saw the connection. Someone had already ripped him off for the information about Toth. Who do you think it was? *Rafer.*"

"Rafer," I said. I was nodding. I could see what he was saying. I'd been thinking the same thing. Tom's friendship with Rafer was such that he'd think long and hard before he turned him in to the authorities. A conflict of that magnitude would have caused him extreme distress. My brain was clicking and buzzing. *Click, click, click.* Like pool balls. Why didn't the clerk at the Gramercy tell me the phony plainclothes detective was black? You'd think he'd remember something so obvious. My mind kept veering. I wished I'd talked to Leland Peck before I left Santa Teresa. I was feeling very weird. So anxious. Sound fading in and out.

Brant was still talking. He seemed to be speaking gibberish, but it all made a peculiar sense. "Pinkie went after Barrett. She was hiking in the mountains and stumbled across their fishing camp. Barrett was assaulted. He put a gun to her head. She was raped. She was attacked and sexually abused. Pinkie hurt her. He forced her to perform unspeakable acts. Alfie did nothing—offered her no assistance—ran off, leaving her to Pinkie's mercy. Barrett came back hysterical, in a state of shock. Rafer went after Pinkie. He strung him up from the limb of a tree and let him die slowly for what he had done to her. He would have killed Alfie, too, but Alfie escaped and blew town. Rafer thought he was safe all these years, and then Pinkie's body turned up and Dad found the link. He drove all the way to Santa Teresa, but Rafer got there first. He hung Toth the same way he hung Pinkie." Brant was looking at me earnestly. "What's wrong with your eyes?"

"My eyes?" Once he mentioned it, I realized my field of vision had begun to oscillate, images sliding side to side, like bad camera work. I felt giddy, as if I were on the verge of fainting.

"Are you okay?"

"Fine." I saw Rafer with the noose. I saw him tighten it on Pinkie's neck. I saw him hang Alfie in the wilderness. I felt his rage and his pain for what they'd done to his only daughter. I said, "How do you know all this?"

"Barrett told me, Kinsey. That's why I broke up with her. I was twenty years old. I couldn't handle it," he said, anguished.

"I'm sorry. I'm sorry," I said.

Brant's tone became accusatory. "You're loaded. I don't believe it. What are you high on?"

"I'm high?" Of course. Daniel playing the piano. My ex-husband. Eyes like an angel, a halo of golden curls, and how I'd loved him. He'd given me acid once without telling me, and I watched the floor recede into the mouth of hell.

Brant's head came up. "What's that?" he hissed.

"What?"

"I heard something." His agitation washed over me. His fear was infectious, as swift as an airborne virus.

"Hang on." Brant strode down the hall. I saw him look out the small ornamental window in the front door. He pulled back abruptly. "A car cruised by with its lights doused. He's parked across the street about six doors down. You have a gun?"

"I told you someone stole it. What's happening?"

"Rafer," he said grimly. He crossed to the drawer in his mother's kitchen desk, where she did her menu planning. He pulled out a gun and thrust it in my hand. "Here. Take this."

I stared at it with bewilderment. "Thanks," I whispered. The gun was a basic police revolver, Smith & Wesson. I'd nearly bought one like it once, .357 magnum, four-inch barrel, walnut stocks.

"Rafer will come in with guns blazing," Brant was saying. "No deals. He's told everyone that you're a killer, that you do drugs, and here you are stoned on something."

"I didn't do anything," I said, mouth dry. The brownies. I was higher than he knew. I racked back through my memory, classes at the police academy, my years in uniform on the street, trying to remember symptoms. What had I ingested? Confusion, paranoia, slurred speech, nystagmus. I was out of my brain on speed.

"You found him out. He'll have to kill you. We'll have to shoot it out," Brant said.

"Don't leave me. Talk to him. I can get away," I burbled.

"He's thought of that. He'll have help. Probably Macon and Hatch. They both hate you. We better get down to business."

When Brant peeled off his jacket, I smelled stress sweat, the scent as acrid and piercing as ammonia. I glanced at his hands.

Given any visual field, the eye tends to stray to the one different item in a ground of like items. Even bombed, I caught sight of a blemish on his right wrist, a dark patch shaped like the prow of a ship. The blot stood out like a brand on the clean white surface of his skin. Sizzling, my brain zapped through the possibilities: scar, smudge, scab, birthmark. The mark was a burn, a match for the tip of a ticking-hot iron. Adrenaline rushed through me. Something close to euphoria filled my flesh and bones. My mind made an odd leap to something else altogether. I'd been struggling to break the code with logic, when the answer was really one of spatial relationships. Vertical, not horizontal. That's how the numbers worked. Up and down instead of back and forth.

I put the gun on the kitchen table. "I'll be right back," I said. With extraordinary effort I propelled myself into Tom's den. 8, 12, 1, 11, and 26. I looked at the calendar Tom had drawn: twenty-eight days with the first falling on a Sunday, and the last two Saturdays, the twenty-first and the twenty-eighth, crossed out.

I found a pencil. I wrote the alphabet, inserting one letter per day, using vertical rows this time. If my theory was correct, then the code would confirm what I already knew: 8 would represent the letter B. The number 12 would stand for the letter R. The number 1 would be A, and 11 would represent N, and the 26 would be T. BRANT.

Brant.

I could feel a laugh billow up. I was stuck in the house with him. He would have had easy access to his father's notes. The search of the den, the broken window—both had been a cover, suggesting someone from the outside had entered the house in hopes of finding the notes. It wasn't Barrett at all. Pinkie hadn't raped Barrett. It was Brant he'd humiliated and degraded.

"What are you doing?"

I jumped. Brant was standing in the doorway. The sight of him wavered, shimmering. I couldn't think of a way to answer. Nystagmus. Something in the brownies. I was smarter than him. Oh, much smarter. I was smarter than anyone that day.

"What are you looking at?"

"Tom's notes. I can't make heads or tails of them."

He stared at me. I could tell he was trying to determine if what I'd said was true. I kept my mind empty. I don't think I'd ever seen him looking so lean and young and handsome. Death is like that— a lover whose embrace you sink into without warning. He held out his hand. "I'll take the notes."

I passed the notebook across to him, picturing the Smith & Wesson. Where had I heard about a gun like that before? There was no way he would give me a gun unless he intended to see that I was killed with it. Rafer LaMott wasn't outside, and neither was anybody else. I envisioned the scene—the two of us skulking through the house, ostensibly waiting for an attack that would never come. Brant could shoot me anytime he chose, claiming later he'd mistaken me for an intruder, claiming self-defense, claiming I was stoned out of my gourd, which I was. Even as the thought formed, I felt the drugs kick up a notch. I could outsmart him. He was strong, but I had more experience. I knew everything he knew, plus some.

"Is the car still out there?" I asked.

Brant dropped back into his fantasy. He moved to the window, peering off to the right. "Down half a block."

"I think we should turn the lights out."

He studied me for a second, picturing the house black as pitch. "You're right. Hit the switch. I'll take care of all the other lights."

"Good." I turned the den light out. I waited until I heard him moving down the hall toward the front. Then I eased to the window, flipped the lock, and pushed the sash up about six inches. I dropped to the floor, felt my way to the lower storage cabinet, and slid myself feet first into the space beneath the bookshelves. Birth in reverse. I was hidden from view. Moments went by.

"Kinsey?" Brant was back.

Silence.

I heard him come to the den. He must have stood in the doorway, allowing his eyes to adjust to the black. He crossed to the window, bumping into cardboard boxes. I heard him force the window open and look out. I was gone. There was no sign of me running across the grass. He slammed the window shut and said, "Damn!" He must have had a gun, because I heard him rack one into the chamber.

He left the den, hollering my name as he went. Now he was mad. Now he didn't care if I knew he was coming. I pulled myself out of the cabinet, crossed to the desk, and opened the bottom drawer as quietly as possible. I took out Tom's handcuffs and tucked them in my back pocket. I could feel myself swell with power. I was suddenly far beyond fear, luminous with fury. As I turned right out of the den into the darkness of the hallway, I could see him moving ahead of me, his body mass blacker than the charcoal light surrounding him. I began to run, picking up speed, my Reeboks making no sound on the carpet. Brant sensed my presence, turning as I lifted myself into the air. I snapped a hard front kick to his solar plexus, taking him down with one pop. I heard his gun thump dully against the wall as it flew out of his hand. I kicked him again, catching him squarely on the side of the head.

I scrambled to my feet and stood over him. I could have crushed his skull, but as a courtesy, I refrained from doing so. I pulled the handcuffs from my pocket. I grabbed the fingers of his right hand and bent them backward, encouraging compliance. I laid the cuff on his right wrist and snapped downward, smiling grimly to myself as the swinging arm of the cuff locked in place. I put my left foot on the back of his neck while I yanked his right arm behind him and grabbed for his left. He was out cold. I double-locked both handcuffs in place. All of this without hesitation. All of this in the dark.

The light in the kitchen was snapped on. Selma appeared in the doorway, still wearing her fur coat. She stood as still as a soldier and took in the sight before her. Brant was now moaning. Blood was pouring from his nose, and he was struggling for breath. "Mom, watch out. She's stoned," he croaked.

Selma backed into the kitchen. I was moving away from her

down the corridor, looking for Brant's gun, when she showed up
with the Smith & Wesson in her right hand.

"Stop right there," she said. She was now holding the gun with
two hands, arms extended stiffly at shoulder height. I went about
my business, ignoring her little drama. She had no way of knowing
I'd been sanctified by angel dust. I was higher than a kite on some
amazing mix of excitation and immortality.

"You're not going to take my son away from me."

As much as anything, I was annoyed with her. "I told you to forget it. You should have left well enough alone. Now you've not only
lost Tom, you've lost Brant as well." I got down on my knees and
felt under the chair. Where the hell was Brant's gun?

"You are completely mistaken. I haven't lost Brant at all," she
said. "Now get up right this minute. Do as I say!"

"Do you see Brant's gun? It's gotta be here somewhere."

"I'm warning you. I'll count to three, and then I'll shoot you."

"You do that," I said. I moved into the dining room, convinced
the gun had somehow become wedged under the hutch. I placed
my shoulder against the floor, reaching as far as the length of my
arm. It was in this awkward position—me spread-eagled on my
stomach, Brant moaning in the hall—that I chanced to look up,
watching in slow-motion amazement as Selma screwed up her face,
closed her eyes, and squeezed the trigger. There was a bright flash
and a large bang. The bullet exited the barrel at a lethal velocity.
The normal football-shaped muzzle flash out the front of the gun
and the vertical fan-shaped flashes at the cylinder gap seemed to be
enhanced—a dazzling yellow. Brant had apparently packed the first
cartridge with an overload of fast powder. I thought I knew now
who Judy Gelson's lover was the night she blew a hole in her husband's chest. The chamber and the top strap ruptured. The blast
unlatched the cylinder and drove it out to the left side of the gun.
The cartridge case shredded, and tiny bits of brass peppered
Selma's hands. Flakes of unburned powder peppered her face as
well. Simultaneously, as though by magic, all the glass in the hutch,
including the crystal goblets and the bone-china plates, exploded

like fireworks and formed a glittering star burst of falling debris.

"Jeez. That was great. You should try that again," I said.

Selma was weeping as I walked to the phone and dialed 911.

LATER the Nota County sheriff gave me permission to read the file on the Ritter/Toth murders. Rafer and I sat down together, and by comparing Tom's notes with other reports submitted in the case, we managed to piece together the course of Tom's investigation. The irony, of course, was that the evidence he'd collected was not only spotty but entirely circumstantial. None of it was sufficient to result in an arrest, let alone a conviction. Tom realized Brant had committed double murder, and he knew it was something he couldn't keep to himself for long. Revealing the truth would destroy his marriage. Concealing it would destroy everything else he valued. Tom had died in silence, and if Selma had been content to leave it there, the case might have died, too.

Brant is currently out on bail on a charge of attempted murder for what he did to me. Selma's hired a fancy-pants attorney who (naturally) advised him to plead not guilty. I suspect if we get to court, this same attorney will find a way to blame the whole thing on me. That's the way justice seems to work these days.

In the meantime Selma's house is on the market, and she's leaving Nota Lake. The town is unforgiving, and the people there never liked her anyway. If I'd been capable of seeing all of these events in advance, I'd have told her to have her teeth capped instead of hiring me. She'd have been better off that way.

Respectfully submitted,
Kinsey Millhone

SUE GRAFTON

Like the heroine of her best-selling alphabet mystery series, Sue Grafton is a maverick at heart. In fact, she says, Kinsey is "the person I would have been had I not married young and had children." Mother of three, Grafton toiled for years as a Hollywood scriptwriter before creating her groundbreaking hard-boiled female private eye in *"A" Is for Alibi*.

Today Grafton and her husband, philosophy professor Steven Humphrey, divide their time between homes in Kentucky and California. Her many fans will be delighted to hear that she doesn't expect to run out of the alphabet anytime soon. It should take her until 2015 to reach Z.

Barbara Delinsky

Coast Road

A marriage can have as many twists and turns as the coast road to Big Sur.

Some marriages are lost on the rocky shore.

But some are as eternal as the ocean itself.

$\mathscr{P}rologue$

WHEN the phone rang, Rachel Keats was painting sea otters. She was working in oils and had finally gotten the right mix of black for the eyes. There was no way she was stopping to pick up the phone. She had warned Samantha about that.

"Hi. You've reached Rachel, Samantha, and Hope. Please leave your name and number, and we'll call you back. Thanks."

Through a series of beeps Rachel applied a smudge of oil with a round brush. Then came a deep male voice that was too old to be calling for Samantha. It belonged to a ticket agent, a friend of a friend, apparently good at his job. "I have in my hand three tickets for tonight's Garth Brooks concert," he said. "San Jose. Gooooood seats."

Rachel made a grab for the phone. "I want them!"

"Heeeey, Rachel. How's my favorite artist?"

"Painting. You need a credit card number, right? Hold on a second." She put the phone down, ran through the house to the kitchen, and snatched up her wallet. She was breathless returning to the studio, breathless reading off the number, breathless hanging up.

She swallowed hard, looked at the canvas on the easel and six others nearby waiting to be finished, thought of everything else she had to do in the next three weeks, and decided that she was crazy. She didn't have time to go to a concert.

But the girls would be absolutely, positively blown away.

She threw the window open and leaned out into clear, woodsy air. "Samantha! Hope!"

Minutes later her daughters came running through the woods, Samantha looking every bit as young as Hope for once, both with blond hair flying and cheeks pink. Rachel shouted the news to them even before they reached her window. The look on their faces was more than worth the prospect of an all-nighter or two.

"Are you serious?" Hope asked. Her eyes were wide, her freckles vibrant, her smile filled with teeth that were still too large for her face. She was thirteen and entirely prepubescent.

Rachel grinned and nodded.

"Awesome," breathed Samantha. At fifteen she was a head taller than Hope and gently curved.

Hope pressed her hands together in excitement. "Are we doing the whole thing—you know, what we talked about?"

Rachel didn't have the time for it. She didn't have the money. But if her paintings were a hit, the money would come, and as for time, life was too short. "The whole thing," she said, because it would be good for Samantha to get away from the phone, Hope to get away from her cat, and yes, maybe even good for Rachel to get away from her oils.

"Omigosh. I have to call Lydia," Samantha cried.

"What you have to do," Rachel corrected her, "is anything that needs to be done for school. We leave in an hour."

Rachel returned to her studio for the hour and accomplished as little as she feared her daughters had. Then they piled into her sport utility vehicle and headed north. The store she wanted was on the way to San Jose. It was still open when they got there, and had a perfect selection. Thirty minutes later they emerged wearing cowboy boots, cowboy hats, and smiles the size of Texas.

Nothing they saw when they got to San Jose brought them down. There were crowds of fans, light shows and smoke, and the man himself, who sang hit after hit without a break. How could Rachel not be into it, with Hope and Samantha dancing beside her? She cheered with them when familiar chords announced a favorite song, and shouted appreciatively with them at song's end. The three of them sang their hearts out until the very last encore was done, and then they left the arena arm in arm, three friends who just happened to be related.

It was a special evening. Rachel loved her hat, her boots, her girls. If she fell behind in her work, it was for a good cause.

SHE wasn't as convinced of it the next morning, when the girls woke up late and cranky and nearly missed the bus. But she worked feverishly through the day, breaking only to meet the girls at the bus stop and have a snack with them.

Afterward Rachel spent another hour in her studio. Half convinced that the sea otters were done, she stopped and put dinner in the oven, then returned to the studio. With alternating glances at a field sketch and photograph, she used the fine edge of her palette knife to add texture to the oil on her canvas. The otters were playing in kelp. Her challenge was to capture the wetness of their fur.

"The buzzer rang, Mom," Hope called from the door.

"Thanks, honey," Rachel murmured, adding several last strokes. "Will you take the casserole out and turn off the gas?"

"I already did." Hope was at her side now, studying the canvas. "I thought you were done."

"Something wasn't right." She stood back for a longer view and was satisfied. "Better." She set her palette aside, reached for a solvent cloth, and wiped her hands. "I'll clean up and be right there." She looked at Hope. "Did Samantha set the table?"

"I did."

"She's on the phone again?"

"Still," Hope said so dryly that Rachel had to chuckle.

"Five minutes," she said, and sent Hope off.

As promised, five minutes later Rachel was in the kitchen doling out lasagna and salad. Twenty minutes after that, Rachel gave out cleanup assignments. Fifteen minutes after that, having showered and put on fresh clothes, she paused and looked wildly around for the book she had read the weekend before.

She searched her bedroom without success. Thinking she might have already set it out, she returned to the kitchen. "Is my book in here? I remember having it in my hand."

The girls were doing the dishes.

"You're not organized," Samantha charged. Rachel regularly preached the merits of organization.

"Oh, I am," she mused. "I just have a lot on my plate right now."

That was putting it mildly. With her show three weeks away, she was feeling the crunch. Okay. She had finally hit gold with the sea otters. But there was still the background to do for that one and six others, and eighteen in all to frame. And there was a dress to buy with Samantha for her first prom, an end-of-the-year picnic to run for Hope's seventh-grade class, a birthday party to throw for Ben Wolfe, who owned the art gallery and was a sometime date.

She had splurged last night. She shouldn't be going anywhere tonight. But she wasn't missing a book club meeting. She loved the women, loved the books.

Hope materialized at her shoulder, holding her cat, Guinevere. "I think it's in your studio."

Closing her eyes, Rachel conjured up the studio, which lay at a far end of her rambling house. She had left the room for the day, then returned for an unexpected little while. Yes, she'd had the book in her hand and set it down there.

"Thanks, sweetheart." She cupped Hope's chin. The child looked forlorn. "Guinevere will be fine. She ate, didn't she?"

Hope nodded.

"See there? That's a good sign." She kissed Hope's forehead. "I'd better get the book. I'm running late."

The book was where Rachel had left it, on a corner of the large worktable. She retrieved it and hurried back through the house. She gave the girls quick kisses and went out to her car.

WHEN Jack McGill's phone rang at two in the morning, the sound cut sharply into the muted world of a soupy San Francisco night.

In the time that it took him to grab for the phone, a dozen jarring thoughts came and went. "Yes?"

"Is this Jack McGill?" asked a voice he didn't know.

"Yes."

"I'm Katherine Evans, one of Rachel's friends. There's been an accident. She's at the hospital in Monterey. I think you should come."

Jack sat up in bed. "What kind of accident?"

"Her car was hit and went off the road."

His stomach knotted. "What road? Were the girls with her?"

"Highway 1, and no, she was alone." Relief. The girls were safe, at least. "She was near Rocky Point, on her way to Carmel. A car rammed her from behind."

His feet hit the floor. The knot in his stomach tightened.

"She's alive," the friend went on. "Only a few broken bones, but she hasn't woken up. The doctors are worried about her brain."

He pushed a hand through his hair. "The girls—"

"Are still home. Rachel was on her way to our book group. When nine o'clock came and she hadn't shown up, I called the house. Samantha said she'd left at seven, so I called the state police. They told me there'd been an accident and ID'd her car, so I called her neighbor Duncan Bligh. He went down to sit with the girls. I didn't know whether to tell Duncan to drive them up here to the hospital. That's not my decision to make."

No. It was Jack's. Divorce or no divorce, he was the girls' father. Clamping the phone between shoulder and jaw, he reached for his jeans. "I'm on my way. I'll call Samantha and Hope from the car."

He hung up. "Unbelievable," he muttered as he zipped his jeans and reached for a shirt. Things were bad at the office and bad in the field. He was living an architect's nightmare, needed in both places come morning, and then there was Jill. Tonight was the charity dinner that she had been working on for so long. She was expecting him at five.

But Rachel was hurt. You're not married to her anymore, his alter ego said. You don't owe her a thing. She was the one who walked out. But she was hurt, and depending on what he found in Monterey, there would be arrangements to make for the girls.

He tossed cold water onto his face and brushed his teeth. Minutes later he entered his studio—and in a moment's dismay wondered why he still called it that. It had become more a place to do business than to create art. What few drawings he had done were buried under proposals, spec sheets, and contracts—the refuse of an insane number of construction projects in various stages.

He crammed his briefcase with his laptop and as many vital papers as would fit, and his portfolio with multiple versions of the Montana design. Tucking both under an arm, he made his way down to the garage. Within minutes he was backing out his BMW and speeding down Filbert. His headlights cut a pale gray swath in the smoky night, lighting little of Russian Hill.

Pressing numbers by feel on his car phone, he called information. He was heading south on Van Ness by the time he got through to the hospital in Monterey. "This is Jack McGill. My wife, Rachel Keats, was brought in a little while ago. I'm on my way there. Can you give me an update?"

"Hold on, please." Several nerve-racking minutes later he connected with a nurse in the emergency room. "Mr. McGill? She's in surgery. That's about all we know at this point."

"Is she conscious?"

"She wasn't when they took her upstairs."

"What's the surgery for?"

"Would you hold on a minute?"

"I'd rather not—" The sudden silence at the other end said he had no choice. He'd had no choice when Rachel moved out six years ago, either. She had said she was going, had packed up the girls and their belongings while he was away on business. He had come home to an echoing house, feeling as thwarted and helpless then as he felt now.

"Mr. McGill?" came a male voice, choppy over the speaker but audible. "I'm Dr. Couley. I treated your wife when she arrived."

"What's the surgery for?" he shouted, gripping the wheel.

"To set her left leg. Compound fractures, both femur and tibia. They'll be inserting pins—"

"I was told there were head injuries," he cut in. "Has she regained consciousness?"

"No. There's some cranial swelling. We don't yet know what direction it'll take. When will you be here?"

"I'm just leaving San Francisco."

"Two hours, then?"

"Less," Jack said. "Here's my cell number." He rattled it off. "Call me if there's any change, will you?" When the doctor agreed, Jack punched out another set of numbers. He wasn't as quick to press SEND this time, though. He didn't know what to say to the girls.

They had mentioned Duncan Bligh, and more than once. He was the rancher who shared Rachel's canyon. The meadow where his herd grazed lay above her redwood forest. Both meadow and forest were part of the Santa Lucias, rising east of the Big Sur coast.

Jack had a bad feeling about Duncan. He didn't like the affectionate way the girls described his cabin, his beard, or his sheep. He didn't like the way they grinned when he asked if Rachel was dating him. Oh, sure. He knew they were trying to make him jealous. The problem was that he could see Rachel with a man like that. Mountain men had a kind of rugged appeal. Not that Jack was a slouch. He was tall. He was fit. But he didn't shear sheep or shoot deer.

He pressed SEND.

The first ring was barely done when there came a fast "Hello?"

He lifted the phone. "Hi, Sam. It's Dad. Are you guys okay?"

"How's Mom?"

"I don't know." He kept his voice light. "I'm on my way to the hospital. I just talked with the doctor. They've taken her into surgery. It sounds like she smashed up her leg pretty good."

"Katherine said it was her ribs, too."

"It may be, but the leg is the thing that needs setting."

"Dad, we want to go to the hospital, but Duncan won't take us."

"Is he there now?"

"He's asleep on the chair. I'll put him on. Tell him to drive us up." She shouted away from the phone, "Duncan, pick up the phone. It's my father."

"Samantha," Jack called to get her back.

Her reply was muffled. "No, Hope, Mom is *not* dead, but that cat will be if you don't let her go. You're holding her too tight. You'll hurt her." She returned to Jack. "Hope wants to talk."

"Daddy?" The voice was a fragile wisp.

Jack's heart shifted. "Hi, Hope. How're you doin', sweetie?"

"Scared."

"I figured that, but your mom's doing fine right now. I'm on my way to the hospital. I'll know more when I get there."

"Come *here,*" begged the small voice.

"I will," he said. "But the hospital's on the way, so I'll stop there first. Then I'll have more to report when I see you."

"Tell Mom—" She stopped.

"What, sweetie?"

Samantha came on. "She's crying again. Here's Duncan."

"Duncan Bligh here." The voice was curt. "What's the word?"

"The word is that I don't know much. I'll be at the hospital within the hour. Don't drive them up."

"I wasn't about to."

There was a muted protest in the background, then an aggrieved Samantha returned. "Daddy, it's sick sitting around here while she's there. She's our *mother.*"

"She's in surgery, Samantha. Even if you were at the hospital, you wouldn't be able to see her. Look, if you want to do something, help your sister. She sounds upset."

"And I'm not?"

Jack could hear the tight panic that was taking her voice a step beyond brash. But Samantha wasn't Hope. Two years apart in age, they were light-years apart in personality. Samantha was fifteen going on thirty, a little know-it-all who didn't take kindly to being treated like a child. Thirteen-year-old Hope was sensitive and silent. Samantha would ask the questions; Hope would see every nuance of the answers.

"I'm sure you're upset, too," he said, "but you're older than she is. Right now the one thing you can do to help your mother most is to reassure your sister. And get some sleep. Both of you."

"Yeah, right," Samantha muttered.

JACK concentrated on driving. He willed the car phone to ring with the news that Rachel had awoken from surgery and was just fine. But the phone remained silent.

He would have calls to make come morning, meetings to reschedule. Or if Rachel woke up, he might be back in the office by noon. That was likely, the more he thought about it. Rachel was the strongest woman he knew—strongest, healthiest, most independent and self-sufficient. She didn't need him. Never had. Six years ago she had reached a fork in the road of her life and gone off in a different direction from him. Her choice. Her life. Fine.

So why was he heading south? Why was he postponing even one business meeting to run to her bedside? She had left him. She had taken ten years of marriage and crumpled it up.

He was heading south because it was his job as a father to help out with the girls. And because he was terrified that Rachel might die. He was heading south because his life with her had been better than anything before or since, and he still owed her for that.

THE very first time Jack had laid eyes on Rachel, he decided that she wasn't his type. Oh, he liked blond hair, and she had endless waves of that, but he usually went for model types. Rachel Keats didn't fit that bill. She looked too pure. No long eyelashes, no glossy mouth, just dozens of freckles scattered over her nose and cheeks, and eyes that were focused intently on the most boring professor Jack had ever heard.

The subject was rococo and neoclassic art. The professor, renowned in his field, was the man whose grant was paying for Jack's architectural degree. In exchange Jack graded exams and papers and helped the professor with research.

Jack was only marginally interested in rococo and neoclassic art and even less interested in moving from Manhattan to Tucson, but the slot had been the only one open that offered full tuition plus a stipend. Being penniless, Jack needed both.

The job wasn't taxing. The professor in question had been delivering the same lectures for twenty-plus years. Since Jack read the lectures beforehand, his presence in the lecture hall was more for the sake of fetching a forgotten book or paper for the professor than anything educational for himself. He sat far off to the professor's side, where he could easily be accessed.

Rachel Keats attended every class, listened raptly, took notes. An art major, she lived in an apartment complex not far from Jack's. She was a loner by all accounts, and if the easygoing expression she wore meant anything, she was content.

Not only wasn't she his type, but he was dating someone who was. Celeste was tall and leggy and made precious few demands. She cooked and cleaned for him, but he hadn't been able to con her into doing his laundry. That was why he found himself in the Laundromat on a Tuesday night when Rachel came through the door.

Those waves of blond hair were gathered up in a turquoise ribbon that clashed with her purple tank top, but her shorts and sandals were white and as fresh as the blush that stained her cheeks when she saw him there.

In the extra-long heartbeat that she spent at the door, he could have sworn she was debating turning and leaving. Not wanting her to do that, he said, "Hey, how're you doing?"

She smiled. "Great." The blush remained. Hugging an over-stuffed laundry bag, she looked down the row of washers for raised lids. "Ah," she said, spotting two side by side. She smiled at him again and headed toward them.

Jack's heart was pounding. He didn't know why. But he slid off the dryer he'd been sitting on, followed her, and leaned up against a machine that backed on one of those she had chosen.

"Rococo and neoclassic art?" he prompted.

She acknowledged the connection with a simple "Uh-huh." She was still blushing, pushing dirty laundry into the washer.

He watched her for a minute, then said, "Mine's in the dryer."

It was probably the dumbest line he'd ever handed a woman. But he couldn't tell her that she was pushing reds and whites together into her machine. He couldn't ask if the reds were shirts, bras, or briefs. He couldn't even look directly at those things, because she would have been mortified. Besides, he couldn't take his eyes from hers. They were hazel with gold flecks and more gentle than any eyes he had ever seen.

"You're Obermeyer's teaching assistant," she said as she filled the second machine. "Are you training to teach?"

"No. I'm in architecture."

She smiled. "Really?"

"Really," he said, smiling back.

"What kind of things do you want to build?" she asked, sounding genuinely interested.

"Homes, for starters. I come from a two-bit town, one little box after another. I used to pass those little boxes on the way to school and spend my class time doodling them into something finer."

"I was a doodler, too," she said almost shyly.

He liked the shyness. It made him feel safe. "Where?"

"Chicago, then Atlanta, then New York. My childhood was mobile. My dad takes old businesses and turns them around. We move when he sells. How about you?"

"Oregon. You won't have heard of the town. It doesn't make it onto maps. What did you doodle?"

"Oh, people, birds, animals, fish—anything that moves."

"Are you still doodling?" he asked.

"I like to think it's more. I'm hoping to paint for a living."

"With or without a day job?" Jack asked.

She wrapped her arms around her middle. Quietly, almost sadly, she said, "I'm lucky. Those businesses keep selling. My parents think I'm crazy to be here doing this. Art isn't business. They want me back in the city wearing designer dresses and imported boots." She took a fresh breath. "Do you have siblings?"

"Five brothers and a sister," he said.

Rachel's eyes lit up. "Six? That's great. I don't have any."

"That's why you think it's great. There were seven of us born in ten years, living with two parents in a three-bedroom house. The others are all back home. I'm the only one who made it out."

Her eyes grew. "Really? How?"

"Scholarship. Work-study. Desperation. I had to leave. I don't get along with my family."

"Why not?" she asked.

"They're negative. Always criticizing to cover up for what they lack, but the only thing they really lack is ambition. My dad could have done anything he wanted—he's a bright guy—only, he got stuck in a potato-processing plant and never got out. My brothers are going to be just like him, same wasted potential. I went to college, which makes what they're doing seem smaller. They'll never forgive me for that."

"Then you don't go home much?"

"No. And you? Back to New York?"

She crinkled her nose. "I'm not a city person."

"What's your favorite thing in Tucson?"

"The desert," she said. "What's yours?"

"The Santa Catalinas."

Again those eyes lit, gold more than hazel. "Do you hike?" When he nodded, she said, "Me, too."

They talked nonstop until Rachel's clothes were clean, dry, and folded. When, arms loaded, they finally left the Laundromat, he knew three times as much about her as he knew about Celeste.

Taking that as a message of some sort, he broke up with Celeste the next day, called Rachel, and met her for pizza. They picked up right where they had left off at the Laundromat.

Jack was fascinated. He had never been a talker. He didn't like baring his thoughts and ideas, but there was something about Rachel that felt safe. She was gentle. She was interested. She was smart. As much of a loner as he was, she seemed just as startled as he to be opening up to a virtual stranger, but they gave each other permission. He trusted her instinctively. She seemed to trust him the same way right back.

As simply as that, they became inseparable. They ate together, studied together, sketched together. They went to movies. They hiked. She was his angel, and he was in love.

THE surgical waiting room was on the second floor at the end of a very long hall. Dropping into a seat there, Jack realized that he wasn't alone. A woman was watching him from the end of a nearby sofa. She looked wary, but she didn't blink when he stared.

"Are you Katherine?" he finally asked.

"Why the surprise?"

"Because you don't look like my wife's type," he said. Rachel was all natural—hair, face, nails. This woman was groomed, from dark lashes to painted nails to hair that was a dozen different shades of beige and moussed into fashionably long curls.

"It's ex-wife," Katherine said, "and looks can deceive. So you're Jack?"

He barely had time to nod when the door opened and a doctor emerged. His scrubs were wrinkled. Short, brownish gray hair stuck up in damp spikes.

Jack was on his feet and at the door before it had swung shut. "Jack McGill," he said, extending a hand. "How is she?"

The doctor met Jack's grip. "Steve Bauer. She's in the recovery room. The surgery went well. Her vital signs are good. She's breathing on her own, but she hasn't regained consciousness."

"Coma," Jack said. He needed the doctor to deny it.

To his dismay Steve Bauer nodded. "She doesn't respond to stimuli—light, pain, noise." He touched the left side of his face. "She was badly bruised here. There's external swelling. Her lack of response suggests that there's internal swelling, too."

Jack pushed his hands through his hair. "Will she die?"

"I hope not."

"How do we prevent it?"

"We don't. She does. When tissues are injured, they swell. The more they swell, the more oxygen they need to heal. Unfortunately, the brain is different from other organs because it's encased in the skull. When brain tissues swell, the skull prevents the expansion they need, and pressure builds. That causes a slowing of the blood flow, and since blood carries oxygen, a slowing of the blood flow means less oxygen to the brain. Less oxygen means slower healing. Her body determines how slow."

Jack needed to know more. "Worst-case scenario?"

"Pressure builds high enough to completely cut the flow of blood, and hence oxygen, to the brain, and the person dies. That's why we'll be monitoring your wife. If we see the pressure when it first starts to build, we stand a better chance of relieving it."

"What's the time frame here?"

"The next forty-eight hours will be telling."

"Will there be permanent damage?" Jack asked.

"I don't know."

"Is there anything you can do to get the swelling down?"

"She's on a drip to reduce it."

"What can we do to help?" Katherine asked from behind Jack.

"Not a whole lot," Bauer replied. "But ask nurses specializing in coma, and they'll say you should talk to her. They say comatose patients hear things and can sometimes repeat those things with frightening accuracy when they wake up."

"Do you believe that?" Jack asked.

Bauer lowered his voice a notch. "My colleagues pooh-pooh it. Me, I don't see that talking to her does any harm."

"What about the girls?" Jack asked. "We have two daughters. They're thirteen and fifteen. Should I keep them away?"

"No. Bring them. Their voices may help her focus."

"How does she look?" he asked. "Will they be frightened?"

"The side of her face is swollen and scraped. It's starting to turn colors. Her leg is casted and elevated, and we've taped her ribs to prevent damage if she becomes agitated, but that's it."

Jack tried to ingest it all. "When can I see her?"

"Once she's stable, we'll transfer her to intensive care." He glanced at the wall clock. It was four ten. "Give us an hour."

JACK and Katherine weren't alone in the cafeteria. A handful of medical personnel were scattered at tables, some eating an early breakfast, others nursing coffee. Voices were muted.

Jack had paid for one coffee, one tea, and one thickly coated sticky bun. The coffee was his. The rest was Katherine's. Her polished fingernails glittered as she pulled the warm bun apart.

Jack watched her for a distracted minute, then studied his coffee. He needed the caffeine. He was feeling tired all over. Rachel dead was unthinkable; Rachel brain-damaged came in a close second.

"I can't picture her here," he said. "She hates hospitals. When the girls were born, she was in and out. If she'd been a farmhand, she'd have given birth in the fields."

Katherine nodded. "I believe it. Rachel's one of the free spirits of the group."

The group. Jack had trouble seeing Rachel in any group. During the years of their marriage she had been a rabid nonjoiner. She had rejected it all, had rejected him, had packed up her bags and moved three hours south to Big Sur, apparently to do some of the very things she had refused to do under his roof.

Stung by that thought, he muttered a snide "Must be some group."

Katherine stopped chewing on her sticky bun for an instant, then swallowed. "What do you mean, 'some group'?"

"For you to be here—what—all night?"

She returned a piece of the bun to her plate and carefully wiped her hands on a napkin. "Rachel's my best friend. It didn't seem right that she should be in the operating room with no one waiting to learn if she lived or died."

"Well, I'm here now. You can leave."

She looked at him for a minute. With a small, quick headshake she gathered her cup and plate and picked herself up. "You're an insensitive jerk, Jack. No wonder she divorced you."

By the time she had relocated to the far side of the room, Jack knew she was only partly right. He was insensitive *and* ungrateful. Topping that off with rude, he could begin to see why the two women were friends. If he had used that tone on Rachel, she would have walked away from him, too.

Taking his coffee, he went after her. "You're right," he said very quietly. "I was being insensitive. You're her friend, and you've been here for hours, and I thank you for that. I'm feeling tired, helpless, and scared. I guess I took it out on you."

She stared at him, then turned back to her roll.

"May I sit?" he asked, suddenly wanting to badly. "Misery-loves-company kind of thing?"

It seemed an eternity of pending refusal before she gestured toward the table's free chair. "For the record," she said, "you're not the only one around here who's tired and helpless and scared."

He could see it then, threads of fatigue behind the neat façade. He was glad for Rachel, having a close friend like this. No doubt Katherine knew more about who Rachel was today than he did. He was curious. "Rachel never told me she was in a book group."

"She helped form the group. We organized five years ago."

"How often do you meet?"

"Once a month. There are seven of us. Local women. One is a travel agent, one sculpts, one owns a bakery, two golf. They were all here earlier. Needless to say, we weren't talking books."

No, Jack realized. They were talking about an accident that shouldn't have happened. Turning to that, he said, "Who hit her? Was the guy drunk? Did the cops get him, at least?"

"It wasn't a guy. It was a gal, and yes, she was drunk. The cops got her, all right. She's in the morgue."

Jack's breath caught. In the morgue. The fact of death changed things, made Rachel's situation feel more grave. He let out a long, low groan. His anger went with it.

THEY agreed that Jack should be the one to see Rachel first, and he was grateful. Entering a starkly sterile room whose railed bed held the shadow of the woman whose personality had always been brightly colored felt bad enough in private. Having his own uncertainties on public display would have made it worse.

Quietly he approached the bed. His mind registered one machine against the wall and multiple IV poles beside the bed, plus Rachel's casted, elevated leg. But his eyes found her face fast and held it. The doctor had warned him well. Even in the low light coming from behind her, he could see that around a raw scrape the left side was swollen and starting to purple. Her eyes were closed, her lips pale, her skin ashen, her freckles out of place.

He reached for the hand nearest him, the right one. Her fingers were limp, her skin cool. Carefully he folded his own around it. "Rachel?" he called softly. "It's me. Jack."

She slept on.

"Rachel? Can you hear me?" He swallowed. "Rachel?"

She didn't move. She showed no sign of having heard him.

Lifting her hand to his mouth, he kissed it, then held it to his chest. With the slightest shift it covered his heart. "Feel that?" The beat was heavy and fast. "It's been that way since I got the call. Samantha and Hope are scared, too."

She said nothing.

"Wake up, Rachel," he begged, suddenly frightened. He had lived without her for six years, but all that time he had known where she was. Now he didn't. Not really. "I need to know how you're feeling," he said in a slightly frantic singsong. "I need to know what to tell the girls. I need you to talk to me."

When she remained silent, he grew frustrated. Frustrated that he couldn't rouse her. Frustrated, too, that the offending party was dead and beyond punishment, but he couldn't say that to Rachel, not if there was a chance she could hear. She was a softhearted woman—hardheaded but softhearted. She would be crushed to learn that someone had died. If she needed to hear upbeat things, that wasn't the news to tell.

And what was? *You'll be pleased to know that my firm's falling apart.* But Rachel wasn't vindictive, so that wouldn't do it. Nor would, *I've lost the touch; nothing I design is right anymore.* Rachel had no taste for self-pity. Nor was she one for jealousy, which meant that he couldn't tell her about Jill. Besides, what would he say? Jill was nearly as softhearted as Rachel. She was nearly as pretty and nearly as bright. She was nowhere near as spirited or as talented or as unique. She would always pale by comparison.

What was the point of telling Rachel that? She had left him. They were divorced.

Feeling useless and suddenly more tired than he would have thought possible, he said, "Katherine is here. She wants to see you, too. I'm going to talk to the doctor. Then I'll go get the girls. We'll be back in a couple of hours, okay?" He watched Rachel's eyelids for even the slightest movement. Nothing.

Discouraged, he returned her hand to the stiff hospital sheet. Leaning down, he kissed her forehead. "I'll be back."

DAWN was breaking to the east of Monterey when he left the hospital. By the time he reached the Santa Lucia Range and Highway 1 began to wind, a morning fog had risen from the water and was bathing the pavement with a shifting mist.

Jack kept his headlights on and his eyes peeled, but neither was necessary. He couldn't have missed the accident site. Traffic was alternating along one lane while wreckers worked in the other. One mangled car had already been raised, but it wasn't Rachel's sturdy 4 × 4. A mauled section of guardrail lay nearby.

Feeling sick to his stomach, he pulled up behind the wreckers and climbed out. Rachel's car lay against boulders a distance below.

Its top and sides were dented and scraped. Water shot up from the rocks not ten feet away, but the car itself looked dry.

"Better move on, sir. If one stops, others do. Before we know it, we have a jam."

Jack pushed shaky hands into his pockets. "My wife was in that car. Looks like it went head over tail. It's a miracle she's alive."

"She's all right, then?" the trooper asked in a more giving tone. "We never know, once they leave the scene."

"She's alive."

The workers were struggling to hitch cables to Rachel's car.

"When'll those guys be done?" Jack asked. "I'll be bringing our daughters back this way, and I'd rather they not see this."

"Couple of hours, I guess. Can you wait that long?"

Jack hadn't planned to, but he could. If he found the girls asleep, it might actually work out fine. He could use the time to figure out the most sensitive way to break the news about their mother's coma.

Chapter Two

THIRTY minutes south of the accident scene Rachel's canyon rose from the sea. Its road was marked by an oak grove and a bank of mailboxes nine deep. Only one of the nine was painted, the fourth from the left. This year it was fire-engine red—Hope's choice. Last year it had been Rachel's butter yellow; the year before that, Samantha's purple.

Jack turned off the highway, downshifted, and began the climb. The road hugged the hillside and wound steadily upward, broken only by driveways that careened down and around into private homes. As he drove higher, oak yielded to sycamore and madrona, which mixed farther on up with cedar. Redwood had replaced that by the time he reached Rachel's.

Her home was a cabin of weathered cedar shingles. Pulling in on a rough gravel drive, he climbed from the car and stretched. He needed a shave, a shower, and some sleep.

The front door opened before he reached it. The man filling its frame was far older than Jack had expected—mid-sixties, he guessed from the pure white of his hair and beard.

"The girls are asleep," Duncan Bligh said in the same hard voice he had used on the phone. "How is she?"

"Comatose," Jack replied. "Her condition isn't critical. Her body is working okay. The bang on the head is the problem."

"Prognosis?"

Jack shrugged and hitched his chin toward the inside of the cabin. "They calmed down, I take it?"

"No." Duncan pushed beefy arms into a flannel vest. "They just wore themselves out." He strode past Jack. "I got work to do."

Jack raised a hand in thanks and good-bye, but Duncan had already rounded the house and was striding up the forested hillside. "Nice meeting you, too, pal," he muttered. Going inside, he quietly shut the door and leaned against it to get his bearings. He could count on one hand the number of times he had been to the cabin, and then, only to the door.

From there he'd had glimpses of color. Now the glimpse became a blur of natural wood, furniture that was green and lilac, purple planters, wild colors framed on the wall. The living room opened into a kitchen, but the back wall of both rooms was a window on the forest. Pale shafts of sun broke through the redwoods.

Mounting several steps to the left of the living room, he went down a hall and peered into the first room. Between the guy posters on the wall and a general sense of chaos, it had Samantha's name written all over it. The bed was mussed but empty.

Up several more steps and on down the hall, another door was ajar. This room had watercolors on the wall and a softer feel entirely. Both girls were asleep in Hope's bed. Hope was in a ball; Samantha was sprawled. In a gully between them was a puff of orange fur that had to be the cat.

When none of the three showed sign of waking, Jack returned to the living room and called the hospital. Speaking with the ICU nurse, he learned that Rachel's condition hadn't changed.

Next he called his business partner at home. In response to a breathless greeting, he said, "Working out?"

"Treadmill," David Sung gasped.

"Sorry to interrupt," Jack said, "but I have a problem. Rachel was in a car crash last night. I'm down here with the girls."

"Down where? In Big Sur?" The beat on the treadmill slowed. "We have a big meeting here in two hours. What kinda car crash?"

"A bad one." Jack kept his voice low. "She's in a coma."

"A coma," David repeated. "Is she on life support?"

"No. But I can't get to that meeting."

"We can't cancel. We've already rescheduled twice." There was a pause. "You're not ready for the presentation, are you?"

"Oh, I'm ready," Jack said, "but they won't like what I have this time any more than they did last time."

He had been hired to design a luxury resort in Montana. The client wanted something with reflective surfaces that would disappear under that big open sky, but Jack had been to Montana. Glass and steel were all wrong. He wanted wood.

When his first design was rejected, he incorporated granite with the wood. When that was rejected also, he had tried fieldstone and torn it up, glass and torn it up, steel and torn it up. The best rendition was the very first.

Only, that was beside the point. "Look," he told David, "I need your backup. I can't be there. This is a family emergency."

"There's one hitch. You're divorced."

"Not from my kids."

"Okay. I get that, Jack, but these guys have been waiting, and there's many millions at stake. If I tell them you can't be there because you have to be with your kids, they won't buy it."

"Then you take it over."

"They want you. They want you, and you've lost your edge."

Jack was suddenly so weary that his bones ached. "I can't handle this now. Tell them whatever, but I can't be at that meeting. I'll call in when I know more." He hung up. Dealing with Rachel's accident was all he could handle just then.

But Rachel and the girls were all sleeping. Stretching out on the sofa with one arm over his eyes, he followed suit.

HOPE came awake as she always did, slowly growing aware, listening and thinking before she moved a muscle. She listened to the soft sound of Guinevere's purring close behind her neck. She began to think, and her eyes flew open.

Swinging her head around, cheek into cat fur, she saw her sister sleeping beside her, and it was suddenly real—what had happened last night. Moving the mattress as little as possible, she sat up and carefully drew the cat into her arms. Silently she pushed her feet into her cowboy boots and tiptoed from the room.

The sight of her father in the living room brought instant relief. She had wanted him there so badly. Samantha had said that he wouldn't come—that he hadn't been there when they needed him for ages. But Hope had sensed he would come. She did that sometimes—sensed things. She had felt an unease when her mother left. She had thought it was about Guinevere. The vet had warned that the end would be silent and swift, and Hope was prepared. She had been the one to insist that Guinevere die at home, with her. But she wanted her mother to be there when it happened.

Lowering herself to the rug not far from her father, Hope folded her legs and gently settled Guinevere into her T-shirted lap.

Her father was sleeping. That said something. If Rachel was dead, he would have woken them up, wouldn't he have?

She was debating waking him, when his whole body suddenly jerked awake. "You should have woken me," he said.

"I figured that if you could sleep, Mom's okay."

"She's okay. She just needs to do a lot of mending."

"Did you talk with her?" Hope asked.

"No. She was sleeping. But I think she knew I was there."

"She isn't dead?"

"She isn't dead."

"You're sure?" Hope was thirteen. If her mother was dead, she wanted to know. She could handle the truth.

"No, Hope, she isn't dead. I'd never lie to you about that."

She nodded, breathing again. "When can we go?"

"Later this morning." He looked at the cat. "So this is the thing that showed up at the front door one day all bitten and bruised?"

Hope fingered the tabby's ear. "The bites healed."

"Gwendolyn, is it?"

"Guinevere." Hope lowered her head and began to smooth the cat's ruff when Samantha's voice came from the door.

"When did you get here?" she asked Jack.

He looked up and, for a minute, muddled by fatigue and nerves, thought he saw Rachel. It was partly the hair—blond but no longer as fine as Hope's, now as wavy and textured as Rachel's when they had first met. It was partly the figure, more defined even in the six weeks since he had seen her last. But it was the voice that clinched it, the echo of caution, even hurt, that he had heard in Rachel on their last married night together—and suddenly he was back in their bedroom that night, sorting through the closet for ties to pack for his business trip while Rachel spoke from the door.

He could see her clear as day. She had just left the studio they shared on the top floor of their pink Mediterranean-style home in the marina and was wearing an old pair of slim jeans and one of his shirts. Her face was pale and held the kind of disappointment that put him on the defensive in a flash.

"I thought you weren't going," she said.

"So did I, but I had to change plans." He pushed ties around on the rack, looking for ones to go with the suits he had laid out.

"I was hoping you'd be here for a while."

He didn't turn, didn't want to see her pallor. "So was I."

"Couldn't you just say no?"

"That's not the way it works," he answered sharply. "I've been hired to design a convention center. A big one. The basic design may be done, but that's the easy part. The hard part is fleshing it

out for function and fit, and to do that, I have to feel the city more."
He tossed down a tie and turned to her, pleading. "Think of your
own work. Your skill sets you apart from other artists. But so do the
choices you make on depth, attitude, medium, and you can't make
those choices without spending time in the field. Well, neither can I."

She kept her voice low, but she didn't back down. "I limit my
time in the field to one week twice a year. You're gone twice a
month—three times if you go to Providence tomorrow."

"This is my work, Rachel."

She looked close to tears. "That leaves me alone here."

Only in a manner of speaking, he knew. "You have the girls. You
could have friends if you wanted to do things besides paint. You
could be out every night if you wanted."

"But I don't. I hate dressing up; I hate small talk; I hate standing
around on spiky heels munching on pretty little caviar snacks."

"Not even for a good cause?" Charity fund-raisers were an inte-
gral part of social life in the Bay Area, particularly for someone like
Jack. He needed to see and be seen.

Sadly she said, "I can't paint here."

And painting was her world. "Every artist gets blocks," he said.

"It's more than that." Those folded arms hugged her middle.
"I'm dried up, creatively dead. I can't see color here. I can't feel
subjects the way I used to. I'm not happy here. I don't feel complete. You and I are apart more than we're together."

He tossed more ties onto the bed.

"Look at those," Rachel cried. "Look at those. They're so conservative. We were going to be different. We were going to do our
own thing, not get caught up in the rat race." She bowed her head.
Her voice low, she said, "I won't be here when you get back."

He sighed. "Come on, Rachel. Try to understand."

"You try to understand," she cried. "If I have to be alone, there
are other places I'd rather be. I'm moving to Big Sur." Softly she
said, "Come with me."

She knew he couldn't move to Big Sur. Big Sur was three hours
from San Francisco. "Are you serious?" he said.

"Very. I've done ten years here for you. Now it's your turn to live somewhere else for me. I need you to come with me."

"Dad!" Samantha's shout brought him back to the present. "How is she?"

He ran a hand over his face and took a steadying breath before telling her about the leg, the ribs. Then he reached out and touched Hope's hair, wanting desperately to ease the blow. "The thing is, her head took a bad hit. She's still unconscious."

Hope's eyes flew to his. "Sleeping?" she asked.

"In a manner. Only, nothing wakes her. It's called a coma."

"Coma," Samantha cried.

"No," Jack hurried to say, "it's not as bad as it sounds. Coma is what the brain does when it needs to focus all its energy on healing. Once enough of the healing's done, the person wakes up."

"Not always," Samantha challenged. "Sometimes people are comatose for years."

"Your mother will wake up," Jack insisted.

"How do you know?"

He didn't, but the alternative was unthinkable. "The doctor had no reason to think she won't. Listen," he began, looking down to include Hope, who was bent over her cat, "we have to be optimistic. We have to go in there and tell your mom that she's going to get better. If we tell her enough, she will."

Samantha made a sound. He looked up in time to see her roll her eyes, but those eyes were tear-lidded when they met his.

"Do you have a better suggestion?" he asked.

Mutely she shook her head.

"Okay. Then this is what I think we should do. I think we should have breakfast and drive up to Monterey."

Hope hugged the cat to her chest. "Maybe I should stay here."

"Don't you want to see your mom?"

Hope raised a tear-streaked face. "What if Guinevere dies while I'm gone?"

"She won't," Samantha said. "The vet said she had time."

"Not much."

"Hope, she's not dying today."

"Am I missing something here?" Jack asked.

"Guinevere has a tumor," Samantha explained. "The vet wanted to put her to sleep, but Hope wouldn't let him."

So the cat was terminally ill. Jack was wondering what else could go wrong, when Hope looked up through her tears and said, "She's not in pain. If she was, I'd let the vet do it. But I love Guinevere, and she knows it. I want her to keep knowing it a little longer. What's wrong with that?"

"Nothing," Jack said.

Samantha disagreed. "Priorities," she told her sister. "Mom's always talking about them. Guinevere isn't dying today. If the accident hadn't happened, you'd have left her home and gone to school. So if you leave her home now, she won't know whether you're going to school or to visit Mom. But Mom will."

Jack was thinking that she had put it well and that maybe there was hope for his elder daughter yet, when she turned to him in distaste and said, "You're gonna shave and stuff before we go, aren't you, Dad? You look gross."

"Thank you," he said. Patting Hope's shoulder, he pushed up from the sofa and, needing fortification after—what?—an hour of sleep, went to put on a pot of coffee.

HAD Jack known of any other road to take back to Monterey, he would have, but there wasn't one. Samantha sat in the passenger's seat, hair wet from the shower, eyes riveted to the road. Hope was stuffed in what passed for the BMW's back seat, her cowboy boots planted on either side of the hump.

Jack slowed the car to take the first of a series of turns.

"Look!" Samantha pointed. "That's where it happened. See where the guardrail's gone? Slow down. I want to see."

Jack kept driving. "There's nothing to see. The car's been towed."

Both girls were looking out the back window. "Katherine said she was hit," Samantha said. "What happened to the other driver?"

"I don't know," Jack lied.

Samantha flopped forward again. "You do, but you're not saying. I can tell by your voice. Mom would want us to know."

"Right now your mother would want you to say good things or nothing at all."

"That's what you'd say, not what she'd say. She'd want us to say what we think, and I think this accident was more serious than you're saying, which means we're all in big trouble. What if Mom doesn't wake up? I'm not going to live in San Francisco."

"Daddy?" came a frightened cry from behind.

Jack found Hope's face in the rearview mirror. "She's not dying, Hope. She'll be okay. She was in an accident barely twelve hours ago. For all we know, by the time we get to the hospital, your mother will be awake and asking for breakfast."

RACHEL wasn't asking for anything. She was as unresponsive when they arrived as she had been when Jack had seen her earlier.

"She's sleeping," Hope whispered, and for a minute he thought she might be right. Aside from the bruise, Rachel looked almost normal.

He approached the bed, hoping, hoping. "Rachel?"

"Don't bother her," Hope cried in a fearful tone.

Backing up, Jack stood at the door with the girls while they adjusted to the scene. He said a quiet "See? No respirators, no life supports. She broke her leg. There's the cast. And the bruises on her face are where she banged it against the car. The IV poles have medicine and food. The TV screen behind her registers things like heart, pulse, and oxygen."

He felt Hope nod against his arm. "Want to go let her know you're here?" The nod became a quick headshake. "Samantha?"

Without defenses Samantha looked as young and frightened as Hope. "What do we say?"

"Whatever you want."

"Are *you* going to talk to her?"

He knew a challenge when he heard it. Leaving them again, he approached the bed. Taking Rachel's hand, he leaned over and kissed her forehead. "Hi, angel. How're you doing? See, I said I'd be back, and here I am. Got the girls with me. They're over by the door. They're feeling a little intimidated by the machines and all."

"I am not intimidated," Samantha said, and was suddenly beside him. "Hi, Mom. It's me. Sam." From the corner of her mouth she whispered, "This is dumb. She can't hear."

"Do you know that for sure?"

"No."

"Then don't assume it." Jack looked around for Hope, who was still at the door. When he invited her over with a hitch of his head, she shrank back.

"What are they doing to wake her up?" Samantha asked.

"See that drip?" He pointed to one of the bags. "That stuff keeps the swelling in her head down so that blood and oxygen can flow and heal the injured tissues."

"Why can't they just give her a shot to wake her up?"

"It doesn't work that way."

"Did you ask?"

"No," Jack said, giving Samantha a stare. He preferred his daughter when she was too frightened to be a smart mouth. He didn't know whether it was her age or whether he just brought out the worst in her.

"Tell you what," he said. "I'm going to leave you here to talk with your mother. Don't be bashful. Tell her how awful I am. Tell her that she'd better wake up because you're *not* moving to the city. Tell her that I don't know anything. Get it all off your chest. I have some calls to make." He turned to find that Katherine Evans had arrived and was standing with an arm around Hope. "Hey, Katherine. I'll be down the hall." As he passed, he told Hope, "Right down the hall. I won't be long."

He felt like a deserter, but what was the point of staying?

"Is Dr. Bauer around?" he asked at the nurses station.

"Tuesday mornings he teaches in the city," said the nurse.

"Are you Mr. McGill?" asked a woman doing paperwork nearby.

She wore a silk blouse under her lab coat and large pearl earrings. Power pearls. Jack suspected they were supposed to make her look older than the barely thirty he guessed she was.

"Yes, I'm Jack McGill."

She extended a hand and said, "I'm Kara. Dr. Kara Bates. I'm in neurology, second under Dr. Bauer. He checked your wife before he left. She's holding her own."

"But not awake yet. Isn't there anything else we can do?"

"Not yet," Kara said.

Turning, Jack strode down the hall to the phone.

HE MADE two calls, both to San Francisco.

"Sung and McGill," said Christina Cianni. She had been with Jack since the firm's inception, back then as receptionist and over-all gofer. Now she manned the front phone only when the regular receptionist was on break. She divided the rest of her time between keeping the books and doing PR. The most precious of her traits was her undying loyalty to Jack.

"Hi," he said in relief when she answered.

"Jack, I'm so sorry to hear about Rachel. How is she?"

"Comatose. Her injuries wouldn't be all that serious if it weren't for the one to the head."

"I'm so so sorry. How are the girls?"

"Scared."

"Do you think she'd be better off at a hospital up here?"

"Not yet. This team seems on top of things. But I want a specialist to tell me for sure. Can you get me the name of the best neurologist in the city?"

"Done," she said with blessed confidence.

"What's happening there?"

There was a pause, then, "You don't want to know."

"We lost Montana?"

"Worse. We didn't. They rescheduled for next Tuesday."

He was tired enough to laugh. Only Tina understood him enough to put it that way. She had seen him through years of increasing success, when the adrenaline was rushing and wild dreams were coming true. But something had happened to the joy. Lately it was harder to come by. Lately there was less actual designing, less creative satisfaction, and more business meetings.

"I should be flattered," he said. "What about Napa?" He had designed a restaurant there and was scheduled to meet with the owner, an electrician, a plumber, and a kitchen consultant.

"Next Wednesday. You're supposed to be in Austin on Friday." After the space of a breath she asked, "Think you'll make it?"

Jack closed his eyes and massaged tired lids. "Who knows. She could wake up later today. Or tomorrow. Or next week."

"Are you staying down there with the girls?"

"Yeah. For a night or two, until we know what's going on." He pushed a hand through his hair. "Austin on Friday may be tight, but leave it for now. Clear my appointment book for tomorrow."

"David won't be happy."

"No, I don't suppose he will." But Jack couldn't worry about David. There were now more urgent players in his life.

The second call he made was to one of those.

"Jack!" It came through with the delighted smile in her voice that he thrived on. "It's early," she said. "Is your meeting done?"

"Never took place. I have a problem, Jill. Rachel's been in a car accident. She's in intensive care. I'm here with the girls."

There was a pause, then, minus the smile, "In Big Sur?"

"In Monterey. She's in a coma." He passed on the basics of the case. "The girls are terrified. I can't leave them alone right now."

Another pause. Finally Jill said, "You won't make it to the ball." Her disappointment was as obvious as her delight had been.

"Not unless Rachel wakes up within the next few hours. I'm sorry, Jill. I really am. I know what you've put into tonight, but you're not the only one I'm canceling out on. It's a stinking, lousy waiting game."

"Isn't there someone who can stay with the girls tonight?"

"The girls are my responsibility. I can't leave them, Jill. Not today. The situation is too shaky. I can't just drive off."

"But I wanted you there. I'm the cochair." It wasn't whiny, mere statement of fact.

"I know, Jill. If I could be in two places at once, I would."

"She isn't your wife anymore."

This, too, was softly spoken, another simple statement of fact. What Jack heard was something entirely different. What he heard was, I've dated you for two years, Jack. Haven't I finally come to mean more to you than your ex-wife?

David had said something similar. Jack answered her now in kind. "She may be my ex-wife, but there's nothing ex about my daughters. How can I leave them alone here so that I can go back to the city to party?" He caught sight of Katherine heading his way. "Hey, I gotta go. I'm really sorry, Jill. I'll call you later, okay?" He hung up the phone and drew himself up. Katherine's expression was all business.

"Are the girls still with Rachel?" he asked.

"They are. Are you heading back to the city?"

"No. I just canceled everything so that I can be here."

She looked startled by that.

Jack pushed off from the phone booth. When Katherine fell into step beside him, he said, "You didn't think I'd stay?"

"I didn't know what to think. All I know about you is what I've heard from Rachel. And it sounded like you were better at leaving than staying put. She felt abandoned."

He stopped. Katherine did the same. "Abandoned?" he echoed. "I didn't walk away from the marriage. Rachel did."

Katherine was silent for a minute. When she spoke, there was challenge in her eyes. "The way Rachel sees it, you'd already left. Her moving on was just in response. San Francisco stifled her. She couldn't paint there. She was frustrated and bored."

"If she was bored, it was her own fault. There were dozens of things she could have done and didn't."

Katherine gave a small shrug. "The only person she wanted to do things with in the city was you, but you weren't around."

"No, I wasn't. I was working my tail off to build a successful practice so that I could keep us housed and fed and, P.S., let her paint without worrying about earning money. She wouldn't take money from her parents. I wanted to give her everything I thought she deserved."

"She knew that," Katherine conceded. "But to hear her tell, you were on the road more often than not."

Jack turned away, swearing under his breath, then turned back in the very next beat. "Rachel told you all that? Who are you, to be coming between my wife and me?"

"It's ex-wife," Katherine said, "and you asked. Who I am is Rachel's friend. I love her and the girls. They're like family. I don't want them hurt."

"And I do?" This time when he set off, he kept going.

IF SIMPLY to spite Katherine Evans, Jack stuck to his daughters like glue. He stayed with them at Rachel's bedside for a time, took them to breakfast, returned with them to sit with Rachel again, took them to lunch. In between he spoke with a neurologist from the city, who agreed to see Rachel the next day.

Of the medical personnel who came and went from Rachel's room, the nurse heading the case was the most encouraging. Her name was Cindy Winston. She wore white leggings, a long blouse to hide plumpness, and thick glasses, but there was a quietness to her, an endearing shyness. She spoke softly and seemed kind as could be. The girls hung on her every word.

"Keep talking to your mom," she told them. "Tell her what you've been doing." She looked at Rachel. "Tell her jokes. Tell her you're sad. Or angry. You can laugh or cry. Those are all normal things. She'll understand them."

"What if we run out of things to say?" Samantha asked.

"Then touch her. That's important."

JACK wanted to know when Rachel was going to wake up, but no one was saying.

He drank so much coffee to stay awake that by late afternoon he was starting to shake. When Katherine arrived with several friends, he barely heard the introductions. As soon as they were done, he ushered the girls to the car.

They had just hit the road when, in a big, bold voice, Samantha said, "So who's taking care of us?"

"Me. If there's no change by tomorrow, I'll drive up for clothes while you guys are in school."

Sam was horrified. "We can't go to school."

"You can't not go. It's the end of the year. Aren't exams coming up?"

"Yes, but—"

"I'll pick you up at school." Since the school in Big Sur went only to sixth grade, the girls were bused to Carmel. From Carmel to the hospital in Monterey was a ten-minute drive. "You can spend the rest of the day at the hospital."

"Like I can concentrate on classes?"

"I really think you should try. Look, your mom's apt to wake up anytime now. This won't go on forever."

"How do you know?" came Hope's small voice from behind.

"Because your mother is young and healthy. She'll heal."

"You don't know it for sure," Samantha argued.

"No. But would you rather assume she's going to die?"

"No. I just don't know what's happening. There's a mess of things we're supposed to be doing. Doctor and dentist—"

"My picnic—"

"My prom, for which I have no dress. Mom was taking me shopping this week, but if she's in the hospital, who'll do it?"

"Me," Jack said.

Samantha sagged into the seat and looked out the window. "Yeah, right. You don't have time. You never have time."

"I'll make time," was all he could say.

The rest of the ride was accomplished in silence. The instant they pulled up at the cabin, Hope said something about seeing Guinevere and raced from the car. Samantha followed, squawking about urgent phone calls. Jack went in to see about dinner.

*S*AMANTHA woke up with a crick in her neck. It wasn't until she clamped the phone to her ear with a shoulder and winced that she knew its cause. Repetitive tongue disorder, her mother called it. But what could she do? She'd had to call Shelly about math, John about science, Amanda about Spanish, and by the time that was done, Brendan was calling to talk, and then there was Lydia. What time had they hung up? Twelve thirty? One?

"ICU, please," she told the hospital switchboard operator. When a nurse came on, Samantha identified herself. "How's my mom?"

"She's doing just fine."

Samantha's hopes soared. "She woke up?"

"No, not yet."

So what is "just fine" supposed to mean? Samantha thought. "Thank you," she said with more disappointment than grace, and hung up the phone.

THE first thing Jack did when he woke up was grab the phone. It was only a minute before he learned with relief that Rachel was still alive, with fear that she was still comatose, and with unexpected pride that Samantha had had the wherewithal to call the hospital on her own.

Pushing the covers aside, he went to the window and peered out. Morning fog filled the canyon, but it was different from the fog that filled his courtyard in the city. This one was softer, gentler.

"Daddy?" He looked over his shoulder at the door. Hope's face was all that showed through a narrow wedge of space. "I don't feel good, Daddy. My stomach hurts."

Jack went to the door and touched her cheek. "You don't feel feverish. Think it was something you ate?"

"I don't know. But if I go to school and start feeling sick, they'll have to call you, and if you're in the city, you can't come, so maybe I should just stay in bed."

She didn't look sick. "Don't you want to see your mother?"

"If I sleep this morning, I can go when Sam goes, can't I?"

It had to be the cat. "Where's Guinevere?"

Bingo. He saw instant worry. "In bed. I don't think she feels good, either. If I stay here with her, the two of us will feel better."

Jack put an arm around her shoulders. They felt small and frail under a T-shirt that reached her knees. Bare bits of skinny leg showed between where the T-shirt ended and her cowboy boots began. "Would your mom let you stay home from school?"

"No. But she'd be here to check on Guinevere."

And he wouldn't. It went without saying. He was dropping the girls at school in Carmel, heading north to Monterey and the hospital, driving farther north to San Francisco, back down to get the girls at school, up to the hospital again.

"I can't leave Guinevere alone, Daddy," Hope begged. "Not all day. Not when she's so sick."

He really didn't want Hope missing school. There had to be another way. "What about Duncan? Think he'd check on her?"

Hope brightened marginally. "I could ask."

DUNCAN had an offer that Hope liked even better, though Jack had no idea why. He didn't understand why Guinevere would be better off spending the day at Duncan's than at her own house.

"He has faith," was all Hope said when Jack asked, and he didn't push. He had been hearing about Duncan's faith for years.

So Duncan was religious. Fine. What mattered more to Jack was that in the rush to get dressed and drive the cat three minutes up the road, Hope forgot about her stomachache.

Jack waited by the car while she got Guinevere settled. When Duncan came out, Jack said, "Thanks. This means a lot to her."

"How's her mother?"

"The same. I'm heading there now."

"Better call Ben."

"Who's Ben?" Jack asked, but before Duncan could answer, Hope had taken the big man's hand and was looking up at him with reverence.

"I'll come for her later," Hope was saying.

Duncan nodded and gave her hand a squeeze.

WHEN Jack arrived at the hospital, Rachel was freshly bathed, lying on crisp white sheets. He had brought a tube of cream from her bathroom and began rubbing it onto those stretches of her skin that were bare. He touched lotion to her cheeks, working carefully around the bruise. "I'll bet you have a headache," he said.

She didn't respond. Her hand lay limp, her arm dead weight. He studied her eyes for a sign of movement behind the lids. When there was none, he left the room in a fit of frustration.

He found Kara Bates in the hall. The pearl earrings had been replaced by onyx squares, powerful in their own right.

"Shouldn't Rachel be reacting to something by now?" he demanded. "It's been a day and a half."

"These things take time, Mr. McGill," the doctor said. "Your wife isn't getting worse."

"I have a neurologist coming from the city sometime today."

Kara reached behind the desk and produced a business card. "He was already here. He suggests that you call him midafternoon. He doesn't feel that anything else should be done right now."

Jack ran a hand through his hair. Another hope thwarted. "If you were to make a guess as to when she'll wake up—"

"I can't do that. I'd like to give you hope, but I just don't know. Head injuries are like that. The best I can do is to say that Rachel is a good candidate for recovery."

That was only part of what Jack wanted to hear.

HE SHOULD have felt better, driving north toward San Francisco. It was where his home was, where his business was, where Jill was. But his middle grew tighter the closer he got.

He stopped at his house first, hoping to get his bearings there, but the place felt cold. He tossed a duffel onto the bed and quickly filled it with clothes. In the studio he stuffed a briefcase with papers, then started out the door, stopped short, and returned. Standing in the front hall, he called Jill.

"How'd it go?" he asked as soon as she said hello.

"Jack, where are you?"

"My place, but not for long. Rachel is still comatose. How was last night?"

"It was fine. Successful."

"I knew it would be. You do things like that so well." She was a warm, generous hostess, whether entertaining at home, at a restaurant, or in a ballroom. "How much did you raise?"

"It looks like we topped a quarter of a million."

"That's great, Jill. Good for you. You must be thrilled."

"I missed you," she said. "When will you be back again?"

She had asked that question often during the past two years. But she didn't nag, and she wasn't nagging now, though the question sounded different this time. He could have sworn he sensed fear.

Usually he skirted the issue by blaming his work. This time he simply said, "I'll be back as soon as I can. Pray for Rachel."

Knowing that she would probably do just that, he drove to the office, but the minute he pulled into his space, he had the urge to flee. But this was his firm. As a name partner, he had a responsibility to the twenty-odd people he and David employed.

Taking the stairs two at a time, he headed straight for Tina Cianni's office. She was on the phone, but she hung up within seconds. "How is Rachel?"

"Alive but still comatose."

Tina released a breath. "How are the girls?"

"Hanging in there. What's doing?"

She gave him a warning look. "You don't want to know."

Again? "Is it worse than a coma?"

"David would say it is," she said dryly. "Michael Flynn was supposed to have revised plans done for Buffalo last night. But he ran out of here at three yesterday to take his two-year-old to the doctor. He tripped and fell down a flight of stairs and thinks he broke his ankle. He's going for X rays."

Jack should have been irate, but he felt numb. "What else?"

"Boca. Back to the drawing board again."

The project in Boca was a combined office building and shopping mall. Jack had already revised the design three times to satisfy the quirks of one vocal member of one crucial committee. He had already compromised to the limit. Was the money worth it?

"Shall I cancel you out for tomorrow?" Tina asked.

"Yeah." He couldn't focus on Buffalo, couldn't focus on Boca. But he was a leader of the firm, and morale was low.

So he walked down the hall and stopped at one cubicle after another, making his presence felt in the barest way—a question here, a suggestion there. He was responsible for three quarters of the design work the firm did. It was good work, increasingly important work. *Metropolitan Home* had photographed his museum in Omaha; *Architectural Digest* was doing a piece on his library in Memphis. Still, Jack felt detached, angry to be in the office. Maybe he was burning out. There had to be an explanation for the revulsion he felt.

Then again, the revulsion could be from fatigue. Or worry. Any normal person would feel shell-shocked given the recent turn of events. Pocketing a pile of telephone messages, he returned to the front desk and told Tina to cancel Austin.

Then he headed south to Monterey.

FOR a petite woman, Rachel had incredibly elegant arms and legs. Jack was smoothing lotion along her forearm when Katherine Evans arrived.

"Hi," he said, determined to be kind. "How's it going?"

"It'd be better if Rachel woke up. She looks the same. Is there any change medically?"

"None. I was hoping she'd be awake by now."

Katherine took a hairbrush from the bed stand. She began brushing Rachel's hair. "Are the girls in school?"

"Yup. I'll pick them up in an hour. They'll see her then." He eyed the monitor. "This is hard for them."

Katherine gently raised Rachel's head and began brushing the hair in back. "I have a hunch this is only part of it."

He paused. "What do you mean?"

"I have a hunch that your being here raises other issues."

"The divorce? I don't think so. They're worried about their mother. They're worried about who's cooking dinner tonight. They're not thinking about the divorce. The divorce is old news."

"They're thinking about it," Katherine insisted. "I'd wager Samantha's obsessed with it. She's resenting authority anyway, and now you're taking over after being out of her daily life for so long. She's probably thinking you don't have the right to tell her what to do."

"Did she say that?"

"No. But I'd guess she's wondering why you're here." Katherine raised her brows. "I've wondered it myself."

Jack stared at her for an astounded minute. "My wife is in a coma. Where else would I be?"

"Rachel's your ex-wife. You keep forgetting that."

"We share more than a decade together and two children. It's only natural that I'm here. Don't make more of it than it is."

"It *is* more if you still love her."

He did not. "We've been divorced for six years. I barely know who she is now. How can I love a woman I don't know?"

She stopped her brushing. "Know what I think? I think you're here out of guilt, to make up for all you didn't do back then."

"Guilt? What are you? A shrink?"

"Close." She set the brush on the bed stand. "I'm a hairdresser."

"You're kidding. You don't look like a hairdresser."

She laughed. "Like I didn't look like a friend of Rachel's?"

"A hairdresser." He couldn't believe it. "The last time my wife stepped foot in a hair salon was on the day of our wedding. She swore she'd never do it again."

Katherine gave him a tiny shrug. "Apparently she saw the error of her ways."

JACK MCGILL REMINDED Katherine of her ex-husband. Roy had the same arrogance, the same myopia. To this day he thought the divorce was about her being unable to fill his needs.

Unable to fill his needs? Not quite. Unwilling was more like it. He had refused to acknowledge her needs, which had been just fine for years. She had a career. She had friends. She found loyalty, sensitivity, intellectual stimulation elsewhere. But the one time she had needed him, he hadn't been there for her. After that, being his personal maid had grown old fast.

Arms folded, eyes down, she tried to put the thought of Roy aside as she took the elevator to the coffee shop, but the setting didn't help. She didn't like hospitals in general, and this one in particular. But she did know her way around. Heading straight for the tea bags, she grabbed an Earl Grey, filled a Styrofoam cup with hot water, paid, and took a seat at one of the small tables.

She was dunking the tea bag when a voice said, "Excuse me. Haven't we met before?"

She looked up. The man regarding her wore a blazer, shirt and tie, and jeans. His hair was more pepper than salt, thick, and well cut. Katherine noticed things like that. It went with her work. She also noticed that he was good-looking. But then, so was she. And he'd just handed her the oldest line in the book.

"I think it was yesterday morning. Early, early morning." He extended a hand. "Steve Bauer."

Ah. Rachel's neurologist. She offered her hand. "Katherine Evans. I'm Rachel's friend. Have you seen her today?"

"Early." He slid into a seat. "Have you?"

"Yes. Isn't there anything more that can be done?"

"Not yet. The fact is, she's not getting worse. That's good." He sat back in the chair. "Do you live nearby?"

"Not terribly," she said, realizing where *his* mind was.

"You look familiar." He seemed genuinely puzzled. "Maybe I'm wrong. Sometimes when you see a face that sticks in your mind, you start thinking you remember it from further back. You've never worked here?"

"No. I'm a hairdresser."

He looked intrigued. "Well, you have spectacular hair."

She shot a beseeching glance skyward. "I'm sitting here upset because my best friend is in a coma and there's nothing you or your staff can do to help her, and you're noticing my hair?"

He backed off. "It was an innocent comment."

"It was inappropriate."

"No. What would be inappropriate is if I discussed the medical details of your friend's case with you or, worse, made empty promises about her recovery. In lieu of that, I made an observation. You do have spectacular hair. Is it your own shop?"

It was, but she wasn't saying so. She didn't know why doctors felt they could ask all the questions. "Where do you live?" she asked, doubting he would answer.

But he did. "Pacific Grove."

Oh, my. Pacific Grove was posh.

"I bought a little house there seven years ago," he said. "It's right down the street from the water."

"Do you have family?"

"One ex-wife. Plus two sons and a daughter, all grown."

That surprised her. Despite the graying hair, she would have put him in his mid-forties. "How old are you?"

"Fifty-three. How old are you?"

Feeling suddenly off balance, she sighed and rose with her tea. "Old enough to know I'd better be getting back to Rachel. Bye."

THERE were ten teenagers waiting for Jack when he pulled up at the school. Hope opened the car door first and scrambled into the tiny back seat. "How's Mom?" she asked.

He tried to keep his answer light. "Pretty good. Still asleep."

Samantha slipped into the passenger's seat, pointing at the others crowding on the curb. "These are my friends—Joshua, Adam, Shelly, Heather, Brendan, Amanda, Seth, and Lydia. They want to know how Mom is. Did she wake up?"

He had raised a hand in general greeting. "Not yet."

"Is she getting better?" asked the girl leaning in closest to Samantha. He guessed it was Lydia, whom he knew only by name.

"The doctors say she's healing," he answered.

A boy's face materialized among the girls. "I'm Brendan. My mom says to tell you she's totally on top of plans for the prom, so you shouldn't worry about a thing. She talked with Samantha's mom on Monday, and everything's set."

Samantha slammed the door. "We have to go."

"What's set?" Jack asked.

"Prom plans. Let's leave. I want to see Mom."

He pulled away from the school. "What prom is this?"

"The one I need a dress for. I told you about it."

She might have, but he'd had a lot on his mind. "What prom? You're only fifteen."

From behind him came a pleading explanation, clearly meant to ward off a fight. "Ninth and tenth have a prom."

"When?"

"A week from Saturday," Samantha said. "I need to buy a dress this weekend. You said you'd take me."

"Daddy?" from the back seat. "What're we going to do about my picnic? Mommy was supposed to run it."

Jack felt like he was holding an armload of bricks, staggering with the addition of one, then another and another. He could handle buying a dress. That meant standing in a store, saying yes or no, and producing a credit card. Running a picnic was something else. He figured he could fill the car with two-liter bottles of soda and get them to a designated spot, maybe even buy a couple dozen subs. But run the whole thing? There had to be another parent who could do it.

"I'll call your teacher tonight. Do you have the number?"

"Mommy does."

"What about her show?" Samantha asked.

"What show?"

"Mom's supposed to have a show at P. Emmet's. It's a gallery here in Carmel. The opening is two weeks from Sunday. What if she isn't awake by then?"

"She'll be awake," he decided.

"But what if she isn't? Or what if she doesn't wake up until a week before? The paintings aren't done. She was kind of freaking out about that. I think you need to talk with Ben."

"Ben?"

"Ben Wolfe. He manages the gallery. He's the one who set up the show for Mom. They've been dating," she added—smugly, he thought. "Ben sells more of Mom's work than any of the other galleries do. He's giving her a solo show."

Jack whistled, doubly impressed.

"What if her paintings aren't done?" Samantha asked. "This is the only solo slot he has for months. She really wanted it."

"I'll talk with Ben," Jack said, and tucked the thought away, back behind a growing need for Rachel to wake up, and fast.

BEN Wolfe was at the hospital when Jack and the girls arrived. He had auburn hair and wire-rimmed glasses, an average-looking man with regard to height, weight, and presence—certainly not the offbeat personality Jack would have guessed Rachel would go for. And she had thought *Jack* was conservative? Ben Wolfe was the epitome of it, but it worked for him. Between his crisp white shirt, neatly tucked into tailored gray slacks, and the reputation of the gallery, Jack guessed he had to be capable enough.

The woman with him was something else. Everything about her screamed rebel, from the pink streaks in her hair to the half-dozen earrings she wore in one lobe. Jack had her pegged as the sculptress in Rachel's book group even before they were introduced.

Ben Wolfe. Charlene Avalon. Jack nodded his way through the introductions but quickly focused on Rachel. Her face was peaceful, pale, and still. He took her hand. Holding it made him feel better, as though he had every right in the world to be there.

To Hope, at his elbow, he said, "Want to tell Mom what you did in school today?"

"Hi, Mommy," Hope said in her timid little voice. "It's me, Hope. I'm still wearing my lucky boots."

"That is so dumb," Samantha said.

"It is not. They make me think about the concert Sunday night. I'm wearing them until she wakes up." To Rachel she said, "Guinevere is at Duncan's. I hope she's okay." She raised frightened eyes to Jack. "Charlie knows Duncan. She visits him a lot."

Charlene nodded. "Duncan has a shed filled with rusty old stuff," she said. "He lets me take what I want for my work." She smiled at Jack. "Ben and I were wondering what to do about the show. You do know there's one planned?"

"Of course," Jack said as though he had known about it all along. "The opening's in two weeks. I'm guessing she'll be awake long before then." He caught Ben Wolfe's eye. "Can we talk a minute?"

Drawing Samantha into his place beside Rachel, Jack went into the hall. When Ben joined him there, he asked, "Any chance of delaying the show?"

Ben shook his head. "I've called everyone else who's scheduled to show, and none of them can be ready this fast."

"How many of Rachel's pieces are ready?"

Ben nudged his glasses higher. "I'm not sure. She promised me eighteen. Maybe if I drive down and take a look at what she has, I'd get a better feel for where we stand."

Jack was surprised the man hadn't already done that. If Ben and Rachel were seriously dating, he would have spent time in her studio. Jack always had.

"No need for you to do that," Jack said now. Ben Wolfe was too tepid for Rachel. He would never challenge her spirit. He was too neat, too pale.

Feeling dominant, Jack said, "I'll take a look. Got a business card?" Minutes later he had one in his hand. "I'll let you know what I find."

WHAT Jack found were photographs. He came across them that evening—after cleaning up the remnants of pizza, calling Hope's teacher to beg for help with the picnic, spending two hours at his laptop grappling with design problems faxed to him from Boca—

when, too tired to face Rachel's studio, he settled for searching her drawers. Cindy Winston, the head nurse, had suggested that she might be more comfortable in a familiar nightgown.

Propriety wasn't an issue. Rachel's nightgowns were prim flannel affairs. He had to hand it to her, though. They were vivid. He had chosen a purple one and a chartreuse one, when, pushing aside a poppy red one, he found the three frames. They were facedown, covering the entire bottom of the drawer.

He turned over the largest first. It was in the kind of elaborate gold frame that only Rachel's mother would have bought. Inside was the formal picture taken at their wedding, of bride and groom standing dead-center, flanked by two sets of happy parents. Jack and Rachel had both hated this picture. They looked all done up and unlike themselves.

Rachel's parents were both dead now, but at the time, Victoria Keats had had her heart set on giving her only child the dream wedding she had never had, and Eunice McGill had gone right along.

Rachel and Jack's engagement picture was better, but what a fight they'd had over that. It was totally casual, totally them—and totally unlike what Rachel's mother had wanted for the newspapers, but they had held out. Jack touched it now, the simple wood frame onto which Rachel had shellacked bright foils and decorative paper. Seventeen years younger, their faces were vibrant, defiant, happy.

And the other picture? It was his favorite. Framed in a rustic stone frame, the photo was one that Rachel had snapped a year before the divorce. It showed the girls and him tumbling together in the tiny yard behind their Pacific Heights home, with Rachel behind the lens but so clearly involved in the scene that she might have been its subject. Three smiles, three laughing faces were looking straight at Rachel with varying amounts of daring and love.

Setting the little stone frame carefully back in the drawer, Jack followed it with the engagement picture, but when it came to putting the wedding picture in place, he couldn't help but think it contaminated the other two.

He buried it alone in the very bottom drawer.

Chapter Four

W HEN Jack arrived at the hospital the next morning, Rachel
was lying on her side with her back to the door. His heart
began to pound. Awake! He crept forward cautiously.

"Rachel?" he whispered, watching her eyelids for a flicker.

Kara Bates turned into the room. "We've started rotating her.
Two straight days on her back is enough. We've also put a pressure
mattress under her sheet. It adds a measure of mobility."

Jack swallowed down a throatful of emotion. Disappointment
was there, along with fear, because what the doctor was saying suggested that with Rachel still comatose after forty-eight hours, they
were looking further down the road.

"Is there any change at all?" he asked, studying the monitor.

"Not up there. I think her face looks better, though."

Jack agreed. "But if the swelling is going down out here, why
isn't it going down inside?"

"The swelling inside is encased, so the healing is slower," Kara
said, peering into the small overnight bag Jack had placed on the
bed. "What did you bring?"

"Nightgowns. Rachel likes color."

"I was starting to guess that," the doctor remarked, arching a
brow at the windowsill. It was crammed with flowers.

There were five arrangements—vases and baskets filled with
flowers whose names Jack didn't know but whose colors he did.
They were Rachel's colors: deep blues, vivid reds, rich greens, brilliant yellows. She liked basic and bright. Each arrangement had a
card. "We need you, Rachel. Heal fast," wrote Dinah and Jan.
There was a bouquet of hot-red flowers from Nellie, Tom, and Bev;
a tall blue arrangement from the Liebermans; and a vase of yellow
roses whose card read, "With love, Ben."

As Jack was thinking that he could do without Ben Wolfe and his love bouquet, Katherine swept into the room. Her eyes widened, and her mouth formed a hopeful O when she saw Rachel on her side. Jack shook his head.

She swore softly and came to the bed. "I was hoping . . ."

"So was I."

She leaned down and talked softly to Rachel, then straightened and looked at him. "I wasn't sure you'd still be here."

"Oh, I'm here," he said, but he wasn't in the mood for sparring. He was wondering about those flowers, wondering about the friends Rachel appeared to have made since she had left him. In San Francisco she had been a loner—independent, focused solely on her art, the kids, and him. "Who are Dinah and Jan?"

"Dinah Monroe and Jan O'Neal. They're in our book group. You met them yesterday."

He had met lots of people yesterday. One face blended into the next. "Who are Nellie, Tom, and Bev?"

"Bridge friends."

He had to have heard wrong. "Bridge? As in the game?"

"Cards. That's right."

He tried to picture it but couldn't. "That's a kicker. The last thing Rachel would have done in the city was play bridge. It stood for everything her mother used to do."

Katherine smiled. "You're right. Rachel hated what bridge stood for in her mother's life, but she had been taught to play, and soon after she moved down here, she met Bev, a bridge player who does the most incredible stuff with acrylics on rattlesnake skin, and somehow playing with her didn't sound so bad."

"And the Liebermans?"

Katherine smiled with genuine warmth. "Faye and Bill. Faye's in our book group. She's one of the golfers. Jan is the other, and a young mother to boot. She'll be by later."

"And you and Rachel? How did you meet?"

"In the gynecologist's waiting room," Katherine said. With a glance at her watch and a look of concern she leaned over Rachel's shoulder. "I have a nine o'clock, so I can't stay long. But I've cleared an hour midafternoon to come by and do your hair." She asked Jack, "Shall I get the girls at school and bring them here?"

Jack was feeling possessive. "I'll do it. They are my responsibility."

"Good morning," Steve Bauer said, crossing the threshold.

Katherine straightened and pushed off. "Bye," she said with an open-handed wave to no one in particular.

The doctor watched her exit. "Don't leave on my account."

But she was already out the door before Jack could wonder why the sudden rush.

JACK needed to work. His laptop was full of messages each time he booted it up. He had driven north from Big Sur that morning intending to drop the girls at school in Carmel, visit Rachel in Monterey, and continue up to San Francisco. But now that he was with Rachel, the sense of urgency had left him.

Bracing his elbows on the bedrail, he studied her face. Even with the fading purple on the left side, he thought it beautiful. Always had.

"What happened to us, Rachel? I never did understand. Never did figure it out." He paused. "Is this payback time for the traveling I did? You want me to spend more time with the girls? Well, I gotta tell you, I'm spending time with them, and we're doing just fine. I love my daughters. I always did. Believe you me, when you packed them up and took them away from me, it was hard."

He put his face in close to hers and spoke softly. "Fine. It's over. We're divorced. But this coma is something else. One day or two, okay. But three days? Wake up, Rachel. I'm doing the best I can, but the girls need you. I'm just filling in. How long are you planning to let this go on?"

She didn't blink, didn't flinch, didn't answer.

He didn't know how long he stood scowling at her. But the scowl slowly faded, and in time he pulled up a chair and sat down.

KATHERINE'S one o'clock was late, and she was late taking her one forty-five. So she didn't reach the hospital until four. She felt a letdown the instant she saw that Rachel was still comatose.

Hope was reading a book on the bed, inside the rail, legs folded, boots on the floor. Jack stood facing the window with one hand on his hip and the other tossing a cell phone. The tray table beside him was covered with papers.

Katherine gave Hope a hug. "How's your mom?"

The child lifted a shoulder. "Okay."

Jack turned around. "How're you doing?" he asked, but headed off before Katherine could answer. "I'll be back."

She watched him go, then turned questioning eyes on Hope.

"They wouldn't let him use the cell phone in here," Hope explained. "It messes up the monitors."

"Ah. He seems distracted."

"Uh-huh." Hope focused on Rachel. "Do you think she knows I'm here?"

"Definitely."

Hope considered that, then said, "Sam's down the hall."

"I know. I passed her on my way in." Samantha had been tucked up in a phone booth with an algebra book in her lap, a pencil in her hand. The sudden cessation of talk and the too wide grin she gave Katherine suggested that she wasn't doing math.

Hope glanced cautiously toward the hall, then whispered an urgent, "Sam is scaring me."

Katherine leaned closer. "Scaring you how?"

"The prom," Hope whispered. "I think they're planning something. I can't say anything to Daddy, because he'll get angry at her and then she'll get angry at me. And it's not like I know anything. I just feel it." She hunched her shoulders, which made the rest of her look even smaller.

"Tell you what," Katherine suggested. "How about I drop a few hints to your dad? No one needs to know you said anything. Trust me?" she asked Hope just as Jack returned. When Hope gave her a wide-eyed nod, Katherine smiled and pulled a five-dollar bill from her pocket. "I'm desperate for tea. Would you run down and get me an Earl Grey? Maybe your dad would like coffee."

Jack asked Hope for anything strong and black. Katherine waited until she had left before eyeing the work on the table. "I thought you were driving up to the city."

He tossed the phone onto the table. "I changed my mind."

"Why?"

"Beats me." He pushed his hands through his hair.

Katherine had to admit that he seemed tired, and felt a trace of sympathy. He had a lot on his mind. She hated to add to it, but had no choice. "Hope seems worried, but I think she'll be okay. How's Sam?"

"Actually," he said, "she was pretty sweet this afternoon."

"That could mean trouble."

"Yeah, well, I'm not looking a gift horse in the mouth."

"Maybe you should," she said, only half teasing. "Teenage girls are wily. Is she all set for the prom?"

"We're shopping for a dress this weekend."

"Is she still going to the prom with Brendan?"

"In a manner of speaking," Jack said, but he looked puzzled. "I can't get a feel for how paired up this is. In my day you had a spe-cific date, but Sam's pretty vague about who's with who. There are ten of them going in the limo from Lydia's house. The girls are spending the night there after the prom."

"Are you sure it's only girls?"

"Samantha says it is. She says Lydia's parents will be there."

"I think," Katherine said, making a show of debating it herself, "that Rachel might want you to give them a call."

"If I did that, it would suggest I didn't trust my daughter."

"This isn't about trust. It's about being involved."

"I take it you've been through this. How old did you say your kids were?"

Katherine didn't have kids, and it hit home. There had been a time when having a child had meant the world to her. Then Roy had left. And suddenly she was forty-two.

"Low blow," Jack surprised her by saying. "Sorry, but I'm going through a tough time here. Samantha and I don't exactly have a love fest going on down there in Big Sur. She doesn't like what I bring in for dinner, doesn't like my talking on 'her' phone or sleeping in Rachel's bed. As far as she's concerned, I'm a major inconvenience in her life. She's given me lip about almost everything I've done—but maybe, just maybe we've turned a corner. She actually smiled at me when I picked her up at school." Pleading, he paused for a breath. "Let me enjoy it for a little bit, huh?"

FRIDAY morning came, and there was still no change in Rachel's condition.

From the bank of phones down the hall from her room, Jack called Jill. At the sound of her voice he felt a guilty tug. "Hey."

"Hey yourself," she said with pleasure. "I was wondering when you'd remember I was here."

His guilt increased. "It's been a rough couple of days. The girls are pretty upset. Rachel hasn't woken up."

"I know."

"Ah. You called my office."

"No." She sighed. "I didn't want Tina to know that you hadn't called me, so I called the hospital."

He felt even worse. "I'm sorry, Jill. I've had a lot on my mind."

"One phone call, Jack. It would have taken ten seconds. But I think you forgot. I think it didn't matter enough to you to talk with me."

"No." He sighed. "This isn't a good time, Jill. I'm grappling with something difficult. I need a little time."

"You always need time."

"You knew when we met that I had a demanding life."

"I didn't count on the demands coming from your ex-wife," she said, then caught herself. "I'm sorry, Jack. That was selfish of me. She's in a coma. She may die."

"She's not dying. My guess is she'll wake up by the first of the week."

He heard a cautious "I won't see you until then? Not even tomorrow night?"

"Can't do it. I have to be there for the girls."

Jill said, "I see."

But she didn't. He heard hurt between those two little words. "Maybe Monday, when they're at school. Want to plan on lunch?"

The smile returned to her voice. "I'd like that."

"Say, one o'clock at Stars?"

"Not Stars. Here. I'll make lunch."

"Sounds good," he said. "Thanks for being understanding, Jill. That's the biggest help to me right now."

He hung up the phone feeling like a total heel. The feeling followed him right back into Rachel's hospital room.

JACK actually dozed off sitting in the chair by Rachel's bed. One minute he put his head down beside her hand, the next he woke up with a jolt.

"I'm sorry. I didn't mean to wake you."

He looked groggily at the woman who had arrived. She wasn't a natural beauty. Her face was too narrow, her silver hair too thin. But she was put together nicely, wearing a silk tunic and slim pants, and there was a gentleness to her. There was also a wonderful smell. It came from the large zippered container she held.

He stood. "I've met you, haven't I?"

Her eyes smiled. "I'm Faye Lieberman. I've been by before. Rachel and I are in book group together." She set the zippered container on the tray table. "This is dinner. I figured you could use a little something homemade by now."

"Bless you," he said. "That's very sweet."

"It's nothing." Faye went to the bedrail and touched Rachel's arm. "I'm here, Rachel. I brought food for your family." She glanced at Jack. "How are the girls?"

The girls! Jack shot a look at his watch. "Waiting to be picked up at school as we speak." He eyed the container. "You're a good soul to remember us."

She waved off his praise. "It's in the genes. This is what Jewish mothers do best. Enjoy."

THEY DID THAT—ALL FIVE OF them. Samantha had invited Lydia and Shelly to stay overnight in Big Sur, a fact that Jack didn't learn until the two additional girls were jammed into the BMW, at which point it seemed more of an effort to say no and pry them out. Maybe it was time to think about buying a bigger car.

The insulated bag held chicken in a wine-and-tomato sauce, with carrots and potatoes. To a person, they ate well and with good humor. Samantha and her friends chatted about everyone and everything that came to mind. Hope, with Guinevere purring on her lap, listened to them with something like awe.

It wasn't until the next morning, though, that Jack understood the deeper implication of the sleepover. "Of course they're coming shopping with me," Samantha said when he had the temerity to suggest that he drop the two girls at their homes on the way. "That's the whole point. I can't pick out a dress myself, and you're not a woman. If Mom can't be here, I want my friends."

They hit Saks. They hit Benetton. By the time they hit the three other specialty stores, he was getting antsy. Hope was getting antsy.

"One more stop," he informed them when they were standing on the street corner, debating which way to go. "The next place is it. So think hard. There was a perfectly good dress back at Saks."

The girls held a prolonged three-way summit and finally agreed to return there. Jack exchanged a smug look with Hope, but it disappeared when the dress Samantha carried to the cash register wasn't the baby blue one he had meant. This one was short, slim, and black.

"Would your mother like this dress?" he asked.

"She would love it," Sam said, and with a sudden killer broad smile held out a hand for his credit card.

AT THE hospital Jack lingered with Rachel. He brushed her hair. He studied her face.

The girls knew their way around the hospital well enough to take themselves to the cafeteria for cold drinks. A while after that, Lydia's mother came to visit and left with Lydia and Shelly. Katherine came and went, as did Ben Wolfe.

When others were in the room, Jack backed off. These people were part of the life that Rachel had made without him. The situation was as awkward for them as it was for him. He was the bad guy in a roomful of good guys.

Still, he outstayed them all. He helped the weekend nurse bathe Rachel and exercise her limbs. When her head looked uncomfortably angled, he propped it with pillows.

"When are we leaving, Daddy?" Hope asked every hour or so. Guinevere was with Duncan. She wanted to get her.

Jack understood that; still, he put it off. He felt better when he was with Rachel, felt decent being with her, felt calmer.

But Samantha was due at a friend's for an overnight, and Hope was giving him beseeching little looks, so he finally trundled them off.

AFTER dropping Hope at Duncan's, Jack drove to the local market for groceries. He put a load of laundry in the washing machine, then sat out under the redwoods, breathing woodsy air. It was a clear, cool, sweetly fragrant late afternoon.

Hope joined him, and they sat together for a while. He ran his hand along Guinevere's back, feeling warmth and weakness. He prayed that the cat wasn't suffering. He knew Hope was.

Jack still hadn't looked through Rachel's work. Her studio still waited.

He put dinner on the table and took his time eating. Between bites he told Hope he was proud of the way she was taking care of Guinevere, and when she burst into tears, he leaned over her chair and wrapped his arms around her. He couldn't think of anything to say to make her feel better, so he just held her. When her tears slowed, he said, "Hey. Want to give me a hand?"

"W-with what?" she asked against his arm.

"Mom's paintings. We have to see what's what so we can tell Ben what to do about her show."

Hope looked up at him, her eyes wet but wide. "Mom was doing sea otters on Monday. Want to see?"

He smiled. "If you take me."

THEY SPENT AN HOUR IN THE studio. Rachel had made things easy. Tacked to her board was a list of the paintings that she had planned to include in the show. The ones she had been working on just prior to the accident stood closest to the easel. Other pieces stood in clearly marked stacks. Jack studied each piece. Rachel painted wildlife. In addition to the sea otters, there were deer in snow, gray whales and Arctic wolves, egrets, quail, and loons. There was a coyote, looking Jack in the eye with such a vivid mix of fear and warning that he nearly backed off.

Whether she used oils, watercolors, acrylics, or pastels, Rachel always caught something so real and direct that he felt it—a look, a mood, a need. There was no mystery to why her following was growing. In a state and age where environmental concerns were rising, she captured the vulnerability of the wild.

Eleven of the paintings were done and ready to frame. Seven, including the otters, were finished except for the background, which held sketchy forms but no more. Field sketches and photographs were affixed to the back of each piece.

His best guess? Rachel would need a week and a half to finish the seven. And the framing? The moldings were stacked in long strips by the baseboard. Pushing it, she could do the framing in several days.

Two weeks of work for a show two weeks away. It would have been a cinch if the artist weren't in a coma.

HE HAD planned to tell Ben Wolfe exactly that when he drove up to Carmel and stopped at the gallery on Sunday afternoon, but before he could say a word, Ben led him into an adjoining room. Three paintings hung in an alcove.

"We had four," Ben explained. "One of them sold last week. Another isn't for sale at all. Rachel won't let it go. Not that I blame her. It's my all-time favorite." He was looking at the one he meant, but Jack had already picked it out.

The painting that Ben loved, that Rachel refused to sell, was one that she and Jack had done together. The subject was a pair of bobcat cubs on a fallen log, the background a meadow surrounded by trees. She had done the cubs, he the background.

"What do you love about it?" Jack asked Ben.

Ben, in his innocence, didn't hesitate to tell him. "The background is complimentary to the rest, but different, very subtlely different. It makes the bobcats more striking."

"Have you told Rachel that?"

"Many times."

"What does she say?"

"Just that it was done a long time ago. So where do we stand? Do we have a shot at the show?"

"I, uh, I think . . . Yeah, actually, I think we do," Jack said, because they definitely had a shot at it. That wasn't the real question. The real question was how Rachel would feel if Jack picked up a brush and collaborated with her again.

THE phone was ringing when he walked in the door. It was David Sung.

David had been sending messages all week. He wanted work done, but Jack's mind was elsewhere. "How're you doing, David?"

"Jack? Jack? Is it really you?"

Jack looked out the window. The early evening sun snagging the tops of the redwoods spilled a glow through airy needles and on down densely scaled bark. There was something settling about it. His voice was more forgiving than it might otherwise have been. "It's been a long day, pal."

"No change, then?"

"No change. What's up?"

"I just got a call. Flynn's gone to Walker, Jansen, and McCree."

Walker, Jansen, and McCree. The competition. Michael Flynn had defected. He was the third one in six weeks.

"Will you be long?" an aggrieved Samantha asked.

Jack held up a hand to silence her and said to David, "Okay. We can live with this. It makes sense. WJM's work is more local than ours. Michael has young kids and doesn't want to travel."

"I agree with you there, but what about you? We have work to do, Jack. It'll only wait so long."

"Dad, I need the phone," Samantha whined.

He turned his back. "I'm driving up tomorrow morning."

"Have you talked with Boca?"

"Oh, yeah, I've talked with Boca. We need to alter the whole design." His stomach churned just thinking about it. "Listen, David, I have to get off the phone."

"To do what? You *are* working down there, aren't you? The girls are in school, and there isn't a whole lot you can do for Rachel."

"Actually, there is. I can paint. Hey, my daughter needs the phone. I have to go, Dave. Later." He hung up the phone.

"Paint what?" Samantha asked.

"Your mom's stuff," he answered.

She screwed up her face in horror. "You can't do that. Mom's stuff is hers. You can't mess with it."

"I wasn't planning to 'mess' with it. I was planning— I was toying with the idea of finishing a few of those pieces so that Ben can go ahead with the show."

"Mom wouldn't want you doing that."

"Know the picture of the bobcat cubs in the meadow?"

"Of course I know it. It's Mom's favorite."

"Right," he said. "Do you know that I helped paint it?" Samantha's withering look said that not only didn't she know it but that she didn't believe it for a minute. "You were six years old. Your mother and I went hiking in the mountains not far from here. When we came back, that was one of the pictures we painted."

"If you did part of it, why would Mom have it hanging in the living room? She divorced you. She wanted you out of her life!"

She stomped off, leaving Jack feeling empty again.

"MY FATHER is a jerk," Samantha told Lydia. She was breathing hard. "Who does he think he is, barging in here and taking over?"

"I thought he was pretty nice."

"That was what he wanted you to think. It was an act."

"He seems really worried about your mother."

"Yeah. Because if she doesn't get better, he'll be stuck with us. That'd cramp his style. Why are you sticking up for him?"

Call waiting clicked. "Hold on." Sam pressed the button. It was Brendan. Normally, talking with Brendan wouldn't hold a candle to talking with Lydia, but Samantha was furious with Lydia just then, so she took the call. "Lydia's being a dweeb," she told Brendan.

"So you know about the party?"

"Know what?"

"Didn't Lydia tell you? She was supposed to."

"Tell me what?"

There was a pause, then a meek "Maybe you should call her."

"Brendan, *tell* me."

"Her parents are staying home," he blurted out.

"What?"

"Lydia let it slip that the guys were coming back afterward, too, so they changed their plans. They're gonna be there all night."

"Lydia let it slip?" Samantha sighed in disgust. "How could she *do* that?"

"Some of the other parents started calling her parents, so they started asking her questions, and it slipped out."

"I should have known." Lydia had been her best friend since third grade, but all along she had been nervous about the party. She was scared that someone would throw up, her parents would find out why, and she'd be the one punished. So now everyone would miss out. "She *is* a dweeb. This ruins the whole thing."

"Why?"

"Forget the beer if her parents are there."

"It won't be so bad. Besides, her parents'll stay in the other room."

"Oh, yuk. You're as pathetic as Lydia is." When he had nothing to say about that, she made a guttural sound. "This prom is going to be totally boring. I'm not sure I want to go."

He was silent for a long minute. "What do you mean?"

"I may not go."

After another silence he said, "What about me?"

"I think you should take Jana," she decided.

"You do?"

"Yes." She wasn't going with a wimp.

He couldn't think of a thing to say to that but a weak "Oh. Okay. See you tomorrow."

Samantha hung up the phone and fumed. She had been waiting forever for a prom, for limos and all-night parties and beer. Thank you, Lydia. Thank you, Brendan. Both of them were big babies. Was she the only one who wasn't?

She knew of another person who wasn't. Picking up the phone, she pressed in his number. She knew it by heart, had called it many times. Before, she hadn't done anything but listen to his voice.

Her pulse raced when it came to her now, a deep, cool seventeen-year-old. " 'Lo?"

"Hi, Teague. It's Samantha. You know, from the school bus?"

The voice turned smooth around a smile. "I know Samantha from the school bus, only she hasn't been there all week."

"My mom's been sick, so my dad's been driving me up."

"Hey. Was it your mom who had an accident?"

"It was," Samantha said, feeling important. "She was driving up to Carmel when someone hit her. The car went off the road and over the cliff. She's in a coma. We've been spending every minute we can in her hospital room."

"Is it gross?"

Samantha straightened her shoulders. "It's actually fine. After a while you forget about the machines and tubes. The thing is, I've been so obsessed with my mom that I haven't been thinking about anything else, but my dad said that my mom would want me to go to my prom—it's Saturday night—only I haven't asked anyone yet. So what do you think? Want to go with me?"

"Where is it?"

"It's at school, but we don't have to stay there long. I mean, it's going to be a dumb little prom. But I have a gorgeous black dress that my dad says is too sexy for someone my age—which shows how much he knows. So do you want to go?"

"Sure." His voice was smiling again. "I'll go."

She smiled back. "Awesome!"

HOPE sat on her bedroom floor. Guinevere was on her lap, curled in a limp little ball, making precious few sounds.

Carefully cradling the cat, she rose and went out in her stocking feet to find her father. She found him in the studio, studying canvases that he had lined up on the opposite side of the room.

"Hi, sweetie," he said, and looked at her feet. "Where are the boots?"

"In my room. Are you really going to finish Mom's pictures?"

"Do you think your mother would be angry with me if I did?"

Hope didn't think so. She hadn't ever heard Rachel say anything bad about Jack. Sam told her she just wasn't listening, but she was. "Daddy?"

"What, sweetie?"

"It'll be a week tomorrow. Do you think Mommy's going to wake up?"

"I do. It's just taking longer than we had hoped it would."

"Guinevere's getting worse. She's going to die soon, Daddy."

Jack crossed the room and rubbed Guinevere between the ears. "Is she in pain?"

"No. She'd meow if she was." Hope swallowed. "Daddy, what'll I do when she dies?"

He thought for a minute. "You'll be sad. You'll grieve for her."

That wasn't what Hope meant. "What will I do with her? I mean, I can't just . . . throw her out like she was chicken bones."

He frowned. "What do you want to do?"

"I want to bury her."

He glanced out the window. "Okay," he said, surprising her. "We could bury her in the forest. Somewhere close. Would you feel better if we did that?"

Much, Hope thought, nodding.

"Done," he said, and pulled her close.

She didn't say anything for a minute. Sam was wrong. He did understand. That meant he cared. "Daddy?" she whispered. "You won't leave us alone, will you?"

"How could I do that?"

"If Mommy doesn't wake up and you have to go back to the city to work, you could hire someone to stay here."

"I won't. I promise."

With the smallest bit of breath she said, "I love you."

He didn't answer, but she felt his cheek against the top of her head, and in that instant the clock turned back and she believed him.

When she woke up the next morning, Guinevere hadn't moved from the spot where Hope had put her the night before. Frightened, she leaned close, close enough so that the cat would feel her breath. "Guin?" she whispered, rubbing the cat's cheek with a fingertip. When she felt the smallest movement against her finger, she let out a breath.

She draped an arm around the cat and lay close, thinking, I love you, Guinevere, and heard the whisper of an answering purr. Then it stopped. For several minutes Hope didn't move. "Guin?" she whispered. She stroked the cat's head and waited for a purr, stroked again, waited again. When there was nothing, she buried her head in Guinevere's cooling fur and began to cry.

"Hope?" Jack called, coming to the door. "Are you up?"

Gulping sobs bubbled up from inside. She pulled Guinevere closer, hoping she was wrong. Only, she knew better. She could feel it—a giant emptiness, a big hole, a huge aloneness.

"Sweetie?" He touched her head. "Hope, what is it?" He touched the cat, left his hand there a minute, and just when she was thinking that she didn't know what she was going to do, because everything she loved always left her, he slipped his arms around her and Guinevere both and leaned over close.

He didn't say anything, just sat there sheltering them, and when Samantha came in asking when they were leaving, he said, "Hope's not going today. Guinevere just died."

"I'm sorry, Hope," Samantha said, softly now, close by.

"We're burying her here," Jack said. "Want to take the bus today?"

Hope didn't hear an answer. She had started crying again. Besides, Samantha wasn't the one she wanted just then. The one she wanted was holding her tight.

IF ANYONE had told Jack that while his wife was in a coma and his firm was floundering he would be splitting firewood into planks to build a tiny coffin for a cat, he would have had them committed. But it seemed like the best thing to do.

Hope sat on the ground nearby. Guinevere was wrapped in the wash-worn baby afghan that Rachel had crocheted and that Hope had slept with for the first eight years of her life. She held her bundle as though it were gold.

When the small coffin was finished, Jack dug a grave. It felt good to work. The exertion tired him out enough so that when Hope placed her little bundle in the coffin and he nailed it shut, put it in the hole, and began covering it with dirt, he didn't feel quite so raw.

Hope cried. It was inevitable. Jack held her against his side and let her get it all out. Then they sat, just sat for a bit—and again it was absurd. The last thing Jack had time for was lingering in the forest on a Monday morning. He had to shower and visit Rachel, then drive on into the city to work. But Hope seemed to want him to do this. And he had to admit there was a peace to it.

Chapter Five

THE drive from Big Sur to the hospital on a Monday midmorning took an easy forty-five minutes. Jack arrived feeling mellow—only to find another patient in Rachel's room. His heart stopped for the fraction of a second it took for him to reason that he would have been called if Rachel had died.

Holding Hope's hand, he strode to the nurses station. "Where's my wife?" he asked, and spotted Cindy emerging from a room at the far end of the corridor. He headed there with Hope in tow. "Where's Rachel?"

Cindy waved them along and into the room from which she had just come. It was a regular hospital room, with a TV, a bathroom, and several easy chairs. Katherine was in one of those chairs. Rachel was lying on her side facing her, and Jack thought the change meant she had woken up.

But Katherine's expression told him that it wasn't so.

"It's been a week," Cindy said. "Rachel's condition has been steady, so the doctors thought she could be moved."

Kara Bates's voice came from the door. "This is what we call an observation room," she said, entering.

Hope climbed onto Rachel's bed, cowboy boots and all, and sat by her mother's hip. She didn't say anything. After a minute she gingerly lifted Rachel's hand and put it in her lap. Her head was down. She curled into herself. When she started to sniffle, she lifted Rachel's hand to cover her tears.

Jack caught Katherine's look of alarm. "Guinevere," he mouthed. She winced and nodded.

He touched Hope's bowed head, but a sinking feeling was starting to take form inside him. He gestured Kara into the hall. "You're giving up on her," he accused. "You've taken her out of ICU because you don't think she's waking up for a while."

"That's not it. We're simply saying that since the accident was nearly a week ago and there haven't been any complications, the chances of one occurring now are low. Cindy will still be her nurse. Same with Steve and me. The fact is, she isn't critical."

"The fact is, she isn't conscious," Jack muttered, but more to himself than to Kara. She patted his elbow and set off down the hall. Cindy and Katherine replaced her.

Since he hadn't gotten anywhere with Kara, he turned on Cindy. "There has to be more we can do."

"I've been talking to people," Katherine said. "There are other things we might try. We could read to her, play her favorite music.

We could burn incense that smells like the woods near her house. That might snap her out of it."

Jack wanted to argue but couldn't. Even now, miles away, he could smell those woods. There was a power to that smell. "Would it work?" he asked the nurse.

"It can't hurt," Cindy said as she had so often before. She put on a smile. "Here's Dr. Bauer."

"I'll go visit with Hope," Katherine said, but before she could leave, someone called her name. She looked past Steve Bauer, broke into a grin, and set off to greet a young, good-looking guy wearing purple scrubs.

Watching her, Jack couldn't help but think that there was something to be said for living in a smaller place than San Francisco. People saw one another around town. Familiar faces were everywhere. It was kind of nice when life was shaky.

JACK called Jill from the phone down the hall and explained about Guinevere's death, about getting a late start from Big Sur, about Michael Flynn's defection. As gently as he could, he said, "I can't do lunch, Jill. Hope's with me, and we don't have much time. I'm sorry. I'll bet you made something incredible."

"Not yet. I was going to do risotto primavera right before you came. The ingredients will hold. Will you come tomorrow?"

"I won't be in the city until later in the week."

There was a pause, then a quiet "Why?"

He felt it coming. The deep stuff. And he didn't want it. So he said, "Because my being here with Rachel could make a difference, Jill. I want her well."

Jill relented with a sigh. "I know."

"Thursday," he suggested. "Will the veggies hold until then?"

"It's not about the veggies."

"I know." It was about commitments. "Thursday. I promise."

THEY stopped at Jack's house before heading for Sung and McGill. While he filled a large duffel with clothes, he had Hope pile mail into a shopping bag. In the midst of putting everything in the car, Jack had a thought. Returning to his bedroom closet, he pushed sweaters aside on the top shelf and pulled down two framed photographs. One was of Rachel and the girls, one of Rachel alone. Slipping them into a bag, he rejoined Hope. Then they headed for the office, where he spent the bulk of the next three hours arguing with contractors, apologizing to clients, and assigning tasks to associates.

It was late afternoon by the time they returned to the hospital. Katherine had picked up Samantha at school and returned with a CD player, which was now running softly on the bed stand not twelve inches from Rachel's head.

"Garth," Samantha told Jack.

"Your mother's a Garth fan, too?"

"A big fan," Samantha said.

Hope confirmed it with a nod, which didn't leave much for him to do but to set up the pictures he had brought.

Samantha was immediately drawn to them. "Where'd you get those?"

"I've had them. I want the doctors and nurses who walk in and out to see your mother as a living, breathing, feeling individual."

JACK was feeling pensive when he started the drive back to Big Sur, but the coast did its thing. By the time they passed Big Sur, a mist had risen to buffer him from the world.

When they got to the house, the girls went to their rooms, leaving him to his own devices. He told himself to work. Instead, needing more of Rachel, he went to her studio. The canvases he had placed against the wall the day before hadn't moved. He sat down on the floor and studied them.

After a bit he began rummaging through Rachel's supplies. She had oils and acrylics in tubes, neatly arranged on a work desk. Brushes of varying widths lay on a cloth with several palette knives.

Snooping idly, he pulled out a thin portfolio that was stashed between the file cabinet and the wall. Squatting down, he set it against the front of the file cabinet, opened it, and sat back.

The first page was blank, a title page without a title. He turned to the next page and saw something that looked like a baby in the very first stages of development. An embryo. He turned to the next and the next, watching the embryo develop into a fetus with features that grew increasingly human. Page by page the fetus grew into a baby. It was a little boy.

On the last page the baby had his eyes open and was looking directly at Jack. He studied the infant, feeling the utter reality of the child, though it was drawn with nothing more than blue pen. Jack felt a chill on the back of his neck. So real. So familiar. He had an eerie thought. He pushed it aside, gathered the pages together, and returned the sheaf to the portfolio. Closing it tightly, he stashed it back between the file cabinet and the wall.

Still he saw that last picture. It haunted him through the night and woke him at dawn.

Watching the girls in the car, he wondered if they knew anything about a baby, but he couldn't ask. Whether he was wrong or right, mentioning it would open a can of worms.

Rachel knew. But Rachel wasn't saying. That left Katherine.

NATURALLY, Katherine wasn't at the hospital when he arrived, but that was fine. Jack had taken her phone number from Rachel's address book—both numbers, work and home. Standing just outside Rachel's room, he called the work number on his cell phone.

"Color and Cut," came a bubbly young voice.

"Katherine Evans, please."

"I'm sorry. She's with a client. Can she return your call?"

He gave the sweet young thing his number, pushed the phone into his pants pocket, and returned to Rachel. Drawing up a chair, he put his elbows on the bedrail.

"Rachel? Are you there? Can you hear me? It's been a week, a whole week. Hope needs you to help her with Guinevere's death. She disappeared this morning, didn't show up for breakfast and wasn't in the house at all. I ran to Guinevere's grave. No Hope. I was getting ready to panic, when she came down from Duncan's.

That's starting to make me nervous. I mean, he's a big guy living alone. Could be he's a pervert." Rachel didn't look upset. Neither had Hope when she returned from Duncan's. "She says she needs his faith. If that's the extent of it, I still feel inadequate. We never talked about religion, you and me. Maybe we should have. Maybe the kids need a faith of their own for times like these."

He stood, bringing her arm up with him, and began to gently put it through its paces. The ring of the phone was muffled by his jeans. Gently he set her arm down. Less gently he flipped the phone open as he walked to the door. "Yeah?"

"It's Katherine. What's up?"

"I need to talk with you," Jack said. "I found a pack of drawings in Rachel's studio. Of a baby. I need to know what those drawings meant, Katherine. That baby had my eyes."

"I'll be over in forty-five minutes," was all she said.

BY THE time she arrived, Jack had listened to Garth Brooks from start to finish and had asked himself a dozen questions about the baby whose existence Rachel's best friend hadn't denied.

Katherine entered the room looking wary. She kissed Rachel's cheek. "Mmm. You smell good. So he's been rubbing in cream?"

Out of the gate at the crack of the gun, Jack asked, "So was Rachel really pregnant?"

Katherine looked torn.

"Come on, Katherine," he warned. "You're not denying it, which means she was. Unless I misinterpreted those drawings, she lost the baby."

Katherine's eyes fell to Rachel. "Yes, she was pregnant."

Suddenly real, it took his breath. He looked at Rachel, trying to imagine it. The pain he felt was gnawing. "How could she pick up and leave me if she was pregnant?"

"Oh, no. She wasn't pregnant when she left. It was before."

"Before." That made even less sense. "No. I would have known."

"From what she told me, she barely knew it herself. Things weren't going well between you. She didn't know what to do."

"But she would have told me," he argued.

Katherine sighed. "She tried. You were on a trip when she started feeling sick. She called and asked you to come home. You wouldn't."

Swallowing, he struggled again to think back. There had been a trip to Toronto two weeks before the split. Yes, she had called, not feeling well, wanting him home. But the trip had been an important one. A large contract had hung in the balance. Turning to Rachel, he said, "I kept asking you what was wrong. You said, nothing terrible. You had stomach pains. Maybe the flu." He looked back at Katherine. "She was miscarrying?"

Katherine nodded.

He made himself remember more. "She was pale as death when I came home, but she said she was getting better. I was home for four days. Not once did she mention a baby." He felt shaky, close to tears. "Then there was a bunch of trips in close sequence." And an ultimatum before the last one. "Why didn't she tell me?"

"She couldn't."

"She lost a baby I didn't know about, then left because I hadn't somehow figured it out?"

When Katherine looked reluctant to speak, he wiggled his fingers. "Come on, Katherine. Talk to me. Tell me what she said."

"She said it wasn't just the miscarriage. It was everything about your relationship. The miscarriage was only the clincher. She saw it as a sign that the marriage wouldn't work."

He felt an overwhelming sadness. "Ahh, Rachel," he breathed, lifting her hand to his chest, "you should have told me."

"Would it have made a difference?" Katherine asked.

"I don't know," he murmured. "Maybe." If he had known she was pregnant, they might have talked.

"For what it's worth," Katherine said, "she would have lost the baby whether you were there or not. She didn't blame you for the miscarriage, only for not being with her when it happened."

He sighed. So now he knew what had actually caused that final break. Not that it helped. He still felt abandoned.

He turned to Katherine. "You said that you met her at the gynecologist's office. Did she have more trouble after she left the city?"

"No. She was just getting to know a local doctor. We got to talking. There was instant rapport. She was very supportive."

He would have thought it was the other way around. "*She* was supportive?"

Katherine paled. "I'd just been diagnosed with breast cancer."

His eyes widened. It was all he could do not to look at her chest. "Bad?"

"Nothing had spread. The lymph nodes were clear. What they found in me was microscopic, tiny in situ ductal carcinomas. I'm living proof of the miracle of early detection." She took a tiny breath. "That was the good news. The bad news was that I had tiny little grains of it in both breasts." She made a gesture that would have suggested beheading had it been eight inches higher.

Jack did look this time, because not once had he thought her body was anything but that of an attractive, shapely fortysomething female.

She chuckled. "Your mouth is open."

"I know . . . it's just . . . I don't see—"

"Reconstruction."

"Ah." He was embarrassed. "Good as new."

"From the outside," she said. Her defensiveness was back. "Rachel was there the entire time—before, during, and after."

"You have no family nearby?"

"Have? No. Had? Yes. I was married at the time. My husband had a squeamish stomach."

"He wasn't there at all?"

"Well, he was. In a way." Her tone was wry, bitter. "Roy was a golf pro. He ran tournaments at a club in Pebble Beach. He didn't have the time to sit in doctors' offices holding his wife's hand." She tipped her head, still wry, still bitter. "I didn't push. I did everything with only a minimal involvement on his part—the doctors, the surgery, the follow-up appointments. Rachel drove me to some. Other friends drove me to others.

"I recovered from the surgery. It was slower than I had expected—they don't tell you the half. But I gradually gained strength and felt better. I told myself I'd been given a gift of life."

She stopped. Looking at Jack, she was wryness personified.

Treating her with care now, he said a cautious "What then?"

"Roy treated me like a leper. And then I learned he was seeing a little redhead from Santa Cruz." She rubbed Rachel's shoulder with her fingernails. "So we had that in common, too."

"Hey, I never cheated on Rachel."

"No. But you left her alone."

"Not when I was home. So maybe I underestimated what she was feeling when I was gone."

"That's putting it mildly."

Jack was feeling too raw to be criticized. "You're taking your anger toward Roy out on me. That's unfair. I'm not Roy."

"Would you be attracted to a woman with no breasts?"

"I'm attracted to a woman in a coma," he said before he could censor the thought. Quickly he added, "Forget Roy. There are other men in the world."

She gave a dramatic sigh. "Yes, well, I told myself that, too, and along came Byron. I met him at a hair show in New York. He was gorgeous, and there was a definite spark. He flew out here to see me. That's when I told him."

Jack waited.

She remained composed. Only her eyes showed the pain. "Oh, it was gradual, his withdrawal. The phone calls came fewer and further between. After a while it was me making the calls. When I stopped, that was it." She took a shuddering breath. "Rachel helped me through that, too."

Jack had a sudden thought. "That young guy the other day in purple scrubs?"

"My anesthesiologist. He had a crush on me."

"And Steve Bauer? Did you know him before?"

"Nope."

"There's a spark."

"Uh-huh. But it isn't going anywhere. In the first place, he's a doctor, and I've had enough of those to last a lifetime. In the second place, he's a man. I'll be very happy to keep those at arm's length for a while."

"We're not all bad," Jack said. "I'm here, aren't I?"

She thought about that for a minute. "Have you thought about the possibility that Rachel may only partially recover? What if she wakes up and she can't talk right or walk right?"

"Let's get her woken up first. Then we'll worry about the rest."

Katherine glanced at her watch. "I have to get back to work."

"Thank you," Jack said.

"For what?"

He had to think for a minute. The thanks had startled him, too. "For coming today. For telling me what you did."

"I haven't told many people. I'd appreciate it if you wouldn't—"

"I won't." He hitched his head toward the door and began walking that way. When she joined him, he said, "Thank you for being there for Rachel. She's lucky to have a friend like you."

"That's a nice thing to say."

"I have my moments." On impulse he gave her a quick hug.

"What was that for?" she asked.

"I don't know. It just seemed right." He looked back at Rachel, wondering if she understood the hug. He went still. "Whoa." He strode back to the bed.

Katherine was right beside him. "What?"

"Rachel?" He leaned over her. "I saw that, Rachel."

"What did she do?"

"Blinked. Flinched. Something." He took Rachel's hand. "If you hear me, give a squeeze." He waited, felt nothing. "Try a blink." Again he waited. "I saw something. I know you can do it."

"Rachel?" Katherine tried. "Fight it. Push your way up."

They stood side by side, leaning in over Rachel.

"Maybe I was wrong," Jack said. "I could have sworn . . ."

From behind them came Cindy's voice. "What's happening?" When Jack told her, she leaned in on the opposite side and chafed Rachel's jaw. "Rachel! Rachel!"

They waited and watched, but they didn't see a thing.

"It might have been involuntary," Cindy said, "what we call lightening. It's a gradual waking that starts with the fingers or toes."

"This wasn't finger or toes," Jack said, his hopes up again. "It was her face. Could that still be the start of something?"

The eyes behind Cindy's glasses said maybe or maybe not, and his letdown returned. "What do we do now?" he asked.

The nurse squeezed Rachel's arm from elbow to shoulder. "We keep talking. When you saw this movement, were you saying anything she might have reacted to?"

Jack looked at Katherine. "We had been talking about personal stuff, but we were done. We walked to the door. I hugged you." He arched a brow. "Maybe she was jealous."

From Cindy came a quiet "Lesser emotions than that have pulled people from comas."

FOR a long while after Katherine left, Jack sat on Rachel's bed. He put their hands palm to palm, then fitted her palm to his jaw. He thought about the miscarriage, about the little boy they might have had. He thought about country music and about jealousy. Then he picked up the phone. He called his would-be client in Boca and said that Sung and McGill was withdrawing from the project.

SAMANTHA loaded her backpack with books to bring home, then checked herself out in the mirror inside her locker door. She ran a comb through her hair, wiped a finger under her eye to get rid of runaway liner. Then she straightened and tossed her hair back. Finally, when Lydia didn't show up, she took her baseball jacket from its hook. She was closing her locker when Pam Ardley turned the corner.

"Hey, Samantha," Pam called, breaking into a trot. "Wait up." Cocaptain of the cheerleading squad, she was the most popular girl in the class. Samantha wasn't going anywhere, not when Pam Ardley called.

Pam slowed to a walk, then stopped. "Teague says you asked him to the prom. I think that's awesome. He's hot. We're having a party at Jake Drumble's. Maybe you two want to come."

Samantha couldn't believe it. If Pam was the most popular girl, Jake Drumble was the most popular boy.

"I'd like that," she said without seeming overeager.

"What can you bring?" Pam asked.

Samantha scooped her hair to the side. "What do you need?"

"Whatever you have at home—vodka, gin."

"I may have a problem," Samantha warned. "My mom's been in a coma for a week, so my dad's with us. It's a nightmare. He drives us here and back. He watches us like a hawk. If he gets even the slightest idea that I'm smuggling out vodka—"

Pam waved a hand. "Don't do it. We'll manage without." She stood back and grinned. "Saturday night at six for something before the prom. See you then." She jogged off.

WHEN Jack reached the hospital on Wednesday morning, the only change that had occurred was the arrival of an arrangement of yellow roses from Ben Wolfe.

Taking one of the roses, he moved it under Rachel's nose. "Bright yellow," he said. "And fragrant. Makes me think beach roses in Nantucket. Remember those? Good vacation."

He teased the tip of her nose with the rose. Then he told her about withdrawing from the project in Boca.

"See, it isn't just the money," he said. "Maybe it was, for a while. But it wasn't conscious materialism. It was wanting to be a success. If I got lost in it, I'm sorry. But success has always been a thing for me, more than for you. Back home I was nothing growing up. I still feel that way sometimes. You've always been a success.

"It's like you get started in one direction and pick up speed, and you may forget where you're going and why, but the momentum takes you there anyway. Only, you find out when you arrive that it isn't where you want to be." He wasn't sure if he was talking about work or about the divorce. Since the divorce was a done deed, he focused on work.

"The problem," he said, pulling shop drawings from his brief-case, "is that I can cancel on a project like Boca because nothing's been signed yet, but there are too many others where the commit-ment's been made." He unfolded the drawings. They were the de-signs for Napa overnighted to him in Big Sur. They needed study and approval.

He told Rachel about the project, then talked his way through the shop drawings. She used to look over his shoulder sometimes when he was working with drawings like these. He'd talked her through the plans then. But she would have been bored with these. Why, even he was bored with these. They had more to do with su-pervision than design, and design was his love.

He had barely refolded the drawings and put them away when Ben Wolfe arrived.

Ben made awkward conversation with Rachel. He seemed like a very nice, decent, and attentive man. Jack had the wildest impulse to introduce him to Jill.

When Ben broached the subject of Rachel's show, Jack said that he would be framing her pictures himself. After all, she had all the materials at the house and he had framed pictures before, or so he reasoned. But he wasn't thinking about framing when Ben left. He was thinking about painting.

JACK began painting at eight that evening. He worked until four in the morning, layering Rachel's canvas with a lake bordered by trees, and an early evening sky shot with a whisper of green and pink. When he finally set down his palette and brushes and stepped back from the easel, his eye was drawn more strongly than ever to Rachel's loons.

It was another half hour before he crawled into bed. He woke up after three hours of sleep, tired but pleasantly so. He had worked hard and done well. He hadn't felt as satisfied in a long, long while.

He showered, shaved, and dressed. When he arrived in the kitchen, Samantha was standing at the counter drinking coffee. "Is your sister up?" he asked.

"Up and gone."

"Gone where?"

Samantha didn't have to do more than look in the direction of Duncan's, and Jack made for the door. Hope had gone to Duncan's one time too many. He wanted to see more of where she went.

Jack was a man with a mission as he strode up the hill to Duncan Bligh's.

The house itself was a log box that might have fit neatly into a corner of the adjacent pen. The barn behind it was larger and newer. Sheep clustered between pen and barn, staring at him as he neared.

He crossed the porch and pounded on the door. When Duncan opened up, Jack barged past him. He hadn't taken more than a handful of steps when he stopped short.

The first thing he saw was a large hearth with a healthy fire radiating warmth. The second was Hope's blond hair, but it was down low, resting against something. It was a minute before he identified that something as a small figure in a wheelchair.

"About time you met Faith," Duncan muttered, waving Jack forward. "Say hello to my wife."

The woman in the wheelchair looked up at Jack. Her hair was white, her face creased, her smile as warm as the fire.

"Hello," she said, more mouthing than sound. Her hand lay on Hope's head, which lay against the crocheted afghan covering her legs. "She's sleeping," she whispered.

Duncan's faith. Jack couldn't count the number of times he had heard that phrase uttered in the same breath as solace and peace. The woman and her smile said it all. Duncan's Faith. He extended a hand. "Jack McGill," he said. Her hand was frail in his, but there was a dignity to it. "I'm pleased to meet you."

Faith nodded. "Hope didn't tell you she was coming here?"

"No." He glanced at Duncan, who was regarding his wife with such tenderness that Jack was all the more humbled. Duncan's Faith. Why hadn't he known?

He hadn't known, because he was thickheaded, because he was driven by jealousy where his family was concerned, because he jumped to conclusions at the drop of a hat. And maybe because the girls had hoodwinked him.

Duncan walked off. Jack hunkered down in front of the fire so that Faith wouldn't have to look up.

"How is Rachel?" she asked.

"She's the same. Do you know I had no idea you existed? The girls talked about 'faith' like it was a religion. I'm afraid I've been rude not coming to thank you before this."

"Thank me for what?"

"For being kind to the girls. For taking care of Guinevere. I couldn't quite understand why the cat would be better off up here if Duncan was out in the fields all day. Now it makes sense."

"He comes back to check on me every few hours." She smiled again. "Not that I'm going anywhere."

"Do you go outside?"

"Oh, yes. I can wheel myself out to the porch. There's a beautiful view of the valley. Some people think I'm crazy living up here, but I've always loved these hills. Duncan and I used to vacation here before the accident."

"How long ago was that?"

"The accident? Twelve years. A ski lift collapsed. My legs were broken in so many places that walking would have been an ordeal even if my spine hadn't been injured, which it was."

"I'm sorry."

"Don't be. Three died that day. I could have been one of those, and then I would have missed out on the life we've found here." Her eyes sparkled. "My Duncan used to drive a truck. I never saw him. Now I do."

Hope moved her head. She opened her eyes slowly and saw Jack. "Daddy," she breathed, and quickly sat up.

"I was worried," he said gently.

"Mom always knows I'm here."

"Well," he said, pushing himself up, "now I'll know, too." He held out a hand. "You have school. Samantha's waiting."

"Hope had breakfast with us," Faith said fondly.

"I'm sorry for that. We've imposed enough."

"Imposed? Oh, no. Hope is no imposition. She's a joy. This is the least I can do after all Rachel has done." She reached for Hope's free hand. "Give your mother a kiss for me, will you?"

"OKAY," he told the girls as he hustled them to the car. "The joke's up. Tell me about your mom and the Blighs."

"They're good friends," Samantha said. "Can we talk about my prom?"

"Not yet," Jack answered, shifting to drive down the hill. "You guys let me think your mother was dating Duncan."

"We never said that."

Hope said, "The thing about Duncan and Faith is that it never seems right talking about them. Mom helps them out, doing marketing and stuff. She always says that Faith was like a favorite aunt. She has coffee up there a lot. They sit and talk."

Samantha's voice was a jarring intrusion. "Dad, we need to talk about my prom. There's been a change in plans."

Jack would have liked to hear more about Faith, because even picturing her brought calm, but Samantha had an agenda of her own and he was learning that car time was good time. She couldn't stomp off when she didn't like what he said.

He turned north onto Highway 1. "What's the change?"

"I'm not going with Brendan. I'm going with Teague."

"Teague?"

"Teague Runyan. He's a great guy."

"Are you still leaving from Lydia's house?"

"No. That's another change. Teague's picking me up here."

Jack felt something by his arm closest to the door. Hope was crowded against the window there. "How old is this Teague?"

"Seventeen. He's a good driver, and he has a truck. It's, like, indestructible."

Jack liked the sound of indestructible. What he didn't like was the sound of seventeen. Seventeen was a dangerous age. "Okay. So I'll meet him when he comes?"

"Uh-huh," Samantha said a little too brightly.

"Is that it for changed plans? You're still doing the limo thing from Lydia's house and back?"

"The party's at Jake Drumble's."

"Who is he?" Jack said a little less easily. "And what happened to Lydia's party?"

"Oh, boy, here we go," Samantha cried. "Like it's the Inquisition. It's no big thing. The only difference is that Teague will pick me up Saturday and drop me back Sunday."

"Yeah, well, that leaves a whole lot of hours unaccounted for," Jack said. He felt Hope shift position. Deliberate? "So the party's at Jake's. Before and after?"

"I think so. It's not definite about after."

"But you're going back to Lydia's to sleep."

"No." She was suddenly impatient. "I'm not *going* with Lydia."

"Not at all?"

"That's the *point*. Like, this is a whole different group. Lydia'll be with Brendan and Jana and Adam and Shelly, and I'll be with Teague and Pam and Jake and Heather."

He was getting the picture. "But Lydia's your best friend."

"So?"

He slid her a glance. "So that doesn't sound right."

"Lydia just isn't sophisticated. If I'm with her, I can't be with other kids who are."

Jack thought about that as he drove. "You seemed happy enough with her last weekend. Was that an act?"

"No." She made a disgruntled sound. "You don't understand."

"I'm trying to, but it doesn't feel right."

"This is a prom," Samantha said. "It's one night."

"Sounds to me like it's more than that," he said. "There's something to be said for loyalty. What feels right to you, Sam? Going to the prom with friends you know and trust, or blowing them off to be with a whole other group?"

"This is hopeless," she grumbled. "You don't understand."

"No," he sighed, feeling defeated, "I guess I don't."

JILL LIVED IN A MODEST HOUSE in Seacliff, which was in northwest San Francisco, overlooking the Pacific. When Jack arrived at one, he felt a sense of dread. Jill was perfect, her blond hair adorably layered. She had decided against the risotto that she would have cooked Monday and, instead, had made a warm Oriental salad with fresh tuna, spaghetti-thin wonton crisps, a light herb dressing, and warm home-baked olive bread. The kiss she gave him tasted of relief, which made him feel worse.

They sat side by side on tall stools, thighs touching, arms occasionally entwined. Jill asked about Rachel and listened in concern while he tried to verbalize the jolt he still felt each morning walking into that hospital room and seeing her lying inert.

Then Jill asked him about work. Fresh from two hours at the office, he talked about that for a while. David had been upset over Boca, but they had worked it through. More worrisome to Jack was his partner's lukewarm response to his latest Montana design, which he described to Jill to her nodding approval. He then asked Jill about her tennis lessons and how her diabetic mother was doing.

When they stopped talking, Jill slipped her arms around his waist. She rested her head on his shoulder, then raised her face. They kissed once, and again. She slipped off her stool, stood in front of him, and wrapped her arms around his neck. As she kissed him again, she undulated ever so slowly.

Jack tried to get into it. He told himself that Jill was an incredible woman, that he would be a fool to let her go. He tried to feel, but nothing came, so he gently disengaged. "This isn't working," he said quietly. "I . . . can't."

She drew back, frightened, studied his face. "Is it Rachel?"

"It's everything."

"Do you love her?" Jill asked.

"I don't know. My life just seems to be turning on end."

"You need space. That's okay. I'll wait."

Clasping her hands together in his, he said, "I can't do this anymore, Jill. It isn't fair to you."

Her voice went high, urgent. "Am I complaining?"

"No. You've been patient, waiting, wanting it to happen, but it isn't going to."

"But—"

"Shh." He pressed a finger to her lips. He spoke in a half whisper. "Listen to me. Please. I love you, Jill, but as a friend. It won't ever end in marriage, which is what you want, what you should have."

Her eyes were teary. "Why? What's missing?"

"Nothing. Nothing in you. It's me. I'm just . . . I'm just . . ."

"Still in love with Rachel?"

He released a breath. "Maybe. I don't know. But I don't feel free now. My marriage is still there. Unfinished business."

"Rachel ended it. She left you. You always told me that."

"It helped keep me angry, but there are reasons why she left, things I didn't know about until now. I have to talk with her, Jill. I won't know where I'm going until I do."

Bewildered, Jill asked, "What if she doesn't wake up?"

"Then I'll have the girls. And regrets." He sighed. "Don't add to the regrets, Jill. I could keep this going between us and just take what I want. But I'm trying to do the right thing. Help me. Please?"

"IT'S done," he told Rachel two hours later. Jill had cried at the end. They had agreed to talk from time to time. He was feeling empty, alone. But he had done the right thing. "She was a perfectly lovely woman, but you have a hold on me. You always did."

JACK painted in Rachel's studio again that night. He was up until four in the morning this time, but the satisfaction was worth it. He woke up to have breakfast with the girls, drive them down the road to the bus stop, and to call the hospital for an update on Rachel. Ignoring E-mail from David Sung, he went back to bed and slept until ten. Even then he took the time to drink a leisurely cup of coffee, sitting on the fallen log in Rachel's woods, watching the foraging of half a dozen wild turkeys.

He stopped at the market for a dozen two-liter bottles of assorted sodas and dropped them at school just in time for Hope's class picnic. Then he went on to Monterey.

There was no change. Rachel was still comatose.

THAT evening Jack and the girls had dinner at the River Inn, where he'd been promising to take them. Between Hope's telling him that the drinks were the best part of the picnic and Samantha's telling him that she had aced a biology test and had the neatest lunch with Pam and Heather, there wasn't a moment of silence. By the time they got home, he wanted to paint, and then he was lost.

The night's subject was quail. Rachel had painted a covey roosting low in a sycamore tree. Even before Jack studied the photographs affixed to the back of the canvas, he knew that the background had to be the duller tans and browns of winter, against which the birds would be simultaneously camouflaged and crisp.

He worked with care, but it flowed. He used umbers, ochers, siennas, and grays, mixing and matching until he had the right feel for a background that would highlight the quail.

By the time he was done, the adrenaline was flowing fast and hard. Tired as he was, it was a while before he fell asleep.

Chapter Six

SAMANTHA had planned to sleep her usual Saturday morning late, but she woke up early and couldn't fall back to sleep. Her head was a battlefield of emotions. The prom came first; she was totally excited. But she was angry at Jack for making her feel guilty about Lydia, and she missed Rachel. They disagreed on lots of things, but at least Rachel cared. Samantha wasn't sure Jack did.

Samantha wished she were twenty-one. If she were, she wouldn't be worrying about a prom. She wouldn't be worrying about whether or not to wear the three-inch heels Heather had lent her. Or about what to do if Teague kissed her.

Rachel would have told her what to do. But Rachel wasn't there, only Jack, and that annoyed her.

JACK set off early with Hope to visit Rachel. Samantha had pleaded exhaustion and stayed home, and he had promised to be back by noon with food.

They stopped at Eliza's for hot coffee and brought it along, moving the cup under Rachel's nose in the hope that the smell would reach her. While Hope used a tiny scissors to cut exquisitely detailed snowflakes from white paper she had brought, they talked about the weather, about Samantha's prom.

Then Hope hung the snowflakes from the IV pole and whispered, "Tell her about the quail."

Jack hesitated. He hadn't told Rachel about doing *any* painting. Hope loved what he had done, but Samantha refused even to look. He feared that on this issue Rachel might side with Samantha.

Suddenly it struck him that that might be good. If Rachel didn't want him finishing her paintings—didn't want it bad enough—she would wake up and tell him.

So he told her about the loons he had done Wednesday night, the deer he had done Thursday night, and the quail he had done Friday night. He gained momentum, talking about the colors he had used and the effects he had sought, got caught up in excitement, but he saw no movement.

THE smartest thing Samantha did was to start getting ready for the prom very early. She ended up taking two showers when her hair didn't blow right the first time. Her deodorant took forever to dry; she botched her eyeliner and had to start all over with that; and though she had decided that sheer black stockings looked more sophisticated than none, she still hadn't made up her mind on the bra issue when it was time to put on the dress.

She owned two black bras. Each had straps. If she reached a certain way, which she was bound to do when she danced with Teague, who was at least six two, the straps showed.

She rummaged through Rachel's drawers for a strapless bra. The only things of interest she found were some framed photographs. She didn't know why her mother kept them. Rachel hated Jack. He might talk a blue streak about loyalty, but talk was all it was. They were divorced. That said it all.

She shoved the drawers closed and turned to leave.

"Everything all right?" Jack asked from the door.

Everything is not all right, she wanted to cry. My mother is in a coma, my father is a jerk, and I don't have a strapless bra. "Just fine," she ground out, and brushed past him.

"Doesn't sound it," he said, following her down the hall.

She whirled on him. "I'm nervous. All right? This is a big night. Just leave me alone."

He held up a hand and backed off—and even that angered her. She wanted to argue. She wanted to scream and shout and let off steam. A part of her even wanted to cry, but she wouldn't do that in front of him. Hope cried. Samantha didn't.

Besides, she didn't have time to do her eyes again.

BY SIX Jack was in the kitchen spooning chip dip into a bowl, while Hope arranged crackers on a dish around the bowl. They had barely put it in the living room when the doorbell rang.

"Talk to him," Samantha wailed from her room. "I'm not ready."

Jack opened the door to a young man who was just his height, but dark-haired, dark-eyed, dark-jawed. He was wearing a tux . . . barely. Where a pleated shirt should have been was a white T-shirt; where a cummerbund should have been was a wide leather belt; and the scuffed black shoes sticking out from his pants looked to Jack to be boots.

Jack extended a hand. "I'm Samantha's dad."

The returning handshake was firm, perhaps cocky, even defiant. "Teague Runyan."

Jack drew him into the house with the kind of firm hand that said he had no choice. "Samantha says you live here in Big Sur."

"Up the street a little," he said.

Hope approached with the dip, staring smilelessly at Teague.

"Hey, Hope," Teague said, "did you make this?" He topped a cracker with dip and popped it into his mouth. "Mmm. Good."

Jack waited until Teague had swallowed. "So what's the plan?"

"I don't know. Samantha made the arrangements."

"When can I expect her back?"

Teague looked mystified. "Sometime tomorrow. It depends how late we sleep."

That wasn't what Jack wanted to hear. "Where will this sleeping be?"

Teague shrugged. "It's Samantha's prom."

"Hi, Teague," Samantha said. She stood at the edge of the living room, looking gorgeous enough to take Jack's breath.

"Hey," said Teague by way of greeting. "Ready to go?"

There was no *You look great.* No *Here's a corsage.* Jack didn't like those boots or that wide leather belt. He didn't like the T-shirt, either.

He crossed to Samantha, pointing her back into the hall, and kept going until he was in her bedroom, glancing behind only to make sure she followed.

She did, but she wasn't happy. "I have to go," she hissed.

"You look beautiful," he said, taking her off guard.

"I do?"

"I wish your mother could see. Wait. I'll get a camera."

She grabbed his arm. "No, Daddy, please. Teague's waiting."

He should have had the camera ready. Should have thought ahead. "You really do look spectacular," he said, feeling suddenly terrified. "Can we talk about curfews?"

She looked at him like he had horns. *"Curfews?* This is an all-nighter. You *knew* that."

"I knew you were sleeping at Lydia's, but that's changed. So tell me the plans. I want to know where you'll be."

"The prom is at school."

"That's not the part that worries me." He rummaged through the refuse on her desk for a pen and a scrap of paper. "There are parties before and after. I need phone numbers."

"You can't check up on me," she cried. "If you call, I'll die."

He compromised. "Give me names, then." He could always call information. "The party before is at Jake's— Is it Jake Drummer?"

"Drumble."

"Where's the party after?"

"Pam's, I think, but it depends on who leaves the prom when, whether we want something to eat, and what we feel like after that, so I don't know."

"Would your mother be satisfied with that answer?"

"Yes. She trusts me."

"So do I. It's the other kids I don't trust." He had another idea. "Take my cell phone."

Again, that where-are-*you*-from look. "Why?"

"So we can be in touch."

She looked horrified. "Kids don't take cell phones to proms. Besides, where would I put it? This dress does *not* have pockets."

"A purse?"

She held up a thin thing on even thinner straps.

He sighed. "Okay. No phone. What's Pam's last name?"

She gave it grudgingly. He had barely begun scribbling it down when she started out of the room. "Wait," he said, because he was uneasy still.

She turned back with an impatient "What?"

"Call me if there's a problem." He approached her. "I'd like a call by ten tomorrow morning, please."

"Fine," she said, and disappeared into the hall.

He followed her back to the living room, arriving just as she swept Teague to the door.

"Bye," she said with a wave, and they were gone.

JAKE Drumble's house was a zoo. Samantha had never seen so many kids in such a small place in her life.

"Do you know these people?" Teague asked, snapping up two beers from the bar and putting one in her hand.

"I think they're football buddies of Jake's," she said. "Hey, there's Pam. Pam!" She led Teague through the crowd, stopping now and again when she felt resistance against her hand, to look back and find him talking to one girl or another. She couldn't blame those girls. He was the coolest guy in the place. She hooked an elbow through his when they reached Pam so that no one would doubt that he was Sam's for the night.

They talked and laughed with Pam and Jake. They munched on nachos and drank beer, ate popcorn and drank beer. Teague was the perfect date, always knowing when she needed a refill.

"How're you doing?" he said with a grin as he backed her into a corner.

She was feeling light-headed and free. "I'm doing fine."

Putting his hands on either side of the wall, he gave her the weight of his body. His mouth was inches from hers. "You're sweet." He erased those inches with a kiss that was so soft and gentle that all of her earlier worries seemed absurd.

"Nice?" he asked.

She grinned. "Mmmm."

"More?"

"Um-hm."

It was a deeper kiss this time, more mobile and open. Breathing hard, he made a guttural sound and put his forehead to hers. "Whooh. We gotta go somewhere."

Samantha was barely beginning to understand what he meant, when the room began to empty. "The prom," she managed to say.

"No. Somewhere alone."

"The prom," she insisted. She wasn't missing her first prom—and dancing with Teague Runyan—for the world.

JACK and Hope stood in Rachel's studio, surrounded by wood moldings that would soon be frames.

"Are you sure you know how to do this?" Hope asked.

"You bet," Jack said. "Those lengths of wood"—he pointed their way—"have to be cut to size with that"—his finger shifted—"miter saw. Then you predrill nail holes, apply wood glue, hammer in nails, clamp in that"—he pointed toward a heavy metal contraption—"miter vise. Piece of cake."

Hope grinned. "Piece of cake."

"I was thinking you'd help. It isn't hard. Want to?"

Hope's eyes told it all, even before she said an excited "Yes."

"Which picture first?" he asked.

Hope pointed to the loons. "That's my favorite."

The loons were Jack's favorite, too. When he projected himself into the scene, he felt closer to Rachel, which was something he very much wanted to feel on this night.

He didn't think he had handled Samantha well. Maybe Rachel would have known what to do and say. Then again, maybe not. In any case, he would have liked her input.

SAMANTHA and Teague left the prom shortly after ten and followed Pam and Jake to Ian McWain's house. The music was canned, but there was pizza, beer, and a punch that was incredibly sweet. Teague was treating her like she were gold, bringing her drinks, dancing body to body regardless of how fast the beat. Minute by minute the kids grew looser and louder, the music faster, the dancing wilder than it had been at school.

Samantha was high, feeling part of the crowd, part of the fun, part of Teague Runyan even, so that when he swiped a fresh longneck with one hand and led her outside to his truck, she went right along.

Pulling her close on the front seat, with an arm around her and his beer dangling between her breasts, he started driving.

"Where to?" she asked.

"Somewhere quiet," he said. "You're too special to share."

There was nothing she could say to that, so she smiled, closed her eyes, and buried her face in the rough spot under his jaw where his beard was a darkening shadow.

They hadn't driven far when he pulled the truck off the road.

Killing engine and lights, he took a long drink, put the bottle on the floor of the cab, and turned to her. He didn't say anything, just caught her face and held it while he kissed her.

He held her face until she was into the kiss; then he lowered both hands to her breasts. She made a sound of protest, feeling dizzy and high and confused.

"Ride with it," he whispered, and shifting, lowered her to the seat.

"Teague, I don't . . . This isn't—"

"Sure it is," he said in that grown-up, sexy way he had.

"No," she said, trying to slip out from under him. But she was on her back and he was pinning her down, hurting her.

"Let me go!" She found his hair and pulled.

"What the . . ."

Kick him in the groin, her mother had always said, and Samantha did just that. It didn't matter that she couldn't do it very hard, but it moved him enough for her to wriggle free, tug at the truck door, and fall out.

"Why'd you do that?" he yelled through the open door.

But she'd had more than enough of Teague Runyan, and she ran. She stumbled when her heels caught in the grass; then she caught herself and barreled on. She ran through a small wooded stretch, ran until she couldn't breathe, then stopped and was violently ill in someone's backyard. Holding her stomach, she backed up to the dark house, slid to the ground, and drew her knees close.

She took shallow breaths, listening hard in between. She couldn't hear Teague, couldn't see him. Finally she pushed up and away from the house. When she searched the street from behind a tree and saw no sign of the truck, she ran in what she hoped was the opposite direction. She turned a corner and sat on the edge of the road to regain strength in her legs, then forced herself up and ran until she rounded another corner. She sank to the ground, praying that no one would see her. She was in a residential area, but she had no idea which one. She felt sick and embarrassed and scared.

She started off again, trying to recognize the names on street signs and failing. She turned one corner just as a pickup approached, and she ducked behind a shrub, but it wasn't Teague's truck. She walked on, wondering what she was going to do. She wanted to lie down, just lie down and sleep while her mother kept watch, only her mother was in the hospital in a coma.

She walked another block. She imagined wandering around all night, freezing in the night air, making it to morning and not knowing what to do then.

More frightened by the minute, wanting only to be home, she began to cry softly. She was nearly frantic by the time she reached the end of another block and recognized the name on the street sign. "Thank God, thank God, thank God," she murmured, and started running again. It wasn't more than five minutes before she found a phone booth. She lifted the receiver, dialed the number, and waited for her father to answer.

JACK was painting when the phone rang, and felt an instant jolt. Dropping his palette and brush, he grabbed the phone. "Hello?"

There was a pause, then a broken "Daddy? Come pick me up."

He swallowed hard. "Where are you? What happened?"

"I feel sick. Can you come?"

"Right now. Tell me where you are." When she gave him a set of cross streets, he asked for the house address.

"It's a pay phone," she cried. "Can you come soon?"

He could do the drive in thirty-five minutes if he pushed it, but a pay phone? "Are you alone?" Where was her date? And what had he done?

"Hurry, Daddy."

"Samantha, do I need to call an ambulance? Or the police? Is there trouble—"

"I just want to come home!"

"Okay, sweetheart, okay. I'm on my way. Just stay there. Don't move. And if anyone stops, call the cops, okay?"

She said a shaky "Okay."

He had a thought. "Give me five minutes, then call me in the car." He wasn't sure what all had happened, but he didn't want to hang up and imagine her alone and sick for the length of his drive. Better to talk her through the time. That way, if she passed out or ran into more trouble, he could call an ambulance himself.

"I don't know the number," she wailed.

He told her and made her repeat it. "Five minutes, okay?"

"Okay."

He hung up, to find a wide-awake Hope inches behind him. "Can I come?"

He didn't answer, just took her hand and, snatching up his wallet in the kitchen, ran with her out to the car.

FIVE minutes passed, then ten, and the car phone didn't ring. He gripped the wheel and drove as fast as he could through a shifting fog, praying that she would still be there when he arrived.

"Okay," he said to Hope. "What do you know that I don't?"

"Nothing. Sam knew I didn't like what she was doing, so she didn't tell me. You were the one who was supposed to ask where she was going."

"I did, and it didn't get me very far." Hope was right. It was his job, and he had bungled it.

At least Samantha had had the sense to call.

IT WAS after two in the morning when he reached Carmel. The streets were deserted. He found the intersection Samantha had named, spotted the phone booth, pulled up fast, and saw nothing. He left the car, looking in every direction, when he heard her call.

"Daddy?" She was huddled on the floor of the phone booth, her tear-streaked face looking green in the night light. "I couldn't remember the number," she cried. "I tried everything."

He knelt, lifted her up and into his arms. Hope ran beside him and helped him fit her into the front seat and strap her in, then ran around the car and snaked behind the driver's seat into the back. He slipped off his jacket and covered Samantha up, because she was trembling. Then he put a hand on the top of her head.

"Do we need a hospital?" he asked softly.

She shook her head. "I just drank too much."

"Where's your date?"

She began to cry. "He wanted to do things I didn't."

Jack's heart ached. "Good girl," he said. Leaning over, he kissed the crown of her head, then turned the car for home.

WHEN they got to Big Sur, he carried Samantha to her room. While she showered, he stared out at the forest through the living-room glass, wondering exactly what had happened.

The water went off. He gave her enough time to get into bed, then went to her room to make sure she was all right.

She had the quilt up to her chin, but she wasn't sleeping. He hunkered down by her face. "What I need to know most," he said gently, "is whether he . . . touched you in ways he shouldn't have." He wasn't sure how else to ask.

She didn't answer at first. So he said, "If it was rape—"

"No."

He waited for her to say more. When she didn't, he said, "Talk to me, Sam. I'm worried. I want to help." After another minute he said, "If your mother was here, she'd be sitting right here talking to you. It's not prying. It's not accusing or finding fault."

She closed her eyes. One tear, then another slid out of the down-ward corners. He felt the pain of each. When she covered her face with a hand and broke into long, deep sobs, he felt those, too.

Sitting back on his heels, he continued to stroke her head until her crying slowed. Then he blew out a breath. "I wouldn't want to be your age for all the tea in China."

She sniffled. "Why not?"

"It's in between nowhere." How well he remembered. "You aren't a child anymore, so you can't just play dumb when things go wrong. You're expected to do a lot of grown-up stuff because you need the experience, only you don't have the experience, so half the time you don't know what you're doing. No. I'd like to be twenty-seven again. But fifteen? Not on your life."

"What was so great about twenty-seven?"

He thought about that. "Your mom."

Samantha started to cry again. "I need her."

"I know. But she isn't here, so we're going to try to work this through together the way she would. Want to tell me about tonight? I want to hear."

"That's because you love knowing"—her voice caught—"what a loser I am."

Fiercely he said, "You aren't a loser. If you were, you'd still be at some party with kids making fools of themselves, drinking and dancing on tables and taking off their clothes—"

Her eyes went wide. "How did you know?"

"I've been there, sweetie."

"Did you know Teague would have beer in his car?"

"No. But it doesn't surprise me."

"You didn't like him."

"How could I? He didn't even tell you how pretty you looked. And you looked pretty, Sam. So did he just leave you at the phone booth or what?"

"I ran there. He probably went back to the party."

"Nice guy," Jack muttered. "If he was cool, he'd have followed you and driven you home. If he was really cool, he'd have kept his hands to himself in the first place."

"It wasn't all his fault. I let him a little."

Jack had figured that. Quietly he said, "Letting him, a little, is okay as long as you trust the guy and there isn't booze involved. Drinking makes people do dumb things. It makes them do tragic things. Anyway, it's over and done. A big part of growing up is learning when to be cautious. It's realizing that you're held accountable for your actions."

She was quiet for so long that Jack wondered if she had fallen asleep. He should have known better.

In the same quiet, very grown-up voice he had used, Samantha asked, "How does that fit in with the divorce? Are you accountable for your actions in a marriage, too?"

It was a minute before he said, "Yes."

"Then you accept the blame for the divorce?"

"No. It takes two to make a marriage and two to break it."

"But how could you guys just let it go?" Samantha asked, and there were tears in her voice again.

"We didn't."

"You did," she cried. "You didn't argue about it; you just split," she charged. "What was your side of the story?"

He wasn't sure he should say, but Samantha needed an answer. "I felt," he began, "that your mother didn't want me. That we had grown apart, maybe needed different things. I was tied to the city because of work, and that was the last place she wanted to be."

"But you loved her."

"Yes."

"Do you still?"

He thought about the hand-around-the-heart feeling he experienced walking into that hospital room every day. "Probably."

"So why didn't you fight to keep her? Wasn't it worth it? Weren't *we* worth it?"

The question stunned him. "Yes. Yes."

"I kept thinking about that when I was waiting for you to come get me. That you were right; we weren't worth it. Especially me."

"Are you crazy?"

"See?" she cried. "You'd never say that to Hope."

"No, I'd say other things to Hope, because Hope and you are different people. Different. Not better or worse."

"She's lovable and I'm not. I say too much."

"That's one of the things that makes you lovable. I always know where I stand. That's a real plus in a relationship. Honesty. Trust. Ease. Well, sometimes we don't have ease, you and me, but that's because you're your age and I'm—"

"Old."

He sighed. "I guess. So, see, we can talk about that, too."

She turned onto her back and stared at the ceiling. "I couldn't talk to Teague. I was afraid he'd think I was a kid."

"Teague's crud," Jack said. "You can do better, Sam."

"I thought he *was* better. Shows how much *I* know."

"You learned. That's what growing up is about. What went wrong with Brendan and Lydia?"

Unexpectedly, Samantha started crying again. Then, between sobs, she said, "I blew them off, so now I don't have them—and I won't have Pam and Heather, because Teague must have gone back there and told them what happened. I'm not going to be able to show my face in school again, not *ever*. I am such a loser."

"No. No, you're not, but I think you should call Lydia later."

"I can't. She's not going to want to talk to me."

"You could apologize. Lydia strikes me as a forgiving person."

Samantha started to cry again.

"What's wrong now?" he asked.

"I miss Mom."

Feeling a wrenching inside, he smoothed the hair back from her face. "Me, too," he said, and realized that he did, very much.

He continued to stroke her hair until she fell asleep.

HE WOKE up Sunday morning to the peal of the phone. "Jack? It's Kara Bates. Rachel's thrown a clot."

" 'THROWN a clot.' What does that mean?" Samantha asked. They were in the car, speeding back to Monterey.

Hope had her lucky boots back on and was leaning forward between their seats, waiting for his answer.

Jack repeated what Kara had told him. "On rare occasions a broken bone—in Mom's case, her leg—creates a clot, a wad that enters the bloodstream and moves through the veins. Sometimes it gets stuck in the head or the heart, sometimes the lungs. That's where your mom's got stuck."

"Like, could she die from this?" Samantha persisted.

"She could, Sam," he said, "but she won't, because we've got Bauer and Bates with her right now. The problem is, a clot can cut the flow of blood. In your mother's case that's the last thing they want. Her brain is healing. It needs all the oxygen it can get, and since blood carries oxygen, they don't want anything slowing the flow."

"So do they operate and cut it out?"

"They're treating it with medication—something they call a clot buster. It's heavy-duty stuff that will break up the clot."

"What if it doesn't?"

"Sam"—he took her hand—"it doesn't do any good to think the worst. And we're due for a break, aren't we?"

"Yes," she whispered, and closed her eyes.

He held her hand for a while. It comforted him, as did the weight of Hope's cheek against his shoulder.

RACHEL was back in ICU. Her lips and the area surrounding them were blue. That would have been frightening enough without the gasping sound she was making.

"What's happened," Kara explained as Jack and the girls watched Rachel in horror, "is that because there's a block, blood carrying oxygen can't get to her lungs to exchange with blood carrying carbon dioxide. The gasping you hear is her attempt to get more oxygen to her lungs. She sounds a lot worse than she is."

To Jack's ears Rachel sounded on the verge of death. He was appalled. "How long until the medicine starts working?"

"We're hoping to see results within a few hours."

THE first hour crept by. Jack was frightened and unsure, as terrified by the gasping, grating sounds Rachel was making as he was by the tinge of her skin. For a time he simply stood with an arm around each of the girls, but they were all tired. Eventually they sat down on the bed, the girls on one side of Rachel, Jack on the other.

The second hour began, and Katherine arrived looking pale and upset—totally different from any other way Jack had seen her. Her face was washed clean, her curls caught up in a ponytail. She wore a lightweight warm-up suit and sneakers.

Jack took comfort in her presence. She was his friend now, too. They were allies in the same war.

When he sent the girls to the cafeteria for drinks, she said, "Thanks for calling. I was working out. I got your message as soon as I got back. Just took time to shower."

"You look great," he said. When she gave him a skeptical look, he added, "I'm serious. All natural. Very Rachel. Thanks for coming." He touched Rachel's lips. They were parted, air grating in and out. "I don't want to lose her, Katherine. Do you think she wants to hear that?"

Katherine looked at him and sighed. "You're not a bad-looking guy. Need a haircut. Need a shave. But you clean up good. So, yeah, she'd want to hear it. What woman wouldn't?"

"HI, THERE."

Jack had left to join the girls in the cafeteria for breakfast. Katherine was leaning over the bedrail, letting Rachel know she was rooting for her, when Steve Bauer walked in. She had known he would appear, had felt it in her gut well before she decided to forgo makeup and mousse. She figured it was time to give him a preview of her less glamorous side.

"What's happening here?" she asked, straightening.

"Clot. Drip. Wait."

"Ah. Thanks."

He approached the bed, studied Rachel, then the monitor. He adjusted the solution dripping from the IV bag.

Katherine sensed his worry. "How does something like this affect the coma? Can it snap her out of it?"

"It can. It may not." He turned his blue eyes on her, along with a small smile. "How are you?"

"Nervous about Rachel."

"How far back do you two go?"

"Six years, but I feel like I've known her forever, we're so alike."

"You look more alike now than usual."

"Ashen skin? Blue lips?"

"Unadorned. You look pretty."

Jack had said the same thing, but it felt different coming from

Steve. She squeezed Rachel's hand. "He's hitting on me again."

"No. Just saying I'm in for the long haul." Before she could begin to analyze *that,* he said, "So you and Rachel are alike. Tell me how."

Katherine could do that. "She's an only child. So am I. She grew up in the city. So did I. She hated it. So did I."

"Why?"

"I felt lost. I like bumping into people I know."

"Like Rick Meltzer?"

Rick was the anesthesiologist who had called out her name. "Like Rick," she admitted.

"Does she like movies?"

"Good ones." She arched a brow. "Don't even suggest it."

"I wasn't about to. You'd feel guilty going to a movie with Rachel struggling in here, but you have to eat, and I can't go far from the hospital. I was thinking something quick and easy, like grilled salmon sandwiches on Fisherman's Wharf."

Katherine couldn't help but grin. "With the tourists?"

"It's quick. It's easy. Tell you what. I'll be in and out of here for another few hours. If you're hungry at two, meet me out front. My car is the dark green CJ-Seven." He briefly turned away to check the speed of the drip, then, with an endearingly vulnerable glance at Katherine, left the room.

WHEN Jack returned with the girls, he was discouraged to find that nothing had changed.

"Bauer was just here," Katherine said. "He didn't seem overly concerned."

But Jack was. Rachel was fading away before his eyes. It struck him that this was his punishment. He had let Rachel walk out of his life. Had *let* her. Samantha was right. He hadn't fought. He had let the silence win.

"Dammit," he muttered, and suddenly his eyes filled with tears.

"Hey, guys," Katherine said to Samantha and Hope, "let's take a walk. Your parents need some private time."

Jack didn't look, but he knew when they were gone. Taking a steadying breath, he whispered his thumb over Rachel's eyelids. "I want to talk about what happened. We never did that. We just kind of split up and went separate ways. Fell back into who we were before we met, but that wasn't us. It was me. It was you. It wasn't us."

He took a shuddering breath and said fiercely, "We had a darn nice marriage, Rachel. I want it back. Don't you die on me now."

She didn't move, just took one gasping breath after another.

Frightened, he pulled up a chair and sat down.

HE WAS in the same chair when Samantha and Hope came back into the room an hour later. Noon had come and gone. Rachel was still blue, still gasping.

"I keep thinking about Lydia," Samantha said softly. "I should tell her about Mom."

Jack pulled the cell phone from his pocket and held it out.

She took it. "What if she hangs up when she hears my voice?"

"She won't hang up." If she did, he would never forgive her. Samantha was headed in the right direction. He didn't want her derailed. "Do it now, Sam. If you know something's right, don't let it go. That's a lesson we all have to learn."

SAMANTHA wanted privacy to call Lydia. So she walked to the end of the corridor and wedged herself in a lonely corner. If Lydia refused to talk, she didn't know what she'd do. But Rachel had given her a perfect excuse. The blood clot was something to tell Lydia. Lydia adored Rachel. All of Samantha's friends adored Rachel.

She pressed in Lydia's number. When Lydia's mother answered, Samantha's throat closed. In that instant, she would have given anything to hear her own mother's voice.

She cleared her throat. "Hi, Mrs. Russell. Is Lydia up?"

"Samantha. We missed you last night. I thought for sure you'd stop over. Did you have fun?"

Samantha's eyes teared up. "No. It wasn't . . . what I thought. Is everyone still there?"

"Shelly just left. I think Lydia's in the shower. Hold on."

Samantha turned in against the wall and waited.

"Yes, she's in the shower," Mrs. Russell said. "Is there a message?"

"Um, it's kind of important. My mom is worse."

There was a gasp. "Hold on, Samantha. Let me get her out."

Samantha pressed her head to the wall. It seemed forever until Lydia's voice came through. "What happened to your mom?"

Acting as though nothing had ever come between them, Samantha told her about the clot and ended with "She's making an awful sound. It's very scary."

There was a silence on the other end, then a wary "Do you want me to come?"

"Yes."

"Okay."

The line went dead before Samantha could say another word. She felt humbled. Lydia hadn't sounded young or stupid. She had taken the phone call when she had every right not to. Maybe her father was right. Maybe there was a lesson here.

KATHERINE had no intention of going to the Wharf for lunch. It felt wrong, with Rachel so weak. She wanted to be at the hospital, rooting, supporting, fighting for her, right by her side. But Jack and the girls were doing that—Jack surprisingly well. And they were family. Besides, she was hungry.

She went down to the front door, assuming that a CJ-7 was a snappy sports car. The dark green car that waited, though, was an old-fashioned Jeep with a roll bar on top, neither roof nor windows, and what looked like tin for doors.

"Wow," she said, fastening her seat belt. "Quite a car."

Steve grinned. "Thanks." He stepped on the gas, and the car headed out. "CJ means civilian Jeep. Know any Jeep history?"

"Uh, no. Beauty school doesn't go that far."

He laughed. "Neither does med school. Jeeps go back to World War Two—1941—when the army needed a reconnaissance vehicle that would go anywhere. Lore has it that the name Jeep is a derivation of GP—general purpose. The first CJs hit the road as early as '46. So there's your trivia for the day."

He took his time driving—enjoying the fresh air, she imagined, because she surely was. The May sun was relaxingly warm, the ocean air a far cry from the hospital's sterility.

Despite his promise to make it quick, he parked a distance away, and they walked to the Wharf. Without the lab coat he looked totally casual—sport shirt, old jeans, sneakers.

They passed storefront after storefront as they ambled down the pier. They reached its end just as a bench opened up. Steve parked her there and left, returning several minutes later with cups of clam chowder, grilled-salmon sandwiches, and iced tea.

Katherine ate every last bit of her portion, not in the least embarrassed, since Steve ate every last bit of his, and with the very same grinning gusto.

Walking back up the pier, he guided her to the car.

He didn't immediately start it, but turned to her and sat back. "That didn't hurt, did it?"

She laughed. "No, Doctor."

"I'm serious." She could see that he was. Then quietly he said, "I'm a good guy, Katherine. You can trust me.

"I've been divorced for ten years," he continued. "I've had it with dating. So if I come on faster than you want, it's because I don't see the point in beating around the bush when someone appeals to me. Few women have. You do."

The air grew charged.

"Say the word, and I'll get lost," he said.

She wanted to say the word, wanted to say any word, but none came.

"Either tell me to get lost," he said, "or give me a kiss."

"That's not a fair choice."

"Look, I know the timing of this stinks, but I'm fifty-three. I'm too old to play games. Do you want me to get lost?"

"No."

"Then kiss me."

"Why?"

"I want to see if it works."

"What a male thing to say."

"And because I said it, you're totally turned off."

"I should be." But she wasn't, because it went two ways. If his kiss left her cold, she wouldn't have to worry about the rest. They could be friends without the threat of anything more.

"Okay," she said, and looked at her watch. "One minute. Then we have to leave." She leaned over and put her lips to his, moved them a little, backed off. "Am I doing a solo here?"

Smiling, he shook his head. He slid one hand around her neck and moved gentle fingers into her hair, slid the other around her shoulder. His eyes touched her lips. He took his time, moved closer, tipped his head, took more time. His mouth was an inch from hers when, with a less-than-steady breath, he drew back, faced front, cleared his throat, and turned the key in the ignition.

Katherine stared in disbelief. "What are you doing?"

"Minute's up." Shifting in his seat, he headed out of the parking lot. "It works. Wasn't that the point of the exercise?"

"Works for who?" she cried. She jabbed a finger at her lips. "Is that your idea of a kiss? I didn't feel a thing."

He shot her one look, then, when she didn't relent, shot her another. Seconds after that he pulled over to the curb, took her into his arms, and gave her a kiss that spelled trouble.

SAMANTHA stood beside Rachel's bed watching the door. It was thirty minutes since she had called Lydia. Jack had his elbows on the bedrail. He was staring at Rachel. Hope was looking around the room, sitting cross-legged with her butt against Rachel's cast.

Hope straightened her legs and slid off the bed. Her boots hit the floor with a thunk. "I'm getting stuff from the other room. This room could be anyone's." She strode into the hall.

"She shouldn't do that," Samantha warned. "The point is getting Mom back there as soon as the medicine works."

Jack had straightened. "That is the point. But then there's Murphy's Law. It says that as soon as we move everything here, she'll be ready to move back. Hold the fort," he said, and left.

Samantha curled her fingers over the bedrail. Just thinking about the fiasco of the prom, she felt lost and scared. The best part was getting home. She didn't know how many of the other dads would have been as supportive as hers had been.

"Sam?"

She whirled around. Lydia's eyes were on Rachel, reflecting the same horror Samantha had felt seeing her mother like this for the first time.

"Can't they *do* something?"

Samantha waved at the IV pole. "It's up there. We have to wait for it to work."

"Oh. Does she know about last night?"

"You mean, did my telling her cause this?" It wasn't the vote of confidence Samantha needed. "No, Lydia, I haven't told her. She did this all on her own."

"Don't get angry. She'd be upset about last night, and you know it."

Samantha looked at her. "What do you know about last night?"

Lydia kept her eyes on Rachel. "You went to Ian's but left with Teague and got so sloshed you passed out, so he drove you home. At least, that's what Teague's been telling everyone. Is it true?"

"No, it is not true. I didn't pass out, and Teague didn't drive me home. He came on so strong that I could nail him for rape—only it never got past the attempted stage. I ran away before it did. Me sloshed? Try Teague. My father came and got me."

Lydia's eyes were wide. "You had to *call* him?"

"I wanted to call you, but I didn't think you'd care."

Lydia looked close to tears and totally like the sweet person Samantha loved. "You're stupid, you know that?" Lydia cried.

Samantha was about to say she was right, when Hope walked in loaded down with cards and pictures. Jack followed with vases of flowers. Samantha said to Lydia, "We're counting on Murphy's Law. Want to help?"

STEVE BAUER AND KATHERINE arrived minutes later. He checked Rachel's chart, the monitor, and the IV drip, then ordered another lung scan. Within minutes the necessary equipment was wheeled in. Jack sent the three girls outside to walk around in the sun. He and Katherine waited in the hall.

"She'll make it," Katherine insisted. "There are too many people working too hard to make her live."

"The point isn't just to make her live. It's to make her wake up and be well. She could wake up not whole. You asked me once what I'd do then. I think I'd be destroyed."

"Would you leave?"

"No." It was a sober admission. "No, I couldn't." When Katherine said nothing, he met her gaze. It was open and warm. "What?" he asked.

"Man has risen to the occasion," she declared, her eyes flying toward Rachel's room.

Jack followed her gaze. All he could see was Steve Bauer, alternately watching the technicians and looking out into the hall at them. And there was Katherine, with windblown hair and warm apricot cheeks.

"Did I miss something?" he asked.

She bowed her head. "Don't ask. This is *so* not the right time."

He disagreed. "I could use a lift. Make me smile."

She raised her head. "He's a great kisser. What should I do?"

Jack did smile. He liked the doctor. The smile faded when he realized what she meant. "Ah. The old breast thing."

She nodded.

He understood. It had to be hard for Katherine to open herself to the kind of rejection she had already experienced twice. "But breasts are only a small part of a woman. Intelligence is more constant. So is warmth and humor. So is loyalty. Look at Steve in there with Rachel. He doesn't have to be here. It's Sunday. Give a guy like that the choice between a bimbo with natural breasts and an intelligent, warm, funny, loyal, beautiful woman with rebuilt ones—no contest. Why, I'd go after you myself if I weren't still in love with my wife."

RACHEL REMAINED unresponsive to the clot buster. The scan showed no noticeable improvement in the passage of air through her lungs. The doctor said it would take longer.

Sitting with her that afternoon, Jack thought about love. Having admitted that he loved Rachel, he wanted to do something. He wanted to believe she would wake up, and wanted things to be right when she did. But right now he needed to paint. He needed to frame. And, he decided, he needed to buy a new car.

Chapter Seven

THE car Jack bought was technically a truck. It was a large, loaded, four-wheel-drive vehicle with power, luxury, and class. He wanted the best for Rachel and the girls.

And he could afford it. How well, he discovered in Rachel's studio that night. He hadn't planned on scrutinizing his finances, had hooked his laptop to the modem for the sole purpose of transferring money from one account to another for the car. Then he set about framing more of Rachel's pieces. The girls were helping. His mind wandered. Transferring money had put a bug in his ear. So when it was time for a break, he went back to the laptop and accessed his bank records and investment accounts.

He hadn't deliberately saved money in the years since his divorce; he simply hadn't spent much. He also discovered, several links later, that San Francisco real estate was at a healthy high, which meant the value of his house had appreciated considerably.

He was, it seemed, fairly well off. For a guy who had started with nothing, he had done well.

When Hope put her head down on the worktable, he sent her to bed. Samantha worked a while longer. By the time she finally went off to her room, six paintings were one step away from being done and ready to hang.

Alone, Jack went to work on a wolf. It was a beautiful thing, lying low in a carpet of khaki-green summer grass, with the top of its head and body outlined, white fur backlit by the sun.

It was nearly five in the morning when he finally finished. He slept for two hours and awoke exhausted. Samantha said she was too tired for school. Hope said she wanted to be with Rachel.

He pushed his hands through his hair. "Your mother would want you in school, and it would do my mind good to know you're there. I'll pick you up right after. You can see her then."

Sam argued as they drove, but he held firm. When he pulled up at the school, she didn't budge. Where a mutinous pout would have been days before, now there was an expression of sheer apprehension.

He tried to understand what she was feeling. "Lydia had no problem with this."

"There's all the other kids. And Teague. It's mortifying."

"Yes." He sighed. "But the sooner it's done, the sooner it's done, if you get my drift."

She scooped her hair back. "Here goes nothing," she mumbled. She opened the door and had barely stepped out when Lydia came toward her. The door closed with a solid new-car thud.

One down, Jack thought, and looked back at Hope. She seemed a great distance behind him, belted safely in, but too far away. When he motioned her forward, she unbuckled herself, shimmied into the passenger's seat, and sat.

So softly it was nearly a whisper, she said, "I have a funny feeling."

"Funny feeling?"

"I want to be with Mom. Like I was with Guinevere."

Jack's heart buckled. He reached over and pulled her into a hug over the center console. "Your mother isn't dying," he said into her hair. "We'll fight harder than ever to wake her up."

"How?" came her small voice.

"I don't know. I don't know, but we'll think of a way."

JACK sat on Rachel's hospital bed and exercised her hands and arms. He told her the medicine was working in places they couldn't see and that it was only a matter of time before she would wake up.

"Sounds like a course in the power of positive thinking," David Sung said from the door. He wasn't a tall man, but he wore his suits well. Today's was a light gray plaid.

He entered the room and put the heels of his hands on the bedrail across from Jack. "I thought I'd come see for myself what's happening here, give you a little support. Is she showing any improvement?"

Jack blew out a breath. "Nah. Not yet."

In the silence that followed, Jack didn't look at his partner. He didn't want to talk business, but business was all they shared.

David cleared his throat. "Listen, Jack, I don't mean to be the heavy, but the truth is, I'm worried. Something's going on here that I don't get."

Jack threaded his fingers through Rachel's. They looked bare. He wondered what she had done with her wedding ring.

"We had no business losing Boca," David said. "We can't afford things like that any more than we can afford to take on the kind of house designing we did ten years ago. This isn't where I want to be at this point in my life."

"Me, neither," Jack said.

"So, okay, we lost Boca. It was more trouble than it was worth. But we need Montana, and"—he grew expectant—"we need Atlantic City."

"What's in Atlantic City?"

"A new hotel," he said with glee. "Big press, big bucks."

Jack raised Rachel's arm, angled it slowly across her chest.

"Well?" David said. "Are you in?"

Jack raised his eyes and slowly shook his head. He was tired of doing projects he didn't like. He was tired of traveling. "It's not working for me anymore," he said. "I want out."

David looked startled. "Out? Out of the firm?"

"Wasn't that what you asked?"

"Yeah, but I didn't expect you'd chuck it. This is your firm as much as it's mine."

"Actually," Jack said with a sigh, "it hasn't been mine for a while.

Isn't that what's been wrong between you and me? It's more yours than mine. I've been pulling back for a while."

David continued to look stunned.

"Regardless of what happens with Rachel," Jack said, "I want to downsize. I want to represent people; you want to represent conglomerates. It's time we split."

"Just like that?"

Jack rubbed his forehead. "Not just like that. There were good years. And there are details. People to reassure. Assets to split." Still, David was stunned. "Why are you surprised? You're here now. You see. This is not a vacation. It's my life."

Perplexed now, David said sharply, "Are you gonna open your own firm or what?"

Jack's voice rose. "I don't know."

David stared at him for the longest time, then turned on his heel. The last Jack saw of him he was shaking his head and picking up the pace of his shiny black shoes. Only when he was completely gone from sight did the enormity of what Jack had done hit him, and then he was as stunned as David had been. Stunned, but relieved. He was suddenly breathing easier.

Then it struck him that he wasn't the only one who was. He looked at Rachel, listened. The gasping was easing. Holding his breath that he wasn't imagining it, he rang for the nurse.

BAUER hurried in. So did Bates, Winston, and everyone else on the floor who had been involved with Rachel's care. The monitor showed improved oxygenation; the gasping was softer, and her lips were definitely less blue.

There were high-fives all around. Rachel might still be comatose, but everything in medicine was relative.

Long after they were gone, Jack was still grinning, breathing one loud, relieved sigh after another. Then, because he needed to hug her and it had been too long, he slid his arms under, carefully drew her up, and fitted her body to his. He closed his eyes on unwanted tears and gave several more immense sighs.

He didn't know how long he held her. There was no rush, no rush at all. When he opened his eyes, Katherine was smiling. Very gently he settled Rachel into the pillows.

"Steve called and told me the news," she said. "He was nearly as excited as I was." She came to the bed. "This is a good sign."

As far as the doctors were concerned, the medicine had finally kicked in. As far as Jack was concerned, Rachel had been listening in on his conversation with David and had reacted with a show of support. He was grinning again, grinning still. He felt so tired, so good, so shocked. "Katherine, I just deep-sixed my job."

"You what?"

He told her about David's visit. "We'll be dissolving the firm."

"Wow," she said, then, "Good for you. You can work on your own, whenever, wherever."

"Yeah, well, I want to work out of Big Sur, but that's Rachel's turf. For all I know, she wants no part of me."

"Is that what you think?"

"I don't know what to think, since she isn't talking. You're her best friend. Do you think she'd consider giving it another try?"

Cautious, she said, "A try, as in living together? Remarrying?"

"Remarrying," Jack said. "Come on, answer me. I'm a big boy."

Katherine held up her hands. "Not my place to say."

KATHERINE had to return to work, Jack had to call his lawyer, and then it was time to get the girls. When they returned to the hospital, Rachel had been moved back to a regular room. Jack talked with his lawyer again while the girls were busy with Rachel; then he told Rachel about dissolving the firm. He drove the girls back to Big Sur, cooked dinner, and went to the studio.

Samantha worked with him for a while before heading off to make calls. Jack was relieved that she was back to normal. Hope continued to work by his side until he finally sent her to bed. They had framed another six pictures that night. Twelve were done in all. They couldn't do much more until Jack finished painting.

He chose a canvas depicting a great egret spreading its wings for takeoff. His task was to fill in the murky dusk of the Florida Everglades against which the white bird was poised. He went to work.

JACK should have been used to being woken by the phone, but he jumped as high as ever when it rang Tuesday morning at dawn.

He reached it on the first grab. "Yes?"

"Mr. McGill?" The voice was authoritative. "This is Janice Pierce. I'm one of the residents—"

"What happened?" he cut in, sitting up.

"Rachel is starting to move her fingers and toes. She may be starting to wake up."

The girls had heard the phone and were beside him even before he hung up. Within five minutes they were on their way.

When they arrived at the hospital, Rachel was propped on her left side. There was no sign of movement. Pillows held her in place. She lay still as ever.

Fearful, Jack eased lank blond hair back from a face that was growing thinner by the day. "Hi, Rachel. Hi, angel. They told us you're moving. Can we see?"

"Hi, Mommy." Hope crowded in beside him. "It's me. We didn't even have breakfast; we just came here first."

"There," Samantha cried, pointing at the sheet. "Her foot."

Jack pulled the sheet away. When there was nothing, Jack tickled her sole.

Hope said a worried "That always makes her laugh."

"How can she not feel it?" Samantha asked.

"She's still comatose," Kara said as she joined them. "The movement isn't conscious. It usually comes in waves, brief periods of activity alternating with periods of rest."

"What do we do now?" Jack asked the power-pearl lady. "How do we get her to do more?"

"Keep doing what you've been doing. Something's working."

JACK drove the girls to school; then he turned around and drove back to Big Sur. He had something urgent to do.

The farmland flanking the road just south of Carmel was green with lettuce and artichoke; the hills beyond were wild-mustard yellow. Granite outcroppings on the shore side of the road were a rich gray, almost slate under an emerging blue sky. Beyond rock the ocean was kelp green, then aqua descending into a deep, dark charcoal blue. The sky was endless and new.

Turning off the highway at Rachel's road, he felt the glow of familiarity. He climbed from the car and stretched, smiled, filled his lungs with air so clear that his body tingled. Then he went to work, moving in and out of the house like a man possessed, carrying framed canvas after framed canvas to the car that was, thankfully, a truck. When twelve were carefully stacked around foam buffers, he closed the hatch and drove to P. Emmet's.

Ben was waiting at the gallery. They quickly carried the pieces inside and stood them against a wall not far from the three paintings already there. Ben's excitement was obvious. He moved in, hunkered down before one, moved on to the next, moved back.

When Jack couldn't bear the suspense, he said, "Well? What do you think?"

"I think she's brilliant," Ben said. "She captured everything I wanted her to. These have the same feeling as the bobcat cubs." He darted Jack a glance. "Nice job with the frames."

Feeling validated and exuberant, Jack grinned. "Thanks."

RACHEL continued to do small things with fingers and toes, occasionally twitching an ankle, elbow, or knee, but there wasn't anything new until that evening. Jack was helping the night nurse turn her, when she moaned. When they repeated the motion, she repeated the moan. Then she settled into silence.

Eventually, at the nurse's urging, Jack drove home. He fell into bed at eleven and slept straight through until Hope shook his shoulder. His eyelids were heavy. With an effort he raised one.

"We're taking the bus," she whispered.

He came awake fast. "No. I'll get ready," he said.

"Sleep longer," Samantha said from the door. "I called the hospital. She's doing the same stuff, but she isn't awake. They promised they'd call when she is."

Jack slept for another three hours. When he woke up, he called the hospital. Rachel hadn't come any further, but she hadn't regressed. The nurses were pleased.

Sipping hot coffee, he stood at the wall of windows overlooking the forest. It was another beautiful, peaceful day.

He turned around. Same with the house. Beautiful. Peaceful. But also fun and full of life, very much the irreverent Rachel he had met so long ago. The Rachel he had married.

With that thought he set off for the bedroom. He searched the dresser, the night table, the closet. He searched the kitchen cabinets. He searched the pantry. He stood in the living room with his hands on his hips and wondered where she would have put it.

If she had kept it.

On a hunch he strode back through the house to Hope's room. Everything here was sweet—and there it was, on the dresser, a fat little ceramic cherub with wings.

He picked up the angel, turned it over, and slipped two small latches hidden under the wings. He lifted off a back panel, pulled out a velvet bag, and emptied its contents into his hand. There were the pearl earrings Rachel had worn at their wedding. And the ring.

JACK and Rachel were divorced. So he felt a little awkward about the wedding ring. Technically he had no right putting it on Rachel's finger. But he wanted it there. He wanted to think it might help. He wanted her to see it when she woke up.

He took her hand while he kissed her cheek, then straightened. Holding her hand close to his chest, he exercised her fingers. Slipping the ring on was part of the motion. No matter that it was looser than it had ever been. It was on.

He ran the pad of his thumb over her face and the scrapes that were nearly healed. *Where are you, Rachel?*

As though in answer to the question, she moved her eyes.

Jack leaned closer. "Rachel?" Her eyeballs were moving behind their lids. "Rachel, wake up. Come on, honey. I know you hear me. Open those eyes. Open those eyes."

The movement continued for a minute, then stopped.

RACHEL didn't move her eyes again, but by the time Jack brought the girls, her lids were ajar. Not much. Just enough to see a tiny rim of white. Jack was frantic with impatience.

"That looks totally gross, Mom," Samantha said.

Hope was ducking down, trying to look under those lids and see something that might see her. She had barely straightened when she saw the wedding band. Her eyes flew to Jack. "Where did you find this?" she asked. "Did she send it to you? I always wondered where it was."

"She kept it," Jack said. Unsure, he looked from Hope to Samantha and back. "I thought it might help. Anyone have a problem with this?"

Neither girl did. They were as restless as he was as the hours passed, and as reluctant to leave Rachel. Ben stopped by. Steve and Kara came in and prodded and tested and talked. Cindy turned Rachel, who moaned, then settled back into place with those same barely open eyes. Steve came again.

By nine Jack and the girls were the only ones left. Hope was pale and yawning; Samantha's mood was sour; Jack was beat. At ten they finally drove home.

Chapter Eight

J ACK sat up in bed and stared into the dark. He thought about how tired he was. He looked at his watch.

It was twelve thirty. He had a sudden urge to drive back to the hospital, but he called there instead and was told that Rachel still hadn't woken.

He lay down again and slept for two hours. He called the hospital, lay down again, slept for three hours this time. He called the hospital. He lay down. He got up and opened the window. And he felt it, felt Rachel.

When he turned away from the window, Hope was at the door. She didn't say anything, just hung on the knob and looked at him.

"Are you sensing things?" he asked.

She nodded.

"Me, too." So maybe they were both going mad, wanting something so much that it became real in their minds. The only thing he knew for sure was that he wouldn't be able to fall back to sleep. "Wanna take a drive?"

HOPE was belted sideways into the back seat. Samantha was in front, with an elbow against the door and a fist to her chin. It was nearly thirty minutes past sunrise on a gray day. Traffic was light. No one spoke.

As they left the car and entered the hospital, Jack tried to stay calm, but he didn't have the patience to wait for the elevator. He found the stairs and took them two at a time, while the girls trotted close behind. They swung onto Rachel's floor, strode quickly down the hall, and stopped just inside her room. Samantha was on his left, Hope on his right. Rachel was on her back, her eyes that same little bit open that they had been the night before.

Jack swallowed. Disappointment lay thick in his throat.

He approached the bed and gave Rachel the lightest, softest kiss on the mouth.

"What happened, Daddy?" Hope asked.

"I guess we got ourselves wound up with wanting, honey."

"This is getting old," Samantha complained.

He let out a breath, then spoke with angry force. "You're toying with us, Rachel. That is not fair." He looked at her long and hard. Something was going on in there. Her eyes were darting around. He saw a pinch between her brows, a tiny frown.

Another frown came. Her eyes began moving more slowly.

Her lids fluttered. They shut, then pressed together. Slowly they rose.

Jack was afraid to breathe. After initial gasps from behind him, there was no sound at all. Rachel's eyes stayed on his face, stayed there so long that he half feared she was still comatose. Then her eyes broke from his and moved past to Hope.

"Mommy?" Hope cried.

Her eyes shifted to Samantha, who said a breathless "Omigosh."

When those eyes returned to him, they were confused. Then she looked at the girls again and smiled. In a voice that was weak but very Rachel, she asked, "What's doing?"

He gave a shout of relief, and suddenly the girls were crowding in, hugging Rachel, talking and laughing at the same time, and though Jack felt the same exuberance they did and wanted to hug her, too, he gave them room. This was the most important thing, after all, Rachel and her girls. She was awake. She was back. With another shout of relief he left to tell the doctors the news.

RACHEL emerged from her coma thinking it was just another day of waking up with Jack on her mind, until she found him there in the flesh, looking worried and involved. Her first thought was that something had happened to one of the girls, but she saw them in her periphery, as alive and intense as Jack. Could she have imagined Big Sur and six years of life without him? She couldn't have dreamed the woods, the cabin, the coast any more than she could have dreamed the aloneness. She was definitely divorced. But there was a wedding band on her finger.

She was clearly in a hospital. But the people she loved were all there and alive. Jack must have been the one who brought the girls. He wouldn't stay. He never stayed.

She mustered a smile for Samantha and Hope. "What's doing?"

Suddenly, like a paused video starting to play, the two of them came to life. Displacing Jack, they began hugging her, laughing, chattering about an accident she didn't remember, a coma she didn't remember, a broken leg, a blood clot.

She didn't remember any of it. She couldn't grasp the fact that she had been lying there for sixteen days—though the doctors and nurses who came in to look and prod confirmed it.

The girls jabbered on about Jack's staying at Big Sur, Jack's driving them to school, Jack's being at the hospital every single day.

She rested a bit. Life was hazy, and she was frightened as well as confused. She asked what day of the week it was and what time. She asked why the girls weren't in school.

"We've waited too long for this," Samantha told her. "Dad said we could skip school."

A nurse cranked up Rachel's head a little, then a little more. She was dizzy, but it passed, and the girls began chattering again. Samantha listed all the people who had come to visit. Hope told her about Katherine's crush on the doctor.

When Samantha told her about the prom, Rachel was heartsick. When Hope told her about Guinevere, Rachel cried.

Jack went off somewhere, which was fine. This was the life she was used to now, just the girls and her. But as soon as he disappeared, the girls started talking about him again.

"He drove down in the middle of the night after the accident."

"He even made a coffin for Guinevere."

"He bought you a new car, Mom. You'll love it."

"He framed your pictures, so the show's going on."

"He hasn't worked in two weeks. I think he's changed."

Rachel smiled and nodded. Before she could ask about the less-than-subtle lobbying, Katherine arrived. Dear, suave Katherine, who actually blushed when the doctor who had earlier introduced himself as Steve returned to the room. The crush Hope had mentioned? *Katherine?* Rachel was overwhelmed. But that wasn't the first thing Rachel asked when she and Katherine finally got a minute alone.

She wiggled her ring finger. "What's with this?"

"Did you ask him?"

"No. Katherine, did you call him after the accident?"

"I did," she said. "I figured you'd want him here."

"Want him here? He shut down on me. You know it still hurts."

"You still love him. That's why it hurts. That's why I called."

"It hurts to see him."

"You don't think he feels that, too? You think he's been here for sixteen days for his health?"

"He feels obligated."

"He cares."

"Caring isn't love, and even if it was, you can love someone and still shut them out." Rachel closed her eyes. "We've been through this, Katherine. You know how I feel."

"So take the ring off," Katherine said.

Rachel didn't, because she was too tired. Besides, the ring might be a charm. She had been wearing it when she had come out of the coma. She figured she would wear it until she got home.

THE girls slept soundly that night. Jack knew, because he looked in on them every few hours. Their ordeal was ending. They were excited enough about Rachel's awakening not to be worried about Jack's future role in their lives, but he sure was. He was worried sick.

Friday morning he went to the hospital alone. Rachel's IV pole was gone. Her hair was damp and waving gently; her face was shiny clean. She was reading the newspaper, looking as thin and small as Hope in a huge magenta T-shirt. The wedding band was still on her finger, but she looked startled to see him.

"How are you feeling?" he asked.

"Better," she said. "Where are the girls?"

"School. They'll be here this afternoon."

She nodded. "When are you going back to the city?"

"I don't know. Not for a while. You'll need some help."

"The girls can help. School will be out in a few weeks."

"Well, between now and then. Unless you'd rather have someone else. If you'd rather have a nurse, I'll hire one."

"That might be best if you have to get back to the city."

A deep, dark hole was eating his insides. He had just said that he didn't have to go, hadn't he? Hadn't anything the girls said registered with her?

"Perfect timing," said Steve Bauer as he slipped past Jack and went to the bed. "I want you taking another walk down the hall. Jack can take you."

"I'm still tired from the last one."

"The more you walk, the stronger you'll be and the sooner you can go home." He held out a hand.

She sighed, took it, and pushed herself to a seated position. When she was steady there, he handed her a furry red slipper. She fitted it to her foot—bending stiffly, Jack thought. Steve gave her a single crutch, helped her up, then gave her the other. When both crutches were in place, she stood with her head down.

"Okay?" Steve asked quietly. Jack envied him the intimacy.

She nodded and took several uneven steps.

"Is she up for this?" Jack asked. He imagined her falling and hurting herself more.

But Steve kept an arm around her, preventing that. "She can't go home until she is." When they reached Jack, he said, "Your turn."

THEY walked slowly and haltingly down the corridor.

"Okay?" Jack asked. Then, after several more steps, "Hanging in there?" When they reached the end, he said, "You're doing great," and when they were halfway back, "Nearly there."

She gave him single-word answers, clearly concentrating on keeping her balance. By the time they were back in the room, she had broken into a sweat. He helped her into bed and asked if she needed anything. She shook her head and closed her eyes.

Jack was devastated.

"HOW'S Mom?" Hope asked as soon as she and Samantha climbed into the car.

"She's great," he said. "She's been up and hobbling around."

"So did you guys talk?" Samantha asked.

He shot her a curious glance. "About?"

"Stuff, Daddy," Hope said, leaning in between the seats. "You know. Your living with us and all."

"No, we didn't talk about that. Your mother's just been through an ordeal. She's concentrating on getting up and eating. Her first priority is getting home."

"What happens then?" Samantha asked.

"What do you mean?"

"Are you staying?"

"That depends."

"On what?"

"On things that your mother and I decide to do," he finally said. "But there's a whole lot of other stuff we need to think about before we think about that, so I'd appreciate it if the two of you backed off. Okay?"

"So Dad's been here all day?" Samantha asked.

They hadn't been there five minutes. Jack was at the window looking out, listening to the girls tell Rachel about school. He hung his head when he heard the question, waited.

"He has," Rachel said.

"I think Dad should stay with us," Samantha said. "You know, like, after you get home."

"We'll talk about that later," Rachel said.

"When later? He's really a good guy, Mom."

"I never said he wasn't."

"Maybe you need to hear his side of the story."

"Samantha," Jack warned, turning to face them.

Hope said, "He did everything while you were sick. I mean, he shopped and cooked and drove us around."

"I'm grateful to him," Rachel said without looking at Jack.

"He left the firm for you," Samantha cried.

Jack said, "No, I didn't, Sam."

Blond hair flying, she looked at him fast. "You did!"

"I left it for me. For me, Sam. It wasn't working for me anymore, so I gave it up. Don't lay that on your mother, too."

"Fine," Samantha said. "But if you go back to San Francisco, I'm going, too."

"Samantha," Rachel cried, sounding totally displeased.

"I can live both places, can't I?"

Jack said, "You're not doing that. Your mother's going to need your help, and besides, I won't be in San Francisco. I'm moving here. I like it here. I'll buy my own place if I have to." The timing was all wrong to say that. The idea would never work if Rachel was against it. He resented his daughter's forcing the issue. This was between Rachel and him.

The fact that Katherine was suddenly standing in the door didn't help. Annoyed, he stalked past her, right out of the room, then realized it was another wrong thing to do. He should have told Katherine to take his daughters away. He needed to tell Rachel what the last few weeks had been like for him.

But he couldn't turn around and go back. Disgusted, he went down the hall to the bank of telephones to call his lawyer.

"WHY didn't you say something?" Samantha asked.

"He loves you, Mommy," Hope said.

Katherine had approached the bed. "Can I talk to your mom, guys?"

"Someone better," Samantha remarked, and with a look of disgust at Rachel, grabbed Hope's arm and hauled her out of the room.

Rachel watched them go. "That was a quick honeymoon."

"Why didn't you?" Katherine asked.

Rachel's eyes flew to her face. "Why didn't I what?"

"Say something to Jack."

"About what?"

"His leaving the firm. His moving here."

Rachel tried to replay the conversation without opening herself to hurt. "Did he ask my opinion?"

"Do you need a formal invitation? Come on, Rachel. The guy hasn't left your side. Help him out a little here."

"Help him with what?" Rachel cried. "Maybe I don't want him

moving here. Fine, the girls are attached to him, but Big Sur is mine. Why does he think he can just barge right in?"

"He loves you, Rachel."

Rachel closed her eyes and turned away.

"Tell him you love him back," Katherine said.

Rachel's heart was aching. "I don't know if I can," she said.

"What are you afraid of?"

Rachel opened her eyes and looked at Katherine hard. "Depending on him and being abandoned again. And he hasn't said he loves me, either, y' know, and don't say he's shown it, because it's not the same. If he loves me, let him say it. Let him go out on a limb and take a risk that I'll say no. Wouldn't you do that if you wanted something bad enough?"

Katherine looked at her a minute longer, then headed for the door. Rachel wanted to ask where she was going, but didn't have the strength.

KATHERINE kept her head down and scowled as she walked. She was frustrated that Rachel was being stubborn, angry at Steve for being persistent, angry at herself for being afraid to take the kind of risk she had just told her best friend to take. She was angry at Jack. And then there he was at the bank of phones.

Jack had made his call and didn't know what to do next. His life was in a limbo—professionally, personally.

"What are you doing?" Katherine asked.

He was feeling raw. He didn't need prodding from her. Pushing away from the booth, he held up a hand and set off for the elevator. "Not now, Katherine."

"If not now, when?" she asked, keeping up with his stride easily. "You told me you loved her and wanted back into the marriage. Why don't you tell her?"

He put a hand over his ear. "Not now, Katherine."

"Then when? What's with you and silence? Haven't you lost enough time? Haven't you learned anything?"

He stopped short and put his face in hers. "Have you?"

That got her fast. She swallowed, blinked, pulled back.

"Yeah," she said, suddenly humble, "I want to think I have. I took a good look at myself, and you were right. What I have isn't so bad." Flattening a hand on her chest, she seemed to be speaking more to herself than to him. "Am I pleased with these? No. But I can live with them."

She dropped her hand, raised her eyes to his, and said with determination, "I'm gonna give it a shot, risk that ole rejection, because maybe there's something that's worth it." She smiled, becoming the friend he wanted, needed. "So what's with you? Can't you just do it, too?"

She made it sound easy. He started walking again. "You're talking apples and oranges."

"I'm talking trust," she said, beside him still.

"Where's hers, Katherine? She knows I'm done with the firm. She knows I'm done with San Francisco. She knows I've been here taking care of her. She hasn't said a word about any of it."

Katherine put a hand on his arm. "Why isn't she talking, Jack?" She tapped her head. "Think."

She looked at him a minute longer, took a deep breath, and started back down the hall.

By THE time she reached the nurses station and asked if Steve was around, Katherine was starting to tremble. There was some confusion and consulting of one another behind the desk. She was starting to wonder if her bravado would hold over for another day, when he emerged from a door far down the hall. He spotted her. His blue eyes smiled, and he closed in fast.

He was still smiling when he reached her.

"Can you take a break?" Katherine whispered.

He spoke briefly with the nurse at the desk, walked Katherine to the elevator, pushed the buttons both outside and inside. The ride to the lowest level was short. Steve stuck a finger toward outside, then a thumb toward a long corridor. "Is this about Rachel?" he asked. When she shook her head, he followed the thumb. Holding her hand, he led her down the corridor, around a corner, and into a small room. He leaned against the door to shut it.

"We have to talk, Steve," she said. "You need to know certain things about me before this relationship goes any further."

He made a humming sound.

"The thing is," she began, "there are never guarantees in any relationship, because no one knows what the future holds. I mean, look at Rachel—perfectly healthy one day and comatose another, through no single fault of her own. We think we'll be here next week, but we don't know for sure. I mean . . . Steve, I have breast cancer."

His voice was deep and sure. "Wrong tense. You had breast cancer. It's gone."

She caught her breath. "Excuse me?"

"Past tense. You're cured."

"You know?"

"You looked familiar when I saw you after Rachel's accident, and you kept bumping into hospital personnel who knew you, too. I put two and two together and checked our database."

"That's a breach of ethics, Steve," she cried.

"Probably, but I was desperate. You were special, and you didn't want any part of me. I had to know why."

"Why didn't you tell me you knew?"

"I couldn't. It had to be this way. I had to know you cared enough about me to share it."

"Well, I do." She swallowed, feeling close to tears. "It's been a long time since I cared enough. Last time I did, he dumped me as soon as he learned."

"It's just not as big a thing as you think, Katherine. We can work with it," he said. He ducked his head and caught her lips in a kiss.

JACK was waiting for Rachel to talk. Rachel was waiting for Jack to talk. It was up to him.

That was what his brain said. His heart said that he couldn't bare all with the girls there.

Evening came. He drove them home. The coast road was bathed in the amber of a setting sun that gilded wildflowers, granite boulders, layer after layer of greening hills. There was a poignance to its beauty, a soft whisper from the surf. *Tell her, ask her, beg her,* it said, repeating its message with the rush of the waves.

At the bank of mailboxes, he turned off the highway and started up the hill. There wasn't a sound from the woods when he climbed from the car, just that nagging whisper all around: *Tell her, ask her, beg her.*

"Uh . . ." He stopped on the front porch, turned to the girls. "Listen, can you two look out for yourselves for a while?"

"We're not babies," Samantha said, but kindly. "Where are you going?"

He was already heading back to the car. "I, uh, need to talk with your mom."

RACHEL hovered on the brink of tears. With each hour that passed, the reality of the accident, the coma, sank in deeper. She had never been one to dwell on her own mortality, but it was hard not to now. She was vulnerable. She was human. So there was that, and the girls, and her work, and Jack. And Jack. And more Jack.

Then he appeared at the door to her room, and her heart moved right up to her throat. She swallowed, but it didn't budge.

"Hi," he said. After several seconds on the threshold he came inside. "I dropped the girls back home." He put his hands on his hips and looked around the room. Then his eyes returned to hers.

"I thought maybe . . ." he began, and cleared his throat. "I know it's late . . . well, there's . . ." He took a breath and asked straight out, "Do you want to take a ride?"

She hadn't expected that. The tears hung on her lids. Something more than her throat squeezed her heart. Standing there, all six two of him—with his sport shirt rolled to the elbow, faded jeans, his weathering hair, and unsureness—he looked so dear.

"You haven't been out of this place in two and a half weeks," he went on. "I have the new car downstairs. I won't keep you out long—unless you're too tired—"

"I'm not," she said. She pushed herself up, carefully easing her casted leg over the side. Her nightgown fell to her ankles. She reached for her crutches.

"If I carry you, you won't wear yourself out," he said with such gentleness that the tears returned. She brushed them away with the heels of her hands and nodded. He lifted her with the same exquisite gentleness that had been in his voice.

She held herself stiffly at first.

"Not comfortable?" he asked as he headed for the door.

"Awkward." She wanted to wrap her arms around his neck, bury her face against his throat, but she was frightened.

He set off down the hall.

Minutes later, permission granted, they were outside. The night was warm and clear. It no sooner enveloped Rachel than her eyes filled with tears again. She took a deep breath, then gasped when she saw where Jack was headed. A tall halogen light lit the car well. "It's red," she cried. "The girls didn't tell me it was red. I haven't had a red car since—"

"Since the VW you had when we met. I thought it was time." He freed a hand enough to open the door and carefully settled her inside.

"Why did you think it was time?" Rachel asked when he slid behind the wheel.

He left the parking lot and drove several blocks before he said, "Because you loved that car."

Rachel rolled down her window and put her face to the warm breeze that blew in as he drove. Her lungs came alive, hungry for more. "Where are we going?"

"P. Emmet's."

The show! Exciting. But "At *this* hour?"

"It's Friday night. They're open late."

"It's nearly ten."

"No, it's not," Jack said. But it was. He looked at the clock and swore. "We're going anyway. I want you to see the paintings."

She didn't argue, didn't have the strength. Laying her head against the headrest, she said, "I haven't thanked you for doing the framing. I'm grateful."

"You had everything there. The girls helped."

She rolled her head to look at him. Six years hadn't changed his profile. She had always thought him beautiful. That hadn't changed. "Thank you for staying with them," she said.

He nodded but didn't speak, simply drove on through the back streets of Carmel and pulled up in front of the gallery. The place looked dark and deserted. He left the car and peered in the front window. He knocked on the glass, went to the door, and knocked harder.

"Custodian," he called to Rachel. He knocked again, then turned to her and raised a victorious fist. Seconds later a man was on the inside of the door, waving a hand no, shaking his head.

Jack spoke loudly. "My wife is the artist whose show is about to open. She's been in the hospital in a coma. I stole her out to show her this. Two minutes. That's all we'll need."

The man opened his hands in a helpless gesture.

Jack held up a finger, telling him to wait. In two long steps he was at the car, lifting Rachel out, carrying her to the door.

"See her cast?" he yelled through the glass. "This is legitimate, bud."

"Show him ID," Rachel tried.

Her arms were around Jack's neck. He looked at her, so close, so tender. "My name, not yours," he said with regret.

The man opened the door, but his head had a constant shake. "Place is closed. No one's s'posed to be here but me."

"This is the artist. Her name's Rachel Keats. Look." Jack thumbed the window. "See this notice? Rachel Keats. Go inside and look for a flyer. Check out the picture. It's her face."

The man scratched his nose. "I don't know."

Jack shouldered the door open and carried Rachel into the gallery. She felt a little naughty, but excited.

"Mr. Wolfe won't like this," came a complaint from behind, but Jack went right on through to the room where shows were hung. It was dark, almost eerily silent. Rachel held her breath there in his arms, catching it when he suddenly turned and went back to the wall. She held on tighter when he angled himself to snag the lights with an elbow. When they came on, he carried her to the center of the room and carefully lowered her. Standing behind her, he slipped his arms around her waist and put his chin on her head.

She barely breathed. Her eye ran around the room, not knowing where to settle, wanting to see everything at once. She began with the bobcats. That canvas was her favorite. She had already seen it framed and hung, but then came the egrets and the gray whale. And her lone Arctic wolf.

She gasped. She hadn't finished the Arctic wolf. She hadn't finished the quail or the deer or the great egret, either. "Oh, my." The loons. The loons, sitting on that mirrored surface of a lake at dusk. Jack had done this. No one else could have. He had done it for her so beautifully, so beautifully.

Her tears came hard and fast along with huge, wrenching sobs. She was touched and lonely and needy and wanting and afraid.

When Jack turned her into his chest, she coiled her arms around his neck and clung. "Don't cry, angel," he begged. "Please don't cry. I only want you to be happy."

She wanted to say that what he had done was so beautiful that she was more happy than she would ever ever be again. She wanted to say she loved him, only she couldn't stop crying.

She had never cried like this. She had never cared like this.

She felt his arms around her, felt movement, and the next thing she knew they were sitting on the floor. He cradled her close, absorbing the spasms of her weeping with a soft rocking.

Then he began to speak. His head was bowed over hers, his voice beseeching but loud enough to carry over her sobs. "It wouldn't have occurred to me if I hadn't come in here and seen the bobcats. Ben was raving about them, saying that the canvas was his all-time favorite, and I remembered how we'd done it together. He didn't know that, so he wouldn't know if I did it again, and I was torn, Rachel, totally torn. I wouldn't have done a thing if you'd shown signs of waking up, but you didn't."

He held her head to his chest. "I've been dreaming," he said. "Know what of?"

She shook her head under his hand, against his chest, all too aware of her own dreams and wanting, wanting so badly.

"Of us doing more of this. I don't want a name role in it. You keep the name. I'll still design, but smaller things again, houses for people who can smile at me and love what I've done. I had that in the beginning, but it's been gone for so long that I barely remember it. What you barely remember, you don't miss until something happens to jog your memory. That's what sitting at your bedside did, Rachel. I remembered things about my work and things about us, things that maybe I didn't want to remember, because they were so good, and they were gone."

Rachel knew what he meant.

"So I want to design houses and paint your backgrounds. I want to live in Big Sur, Rachel. I want us to be married."

Rachel drew herself up against him. Her tears wet his neck, but she held on tightly, held on until she needed a kiss.

His mouth moved on hers, reinforcing everything he had said. When he finally broke the kiss and framed her face with his hands, he whispered, "I never stopped loving you. Never."

"You shut me out," she accused in a nasal voice.

He threw back an accusation. "You walked away."

"I was hurting. I had to distance myself from the source of the pain."

"I didn't know you were pregnant when you called me that time. I should have come. I'm sorry you lost the baby. It would have been something."

"Yes." She had mourned that child. It would have been something.

"Do you mind that I finished your pictures?"

"I love that you finished my pictures. What's with Jill?"

"Over. I knew there was no future. What's with Ben?"

"Nothing. Nothing. Nothing."

"I like your friends."

"They like you. What'll you do with your house?"

"Sell it. We could buy something bigger, but I like the place you have."

"Really? Are you sure? You're not just saying that?"

"Really. I'm sure. I'm not just saying that."

"Will you like it in five years?" she asked, knowing he knew what she meant. It was there in his eyes, with his love.

"I've been alone. Five years, ten years, twenty years living with you in that house is so much more than what I was facing before . . ." His voice broke. His eyes were moist.

Rachel touched his lips. "I love you," she mouthed, and said it again in a kiss. When it was done, he gave a huge sigh of the relief she felt and hugged her with arms that shook.

From somewhere off to the side came an edgy "Mr. Wolfe won't like this."

No, Rachel figured, he wouldn't. She also figured he had known all along that something was missing in her life. She suspected that in his own kind way he would be pleased to know she had found it again.

BARBARA DELINSKY

"*Coast Road* was born of three things I admire," explains Barbara Delinsky, "the Big Sur coast, people with artistic ability, and men who rise to the occasion." She also drew on her years-long membership in a book group—a connection she shares with her book's heroine. Delinsky says that she reaps huge personal rewards from the group's meetings. "I rarely see these women from meeting to meeting, and because of that, there's a kind of immunity that allows for intimate discussion. We blurt out things we might not say to co-workers, neighbors, or even longtime friends." Delinsky is the author of sixty-six novels. She and her husband, both lifelong New Englanders, have three adult sons.

"There isn't a better
storyteller alive."
—Larry King

COMMANDMENT

JEFFREY ARCHER

For everyone else there are Ten Commandments.

For CIA hero Connor Fitzgerald it's the Eleventh Commandment that counts: Don't get caught.

As HE opened the door, the alarm went off.

The sort of mistake you would expect an amateur to make, which was surprising, since Connor Fitzgerald was considered by his peers to be the professional's professional.

Fitzgerald had anticipated that it would be several minutes before the Bogotá *policía* responded to a burglary in the San Victorina district. There were still a couple of hours to go before the kickoff of the annual soccer match against Brazil, but half the television sets in Colombia would already be switched on. If Fitzgerald had broken into the pawnshop after the game had started, the *policía* probably wouldn't have followed it up until the referee had blown the final whistle. It was well known that the local criminals regarded the match as a ninety-minute parole period. But his plans for that ninety minutes would have the *policía* chasing their own shadows for days. And it would be weeks, probably months, before anyone worked out the real significance of the break-in that Saturday afternoon.

The alarm was still sounding as Fitzgerald closed the back door and made his way quickly through the small storeroom toward the front of the shop, ignoring the rows of watches on their little stands, the emeralds in their cellophane bags. He swept aside the bead curtain that divided the storeroom from the shop and paused behind the counter. His eyes rested on a battered leather case on a stand in the center of the window. Printed on the lid in faded gold letters were the initials DVR. He remained absolutely still until he was certain that no one was looking in.

When Fitzgerald had sold the handcrafted masterpiece to the pawnbroker earlier that day, he had explained that as he had no intention of returning to Bogotá, it could go on sale immediately. Fitzgerald was not surprised that the piece had already been placed in the window. There wouldn't be another one like it in Colombia.

He climbed over the counter and walked to the window, glancing up and down the road to check for any casual observers, but there were none. He removed the leather case from its stand, leaped back over the counter, and moved quickly toward the storeroom. He pulled aside the bead curtain and strode on toward the closed door. He checked his watch. The alarm had been blaring away for ninety-eight seconds. He stepped into the alley, listened, then turned right and walked casually in the direction of Carrera Septima.

When Connor Fitzgerald reached the sidewalk, he glanced left and then right, wove through the light traffic, and crossed to the far side of the street. He disappeared into a crowded restaurant, where a group of noisy fans were seated around a large-screen television.

Nobody gave him a glance as he took a seat at a corner table. Although he couldn't see the television screen clearly, he had a perfect view across the street. A battered sign with the words J. ESCOBAR. MONTE DE PIEDAD, ESTABLECIDO 1946 flapped in the afternoon breeze above the pawnshop.

Several minutes passed before a police car screeched to a halt outside the shop. Once Fitzgerald had seen the two officers enter the building, he left his table and walked nonchalantly out the back door onto another quiet Saturday afternoon street. He hailed a taxi and said in a broad South African accent, "El Belvedere on the Plaza de Bolívar, *por favor.*" The driver nodded and turned up the radio.

Fitzgerald checked his watch again. Seventeen minutes past one. He was running a couple of minutes behind schedule. The speech would have already begun, but as they always lasted for well over forty minutes, he still had more than enough time to carry out his real reason for being in Bogotá. He moved a few inches to his right, so as to be sure the driver could see him clearly in the rearview mirror.

Once the *policía* began their investigations, Fitzgerald needed everyone who had seen him that day to give roughly the same description: male, Caucasian, fiftyish, a shade over six feet, about two hundred and ten pounds, unshaven, dark unruly hair, dressed like a foreigner with a foreign accent, but not American. He hoped that at least one of them would be able to identify the South African nasal twang. Fitzgerald had always been good at accents. In high school he had regularly been in trouble for mimicking his teachers.

When the taxi drew up outside the El Belvedere, Fitzgerald handed over a ten-thousand-peso note and had slipped out of the cab before the driver could thank him for such a generous tip.

Fitzgerald ran up the hotel steps. In the lobby he headed straight for the elevators, rode to the eighth floor, and walked down the corridor to room 807. He pushed a plastic card into the slot. As soon as the door opened, he placed the FAVOR DE NO MOLESTAR sign on the outside knob, closed the door, and bolted it.

He checked his watch yet again: twenty-four minutes to two. By now he calculated that the *policía* would have left the pawnshop, having concluded that it was a false alarm. They would phone Mr. Escobar to inform him that everything appeared to be in order, and would suggest that he let them know on Monday if anything was missing. But long before then, Fitzgerald would have put the battered leather case back in the window. On Monday morning the only items that Escobar would report stolen would be the several small packets of uncut emeralds that had been removed by the *policía* on their way out. How long would it be before Escobar discovered the only other thing that was missing? A day? A week? A month? Fitzgerald had already decided he would leave the odd clue to help speed up the process.

Fitzgerald picked up the remote control from the bedside table. He pressed the ON button and sat down on the sofa in front of the television. The face of Ricardo Guzman filled the screen. The favorite in the upcoming presidential election, Guzman was the boss of the Cali cartel, which controlled eighty percent of the New York cocaine trade and made over a billion dollars a year.

"The first action I shall take as your President will be to nationalize any company in which Americans are the majority shareholders." The crowd that surrounded the steps of the Congress building on the Plaza de Bolívar screamed its approval.

Fitzgerald estimated that there were about six minutes' of the speech left. He had already heard Guzman's words at least a dozen times—in crowded halls, in half-empty bars, on street corners. He pulled the leather case off the bed and onto his lap.

"Antonio Herrera is not the Liberal candidate," hissed Guzman, "but the American candidate. His every word is chosen for him by the man who sits in the Oval Office." Herrera was the Vice President and Guzman's main rival in the upcoming election. The crowd cheered again.

Fitzgerald opened the case and stared down at the Remington 700 that had been out of his sight for only a few hours.

"How dare the Americans assume that we will always fall in line with whatever is convenient for them?" Guzman barked. "And simply because of the power of the God Almighty dollar. To hell with the dollar!" The crowd cheered even more loudly as the candidate took a dollar bill from his wallet and tore it into shreds.

Fitzgerald removed the fiberglass stock from the leather case.

"In two weeks' time the citizens of Colombia will be given the opportunity to let their views be heard right across the world."

"Four minutes," murmured Fitzgerald as he took the stainless steel barrel from its resting place and screwed it firmly into the stock. It fitted like a glove.

"Within a year I will have the Americans treating Colombia not as a Third World country, but as their equals."

The crowd roared as Fitzgerald lifted the Leupold 10X sniperscope from its place and slid it into the two little grooves on the top of the barrel.

"When I am your President . . ."

Fitzgerald slowly nestled the stock of the Remington 700 into his shoulder. It felt like an old friend. But then it should have: Every part had been handcrafted to his exact specifications.

He raised the telescopic sight to the image on the television screen and lined up the little row of mil dots until they were centered an inch above the heart of the candidate.

Three minutes. Fitzgerald breathed out. He lowered the rifle and rose from the sofa. It would be another ninety seconds before Guzman reached his ritual condemnation of U.S. President Tom Lawrence.

He removed one of the hollow-point bullets from its little leather slot inside the lid of the case. He broke the stock and slipped the bullet into its chamber, then snapped the barrel shut.

"This will be a last chance for the citizens of Colombia to reverse the disastrous failures of the past," cried Guzman.

"One minute," murmured Fitzgerald. He walked slowly across the room to the French windows, pulled back the lace curtain, and stared across the Plaza de Bolívar to where the presidential candidate was standing. He waited patiently.

"Viva la Colombia!" Guzman cried. *"Viva la Colombia!"* the mob screamed back in a frenzy.

Fitzgerald pushed open the French windows to be greeted by the full volume of the masses. For a second time he pulled the stock of the Remington 700 slowly up into his shoulder. Every eye was looking at the candidate as he boomed out the words *"Dios guarde a la Colombia!"* The noise became deafening as Guzman raised both arms high in the air to acknowledge the roars of his supporters shouting back, *"Dios guarde a la Colombia!"* Guzman's hands remained triumphantly in the air for several seconds, as they did at the end of every speech. And, as always, for a few seconds he remained absolutely still.

Fitzgerald breathed out as he tightened the fingers of his left hand around the stock. "Three . . . two . . . one," he murmured under his breath before gently squeezing the trigger.

Guzman was still smiling as the boattail bullet tore into his chest. A second later he slumped to the ground like a stringless puppet.

Fitzgerald lowered the rifle, broke the stock, and quickly closed the French windows. His assignment was completed.

His only problem now was to make sure he didn't break the Eleventh Commandment.

"SHOULD I send a message of condolence to Ricardo Guzman's wife and family?" asked Tom Lawrence.

"No, Mr. President," replied Larry Harrington, the Secretary of State. "I think you should leave that to an assistant secretary for inter-American affairs. It now looks certain that Antonio Herrera will be the next President of Colombia, so he'll be the person you'll have to do business with."

The President nodded.

"If you have a moment," continued Larry Harrington, "I should brief you in greater detail on our present policy in Colombia. The press may want to question you on the possible involvement of—"

The President was about to interrupt Larry when there was a knock on the door and Andy Lloyd entered the room.

It must be eleven o'clock, thought Tom Lawrence. He hadn't needed a watch since he had appointed Lloyd his White House chief of staff.

"Later, Larry," said the President. "I'm about to give a press conference on the arms reduction bill, and I can't imagine many journalists will be interested in the death of a presidential candidate in Colombia, a country that—let's face it—most Americans couldn't even place on a map."

Larry Harrington said nothing. He didn't feel it was his responsibility to point out that most Americans couldn't place Vietnam on a map either. He left the Oval Office without a word.

The President flicked open the blue file marked IMMEDIATE that Andy had left for him earlier that morning. He began to go over the questions his chief of staff considered the most likely to be asked at the midday press conference: How much taxpayers' money do you anticipate saving by this measure? How many Americans will lose their jobs as a result?

Lawrence ran his finger down the list of anticipated questions. He stopped at number seven: Isn't this another example of America losing its way?

He looked up at his chief of staff. "Sometimes I think we're still living in the Wild West, Andy, the way certain members of Congress have reacted to this arms reduction bill."

"I agree, sir. But as you know, forty percent of Americans still consider the Russians our biggest threat, and nearly thirty percent expect us to go to war with Russia in their lifetime."

Lawrence cursed and ran a hand through his thick, prematurely gray hair as he continued to go down the list of questions, stopping again when he reached nineteen.

"Surely there's no chance of Victor Zerimski becoming the next President of Russia?"

"Probably not," said Andy Lloyd, "but he's moved up to third place in the latest poll, and though he's still well behind Prime Minister Chernopov and General Borodin, his stand against organized crime is beginning to make a dent in their leads."

"Thank God the election's still a couple of years away. If it looked as if that fascist Zerimski had the slightest chance of becoming the next President of Russia, an arms reduction bill wouldn't get past first base in either house."

Lloyd nodded as the President continued to read the questions. When he reached the final one, he said, "My hunch is that if Chernopov promised the Russian voters that he intended to spend more on health care than on defense, he'd romp home."

"You may be right," said Lloyd. "But you can also be certain that if Zerimski's elected, he'll start rebuilding Russia's nuclear arsenal long before he considers building new hospitals."

"That's for sure," said Lawrence. "But as there's no chance of that maniac being elected . . ."

Andy Lloyd remained silent.

CONNOR FITZGERALD KNEW THAT the next twenty minutes would decide his fate. He walked quickly across the hotel room and glanced at the television. The crowd was fleeing from the square in every direction. Noisy elation had turned to blind panic.

Fitzgerald retrieved the spent cartridge and placed it in its slot inside the leather case. Would the owner of the pawnshop realize that one of the bullets had been used?

Fitzgerald unclipped the viewfinder and placed it in its sculpted slot. He then unscrewed the barrel, slipped it into position, and finally replaced the stock in the leather case.

He glanced at the television screen for the last time and watched the *policía* pouring into the square. He grabbed the gun case, pocketed a book of matches from an ashtray on top of the television, then crossed the room and opened the door.

He looked up and down the empty corridor, then walked quickly in the direction of the freight elevator. He jabbed the little white button on the wall several times. When the heavy doors slid open, he came face to face with a young waiter carrying an overloaded lunch tray.

"No, señor, perdone, no puede entrar," the waiter tried to explain. But Fitzgerald brushed past him and jabbed the button marked PLANTA BAJA. The doors had closed long before the waiter could tell him that that particular elevator ended up in the kitchen.

When he reached the basement, Fitzgerald moved deftly between the stainless steel tables covered with hors d'oeuvres. He had pushed his way through the swinging doors at the far end of the kitchen before any of the staff could think of protesting. He ran down a poorly lit corridor—he had removed most of the lightbulbs the previous night—to a heavy door that led to the hotel's underground garage.

He headed straight for a small black Volkswagen parked in the darkest corner. He removed a small key from his jacket pocket, unlocked the car's door, slipped behind the wheel, placed the leather case under the passenger seat, and turned on the ignition. The engine sprang to life, and Fitzgerald maneuvered the vehicle unhurriedly up the steep ramp out onto the street. At the top of the slope he turned left and headed slowly away from the Plaza de Bolívar.

And then he heard the whining sound behind him. He glanced at the rearview mirror to see two police escorts bearing down on him, their lights flashing on high. He pulled over as the escorts and the ambulance carrying Guzman's lifeless body sped past him.

He took the next left down a side street and began a long circuitous route to the pawnshop, often doubling back on himself. Twenty-four minutes later he drove into the alley behind the shop and parked. He retrieved the battered leather case from under the passenger seat and left the car unlocked. He planned to be back behind the wheel in less than two minutes.

Once again, as Fitzgerald was entering the building, the alarm went off. But this time he was not worried about the speedy arrival of a passing patrol. Most of the *policía* would be fully occupied, either at the stadium, where the game was due to kick off in half an hour, or arresting anyone who was still within a mile of the Plaza de Bolívar.

Fitzgerald closed the back door behind him. For the second time that day he moved quickly through the pawnshop and returned the battered leather case to its original place in the window. How long would it be before Escobar discovered that one of the six boattail bullets had been fired and that only the casing remained in place? And even then, would he bother to pass the information on to the police?

Fitzgerald was back behind the wheel of the Volkswagen in less than ninety seconds. He could still hear the clanging alarm as he began to follow the signs for the airport.

Once Fitzgerald reached the highway, he stuck to the center lane, never once exceeding the speed limit. At the exit for the airport he left the highway, and after a quarter of a mile he suddenly swung right and drove into the parking lot of the San Sebastián Hotel. He opened the glove compartment and removed a much stamped South African passport. With the book of matches he had taken from the El Belvedere, he set Dirk van Rensberg alight. When his fingers were about to be burned, he opened the car door, dropped the remains of the passport onto the ground, and stamped out the flames, making sure the South African crest was still recognizable. He put the matches on the passenger seat, grabbed his suitcase from the back, and slammed the door closed. He walked toward the front door of the hotel and deposited the remains of Dirk van Rensberg's passport in the trash can at the bottom of the steps.

Fitzgerald pushed through the revolving doors behind a group of Japanese businessmen and remained in their slipstream as they were ushered toward an open elevator. He was the only passenger to step out on the third floor. He headed straight for room 347, where he extracted another plastic card that unlocked a room booked in yet another name. He tossed the suitcase onto the bed and checked his watch. One hour and seventeen minutes until takeoff.

He removed his jacket and threw it over the only chair before disappearing into the bathroom to shave off his week-old beard. Then it took twenty minutes under the warm shower to return his hair to its natural wavy state and sandy color.

Back in the bedroom, Fitzgerald put on a clean pair of Jockey shorts, then walked over to the chest of drawers, pulled open the third drawer, and felt around until he found a packet taped to the drawer above. Although he hadn't occupied the room for several days, he was confident that no one would have come across his hiding place.

Fitzgerald ripped open the brown envelope and quickly checked its contents. Another passport in yet another name, five hundred dollars in used notes, and a first-class ticket to Cape Town. Escaping assassins don't travel first class.

Five minutes later Fitzgerald was strolling across the hotel lobby, confident that no one would give a fifty-one-year-old man in a blue denim shirt, sports jacket, and gray flannels a second look. He made no attempt to check out. When he'd arrived eight days earlier, he had paid cash in advance for the room.

He only had to wait for a few minutes before the shuttle bus swept up to the hotel entrance. He checked his watch. Forty-three minutes to takeoff.

At the airport he was not surprised to be told that Aeroperu's flight 63 to Lima had been held up by more than an hour. Several *policía* in the overcrowded, chaotic departures building were suspiciously eyeing all passengers, and although he was stopped and questioned several times, he was eventually allowed to proceed to gate 47 for his flight, which would connect with flights to Buenos Aires and then Cape Town.

When Fitzgerald joined the line that led to passport control, he repeated his new name under his breath. The blue-uniformed official in the little cubicle flicked open the New Zealand passport and studied the photograph inside, which bore an undeniable resemblance to the smartly dressed man standing in front of him. He handed back the passport and allowed Alistair Douglas, a civil engineer from Christchurch, to stroll through to the departure lounge. After a further delay the flight was finally called. A stewardess guided Mr. Douglas to his seat in the first-class section. "Would you care for a glass of champagne, sir?"

Fitzgerald shook his head. "No, thank you. A glass of water will be just fine," he replied, trying out his New Zealand accent.

He fastened his seat belt, sat back, and pretended to read the inflight magazine as the aircraft began its slow progress down the runway. When the 727's wheels finally left the ground, Fitzgerald started to relax for the first time that day.

Once the aircraft had reached its cruising altitude, he disposed of the magazine, closed his eyes, and began to think about what needed to be done when he landed in Cape Town.

"This is your captain speaking," said a somber voice. "I have an announcement to make that will cause some of you considerable distress." Fitzgerald sat bolt upright. The one eventuality he hadn't planned for was an unscheduled return to Bogotá.

"My friends, a national tragedy has taken place in Colombia today," the captain declared gravely. "I'm sorry to have to inform you that the Colombian team has been defeated by Brazil by two goals to one."

An audible groan went through the cabin, as if crashing into the nearest mountain would have been a preferable alternative. Fitzgerald allowed the suggestion of a smile to cross his lips.

The stewardess reappeared by his side. "Can I fix a drink for you now that we're on our way, Mr. Douglas?"

"Thank you," Fitzgerald replied. "I think I'll have that glass of champagne after all."

As Tom Lawrence entered the room, the press corps rose to its feet. "The President of the United States," declared the press secretary, just in case there was a visitor from outer space.

Lawrence climbed the one step up to the podium and placed Andy Lloyd's blue file on the lectern. He waved at the assembled journalists to let them know they could resume their seats.

"I am delighted to announce," he began, sounding relaxed, "that I will be sending to Congress a bill I promised the American people during the election campaign."

The President went on to remind the correspondents seated in front of him that the passing of an arms reduction bill would allow him to release more revenue for long-term health care, so that elderly Americans could expect a better standard of living during their retirement.

Shouts of "Mr. President!" came from every direction as Lawrence opened his blue file and glanced down at the thirty-one likely questions. He looked up and smiled at a familiar face in the front row. "Barbara," he said, pointing to the veteran UPI journalist whose right it was, as the doyenne of the press corps, to ask the first question.

Barbara Evans rose to her feet. "Mr. President, are you able to confirm that the CIA had no involvement in the assassination of the Colombian presidential candidate Ricardo Guzman?"

A buzz of interest rippled around the room. Lawrence stared down at his file and wished he hadn't dismissed the Secretary of State's offer of a more detailed briefing quite so casually.

"I'm glad you asked that question, Barbara," the President responded without missing a beat. "Because I want you to know that while I'm President, such a suggestion doesn't even arise.

This administration would never in any circumstances interfere with the democratic process of a sovereign state."

Before Evans could follow up with a second question, the President turned his attention to a man standing in the back row, who, he hoped, would have no interest in the presidential election in Colombia. But once the man asked his question, Lawrence began to wish he had. "What chance does your arms reduction bill have of becoming law if Victor Zerimski is elected as the next Russian President?"

For the next forty minutes Lawrence answered questions about the arms reduction bill, but they were interspersed with demands to be told about the CIA's current role in South America and how he would deal with Victor Zerimski should he eventually become President of Russia. Then, without warning, Lawrence wrapped up the press conference and left the room, heading quickly in the direction of the Oval Office.

The moment Andy Lloyd caught up with him, the President growled under his breath, "I need to speak to the Secretary of State immediately, and I want the director of the CIA in my office within the hour. If I find out that the CIA had any involvement in that assassination in Colombia, I'll hang Helen Dexter out to dry."

CONNOR Fitzgerald handed over his passport to the Australian customs official. For the first time in three weeks he was using his real name. The uniformed officer stamped the tourist visa and said, "Hope you enjoy your visit to Australia, Mr. Fitzgerald."

Connor thanked him and walked through to baggage claim, where he took a seat and waited for his luggage to appear. He never allowed himself to be the first to pass through customs, even when he had nothing to declare.

When he had landed in Cape Town the previous day, Connor had been met at the plane by his old friend and colleague Carl Koeter. Carl had spent the next couple of hours debriefing him before they enjoyed a long lunch together, discussing Carl's divorce and what Maggie and Tara were up to. It was the second bottle of 1982 Rustenberg cabernet sauvignon that nearly caused Connor to miss his flight to Sydney. In the duty-free shop he hurriedly chose presents for his wife and daughter that were clearly stamped MADE IN SOUTH AFRICA. Even his passport gave no clue that he had arrived in Cape Town via Bogotá, Lima, and Buenos Aires.

Now, as he sat in the baggage claim area of the Sydney airport, he began to think about the life he had been leading for the past twenty-eight years.

Connor Fitzgerald had been brought up in a family dedicated to the cause of law and order. His paternal grandfather, Oscar, had immigrated to America from Kilkenny at the turn of the century. Within hours of landing at Ellis Island he had headed straight for Chicago to join his cousin in the police department. Oscar sired five sons, three of whom also joined the Chicago PD. The youngest, Connor's father, joined the FBI.

Connor was born in Chicago on February 8, 1951, and even before he was old enough to attend the local Catholic high school, it had become clear that he was going to be a gifted football player. In time he won a scholarship to Notre Dame.

The combination of a father who stood whenever a woman entered the room and a mother who verged on being a saint had left Connor, despite his physical prowess, shy in the presence of women. That changed during the first few days of his sophomore year at Notre Dame.

When Connor turned up for his weekly session at the Irish Dance Club, she was putting on her shoes. He couldn't see her face, but that didn't matter much, because he was unable to take his eyes off those long, slim legs. As a football hero, he had become used to girls staring at him, but now the one girl he wanted to impress didn't seem aware that he even existed. To make matters worse, she was partnered by Declan O'Casey, who had no rival as a dancer. They both held their backs rigidly straight, and their feet moved with a lightness Connor could never hope to match.

When the dancing came to an end, Connor still hadn't discovered her name. And worse, she and Declan left before he could find some way of being introduced to her. In desperation he followed them back to the women's dorms, walking in the shadows fifty yards behind them. When they reached Le Mans Hall, she kissed Declan on the cheek and disappeared inside.

After Declan headed off, Connor began to stroll casually below the dormitory windows. He finally caught a glimpse of her in a robe as she drew the curtain, and he hung around for a few more minutes before returning to his room.

During the week he tried to find out as much as he could about her, but he picked up very little other than that she was called Maggie Burke, had won a scholarship to St. Mary's, and was in her first year of studying art history. Declan, it turned out, was not only the best dancer in the club but he was also considered the university's brightest mathematician.

Connor was the first to turn up at the dance club the following Thursday, and when Maggie appeared from the dressing room in her cream cotton blouse and short black skirt, the only question he had to consider was whether to stare up into those green eyes or down at her long legs. Once again Maggie was partnered by Declan all evening, while Connor sat mutely on a bench. After the final number Connor followed them back to Le Mans Hall again.

After a long chat and another kiss on the cheek Declan disappeared in the direction of the men's dorms. Connor slumped down on a bench opposite Maggie's window and stared up at it. He decided to wait until he had seen her draw the curtains, but by the time she appeared at the window, he'd dozed off.

The next thing he remembered was waking from a deep sleep in which he had been dreaming that Maggie was standing in front of him, dressed in pajamas and a bathrobe.

He woke with a start, stared at her in disbelief, jumped up, and thrust out his hand. "Hi, I'm Connor Fitzgerald."

"I know," she replied as she shook his hand. "I'm Maggie Burke. Any room on that bench?"

From that moment Connor never looked at another woman. They were married two weeks after Maggie graduated summa cum laude, but they ended up having time only for a four-day honeymoon before Second Lieutenant Fitzgerald left for Vietnam in July 1972.

Those two years in Vietnam were now a distant memory for Connor. Being promoted to first lieutenant, being captured by the Vietcong and escaping while saving another man's life—it all seemed so long ago now. Five months after he returned home, the President awarded him the Medal of Honor, but after eighteen months as a prisoner of war in Vietnam he was just happy to be alive and reunited with Maggie and Tara, who had been born while he was in Vietnam.

Within a week of returning to the States, Connor began to look for a job. He had already been interviewed for a position at the CIA's Chicago field office when Captain Chris Jackson, his old platoon commander from Vietnam, invited him to be part of a special unit that was being set up in Washington. Connor was warned that should he agree to join Jackson's elite team, there would be aspects of the job he could never discuss with anyone, including his wife.

When Maggie was suddenly offered a job at the admissions office at Georgetown University, Connor realized just how determined Jackson was to recruit him. He agreed to join "Maryland Insurance" as an executive trainee.

That was when the deception had begun.

"DO YOU expect me to believe that the CIA didn't even *know* that an assassination attempt was being considered?"

"That's right, sir," said CIA director Helen Dexter.

The President began to pace around the Oval Office, which he found gave him more time to think and usually made his guests feel uneasy. Most people who entered the Oval Office were nervous. But if a bomb had gone off in the Rose Garden, Helen Dexter would probably have done no more than raise a well-groomed eyebrow. Her career had outlasted three Presidents so far, all of whom were rumored at some point to have demanded her resignation.

"And when Mr. Lloyd phoned to tell me that you required more details," said Dexter, "I instructed my deputy, Nick Gutenburg, to contact our people in Bogotá and to make extensive investigations as to what happened on Saturday afternoon. Gutenburg completed his report yesterday." She tapped the file on her lap.

Lawrence stopped pacing and came to a halt under a portrait of Abraham Lincoln that hung above the fireplace. He looked down at the director. She continued to face straight ahead.

Helen Dexter was dressed in an elegant, well-cut dark suit with a simple cream shirt. She rarely wore jewelry, even on state occasions. Her appointment by President Ford as deputy director at the age of thirty-two was meant to have been a stopgap to placate the feminist lobby a few weeks before the 1976 election. As it was, Ford turned out to be the stopgap.

Dexter began her life with the Agency in the office of the directorate of operations. By the time she had risen to deputy director, she had made more enemies than friends, but as the years passed, they seemed to disappear, or were fired, or took early retirement. When she was appointed director, she had just turned forty. The Washington *Post* described her as having blasted a hole through the glass ceiling, but that didn't stop the bookies from making odds on how many days she would survive. Soon they altered that to weeks and then months. Now they were taking bets on whether she would last longer at the helm of the CIA than J. Edgar Hoover had at the FBI.

Andy Lloyd had warned Lawrence on several occasions that if he ever tried to remove Dexter from her job, he had better have the sort of proof that would convince the public that Mother Teresa had held a secret bank account in Switzerland regularly topped off by organized crime syndicates.

The President had accepted his chief of staff's judgment. But he now felt that if he could prove the CIA had been involved in the assassination of Ricardo Guzman without even bothering to inform him, he could have Dexter clearing her desk within days.

He returned to his chair and touched the button under his desk that would allow Andy to listen in on the conversation or pick it up off the tape. Lawrence realized that Dexter would know exactly what he was up to, and he suspected that the legendary handbag that never left her side had already recorded every syllable that had passed between them. Nevertheless, he still needed his version of events for the record.

"Since you seem to be so well informed," the President said as he sat down, "maybe you could brief me in more detail on what actually happened in Bogotá."

Helen Dexter ignored his sarcastic tone and opened the file on her lap. It was marked FOR THE PRESIDENT'S EYES ONLY. "It has been confirmed by several sources that the assassination was carried out by a lone gunman," she read.

"Name one of these sources," snapped the President.

"Our cultural attaché in Bogotá," replied the director.

Lawrence raised an eyebrow. Half the cultural attachés in American embassies around the world had been placed there by the CIA simply to report back directly to Helen Dexter at Langley without any consultation with the local ambassador, let alone the State Department. Most of them would have thought the "Nutcracker Suite" was a dish to be found on the menu of an exclusive restaurant.

The President sighed. "And who does *he* think hired the assassin?"

Dexter extracted a photograph from the file and pushed it across the Oval Office desk. The President looked down at a picture of a well-dressed, prosperous-looking middle-aged man.

"That's Carlos Velez," Dexter said. "He runs the second-largest drug cartel in Colombia. Guzman controlled the biggest."

"And has Velez been charged?"

"Unfortunately, he was killed only a few hours after the police had obtained a warrant to arrest him."

"How convenient. And did this lone gunman have a name? Or did he also die only moments after a court order was—"

"No, sir, he's still very much alive," the director replied firmly. "His name is Dirk van Rensberg. He's South African. After the assassination he went underground."

"Do we know anything of van Rensberg's movements following the assassination?"

"He's reported to have taken a flight to Lima in the name of

Alistair Douglas, and then continued on to Buenos Aires, using the same passport. We lost track of him after that."

"And I doubt if you'll ever find him again."

"Oh, I wouldn't be that pessimistic, Mr. President."

"Well," said Lawrence, "let me assure you that in this case I intend to keep the heat on. When we next meet, I may well have a report of my own for you to consider."

"I'll look forward to reading it," said Dexter, rising from her place. She put the file on the President's desk, picked up her handbag, and left the office without another word.

A moment later Andy Lloyd entered the room.

"I don't believe a word of it," the President said to his chief of staff. "I guess the best we can hope for is that we've put the fear of God into her and that she won't consider carrying out another operation like that while I'm in the White House."

"I wouldn't put a whole lot of money on that, Mr. President."

"I can hardly employ an assassin to remove her, so what do you suggest I do?"

"In my opinion you have two choices, Mr. President. You can either fire her and face the inevitable Senate investigation, or accept defeat, go along with her version of what took place in Bogotá, and hope you can get the better of her next time."

"There could be a third way," the President said quietly.

Lloyd listened intently. It quickly became clear that the President had given considerable thought to how he might remove Helen Dexter from her post as director of the CIA.

CONNOR Fitzgerald collected his thoughts as the belt began to spew out the luggage from his flight. His suitcase finally appeared in front of him. He grabbed it and headed for customs.

When he stepped out into the arrivals building, he immediately spotted his wife and daughter standing among the crowd. He quickened his pace and smiled at the two women he adored.

"How are you, my darling?" he asked, taking Maggie in his arms.

"I always come alive again whenever you're safely back from an assignment," she whispered. He tried to ignore the word "safely" as he released her and turned to the other woman in his life: a slightly taller version of the original, with the same long red hair and flashing green eyes. Connor's only child gave him a huge kiss on the cheek that made him feel ten years younger.

"How was South Africa?" Maggie asked.

"It's become even more precarious since Mandela's death," Connor replied. He'd had a full briefing from Carl Koeter on the problems facing South Africa over their long lunch in Cape Town.

How often Connor had wanted to tell Maggie the whole truth. But he had always accepted the code of total silence and tried to convince himself that it was in her best interests not to know the truth. But when she unthinkingly used words like "assignment" and "safely," he was aware that she knew far more than she admitted. Soon, though, it would no longer be necessary to lie. Bogotá had been his last mission. During the coming vacation he would drop a hint about a promotion that would mean far less traveling.

They walked out of the arrivals building into the warm Australian summer and headed for the parking lot.

ANDY Lloyd hailed a taxi and jumped in.

"AV's, on New York Avenue," he said.

The taxi turned left on Pennsylvania, then headed north up 6th Street. He tried to marshal his thoughts into some sort of coherent order, grateful that the driver didn't want to spend the journey offering him his opinions on the administration or, particularly, on the President.

They swung left onto New York Avenue, and the taxi immediately began to slow down. He handed a ten-dollar bill to the driver, then stepped out without waiting for the change.

He passed under a red-white-and-green awning that left no doubt of the restaurant proprietor's Italian origins and pushed open the door. He was relieved to find that the place was empty except for a solitary figure seated at a small table at the far end of the room, toying with a half-empty glass of tomato juice. His stylish, well-cut suit gave no indication that he was unemployed. Although the man still had the build of an athlete, his prematurely balding dome made him look older than the age given in his file. Their eyes met, and the man nodded. He walked over and took a seat.

"My name is Andy . . ." he began.

"The mystery, Mr. Lloyd, is not who you are, but why the President's chief of staff should want to see me in the first place," said Chris Jackson.

"AND what *is* your special field?" Stuart McKenzie asked.

Maggie glanced at her husband, knowing he wouldn't welcome such an intrusive question.

Connor realized that Tara couldn't have warned the latest young man to fall under her spell not to discuss her father's work.

Until that moment Connor couldn't remember enjoying a lunch more. Fish that must have been caught only hours before they had sat down at the corner table in the little beach café at Cronulla. Fruit that had never seen preservatives or a can, and a beer he hoped they exported to Washington. He took a gulp of coffee before leaning back in his chair and watching the surfers only a hundred yards away—a sport he wished he'd discovered twenty years before. Stuart had been surprised by how fit Tara's father was when he tried out the surfboard for the first time. Connor bluffed by telling him that he still worked out two or three times a week. Two or three times a day would have been nearer the truth.

Although he would never consider anyone good enough for his daughter, Connor had to admit that over the past few days he had come to enjoy the young lawyer's company.

"I'm in the insurance business," he replied, aware that Tara would have told Stuart that much.

"Yes, Tara said so, but she didn't go into any details."

Connor smiled. "That's because I specialize in kidnap-and-ransom, and have the same attitude to client confidentiality that you take for granted in your profession." He hoped that would stop the young Australian from pursuing the subject.

In case it didn't, Maggie rose from her place, turned to Connor, and said, "I'm going for a swim. Anyone care to join me?"

"No, but I'd like another go on the surfboard," said Tara, eagerly assisting her mother's attempt to end the interrogation. She grabbed Stuart by the arm. "Let's go, Superman. I'll give you the chance to rescue me and look heroic."

Stuart leaped up, and they ran down the beach toward the surf.

"He's a nice young man," said Maggie, taking Connor's hand as they, too, began heading toward the waves.

As they walked, Maggie thought back to their early years together and smiled. When Connor had signed up with Maryland Insurance as a management trainee, she had been puzzled by his decision. She had always thought that, like his father, Connor would want to be involved in law enforcement. That was before he explained who he would really be working for. Although he didn't go into great detail, he did tell her who his paymaster was and the significance of being a nonofficial cover officer, or NOC. She had kept his secret loyally over the years, though not being able to discuss her husband's occupation with friends was sometimes awkward. But she decided this was a minor inconvenience compared with what so many other wives were put through by husbands only too happy to discuss their work in endless detail. It was their extracurricular activities they wanted to keep secret.

All she really hoped was that one day Tara would find someone willing to wait on a bench all night just to see her draw a curtain.

CHRIS Jackson lit a cigarette and listened carefully to every word the man from the White House had to say. He made no attempt to interrupt him.

When Andy Lloyd eventually came to the end of his prepared

piece, he took a sip of mineral water and waited to hear what the former CIA deputy director's first question would be.

Jackson stubbed out his cigarette. "May I ask why you thought I was the right person for this assignment?"

Lloyd told the truth. "We know that you resigned your post with the CIA because of a . . . difference of opinion"—he emphasized the words—"with Helen Dexter, despite the fact that your record with the Agency had been exemplary. Since resigning eight months ago for reasons that on the face of it seem somewhat bizarre, you haven't been able to find a job worthy of your qualifications. We suspect that Dexter also has something to do with that."

"It only takes one phone call," said Jackson, "off the record, of course, and suddenly you find you've been removed from any short-list." He lit another cigarette. "You see, Dexter believes that Tom Lawrence has the second most important job in America and that *she* is the true defender of the faith. To her, elected politicians are nothing more than temporary inconveniences who will sooner or later be ejected by the voters. You can be sure that Dexter has a file on your boss filled with reasons why he isn't qualified for a second term."

"Then we'll have to start building up our own file, Mr. Jackson. I can think of no one better qualified to carry out the task."

"Where would you like me to begin?"

"By investigating who was behind the assassination of Ricardo Guzman in Bogotá last month," said Lloyd. "We have reason to believe that the CIA might have been involved."

"Without the President's knowledge?" asked Jackson.

Lloyd nodded, removed a file from his briefcase, and slid it across the table. "Take your time," he said, "because you're going to have to memorize everything."

Jackson flipped the file open. When he had finished reading, he said, "How long have I got?"

"The new President of Colombia is visiting Washington in three weeks' time. It would help if we had something by then."

"It's already beginning to feel like the old days," said Jackson as he stubbed out his cigarette. "Except this time there's the added pleasure of Dexter being officially on the other side." He lit another cigarette. "Who will I be working for?"

"Officially you're freelance, but unofficially you work for me. I'll contact you whenever—"

"No, you won't, Mr. Lloyd," said Jackson. "I'll contact you whenever I have anything worthwhile to report. Two-way contacts only double the chance of someone stumbling across us. All I'll need is an untraceable phone number."

Lloyd wrote down seven figures on a napkin. "This gets straight through to my desk. After midnight it's automatically transferred to a phone by my bed. You needn't bother about the time difference when you're abroad, because I don't care about being woken up."

"That's good to know," said Jackson. "Because I don't think Helen Dexter ever sleeps."

Lloyd smiled. "Have we covered everything?"

"Not quite," said Jackson. "When you leave, turn right and then take the next right. Don't look back, and don't hail a taxi until you've walked at least four blocks. From now on you're going to have to think like Dexter, and be warned, she's been at it for thirty years. There's only one person I know who's better than she is."

"I hope that's you," said Lloyd.

"I'm afraid not," said Jackson.

"Don't tell me he already works for Dexter."

Jackson nodded. "Even though he's my closest friend, if Dexter ordered him to kill me, there isn't an insurance company in town that would take out a policy on my life. If you expect me to beat both of them, you'd better hope I haven't gone rusty over the past eight months."

The two men rose. "Good-bye, Mr. Lloyd," said Jackson as they shook hands. "This will be our first and last meeting."

"But I thought we agreed—" said Lloyd, looking anxiously at his new recruit.

"To work together, Mr. Lloyd, not to meet. You see, Dexter wouldn't consider two meetings a coincidence."

Lloyd nodded. "Then I'll wait to hear from you."

"THIS IS THE LAST CALL FOR United Airlines flight 816 to Los Angeles," said a voice that echoed around the Sydney airport. "Will all ticketholders please make their way immediately to gate 27."

Connor and Maggie began walking in the direction of the gate, trying to stay a few paces in front of Tara and Stuart, who were locked together as if they were in a three-legged race. During the past two weeks Connor and Maggie had come first to like, and later to respect, Stuart. All in all, Connor reflected now, this had been one of the most enjoyable vacations he could remember.

Once he and Maggie had gone through passport control, Connor hung back while Maggie carried on toward the departure lounge to tell the gate agent that the last two passengers would be following shortly. When Tara reluctantly appeared around the corner a few moments later, Connor placed an arm gently around her shoulder. "Your mother and I think Stuart's . . ." Connor hesitated.

"I know," Tara said between sobs. "As soon as I get back to Stanford, I'm going to ask if they'll allow me to complete my thesis at Sydney University." Connor spotted his wife talking to a stewardess by the gate to the aircraft.

"Is she that afraid of flying?" the stewardess whispered to Maggie when she saw the young woman sobbing.

"No. She just had to leave something behind that they wouldn't let her take through customs."

"ARE you certain Chris Jackson can be trusted?"

"No, Mr. President. But I am certain of one thing: Jackson loathes—I repeat, loathes—Helen Dexter as much as you do."

"Well, that's as good as a personal recommendation," said the President. "What else made you pick him?"

"Jackson has the other attributes I was looking for. There's his record as an officer in Vietnam and as head of counterintelligence, not to mention his reputation as deputy director of the CIA."

"Why did he suddenly resign from the CIA when he still had such a promising career ahead of him?"

"I suspect that Helen Dexter felt it was a bit too promising, and he was beginning to look like a serious contender for her job."

"If Jackson can prove that she gave the order to assassinate Ricardo Guzman, he still might be a serious contender. So let's hope he can supply us with enough rope to hang Dexter publicly. And while we're at it, let's hold the execution in the Rose Garden."

MAGGIE began dialing the San Francisco number minutes after she had turned the key in the lock of their house in Georgetown. Connor started to unpack, listening to one end of the conversation between his wife and his daughter. They had said good-bye at the Los Angeles airport, where Tara had boarded a flight to San Francisco.

"Everything all right at your end?" asked Maggie.

"Yes, fine," Tara said, before spending the next few minutes trying to assure her mother that she wasn't about to do something impetuous. Eventually she asked, "Is Dad around?"

"He's right here." Maggie handed the phone to Connor.

"Can you do me a favor, Dad? Please explain to Mom that I'm not about to do anything silly. Stuart's planning to come over for Christmas, and I'm pretty sure I can hang on until then. By the way, Dad, I already know what I'd like for Christmas."

"And what's that, my darling?"

"That you'll pay for my overseas calls for the next eight months. I have a feeling that might end up being more expensive than buying that used car you promised me if I got my Ph.D."

Connor laughed. "Okay. Bye, darling." He hung up and gave Maggie a reassuring smile. He was about to tell her to stop worrying, when the phone rang again. He picked up the receiver.

"Sorry to call the moment you arrive back," said his secretary, Joan Bennett, "but I've just heard from the boss, and it sounds like an emergency. How quickly can you come in?"

Connor checked his watch. "I'll be with you in twenty minutes."

"Who was that?" asked Maggie when he hung up.

"Joan. She needs me to sign a couple of contracts."

Connor quickly left the room and ran out of the house before Maggie could ask any more questions. He got into the old family

Toyota and eased it out onto 29th Street. Fifteen minutes later he was disappearing down a ramp into an unmarked underground garage.

As Connor entered the building, the security guard said, "Welcome back, Mr. Fitzgerald. I wasn't expecting you until Monday."

"That makes two of us," said Connor, returning the mock salute and heading toward the elevators. He took one to the seventh floor. When he stepped out into the corridor, he was greeted by a smile from the receptionist who sat at a desk below the boldly printed caption MARYLAND INSURANCE COMPANY.

"You have a visitor, Mr. Fitzgerald," she said.

Connor smiled and continued down the corridor, turned the corner, and strode into his office. Sitting on the other side of his desk was someone he'd never known to take a day off.

"We have a problem," was all Helen Dexter said, pushing a file across the desk.

"GIVE me one decent lead; I'll do the groundwork," said Jackson.

"I wish I could, Chris," replied Bogotá's chief of police. "But it has been made clear to me that you are now *persona non grata*."

"I've never thought of you as someone who cared about such niceties," said Jackson, pouring the chief a whiskey.

"Chris, you have to understand that when you were a representative of your government, it was all aboveboard."

"Including your kickbacks?"

"But of course," said the policeman nonchalantly. "You'll be the first to appreciate that expenses still have to be met."

"Am I to understand," said Jackson, "that the rate remains the same even if one is *persona non grata?*"

The chief downed his whiskey and said, "Chris, Presidents come and go in both our countries—but not old friends."

Jackson gave him a thin smile before removing an envelope from his pocket and sliding it under the table. The chief of police glanced inside it and slipped the envelope into his tunic pocket.

"I see that your new masters have not, alas, allowed you the same degree of latitude when it comes to expenses."

"One decent lead, that's all I ask," repeated Jackson.

The chief of police smiled. "I have always believed, Chris, that if you're looking for a bargain, there's no better place to start than a pawnshop." He rose from the table. "And remembering the dilemma you're facing, my old friend, I'd begin in the San Victorina district. I wouldn't bother to do much more than window-shop."

ONCE Connor Fitzgerald had finished reading the details of the confidential file, he passed it back to the director.

Her first question took him by surprise. "How long is it before you're due to retire from the service?"

"I come off the active list on January first of next year, but naturally, I hope to remain with the Company."

"It may not be quite that easy to accommodate your particular talents at the present time," Dexter said. "However, I do have a vacancy as director of our Cleveland office."

"Cleveland?"

"Yes."

"After twenty-eight years' service I was hoping you might find me something in Washington. I'm sure you know that my wife is the dean of admissions at Georgetown."

"I'd like to help," Dexter said matter-of-factly, "but there's nothing suitable for you at Langley at present."

Connor stared across the table at the director, painfully aware that she was now using the same lethal blade on him as she had on so many of his colleagues in the past. But why? He glanced at the file. Had the President demanded that someone be sacrificed after he had been questioned so closely about the CIA's activities in Colombia?

"Is there any alternative?" he asked.

"You could always opt for early retirement." Helen Dexter rose from her place. "Perhaps you'll let me know when you've reached a decision." She left the room without another word.

Connor sat alone at his desk for some time, trying to take in the full implications of the director's words. He recalled that Chris Jackson had told him of an almost identical conversation he'd had with her eight months before. How many other good officers had been sacrificed over the years, he wondered, on the altar of Dexter's ego?

As CHRIS Jackson opened the front door, a bell rang to warn the shopkeeper that someone had entered the premises.

There are more than a hundred pawnshops in Bogotá, most of them in the San Victorina district. Jackson hadn't done so much footwork since he had been a junior agent.

Escobar looked up from his evening paper. "Good evening, sir," the old man said, rising from his stool. "How may I assist you?"

"The gun in the window . . ."

"Ah, yes. A collector's item." Escobar lifted the counter lid and walked to the window. He removed the case, placed it on the counter, and allowed his customer to have a look at its contents.

Jackson needed only a cursory glance at the handcrafted rifle to know its provenance. He wasn't surprised to find that one of the cartridges had been fired. "How much are you asking for it?"

"Ten thousand dollars," replied Escobar.

Jackson was in no mood to bargain, but he didn't have that amount of cash on him. "Can I leave a down payment," he asked, "and pick it up first thing in the morning?"

"Certainly, sir," said Escobar. "Although for this particular item, I would require a ten percent deposit."

Jackson nodded and removed a wallet from his inside pocket. He extracted ten hundred-dollar bills and passed them across the counter to Escobar, who wrote out a receipt.

Jackson looked down at the open case, smiled, removed the spent cartridge, and put it in his pocket.

The old man was puzzled, not by Jackson's action, but because he could have sworn that all six bullets had been in place when he had bought the rifle.

WHEN he opened the door, the alarm went off. He swept aside the bead curtain and stepped into the shop. He stared across at the stand in the window. The rifle was no longer in its place.

It took him several minutes to find it, hidden under the counter.

He checked each item and noted that one cartridge was missing, placed the case under his arm, and left quickly. Not that he had any anxiety about being caught: The chief of police had assured him that the break-in would not be reported for at least thirty minutes.

The chief of police could hardly be blamed if his old friend didn't have enough cash on him to buy the rifle. And in any case, he did so like being paid twice for the same piece of information. Especially when the currency was dollars.

SHE poured him a second cup of coffee.

"Maggie, I'm considering resigning from the company and looking for a job that means I don't have to travel so much." He glanced across the kitchen table to see how his wife would react.

Maggie replaced the coffeepot on the warmer. "Why now?"

"I'm to be taken off kidnap-and-ransom and replaced by a younger man. It's company policy at my age."

"But there must be plenty of other jobs in the company."

"The chairman did come up with a suggestion," said Connor. "She offered me the chance to head up our office in Cleveland."

"Cleveland?" said Maggie in disbelief. "Why is the chairman suddenly so eager to see the back of you?"

"Oh, it's not that bad. I'm still eligible for a full retirement package," said Connor, making no attempt to answer her question.

"Don't you think the time has come to tell me the whole truth?" said Maggie. "You've never hidden the fact that Maryland Insurance is nothing more than a front for the CIA. And I've never pressed you on the subject. But lately even your well-disguised trips have left a little mud on your shoes."

"I'm not sure I understand," Connor said lamely.

"When I picked up your suit from the cleaners, they told me they'd found this in the pocket." Maggie placed a tiny coin on the table. "I'm told it has no value outside Colombia."

Connor stared at a ten-peso piece. "I promise you, Maggie—"

"I know, Connor. I've always accepted that there had to be a good reason why you haven't been completely candid with me over the years." She leaned across, took her husband's hand, and said, "But if you're about to be dumped on the scrap heap for no apparent reason, don't you feel I have a right to be told exactly what you've been up to for the past twenty-eight years?"

CHRIS Jackson asked the taxi driver to pull up outside the pawnshop and wait. He would only be a few minutes, he said, and then he wanted to be taken to the airport.

As soon as he entered the shop, Escobar came scurrying through from the outer office. He looked agitated. When he saw who the customer was, he pressed a key on the cash register and pulled open the drawer. Without a word he extracted ten hundred-dollar bills and handed them across the counter.

"I must apologize, sir," he said, "but I fear the rifle was stolen at some time during the night."

Jackson said nothing. Escobar couldn't help thinking, after his customer had left, that he hadn't seemed all that surprised.

As the taxi headed toward the airport, Jackson removed the spent cartridge from his jacket pocket. He might not be able to prove who had pulled the trigger, but he was now in no doubt who had given the order to assassinate Ricardo Guzman.

THE helicopter landed softly on a patch of grass by the Reflecting Pool between the Washington Monument and the Lincoln Memorial. As the rotor blades slowed, a short flight of steps unfolded. The door of the Nighthawk swung open, and President Herrera appeared, sporting a full-dress uniform that made him look like a minor character in a B movie. He returned the salute of the waiting marines, then walked to his armored Cadillac limousine.

President Tom Lawrence, Secretary of State Larry Harrington, and White House chief of staff Andy Lloyd were waiting at the South Portico of the White House to greet the new Colombian President. The better-tailored the outfit, the more numerous the medals, the less significant the country, Lawrence thought as he stepped forward to greet his visitor.

"Antonio, my dear old friend," said Lawrence as Herrera embraced him, though they had met only once before. After the requisite three-minute photo-op, the President ushered his guest into the Oval Office. While Colombian coffee was being served and yet more photographs taken, they discussed nothing of significance. When they were eventually left alone, Lawrence spoke authoritatively about extradition agreements, this year's coffee crop, the drug problem. But as the Secretary of State broadened the discussion to take in the repayment of extended dollar loans, the President found his mind wandering.

The arms reduction bill was getting bogged down in committee, and the votes just weren't stacking up. He would probably need to see several Congressmen individually if he was to have any chance of pushing it through.

Lawrence was brought back to the present with a jolt when Herrera said, "And for that I must thank you personally, Mr. President." A large smile appeared on Herrera's face as the three most powerful men in America stared at him in disbelief.

"Would you care to repeat that, Antonio?" said the President, not quite sure that he had heard his visitor correctly.

"As we are in the privacy of the Oval Office, Tom, I wanted to say how much I appreciated the personal role you played in my election."

"How long have you been working for Maryland Life, Mr. Fitzgerald?" asked the chairman of the board. It was his first question in an interview that had already lasted for over an hour.

"Twenty-eight years in May, Mr. Thompson," replied Connor, looking directly at the man who sat at the center of the large table, facing him.

"Your record is most impressive," said the woman sitting on the chairman's right. "Why do you want to leave your present job?"

"My only chance of promotion would have meant moving to Cleveland," he answered truthfully, "and I felt I couldn't ask my wife to give up her job at Georgetown University."

The third member of the interviewing board nodded. Maggie had briefed him that one member of the panel had a son at Georgetown.

"We needn't detain you any longer," said the chairman. "I'd just like to thank you, Mr. Fitzgerald, for coming to see us."

"My pleasure," said Connor, standing to leave.

The chairman rose from behind the long table and came around to join him. "Would you and your wife care to have dinner with us one evening next week?" he asked as he escorted Connor to the door.

"We'd be delighted, sir," Connor replied.

"Ben," said the chairman, "nobody at Washington Provident calls me sir." He shook Connor warmly by the hand. "I'll ask my secretary to phone your office tomorrow and fix a date. I look forward to meeting your wife. Maggie, isn't it?"

"Yes, sir," Connor replied. He paused. "And I look forward to meeting Mrs. Thompson, Ben."

ANDY Lloyd picked up the red phone but didn't immediately recognize the voice.

"I have some information. I'm sorry it's taken so long."

Lloyd quickly grabbed a blank yellow pad and a pen. He didn't need to press any buttons. Every conversation that took place on that particular phone was automatically recorded.

"I've just returned from ten days in Bogotá, and someone down there was making sure that doors were not only slammed in my face but locked and bolted."

"Dexter must have found out what you were up to," said Lloyd.

"Within minutes of my speaking to the local chief of police would be my bet."

"Does that mean she also knows who you're working for?"

"No. I covered myself on that front, which is why I've taken so long getting back to you. But all the evidence suggests that the CIA was behind the assassination."

"How can you be so sure the CIA was involved?"

"I saw the rifle that I'm confident was used to kill Guzman. I even got hold of the spent cartridge of the bullet that hit him. What's more, I know the man who made the gun. He's contracted to work for a small number of NOCs."

"NOCs?"

"Nonofficial cover officers, unattached to any government agency. That way the CIA can deny all knowledge of their activities if anything goes wrong."

"So the assassin is a serving officer of the CIA," said Lloyd.

"It looks that way. Unless it turns out to be the one Dexter pensioned off a few days ago."

"Well, that's one person we ought to have on our payroll."

There was a long silence before Jackson finally said, "Mr. Lloyd, this man wouldn't betray a former employer, however large a bribe you offered him. He served under me in Nam, and even the Vietcong couldn't get anything out of him. He's about the only reason I'm still alive. In any case, Dexter will have convinced him that her orders came straight from the White House."

"We could tell him she was lying," said Lloyd.

"That would only put his own life in danger. No. I have to be able to prove Dexter's involvement without him finding out what we're up to. And that won't be easy."

"So how do you intend to do it?"

"By going to his retirement party. There'll be one person there who loves him even more than she loves her country. And she just might be willing to talk. I'll be in touch."

The phone went dead.

WHEN Nick Gutenburg, the deputy director of the CIA, entered the Fitzgeralds' living room, the first person he saw was his predecessor, Chris Jackson, deep in conversation with Joan Bennett. Was Jackson telling her who he'd been working for in Bogotá? Gutenburg would have liked to overhear what they were talking about, but first he had to say hello to his host and hostess.

"I'll do another nine months with the company," Joan was saying. "By then I'll be eligible for my full pension. After that, I'm hoping to join Connor in his new job."

"I've just heard about that," said Jackson. "It sounds ideal."

"His appointment isn't official yet," said Joan. "But since Ben Thompson, the chairman of Washington Provident, has invited him and Maggie to dinner, I think he's landed the job."

"Good of you to come, Nick," said Connor warmly, passing him a glass of Perrier. He didn't need to be reminded that Gutenburg never allowed alcohol to pass his lips. Turning to his wife, he said, "Maggie, this is Nick Gutenburg, a colleague of mine. He works in—"

"Loss adjustment," Gutenburg interjected quickly. "We're all going to miss your husband at Maryland Life, Mrs. Fitzgerald."

"Well, I'm sure your paths will cross again," said Maggie, "since Connor's taking up another job in the same line of business."

"It hasn't been confirmed yet," said Connor. "But as soon as it is, Nick, you'll be the first to hear about it."

Nick Gutenburg's eyes returned to Jackson, and when he moved away from Joan Bennett, Gutenburg slipped across the room to join her. "I was delighted to hear that you'll be staying with the company, Joan," were his opening words. "I thought you might be leaving us to join Connor in his new job."

"No. I'll be remaining with the firm," said Joan, uncertain how much the deputy director knew.

"I just thought since Connor will be continuing in the same line of business . . ."

You're on a fishing trip, thought Joan. "I wouldn't know," she said firmly.

"Who's Chris Jackson talking to?" Gutenburg asked.

Joan looked across the room. "That's Tara, Connor's daughter."

"And what does she do?" asked Gutenburg.

"She's completing a Ph.D. at Stanford."

Gutenburg realized that he was wasting his time trying to get any real information out of Connor's secretary, so when Tara went over to the bar to refill her glass, Gutenburg left Joan without another word.

"My name's Nick Gutenburg," he told Tara, thrusting out his hand. "I'm a colleague of your father's."

"I'm Tara," she said. "Which branch do you work for?"

"Loss adjustment. It's rather boring compared with what your father does," he said, letting out a little laugh. "By the way, I was delighted to hear about his new appointment."

"Yes. It's still not official, but—" Tara stopped talking when she heard a sharp noise. She turned to see Chris Jackson banging the table to bring the guests to order.

"Ladies and gentlemen," Chris began. "It's my privilege to propose a toast to two of my oldest friends, Connor and Maggie. Over the years Connor has consistently proved to be the one man most likely to get me into trouble. But once you're in trouble, I don't know anyone better to get you out of it." This was greeted by warm applause.

Gutenburg felt his pager buzz and quickly pulled it off his belt. TROY ASAP, it read. He slipped out of the room, picked up the nearest phone, and dialed a number that wasn't in any directory. It hadn't even rung before a voice said, "The director."

"I got your message, but I'm on a nonsecure line."

"Yeltsin died of a heart attack seventeen minutes ago," said Helen Dexter. "Report to my office immediately." The line went dead. No call from a nonsecure line to Dexter's office lasted more than forty-five seconds. She kept a stopwatch on her desk.

Gutenburg replaced the phone and slipped out the front door without bothering to say good-bye to his hostess. He was on his way back to Langley by the time Chris raised his glass and said, "To Connor and Maggie, and whatever the future holds for them."

All the guests raised their glasses. "To Connor and Maggie."

"I'LL tell you exactly where my information came from," said Tom Lawrence. "From the President of Colombia himself. He thanked me personally for the role I played in his election."

"That's hardly proof," Helen Dexter said, showing no sign of emotion. "But if you're accusing the Agency of carrying out covert operations without your knowledge, I hope it's not going to be simply on the word of a South American politician."

The President leaned forward. "I suggest, Helen, that you listen carefully to a recording of a conversation that took place in this office quite recently."

Nick Gutenburg, seated on Dexter's right, shifted uneasily in his seat. Andy Lloyd pressed a button on a remote control. A tape began to play from somewhere in the room.

"Do you have *any actual* evidence to link Guzman's assassination with the CIA?" It was the President's voice.

"The bullet that killed him was traced to a rifle that had been sold to a pawnshop before the lone assassin fled the country," said Herrera. "The rifle was later removed from the shop by one of your operatives and shipped back to America via diplomatic pouch."

"How can you be sure of that?"

"My chief of police is obviously a lot more forthcoming with me than the CIA is with you."

Andy Lloyd flicked off the tape recorder. Helen Dexter looked up to find the President's eyes boring into hers.

"From that conversation there is absolutely no proof of any CIA involvement in Guzman's assassination," she said evenly. "All it suggests to me is that Herrera is trying to shield the person who carried out his orders."

"I assume you're referring to the 'lone assassin,' who has since conveniently disappeared somewhere in South Africa," said the President sarcastically.

"The moment he surfaces, Mr. President, we'll find him," said Dexter. "And when I produce the man responsible for the assassination, there won't be any doubt about who he was working for." There was a slight edge to her voice.

"If you fail to do so," said the President, "I wouldn't be surprised if this tape"—he tapped the recorder—"ended up in the hands of the Washington *Post*. Then you'll have to answer an awful lot of awkward questions."

"If that happens, you might have to answer one or two yourself, Mr. President," said Dexter, not flinching.

Lawrence rose angrily from his chair. "Let me make it clear. I require positive proof of the existence of your missing South African. And if you fail to produce it within twenty-eight days, I'll expect both of your resignations. Now get out of my office."

The director and her deputy rose and left the room. Neither of them spoke until they were seated in the back of Dexter's car.

"Have you talked to Connor Fitzgerald yet?"

"No," replied Gutenburg. "I plan to call Fitzgerald on Monday, after he's heard from Washington Provident."

"WE ARE sorry to inform you . . ."

Connor was reading the letter for the third time when the phone on his desk rang. He felt numb with disbelief. What could have gone wrong? Dinner at the Thompsons' home couldn't have been more agreeable. When he and Maggie left a few minutes before midnight, Ben had suggested golf at Burning Tree the following weekend, and Elizabeth Thompson had asked Maggie to drop by for coffee while the men were out chasing little white balls. The next day his lawyer had called to say that the contract Washington Provident had sent for his approval didn't need more than a few minor adjustments.

Connor picked up the phone. "Yes, Joan."

"I have Nick Gutenburg on the line."

"Put him on," he said wearily.

"Connor?" said a voice he had never trusted. "Something important has come up, and the director's asked me to brief you immediately. Shall we make it three o'clock, the usual place?"

"Of course," said Connor, not really taking in Gutenburg's words. He read the letter for a fourth time and decided not to tell Maggie about it until he had been short-listed for another job.

CONNOR was the first to arrive in Lafayette Square. He sat down on a bench facing the White House. A few minutes later Nick Gutenburg took a seat on the other end of the bench.

"The President himself requested that you should take on this assignment," murmured Gutenburg. "He wanted our best man."

"But I'm leaving the Company in ten days' time," said Connor.

"The President insisted that we do everything in our power to convince you to stay until this assignment is completed."

Connor remained silent.

"Connor, the outcome of the elections in Russia could affect the future of the free world. If that lunatic Zerimski is elected, it would mean a return to the cold war overnight."

"But Zerimski's still way behind in the polls," said Connor. "Isn't Chernopov expected to win comfortably?"

"That's how it may look right now," said Gutenburg. "But there are still three weeks to go. The President wants you out there, just in case your particular expertise is needed."

Connor didn't respond.

"If it's your new job you're worrying about," continued Gutenburg, "I'd be happy to have a word with the chairman of the company you're joining and explain to him that it's only a short-term assignment."

"That won't be necessary," said Connor. "I'll take the assignment, but on one condition. I want proof that the operation has been sanctioned by the President."

There was a long silence before Gutenburg said, "I'll inform the director of your request." He rose and walked away. Three minutes later Connor strolled off in the opposite direction.

ANDY Lloyd picked up the red phone. This time he recognized the voice immediately.

"I'm almost certain I know who carried out the assignment in Bogotá," said Chris Jackson. "And he *was* working for the CIA."

"Do you have enough proof to convince the congressional Select Committees on Intelligence?" Lloyd asked.

"No. Almost all the evidence I have is circumstantial. But when it's all put together, there are far too many coincidences."

"For example?"

"The agent who I suspect pulled the trigger was fired shortly after the President demanded to know who was responsible for Guzman's assassination."

"Not even admissible as evidence."

"Maybe not. But the same agent was about to start a new job with Washington Provident when suddenly, without any explanation, the job offer was withdrawn. Three days later Gutenburg gave the agent in question a one-time assignment."

"Do we have any idea what that assignment is?"

"No. But don't be surprised if it takes him a long way from Washington."

"Okay," said Lloyd. "What do you think Dexter is doing right now to cover her tracks?"

"Before I could begin to answer that, I'd need to know the outcome of her last meeting with the President," said Jackson.

"The President gave her and Gutenburg twenty-eight days to prove that the CIA wasn't involved in Guzman's assassination and to provide cast-iron proof of who *did* kill him. If they fail, he'll demand their resignations and release all the evidence in his possession to the Washington *Post*."

There was a long silence before Jackson said, "That means the agent in question has less than a month to live."

"She'd never eliminate one of her own people," said Andy Lloyd in disbelief.

"Don't forget he's an NOC. The section of the CIA he works for doesn't even exist officially, Mr. Lloyd."

"This guy's a good friend of yours, isn't he?" said Lloyd.

"Yes," replied Jackson quietly.

"Then you'd better make sure he stays alive."

"SO HOW does it work?" asked the director.

"It's quite simple, really," said Professor Ziegler, the CIA's director of technical services. He turned to a bank of computers and pressed some keys. Tom Lawrence's face appeared on the screen.

After Dexter and Nick Gutenburg had listened to the President's words for a few moments, she said, "What's so remarkable about that? We've all heard Lawrence making a speech before."

"Maybe, but you've never heard him make that particular speech," said Ziegler.

"What do you mean?" asked Gutenburg.

An almost childlike smile of satisfaction spread across the professor's face. "I have stored in my computer—code-named Tommy—over a thousand speeches and interviews the President has given during the past two years. Every word or phrase he has used in that time is stored in this memory bank. That means I can make him deliver a speech on any subject you choose. The program was set up in case the President died while the United States was at war, and we needed the enemy to believe he was still alive."

Dexter began to consider the possibilities. "If Tommy were to be asked a question, could he give a convincing reply?" she asked.

"Not spontaneously," admitted Ziegler. "But if you had some idea of the questions he might be expected to answer, I believe I could fool Lawrence's own mother."

"So all we have to do," said Gutenburg, "is anticipate what the other party is likely to say."

"Which may not be as difficult as you think," said Ziegler. "If you were to prepare opening and closing remarks, as well as—say—the fifty questions or statements he was most likely to have to respond to, I could almost guarantee he could conduct a plausible conversation."

"How long would it take you to prepare a specific program?" Gutenburg asked.

"How long will it take you to work out what the President needs to say?" replied Ziegler.

SHE kept her finger on the buzzer until Connor finally picked up the phone on his desk.

"What's the problem, Joan? I'm not going deaf."

"The President's personal secretary is on the line."

The next voice Connor heard was a woman's. "Mr. Fitzgerald? I have the President on the line for you."

Connor heard a click. "Good afternoon," a familiar voice said.

"Good afternoon, Mr. President."

"I think you know why I'm calling."

"Yes, sir, I do."

Professor Ziegler pressed OPENING STATEMENT. The director and deputy director held their breath.

"I felt I had to call and let you know just how important I consider this assignment to be." Pause. "Because I have no doubt that you're the right person to carry it out."

Ziegler pressed the WAIT button.

"I appreciate your confidence in me, Mr. President," said Connor, "and I'm grateful to you for phoning personally."

"Number eleven," said Ziegler, who knew all the replies by heart.

"I felt it was the least I could do in the circumstances." Pause.

"Thank you, Mr. President. I felt unable to take on the assignment unless I was certain the order had come directly from you."

"Number seven."

"I can quite understand your anxiety." Pause.

"Number nineteen."

"Perhaps when this is all over, you and your wife would come and visit me at the White House." Pause.

"We would be honored, sir," Connor said.

"Closing statement," said Ziegler.

"Good. I'll look forward to seeing you as soon as you return." Pause. "It was good talking to you. Good-bye."

"Good-bye, Mr. President."

Connor was still holding the phone when Joan came into the room. "So that's another myth exploded," she said. Connor looked up at her and raised an inquiring eyebrow.

"That the President always calls everyone by their first name."

GUTENBURG handed him an envelope containing four passports, three airline tickets, and a bundle of bills in different currencies.

"Don't I have to sign for all this?" asked Connor.

"We'll deal with the paperwork when you get back. Once you

arrive in Moscow, you're to go to Zerimski's headquarters and produce your credentials as a reporter from South Africa. They'll give you a press kit detailing his campaign schedule."

"Do I have a contact in Moscow?"

"Yes. Ashley Mitchell." Gutenburg hesitated. "It's his first big assignment. He's been instructed to get in touch with you only if it's a green light, in which case he'll supply you with the weapon."

"Make and model?"

"The usual custom-made Remington 700," said Gutenburg. "But if Chernopov stays ahead in the polls, I don't expect your services will be needed, and you'll return to Washington the day after the election."

"Let's hope so," said Connor, and left the deputy director without shaking hands.

"CAN you be absolutely sure there'll be no trace of his ever having existed?" asked Helen Dexter.

"No trace whatsoever," said Gutenburg. "Don't forget that as an NOC, he was never on the Company's books in the first place."

"But what about his wife?"

"Why should she suspect anything? As far as she's concerned, he couldn't say no to one last assignment for Maryland Insurance."

"There's still his former secretary."

"I've had her transferred to the Middle East division at Langley. She'll have to be at the office during their working hours, from six in the evening until three in the morning. And I'll work her so hard that she'll be too tired to think about anything but what she's going to do once she retires."

"Good. Where's Connor Fitzgerald right now?"

Gutenburg checked his watch. "Halfway across the Atlantic. He'll be landing at London Heathrow in about four hours. He's traveling under the name of Martin Perry."

"You seem to have thought of everything except what happens when he returns to Washington," said the director.

"He isn't going to return to Washington," replied Gutenburg.

"AND HOW'S STUART?" Maggie asked.

"Still hanging in there," Tara replied. "He arrives in L.A. in fifteen days. I can't wait."

"Will you both be flying straight here?"

"No, Mom," said Tara, trying not to sound exasperated. "I told you, we're going to rent a car and drive up the West Coast."

"Drive carefully, will you?"

"Mother, I've been driving for nine years without even a ticket. Now stop worrying and tell me what you're doing this evening."

"I'm going to hear Plácido Domingo in *La Bohème*. I decided to wait until your father was out of town and go on my own because I knew he'd fall asleep before the first act was over."

"Why don't you ask Joan to go with you?"

"I called her at the office, but the number seems to be out of order. I'll try her at home later."

"Okay. Bye, Mom. Talk to you tomorrow," said Tara. She knew her mother would call every day while Connor was away.

Whenever Connor traveled abroad, Maggie would catch up with some of her university activities. Anything from the poetry society to the Irish dance class, where she gave lessons. The sight of the young students dancing brought back memories of Declan O'Casey. He was now a distinguished professor at the University of Chicago. He had never married and still sent her a card every Christmas and an unsigned one on Valentine's Day. The old typewriter with the crooked *e* always gave away his identity.

She picked up the phone again and dialed Joan's home number, but there was no reply. She fixed herself a light salad, then set off for the Kennedy Center. A single ticket was always easy to come by, however celebrated the guest tenor happened to be.

Maggie was transfixed by the first act of *La Bohème*, and when the curtain came down, she joined the throng heading for the foyer. As she approached the crowded bar, she thought she caught a glimpse of Ben and Elizabeth Thompson.

When Ben Thompson turned and caught her eye, Maggie smiled and walked over to join them.

"How nice to see you, Ben," she said.

"And you too, Mrs. Fitzgerald," he replied, but not in the warm voice she remembered from dinner two weeks earlier. And why hadn't he called her Maggie?

Undaunted, she plowed on. "Domingo is magnificent, don't you think?"

"Yes, and we were lucky to lure Leonard Slatkin from St. Louis," Ben Thompson replied. Maggie was surprised that he didn't offer to buy her a drink, and when she finally ordered an orange juice, she was even more puzzled when he made no attempt to pay for it.

"Connor is really looking forward to joining you all at Washington Provident," she said, taking a sip of her juice. Elizabeth Thompson appeared surprised but didn't comment.

The three-minute bell sounded. "Well, we'd better get back to our seats," said Ben Thompson. "Nice to have seen you again, Mrs. Fitzgerald." He took his wife firmly by the arm and guided her toward the auditorium. "I hope you enjoy the second act."

Maggie didn't enjoy the second act. The conversation that had just taken place in the foyer kept running through her mind. She simply couldn't reconcile it with what had happened at the Thompsons' only two weeks ago. If she had known how to get in touch with Connor, she would have broken the rule of a lifetime and phoned him. So she did the next best thing. The moment she arrived home, she called Joan Bennett again.

The phone rang and rang.

THE following morning, at seven forty, Connor Fitzgerald boarded Swissair flight 839 from London to Geneva. The flight took just under two hours, and he readjusted his watch to ten thirty as the wheels of the aircraft touched the ground.

During the stopover in Geneva he took advantage of Swissair's offer to take a shower. He entered the "exclusive facility"—the description in their in-flight magazine—as Theodore Lilystrand, an investment banker from Stockholm, and emerged forty minutes later as Piet de Villiers, a reporter with the Johannesburg *Mercury*.

Connor still had more than an hour to kill, so he bought a croissant and a cup of coffee from one of the most expensive restaurants in the world.

Eventually he walked across to gate 23. There wasn't a long line for the Aeroflot flight to St. Petersburg. When the passengers were called a few minutes later, he made his way to the back of the plane. He began to think about what needed to be done the following morning, once the train had pulled into Moscow's Raveltay station. He went over the deputy director's final briefing again, wondering why Gutenburg had repeated the words "Don't get caught. But if you are, deny absolutely that you have anything to do with the CIA. Don't worry—the Company will always take care of you."

Only raw recruits were reminded of the Eleventh Commandment.

"GOOD morning. This is Helen Dexter."

"Good morning, Director," replied Andy Lloyd stiffly.

"I thought the President would want to know that the man he asked us to track down in South Africa is on the move again."

"I'm not sure I follow you," said Lloyd.

"Guzman's killer boarded a South African Airways flight to London two days ago. He was carrying a passport in the name of Martin Perry. He only stayed in London overnight. The following morning, using a Swedish passport in the name of Theodore Lilystrand, he flew to Geneva, where he boarded an Aeroflot flight to St. Petersburg. This time he was carrying a South African passport in the name of Piet de Villiers. From St. Petersburg he took the overnight train to Moscow."

"Moscow? Why Moscow?" asked Lloyd.

"If I recall correctly," said Dexter, "an election is about to take place in Russia."

WHEN the plane landed in St. Petersburg, Connor's watch claimed that it was five fifty. He waited for the aircraft to taxi to a halt before altering the hands to local time. He looked out the window at an airport that was in semidarkness because half the light-bulbs were missing. The hundred weary passengers had to wait another twenty minutes before a bus arrived to transport them to the terminal. Some things simply didn't change, whether the KGB or organized criminals were in charge. Americans had come to refer to them as the Mafya to avoid confusion with the Italian version.

Connor was the last to leave the aircraft and the last to get off the bus. A man who had traveled first class on the same flight shadowed him through immigration and customs. When Connor left the airport thirty minutes later, he hailed the first available taxi and asked to be taken to Protsky station.

The first-class traveler followed Connor into the reservations area, which looked more like an opera house than a railway station. He watched closely to see which train Connor would be boarding. But there was another man standing in the shadows who even knew the number of the sleeping compartment Connor would be occupying.

The American cultural attaché in St. Petersburg had passed up an invitation to the Kirov Ballet that evening so he could inform Gutenburg when Fitzgerald had boarded the overnight train to Moscow. It wouldn't be necessary to accompany him on the journey, as Ashley Mitchell, his colleague in the capital, would be waiting on platform 4 the following morning to confirm that Fitzgerald had reached his destination.

"One first-class sleeper to Moscow," said Connor in English to the booking clerk.

The man pushed a ticket across the wooden counter. Connor checked it before making his way toward the Moscow express. He walked down the crowded platform, passing several old green carriages that looked as if they predated the 1917 Revolution, stopped at coach K, and climbed aboard.

He strolled down the corridor, looking for compartment 8. Once he found it, he switched on the light and locked himself in. He needed to change his identity once again.

He had seen the fresh-faced youth standing under the arrivals board at the Geneva airport, but didn't bother trying to spot the

CIA agent in St. Petersburg. He knew someone would be there to check on his arrival and someone else would be waiting on the platform in Moscow. Gutenburg had already briefed him fully on Agent Ashley Mitchell, whom he had described as fairly raw and not unaware of Fitzgerald's status as an NOC.

The train left St. Petersburg at exactly one minute to midnight, and the gentle, rhythmic sound of the carriage wheels clattering over the tracks soon made Connor feel drowsy. He slept fitfully until the train pulled in to Moscow's Raveltay station at eight thirty-three that morning.

"WHERE are you?" asked Andy Lloyd.

"A phone booth in Moscow," Jackson replied. "Via London, Geneva, and St. Petersburg. As soon as he got off the train, he led us all on a wild-goose chase. He managed to lose our man in Moscow in about ten minutes. If I hadn't taught him the doubling-back technique myself, he would have shaken me off as well."

"Where did he end up?" asked Lloyd.

"He checked into a small hotel on the north side of the city, left about an hour later, and took a circuitous route to the campaign headquarters of Victor Zerimski."

"Why Zerimski?"

"I don't know yet, but he came out of the building carrying all Zerimski's campaign literature."

"Oh, my God," said Lloyd. "It's going to be Zerimski this time."

There was a long pause before Jackson said, "That's not possible. He'd never agree to carry out such a sensitive assignment unless the order had come directly from the White House."

"Try not to forget that your friend carried out exactly the same assignment in Colombia. No doubt Dexter convinced him that that operation had also been sanctioned by the President."

"There could be an alternative scenario," said Jackson quietly.

"Namely?"

"That it's not Zerimski they're planning to kill but Connor."

Lloyd wrote the name down on his yellow pad.

"AMERICAN?"

"Yes," said Jackson, not looking down at the source of the piping voice.

"You need anything?"

"No, thanks," he said, still watching the front door of the hotel.

"Americans always need something. Caviar? Fur hat? Woman?"

Chris Jackson looked down at the boy for the first time. He was draped from head to toe in a sheepskin jacket three sizes too large for him. His smile revealed two missing teeth.

"How much do you charge for your services?"

"What type of services?" asked the boy, looking suspicious.

"As a runner. A helper. An assistant."

"Ah, you mean partner, like in American movies."

"Okay, wise guy. How much do you charge per hour?"

"Ten dollars."

"That's nothing less than extortion. I'll give you two."

"Six."

"Four."

"Five."

"Agreed," said Jackson.

The boy raised the palm of his right hand high in the air. Jackson slapped it. The deal was done.

"So what's your name?" Jackson asked.

"Sergei," replied the boy. "And yours?"

"Jackson. How old are you, Sergei?"

"Fourteen."

"Cut it out. You're not a day over nine."

"Eleven."

"Okay," said Jackson. "I'll settle for eleven."

"And how old are you?" demanded the boy.

"Fifty-four."

"I'll settle for fifty-four," said Sergei.

Jackson laughed for the first time in days. "How come your English is so good?"

"My mother live with American for long time. He return to States last year but not take us."

This time Jackson believed he was telling the truth.

"So what's the job, partner?" asked Sergei.

"We're keeping an eye on someone staying at that hotel."

"Is friend or enemy?"

"He's a friend, Sergei," said Jackson, just as Connor appeared in the doorway. "Don't move." He placed a hand firmly on the boy's shoulder.

"Is that him?" asked Sergei.

"Yes, that's him."

"He has kind face. Maybe better I work for him."

VICTOR Zerimski was paying a campaign visit to Moscow's Pushkin Museum and was being guided through its galleries by the museum's director. The Pushkin was as crowded as Cooke Stadium for a Redskins game, and wherever Zerimski appeared, the crowds parted as if he were Moses approaching the Red Sea. Connor, meanwhile, had to be careful not to become distracted by the many masterpieces and to concentrate on observing the communist leader.

When Connor had first been sent to Russia back in the 1980s, the nearest any senior politician got to the people was to stare down on Red Square during May Day parades. Now that the masses could vote, it had suddenly become necessary for those who hoped to be elected to move among them, even to listen to their views.

Once Zerimski had walked through half a dozen galleries, he switched his attention from the art on the walls to the journalists following closely behind him. On the first-floor landing he began to hold an impromptu press conference. "Go on, ask me anything you like," he said, glowering at the pack.

"What is your reaction to the latest opinion polls, Mr. Zerimski?" asked the Moscow correspondent of *The Times*.

"Heading in the right direction."

"You now appear to be in second place and therefore Mr. Chernopov's only real rival," shouted another journalist.

"By election day *he* will be *my* only rival," said Zerimski. His entourage laughed dutifully.

"Do you think Russia should return to being a communist state, Mr. Zerimski?" came the inevitable question, delivered with an American accent.

The wily politician was far too alert to fall into that trap. "If by that you mean a return to higher employment, lower inflation, and a better standard of living, the answer must be yes. The Russian people will vote resoundingly for a return to those days when we were the most respected nation on earth."

"And the most feared?" suggested another journalist.

"I'd rather that than continue the present situation, where we are simply ignored by the rest of the world," said Zerimski. Now the journalists were writing down his every word.

"Why is your friend so interested in Victor Zerimski?" whispered Sergei at the other end of the landing.

"You ask too many questions," said Jackson.

"Zerimski bad man."

"Why?" asked Jackson, his eyes fixed on Connor.

"If elected, he put people like me in jail, and we all go back to 'the good old days,' while he's in Kremlin eating caviar and drinking vodka."

Zerimski suddenly began striding toward the museum's exit, with the director and his entourage trying to keep up with him.

"Your man's on the move again," said Sergei. Jackson looked up to see Connor disappearing out of a side entrance of the museum with Ashley Mitchell in pursuit.

CONNOR Fitzgerald sat alone in a Greek restaurant on the Prechinstenka and considered what he had seen that morning.

Although Zerimski was always surrounded by a bunch of thugs, their eyes staring in every direction, he was still not as well protected as most Western leaders. Several of his strong-arm men might be brave and resourceful, but only three of them appeared to have any experience protecting a world statesman. And they couldn't be on duty all the time.

Connor tried to digest a rather bad moussaka as he went over the rest of Zerimski's itinerary, right through to election day. The candidate would be seen in public on twenty-seven different occasions during the next eight days. By the time a waiter had placed a black coffee in front of him, Connor had short-listed the only two locations worth considering if Zerimski's name needed to be removed from the ballot.

The following morning the candidate would travel by train to Yaroslavl', where he would open a factory before returning to Moscow to attend a performance by the Bolshoi Ballet. From there he would take the midnight train to St. Petersburg. Connor had already decided to shadow Zerimski in Yaroslavl'. He had also reserved tickets for the ballet and the train to St. Petersburg.

Connor knew that if he was required to carry out his assignment, he would have to rely on a high-powered rifle in an open space. Nick Gutenburg had assured him that a customized Remington 700 would be safely in the U.S. embassy long before he arrived in Moscow—another misuse of the diplomatic pouch. If Lawrence gave the order, they would leave it to Connor to decide the time and place.

As Connor sipped his coffee, he tried not to laugh when he thought about Ashley Mitchell at the Pushkin, slipping behind the nearest pillar whenever Connor had glanced in his direction. He had decided that he would allow Mitchell to follow him during the day—he might prove useful at some point—but he wouldn't let him find out where he slept at night. He glanced out the window to see the cultural attaché seated on a bench, reading a copy of *Pravda*. He smiled. A professional should always be able to watch his prey without being seen.

MAGGIE DROVE OUT OF THE Georgetown University parking lot at one minute past one. She always took just an hour for lunch, and if she failed to find a parking place near the restaurant, it would cut down on their time together. And today she needed every minute of that hour.

At least the gods were on her side. A woman was pulling out of a parking spot a few yards from the restaurant where they had arranged to meet. Maggie put four quarters in the meter to cover an hour.

When she entered the Café Milano, Maggie gave the maître d' her name. "Yes, of course, Mrs. Fitzgerald," he said, and guided her to a table by the window to join someone who had never been known to be late for anything.

Maggie kissed the woman who had been Connor's secretary for the past nineteen years on the cheek and took the place opposite her.

"How's Tara?" asked Joan Bennett.

"Hanging in there, to use her own words. I only hope she'll finish her thesis. Connor will be very disappointed if she doesn't."

"He speaks warmly of Stuart," Joan said as a waiter appeared by her side.

"Yes," said Maggie, a little sadly. "It looks as if I'm going to have to get used to the idea of my only child living thirteen thousand miles away." She looked up at the waiter. "Cannelloni and a salad for me."

"And I'll have the angel-hair pasta," said Joan.

"Yes, Connor and Stuart got along well," said Maggie once the waiter had left. "Stuart will be joining us for Christmas, so you'll have a chance to meet him then."

"I look forward to that," said Joan.

"I've tried to call you several times in the past few days," Maggie said. "I hoped you might be able to come for dinner one evening, but I keep missing you."

"Now that Connor's left the company, they've closed the office on M Street and moved me back to headquarters," said Joan.

"It's no secret that he hopes you'll eventually join him at Washington Provident," said Maggie.

"I'd love to. But there's no point in making any move until we know what's happening."

"What do you mean 'happening'?" asked Maggie. "Connor starts his new job at the beginning of January."

A long silence followed before Maggie said quietly, "So he didn't get the job with Washington Provident after all."

The waiter arrived with their meals. "A little Parmesan cheese?" he asked as he placed them on the table.

"Thank you," said Joan, staring intently at her pasta.

"So that's why Ben Thompson cold-shouldered me at the opera last Thursday. He didn't even offer to buy me a drink."

"I'm sorry," said Joan. "I just assumed you knew."

"Don't worry. Connor would have let me know the moment he'd got another interview, and then told me it was a far better job than the one he'd been offered at Washington Provident."

"How well you know him," said Joan.

"Sometimes I wonder if I know him at all," said Maggie. "Right now I have no idea where he is or what he's up to."

"I don't know much more than you do," said Joan. "For the first time in nineteen years he didn't brief me before he left."

"It's different this time, isn't it, Joan?" said Maggie.

"What makes you say that?"

"He told me he was going abroad but left without his passport. My guess is that he's still in the U.S. But why—"

"Not taking his passport doesn't prove he isn't abroad," said Joan.

"Maybe not," said Maggie. "But this is the first time he's hidden it where he knew I would find it."

A few minutes later the waiter reappeared and whisked away their plates.

"Would either of you care for dessert?" he asked.

"Not for me," said Joan. "Just coffee."

"Me too," said Maggie. "Black." She checked her watch. She only had sixteen minutes left. She bit her lip. "Joan, I've never asked you to break a confidence before, but there's something I have to know."

Joan looked out the window and glanced at the good-looking

young man who had been leaning against the wall across the street for the past forty minutes. She thought she'd seen him before.

When Maggie left the restaurant at seven minutes to two, she didn't notice the same young man take out a mobile phone and dial a number.

"Yes?" said Nick Gutenburg.

"Mrs. Fitzgerald has just finished lunch with Joan Bennett at Café Milano on Prospect. They were together for forty-seven minutes. I've recorded every word of their conversation."

"Good. Bring the tape to my office immediately."

As Maggie ran up the steps to the admissions office, the clock in the university courtyard was showing one minute to two.

IT WAS one minute to ten in Moscow. Connor was enjoying the finale of *Giselle,* performed by the Bolshoi Ballet. But unlike most of the audience, he didn't keep his opera glasses trained on the prima ballerina's performance. From time to time he would glance to the right and check that Zerimski was still in his box.

It had been another long day of campaigning for Zerimski, and Connor was not surprised to see him stifling the occasional yawn. The candidate's train had left for Yaroslavl' early that morning, and he had not returned to Moscow until shortly before the ballet began.

When the performance finally ended and Zerimski left the theater, a line of cars was waiting to whisk him and his entourage off to another train station. Connor noted that the number of motorcycle outriders had been increased from two to four.

Other people were obviously beginning to think Zerimski might be the next President of Russia.

CONNOR arrived at the station a few minutes after Zerimski. He showed a security guard his press pass before purchasing a ticket for the eleven fifty-nine to St. Petersburg.

Once he was inside his sleeping compartment, he locked the door, switched on the light over his bunk, and began to study the itinerary for Zerimski's visit to St. Petersburg.

In a carriage at the other end of the train the candidate was also going over the itinerary with his chief of staff.

"Another first-thing-in-the-morning-to-last-thing-at-night sort of day," he was grumbling. And that was before Titov had added a visit to the Hermitage.

"Why should I bother to go to the Hermitage?"

"Because you went to the Pushkin, and not to go to Russia's most famous museum would be an insult to the citizens of St. Petersburg."

Zerimski knew that by far the most important meeting of the day would be with General Borodin and the military high command. If he could persuade the general to withdraw from the presidential race and back him, then the military—almost two and a half million of them—would surely swing behind him, and the prize would be his. And just to make sure, Zerimski intended to offer Borodin something he would find irresistible.

Connor also realized that tomorrow's meeting with the general might decide Zerimski's fate. He switched off the light above his bunk a few minutes after two a.m. and fell asleep.

Ashley Mitchell had turned off his light the moment the train had pulled out of the station, but he didn't sleep.

Sergei had been unable to hide his excitement at the thought of traveling on the Protsky express. He had followed Jackson to their compartment like a contented puppy. When Jackson opened the door, Sergei announced, "It's bigger than my apartment." He leaped onto one of the bunks, kicked off his shoes, and pulled the blankets over him without bothering to take off any clothes.

As Jackson prepared for bed, Sergei rubbed the steamed-up window with an elbow, making a circle he could peer through. He didn't say another word until the train began to move slowly out of the station.

Jackson climbed into his bunk and switched his light off.

"How long will it take us to get to St. Petersburg, Jackson?"

"Eight and a half hours. We've got another long day ahead of us, so try to get some sleep."

Sergei switched off the light, but Jackson remained awake. He was now certain that he knew why his friend had been dispatched to Russia. Helen Dexter obviously wanted Connor out of the way, but Jackson didn't know how far she would go to save her own skin.

He had attempted to call Andy Lloyd earlier that afternoon on his cell phone but hadn't been able to get through. He didn't want to risk calling the White House chief of staff from the hotel, so he decided to try again after Zerimski had delivered his speech in Freedom Square the following day. Once Lloyd knew what was going on, Jackson was sure he would be given the authority to abort the whole operation before it was too late. He closed his eyes.

"Are you married, Jackson?" asked Sergei.

"No. Divorced," he replied.

"What about children? You have any?"

"None," said Jackson.

"Why don't you adopt me? I go back to America with you."

"Go to sleep, Sergei."

"Tell me, why is this man so important to you, Jackson?"

Jackson waited some time before answering. "Twenty-nine years ago he saved my life in Vietnam, so I guess you could say I owe him for those years. Does that make any sense?"

Sergei would have replied, but he'd fallen fast asleep.

VLADIMIR Bolchenkov, St. Petersburg's chief of police, had set up a whole department to deal with the threat of terrorism during the election campaign. If any of the candidates were going to be assassinated, it wouldn't be on his territory. That week alone, the department had received twenty-seven threats on Zerimski's life. The chief had dismissed them as the usual assortment of weirdos and lunatics—until a young lieutenant had rushed into his office earlier that morning, white-faced and talking far too quickly.

The chief sat and listened to the recording of a telephone call that had come in only moments before.

"There will be an attempt on Zerimski's life this afternoon," said a male voice with an accent that Bolchenkov couldn't quite place.

"While Zerimski is addressing the rally in Freedom Square, a lone gunman hired by the Mafya will make the attempt. I will call back with more details in a few minutes' time, but I will speak only to Bolchenkov." The line went dead. The brevity of the call meant there was no possibility of tracing it.

Eleven minutes later the second call came through. Bolchenkov stubbed out a cigarette and picked up the phone.

"The man you are looking for will be posing as a foreign journalist, representing a South African newspaper that doesn't exist. He arrived in St. Petersburg on the express from Moscow this morning. He is six feet one, has blue eyes and thick sandy hair. But he'll probably be disguised." The line went dead.

The whole department listened to the tapes of the phone calls again and again over the next half hour. Suddenly the chief said, "Play the second tape."

The young lieutenant pressed a button, wondering what his boss had picked up. They all listened intently.

"Stop," said the chief after only a few seconds. "I thought so. Go back and start counting."

Count what? the lieutenant wanted to ask as he pressed the PLAY-BACK button. This time he heard the faint chime of a clock strike twice in the background.

He rewound the tape and listened again. "Two chimes," he said. "If it was two in the afternoon, our informant was calling from the Far East."

The chief smiled. "I don't think so," he said. "More likely the call was made at two in the morning, from the East Coast of America."

MAGGIE picked up the phone by her bed and called Tara.

"It's Mom," she said when her daughter picked up. "And I have a problem, honey. I haven't a clue where your father is."

"There's nothing new about that, Mom."

"Yes, I know. But I have an uneasy feeling about this particular trip," said Maggie. "I discovered an envelope addressed to me hidden in one of his drawers, and on the outside he's written, 'Not to be opened before December seventeenth.' "

"If you're that anxious about it, Mom, I'm sure Dad would want you to open it."

"Not until December seventeenth," Maggie said. "If he arrived home before then and discovered I'd opened it, he'd . . ."

"When did you find it?"

"This morning. It was buried in his sports clothes, in a drawer I hardly ever open."

"I'd have opened it right away," said Tara.

"I know you would," said Maggie, "but I still think I'd better leave it for a few more days before I do anything."

"Mom, why don't you give Joan a call and ask her advice?"

"I already have."

"And what did she say?"

"Open it."

BOLCHENKOV sat on the desk at the front of the operations room and looked down at the twenty handpicked men. "How many people are we expecting in the square this afternoon?" he asked.

"It's only a guess, Chief," said the most senior uniformed officer present, "but it could be as many as a hundred thousand."

"How many officers can you spare me?"

"Every available man will be in the square, Chief, and I've canceled all leave. I've already issued the man's description in the hope that we can pick him up before he even reaches Freedom Square. But not many of my men have any experience with something this big."

"If there are really going to be a hundred thousand people in the square," said Bolchenkov, "it will be a first for me as well. Has anyone picked up any more information?"

"Yes, Chief," replied a younger man leaning against the back wall. "There are three South African journalists officially covering the election. From the description given to us by our informant, I'm confident it's the one who calls himself Piet de Villiers."

"Anything on the computer about him?"

"No," said the young officer. "But the police in Johannesburg were extremely cooperative. They mentioned a Colombian connection."

"What Colombian connection?" queried Bolchenkov.

"A few weeks ago the CIA circulated a confidential memo giving details about the murder of a presidential candidate in Bogotá. It seems they traced the assassin to South Africa, then lost him. I called my contact at the CIA, but all he could tell me was that the man was on the move again and was last seen boarding a plane for Geneva."

"That's all I need," said the chief. "Any more questions?"

No one stirred.

"If any of you picks up anything, I want to know immediately. Heaven help the man who tells me afterward, 'I didn't mention it, Chief, because I didn't think it was important at the time.' "

CONNOR kept the television on while he shaved. Hillary Bowker of CNN was bringing viewers up to date with what was happening in the States. The arms reduction bill had passed the House, squeaking home by a mere three votes. The pundits were warning that the bill would face a far tougher passage in the Senate.

Connor stopped shaving and stared at the screen.

"And now, for more on the upcoming elections in Russia, we go to Clifford Symonds, our correspondent in St. Petersburg.

"The opinion polls show that the two leading candidates, Prime Minister Grigory Chernopov and Communist Party leader Victor Zerimski, are now running neck and neck. The communist candidate will be addressing a rally in Freedom Square this afternoon that the police are predicting could be attended by as many as a hundred thousand people. This morning Mr. Zerimski will have a meeting with General Borodin, who is expected shortly to announce his withdrawal from the race, following his poor showing in the latest opinion polls. It remains uncertain which of the two front-runners he will support, and on that decision could hang the election."

Connor shut off the television. He had decided not to go to the Hermitage this morning. He would concentrate on Zerimski's main public appearance that day. He had already found a convenient restaurant on the second floor of a building overlooking Freedom Square. More important, it had a rear door, so he wouldn't have to enter the square before it was necessary.

Once he had left his hotel, he called the restaurant from a pay phone and reserved a corner table by the window for twelve o'clock. He then strolled into the nearest hotel and slipped the head porter a twenty-dollar bill, explaining that he needed a room for about an hour so that he could take a shower and change his clothes.

When he came back down in the elevator a few minutes before twelve, the head porter didn't recognize him. Connor left a duffel bag with him and said he would pick it up around four. When the porter placed the bag under the counter, he noticed the briefcase for the first time. As each bore a label with the same name, he put them together.

Connor walked slowly up the side street next to Freedom Square. He passed two policemen who were questioning a tall, sandy-haired foreigner. They didn't give him a second glance as he slipped inside and took the elevator to the second-floor restaurant. He gave the headwaiter his name and was directed to a corner table with a bird's-eye view of the square below.

He was thinking about Tom Lawrence and wondering how long it would take the President to make up his mind about the assassination, when a waiter appeared by his side and handed him the menu.

"Could I please take your order, sir? The police have instructed us to close the restaurant before two o'clock."

"Then I'd better have the minute steak," said Connor.

"WHERE do you think he is right now?" asked Sergei.

"He'll be out there somewhere, but he'll be near impossible to find in this crowd," said Jackson. "I'll give you a ten-dollar bonus if you can spot him. Remember, he's likely to be well disguised."

Sergei suddenly took a far greater interest in the crowd milling around in the square. "See that man on the top step in the north corner?" he said. "Talking to a policeman."

"Yes," replied Jackson.

"That's Vladimir Bolchenkov, the chief of police. A fair man, even though he's the second most powerful person in St. Petersburg."

"Who's the first?" asked Jackson.

"Bolchenkov's brother, Joseph. He's the city's Mafya boss."

Jackson laughed. "Where do you get all your information?"

"My mother. She slept with both of them."

CONNOR ordered a cup of coffee. Although there were still thirty minutes to go before the candidate was due to arrive, Freedom Square was already packed. Connor concentrated on the far side of the square. The little stand erected for the press was now the only area that remained unoccupied. He wondered why so many plain-clothes detectives were milling around, far more than was necessary to keep a casual passerby from straying into a restricted area. Something didn't add up. He checked his watch. Zerimski should have finished his meeting with General Borodin by now. Connor wondered if he would be able to tell from Zerimski's manner if a deal had been struck.

He called for the check, and while he waited, he studied the scene below him for the last time. No professional would ever have considered Freedom Square a suitable target area. Despite this, Connor felt that the sheer size of the crowd would give him the best opportunity yet to study Zerimski at close quarters, which was why he had decided not to sit among the press on this occasion.

He paid his check in cash, walked over to the girl seated in the little booth, and passed her a ticket. She handed him his hat and coat, and he gave her a five-ruble note. Old people always leave small tips, he'd read somewhere.

He joined a large group of workers streaming out of offices on the first floor of the building. They had obviously been given time off to attend the rally. Connor found himself being borne along by the crowd as it flowed out onto the sidewalk.

Freedom Square was already packed as Connor tried to squeeze between the bodies and make his way toward the podium. He looked toward the roped-off press enclosure, which seemed to have a considerable amount of activity going on around it. He smiled when he spotted Ashley Mitchell in his usual place, about ten feet from where he himself would normally have been seated. Not today, my friend.

"WHERE is he?" Chief of Police Bolchenkov was asking a sergeant with a walkie-talkie.

"He left the meeting with General Borodin eighteen minutes ago, so he should be with us in about seven minutes."

"Then in seven minutes our problems begin," said the chief. "Our man's out there in that crowd. I feel it in my bones. Don't forget, the last time he tried something like this, it was a standing target in the open. That way it's almost impossible to hit the wrong person— and with a crowd this large you have a better chance of escaping."

Connor was still edging his way slowly toward the platform. He checked the roofs. A dozen or so marksmen were scanning the crowd with binoculars. There were also at least a couple of hundred uniformed police standing around the perimeter of the square.

Once again Connor glanced toward the press enclosure. The police were checking everyone's credentials—nothing unusual about that except that some journalists were being asked to remove their headgear. Everyone being challenged had two things in common: They were male, and they were tall. Then, out of the corner of his eye, Connor caught sight of Mitchell a few paces away from him in the crowd. He frowned. How had the young agent recognized him?

Suddenly a loud roar came from behind him, as if a rock star had arrived onstage. Connor turned and watched Zerimski's motorcade coming to a halt in the northwest corner of the square.

When the candidate finally mounted the steps to the podium a few minutes later, the crowd began cheering even louder, reaching a climax as he walked to the front of the stage. Connor ignored the bedlam all around him, keeping his eye on the police. They were searching for something, or someone, in particular. A thought flashed across his mind, but he dismissed it at once. No, it wasn't possible. Paranoia setting in. He'd once been told by a veteran agent that it was always at its worst on your last assignment.

But if you were in any doubt, the rule was always the same: Get yourself out of the danger area. He looked around and decided he would start moving toward the north end of the square the moment there was a burst of prolonged applause. That way it was less likely that he'd be noticed slipping through the crowd.

"I've just seen your man," said Sergei.

"Where?" demanded Jackson.

"He faces Zerimski, about twenty steps from stage. He has different-colored hair and walks like an old man. You owe me ten dollars."

"How did you pick him out from this distance?" asked Jackson.

"He is the only one trying to leave the square."

Jackson handed over a ten-dollar bill as Zerimski stepped in front of the microphone.

"Comrades," the party leader began resonantly, "it is a great honor for me to stand before you as your candidate. As each day passes, I become more and more aware . . ."

As Connor scanned the crowd, he once again caught sight of Mitchell. He was a few yards closer than when he'd first spotted him.

"The vast majority of our citizens want to see a fairer distribution of the wealth that has been created by their skills and hard work." As the crowd began to cheer, Connor quickly moved to his right. When the applause died down, he froze, not moving a muscle.

"Why is that man following your friend?" asked Sergei.

"Because he's an amateur," said Jackson.

"So far he do everything but kiss him," said Sergei.

"Look at the streets of St. Petersburg, comrades," continued Zerimski. "Yes, you will see Mercedes, BMWs, and Jaguars, but who is driving them? Only the privileged few."

When the crowd burst into applause again, Connor took a few more steps toward the north end of the square.

"I think I've spotted him," said a plainclothes policeman.

"Where, where?" demanded Bolchenkov.

"Twelve o'clock, fifty yards back, not moving a muscle. He doesn't look like his photograph, but whenever there's a burst of applause, he moves too quickly for a man of that age."

"Got him," Bolchenkov said. After a few seconds he added, "Yes, it might just be him. Brief those two at one o'clock to move in and arrest him. Let's get it over with as quickly as possible."

Ashley Mitchell was now only a step away from Connor, who was studiously ignoring him. In a few seconds there would be an extended ovation when Zerimski told the crowd what he intended to do when he became President. No bank accounts supplied by the bribes of dishonest businessmen—that always got the loudest cheer of all. Then he'd make a clean getaway, and he'd make sure that Mitchell was transferred to a desk job in some mosquito-infested backwater.

"Let us never forget," continued Zerimski, "that Russia can once again be the greatest nation on earth."

The crowd erupted into cheers. Connor turned suddenly and began moving to his right. He had taken almost three strides when the first policeman grabbed his left arm. A second later another came at him from the right. He was thrown to the ground but made no attempt to resist. Rule one: When you've nothing to hide, don't resist arrest. His hands were wrenched behind his back and a pair of handcuffs snapped around his wrists. The crowd began to form a little circle around the three men on the ground. Mitchell hung back slightly and waited for the inevitable "Who is he?"

"Mafya hit man," he whispered into the ears of those nearest him. He moved back toward the press enclosure, muttering the words "Mafya hit man" periodically.

"Let me leave you good citizens in no doubt that if I am elected President, you can be sure of one thing."

"You're under arrest," said a man whom Connor couldn't see, because his nose was being pressed firmly against the ground.

"Take him away," said the same authoritative voice, and Connor was bundled off toward the north end of the square.

Jackson never took his eyes off Connor as the crowd divided, making a path to allow the police through.

Zerimski had spotted the disturbance in the crowd, but like an old pro, he ignored it. "Don't do it for me," he continued unfalteringly. "Don't even do it for the Communist Party. Do it for the next generation of Russians."

The police car, surrounded by four motorcycles, began to make its way out of the square.

Jackson looked toward the press enclosure. He could see that the journalists were far more interested in the disappearing police car than in Zerimski's words.

"Mafya hit man," a Turkish journalist informed a colleague—a "fact" she had picked up from someone in the crowd.

Mitchell was looking up at a row of television cameramen who were following the progress of the police car as it disappeared out of sight. His eyes settled on the one person he needed to speak to. He waited patiently for Clifford Symonds of CNN to look in his direction, and when he eventually did, Mitchell waved his arms to indicate that he needed to speak to him urgently. The CNN reporter quickly joined the American cultural attaché among the cheering throng.

Symonds listened carefully to what Mitchell had to tell him. He was due on the air in twelve minutes. The smile on his face became broader by the second as he turned and dashed back toward the press enclosure.

Mitchell slipped away in the opposite direction. There was still one more receptive ear in which he needed to plant the story, and it would have to be done before Zerimski left the stage.

A protective line of bodyguards was barring any overenthusiastic supporters from getting near the candidate. Mitchell told one of the guards in perfect Russian whom he needed to speak to. The thug shouted at the press secretary, who made an immediate sign to let the American through. Mitchell entered the cordoned-off area and joined the secretary. He briefed him quickly, telling him that de Villiers had been disguised as an old man and which hotel he'd been seen leaving just before he'd entered the restaurant.

THE President and his chief of staff sat alone in the Oval Office, watching the early morning news. Neither of them spoke as Clifford Symonds presented his report.

"An international terrorist was arrested in Freedom Square this afternoon during a speech given by communist leader Victor Zerimski. The man is being held in the notorious Crucifix Prison in St. Petersburg. The local police are not ruling out the possibility that this may be the same man who was recently linked to the assassination of Ricardo Guzman, a presidential candidate in Colombia. The man who police have arrested appears to have been following Zerimski for several days while he was campaigning around the country. He is thought to have been offered a million dollars by the Russian Mafya to remove Zerimski from the presidential race."

Tom Lawrence pressed a button on his remote control, and the screen went blank. "And you're telling me the man they've arrested has no connection with the Russian Mafya but is a CIA agent?"

"Yes," said Andy Lloyd. "I'm waiting for Jackson to call in and confirm that it's the same man who killed Guzman."

"What do I say to the press if they question me about this?"

"You'll have to bluff, because we don't need anyone to know that the man they're holding is one of ours."

"But it would finish off Dexter once and for all."

"Not if you claimed you knew nothing about it, because then half the population would dismiss you as a CIA dupe. But if you admit you did know, the other half would want you impeached. So for now, I suggest you confine yourself to saying that you are awaiting the result of the Russian elections with interest."

"You bet I am," said Lawrence. "The last thing I need is for that evil little fascist Zerimski to become President. We'd be back to Star Wars overnight."

"I'd say that's exactly why the Senate is holding out on your arms reduction bill. They won't want to make a final decision until they know the outcome of the election."

Lawrence nodded. "If it's one of ours they've got locked up in that jail, we've got to do something about it, and quickly. Because if Zerimski does become President, then God help the prisoner. I certainly won't be able to."

CONNOR lay on the bunk and looked around the tiny cell, which wasn't much larger than the sleeping compartment he'd traveled in from Moscow. He had spent eighteen months in a far more restricted space in Vietnam. Then his orders had been clear: When questioned by the enemy, give only your name, rank, and serial number. The same rules did not apply to those who lived by the Eleventh Commandment:

> Thou shalt not be caught. But if you are, deny absolutely
> that you have anything to do with the CIA. Don't worry—the
> Company will always take care of you.

Connor realized that in his case he could forget being taken care of. It now all fell so neatly into place.

He hadn't been asked to sign for the cash. And he now remembered the sentence he'd been trying to recall from the recesses of his mind: "If it's your new job you're worrying about, I'd be happy to have a word with the chairman of the company you're joining and explain to him that it's only a short-term assignment."

How did Gutenburg know he'd been interviewed for a new job and that he was dealing with the chairman of the company? The deputy director knew because he'd already spoken to Ben Thompson. That was why Washington Provident had withdrawn its offer.

As for Ashley Mitchell, Connor should have seen through that angelic choirboy façade. But he was still puzzled by the phone call from the President. Why had Lawrence never once referred to him by name? And the sentences had been a little disjointed. He stared up at the ceiling. If the President had never made the phone call in the first place, he realized he had no hope of being released from the Crucifix. Helen Dexter had successfully removed the one person who might expose her.

The cell door suddenly swung open, and a man dressed in a light blue uniform covered in gold braid walked in.

JACKSON remained in the square until the police car was out of sight. He was furious with himself. He finally turned and marched off, leaving the cheering mob behind him, walking so quickly that Sergei had to run to keep up with him. The young Russian was relieved when Jackson stopped and hailed a taxi.

Jackson could only admire how well Mitchell—no doubt guided by Dexter and Gutenburg—had carried out the operation. It was a classic CIA sting but with a difference: This time it was one of their own they had ruthlessly left languishing in a foreign jail.

He tried not to think about what they would be putting Connor through. Instead, he concentrated on the report he was about to make to Andy Lloyd. If only he had been able to contact him the previous night, he might have got the go-ahead to pull Connor out. His cell phone still wasn't working, so he was going to have to risk using the phone in his hotel room. After twenty-nine years he had been given one chance to balance the books. And he had been found wanting.

The taxi stopped outside Jackson's hotel. He paid the fare, ran inside, and bounded up the stairs. Sergei had just caught up with him by the time he opened the door to room 132.

As the young Russian sat on the floor in a corner, he listened to half a conversation Jackson had with someone called Lloyd. When Jackson finally hung up, he was trembling with rage.

Sergei spoke for the first time since they had left the square. "You need to meet Nicolai Romanov. He is another of my mother's customers." That said, he dialed his mother's number, and when the phone was eventually answered, he behaved in a way Jackson had not witnessed before. He was respectful, listened attentively, never once interrupted. Twenty minutes later he put the phone down.

"She'll make the call," he said.

Sergei went on to explain that he had asked that Jackson be granted a meeting with the czar, the leader of the Thieves in Law. The organization, known by Americans as the Russian Mafya, had been founded at the time when Russia was ruled by a real czar, and it had survived to become the most feared and respected criminal body in the world.

"My mother is one of the few women the czar will talk to. She will ask him to grant you an audience," said Sergei.

The phone rang, and he immediately picked it up. As he listened to what his mother had to say, he turned white and began to tremble. He hesitated for some time, but finally agreed to whatever she was suggesting and put the receiver down.

"Has the czar agreed to see me?" asked Jackson.

"Yes," said Sergei quietly. "Two men come to pick you up tomorrow morning: Alexei Romanov, the czar's only son, and Stefan Ivanitsky, Alexei's cousin, who is third in command."

"Then what's the problem?"

"They do not know you, so they make one condition. If the czar thinks you waste his time, the two men will come back and break one of my legs, to remind me not to bother them again."

Jackson wondered if he should cancel the meeting. He didn't want to be responsible for Sergei ending up on crutches. But the boy told him it was too late. He had already accepted their terms.

"CONGRATULATIONS," said Dexter the moment Gutenburg entered her office. "I've just been watching the headlines on ABC and CBS. They've both run with Symonds's version of what took place in Freedom Square. Any feel yet as to how big the press is going to play the story tomorrow?"

"They're already losing interest. By this time tomorrow the story will only be making the front pages in Russia. And if Zerimski's elected, Fitzgerald will never set foot outside the Crucifix again."

"Have you prepared a report for the President?"

Gutenburg took a seat and placed a folder on Helen Dexter's

desk. She opened it and began reading, showing no sign of emotion as she turned the pages. When she reached the end, she allowed a flicker of a smile to cross her face.

"See that it's signed in your name and sent over to the White House immediately," she said. "It's a pity we had to sacrifice Fitzgerald. But if it helps to get Zerimski elected, it will have served a double purpose. Lawrence's arms reduction bill will be rejected by Congress, and the CIA will have far less interference from the White House."

Gutenburg nodded his agreement.

CONNOR swung his legs off the bunk, placed his bare feet on the floor, and faced his visitor. The chief took a long drag on his cigarette. "Filthy habit," he said in flawless English.

Connor showed no emotion.

"My name is Vladimir Bolchenkov. I am the chief of police in this city, and I thought we might have a little chat before we put anything on the record."

"My name is Piet de Villiers. I am South African. I work for the Johannesburg *Mercury*, and I wish to see my ambassador."

"Now there's my first problem," said Bolchenkov. "You see, I don't believe your name is Piet de Villiers, I'm fairly sure you're not South African, and there's no such paper as the Johannesburg *Mercury*. And just so we don't waste too much of each other's time, I have it on the highest authority that you were not hired by the Mafya. Now, I admit that I don't yet know who you are or even which country you come from. But whoever sent you is in serious trouble."

Connor didn't even blink.

"So if you feel unable to cooperate with my investigation, there is nothing I can do except leave you here to rot, while I continue to bask in the glory that is currently being undeservedly heaped on me."

Connor still didn't react.

"I see that I'm not getting through to you," said Bolchenkov, turning toward the cell door. "I'll leave you to think it over. But if I were in your shoes, I wouldn't wait too long."

He banged on the door. "Let me assure you," he added as the door was opened, "there will be no torture here while I'm St. Petersburg's chief of police. I don't believe in torture; it's not my style. But I can't promise you everything will be quite so friendly if Victor Zerimski is elected our next President." The chief slammed the cell door closed, and Connor heard a key turn in the lock.

THREE white BMWs drew up outside the hotel, and Jackson, who was waiting in the lobby, stepped out onto the street. He was ushered toward the back door of the center vehicle and seated between a tall, thin man in a black cashmere coat, who introduced himself as Alexei Romanov, and a more heavily built man who must have been Stefan Ivanitsky, the czar's nephew.

The three cars slipped into the center lane. Once the BMWs had passed the city boundaries, they quickly accelerated to sixty miles per hour. The little motorcade climbed the winding roads up into the hills, meeting few other vehicles.

Suddenly, without warning, the front car swung left and stopped outside a massive wrought-iron gate dominated by a crest with a black falcon's outstretched wings. Two men holding Kalashnikovs stepped forward, and the first driver lowered a smoked-glass window to allow them to peer in. After all three cars had been inspected, one of the guards nodded and the wings of the falcon split open. The motorcade proceeded along a gravel drive that wound through a thick forest. It was another five minutes before Jackson caught his first glimpse of the house—though house it was not. A century earlier it had been the palace of an emperor's firstborn. It was now inhabited by a remote descendant who also believed in his hereditary position.

The cars crunched to a halt outside the front door. A butler in a long black tailcoat stood waiting on the top step. He bowed to Jackson. "Welcome to the Winter Palace, Mr. Jackson," he said. "Mr. Romanov awaits you in the Blue Gallery."

Alexei Romanov and Stefan Ivanitsky accompanied Jackson down a long corridor. The butler stopped when he reached two white doors that stretched almost to the ceiling. He knocked, then opened one of the doors. "Mr. Jackson," he announced, and stood aside to allow Jackson to enter a vast, lavishly furnished room.

From a Louis XIV wing chair of red velvet rose an elderly man in a blue pin-striped suit. His hair was silver, and the pallor of his skin suggested that he had suffered a long illness. His thin body was slightly stooped as he took a step forward to shake hands with his guest.

"It is kind of you to come all this way to see me, Mr. Jackson," he said. "You must forgive me, but my English is a little rusty. I was forced to leave Oxford in 1939, soon after the war broke out." He smiled sweetly.

Jackson wasn't sure how to react.

"Do have a seat, Mr. Jackson," said the old man, gesturing toward the twin of the chair he had been sitting in.

"Thank you," said Jackson. They were the first words he had spoken since leaving the hotel.

"Now, Mr. Jackson," said Romanov, lowering himself slowly into his chair, "if I ask you a question, be sure to answer it accurately. Because should you lie to me—how shall I put it?—you will find that it's not only this meeting that will be terminated."

Jackson knew that the old man was probably the one person on earth who could get Connor out of the Crucifix Prison alive. He gave a curt nod to show that he understood.

"Good," said Romanov. "I can tell at a glance that you work for a law-enforcement agency, Mr. Jackson. And as you are in my country, I assume it has to be the CIA. Am I right?"

"I worked for the CIA for twenty-eight years, until recently when I was . . . replaced." Jackson chose his words carefully.

"It's against the rules of nature to have a woman as your boss," commented Romanov without even the suggestion of a smile. "The organization I control would never indulge in such stupidity."

Romanov leaned across to a table on his left and picked up a small glass of colorless liquid. He took a sip and replaced the glass on the table before asking, "Why did you want to see me, Mr. Jackson?"

"I came on behalf of a friend of mine who, because of my stupidity, is currently locked up in the Crucifix Prison."

"Does your friend work for the CIA?" the old man asked.

Jackson didn't reply.

"Ah, I see. Just as I thought. Well, I think he can be confident Helen Dexter will not be riding to his rescue on this occasion."

Jackson still said nothing.

"Good," said the old man. "So now I know exactly what you expect of me." He paused. "But I am at a loss to understand what you have to offer in return."

"I have no idea what the going rate is," said Jackson.

The old man began to laugh. "You can't believe that I dragged you out here to discuss money, can you? Last year alone my organization had a turnover of one hundred eighty-seven billion dollars. We now have branches in one hundred forty-two countries. No, Mr. Jackson, I do not have enough days left on earth to waste any of them discussing money with a penniless man."

"Then why did you agree to see me in the first place?"

The old man took another sip of the colorless liquid before spelling out exactly what he expected in return for assisting Connor Fitzgerald to escape from the Crucifix.

"You may need a little time to think over my proposition, Mr. Jackson," continued Romanov. "But should your friend agree to my terms and then fail to carry out his side of the bargain, he must be made fully aware of the consequences of his actions." He paused once again and drew a breath. "I have already given orders that my son, Alexei, will accompany you both back to the United States. I have made it Alexei's personal responsibility to see that this particular contract is carried out to the letter. He will not return until the agreement has been honored. I hope I make myself clear, Mr. Jackson."

ZERIMSKI'S office could not have been in greater contrast to the czar's country palace. The communist leader occupied the third floor of a dilapidated building in a northern suburb of Moscow, although anyone who was invited to stay at his dacha on the Volga quickly became aware that Zerimski was no stranger to luxury.

The last vote in the Russian election had been cast at ten o'clock the previous evening. Now all Zerimski could do was sit and wait for the officials to count the ballots. He was confident that since he had come to an agreement with Borodin, and the general had withdrawn from the race, he had a real chance of winning. But he was enough of a realist to know that with the Mafya backing Prime Minister Chernopov, he would need to poll well over half the votes cast to have the slightest chance of being declared the winner. For that reason he had decided to make an ally in the czar's camp.

"That's good news, Stefan," Zerimski was saying from the privacy of his office. "As long as you can take care of the problem of your cousin." He was listening to Ivanitsky's response when there was a knock on the door. He hung up the phone the moment he saw his chief of staff enter the room. He had no desire for Titov to find out whom he had been talking to.

"The press are wondering if you'll speak to them," said Titov.

Zerimski nodded reluctantly and followed Titov down the stairs and out onto the street. He had instructed his staff never to allow a member of the press to enter the building, for fear that they would discover just how inefficient and understaffed his organization was. That was one of the many things that would change once he got his hands on the state coffers. He hadn't even told his chief of staff that if he won, this would be the last election the Russian people would vote in while he was alive.

THE cell door swung open. Bolchenkov entered, carrying a large duffel bag and a battered leather briefcase.

"As you see, I have returned," said St. Petersburg's police chief, sitting down opposite Connor and lighting a cigarette. "I have to tell you that there have been some interesting developments since our last meeting, which I have a feeling you will want to know about."

He placed the duffel bag and the briefcase on the floor. "These two pieces of luggage were reported as unclaimed by the head porter of the National Hotel."

Connor raised an eyebrow.

"Just as I thought," said the chief. "And to be fair, when we showed him your photograph, the porter confirmed that although he remembered a man fitting your description leaving the bag, he couldn't recall the briefcase."

The chief flipped up the knobs of the case and lifted the lid to reveal a Remington 700. Connor stared straight ahead, feigning indifference.

"Although I'm sure you have handled this type of weapon before, I'm confident that you have never seen this particular rifle despite the initials PDV being so conveniently printed on the case. Even a raw recruit could work out that you have been set up."

Bolchenkov dragged deeply on his cigarette.

"The CIA must think we have the dumbest police force on earth. Did they imagine for a moment that we don't know what Mitchell's real job is? Cultural attaché!" he snorted. "He probably thinks the Hermitage is a department store. Before you say anything, I have another piece of news. Victor Zerimski has won the election."

Connor smiled weakly.

"And since I can't imagine he'll be offering you a front-row seat for the inauguration," said the chief, "perhaps the time has come for you to tell us your side of the story, Mr. Fitzgerald."

PRESIDENT Zerimski swaggered into the room. His colleagues immediately rose from their places around the long oak table and applauded until he had taken his seat below a portrait of Stalin resurrected from the basement of the Pushkin, where it had languished since 1956.

"Although I do not officially take office until next Monday," Zerimski began, "there are one or two areas where I intend to make immediate changes." He turned to a short, squat man who was staring blankly in front of him. Joseph Pleskov had been promoted from Zerimski's bodyguard to a full member of the Politburo the day after he had shot three men who had tried to assassinate his boss while he was on a visit to Odessa.

"Joseph, my old friend," Zerimski said, "you are to be my Minister of the Interior." Pleskov beamed at his leader like a child who had been given an unexpected toy.

"Your first responsibility, Joseph, will be to deal with organized crime. I can think of no better way of setting about that task than by arresting Nicolai Romanov, the so-called czar."

Pleskov looked a little apprehensive. It would have been easier if the boss had simply ordered him to kill the man.

Zerimski looked around the table. "Lev," he said, turning to another man, "you are to be my new Justice Minister."

Lev Shulov smiled nervously.

Just then there was a quiet knock on the door, and Dmitri Titov entered. He bent down and whispered in Zerimski's ear.

Zerimski immediately burst out laughing. "The President of the United States is on the line. He wishes to congratulate me."

Zerimski picked up the phone by his side. "Mr. President," he said.

"Is that you, Victor?"

"This is President Zerimski. Who am I addressing?"

"Tom Lawrence," said the President, raising an eyebrow to the Secretary of State and the White House chief of staff, who were listening in on extensions.

"Good morning. What can I do for you?" said Zerimski.

"I was just calling to add my congratulations to all the others you must be receiving after your impressive victory, and to say that I'd like to get to know you a little better, Victor."

"Then you will have to start by understanding that only my mother calls me by my first name."

"I'm sorry," said Lawrence. "How would you like me to address you?"

"The same way you would expect anyone *you* don't know to address you."

"Try a different tack, Mr. President," suggested the Secretary of State, cupping his hand over the phone.

"I was hoping it wouldn't be too long before we could find an opportunity to meet," Lawrence said.

"I'll give that my serious consideration," said Zerimski. "Tell your chief of staff to get in touch with Comrade Titov, who is responsible for organizing my meetings with foreign leaders."

"I certainly will," said Lawrence, feeling relieved.

"Good-bye, Mr. President," said Zerimski.

"Good-bye . . . Mr. President," Lawrence replied.

After Zerimski put the phone down, he turned to his chief of staff and said, "When Andy Lloyd rings, he will propose that I visit Washington. Accept the offer."

Titov nodded.

"I am determined," said Zerimski, "that Lawrence realize as soon as possible what sort of man he is dealing with. I intend to begin by making sure that his arms reduction bill is defeated by the Senate."

He allowed his colleagues to applaud him briefly, before silencing them with a wave of his hand.

"But we must return to our domestic problems, which are far more pressing. You see, I believe it is important that our own citizens are also made aware of the mettle of their new leader."

He turned his gaze to the newly appointed Justice Minister. "Where is that Mafya hit man who tried to assassinate me?"

"He's locked up in the Crucifix," said Shulov.

"We will make him our first public example," said Zerimski.

"But the police haven't come up with any proof that he—"

"Then manufacture it," said Zerimski.

"I understand, Mr. President," said the new Justice Minister. He hesitated. "And the sentence, Mr. President?"

"The death penalty, of course," said Zerimski. "Once the sentence has been passed, you will inform the press that I shall be attending the execution."

"And when will that be?" asked the Justice Minister.

Zerimski flicked over the pages of his diary, searching for a fifteen-minute gap. "Eight o'clock next Friday morning."

ONLY moments after Bolchenkov had left Connor's cell empty-handed the second time, three massive men came charging in. Two of them dragged Connor off the bunk and threw him into the chair recently occupied by Bolchenkov. They wrenched his arms behind his back and handcuffed him.

That was when Connor first saw the cutthroat razor. While two of the thugs held him down, the third took just fourteen strokes of the rusty blade to shave every hair off his head, along with a considerable amount of skin as well. The blood continued to run down Connor's face and soak his shirt long after they had left him slumped in the chair.

He eventually slept, but for how long he could not tell. The next thing he remembered was being pulled up off the floor, hurled back into the chair, and held down for a second time.

The third man used the same degree of delicacy he had shown as a barber to tattoo the number 12995 on Connor's left wrist with a long, thick needle. They obviously didn't believe in names when you booked in for room and board at the Crucifix.

When they returned a third time, they pushed him out of the cell into a long, dark corridor. He tried not to think about what they might have in mind for him. The citation for his Medal of Honor had described how Lieutenant Fitzgerald had been fearless in leading his men, had rescued a brother officer, and had made a remarkable escape from a North Vietnamese prisoner-of-war camp. But Connor knew he had never come across a man who was fearless. In Nan Dinh he had held out for one year, five months, and two days—but then he was only twenty-two, and at twenty-two you believe you're immortal.

When they hurled him out of the corridor and into the morning sun, the first thing Connor saw was a group of prisoners erecting a scaffold. As he stood in the courtyard and stared up at the scaffold, a police car pulled up and one of the thugs shoved him into the back seat. He was surprised to find the chief of police waiting for him.

Bolchenkov leaned forward and addressed the driver. "To the Palace of Justice," he said.

WHEN Joan Bennett checked in for work at Langley that Monday, she headed straight for the library. For the next nine hours she would read through the latest batch of E-mailed newspaper extracts from the Middle East. Her main task was to search for any mention of the United States and, if it was critical, E-mail it to her boss on the third floor. It was tedious, mind-deadening work, but she was determined not to give Gutenburg the satisfaction of seeing her resign.

It was just before her midnight meal break that Joan started studying the Istanbul *News*, the sole English-language paper in Turkey. Suddenly she spotted a headline: MAFYA KILLER TO GO ON TRIAL. The article concerned a South African terrorist on trial for the attempted murder of the new President of Russia. She would have taken no further interest if she hadn't seen the line drawing of the accused man that accompanied the article.

Joan's heart began to thump as she carefully typed a search string into the computer: "Attempt on Zerimski's life." What press reports there were all seemed to agree on one thing—that the man who had been arrested in Freedom Square was Piet de Villiers, a South African hit man hired by the Russian Mafya to assassinate Zerimski. A rifle discovered among his belongings was identified as identical to the one used to assassinate Ricardo Guzman, a presidential candidate in Colombia, two months earlier.

Joan scanned the Turkish newspaper's line drawing of de Villiers into her computer and enlarged it until it filled the entire screen. She was now certain of the true identity of the man about to go on trial in St. Petersburg.

She picked up the phone by her side and dialed a number she knew by heart. It rang for some time before a sleepy voice answered, "Who's this?"

Joan said only, "It's important that I see you. I'll be at your place in a little over an hour," and replaced the phone.

A few moments later someone else was woken by a ringing telephone. He listened carefully before saying, "We'll just have to advance our original schedule by a few days."

CONNOR stood in the prisoner's box and looked around the courtroom. His eyes first settled on the jury. Twelve good men and true? Unlikely. Not one of them even glanced in his direction.

Everyone in the courtroom rose as a man in a long black robe emerged from a side door. He sat down in a large chair in the center of the raised dais, below a full-length portrait of President Zerimski. The clerk of the court rose and read out the charge in Russian. Connor was barely able to follow the proceedings, and he certainly wasn't asked how he wished to plead. The clerk resumed his seat, and a tall, somber-looking man rose from the bench directly below the judge and began to address the jury.

Holding the lapels of his jacket, the prosecutor spent the rest of the morning describing the events that had led up to the defendant's arrest in Freedom Square. He told the jury how the rifle with which de Villiers had intended to assassinate their beloved President had been discovered among his personal belongings in a hotel lobby. "Vanity got the better of the accused," the prosecutor said. "The case that contained the weapon had his initials clearly printed on it."

He completed his monologue with the words "My own conclusion is that having heard the evidence, there can only be one verdict and one sentence." He smiled thinly at the judge and resumed his seat.

Connor looked around the courtroom to see who had been appointed to defend him. Then the judge nodded at a young man who looked as if he wasn't long out of law school. He rose to address the court and simply said, "My client offers no defense." Then he resumed his seat. Connor had never even met his counsel.

The judge nodded again, then turned to the foreman of the jury, a grave-looking man who rose from his place on cue. "Mr. Foreman," said the judge, "how do you find the defendant?"

"Guilty," said the man, delivering his one-word script without consulting any other member of the jury.

The judge looked at Connor for the first time. "By statute, there is only one penalty for your crime." He paused, stared impassively at Connor, and said, "I therefore sentence you to death by hanging. The execution will take place at eight a.m. on Friday."

Connor was surprised only that they were waiting until Friday to hang him.

IT WAS three a.m., and Joan felt drained as she switched on her headlights and drove her brand-new Volkswagen Passat out of the Langley parking lot. She didn't look forward to telling Maggie the results of her detective work. If it really was Connor on trial in St. Petersburg, there wasn't a moment to waste. The Turkish papers were already a couple of days old.

She turned east onto the George Washington Parkway. The road was covered with patchy ice from a storm, and highway crews were working to clear it before the morning rush hour.

Joan was trying to put her thoughts into some logical order when a large green sanding truck cut in front of her. She checked her rearview mirror and eased into the center lane. The truck immediately began to drift across into her path, forcing her to veer sharply into the left-hand lane.

Joan checked her rearview mirror again and was horrified to see a large black Mercedes coming up fast behind her. She slammed her foot down on the accelerator as the highway banked steeply to the left near Spout Run. Her little Passat responded immediately, but the sanding truck also accelerated, and she couldn't pick up enough speed to pass it.

Joan had no choice but to move farther to her left, almost into the median strip. The Mercedes was now close to her rear bumper. She could feel her heart pounding. Were the truck and the car working together? She tried to slow down, but the Mercedes just moved closer and closer. Joan accelerated again, but even with her foot flat on the floor, she just couldn't overtake the truck. She stared up into the cab and tried to attract the driver's attention, but he ignored her waving hand and went on easing the truck farther to his left, forcing her to slow down and fall in behind him. She checked her rearview mirror: The Mercedes was even closer to her bumper.

As she looked forward, the truck's tailgate rose and its load of sand began to pour out onto the road. Instinctively Joan slammed on her brakes, but the little car careered out of control, skidded across the ice-encrusted median strip into the oncoming lane, then hurtled down the grass embankment toward the river. It hit the water like a flat stone and, after floating for a moment, disappeared out of sight. The sanding truck moved back into the center lane and continued its journey in the direction of Washington. A moment later the Mercedes flashed its lights, overtook the truck, and accelerated away.

Two cars that were heading toward Dulles Airport came to a halt at the side of the road. One of the drivers leaped out and slid down the bank toward the river to see if he could help, but by the time he reached the water, there was no sign of the car.

WHEN Connor was bundled into the back of the car, he found the chief of police waiting for him once again. As the driver began the return journey to the Crucifix, Connor couldn't resist asking Bolchenkov a question.

"I'm puzzled that they're waiting until Friday to hang me."

"Bit of luck, really," said the chief. "Our beloved President insisted on witnessing the execution, and he doesn't have a spare fifteen minutes before Friday morning."

Connor gave a wry smile.

"I'm glad you've found your tongue at last, Mr. Fitzgerald," continued Bolchenkov. "Because I think the time has come to let you know that there is an alternative."

ONCE four o'clock had come and gone, Maggie started checking her watch every few minutes. By four thirty she began to wonder if she had been so sleepy when Joan called that she might have misunderstood what she said. Joan was never late.

At five o'clock Maggie decided it was time to give her friend a call at home. No answer, just a continual ringing tone.

Maggie began pacing around the kitchen table, feeling sure that Joan must have some news of Connor. It had to be important, otherwise why would she have woken her at two in the morning? Had he been in touch with her? Did she know where he was? Would she be able to tell her when he was coming home? By six Maggie had decided it was now an emergency. She switched on the television news to check the exact time.

She was wondering if she should break a lifetime's rule and try to call Joan at Langley when a banner appeared under the reporter's image: "GW Parkway crash—sanding truck and Volkswagen—driver of car presumed drowned. Details on *Eyewitness News* at 6:30." The words crawled across the screen and disappeared.

Maggie began trembling. Joan had just bought a new Volkswagen. "Oh, my God. Oh, no!" she said out loud. She switched to Channel 5, where another newscaster was saying, "And now we have more on that accident on the George Washington Parkway. We go live to our on-the-spot correspondent, Liz Fullerton."

"Thank you, Julie. I'm standing on the median of the George Washington Parkway, where the tragic accident took place at approximately three fifteen this morning. Behind me you can see police divers, who have already located the vehicle, a Volkswagen Passat. No one seems to be quite sure exactly what happened, and the identity of the driver is still unknown."

"No, no, no," screamed Maggie. "Please, God, not Joan."

She ran into the hall, grabbed her coat, and rushed out the front door. She leaped into her old Toyota and eased it slowly out onto Avon Place, before accelerating in the direction of the parkway.

If she had checked her rearview mirror, she would have seen a small blue Ford making a three-point turn before chasing after her.

"MR. JACKSON, it is so good of you to come and see me again."
Jackson was amused by Nicolai Romanov's elaborate courtesy,

especially as it carried with it the pretense that he might have had some choice in the matter.

"You'll be glad to hear that with the exception of a single problem that still needs to be resolved, everything required to make good your colleague's escape has been arranged. All we need now is for Mr. Fitzgerald to agree to our terms. Should he find himself unable to do so, I can do nothing to prevent him from being hanged at eight o'clock tomorrow morning." Romanov spoke without feeling. "Allow me to take you through what we have planned so far."

The old man pressed a button in the armrest of his chair, and Alexei Romanov immediately entered the room.

"I believe you know my son," said the czar.

Jackson nodded as the young man pushed aside an exquisite tapestry to reveal a large television set. The first image to come up on the screen was an exterior shot of the Crucifix Prison.

Alexei Romanov pointed to the entrance. "Zerimski is expected at the jail at seven fifty. He will be in the third of seven cars. . . ."

The young Romanov continued to take Jackson through Connor's projected escape plan minute by minute. Jackson noticed that he seemed unconcerned by the one remaining problem, obviously confident that his father would come up with a solution before the following morning. When he had finished, Alexei switched off the television, replaced the tapestry, and gave his father a slight bow. He then left the room without another word.

When the door had closed, the old man asked, "Do you have any observations?"

"One or two," said Jackson. "First, let me say that I'm impressed by the plan and convinced it has every chance of succeeding. But you're still facing one problem."

Romanov nodded. "And do you have a solution?" he asked.

"Yes," replied Jackson, "I have."

BOLCHENKOV spent nearly an hour spelling out Romanov's plan, then left Connor to consider his response. He didn't need to be reminded that he was faced with an unalterable time limit: Zerimski was due to arrive at the Crucifix in forty-five minutes.

Connor lay on the bunk. The terms could not have been more explicit. But even if he did accept those terms, he was not confident that he would be able to carry out his side of the bargain. If he failed, they would kill him, and Bolchenkov had promised that it would not be the quick and easy death of the hangman's noose. He had also spelled out that all contracts made with the Russian Mafya and not honored became the responsibility of the offender's next of kin.

Connor could still see the cynical expression on Bolchenkov's face as he extracted the photographs from an inside pocket and passed them over to him before leaving. "Two fine women," he had said. "It would be a tragedy to have to shorten their lives for something they knew nothing about."

Fifteen minutes later the cell door swung open again, and Bolchenkov returned. This time he didn't sit down. Connor continued to look up at the ceiling as if the chief of police wasn't there.

"I see that our little proposal is still presenting you with a dilemma," said the chief. "Perhaps when I tell you that your former secretary met with an unfortunate car accident on her way to visit your wife, you will change your mind."

Connor sat up and stared at Bolchenkov. "How do you know Joan was on her way to see my wife?"

"The CIA aren't the only people who are tapping your wife's telephone," replied the chief, lighting a cigarette. "We suspect that your secretary had discovered who it was that we arrested in Freedom Square. And I think we can assume that it won't be long before your wife reaches the same conclusion. If that is the case, I fear Mrs. Fitzgerald is destined to suffer the same fate as your late secretary."

"If I agree to Romanov's terms, I wish to insert a clause of my own into the contract."

Bolchenkov listened with interest.

"MR. GUTENBURG?"

"Speaking."

"This is Maggie Fitzgerald. I'm the wife of Connor Fitzgerald, who I believe is currently abroad on an assignment for you."

"I don't recall the name," said Gutenburg.

"You attended his farewell party at our home in Georgetown only a couple of weeks ago."

"I think you must have mistaken me for someone else."

"Then tell me, Mr. Gutenburg, did Joan Bennett ever work for the Agency? Or has she also been erased from your memory?"

"What are you suggesting, Mrs. Fitzgerald?"

"Ah, I've caught your attention at last. Allow me to repair your temporary loss of memory. Joan was my husband's secretary. She was on her way from Langley to see me when she met her death."

"I was sorry to read of Miss Bennett's tragic accident, Mrs. Fitzgerald. But I don't recall ever meeting Miss Bennett, let alone your husband."

"I see I'll have to jog that failing memory of yours a little further, Mr. Gutenburg. As it happens, the party you didn't attend was videotaped by my daughter. She'd hoped to surprise her father by giving him the tape for Christmas. I can assure you that your tête-à-tête with Joan Bennett is there on tape for all to see. This conversation is also being recorded, and I have a feeling that the networks will consider it worth airing."

Gutenburg didn't reply for some time. "Perhaps it might be a good idea for us to meet, Mrs. Fitzgerald," he said eventually.

"I see no purpose in that, Mr. Gutenburg. But if you let me know where my husband is at this moment, and when I can expect to see him again, I will hand over the tape."

"I'll need a little time—"

"Of course you will," said Maggie. "Shall we say forty-eight hours? And Mr. Gutenburg, don't waste your time tearing my home apart searching for the tape, because you won't find it. It's been hidden somewhere that even a mind as devious as yours wouldn't think of."

"But—" began Gutenburg.

"I should also add that if you decide to dispose of me in the same way you did Joan Bennett, I've instructed my lawyers that should I die in suspicious circumstances, they are to immediately release copies of the tape to all the major networks. If, on the other hand, I simply disappear, the tape will be released seven days later. Good-bye, Mr. Gutenburg." Maggie put the phone down and collapsed onto the bed, bathed in sweat.

Gutenburg shot through the connecting door between his office and the director's. "We have a problem," was all he said.

THE condemned man ate no breakfast. He lay on his bunk staring up at the ceiling, not for one moment regretting his decision. Once he had explained his reasons, Bolchenkov had accepted them without comment, even nodding curtly as he left the cell. It was the nearest the chief would ever get to admitting that he admired a man's moral courage.

The prisoner had faced death once before. It didn't hold the same horror for him a second time. Why had he made the decision that had so moved the usually passionless chief of police? He didn't have time to explain to him what had taken place in Vietnam, but that was where the die had been irrevocably cast.

Perhaps he should have faced the firing squad all those years ago in that far-off land. But he had survived. This time there was no one to rescue him at the last moment. And it was too late now to change his mind.

THE chief of police was waiting to greet Zerimski and his entourage at the prison gate. The President had been looking forward to his morning at the Crucifix as others would anticipate an evening at the Kirov.

Bolchenkov led Zerimski into the courtyard where the execution would take place. As they crossed the yard, the small crowd began to applaud. It amused Zerimski that he had awarded Bolchenkov the Order of Lenin on the same day as he had signed an order to arrest his brother, Joseph, the city's Mafya boss.

Bolchenkov came to a halt by a plush eighteenth-century chair that had been requisitioned from the Hermitage the previous day.

The President sank into the comfortable seat directly in front of the gallows and began fidgeting impatiently as he waited for the prisoner to appear. He looked across at the crowd, and his eyes rested on a young boy who was crying. It didn't please him.

At that moment the prisoner emerged from the dark corridor into the stark morning light. The bald head covered in dried blood and the thin gray prison uniform made him look strangely anonymous. He appeared remarkably calm for someone who only had a few more moments to live.

An officer of the guard marched forward, grabbed the condemned man's left wrist, and checked the number: 12995. The officer then turned to face the President and read out the court order.

While the officer went through the formalities, the prisoner looked around the yard: His eyes settled on the boy, who was still weeping. If they had allowed him to make a will, he would have left everything to that child.

The officer, his commission completed, rolled up his scroll and marched away. This was the sign for two thugs to come forward, grab one of the prisoner's arms each, and lead the prisoner to the scaffold.

He walked calmly past the President and on toward the gallows. When he reached the first wooden step, he glanced up at the clock tower. Three minutes to eight. He had waited twenty-eight years to repay his debt. Now, in these final moments, it all came back to him.

It had been a hot, sweaty May morning in Nan Dinh. Someone had to be made an example of, and as the senior officer, he had been singled out. His second-in-command had volunteered to take his place. The Vietcong officer had laughed and decided that both men would face the firing squad the following morning.

That night the same lieutenant had come to his bedside and said they must try to escape. Security at the camp was always lax because to the north lay a jungle occupied by the Vietcong, and to the south twenty-five miles of impenetrable swamp.

The lieutenant said he would rather risk dying in the swamps than face the certainty of death by firing squad. As he stole away into the night, the captain had reluctantly joined him.

By the end of the second day he wished he had faced the firing squad instead of dying in that godforsaken swamp. But on and on he and the young lieutenant went. For eleven days and twelve nights they didn't eat, surviving only by drinking from the endless torrents of rain. On the twelfth morning they reached dry land, and delirious from illness and exhaustion, he collapsed. He later learned that for four more days the lieutenant had carried him through the jungle to safety.

Six months later he had stood on the White House lawn and had listened as the citation that he had written in the army hospital was read aloud. Lieutenant Connor Fitzgerald stepped forward, and the President awarded him the Medal of Honor.

As he began to mount the steps of the gallows, he thought of the one man who would mourn him when he discovered the truth. He had warned them not to tell him, because if he found out, he knew he would break the contract, give himself up, and return to the Crucifix. "You must understand," he had explained to them, "that you are dealing with a totally honorable man. So be sure that the clock has struck eight before he finds out he's been deceived."

The first chime sent a shiver through his body.

On the second chime, the little boy who had been crying ran up to the foot of the gallows and fell on his knees.

On the third, the chief placed a restraining arm on a young corporal who had taken a step forward to drag the child away.

On the fourth, the prisoner smiled down at Sergei as if he were his only son.

On the fifth, the two thugs pushed him forward so that he was standing directly below the dangling rope.

On the sixth, the hangman placed the noose around his neck.

On the seventh, he lowered his eyes and stared directly at the President of the Russian Republic.

On the eighth, the hangman pulled the lever and the trapdoor opened.

As the body of Christopher Andrew Jackson swung above him, Zerimski rose to applaud. Some of the crowd halfheartedly joined in.

A minute later the two thugs carried the lifeless body down from the gallows. Sergei rushed forward to help them lower his friend into the crude wooden coffin that lay beside the scaffold.

The chief accompanied the President back to his limousine, and the motorcade sped out of the prison gates even before the coffin lid had been nailed down. Four prisoners lifted the heavy casket onto their shoulders, and Sergei walked at their side, out of the yard, to a graveyard at the back of the prison.

The pallbearers dropped the casket unceremoniously into a gaping hole that other prisoners had just finished digging. Then, without a prayer or even a moment's pause, they shoveled the recently dug sods of earth on top of it.

The boy didn't move until they had completed their task. A few minutes later the guards herded the prisoners back to their cells. Sergei fell to his knees, wondering how long they would allow him to remain by the grave.

A moment later a hand was placed on the boy's shoulder. He looked up and saw the chief of police standing above him. A fair man, he'd once told Jackson.

"Did you know him well?" the chief asked.

"Yes, sir," said Sergei. "He was my partner."

The chief nodded. "I knew the man he gave his life for," he said. "I only wish I had such a friend."

"MRS. Fitzgerald is not quite as clever as she thinks she is," said Gutenburg.

"Amateurs rarely are," said Helen Dexter. "Does that mean you've got your hands on the video?"

"No, although I've got a pretty good idea where it is," said Gutenburg. He paused. "But not *exactly* where."

"Get to the point," said Dexter.

"Mrs. Fitzgerald doesn't realize that her home and office have been bugged for the past month and that we've had agents watching her since the day her husband flew out of Dulles three weeks ago."

"So what have you found out?"

"Not a lot when the individual bits of information are taken in isolation. But if you piece them together, they start making a picture. For instance, after Mrs. Fitzgerald met with Joan Bennett at the Café Milano, she placed several calls, including one to Chris Jackson's cell phone."

"Why would she do that, when she knew he'd left the Company?"

"They go back a long way. He and Fitzgerald served in Vietnam together. In fact, it was Jackson who recommended Fitzgerald for the Medal of Honor and who recruited him as an NOC."

"Did Jackson tell her about you?" asked Dexter in disbelief.

"No. He didn't have a chance. We blocked his cell phone the moment we discovered he was in Russia." Gutenburg smiled. "We can, however, still identify who's been trying to call him and who he's been trying to call."

"Does that mean you know who he's reporting back to?"

"Jackson has only dialed one number on that line since he landed in Russia—an unlisted number at the White House."

Dexter didn't even blink. "Our friend Mr. Lloyd, no doubt. Is Mrs. Fitzgerald aware that Jackson is reporting directly to the White House?"

"I don't think so," said Gutenburg.

Dexter nodded. "Then we must be certain that she *never* finds out. What's the latest status on the family video?"

"We wouldn't have progressed an inch if it hadn't been for a clue in an intercepted phone call. When Mrs. Fitzgerald knew for certain it was Joan Bennett in that car, she immediately phoned her daughter at Stanford. Perhaps you'd like to hear the conversation for yourself. He touched the PLAY button on the tape recorder.

"Hi, Tara. It's Mom. I'm sorry to call so early, darling, but I have some very sad news. Joan Bennett has been killed in a car crash."

"Joan's dead? Tell me it's not true."

"I'm afraid it is. And I have a terrible feeling that in some way it's connected to the reason Connor hasn't returned home."

"Come on, Mom. Aren't you getting a little paranoid? After all, Dad's only been away for three weeks."

"You may be right, but I've still decided to move that video you made of his farewell party to a safer place. It's the only proof I have that your father ever met a man called Nick Gutenburg, let alone worked for him."

The deputy director touched STOP. "When Mrs. Fitzgerald left the house a few minutes later carrying a videotape, the officer listening in tailed her to the university library. She went straight to the computer section on the first floor. She spent twenty minutes searching for something on one of the computers and left with a printout of about a dozen pages. Then she took the elevator down to the audiovisual research center on the ground floor. She came out after a few minutes without the tape."

"She must have deposited it in the audiovisual center."

"My thought exactly," said Gutenburg.

"How many tapes does the university store in its library?"

"Over twenty-five thousand," said Gutenburg.

"It would take far too long to go through them," said Dexter.

"It would if Mrs. Fitzgerald hadn't made her first mistake."

Dexter raised an eyebrow.

"When she left the library, she was carrying a printout. Our agent followed her to the recycling center, where she dumped the printout in the paper depository."

"Good. So what did you find on it?"

"A complete list of the videos currently on loan and unlikely to be returned until the beginning of next term."

"She must have felt it safe to leave her video in an empty box because no one would come across it for weeks."

"Correct," said Gutenburg.

"How many videos are there that fall into that category?"

"Four hundred and seventy-two," replied Gutenburg. "I've detailed a dozen officers—all recent graduates, so they won't stand out—to check out every one of the titles on that list until they come across a homemade video in what should be an empty box."

"Call me the minute you get your hands on the video. Then there will be nothing to stop us from eliminating the one person who could still—" The red phone on Dexter's desk began to ring, and she grabbed it without completing her sentence.

"The director," she said, pressing a button on her stopwatch. "When did this happen? . . . And Jackson? Where is he?" When she had heard the reply, she immediately put the phone down.

"I do hope you find that videotape within the next forty-eight hours," said the director, looking across the desk at her deputy.

"Why?" asked Gutenburg, looking anxious.

"Because Ashley Mitchell tells me that Connor Fitzgerald was hanged at eight o'clock this morning St. Petersburg time and that Jackson has just boarded a United Airlines flight out of Frankfurt, bound for Washington."

AT SEVEN a.m. the three thugs entered Connor's cell and marched him off to the chief's office. Once they had left the room, Bolchenkov locked the door and without a word went over to a wardrobe in the corner. Inside was a policeman's uniform, which he indicated Connor should change into. Because of his loss of weight over the past week, the clothes hung on him and he was grateful for the suspenders. But with the aid of a wide-brimmed hat and a long blue coat, he managed to look like any of the thousand policemen who would be walking the beat in St. Petersburg that morning. He left his prison clothes at the bottom of the wardrobe, wondering how the chief would dispose of them.

Still without saying a word, Bolchenkov ushered him out of his office and into the courtyard. Connor's legs felt very weak, but he followed Bolchenkov as quickly as he could, past the scaffold to a car on the far side of the yard. Connor was about to open the passenger door when Bolchenkov shook his head and pointed to the driver's seat. Connor took his place behind the wheel.

"Drive up to the gate and then stop," said the chief as he got into the passenger seat.

Connor drove slowly across the yard, stopping in front of two guards posted by the closed gate. One of them saluted the chief and immediately began checking under the vehicle while the other inspected the trunk. When the guards had completed their search, they saluted Bolchenkov once again, taking no interest in the driver. The vast wooden bolts were removed, and the great gates of the Crucifix Prison were pulled open.

"Turn right," said the chief under his breath, and Connor began driving alongside the Neva River toward the city center.

"Cross the next bridge," said Bolchenkov, "then take a left."

Connor continued driving for another couple of hundred meters. Suddenly Bolchenkov said, "Pull over here." Connor brought the car to a halt behind a large white BMW with one of its rear doors open.

"This is where we part company, Mr. Fitzgerald," said Bolchenkov. As he stepped out of the car, the chief added, "You are privileged to have such a remarkable friend."

It was to be some time before Connor understood the full significance of Bolchenkov's words.

"THIS is the first call for Finnair flight 821 to Frankfurt," said a voice over the intercom at the Helsinki airport.

Connor didn't move. In the twenty-four hours since he had left the Crucifix, he hadn't relaxed for one moment. If they had told him the truth, he would never have allowed Chris Jackson to take his place. Now he was trying to piece together everything that had happened after he had left Bolchenkov.

He had got out of the police car and walked as quickly as he could to the waiting BMW. The chief had already begun his return journey to the Crucifix by the time Connor climbed into the back of the car and sat beside a pale, thin young man wearing a long black cashmere coat. Neither he nor the two men seated in the front of the car spoke or even acknowledged his presence.

His keepers had driven him to a safe house across the Finnish border. They had provided him with a complete change of clothes, including a black rabbit-skin hat, a first-class ticket to Dulles International, a thousand U.S. dollars, and an American passport. The passport was in the name of Christopher Andrew Jackson, but there was a photograph of himself.

"What does this mean?" he'd asked the pale young Russian.

"It means you're still alive," answered Alexei Romanov.

"This is the second call for Finnair flight 821 to Frankfurt."

Connor strolled across to the gate agent, handed over his boarding pass, and made his way to the waiting plane. He didn't have to search for the window seat in the fifth row, because Alexei Romanov was already strapped into the aisle seat. It was obviously his job not only to pick up the package but also to deliver it and to make sure the contract was carried out. As Connor stepped over his escort's feet, a stewardess asked, "Can I take your hat, Mr. Jackson?"

"No, thank you." It would take some time for the wounds on his head to heal.

He leaned back in the comfortable seat but didn't relax until the plane had taken off. Then it began to sink in for the first time that he really had escaped. But to what? he wondered. He glanced to his left: From now on someone would be with him night and day until he had carried out his side of the bargain. And he knew that if he tried to escape, they would carry out the threat the chief had so vividly described. He shuddered at the thought of any of those thugs laying a finger on Maggie or Tara.

Connor and Romanov changed planes in Frankfurt, where they boarded a United Airlines flight for Dulles.

In the final hour before they were due to land in Washington, Connor's thoughts returned to Chris Jackson and the sacrifice he'd made. Connor knew he could never repay him, but he was determined not to let it be a worthless gesture.

His mind switched to Dexter and Gutenburg, who must now be assuming he was dead. First they had sent him to Russia to save their own skins. Next they had murdered Joan because she just might have passed some information on to Maggie. How long would it be before they decided Maggie herself had become too great a risk and that she also needed to be disposed of?

MAGGIE checked the arrivals screen at Dulles Airport. The flight from San Francisco was scheduled to land on time.

She picked up a copy of the Washington *Post* from the newsstand, wandered into the nearest coffee shop, and ordered a black coffee. She didn't notice the two men occupying a table in the opposite corner, one of whom also appeared to be reading the Washington *Post*. But however hard she'd looked, she wouldn't have seen the third man, who was taking more interest in her than in the arrivals screen he was looking up at. He had already spotted the other two men in the corner.

A few minutes before the plane was scheduled to land, Maggie slipped off the stool and walked slowly over to the arrivals gate. The three men continued to watch her as she waited for the board to confirm that United's flight 50 from San Francisco had landed. When the message finally appeared, she smiled. One of the three men punched eleven numbers into his cell phone and passed the information back to Langley.

When Tara and Stuart emerged from the Jetway, Maggie hugged them in turn. "It's wonderful to see you both," she said, leading them toward the subway to the main terminal.

One of the men who had been watching her was already waiting in the short-term parking lot, in the passenger seat of a Toyota transporter with a load of eleven new cars. The other two were running across the lot.

Maggie, Tara, and Stuart stepped into the cold morning air and walked over to Maggie's car. "Mom, isn't it time you got yourself something more up to date than this old scrap heap?" Tara asked in mock horror.

"Your father thinks we should hold on to it until he begins his new job, when he'll be given a company car."

The three of them climbed into the old Toyota. Maggie switched on the ignition and pulled out of the parking lot and onto the highway. She glanced in the rearview mirror but didn't notice a non-descript blue Ford about a hundred yards behind her. The man in the passenger seat was reporting in to his superior at Langley.

"Did you enjoy San Francisco, Stuart?" Maggie asked.

"Every moment," he replied.

When Maggie glanced in her rearview mirror again, she saw a Virginia State patrol car coming up behind her, lights flashing.

"Is he following me, do you think? I certainly wasn't speeding," she said, looking down to check her speedometer.

"Mom, it could be anything. Just pull over."

Maggie pulled over and wound down her window as two police-men stepped out of their patrol car and walked toward her. The first officer said politely, "May I see your license, ma'am?"

"Certainly, Officer," said Maggie. She began rummaging around in her bag as a second patrolman indicated to Stuart that he should also wind down his window. Stuart thought this was an odd request, but since he wasn't in his own country, he thought it wiser to comply. He wound down the window just as Maggie located her driver's license. As she turned to hand it over, the second policeman drew his gun and fired three shots into the car.

The two officers walked quickly back to their patrol car. While one eased it into the early morning traffic, the other phoned the man in the passenger seat of the transporter. "A Toyota has broken down and is in need of your immediate assistance."

Soon after the patrol car accelerated away, the transporter carry-ing eleven brand-new Toyotas drew up and stopped in front of the stationary vehicle. The man in the passenger seat, wearing a Toyota cap and blue overalls, jumped down from the cab and ran toward the old Toyota. He opened the driver's door, moved Maggie gently across to the passenger seat, and pulled the lever that controlled the car's hood.

The driver of the transporter then opened the Toyota's hood, swiftly deactivated the tracking device, and slammed the hood closed. His companion was now seated behind the wheel of the Toyota. He turned on the ignition and drove up the transporter's ramp, taking the one space left. He fastened the car's wheels to the ramp and rejoined the driver in the transporter's cab. The entire exercise had taken less than three minutes.

The transporter resumed its journey toward Washington, but after half a mile it took the air freight exit and drove back in the direction of the airport.

The CIA officers in the blue Ford had come off the highway at the next exit, then doubled back and rejoined the morning traffic heading into Washington. "She must have made some minor violation," the driver was saying to his superior at Langley. "It wouldn't be surprising with a car that old."

The officer in the Ford's passenger seat noticed that the Toyota was no longer registering on his screen. "They're probably on their way back to Georgetown," he suggested. "We'll call in when we regain contact."

As the two CIA agents sped toward Washington, the transporter was turning left off the Dulles service road at a sign marked CARGO ONLY. The driver drove down an old runway and into an isolated hangar, where he brought the vehicle to a halt next to an unmarked van. Seven men in white overalls quickly emerged from the back of the van. One of them undid the chains that secured the Toyota to the transporter and allowed it to roll back down the ramp to the ground. The moment it came to a halt, its doors were opened and the bodies were carefully lifted out.

The man in the Toyota cap jumped out of the transporter, took the wheel of the old car, and drove out of the hangar. Meanwhile, the bodies were being gently placed in the rear of the van, where three coffins were waiting for them. One of the men in white overalls said, "Don't put the lids on until you're approaching the plane."

"Okay, Doc," came the reply.

"And once the hold's been closed, remove the bodies and strap them into their seats."

As another man nodded, the transporter backed out and retraced its route down the old runway. When the driver reached the highway, he turned left and headed toward Leesburg, where he would deliver eleven new Toyotas to the local dealer. His fee for six hours' unscheduled work would allow him to buy one of them.

The white van drove out of the hangar and began heading toward the cargo docking area. The driver passed rows of cargo planes, finally stopping at the back of a 747 marked AIR TRANSPORT INTERNATIONAL. The hold was open, and two customs officials stood waiting at the bottom of the ramp. They began checking the paperwork just as the two CIA officers in the blue Ford drove past the Fitzgeralds' home at 1648 Avon Place. After cautiously circling the block, the agents reported back to Langley that there was no sign of the car or the three packages.

The old Toyota came off Route 66 and joined the highway into Washington. Over his earphone the driver listened to the two officers in the Ford being told to go to Mrs. Fitzgerald's office to see if the car was in her usual parking space behind the admissions building.

Once the customs officials had satisfied themselves that the coroner's documents were in order, the men in white overalls carried the coffins up the ramp and laid them side by side in the hold.

The ramp of the 747 was being raised as the old Toyota screeched to a halt in the driveway at 1648 Avon Place.

The driver had already slipped around the side of the house and let himself in through the back door by the time the doctor began checking the pulses of his three patients. The driver ran upstairs to the master bedroom, rummaged through his shirts in the chest of drawers, took out the brown envelope marked NOT TO BE OPENED BEFORE DECEMBER 17, and slipped it into an inside pocket. He pulled down two suitcases from the top of the closet and quickly filled them with clothes. Next he removed a small cellophane packet from his overalls and slipped it into a cosmetics bag, which he threw into one of the cases. He switched on the bathroom light, then the light at the bottom of the stairs, and, finally, using the remote control, the television in the kitchen, turning the volume to high.

He left the suitcases by the back door and returned to the Toyota, raised the hood, and reactivated the tracking device.

The CIA officers had begun slowly circling the university parking lot for a second time when a blip reappeared on their screen. They headed back toward the Fitzgeralds' home.

The man in the Toyota cap returned to the rear of the house, grabbed the suitcases, and let himself out by the back gate. He spotted the taxi parked in front of Tudor Place and jumped into the back just as the two CIA agents returned to Avon Place. A relieved young man called Langley to report that the old Toyota was parked in its usual place and that he could see and hear a television in the kitchen. No, he couldn't explain how the tracking device had been out of action for nearly an hour.

The taxi driver didn't even turn his head. He knew exactly where Connor Fitzgerald wanted to be taken.

"ARE you telling me that all three of them have disappeared off the face of the earth?" said the director.

"It looks that way," replied Gutenburg. "It was such a professional operation that if I didn't know he was dead, I would have said it had all the hallmarks of Connor Fitzgerald."

"Since we know that's impossible, who do you think it was?"

"My bet is Chris Jackson," replied the deputy director.

"Well, if he's back in the country, Mrs. Fitzgerald will know her husband is dead. So we can expect to see her home video on the early evening news any day now."

Gutenburg grinned complacently. "Not a chance," he said, passing a sealed package across the table. "One of my agents finally found the tape in the university library last night."

"That's one problem dealt with," said the director, tearing open the package. "But as long as Jackson and the Fitzgerald women are out there, we still have a problem. If the President finds out what really happened in St. Petersburg, he'll have more than enough excuse to call for someone's resignation. And since it's your signature at the bottom of every relevant document, I would, alas, be left with no choice but to let you go."

Small beads of sweat appeared on Gutenburg's forehead.

STUART THOUGHT HE WAS coming out of a bad dream. He tried to remember what had happened. Tara's mother had been at the wheel when the car was stopped by a traffic cop. And then . . .

He looked around. He was on another plane, but where was it going? Tara's head was resting on his shoulder; on her other side was her mother, also fast asleep. All the other seats were empty.

As Stuart began to go over the facts again, Tara began to stir. When Maggie eventually opened her eyes, Stuart leaned across and whispered, "I haven't a clue why we're here or where we're going, but I have to believe that in some way it's connected with Connor."

Maggie nodded and quietly began to tell them everything she had found out since Joan's death. "But I don't think the people holding us can be the CIA," she said, "because I told Gutenburg that if I was missing for more than seven days, that video would be released to the media."

"Unless they've already found it," said Stuart.

"That's not possible," said Maggie emphatically.

"Then who on earth are they?" said Tara as the plane continued its journey through the night.

ONCE Connor had placed the two suitcases in the hold and checked that all three passengers were alive and unharmed, he left the aircraft and climbed into the back of a waiting white BMW, whose engine was already running.

"We continue to keep our side of the bargain," said Alexei Romanov who was sitting next to him. Connor nodded his agreement as the car began its journey to Washington National Airport.

When the BMW drew up outside the departure entrance of the airport, Connor stepped out, with Romanov a pace behind. Two other men joined them and followed Connor as he strolled calmly into the airport and walked in the direction of a row of telephones. He chose one with occupied booths on either side. Romanov and the two bodyguards hovered a few paces away, looking displeased. Connor smiled at them innocently, then dialed a Cape Town number.

The phone rang for some time before it was answered. "Yes?"
"It's Connor."

There was a protracted silence. "I thought it was only Jesus who could rise from the dead," said Carl Koeter eventually.

"I spent some time in purgatory before I managed it."

"Well, at least you're alive, my friend. What can I do for you?"

Connor was answering Carl's last question when he heard the final call for flight 383 to Dallas. He put the phone down, smiled at Romanov and the bodyguards again, and headed for the gate.

FLIGHT 383 to Dallas landed on time, and when Connor and Romanov stepped out of the airport, another white BMW was waiting for them. Had the Mafya placed a bulk order? Connor wondered. The latest pair of thugs to accompany them looked as if they had been hired from central casting—even their shoulder holsters were bulging under their jackets.

He could only hope that the Cape Town branch was a recent subsidiary, although he found it hard to believe that Carl Koeter, with more than twenty years' experience as the CIA's senior operative in South Africa, wouldn't be able to handle the newest kid on the block.

The trip into downtown Dallas took just over twenty minutes. Connor sat silently in the back of the car, aware that he might be about to come face to face with someone else who had worked for the CIA for almost thirty years. Although they'd never met, he knew this was the biggest risk he had taken since arriving back in the United States. But if the Russians expected him to honor the most demanding clause in their contract, he had to have the use of the only rifle ideal for carrying out such an assignment.

After another silent journey they pulled up outside Harding's Big Game Emporium. Connor slipped quickly into the shop, with Romanov and his two new shadows dogging his every step. He went up to the counter while they pretended to take a keen interest in a rack of automatic pistols on the far side of the store.

Connor glanced around. His search needed to be quick, unobtrusive, but thorough. After a few moments he was convinced there were no security cameras in the shop.

"Good afternoon, sir," said a young assistant. "Can I help you?"

"I'm out here on a shooting trip, and I'd like to buy a rifle."

"Do you have any particular model in mind?"

"Yes, a Remington 700."

"That should be no problem, sir."

"It may need a few modifications," said Connor.

The assistant hesitated. "Excuse me for a moment, sir." He disappeared through a curtain into a back room. A few moments later an older man, dressed in a long brown coat, appeared through the curtain. Connor was annoyed: He had hoped to purchase the rifle without having to meet the legendary Jim Harding.

"Good afternoon," the man said, looking closely at his customer. "What modifications did you have in mind, sir?"

Connor described in detail the gun he had left in Bogotá, watching carefully for any reaction.

Harding's face remained impassive. "I might have something that would interest you, sir," he said, then turned and disappeared behind the curtain. Within seconds he reappeared carrying a familiar leather case, which he placed on the counter.

"This model came into our possession after the owner's recent death," he explained. He opened the lid and swiveled the case around so that Connor could inspect the rifle.

"How much?" Connor asked.

"Twenty-one thousand dollars," Harding said. "Though we do have the standard model should you—"

"No," said Connor. "This one will be just fine."

"And how will you be paying, sir?"

"Cash."

"Then I will require some form of identification," said Harding.

Connor took out a Virginia driver's license he'd bought from a pickpocket in Washington the previous day.

Harding studied the license and nodded. "All we need now, Mr. Radford, is for you to fill in these three forms."

Connor wrote out the name, address, and Social Security number of the assistant manager of a shoe store in Richmond.

As Harding entered the numbers into a computer, Connor was silently praying that Mr. Radford hadn't reported the loss of his driver's license during the past twenty-four hours.

After a few long moments Harding looked up from the screen and said, "That all seems to be in order, Mr. Radford."

Connor turned and nodded to Romanov, who strolled over and extracted a thick bundle of bills from an inside pocket. He spent some time ostentatiously peeling off hundreds, counting out two hundred and ten of them before passing them to Harding. What Connor had hoped would appear no more than a casual purchase, the Russian was fast turning into a show. His sidekicks might as well have stood out on the street and sold tickets for the performance.

Harding wrote out a receipt for the cash and handed it to Connor, who left without another word. One of the hoodlums grabbed the rifle and ran out of the shop onto the sidewalk as if he had just robbed a bank. Connor climbed into the back of the BMW and wondered if it was possible to attract any more attention to themselves. The car screeched away from the curb and cut into the fast-moving traffic. He remained speechless as the driver broke the speed limit all the way back to the airport. Even Romanov began to look a little apprehensive. Connor was quickly discovering that the new Mafia in the States was still amateurish compared with their cousins from Italy.

Fifteen minutes later the BMW drew up outside the entrance to the airport. Connor stepped out and began walking toward the revolving door as Romanov gave instructions to the two men in the car, finally peeling off several more hundred-dollar bills and handing them over. When he joined Connor at the check-in counter, he whispered confidently, "The rifle will be in Washington within forty-eight hours."

"I wouldn't bet on it," said Connor.

WITHIN moments of reading the priority message, Gutenburg was dialing the number in Dallas. When Harding came on the line, the deputy director of the CIA simply said, "Describe him."

"Six feet, possibly six one. Blue eyes. He was wearing a hat, so I couldn't see his hair color."

"Age?"

"Fifty. Could be a year or two either way."

"I'll have an agent with you in under an hour," said Gutenburg. "I'll need a computerized sketch of the suspect."

"That won't be necessary," said Harding.

"Why not?"

"Because the whole transaction was videotaped." Gutenburg couldn't see Harding's smile of satisfaction as he added, "Even you wouldn't have spotted the security camera."

IT'S a long drive from Dallas to Washington. Just after nine o'clock that evening, having covered the first four hundred miles, the two men who had dropped Connor and Romanov at the airport pulled into a hotel on the outskirts of Memphis.

The two senior CIA officers who watched them park their BMW reported back to Gutenburg forty-five minutes later. "They've checked into the Memphis Marriott, rooms 107 and 108. They ordered room service at nine thirty-three and are currently in room 107 watching *Nash Bridges*. The rifle is handcuffed to the wrist of the man booked into room 108."

"Then you're going to need a passkey," said Gutenburg.

Just after ten o'clock a waiter appeared in room 107 and set up a table for dinner. He opened a bottle of red wine, poured two glasses, and laid out the food. He told the guests he would return in about forty minutes to clear the table.

At a few minutes after midnight the waiter went to the parking lot and reported to the CIA officers that both men had gone to bed in their own rooms. He handed over a passkey and in return was given a fifty-dollar bill. What the waiter didn't know was that the man in room 107 had the keys to the handcuffs so as to be sure that no one would try to steal the briefcase from his partner while he was asleep.

When the guest in room 107 woke the following morning, he felt unusually drowsy and was surprised to find how late it was. He pulled on his jeans and hurried through the connecting door to wake his partner. He came to a sudden halt and began to vomit. Lying on the carpet in a pool of blood was a severed hand.

As STUART, Tara, and Maggie stepped off the plane in Cape Town, Stuart was aware of the presence of two men watching their every move. An immigration officer stamped passports they had been given on the plane, and they headed toward the baggage claim area. After only a few minutes luggage began to appear on the carousel. Maggie was surprised to see two of her old suitcases coming down the chute.

Once they had retrieved their bags, Stuart put them all on a cart and they walked toward the customs exit. The two men walked close behind them.

As Stuart was wheeling the cart through customs, an officer stepped into his path, pointed to one of the suitcases, and asked if the owner would place it on the counter. Stuart helped Maggie lift it as the two men following them reluctantly moved on. Once the men were through the sliding doors, they stationed themselves a few feet from the exit. Each time the doors opened, they could be seen peering back through.

"Open the case, please, ma'am," said the customs officer.

Maggie lifted the catches and smiled at the mess that greeted her. Only one person could have packed that case—Connor. The customs officer dug around among her clothes for a few moments and eventually came out with a cosmetics bag. He unzipped it and removed a small cellophane packet, which contained a white powder.

"I'm afraid we'll have to conduct a body search, ma'am," said the officer. "All three of you follow me, and bring the case and the rest of your luggage." He lifted a section of the counter and ushered them through a door that led into a small drab room with a table and two chairs. "One of my colleagues will join you in a moment." He closed the door, and they heard the key turning in the lock.

"What's going on?" said Maggie. "That bag wasn't—"

"I expect we're about to find out," said Stuart.

A door on the far side of the room opened, and a tall, athletic-looking man bounced into the room. He went straight over to Maggie, took her right hand, and kissed it.

"My name is Carl Koeter," he said in a broad South African accent. "This is a great honor for me, Mrs. Fitzgerald. I've wanted for many years to meet the woman who was brave enough to marry Connor Fitzgerald. He called me yesterday afternoon and asked me to assure you that he's very much alive." Carl smiled at Stuart and Tara and bowed slightly. "Perhaps you would all be kind enough to follow me."

He turned, pushed the cart with their luggage through the door, and began to lead them down a steep ramp and along a dark, empty passageway. Maggie quickly caught up with him and immediately began to question him about his phone conversation with Connor. At the end of the tunnel they climbed up another ramp and emerged on the far side of the airport. Koeter guided them through security, where they were met with only the most cursory of checks. After another long trek they arrived in an empty departure lounge, where Koeter handed over three tickets to a gate agent and received three boarding passes for a Qantas flight to Sydney that had been mysteriously held up for fifteen minutes.

"How can we begin to thank you?" asked Maggie.

Koeter took her hand and kissed it again. "Ma'am," he replied, "you will find people all over the world who will never be able to fully repay Connor Fitzgerald."

THEY both sat watching the television screen. Neither of them spoke until the twelve-minute clip had come to an end.

"Could it be possible?" said the director quietly.

"Only if Jackson somehow changed places with him in the Crucifix," replied Gutenburg.

After a long silence Dexter said, "Jackson would only have done that if he was willing to sacrifice his own life."

Gutenburg nodded.

"And who's the man who paid for the rifle?"

"Alexei Romanov, the number two man in the Russian Mafya. We suspect he and Fitzgerald are now working together."

"So it must have been the Mafya who got him out of the Crucifix," said Dexter. "But if he needed a Remington 700, who's the target?"

"The President," said Gutenburg.

"You could be right," replied Dexter. "But which one?"

THE President of the United States and the Secretary of State were among the seventy-two officials lined up on the runway when the Russian Air Force Ilyushin 62 landed at Andrews Air Force Base. The door of the plane opened, and a short, squat man appeared in the doorway. As Zerimski slowly descended the steps, the massed ranks of photographers began clicking furiously.

The U.S. chief of protocol stepped forward to introduce the two Presidents, and Lawrence shook hands warmly with his guest. "Welcome to the United States, Mr. President."

"Thank you, Tom," said Zerimski, immediately wrong-footing him.

The Russian President appeared disarmingly affable and friendly as Lawrence introduced him to each new Cabinet member. When he came to the end of the line, Lawrence touched Zerimski's elbow and guided him toward the podium. "I'll just say a few words of welcome, Mr. President, and then perhaps you'd like to reply."

Lawrence stepped up onto the podium.

"Mr. President," he began. Then, turning toward Zerimski, he smiled and said, "Victor. Today marks the opening of a new era in the special relationship between our two great countries. . . ."

Connor sat in front of three television screens, watching the major networks' coverage of the ceremony. There was a greater security force than he had anticipated. The Secret Service seemed to have turned out a full Dignitary Protective Division for each President. But there was no sign of Gutenburg or of any CIA operatives. Connor suspected that the Secret Service was unaware that a potential assassin was on the loose.

Connor wasn't at all surprised that the rifle he had bought in Dallas had never reached its destination. The two Mafya hoodlums had done everything to tip off the CIA except call their toll-free number.

After the episode in the Memphis Marriott it had become clear that Alexei Romanov wasn't willing to take the blame if anything else went wrong, and Connor now had complete control of all the preparations for the assassination. Those shadowing him kept a respectful distance.

The President came to the end of his welcoming speech. He stepped aside to allow Zerimski to respond, but when the Russian President took his place, he couldn't be seen above the bank of microphones. Zerimski would assume it had been done intentionally to upstage him, and Connor wondered which White House advance man's head would roll later that day.

Shooting a six-foot man would be much easier than one who was only five four, Connor reflected. He studied the Secret Service agents who had been assigned to protect Zerimski. He recognized four of them, each as good as any in the profession.

As Zerimski began to read from his script, Connor glanced down at the four-day itinerary so conveniently catalogued in the Washington *Post*. From the air force base the two Presidents would be flown by helicopter to the White House, where they would immediately go into a session of private talks. After lunch Zerimski would be taken to the Russian embassy to rest before returning to the White House for a black-tie dinner in his honor.

The following morning, Thursday, he would travel to New York to address the United Nations, followed by a visit to the Metropolitan Museum. That night he would return to Washington to attend a performance of *Swan Lake* at the Kennedy Center.

On Friday, Zerimski would address a joint session of Congress, the high point of his four-day visit. Lawrence hoped that the legislators would be convinced that the Russian leader was a man of peace and would agree to back his arms reduction bill.

On Saturday, Zerimski and Tom Lawrence would go to Cooke Stadium in Maryland to watch the football game between the Washington Redskins and the Green Bay Packers. That evening Zerimski would host a dinner at the Russian embassy.

The following morning he would fly back to Moscow—but only if Connor had failed to carry out the contract.

Nine venues for Connor to consider. But he had already dismissed seven of them before Zerimski's plane had touched down. Of the remaining two, the banquet on Saturday night looked the most promising, especially after he'd been told by Romanov that the Mafya had the catering concession for all functions held at the Russian embassy.

A smattering of applause brought Connor's attention back to the welcoming ceremony. The two leaders were now waving to the crowd from the waiting helicopter. Moments later Marine One rose, hovered, then lifted away.

Connor turned off the three televisions and began considering the two most promising venues. The Mafya had arranged for him to visit the Russian embassy that afternoon so he could be taken through the details of Saturday night's banquet.

He checked his watch, put on a coat, and went downstairs. The BMW was waiting for him. He climbed into the back seat.

"Cooke Stadium," was all he said. No one in the car commented.

As the driver eased the car into the center lane, a transporter laden with new cars passed on the other side of the road. Connor thought of Maggie and smiled. He had spoken to Carl Koeter earlier that morning and had been reassured that all three of the kangaroos were safely in their pouches.

"By the way, the Mafya are under the impression that they were sent straight back to the U.S.," Koeter had told him.

"How did you manage to pull that one off?" asked Connor.

"One of their guards tried to bribe a customs officer. He took the money and informed him they'd been caught with drugs and had been 'returned to their port of embarkation.'"

"Do you think they fell for it?"

"Oh, yes," said Koeter. "They were made to pay a lot of money for that piece of information."

Connor laughed. "I'll always be in your debt, Carl. You'll have to let me know how I can repay you."

"That won't be necessary, my friend. I simply look forward to meeting your wife again in more agreeable circumstances."

Connor's Mafya watchdogs had made no mention of Maggie's disappearance, so he couldn't be certain whether they were too proud to admit that they'd lost her, Stuart, and Tara, or whether they were still hoping to catch them before he found out the truth. Perhaps they were afraid he wouldn't carry out the job if he knew his wife and daughter were no longer in their hands. But Connor never doubted that if he failed to honor the agreement, Alexei Romanov would eventually track down Maggie and kill her, and if not Maggie, Tara. Bolchenkov had warned him that until the contract had been completed—one way or the other—Romanov wouldn't be allowed to return to his homeland.

As the driver swung onto the beltway, Connor thought about Joan, whose only crime was to have been his secretary. He clenched his fist and wished that his contract with the Mafya had been to take out Dexter and her conniving deputy. That was an assignment he would have carried out with relish.

The white BMW passed the Washington city limits, and Connor sat back, thinking about just how much preparation still needed to be done. He would have to visit both venues before he could make his final decision. But even then he had no intention of letting Romanov know which one he'd chosen.

TOM Lawrence felt the preliminary discussions with Zerimski had gone well. After lunch Lawrence accompanied the Russian President to his limousine, then hurried back to the Oval Office. A grim-faced Andy Lloyd was standing by his desk.

"We've got a big problem on our hands," Lloyd said, handing Lawrence a file bearing the CIA emblem.

The President began reading. By the time he came to the final paragraph, his face was drained of color. He looked up and said, "I thought Jackson was supposed to be on our side."

"He is, Mr. President."

"Then how come Dexter claims she can prove that he was responsible for the assassination in Colombia, then went to St. Petersburg intending to kill Zerimski?"

"Because that way she clears herself of any involvement and leaves us to explain why we hired Jackson in the first place."

"What about Dexter's claim that Jackson's back in the States and is working with the Russian Mafya?"

"If anything goes wrong during Zerimski's visit, she already has someone lined up to take the rap," said Lloyd.

"She says that a security camera in Dallas recorded Jackson buying a rifle of near-identical specifications to the one used to kill Guzman. How do you explain that?"

"Simple," said Lloyd. "Once you realize it wasn't actually Jackson, everything else falls into place."

"If it wasn't Jackson, then who on earth was it?"

"It was Connor Fitzgerald," said Lloyd quietly. "Jackson took his place."

"Why would he do that?"

"Fitzgerald saved Jackson's life in Vietnam and has the Medal of Honor to prove it. When Fitzgerald returned from the war, it was Jackson who recruited him as an NOC. For the next twenty-eight years he served the CIA and gained the reputation of being their most respected officer. Then, overnight, he disappears and can't be traced on their books. His secretary, Joan Bennett, who worked for him for nineteen years, dies in a mysterious car accident. Then his wife and daughter vanish. Meanwhile, the man we appoint to find out what's going on is accused of being an assassin and double-crossing his closest friend. But however carefully you search through Helen Dexter's numerous reports, you'll never find a single reference to Connor Fitzgerald."

"How do you know all this, Andy?" asked Lawrence.

"Because Jackson called me from St. Petersburg just after Fitzgerald had been arrested."

"Do you have a recording of that conversation?"

"Yes, sir, I do."

"Dammit," said Lawrence. "Dexter makes J. Edgar Hoover look like a Girl Scout."

"If we accept that it was Jackson who was hanged in Russia, we have to assume it was Fitzgerald who flew to Dallas with the intention of buying a rifle for his present assignment."

"Am I the target this time?" asked Lawrence quietly.

"I don't think so, Mr. President. That's the one thing I agree with Dexter about. I believe the target's Zerimski."

"Oh, my God," said Lawrence, slumping into his chair. "But why would an honorable man with a background and reputation as good as Fitzgerald's get involved in a mission like this? It just doesn't add up."

"It does if that honorable man believes that the original order to assassinate Zerimski came from you."

"Pug" Washer—no one knew his real name—was one of those characters who is an expert on one subject. In his case it was the Washington Redskins.

Pug had joined the Redskins' ground staff at the age of fifteen and had later taken over as the team's masseur, becoming the trusted confidant of generations of Redskins. He spent the year before his retirement in 1997 working alongside the contractor who was building the new Jack Kent Cooke Stadium. His brief was simple: to make sure that the Redskins' fans and players had a facility worthy of the greatest team in the country.

At the opening ceremony John Kent Cooke, the Redskins' president, announced that Pug had been elected to the team's Hall of Fame, a mark of distinction normally reserved only for the greatest players.

It took Connor two phone calls to track Pug down at his little apartment in Arlington, Virginia. When he explained to the old man that he had been commissioned to write an article for *Sports Illustrated* on the new stadium, it was like turning on a tap.

They agreed to meet at eleven o'clock on Friday morning so Pug could show Connor around the stadium. Connor arrived at one minute to eleven, and for the next three hours Pug regaled his guest with Redskins lore. Most of the information Pug came up with would be of no practical use to Connor, but he still produced a gem every few minutes. Connor learned that the Sony JumboTrons behind the end zones made up the largest video-screen system in the world, and that a local band would be playing the national anthems of Russia and the United States before tomorrow's kickoff.

As they strolled around the stadium, Connor could see the tight security checks that the White House advance staff were carrying out for the following day's game. The metal detectors through which everyone would have to pass were already in place. The nearer he and Pug got to the owner's box—from where the two Presidents would be watching the game—the more intense the checks became.

When the two men parted, Connor handed his guide an honorarium of one hundred dollars. The old man had told him more in three hours than an entire Secret Service detail would have divulged in a lifetime.

Connor checked his watch to find he was running a few minutes late for his meeting with Alexei Romanov at the Russian embassy. As he was driven away from the stadium, he switched on the radio.

A commentator was describing the atmosphere on the floor of the House as the members waited for the Russian President to arrive. No one had any idea what he was going to say, since the press had not been issued with advance copies of the speech.

Five minutes before the speech was due to begin, Zerimski walked out onto the floor of the House.

"Everyone present," announced the radio commentator, "has risen from their seats and is applauding the guest from Russia."

When Zerimski reached the podium, he carefully placed his papers on the lectern. The members of Congress, the Supreme Court, and the diplomatic corps resumed their seats, unaware of the bombshell that was about to be dropped.

"Mr. Speaker, Mr. Vice President, and Mr. Chief Justice," Zerimski began. "Let me begin by thanking you and your countrymen for your kind welcome and generous hospitality."

Tom Lawrence, who was watching the speech with Andy Lloyd in the Oval Office, began to smile as Zerimski described "the excellent relationship currently enjoyed by our two countries."

That smile was wiped off his face as the Russian President delivered the next sixty-two words of his speech.

"I am the last person on earth who would want our two great nations to become embroiled in another pointless war." Zerimski paused. "To be sure that such a calamity can never befall us again, it will be necessary for Russia to remain as powerful as the United States on the battlefield if it is to carry the same weight at the conference table."

At that moment Lawrence realized that Zerimski had just destroyed any chance of his arms reduction bill becoming law.

As THE white BMW drove up Wisconsin Avenue, Connor switched off the radio. When they reached the gates of the Russian embassy, one of Alexei Romanov's henchmen checked them through security.

Connor could see immediately what Romanov had meant when he said the embassy's internal security was lax. "After all, who would want to murder Russia's beloved President in his own embassy?" he had remarked with a smile.

As they walked down a long corridor, Connor said to Romanov, "You seem to have the run of the building."

"So would you if you'd paid enough into the ambassador's Swiss bank account to ensure that he never had to return to the motherland again."

Romanov unlocked the door to the ambassador's study and let himself in. As they entered the ornate room, Connor was surprised to see a customized Remington 700 resting on the ambassador's desk. He picked it up and studied it closely. He would have asked Romanov how he'd got his hands on it if he thought there was any chance of being told the truth.

Connor gripped the stock and broke the breech. There was a single boattail bullet in the chamber. He raised an eyebrow and glanced at Romanov.

"I assume that from that range you will need only one bullet," said the Russian. He led Connor to the ambassador's private elevator at the far corner of the room. They stepped inside and traveled up to the gallery above the ballroom on the second floor.

Connor checked every inch of the gallery, then squeezed in behind a vast statue of Lenin. He looked through its cocked arm to check the sight line to the spot from which Zerimski would deliver his farewell speech, thinking how easy it all seemed.

"You will have to arrive several hours early and work with the catering staff before the banquet begins," Romanov said.

Connor nodded. As they walked toward the elevator, he said, "I'll let you know when I've decided which venue I've chosen."

Romanov looked surprised but said nothing.

CONNOR phoned Romanov a few minutes after midnight.

The Russian seemed delighted that they had both come to the same conclusion. "I'll arrange for a driver to pick you up at three thirty so you can be at the embassy by four."

Connor put the phone down. If everything went according to plan, the President would be dead by four.

THE ambassador tapped gently on the door of Zerimski's suite, but there was no response. He stiffened his resolve and knocked a little louder, then tentatively opened it.

In the light from the landing the ambassador could see Zerimski stirring in his bed. It was four o'clock in the morning.

"This had better be important," the Russian President said.

"There is a call for you from St. Petersburg," said the ambassador. "A Mr. Stefan Ivanitsky. He says it's urgent."

"Get out," said Zerimski as he picked up the phone by his bed. The ambassador stepped into the corridor and closed the door.

"Stefan," said Zerimski, "why are you calling at this hour?"

"The czar is dead, Mr. President." Ivanitsky spoke without emotion. Nicolai Romanov was his uncle.

"When? Where? How?"

"About an hour ago, at the Winter Palace. The colorless liquid finally got him." Ivanitsky paused. "The butler has been on my payroll for almost a year."

Zerimski was silent for a few moments before saying, "Good. It couldn't have worked out better for us."

"I would agree, Mr. President, were his son not in Washington. There's very little I can do from this end until he returns."

"That problem may resolve itself this evening," said Zerimski.

"Have they fallen into our little trap?"

"Yes. By tonight I shall have disposed of both of them."

"Both of them?"

"Yes," Zerimski replied. "I have learned an appropriate new expression since I've been over here—'killing two birds with one stone.' After all, how many times does one have the chance to see the same man die twice?"

"I wish I was there to witness it."

"I'm going to enjoy it even more than I did watching his friend dangling from a rope," said Zerimski. "All things considered, Ivan, this will have been a most successful trip, especially if—"

"It's all been taken care of, Mr. President," said Ivanitsky. "I arranged yesterday for the income from the Yeltsin oil and uranium contracts to be diverted to your Zurich account. That is, unless Alexei countermands my orders when he returns."

"If he doesn't return, he won't be able to, will he?" Zerimski put the phone down and was asleep again within minutes.

THE wake-up call came through at six. Connor rose, pulled back a corner of the curtain, and checked that they were still there. They were: two white BMWs parked on the far side of the street, as they had been since the previous evening. By now their occupants would be drowsy.

He allowed the cold jets of the shower to needle his body for some time before he grabbed a towel. Then he dressed in a blue shirt, jeans, a thick sweater, black socks, and a pair of black Nikes.

He went into the small kitchenette, poured himself a glass of grapefruit juice, and filled a bowl with cornflakes and milk. He always ate the same meal on the day of an operation. It helped him believe everything would run smoothly.

He checked his watch and returned to his bedroom. He put three hundred-dollar bills, a quarter, and a thirty-minute audiocassette into a back pocket of his jeans. He then left the anonymous apartment for the last time.

At ten minutes to eight he walked slowly across the street to the first of the two BMWs. "I need to go downtown to pick up a couple of things," he said. The man in the back nodded, so the driver put the car into first and joined the traffic on Wisconsin Avenue. The second car followed closely behind them as they turned left onto P Street.

As each day passed, Connor had noticed that his keepers had become more relaxed. At roughly the same time every morning he had jumped out of the BMW at the corner of 21st Street and DuPont Circle, bought a copy of the Washington *Post* from a news vendor, and returned to the car. Yesterday the man in the back seat hadn't even bothered to accompany him.

They crossed 3rd Street, and Connor could see DuPont Circle in the distance. The cars were now bumper to bumper, and traffic had almost ground to a halt. On the other side of the street the traffic heading west was moving far more smoothly. He would need to judge exactly when to make his move.

Connor knew that the lights on P Street approaching the circle changed every thirty seconds, and on average, twelve cars managed to cross during that time. The most he'd counted during the week was sixteen.

When the light turned red, Connor counted seventeen cars ahead of them. He didn't move a muscle. The light switched to green, but the traffic was so heavy that the BMW was able to edge forward only a few yards. Only eight cars crawled through the light.

Connor had thirty seconds. He turned and smiled at his keeper in the back, pointing to the news vendor. The man nodded. Connor stepped out onto the sidewalk and started walking slowly toward the old man. He concentrated on the traffic moving in the opposite direction on the other side of the street, trying to estimate how long the line of cars would be when the light turned red again. When he reached the news vendor, he gave a quarter to the old man, who handed him the *Post.* As he turned and began to walk back toward the first BMW, the light turned red and the traffic came to a halt.

Connor spotted the vehicle he needed. He suddenly switched directions and started running, darting in and out of the stationary traffic on the westbound side of the street until he reached an empty taxi, six cars away from the lights. The two men in the second BMW leaped out of the car and began sprinting after him just as the light at DuPont Circle turned green.

Connor threw himself into the back of the taxi. "Straight ahead," he shouted. "You get a hundred dollars if you beat that light."

The driver pressed the palm of his hand onto his horn and ran the red light. The two white BMWs executed screeching U-turns, but the lights had already changed and their path was blocked.

So far everything had gone according to plan.

The taxi swung left onto 23rd Street, and Connor instructed the driver to pull over. When the car came to a halt, he passed him a hundred-dollar bill and said, "Drive straight to Dulles Airport. If you spot a white BMW behind you, don't let it overtake you. When you get to the airport, stop for thirty seconds outside departures, then drive slowly back into town."

"Anything you say, man," said the driver, pocketing the bill. Connor slipped out of the cab, darted across 23rd Street, and flagged another cab heading in the opposite direction. As he shut the door, the two BMWs swept past in pursuit of the first taxi.

"And where would you like to go this fine morning?"

"Cooke Stadium."

THE THREE MEN STOOD AS Zerimski entered the room. He waved them down and took the chair behind the ambassador's desk. He was surprised to see a rifle where the blotter would normally be, but he ignored it.

"I have some sad news for you, Alexei," said Zerimski. "It appears that your father suffered a heart attack during the night and died on the way to the hospital."

Romanov bowed his head. Zerimski rose, walked slowly over to the young man, and placed a consoling hand on his shoulder. The ambassador and first secretary looked suitably sad.

"I shall mourn him," said Zerimski. "He was a great man." Romanov inclined his head to acknowledge the President's words.

"Now his mantle has passed on to you, Alexei—a most worthy successor," Zerimski said. "Let no one in Russia doubt who is the new czar."

Romanov raised his head and smiled, his mourning over.

"That is," added Zerimski, "assuming nothing goes wrong this evening."

"Nothing can go wrong," said Romanov emphatically. "Fitzgerald has agreed to my plan. He will report to the embassy at four o'clock this afternoon, while you are at the football game."

"Why so early?" asked Zerimski.

"We need everyone to think he's a member of the catering team so that tonight when he slips out of the kitchen just before your farewell speech, nobody gives it a second thought."

"Excellent," said Zerimski. "And then what happens?"

"I will accompany him to this room, where he will collect the rifle. He will take the elevator to the private gallery that overlooks the ballroom and position himself behind the statue of Lenin. He'll remain there until you reach the end of your speech.

"Once Fitzgerald has fired, he will climb out onto the ledge by the cedar tree in the back garden," continued Romanov. "He made us repeat the exercise several times yesterday afternoon, but this evening he will discover there is a small difference."

"And what is that?" asked Zerimski.

"Waiting under the tree will be six of my personal bodyguards. They will have gunned him down long before his feet touch the ground."

"But surely your plan has a minor flaw?" Zerimski said.

Romanov looked puzzled.

"How am I expected to survive a shot from a marksman of Fitzgerald's reputation from such close range?"

Romanov rose from his chair and picked up the rifle. He removed a small piece of metal and handed it to the President.

"What is this?" Zerimski asked.

"The firing pin," Romanov replied.

WHEN the taxi dropped Connor at Cooke Stadium, he walked up the wide gravel path toward the two long lines of people who hung around before every home game in the hope of a day's work. The first line was for those who wanted to work outside the stadium, organizing the parking or selling programs, cushions, and souvenirs. The other was for those who hoped to work inside the stadium. Connor joined that line.

On this particular day a handful of Secret Service men were eyeing the hopeful applicants. Connor kept reading the Washington *Post* as the line moved slowly forward. A wry smile crossed his face as he read in the Metro section of the premature death of a distinguished academic from his hometown.

"Hi," said a voice.

Connor glanced around at a smartly dressed young man in the line behind him. "Hi," he responded briefly, before returning to his paper. He didn't want to get involved in a conversation with someone who might later be called as a witness.

"My name's Brad," the young man announced. "I'm hoping to get a job on one of the lighting towers. How about you?"

"Why the lighting towers?" asked Connor.

"Because that's where the Secret Service's special agent in charge will be stationed, and I want to find out what the job's really like. I'm thinking about joining them when I leave college."

"Next," said a voice.

Connor turned to the man seated behind a trestle table. "What have you got left?" he asked.

"Not much," said the man, looking down at his list.

"Anything in catering?" asked Connor. Like Brad, he knew exactly where he wanted to be.

"Washing dishes or serving meals to employees is all I've got."

"That will be just fine."

"Name?"

"Dave Krinkle," said Connor, handing over a driver's license. The man filled in a security pass and a photographer stepped forward and took a Polaroid of Connor, which seconds later was laminated onto the pass.

"Okay, Dave," the man said, handing it over. "This pass will get you everywhere inside the stadium except the high-security area." Connor nodded and clipped the pass onto his sweater. "Report to room 47, directly below block H."

Connor knew exactly where room 47 was. Once he had passed through the three security checks and was inside the stadium, he ambled along the inner walkway until he came to a stairway with a sign reading ROOM 47, PRIVATE CATERING and an arrow pointing down. Inside the small room at the foot of the stairs he found a dozen men lounging around. He took a seat in a corner and returned to his copy of the *Post*.

"Okay," said a voice, "pay attention." Connor looked up to see a huge man of about fifty wearing a chef's uniform standing in front of them. "I'm the catering manager," he said, "and I can offer you two choices. You either wash dishes or you serve stadium employees and security guys stationed around the stadium. Any volunteers for the dishes?"

Most of the men in the room put their hands up. Dishwashing, Pug had explained, was always popular because not only did the washers get the full rate of ten dollars an hour but for some of them the leftovers were the best meal they had all week.

"Good," the manager said, picking out five of them and writing down their names. When he had completed the list, he said, "Now, serving. You can either serve the senior staff or the security personnel. Senior staff?" he said, looking up from the clipboard. Almost all the remaining hands shot up. Again the catering manager wrote down five names. When he'd finished, he tapped his clipboard and said, "Okay, everyone on the list can now report to work." The old pros rose from their seats and shuffled through to the kitchens. Only Connor and Brad were still in the room.

"I've got two jobs left serving security personnel," said the catering manager. "One great, one lousy. Who is going to get lucky?" He looked hopefully at Connor, who nodded and placed a hand in his back pocket.

The manager walked up to him, not even glancing at Brad, and said, "I have a feeling you'd prefer the comfort of the JumboTron."

"Right," said Connor, slipping him a hundred-dollar bill.

"Just as I thought," said the catering manager with a smile. He pocketed the cash, exactly as Pug had predicted he would.

That man had been worth every cent of his fee.

"Do you know, I've seen the rifle Fitzgerald plans to kill me with," Zerimski said as his nine-limousine motorcade swept out of the embassy gates en route to the game.

Titov looked surprised.

Zerimski put a hand in his jacket pocket. "What do you think this is?" he asked, holding up what looked like a bent nail.

Titov shook his head. "I've no idea."

"It's the firing pin of a Remington 700," Zerimski replied, dropping it back into his pocket. "Has the speech I'm meant to be giving tonight been released to the press?"

"Yes, Mr. President," said Titov. "It's full of the usual platitudes."

"And what about my spontaneous reaction after Fitzgerald has been killed?"

"I have it here, Mr. President."

"Good. Give me a taste of it," said Zerimski.

Titov began reading from a handwritten script: "On the day of my election President Lawrence telephoned me and invited me to visit his country. I accepted. But my outstretched hand has been met not with an olive branch, but with a rifle pointing directly at me. And where? In my own embassy. I then discover that the trigger was pulled by an officer of the CIA. Had it not been for my good fortune—".

"A *former* officer," interrupted Zerimski.

"I thought it prudent for you to make the occasional error. That way no one will suggest you knew what was going on. In America they want to believe that everything is a conspiracy."

"I shall be only too happy to fuel their paranoia," said Zerimski. "Long after Lawrence has been removed from office, I want Americans to be writing copious volumes about how I was responsible for the complete breakdown in relations between the two countries. Lawrence's administration will end up as nothing more than a footnote in the history of the resurgence of the Russian Empire under my presidency." He beamed at Titov. "I shall remain in power until the day I die."

CONNOR checked his watch. It was nine fifty-six, thirty-four minutes before the stadium would be open to the public. As instructed by the catering manager, Connor was standing by the service elevator on the seventh level. He pressed the button beside the elevator and immediately heard the whir of the engine as the elevator began its slow journey from the kitchen up to the seventh level.

Forty-seven seconds later Connor removed a tray from the elevator and pressed the button to let the staff in the basement know he had received it. He then walked quickly along the seventh-floor concourse to a door marked PRIVATE. He extracted from his pocket a key the catering manager had given him. Balancing the tray on one hand, he turned the key in the lock with the other and slipped inside. Then he switched on the light and strode down the covered walkway at the back of the JumboTron. He checked his watch again— eighty-three seconds. Too long, but since the final run would be without a tray, it should be possible to complete the whole exercise, from roof to basement, in under two minutes. If it all went according to plan, he would be out of the stadium and on his way to the airport before they had time to set up any roadblocks.

Connor knocked on the door. It was opened by a tall, heavily built man. "I've brought you a snack," said Connor.

"Great," said the sharpshooter. "Why don't you come in and join me?" He removed a pastrami sandwich from the tray, and Connor followed him along a thin steel platform behind a vast screen made up of 786 televisions. The Secret Service man sat down and sank his teeth into the sandwich. Connor tried not to let him see how closely he was studying his rifle.

The JumboTron was on three floors, one above the steel platform and one below. Connor put the tray down beside the officer, who was sitting in the middle of the flight of stairs that led to the lower ramp. He took more interest in his can of Diet Coke than in Connor's roaming eyes.

"By the way," he said between swigs, "I'm Arnie Cooper."

"Dave Krinkle," Connor replied.

"So how much did you have to pay for the privilege of spending the afternoon with me?" asked Arnie with a grin.

WHEN the limousine carrying President Lawrence and his entourage pulled up at the stadium's entrance, John Kent Cooke, the president of the Redskins, was waiting to greet them.

"This is a great honor, sir," he said, shaking Lawrence's hand.

"It's good to meet you, John," replied the President.

Cooke escorted his guest to his private box, a large, comfortable room positioned above the fifty-yard line, with a perfect view of the whole field. "Mr. President," said Cooke, "I'd like to introduce you to one or two of the folks who have made the Redskins the greatest football team in America. Let me start with my wife, Rita."

"Good to meet you, Rita," Lawrence said. "And congratulations on your triumph at the National Symphony Ball. I'm told they raised a record amount under your chairmanship."

Mrs. Cooke beamed with pride.

"This is Pug Washer," said John Kent Cooke, placing a hand on the old man's shoulder. "Now, he—"

"Is the only man in history to make the Redskins Hall of Fame without playing a single game for the team," said Lawrence.

A huge smile appeared on Pug's face.

"Do you know, Mr. President," said Cooke, "I've never been able to come up with a question about the Redskins that Pug wasn't able to answer."

"Has anyone ever stumped you, Pug?" asked the President.

"They try all the time, Mr. President," Pug replied. "Why, only yesterday a man—"

Before Pug could complete his sentence, Andy Lloyd touched Lawrence's elbow. "I'm sorry to interrupt you, sir, but we've just been informed that President Zerimski is only five minutes away from the stadium. You and Mr. Cooke should make your way to the northeast entrance now so you'll be in time to welcome him."

"Yes, of course," said Lawrence. He turned to Pug and said, "Let's continue our conversation just as soon as I get back."

Pug nodded as the President and his entourage left the room.

"IT'S a bit cramped in here," Connor shouted above the noise of the large ventilation fan in the ceiling.

"Sure is," said Arnie Cooper, finishing off his Diet Coke.

"Are you expecting any trouble today?"

"Nope, not really. Of course, we'll all be on full alert the moment the two Presidents walk out onto the field, but that only lasts for about eight minutes. Although if Special Agent Braithwaite had his way, neither of them would be allowed out of the owner's box until it was time for them to go home."

Connor nodded and asked several innocuous questions, listening carefully to Arnie's Brooklyn accent and concentrating especially on any expressions he used regularly.

As Arnie bit into a slice of chocolate cake, Connor looked through a gap in the rotating advertising boards. Most of the Secret Service officers in the stadium were also taking a snack break. He focused on the lighting tower behind the western end zone. Brad was up there, listening intently to an officer who was pointing to the owner's box. Just the sort of young man the Secret Service needed to recruit, thought Connor. He turned back to Arnie. "I'll see you again at the start of the game. A plate of sandwiches, another slice of cake, and some more Coke okay with you?"

"Yep, sounds great. But go easy on the cake."

A siren sounded to let all the staff in the stadium know it was ten thirty and the gates were about to be opened. The fans began to flood into the stands. Connor placed the empty Coke can on the tray.

"I'll be back with your lunch at the kickoff," Connor said.

"Yup," replied Arnie, his binoculars now focused on the crowd below. "But don't come in until after the two Presidents are back in the owner's box. No one else is allowed in the JumboTron while they're out on the field."

"Okay," said Connor, taking a last look at Arnie's rifle before stepping out onto the covered walkway. He closed the door behind him and placed the empty Coke can on the step.

He checked his watch, then strode quickly down the walkway, unlocked the door at its end, and turned off the lights. When he reached the elevator shaft, he pressed the button. Forty-seven seconds later the service elevator reappeared. He placed the tray inside and pressed the button once again. The elevator began its journey down to the basement.

Connor was dressed in a long white catering coat and a Redskins cap, and no one gave him a second glance as he strolled casually past the concession stand toward the door marked PRIVATE. He slipped inside and locked the door behind him. In the darkness he walked noiselessly back along the narrow walkway until he was a few yards from the entrance to the JumboTron. He stood looking down at the vast steel girder that held the massive screen in place.

Connor gripped the handrail for a moment, then fell to his knees. He leaned forward, grabbed the girder with both hands, and eased himself off the walkway. He stared fixedly at the screen, which, according to the architects' plans, was forty-two feet in front of him. It looked more like a mile.

He could see a small handle, but he had no idea if the emergency trapdoor that had been marked on the engineer's plans really existed. He began to crawl slowly along the girder, inch by inch, never once looking down at the 170-foot drop below him.

When he finally reached the end of the girder, he dropped his legs over the sides and gripped tightly, as if he were on horseback. He took a deep breath, gripped the handle, and pulled. The trapdoor slid back, revealing the promised twenty-two-and-a-half-inch-square hole. Connor slowly hauled himself inside and slid the door back in place.

He lay suspended inside the hollow steel girder 170 feet above the ground for almost forty-five minutes, barely able to turn his wrist to check the time. Nevertheless, as each minute passed, he became more confident that should it prove necessary to fall back on his contingency plan, no one would discover where he was hiding.

ZERIMSKI shook hands warmly with everyone he was introduced to, and even laughed at John Kent Cooke's jokes. He remembered the names of all the guests and answered every question that was put to him with a smile. "What the Americans call a charm offensive," Titov had told him. It would only add to the horror of what he had planned for them that evening.

After the introductions had been completed, Cooke rapped on a table with a spoon. "I'm sorry to interrupt such a pleasant occasion," he began, "but time is marching on, and this is probably going to be the only opportunity I have in my life to brief two Presidents at once." A little laughter broke out. "So here goes." He began reading from a sheet of paper.

"At eleven thirty-six I will lead both Presidents out onto the field. There I will introduce the Presidents to the team captains, coaches, and game officials.

"At eleven forty everyone will turn and face the west stand, where the Redskins band will play the Russian national anthem, followed by 'The Star-Spangled Banner.' I shall then accompany both gentle-men off the field and bring them back here, where I hope everyone will enjoy watching the Redskins defeat the Packers."

CONNOR checked his watch. Eleven seventeen. He slid open the trapdoor and eased himself out of the confined space. He gathered his strength for a moment before swinging his legs over the girder and gripping it with his thighs. Again, he didn't look down as he began the slow forty-two-foot crawl back to the walkway.

Once he had reached the safety of the ledge, he pulled himself up onto the walkway and began a short series of stretching exercises. Eleven twenty-seven. He breathed deeply, then walked quickly toward the JumboTron, pausing only to pick up the empty Coke can he had left on the step.

He banged loudly on the door. Without waiting for a response, he opened it, marched in, and shouted, "It's only me."

Arnie peered down from the ledge above, his right hand moving toward the trigger of his rifle. "Beat it!" he said. "I told you not to come back till the Presidents were off the field."

"Sorry," said Connor. "It's just that I noticed how hot it gets in here, so I brought you another Coke."

He passed the empty can up, and Arnie bent down to take it with his free hand. As his fingers touched the rim of the can, Connor let go of it, grabbed Arnie by the wrist, and, with all the strength he could muster, pulled him down from the ledge.

Arnie let out a terrible scream as he came crashing down, landing headfirst on the walkway, his rifle skidding away across it.

Connor leaped on his adversary before he had a chance to get up. As Arnie raised his head, Connor landed a straight left to his chin that stunned him for a moment, then grabbed for the pair of handcuffs hanging from his belt. As Arnie tried to rise to his feet, Connor landed another punch, this time full on his nose. Arnie's legs buckled. He sank to the ground and lay still.

Connor tore off his clothes and threw them into a pile in the cor-ner. Then he quickly stripped Arnie of his uniform. As he put it on, he found that the shoes were too small and the pants too short. He had no choice but to pull up his socks and stick with his Nikes, which were at least black. He didn't think that in the mayhem he was about to cause, anyone would recall that they had seen a Secret Service agent who wasn't wearing regulation shoes.

Connor retrieved his tie from the pile of clothes and bound Arnie's ankles tightly together. He then lifted up the unconscious man and held him against the wall, placed his arms around a steel beam, and clamped the handcuffs on his wrists. Finally he forced a rolled-up handkerchief into Arnie's mouth.

"Nothing personal," said Connor. He picked up Arnie's rifle: As he'd thought, an M-16. It could do the job. He quickly climbed the steps to the second-floor landing where Arnie had been sitting, picked up his binoculars, and scanned the crowd below.

Suddenly he heard a voice behind him. "Hercules three."

He grabbed the small two-way radio attached to Arnie's belt. "Hercules three, go ahead."

"Thought we'd lost you there for a moment, Arnie," said Special Agent in Charge Braithwaite. "Is everything okay?"

"Yep," said Connor. "Just needed to take a leak and thought I'd better not do it over the crowd."

"Affirmative," said Braithwaite, breaking into a laugh. "Keep scanning your section. It won't be long before Red Light and Waterfall come out on the field."

"Will do," said Connor in an accent his mother would have chastised him for. The line went dead.

Eleven thirty-four. A roar went up from the crowd as the teams entered from the tunnels at the south end of the stadium and jogged slowly toward the center of the field.

Connor raised Arnie's binoculars to his eyes and focused on the lighting towers high above the stadium. Almost all the Secret Service agents were now scanning the crowd below, looking for any suggestion of trouble. Connor's gaze settled on young Brad, who looked as if this was the nearest he'd been to heaven.

Connor swung around and lined the binoculars up on the fifty-yard line. The two captains were now facing each other. *Eleven thirty-six*. Another roar went up as John Kent Cooke proudly led the two Presidents out onto the field accompanied by a dozen agents who were almost as big as the players. One look and Connor could tell that Zerimski and Lawrence were both wearing bulletproof vests.

As the Presidents were introduced to the players, Connor cracked the rifle open to find that it was fully loaded, off-safe, uncocked. He chambered the first round and slammed the breech shut. The noise acted on him like the crack of a starting pistol, and he suddenly felt his heart rate almost double.

Eleven forty-one. John Kent Cooke whispered something into Lawrence's ear. The American President nodded and guided Zerimski to a space between the two teams.

"Ladies and gentlemen," said a voice over the loudspeaker. "Please rise for the national anthem of the Russian Republic."

There was a clattering of seats as the crowd rose from their places to listen to a tune few of them had ever heard before.

Although Connor had stood through the Russian national anthem many times, he found that few bands knew at what tempo it should be played or how many verses ought to be included. So he decided to wait for "The Star-Spangled Banner" before he took his one chance.

When the Russian anthem came to an end, the players began to stretch and jog on the spot in an attempt to calm their nerves. Connor waited for the bandleader to raise his baton once more, which would be his cue to line up Zerimski in his sights. He glanced at the flagpole: The Redskins banner was hanging limp, indicating that there was virtually no wind.

The bandleader raised his baton a second time. Connor placed the rifle through the gap between the triangular ad panel and the video screen, using the wooden frame as a rest. He focused the telescopic sight, lining up the mil dots until the back of Zerimski's head completely filled the center of the rifle's sight.

The opening bars of the American anthem struck up. Connor breathed out. Three . . . two . . . one. He gently squeezed the trigger just as Tom Lawrence's right arm swung across his chest, his hand coming to rest over his heart. Distracted by the sudden movement, Zerimski glanced to his left and the bullet flew harmlessly past his right ear. Seventy-eight thousand out-of-tune voices ensured that no one heard the soft thud as the inch of metal embedded itself in the grass beyond the fifty-yard line.

Brad, lying flat on his stomach on the lighting platform, stared intently down at the crowd through binoculars. His eyes settled on the JumboTron. The vast screen was dominated by a larger-than-life President Lawrence, hand on heart, lustily singing the national anthem.

Brad's glasses swept on. Suddenly he jerked them back. He thought he'd seen something in the gap between the triangular ad panel and the screen. He double-checked—it was the barrel of a rifle, pointing toward the center of the field from the gap where he had earlier seen Arnie. He touched the fine focus and stared at a face he'd seen earlier that day. He didn't hesitate.

"Cover and evacuate. Gun."

Brad spoke with such urgency and authority that Special Agent in Charge Braithwaite and two of his countersnipers instantly swung their binoculars to the JumboTron. Within moments they were focusing on Connor.

"Relax," Connor was murmuring to himself. "You've got plenty of time." Zerimski's head again filled the scope. Connor lined up the mil dots and breathed out again. Three . . . two . . .

Braithwaite's bullet hammered into his left shoulder, knocking him backward just as the national anthem came to an end.

Twenty-eight years of training had prepared Connor for this moment. He immediately began to carry out his escape plan. Trying to ignore the excruciating pain in his shoulder, he struggled to the door, switched off the light, and clambered out onto the walkway. He tried to run to the far door that led out onto the concourse and found he needed every ounce of energy just to keep moving. Forty seconds later he reached the door. He heard a roar from the crowd as the Redskins prepared to kick off.

Connor unlocked the door, staggered to the service elevator, and jabbed the button several times. The pain in his shoulder was becoming intense, but he knew there was nothing he could do about it. The elevator was about fifteen seconds away from him. But then it came to a sudden halt. Someone must be loading or unloading at the executive level.

Connor's instinctive reaction was to fall back on his contingency plan, something he had never before had to do. If he had to hang around for more than a few more seconds, someone would spot him.

He moved as quickly as he could back toward the door that led to the JumboTron and slipped through it, leaving it unlocked. He had to summon up every ounce of willpower in his body to cover the seventy yards along the walkway, but he knew that agents from the Protective Intelligence Division mobile team would be swarming through that door within minutes.

Twenty-four seconds later Connor reached the massive girder that supported the video screen. He gripped the rail with his right hand and eased himself over the edge of the walkway and onto the ledge just as the door to the corridor swung open behind him. He slipped under the walkway and heard two sets of feet pass above him and stop outside the door to the JumboTron itself. Through a gap in the walkway he could see one of the officers, gun in hand, pushing the door open. Without stepping inside, the officer fumbled for the light switch.

Connor waited until the lights went on and the two officers had disappeared inside the JumboTron before he began to crawl along the forty-two-foot girder for the third time that day. But now he could only hold on with his right arm, which meant that his progress was even slower. At the same time, he had to be sure that the blood dripping from his shoulder fell the 170 feet to the ground and not onto the girder for all to see.

When the leading Secret Service agent entered the JumboTron, the first thing he saw was Arnie handcuffed to the steel beam. He unlocked the handcuffs and was lowering Arnie to the ground when a message came over his radio.

"Hercules seven."

"Hercules seven, go ahead."

"Any sign of him?" asked Braithwaite.

"There's nobody here except Arnie, who was cuffed to a beam in his underwear. Both doors were unlocked, and there's a trickle of blood all the way to the concourse, so you definitely winged him. He has to be out there somewhere. He's wearing Arnie's uniform, so he shouldn't be too hard to spot."

"Don't count on it," said Braithwaite. "If it's who I think it is, he could be right under your nose."

THREE men sat in the Oval Office listening to the tape. Two were in evening dress, the third in uniform.

"How did you find it?" asked Lawrence.

"It was in the back pocket of the jeans among the pile of clothes Fitzgerald left in the JumboTron," said Special Agent in Charge Bill Braithwaite.

"How many people witnessed the incident in the stadium?" asked Lloyd, trying not to sound anxious.

"Apart from myself, only five other people were aware that anything happened, and you can be assured of their discretion," said Braithwaite. "Four of them have been on my staff for ten years or more, and the fifth is a college student whose application to join the Secret Service is on my desk as we speak."

The President smiled. He rose from his desk, turned around, and stared out the bay window. Dusk had fallen.

"It's important that you realize one thing, Bill," he said eventually. "It certainly sounds like my voice on that tape, but I have never suggested to anyone, at any time, that Zerimski or any other person should be the target of an assassin."

"I accept that without question, Mr. President, or I wouldn't be here now. But I must be equally candid with you. If anyone in the Secret Service had realized that it was Connor Fitzgerald in the JumboTron, they would probably have helped him escape."

"What kind of man can inspire such loyalty?" asked Lawrence.

"In your world I suspect it's Abraham Lincoln," said Braithwaite. "In ours it's Connor Fitzgerald."

"I would have liked to meet him."

"That's going to be difficult, sir. Even if he's still alive, he seems to have disappeared off the face of the earth—"

"Mr. President," interrupted Lloyd, "you're already running seven minutes late for the dinner at the Russian embassy."

Lawrence shook hands with Braithwaite and gave a wry smile. "I suppose you'll be on duty again tonight," he said.

"Yes, sir. I'm covering the whole of President Zerimski's visit."

"I may see you later, then, Bill. If you pick up any new information about Fitzgerald, I want to hear about it immediately."

"Of course, sir," said Braithwaite, turning to leave.

A few minutes later Lawrence and Lloyd walked to the South Portico, where nine limousines stood in line. As soon as the President was in the back of the sixth car, he turned to his chief of staff and asked, "Where do you think he is, Andy?"

"I have no idea, sir. But if I did, I'd probably sign up with Braithwaite's team and help him escape."

Lawrence turned to look out the window. Something had been nagging at him ever since he had left the stadium, but when he arrived at the Russian embassy, he still hadn't dredged it up from the recesses of his mind.

"What's he looking so angry about?" said Lawrence, spotting Zerimski pacing up and down outside the embassy.

Lloyd glanced at his watch. "You're seventeen minutes late, sir."

"That's hardly a big deal. Frankly, the man's lucky to be alive."

Lawrence stepped out of the car and said, "Hi, Victor. Sorry we're a couple of minutes late."

Zerimski made no attempt to hide his displeasure. After a cool handshake he led his guest of honor silently into the embassy. Then he made a perfunctory excuse and dumped the President of the

United States on the Egyptian ambassador, who tried to interest him in an exhibition of Egyptian artifacts on display at the Smithsonian.

Presently a gong sounded, and dinner was announced. Lawrence found his place—between Mrs. Pietrovski, the Russian ambassador's wife, and Yuri Olgivic, the head of the Russian trade delegation, who didn't speak a word of English.

"Were you able to follow the game?" the President asked Mrs. Pietrovski as a bowl of borscht was placed in front of him.

"Not really," the ambassador's wife replied. "But I was fortunate enough to be placed next to a Mr. Pug Washer."

The President dropped his spoon before he'd taken a sip. He looked across the room at Andy Lloyd and placed a clenched fist under his chin—the sign he always used when he needed to speak to his chief of staff urgently.

Lloyd walked over to the President's side.

"Go and find Bill Braithwaite immediately," Lawrence whispered. "Tell him there's one man who'll know where Fitzgerald's hiding if he's still in the stadium—Pug Washer. Find Pug, and my bet is you'll find Connor Fitzgerald."

WHEN Zerimski eventually rose to address his guests, even his most ardent admirers would have been hard-pressed to describe his efforts as anything other than pedestrian.

Lawrence kept waiting for Zerimski to reinforce his message to Congress the previous day, but he said nothing controversial, sticking to the bland script that had been sent to the White House that afternoon.

"Let me end by thanking the American people for the hospitality I have experienced during my visit to your great country—in particular, from your President, Tom Lawrence."

The applause that greeted this statement was loud and prolonged. Zerimski was standing motionless, staring up at the statue of Lenin. He waited till the applause had ended before he sat down. He didn't look at all pleased, which surprised Lawrence, as in his opinion the speech's reception had been far more generous than it deserved.

Lawrence rose to reply. His speech, which was equally banal, was received with respectful applause, but nothing compared to the ovation Zerimski received.

Once the coffee had been served, Zerimski rose and walked over to the double doors on the far side of the room. He soon began saying "Good night" in a loud voice, making it clear that he wanted his guests off the premises as quickly as possible.

When Lawrence eventually reached the door, Zerimski gave him a curt nod before accompanying him down the stairs. At the foot of the stone steps Lawrence turned to wave to his host, but Zerimski had already disappeared back inside the embassy. If he had taken the trouble to accompany Lawrence beyond the front door, he would have seen Braithwaite waiting in the back of Lawrence's limousine.

Braithwaite didn't speak until the door had been closed.

"You were right, sir," he said as they passed through the embassy gates.

THE first person Zerimski saw as he walked back into the embassy was the ambassador. His excellency smiled hopefully.

"Is Romanov still in the building?" Zerimski bellowed angrily.

"Yes, Mr. President," the ambassador said. "He's been—"

"Bring him to me immediately. I'll be in your study."

Pietrovski scurried away in the opposite direction.

Zerimski marched down the long corridor to the ambassador's study and shoved open the door as if he were thumping a punching bag. The first thing he saw was the rifle, still lying on the desk. He sat down in the ambassador's chair. While he waited impatiently for the ambassador and Romanov to join him, he picked up the rifle. He looked down the barrel and saw that the single bullet was still in place. As he held it up to his shoulder, he could feel its perfect balance and he understood why Fitzgerald had been willing to fly halfway across the United States to find its twin.

It was then that he saw that the firing pin had been replaced.

Zerimski could hear the two men hurrying down the marble corridor. Just before they entered, he lowered the rifle onto his lap.

They almost ran into the room. Zerimski pointed unceremoniously to the two seats on the other side of the desk. "Where was Fitzgerald?" he demanded before Romanov had even sat down. "You assured me nothing could go wrong."

"While my men were escorting him into the city early this morning, the driver was forced to stop at a set of traffic lights. Fitzgerald leaped out of the car, ran to the other side of the road, and jumped into a passing taxi. We pursued it all the way to Dulles Airport, only to find Fitzgerald wasn't inside."

"The truth is that you allowed him to escape," said Zerimski.

Romanov bowed his head and said nothing.

The President's voice lowered to a whisper. "I understand you have a code in the Mafya," he said, clicking the breech of the rifle shut, "for those who fail to carry out contracts."

Romanov looked up in horror as Zerimski raised the gun, smiled, and gently squeezed the trigger. The boattail bullet tore into Romanov's chest about an inch below the heart. The power of its impact hurled his lithe body back against the wall, where it remained for a second or two before slithering down onto the carpet.

Zerimski swung slowly around until he was facing his representative in Washington. "No, no!" cried Pietrovski, falling on his knees. "I'll resign, I'll resign."

Zerimski squeezed the trigger a second time. When he heard the click, he remembered that there had been only one bullet in the breech. He rose from his seat, a look of disappointment on his face, and placed the rifle back on the desk. "I accept your resignation. But before you clear your office, see that what's left of Romanov's body is patched together and sent back to St. Petersburg." He began walking toward the door. "Make it quick. I'd like to be there when he's buried with his father."

Pietrovski was too frightened to open his mouth.

THE snow was falling heavily as Zerimski climbed the steps to the waiting Ilyushin 62. He disappeared through its door without even bothering to turn and give the traditional wave for the cameras.

Tom Lawrence, standing on the tarmac, was the first to turn his back on the departing aircraft as it lumbered toward the runway. He walked to his waiting helicopter, where he found Andy Lloyd, a phone pressed to his ear. As Marine One lifted off, Lloyd concluded his call and briefed the President on the outcome of the emergency operation that had taken place early that morning at Walter Reed Hospital. Lawrence nodded as Lloyd outlined the course of action Braithwaite was recommending. "I'll call Mrs. Fitzgerald personally," he said.

The two men spent the rest of the short journey preparing for the meeting that was about to take place in the Oval Office. The President's helicopter landed on the South Lawn, and neither of them spoke as they made their way toward the White House. Lawrence's secretary was waiting anxiously by the door.

"Good morning, Ruth," the President said for the third time that day. Both of them had been up for most of the night.

"Your ten-o'clock appointment has been waiting in the lobby for the past forty minutes," Ruth informed him.

"Have they? Then you'd better send them in."

The President walked into the Oval Office, opened a drawer in his desk, and removed two sheets of paper and a cassette tape, which he inserted into the recorder on his desk. Andy Lloyd came in from his office, carrying two files under his arm. He took his usual seat by the President's side.

There was a knock on the door. Ruth opened it and announced, "The director and deputy director of the CIA."

"Good morning, Mr. President," said Helen Dexter brightly as she entered the Oval Office with her deputy a pace behind.

"You'll be relieved to know," continued Dexter as she took a seat, "that I was able to deal with that problem we feared might arise during the visit of the Russian President. In fact, we have every reason to believe that the person in question no longer represents a threat to this country."

"Could that possibly be the same person I had a chat with on the phone a few weeks ago?" asked Lawrence, leaning back in his chair.

"I'm not quite sure I understand you, Mr. President," said Dexter.

"Then allow me to enlighten you," said Lawrence. He leaned forward and pressed the PLAY button of the tape recorder.

"I felt I had to call and let you know just how important I consider this assignment to be. Because I have no doubt that you're the right person to carry it out."

"I appreciate your confidence in me, Mr. President."

Lawrence pressed STOP. "No doubt you have a simple explanation as to how and why this conversation took place," he said. "Because it did not emanate from this office."

"Are you accusing the Agency of—"

"I'm not accusing the Agency of anything. The accusation is leveled at you personally."

"Mr. President, if this is your idea of a joke—"

"Do I look as if I'm laughing?" asked the President before hitting the PLAY button again.

"I felt it was the least I could do in the circumstances."

"Thank you, Mr. President. Although Mr. Gutenburg assured me of your involvement, I felt unable to take on the assignment unless I was certain the order had come directly from you."

The President leaned forward once again and pressed the STOP button. "There's more, if you want to hear it."

"I can assure you," said Dexter, "that the operation Fitzgerald was referring to was nothing more than a routine exercise."

"Are you asking me to believe that the assassination of the Russian President is now considered by the CIA to be nothing more than a routine exercise?" said Lawrence in disbelief.

"It was never our intention that Zerimski should be killed."

"Only that an innocent man would hang for it," the President retorted. A long silence followed before he added, "And thus remove any proof that it was you who ordered the assassination of Ricardo Guzman in Colombia."

"I can assure you that the CIA had nothing to do with—"

"That's not what Connor Fitzgerald told us earlier this morning," said Lawrence.

Helen Dexter was silent.

"Perhaps you'd care to read the affidavit he signed in the presence of the Attorney General."

Andy Lloyd opened the first of his two files and passed Dexter and Gutenburg copies of an affidavit signed by Connor Fitzgerald and witnessed by the Attorney General.

"On the advice of the Attorney General, I have authorized the special agent in charge to arrest you both on a charge of treason. If you are found guilty, I am advised that there can be only one sentence."

Dexter remained tight-lipped. Her deputy was now visibly shaking.

Lawrence turned to him. "Of course it's possible, Nick, that you were unaware that the director hadn't been given the necessary executive authority to issue such an order."

"That is absolutely correct, sir," Gutenburg blurted out.

"I thought you'd say that, Nick," said the President. "And if you feel able to sign this document"—he pushed a sheet of paper across the desk—"the Attorney General has indicated to me that the death sentence would be commuted to life imprisonment."

"Whatever it is, don't sign it," ordered Dexter.

Gutenburg ignored her. He removed a pen from his pocket and signed his resignation as deputy director of the CIA.

Dexter glared at him with undisguised contempt, then turned back to face the President. "I won't be signing anything, Mr. President," she said defiantly. "I don't scare that easily."

"Well, Helen, if you feel unable to take the same honorable course of action as Nick," said Lawrence, "when you leave this room, you'll find two Secret Service agents on the other side of the door with instructions to arrest you."

"You can't bluff me," said Dexter, rising from her chair.

"Mr. Gutenburg," said Lloyd as Helen Dexter began walking toward the door, leaving the unsigned sheet of paper on the desk, "I consider life imprisonment with no hope of parole too high a price to pay under the circumstances. Especially if you were being set up. A sentence of six, perhaps seven, years would be more appropriate in your case. But that would of course mean your agreeing to—"

"I'll agree to anything. Anything," Gutenburg spluttered.

"To testifying on behalf of the prosecution."

Gutenburg nodded again, and Lloyd extracted a two-page affidavit from the other file resting on his lap. The former deputy director spent only a few moments reading the document before scribbling his signature at the bottom of the second page.

The director rested a hand on the doorknob, hesitated for some time, then turned and walked slowly back to the desk. She gave her former deputy one last look of disgust before picking up the pen and scrawling her signature on her own resignation.

"You're a fool, Gutenburg," she said. "They would never have risked putting Fitzgerald on the stand. And without Fitzgerald they don't have a case." She turned again to leave the room.

"Helen's quite right," said Lawrence, retrieving the three documents. "If the case had ever reached the courts, we could never have put Fitzgerald on the stand."

Dexter stopped in her tracks.

"Sadly," said the President, "I have to inform you that Connor Fitzgerald died at seven forty-three this morning."

THE cortege continued its slow progress over the brow of the hill. Arlington National Cemetery was packed for a man who had never sought public recognition. The President stood on one side of the grave, flanked by the White House chief of staff and the Attorney General. Maggie Fitzgerald was facing them. On her right stood her daughter; on her left, her future son-in-law.

The three of them had flown from Sydney two days after receiving a personal telephone call from the President. The large crowd assembled at the graveside could not have left Maggie Fitzgerald in any doubt as to how many friends and admirers Connor had left behind.

The funeral procession came to a halt a few yards from the gravesite. The honor guard lifted the coffin from the gun carriage, raised it onto their shoulders, and began the slow march toward the grave. The coffin was draped in the American flag and resting on top were

Connor's battle ribbons. The Medal of Honor lay in the center.

The pallbearers reached the graveside and lowered the coffin gently into the ground. Father Graham, the Fitzgeralds' family priest, made the sign of the cross, bent down, picked up a handful of earth, and scattered it on the coffin.

"Ashes to ashes, dust to dust," intoned Graham as a lone marine bugler played taps. The honor guard folded the flag from the coffin until it ended as a neat triangle in the hands of a young cadet. Normally he would have presented it to the widow with the words "Ma'am, on behalf of the President of the United States." But not today. Today he marched over to the President of the United States and surrendered the flag as the marines fired a twenty-one-gun salute.

Tom Lawrence received the flag, walked slowly around to the other side of the grave, and stood before the widow. "On behalf of a grateful country, I pass to you the flag of the Republic. You are surrounded by friends who knew your husband well. I only wish I'd had that privilege." The President bowed his head and returned to the other side of the grave. As the marine band struck up the national anthem, he placed his right hand over his heart.

Two men who had remained on the top of the hill throughout the service had flown in from Russia the previous day. They had not come to mourn. They would return to St. Petersburg and report that their services were no longer required.

AIR Force One was surrounded by tanks when the President of the United States landed at the Moscow airport.

President Zerimski left us in no doubt that he had little interest in giving Tom Lawrence a photo opportunity for the folks back home. As a grim-faced Lawrence descended the aircraft's steps, he was greeted by the sight of Marshal Borodin standing in the turret of a tank.

When the two Presidents met at the Kremlin later this morning, the first item on the agenda was President Zerimski's demand that the NATO forces that patrol Russia's western borders be immediately withdrawn. Following the heavy defeat of his arms reduction bill in the Senate, President Lawrence knows that he is not in a position to give an inch on NATO's role in Europe, especially since the newly elected Senator Helen Dexter keeps describing him as "the red stooge."

Since Dexter's resignation as director of the CIA last year, in order to "oppose the President's misguided foreign policy," there is already talk of her becoming the first woman President.

Stuart looked up from the front page of the Sydney *Morning Herald* as Maggie walked into the kitchen, dressed in jeans and a sweater. "Good morning," she said. "Anything interesting in the paper?"

"Zerimski's still flexing his muscles at the slightest opportunity," Stuart replied. "And your President is having to put on a brave face."

"Zerimski would drop a nuclear bomb on the White House if he thought he could get away with it," said Maggie, filling a bowl with cornflakes. "Isn't there any brighter news on a Saturday morning?"

"The Prime Minister has announced the date for the election of our first President," said Stuart with a laugh as his wife strolled into the room in her bathrobe.

"Good morning," Tara said sleepily. Maggie slid off her stool and gave her a kiss on the cheek.

"You sit there and have these cornflakes while I make you an omelette. You really mustn't—"

"Mother, I'm pregnant, not dying of consumption," said Tara. "I'll be just fine with a bowl of cornflakes."

"I know, it's just that—"

"You'll never stop worrying," said Tara, putting her arms around her mother's shoulders. "What's the big story this morning?" she asked, looking across at Stuart.

"My case in the criminal court has made the headlines—on page sixteen," he said.

There was a thud on the doormat. "I'll get it," said Stuart, rising from the table.

He collected the mail and started sorting the letters, the bulk of which were for him. He handed a couple over to Tara and two to

Maggie, and pushed his own little pile to one side in favor of the Saturday sports section of the *Herald.*

Maggie poured herself a second cup of coffee before she turned to her mail. Both letters carried U.S. postmarks. She opened the official-looking envelope first.

Neither Tara nor Stuart made any comment as she extracted a check for $227,000, signed by the Treasury Secretary in Washington, D.C. "Benefit in full," the attached letter explained, for the loss of her husband while serving as an officer of the CIA. How could they begin to understand what the words "benefit in full" meant?

She quickly opened the other letter. She had saved it till last, recognizing the ancient typewriter and knowing who had sent it.

Tara nudged Stuart. "The annual love letter from Dr. Declan O'Casey, if I'm not mistaken," she said in a stage whisper. "I must admit, I'm impressed that he managed to track you down."

"So am I," said Maggie, smiling as she tore open the envelope. When she finished reading it, she said, "Good heavens. He's been offered a job as head of the mathematics department at the University of New South Wales, and he's coming over to meet the vicechancellor before he makes a final decision."

"Couldn't be better," said Tara. "After all, he's Irish, handsome, and has always adored you. And as you regularly reminded us, Dad only just managed to beat him off in the first place."

There was a long silence before Maggie said, "I'm afraid that's not altogether accurate. You see, although he *was* handsome and a magnificent dancer, he was also a bit of a bore."

"But you always told me—"

"I know what I told you," said Maggie. "And you needn't look at me like that, young lady."

"So tell me," Stuart said, changing the subject, "when does Dr. O'Casey arrive in Oz?"

Maggie read the letter again. "He's arriving on the fifteenth."

"But that's today," said Stuart. He glanced at his watch. "What time does his plane land?"

"Eleven twenty this morning," said Maggie.

"If we leave in ten minutes, we might still get to the airport in time. You could invite him to join us for lunch at the beach café."

Tara looked across at her mother, who didn't appear at all enthusiastic about the idea. "Even if we do, he'll probably say no," she said. "He'll have to prepare for his meeting tomorrow."

"But at least you'll have made the effort," said Tara.

Maggie folded the letter, took off her apron, and said, "You're right, Tara. After all these years it's the least I can do." She smiled at her daughter and disappeared upstairs to change.

When she came back downstairs ten minutes later, Stuart and Tara were waiting in the car.

As Maggie climbed in, Tara said, "I can't wait to meet Declan. Even his name has a romantic ring to it."

"That's exactly the way I felt at the time," said Maggie. "But it didn't make him any more interesting."

"Isn't it possible," said Tara, "that after all these years, Dr. O'Casey might have become amusing, rugged, and worldly?"

"I doubt it," said Maggie. "I think it's more likely he'll be pompous and wrinkled."

By the time they reached the airport, Maggie was quite apprehensive about meeting her old dancing partner after so many years.

"Do you want me to come with you, Mom?" Tara asked as Stuart pulled up to the curb.

"No, thank you," Maggie replied. She got out of the car and walked quickly toward the automatic doors before she could change her mind.

She checked the arrivals board. United's flight 815 from Chicago had landed at eleven twenty. It was now eleven forty.

She studied the arriving passengers as they came through the gate and began to wonder if she would even recognize Declan. After all, it had been over thirty years since they had last met.

She began to think about a plate of gnocchi and a glass of Chardonnay at the beach café at Cronulla, and then dozing in the sun while Tara and Stuart surfed. Then her eyes settled on a one-armed man striding through the arrivals gate.

Maggie's legs felt weak. She stared at the man she had never stopped loving and thought she might collapse. Tears welled up in her eyes. She demanded no explanation. That could come later. She ran toward him, oblivious of anyone around her.

The moment he saw her, he gave that familiar smile that showed he knew he'd been found out.

"Oh, my God, Connor," she said, flinging out her arms. "Tell me it's true. Dear God, tell me it's true!"

Connor held her tightly with his right arm, his left sleeve dangling by his side. "It's true enough, my darling Maggie," he said in a broad Irish accent. "Unfortunately, although Presidents can fix almost anything, once they've killed you off, you have no choice but to disappear for a little while and take on another identity." He released her and looked down at the woman he had wanted to hold every hour of the past six months. "I decided on Dr. Declan O'Casey, an academic considering taking up a new appointment in Australia, because I remembered your once telling me that you'd wanted nothing more from life than to be Mrs. Declan O'Casey."

Maggie looked up at him, the tears streaming down her cheeks. "But the letter," she said. "The crooked *e*. How did you—"

"Yes, I thought you'd enjoy that touch," said Connor. "It was after I saw the picture of you in the Washington *Post*, standing by the grave opposite the President, that I thought, Declan, my boy, this could be your last chance to marry that young Margaret Burke from the East Side." He smiled. "So how about it, Maggie?" he said. "Will you marry me?"

"Connor Fitzgerald, you've got a lot of explaining to do."

"I have indeed, Mrs. O'Casey. And the rest of our lives to do it."

JEFFREY ARCHER

TERRY O'NEILL

"I am rather an energetic person," says Jeffrey Archer. "Always have been. I think that's probably the secret of my success." It is this well-spring of energy, no doubt, that has enabled him to play a leading role in British Conservative politics while at the same time writing a string of best sellers—ten to date. And as if that weren't enough, Archer has also pursued his other great passion, the theater. He has written two plays and owns a controlling interest in London's Playhouse theater. A British life peer since 1992, Lord Archer is as determined as ever to remain in the public eye. When plans were recently put forward for the creation of the new post of mayor of Greater London, he announced that he would stand as a candidate.

The volumes in this series are issued
every two to three months. The typical volume
contains four outstanding books in condensed
form. None of the selections in any volume has
appeared in *Reader's Digest* itself. Any reader
may receive this service by writing
The Reader's Digest Association, Inc.,
Pleasantville, N.Y. 10570
or by calling 800-234-9000.

Visit our Web site at
http://www.readersdigest.com

ACKNOWLEDGMENTS

Pages 6–7: photo by John Warden/SuperStock.
Pages 292–293: illustration by Robbin Gourley.